PRAISE FOR THE W*

In *The Way of Edan*, Philip Chase has written a highly accomplished first novel. The storytelling is top-notch. There's a gravitas in the writing that put me in mind of Tolkien, with definite shades of Katherine Kerr, along with John Gwynne. This is a novel born of love for the story.

— MARK LAWRENCE

What a wonderful read! Prose that is smooth and accessible, a world with a weight and depth to it, and a gripping and emotional story. There's a lot to love here. Lovely to see the Anglo-Saxon influences that gave me a real sense of time and place, and the storytelling was done with a deft, assured hand.

— JOHN GWYNNE

The Way of Edan encompasses an expanding war driven by voracious religious fanaticism. Young heroes emerge, bonded by loyalty, in an age of ripening prophecy. Traditional fantasy readers will find elves with a fresh spin expanding the familiar bounds of individuality, and women, old and young, who wield magic in positions of power.

— JANNY WURTS

An impressive debut novel. Chase deftly weaves mystery and action with profound world-building. Deeply realized and compelling

— IAN ESSLEMONT

PRAISE FOR THE WAY OF EDAN (CONTINUED)

A classic feeling tale about connection. Connection to each other, to the earth, and to the creatures that live in it, as well as connection to life and death. A story that feels familiar, yet very much belonging to Philip Chase. I loved my time with it.

— MERPHY NAPIER

Gemmell's characters have invaded the landscape of Tolkien in this immersive, addictive, poetic read. An instant classic that will have fantasy and historical fiction fans desperate for more.

— ED FROM THE BROTHERS GWYNNE

Every element of storytelling comes together to weave an engaging and immersive story that is an absolute joy to follow.

— WILL FROM THE BROTHERS GWYNNE

A spectacular debut reminiscent of Ken Follett and Tad Williams.

— MIKE FROM MIKE'S BOOK REVIEWS

PRAISE FOR THE WAY OF EDAN (CONTINUED)

Every word is worth savoring in *The Way of Edan*, the masterful debut epic fantasy from Philip Chase. Lyrical and evocative . . . the most perfectly conceived and executed debut fantasy that I have read since *The Name of the Wind* by Patrick Rothfuss.

— JOHN MAURO FOR GRIMDARK MAGAZINE

This is a marvelous debut penned by a seemingly veteran author with a lot of love for the genre. A magnificent mix of classic and modern . . . it is a lyrical and traditional epic fantasy oozing with mythical quality due to its world-building. *The Way of Edan* might become my favorite fantasy debut of the year.

— PETRIK LEO FOR NOVEL NOTIONS

The Way of Edan is a compelling debut fantasy novel rich in setting, lore, history, and song. Well-seasoned fantasy readers may notice nods to Tolkien, *Beowulf*, and medieval sources, but the incorporation of Buddhist-inspired magic and enigmatic elf portrayals provides a razor-edge balance between beauty and peril. Refined and impactful prose immerses the reader into intimate character conflicts amidst an expanding holy war and into explorations of faith, doubt, duty, loyalty, and particularly empathy.

— JOHANNA FROM JOHANNA READS

THE PROPHET OF EDAN

Book Two of The Edan Trilogy

PHILIP CHASE

Copyright © 2023 by Philip Chase

All rights reserved.

No part of this book may be reproduced in any form or by any electronic or mechanical means, including information storage and retrieval systems, without written permission from the author, except for the use of brief quotations in a book review.

❦ Created with Vellum

ACKNOWLEDGMENTS

I am more grateful than I can express in words to the family, friends, colleagues, and students who have supported me over the many years of toil on this story. Friends I have been so fortunate to make on "BookTube" in the last several years have played a vital part in aiding me to get The Edan Trilogy into the hands of readers.

Two individuals in particular helped me to improve my storytelling, and my gratitude to Simon Lipskar and A.P. Canavan is immense.

Kyra Gregory and Jack Shepherd have once again combined their considerable talents to deliver a stunning cover, and Jack's map makes me long to live in Eormenlond, though preferably not with any dragons as neighbors.

For Rohana

Outer Isles
Hemeldowns
Frost Bar
North Downs
Hrones Sea
The Mark
hwitwater
Farwick
Northweald
(Iltharwyn)
Norfast
Rimdale
Wolvendon
withweald
Kinsford
folkwater
folkmere
Birch Bar
Southweald
(Iltharwyn)
DWEORG BARROWS
anrod
Erinstone
theodamar
The Dweorghlithes
Woodbury
Torrlond
ORMETBERG
Ellordor
Bay of Harlon
Hasumere
Gorifaen Hills
Torrhelm
ea
Sundering Sea
Beltlam
stramas
Derwyn
Caltrilion
glas
BALNOR PASS
Gadomiel
gilion
Marar Mtns
Culvor Sound
maranant
Adanon
Asdralad
Palahon
Dirgal
Dwarioth
Isles of Yaladir
Gulf of Gath
Kiriath
Halion Sound
Firdal
Isthmus of Lod
Yalawyn
25 50 75 100 150 200 300
scale in miles
Hormenlond or Andumedan

Map

- Enga Isle
- Bjornholm
- Savage Sea
- Ironwood
- The Wildlands
- Sirukinn's Wall
- Amlar Mtns
- Edwend Downs
- Sea of Morthul
- nurgleth
- kuralas
- Nahan
- Slith (The Great Fen)
- diadas
- Shohan
- Sildharan
- Holupad
- Golzay
- lannad
- Orudwyn
- sannodi
- ulnodi
- Shinan
- Ketzaon
- Suindara
- Gulf of Bahan
- Glirdan
- Tinubor

CONTENTS

Prologue	1
1. The Burden	17
2. Up in Flames	43
3. The Last Survivor	68
4. Using One's Gift	92
5. A Reason to Fight	118
6. Finding an Advantage	144
7. An Announcement	163
8. Plots Beneath Plots	184
9. Hanging by a Thread	202
10. The Triumph of the Way	228
11. The Council of Kiriath	249
12. Fire and Ruin	268
13. Captives	295
14. Origins	318
15. To Be a God	340
16. The Embrace	357
17. The Homecoming	375
18. Sildharan's Pride	393
19. Seeing the Hidden	410
20. The Fury of the Ilarchae	430
21. Taken by Surprise	450
22. Wrath and Destruction	472
23. Ascension	493
24. Dragonbane	512
25. Seeking the Eldest	528
26. The Prophet of Edan	542
27. The Final Parting	571
Epilogue	592
About the Author	595

PROLOGUE

Gnorn lay staring at the grave-like darkness. His small chamber in the guest quarters of King Balch's castle included no windows, but he imagined the night-shrouded streets of Palahon outside the thick walls were quiet in any case. Though his straw mattress was more comfortable than most places he had slept in the last few weeks, he found his mind restless and full. Full of loss. Of what was to come. No one shared the little cell with him, but he mumbled aloud as he lay there.

"I'm sorry. So sorry. Had to leave you there."

A moment of silence. The Dweorg continued as if he had been listening to someone, and now it was his turn to speak again. "I know. It's not why we joined. But things have changed. It's as I told you back in Etinstone. Something about that boy. He has a purpose."

Another pause, and then Gnorn sighed.

"Don't know. Can't put it into words. But somehow I feel wrapped up in it now. Mayhap I feel protective. He's a good lad. He sees people. Sees right into them. But not just that. He feels their joy and pain like they're his own. If he were shorter and hairier, he could fool me into thinking he's a Dweorg."

He chuckled before resuming his conversation. "You'll see. He's no ordinary boy. Mayhap I'm also curious to see what he becomes. But I tell you: He's meant to be someone the loremasters will write about for centuries."

A few heartbeats went by, and this time, when Gnorn answered the imagined voice, his tone grew excited.

"Might be. You may have the right of it, Brother. Someone must follow the lad and record everything when it's all over. Why not a Dweorg? We are the witnesses to the history of this land, and that boy will be a great part of it somehow. And why not me? I am a loremaster trained, the last of my people. The Dweorgs of the Fyrnhowes may be a dying race, but I will give the world one last tale to remember and tell over the fire."

Gnorn waited again.

"Yes. Do you know, Brother, I believe you have it. The boy's given me a purpose. It's been so long since I felt anything like that. I only wish you were here to feel it too. I only wish . . ."

A sob escaped the Dweorg, and a long moment of silence went by.

"No. I know. None of that. You met your end like a Dweorg of old. You're with the ancestors now. It's as you wished. But I must go on. I have a task, and I'll see it done. For Dayraven."

A mighty rumble interrupted the Dweorg's conversation, and vibrations reached him through the stone of the floor and walls. Muffled screams within the castle followed a few moments later.

Gnorn sat up in his bed. "What's this?"

A giant boom exploded somewhere in the night. More rumbling shook the stones of the castle. More screams came.

"What in all of Eormenlond?"

The Dweorg jumped off his bed and felt in the darkness for his boots, which he had left on the floor. The chamber was small, so it was not difficult to find his byrny, kirtle, helm, and axe. As he dressed, the rumbling and screams grew in frequency and intensity. Though he could not see, he glanced up at the ceiling. *Let's hope the castle doesn't crash down on my head.* As soon as Gnorn was clothed and ready, he threw open the door to his chamber and burst out of his room.

He stood alone in a hallway in the guest quarters, where torches set in sconces provided a little ruddy light. Terrified screams came from some distant part of the castle. "Where now?"

A boom and rumble vibrated the floor, and a chunk of stone from the ceiling cracked near his feet, dust trickling down in its wake.

"Dayraven." He bolted down the hallway.

After turning down another passage, Gnorn ran a few more feet until he reached the young man's chamber. The door was open, and he rushed inside.

Orvandil was already there. The tall Thjoth was holding Dayraven's limp form in his arms. Sequara was there too, bearing a torch.

"We must leave now. Palahon's under attack." The sorceress kept her words calm, but she could not hide the urgency beneath them.

A massive blast thundered against the exterior wall of Dayraven's chamber, and gouts of fire burst through the window, consuming the wooden shutters in a moment and gushing inside. Gnorn grunted as the floor smacked into his side. When he looked up, he saw Orvandil had leapt toward the door and shielded Dayraven with his body. The bed was alight with flames.

Sequara crouched and screamed something in a language Gnorn did not understand, though he recognized the tongue of magic. She made a sweeping motion with her hand, and the growling flames on the bed all died at once. The room reeked of burnt straw, sulfur, and a tinge of singed hair. Hovering smoke clawed at the Dweorg's throat.

"Go," the sorceress commanded in a hoarse voice.

Gnorn scrambled back on his feet. On his way out, he glimpsed Sweothol in its baldric leaning against the far wall. "Wait!"

He ran past Sequara and grabbed the sword, and then he slipped the baldric's strap over his head. The scabbard nearly dragged on the floor. Gnorn knew he looked ridiculous, but it would have to do.

Sequara nodded at him, and they both ran for the door.

In the hallway stood Orvandil holding Dayraven, who groaned in his sleep as if troubled by a nightmare. Abon rushed round the corner and hurried to join them. Like the others, he was fully dressed and armed, his harp in its sack slung on his back.

"Where are we heading?" asked the shaper.

Another huge blast shook them and sent small pieces of the ceiling down on their heads.

Abon looked up. "Shit. The place is falling to pieces."

"The stables," said the sorceress. "We need a cart for Dayraven."

"This way," said Abon. He ran down the hallway, followed by Sequara and Orvandil, who bore Dayraven. Gnorn came last.

Down the stone steps of a steep spiral staircase they fled. Gnorn almost fell and rolled down them as he hastened to keep up with the longer legs of the others. While they leapt over two steps at a time, he was forced to bounce down each one in quick succession. Then his feet got tangled up with Sweothol, and he narrowly avoided planting his face on the stairs. "Damnation! They didn't build this place for Dweorgs' legs."

A massive reverberation threw him off balance and knocked him off his feet, and he clung to the wall to hold himself up. Chunks of stone fell all around him, one pinging off his helm. "By the ancestors' beards!" He coughed amidst a cloud of dust. "We'll be buried here!"

The light of Sequara's torch disappeared down the staircase. Gnorn shot up and ran after it. A moment later, a huge block of stone fell with a groan and shattered the steps where he had been sitting, sending down an avalanche of bouncing rocks and pebbles and thickening the billowing dust. "Wait for me!"

When Gnorn came tumbling out the bottom of the staircase, he caught a glimpse of Orvandil's back as the large Thjoth disappeared through a doorway at the end of a hall. Gnorn ran for the doorway, remembering that it led outside to a courtyard, across which were the stables. He reached the doorway panting and sweating. When he emerged from it, he stumbled backwards.

A wall of heat slapped Gnorn's face and stung his eyes. The Dweorg gawped before him, blinking at the roaring inferno that was devouring the castle on every side. Fire roiled and ascended, licking the night air and illuminating the courtyard in ghastly shades of red. Wind and heat combined to form bizarre funnels of flame that coiled and spiraled upward. Horses screamed. Men and women ran and yelled, some clothed and others as naked as when they were sleeping. Some were ablaze, and their cries of horrible agony drove Gnorn to clasp his hands over his ears. Madness and chaos held sway, and no one seemed to know where to go or what to do. Gnorn coughed and choked on the thick smoke, through which he could make out the silhouettes of Sequara, Abon, and Orvandil, the last of whom still bore Dayraven.

The sorceress raised her arms and yelled something. Across the courtyard from her, where the stables were ablaze, the flames died. She and the others ran toward the smoking structure. Gnorn hastened to follow.

Before they reached their goal, something massive swept down from the dark sky, bearing down on Sequara and the others. The glow of the flames revealed it for an instant: an enormous blur of red stabbing through air. Fifty feet of gleaming scales and jagged spikes on its back. Leathery wings like the sails of a ship. Curved claws like twisted sword blades on its splayed feet. Long neck connected to huge jaws. Horns jutting from its brow, and wrathful amber eyes. Its vast maw gaped open, exposing rows of sharp yellowed teeth like glistening spearheads.

Eyes widened in shock, Gnorn screamed through the hoarseness in his voice, "Look out! Above you!"

Sequara turned.

A torrent of roiling flames vomited from the creature's mouth, raging toward the sorceress and the other companions.

Sequara yelled and swept her arms to her left, away from the stables. The flames obeyed the sorceress's spell and changed direction, curving away from her, Abon, Orvandil, and Dayraven. They roared straight toward Gnorn.

"Whoa, now!" cried the wide-eyed Dweorg. He dove. The cobbled ground jarred his body as a wave of heat bellowed over him and smashed into the doorway behind, consuming it in an explosive instant and showering sparks and bits of rock all around him.

Greedy fire growled and consumed the wall. Gnorn crawled away from its intense heat. When he looked up, there was no sign of the monster. The night sky behind all the smoke had swallowed it. "Was that . . .?"

"A dragon. Yes," said Sequara above him. She extended her hand, and he took it as he rose. "It will return. Let's go."

PHILIP CHASE

They ran for the charred stables, inside of which they found Orvandil and Abon. A torch in a wall bracket and the flames outside gave enough light to see by, but in the shadows the terrified animals whinnied and neighed. The scents of horse, sweat, straw, dung, and smoke permeated the air, but Gnorn could almost smell the fear as well.

Orvandil had laid Dayraven on the straw-covered floor, where the unconscious young man stirred and groaned. The Thjoth and the shaper were trying to lead two horses to an open cart they had wheeled into the large aisle between the stables. Too frightened to cooperate, the horses were snorting and neighing.

"They're too spooked," growled Abon. "Can't get them to budge."

Sequara murmured a spell, "Hrondin ar dwinnor uthanash in haldir. Innin im gwalor runash ni shardir." All the horses in the stables ceased whinnying at once. The beasts grew still. Save for the muffled screams of women and men in the distance, the place grew eerily quiet.

"Release the others," said Sequara to Gnorn. "The dragons will return, and they'd have no chance in here."

"Dragons? There's more than one?" Gnorn set about opening the stable doors and freeing the beasts. "Go on. Out with you all." He patted and encouraged them, after which they neighed and trotted out. By the time he had finished, Abon and Orvandil had their two horses hitched to the cart. Sequara was at the stable doors watching the smoke billowing up into the night sky. Across the courtyard, a blinding inferno ascended high over Balch's castle. Frightened people outside were still screaming, and shadows danced and careened as fire ruled the night. Gnorn approached the sorceress to await her commands. Tears rolled down her cheeks, though she appeared otherwise composed.

"There are several of them. Perhaps a dozen. I can't control them. Not even one. I tried. I can't wield the song of origin. The creatures are too large, too ancient. Too clever. It's beyond me. Either that, or Bledla's power over the dragons is too strong. And I can't quench all the fires. So many. The whole city's burning. People are dying. Their pain is . . ." She shook her head.

"My lady." Gnorn swallowed. "You must keep your strength to get us out of here. We must save Dayraven."

Sequara looked at the Dweorg and nodded. Her face was like stone, if stone could weep.

"Ready," said Orvandil, who lowered Dayraven into the rear of the cart. "Everyone in."

The Thjoth climbed to the driver's seat and took the reins. Abon sat next to him. Gnorn scrambled up and joined Sequara in the rear of the cart, where she knelt next to Dayraven. The young man was mumbling something, but his eyes were still closed.

"He'll awaken soon," said Sequara as she stroked his forehead. She looked into Gnorn's eyes. "When he does, you must explain to him. Keep it simple. Tell him where he is, and who is with him. Tell him we're going to Urd."

Gnorn nodded, and he grabbed the side of the cart as it lurched forward. When they rolled out the stable doors, he found the chaos and terror had receded, as if the dragons were attacking another part of Palahon now. The courtyard was empty of people and beasts. Most of the castle was still engulfed in fire. "Let's hope we keep clear of the monsters," the Dweorg murmured.

The horses' hooves clopped on the cobbles. The cart rumbled and squeaked. Gnorn peered into the night sky, hardly daring to breathe. They had covered half the courtyard when, from darkness into the flame-glow, a massive dragon emerged. The beast of terror swooped down on them and spouted a column of churning fire.

Sequara surged to her feet, her arms already in motion, as she commanded the gout of fire, sweeping it aside to collide with a roar and a shower of sparks into the inferno devouring the castle. A gust of wind tore at her hair and tunic as the monstrosity blurred by overhead. Crouching low, Gnorn held his helm on with one hand and Dayraven with the other. He could hear the sorceress chanting to keep her hold strong over the song of origin. *I hope her strength will hold too.*

Orvandil whipped the horses toward an open gate at the end of the courtyard. Gnorn fought the temptation to close his eyes and hide. *Keep your wits about you, old fellow.* They rolled on, the wheels clacking on the cobbles, and the gate grew nearer. He dared to hope they might make it. Just a few more moments. Perhaps the dragons would leave them alone if they could leave the castle behind.

Red flashed from the dark sky and descended with a blast of warm wind. A vast collision boomed and shook the ground as a monstrosity more terrible than Gnorn's worst nightmare landed in front of the gate and barred their way. Its clawed feet dug into the cobblestones of the courtyard as it splayed on all fours, ready to spring. Huge muscles bulged under thick scales gleaming in the firelight. Black-slit amber eyes beheld them as prey. The lingworm snapped its long neck forward and unfastened its colossal jaws to let loose a gravelly roar like giant boulders grinding each other to bits, mightier than the Dweorg could have conceived. Its breath followed the roar as a rush of fetid heat, warping the air and causing the Dweorg's stinging eyes to squint and his beard to flap.

The horses screamed and bucked. Orvandil jerked on the reins, and the cart came to an abrupt halt, sending Gnorn bouncing off the side of the bed and rolling in it.

The dragon vomited a torrent of flames.

Sequara stood ready. She motioned with her arms to fling aside the fire, which arced off to the side again and slammed into the wall of the burning castle with an explosion of flames and sparks.

The serpent of the air gave vent to a wrathful roar, but then the cunning of a predator lit up its eyes. It lifted its massive foreclaw and lurched forward. In the next instant, the monster was barreling straight for them, and the earth trembled with its charge.

In the driver's seat, Abon cringed at the approaching beast and screamed, "Fuck me bloody!" Orvandil stood, drew his sword, and yelled defiance.

Just as Gnorn was going to dive for Dayraven to throw the young man from the doomed cart, a group of men arrived shouting from their left. A score of fully armed Adanese soldiers hurled themselves toward the dragon. "Adanon! Adanon!" One in front yelled, "Dayraven!"

Gnorn recognized Imharr's voice.

Spears flew toward the lingworm and ricocheted off its scales in a series of clatters. It halted its charge at the cart and spun its massive head toward the newcomers, who unsheathed their swords and rushed toward death.

The dragon unleashed its fire on the soldiers, but Sequara shouted and turned aside the flames. Her teeth were clenched in a strained grimace, and sweat beaded on her brow. Feeling like a useless bundle, Gnorn prayed to his ancestors to give the sorceress strength.

The Adanese kept running to the attack, and the foremost leapt at the beast with their swords raised. With one muscled foreclaw, the monster swept aside the first three soldiers. Limbs flailing, two flew over the cart with streams of blood trailing behind them. One slammed into the cart's side and shook it with the impact. He grunted and collapsed next to it, his blade clanging on the cobbles. It was Imharr.

The lingworm's head surged toward the oncoming soldiers, and one disappeared when its jaws snapped down on him. Two legs dropped from its mouth amidst a spray of blood. The rest of the men attacked, hacking at the beast with their blades, which rang as they bounced off the scales.

One of the soldiers broke off from the others and ran toward Imharr, who lay under the cart groaning. Gnorn was sure it was Duke Anarad. Next to the Dweorg, Sequara stood in the cart and began to weave a new spell. She cried out, "Alakathon indomiel ar galathon anrhuniae! Vortalion marduniel im paradon khalghoniae!" Energy erupted into life and buzzed around the sorceress, and bright blue bolts of it writhed in the air. She swept her arms towards the beast and prepared to unleash her power.

The cunning dragon turned its head in Sequara's direction. It raised one of its massive wings and swooped it down towards her with a deafening whoosh. Its wind rocked the cart and tore at the neighing horses, which struggled to keep their footing as their manes flowed. The mighty gust swept the sorceress out of the cart, thrusting her yards backwards to land hard on the ground with a grunt. Orvandil and Abon too were sprawled on the cobbles, leaving Gnorn alone with Dayraven in the back of the cart.

Soldiers screamed and attacked the serpent of the air, and one of them managed to pierce the monster's outstretched wing with his blade. The beast roared and crushed the man in its jaws, twisting and flinging away the body like a rag. Then it turned to face the other soldiers.

Gnorn knelt next to Dayraven, clutching the cart's side with one hand and the young man with the other. He raised himself and thought about leaping out to help the prostrate sorceress. Orvandil pulled Abon up by the arm from the ground. The Thjoth screamed at the shaper, "Get back in and drive away! I'll help Sequara fight the dragon! She's our only chance!" The Thjoth ran toward her. At the same moment, a weak voice came from behind Gnorn.

"Gnorn?"

"Dayraven!" The Dweorg rushed to the young man's side. He was trying to prop himself up with his elbows. "Not now. You must stay down. We must leave this place."

The soldiers screamed as the growling dragon clawed and devoured them.

"Where am I?" Dayraven sat up. His eyes crossed, and he blinked them as if he could not make them focus. He wobbled and reached out with shaking hands.

Gnorn caught him before he fell and eased him down. "Not to worry, lad. Abon will drive us away any moment."

The shaper was still struggling to get back on the driver's seat of the cart. His grip slipped and he winced. Blood trickled down the man's bald scalp onto his forehead.

"Hurry, Abon!" said Gnorn, waving his hand. Only three soldiers remained standing, and the dragon would slaughter them soon.

On the other side of the cart, Imharr stood up with Duke Anarad's help. He grasped the cart and leaned on it. His eyes focused, and he looked at Dayraven. "Day."

From where he was lying, Dayraven's head jerked toward his friend. "Imharr? What's happening?"

Imharr smiled as if he were home in the Mark, jesting with his little brother. "I won't fail you this time."

Dayraven's friend raised Wreaker, and he turned toward the dragon, which finished off the last of the Adanese soldiers by crushing him with its foreclaw.

Duke Anarad shouted, "Imharr, no!"

His nephew ignored him and sprinted toward the gigantic lingworm. Duke Anarad ran behind him. Gnorn could not help but reflect on how tiny and frail they appeared before the enormity of the dragon, yet they rushed toward it with swords brandished. He wanted to look away, but he could not.

The monster turned towards the cart. Its neck craned forward and maw yawned open as it prepared to belch its fire and burn them all to ashes. *This is the end, then,* thought the Dweorg. *Flames and destruction will consume us all.*

Swinging Wreaker above him, Imharr yelled and leapt toward the gaping jaws of death. He was still in mid-air as the dragon-fire began to boil out. Imharr plunged the sword downward. The blade's tip pierced the monster's tongue and mouth with a spray of blood, and the serpent of the air choked. The burst of flames dissipated, and the beast's shriek split the night air like a peal of thunder.

Gnorn clapped his hands to his ears and watched the end.

Imharr had landed on his feet. He crouched low and clutched his withered and blackened sword hand, which had burned in the heat of the dragon's mouth. At a full sprint, Duke Anarad reached toward his nephew, yelling as he leapt at him in a seeming attempt to tackle him away and shield him.

With Wreaker still lodged in its mouth, the dragon roared and disgorged a column of fire straight down, where Anarad and Imharr disappeared beneath the flames. The sword glowed red with the unbearable heat surging around it, and there was no sign of Imharr or his uncle amidst the terrible, engulfing inferno roiling over the cobbles.

Gnorn looked on, gape-mouthed and unblinking.

"Imharr!"

Dayraven's scream startled the Dweorg, and he jerked toward him. Painted red in the flame-glow, the young man slowly rose to his feet, and Gnorn flinched away. His eyes. In them was no fury, no sorrow, no fear. It was the power of life and death that emanated from them, the force quickening all beings and to which they would all return. The sight at once fascinated and chilled the Dweorg, stripping him bare until he marveled at his own minuteness next to the infinite energy underlying the fleeting world of forms. Gnorn gaped at the terrible and blessed wonder of it.

When the dragon finished disgorging its deadly burst, the courtyard dimmed and quieted. The beast shook its head until the glowing metal lodged in its tongue flew loose, clanging on the cobbles a moment later. Seeming to sense the movement on the cart, its head pivoted on its long, sinuous neck to face Dayraven, who stood erect with no display of fear at the monster towering over him.

Unleashing the elvish power within him, Dayraven raised his arms and pointed them toward the dragon. Just as when Sequara had sung the song of origin, energy exploded around Dayraven and danced in jagged currents. Only this time, the explosion was so massive that it dazzled the Dweorg's eyes and throbbed in his ears. Its heat singed his beard and warmed his flesh.

Gnorn had only a moment to leap from the cart. His body floated until the cobblestones punched into and jolted his back. Above him, a vast eruption of energy detonated and shattered the fabric of the world with its thunderous crack. Save for a continuous, shrill ringing, a blurry silence filled the Dweorg's ears, and the pain seemed to split his skull in half. The ground beneath his body vibrated as a massive trunk of wizard's fire streaked from Dayraven's bright form toward the dragon, which met it with a huge column of flames in a collision that ruptured the night. The energy burst apart the flames in an explosion, and red tongues of fire scattered across the dark sky. The dragon writhed as the thick shaft of wizard's fire slammed into its head and branched and snaked all over its body in hissing currents. As he lay cringing on the ground, Gnorn shielded his eyes from the otherworldly brightness. The world was half piercing whiteness and half eerie shadow. A shriek of dismay and terror escaped the lingworm's throat. It beat its wings and vaulted into the air.

Dayraven bombarded the agonized creature with his sublime power, but as it rose, his body swayed. A moment later, the energy blinked out, leaving a giant red afterglow across the dim night. The ruddy blush of the fires returned, and Dayraven collapsed to the cart's bed. With tendrils of smoke curling from its scales, the dragon flapped its wings, wobbling in erratic flight as it disappeared into the darkness above with a final wail.

Save for the muted roaring of the fires and the high-pitched squeal in Gnorn's ears, all was silent.

"Dayraven! Dayraven, lad!" His own voice sounded distant. The Dweorg leapt back up and scrambled over the side of the cart to land in its bed. The young man lay on his back. His eyes were closed.

Red swirls floated before Gnorn's dazzled eyes, and he hardly trusted his senses. He fumbled his hand onto Dayraven's chest and placed his face next to the young man's mouth. The chest rose and fell, and a faint breath brushed his cheek. "He lives." The Dweorg's body shuddered, and tears streamed down his stinging cheeks, blurring his vision further. He shook his head to collect himself and looked up.

Abon looked on from the driver's seat. Sequara and Orvandil approached the cart.

"We must leave," said the sorceress. Blood ran down her face from a cut on her head, and she was limping, but she walked unaided.

"It's quieter now," remarked Abon. His voice was fuzzy, and everything seemed slow to Gnorn.

The roars and screaming had ceased, though the ruddy luminosity of many fires consuming Palahon still penetrated the night and glowed over the city like a dome. Nearby, flames growled and devoured the castle, whose timber and stones groaned and tumbled down. The network of structures crashed inward and released sparks that floated and winked out in the darkness.

"The dragons have retreated," said Sequara. "All of them. I no longer feel their presence. My guess is the supreme priest recalled them when he sensed one in mortal danger. But they will return soon, and Torrlond's army will be with them. We must cover a great distance before they arrive. But first, are any of the Adanese soldiers alive?"

Gnorn swiveled around and squinted at the many corpses strewn all over the courtyard. Mangled and broken bodies lay still, with puddles and spatters of blood glistening in the fire light. Limbs and viscera also littered the ground, so frenzied had been the slaughter the dragon wrought. But movement among the bodies caught the Dweorg's eye. Not far from the circle of blackened cobbles that the dragon's flames had scorched, a hunched form resolved into two bodies, one of which aided the other to rise. Gnorn gasped with disbelief and sudden hope.

Duke Anarad stood up and held an arm around Imharr, who clutched his own forearm above his trembling hand as the pair walked toward the cart. The duke's tackle must have pushed Imharr beyond the dragon's column of fire. Gnorn did not need to see the grimace on Imharr's face to know his burned hand was excruciating. Where the hand was not red with oozing blood, it was blackened.

"Imharr! You're alive! Thank the ancestors!" If Gnorn had not been cradling Dayraven's head, he would have leapt down from the cart to embrace his wounded friend.

"Yes," said Imharr between clenched teeth, whence air escaped in a pained hiss. "Thank the ancestors, and . . . Ow! . . . thank my uncle as well. Ah, by all the gods, it hurts!" When the pair got closer, the stench of singed hair reached Gnorn, and he could see scorch marks on the duke's cloak.

"Come here." Masking her fatigue by standing straighter, Sequara approached Imharr and Anarad. She could not entirely disguise her limp. "Hold out your hand."

Imharr winced as he glanced at Sequara's blood-streaked face. "You're hurt yourself."

"A minor cut. Scalp wounds bleed. My hip will be fine as well. Bruised, not broken. But you'll never be able to use that hand again if you don't hold it out to me now."

"Go on, son." Anarad nodded. "Give her the hand."

Imharr hesitated only a moment longer before nodding and holding out his scorched hand.

"I must touch it, which will hurt. But the pain won't last long." Sequara mumbled a song of origin beneath her breath. Gnorn could not make out the words, but he saw the change come over her body, which somehow lost any sign of fatigue as she reached for Imharr's hand. The otherworldly look in her eyes was a distant echo of what the Dweorg had seen in Dayraven's, and though not nearly as frightening, it was chilling nonetheless.

Imharr gasped when the sorceress touched his hand, but a moment later his trembling ceased, and his eyes widened with awe as they gazed at Sequara. The sorceress continued to chant beneath her breath.

When Sequara ceased chanting and let go of the wounded hand, Imharr's mouth hung open while he gawped at her. He shook his head as if in disbelief. "I don't know how to thank you for this . . . this gift." Gnorn had a strange feeling he was talking about something more than just the healing.

Sequara's eyes revealed that she had returned to the mundane world. She shook her head. "No thanks. You saved us all. It was the bravest and most foolish thing I've ever seen."

Imharr smiled and chuckled. "Might be it was." He held up his hand to his face as if it were an afterthought and wiggled his fingers. Flakes of charred dead skin fell away. Gnorn could see it was scarred beneath the grime and dried blood, but it appeared to be completely healed. Imharr focused on it for a moment. "A little stiff, but it works well enough." A puzzled frown took over his face as he flexed the hand. "In fact, it feels stronger than it should. And why is it silver?"

Gnorn squinted and saw what Imharr meant. Beneath the blackened blood, the flesh appeared to have a strange sheen.

Looking as baffled as the others, Sequara shook her head. "When you stabbed the dragon's mouth, did any of its blood spatter your hand?"

Imharr nodded. "It was hot. Burned almost as much as the flames." He wiggled his fingers again.

"If any of its blood entered your flesh, it might have changed it somehow." Sequara still appeared uncertain. "That is my best guess."

"Imharr Silverhand." Gnorn chuckled. "A good name."

Imharr smiled at the Dweorg. "As long as it works, I suppose it matters little what color it is. But best we not linger here, I think." He returned his gaze to Sequara and looked her in the eyes. "Thank you. For this, and . . . I understand now. I know you'll take good care of him. May the Mother and Father bless you wherever you go."

The sorceress nodded. "And may you walk under their protection. Adanon will need fighters like you." She turned to Imharr's uncle. "And you as well, Duke Anarad. My thanks to you for everything."

The duke glanced at Imharr's healed hand. "It is I who owe you thanks, Lady Sequara. But you must go. We will hold off the Torrlonders to give you time to reach the coast. King Balch and Queen Rona have escaped, I believe. Once I gather my remaining soldiers and find them, the resistance against the Torrlonders will begin."

"There will be many deeds ahead." Sequara glanced at Imharr before looking again at Duke Anarad. "I hope we will meet again."

When she turned and limped toward the cart, she closed her eyes as a brief look of sorrow passed over her face, or perhaps it was only fatigue.

I

THE BURDEN

A blur of red stabbed through the azure sky. Wheeling and twisting, the object plummeted towards the earth in a gyre. As it descended, its wings grew visible, but no one could have mistaken it for even the largest of birds. Circling lower, its enormous size grew apparent as it flew above a low hillside: From its head to its writhing tail's tip, it spanned at least fifty feet long.

It soared closer still to the ground. Orange tinged the red scales on its belly, while the gleaming scales covering the rest of the body were darker crimson. Jagged spikes fanning up from its back cut the air. As the beast blocked out the sun, light behind it exposed thick veins in the two huge, leathery wings, which stirred loud gusts of wind as they flapped to lower the colossal body to the earth.

It landed with a reverberating boom on all four of its splayed feet, each with three curved claws in front and one foot-long claw behind. At the end of its long neck, thick jaw muscles supported its sleek head. Beneath two horns jutting backward from its brow, the creature's amber eyes with dark slits spoke of the cunning and coiled wrath of a predator. Its jaw gaped open, revealing rows of dagger teeth and a glistening, forked tongue. The dragon's deep roar pierced the air, which wavered with the heat pouring from the enormous maw.

The lingworm had landed some twenty paces from a lone figure on a rising in the flat landscape. Few could abide the presence of such a beast, but the white-robed man whom the dragon gazed at looked back at it with his cold blue eyes and smiled.

Stroking his long white beard, the Supreme Priest Bledla walked toward the beast, whose mind he knew since it was under his command. Beneath its huge shadow he appeared small and frail, but he did not hesitate to approach. As their master through his unequalled power in the gift, Bledla understood dragons in a way that no one else in all of Eormenlond or in all the kingdoms of the world could. No one but he could know of the years of pain and toil it took to find, entrap, and master the serpents of the air. No one but he could know the labor he went through to ensure their secrecy until their unveiling. And no one but he could wield the song of origin of dragons.

As he knew his own body he knew them. He grasped their power and their cunning. Deep in the tissues of his organs dwelled the vast strength of their primal urges, the intense heat of their inner fire, and the ferocity of their wrath. Of tenderness too they were capable, at least towards their own kind, yet they were for the most part solitary, territorial creatures. The twelve that he wielded, however, had no choice but to brook each other's company. They were the tools of the Way, the harbingers of Edan's righteousness. Through them Bledla would fulfill his purpose of bringing to fruition the Kingdom of the Eternal, which, through the offering of Edan's mercy, was humanity's salvation.

Even now, as he reached out to stroke the scales on the dragon's lowered neck and felt their heat beneath his bony, veined hand, Bledla viewed the irrefutable proof of Edan's blessing. The smoking ruins of Palahon lay beneath his gaze. It had not been large in comparison to Torrhelm, but its inhabitants had toiled long to make it fair and graced it with spires and domes, most of which lay in heaps or still burned. Its thick walls, long deemed too strong for any foe to overcome, were charred and crumbled in many places — a testament to the futility of opposing Edan's will. The red tiles of its remaining roofs were scorched and blackened, and gaping holes yawned over many of the dwellings that once sheltered Palahon's people. The River Maranant, which skirted the city, ran muddy and crimson. Scores of dark, bloated corpses bobbed on its banks. Many found death there while fleeing from the flames, the beasts of battle, and the soldiers. Black plumes billowed in dozens of places from the still burning fires consuming the bones of the city.

Bledla did not allow sorrow at the sight of such ruin and despair. On the contrary, triumph leapt out of his bright blue eyes. Such destruction, as painful as it might be in the moment, meant progress toward a goal more important than any city or mortal kingdom. Humanity's salvation! The broad smile playing across the Supreme Priest Bledla's face conveyed absolute, ecstatic victory.

Palahon was nearly empty of people. The streams of haggard refugees had lessened to a trickle. Even from a distance, the air carried the wailing of men and women and the cries of children as they limped out of the ashes. Most were covered in soot. Some were half clothed or nearly naked. Grey-kirtled soldiers with gleaming helms flanked the lines of the wretched, shivering survivors and barked orders as they herded them toward pens on the outskirts of the massive encampment of Torrlond's peerless army, whose tents and campfires filled the plain around the city. Those Adanese that renounced their worship of their false gods, the demons Oruma and Anghara, would find the offer of life. Food and shelter awaited them, and a chance at eternal salvation. Edan was merciful. Those that refused to submit to the Way would have one last choice to make: axe or rope. There was no place in the Kingdom of the Eternal for unbelievers.

Words seared in his heart came to Bledla's lips, a passage from the Book of Aldmund. "'In death lieth life. From destruction cometh birth. The one who wieldeth Edan's power bringeth to an end the oaths and ties of humankind. This one breaketh to renew, and those who dwell in darkness fear the light's coming. The kingdoms and powers tremble when Edan's power cometh, for they knew Him not. Their wisdom turneth to folly, and their might to ashes.'" The supreme priest closed his eyes for a moment and took deep, long breaths. "The spirit of Edan truly guided your mind and your hands when you recorded your words for us, most holy prophet." Bledla opened his eyes and gazed at his own hands in rapt fascination, as if seeing them for the first time.

A deep, gravelly rumble vibrated from the dragon's throat. Bledla smiled. He looked up. In the sky the distant specks of some of his other eleven dragons circled on the lookout for escapees. Companies of soldiers also scoured the countryside around Palahon. They especially sought Adanon's former king, the fool Balch, who dared to defy Edan in words unfit even for a common soldier. The blasphemer's castle was a heap of charred stones, and at first Bledla supposed the man lay buried in it somewhere. But one captive had confessed to seeing the king and queen leave the city just before the dragons' arrival, and long before Torrlond's army came. It seemed Balch had escaped. It would be important to find and execute the man before any resistance could coalesce around him. Otherwise, there was a risk of delaying the Way's conquest of Eormenlond. He needed to accomplish Edan's will with swiftness.

The supreme priest frowned and allowed a quiet sigh to escape. In truth, Balch's life little concerned him. The Torrlonders would deal with the fool one way or another. It was the possibility that another lived that ate at his mind. Someone with immense power in Palahon had struck the dragon next to him with wizard's fire. The beast had required his healing, and it was still rattled from the ordeal. To think that such mighty creatures, Edan's chosen tools, could be vulnerable put an itch in Bledla's mind, an itch that disturbed him with the lack of faith it implied. The beast's blurry memory – he was still not accustomed to the differences in perception of dragons' minds – suggested that one with incredible power in the gift had assaulted it. He growled as the itch flared.

Joruman had insisted the boy was dead, but Bledla suspected his high priest's sincerity and his motives. The supreme priest's fists clenched. Perhaps the boy's corpse truly was rotting on a slope outside Iarfaen in Caergilion. Always in the past, Edan had spoken to Bledla with such clarity. But this boy . . . The power in him was like nothing he had ever experienced. What could it mean? "Edan give a sign," he said.

He closed his eyes in prayer, and he begged Edan for some clear declaration. *A sign, my Lord and Creator . . . If the boy Dayraven is dead, give Your servant some assurance.* He waited. Nothing happened. He clenched his teeth and shook his head, reproaching himself for such weakness. *Fool. Weakling. It is not your place to doubt or to demand a sign of the Almighty.*

Bledla sighed and gazed ahead at the smouldering ruins of Palahon. "I am sorry, mighty and glorious one. My weakness, my lack of faith, grieves me to my core. Your chastised servant humbles himself before You. It is enough. It is enough that You have given us such glory in battle as this. It is enough that You have given your servant power that no one has seen since the days of Aldmund. So many signs You have given. I am a feeble fool for asking for more. For I wield dragons. In Your name, mighty Edan, I command the serpents of the air to humble Your foes. In Your name, merciful Edan, the lingworms grind the unbelievers into dust."

A gasp escaped the supreme priest, and his face tilted upward as an ecstatic smile played across it. The dragon crouching next to Bledla roared and let loose a torrent of roiling flames from its jaws toward the destroyed city. The heat radiating from the fire bathed the supreme priest's body, and in his mind steel conviction took root even as his energy tore away from him and expanded beyond his body, beyond the dragon whose mind he wielded, beyond the ruined city and the lives of the soldiers and wretched survivors, all tools of the Almighty. With Edan his energy soared. One with the Creator he was, and his frail mortal body groaned as the bliss strained at it and radiated from every corner of his being.

"Yes, Edan. You are the one true God. Our triumph confirms it. And this is only the beginning. Caergilion first. Then Adanon. Then onward to the east. One by one they will come under Your blessed rule. The other kingdoms of Eormenlond will all fall unless they worship You freely. Once all of Eormenlond cleaves to the Way, Your kingdom, the Kingdom of the Eternal, will begin. Your servants will dwell with You in bliss, and no other kingdom of this world, whether on these shores or in the distant lands that lie over the vast seas, will have seen such glory."

The dragon bellowed in triumphant confirmation. Far below the supreme priest, the conquered and forlorn people of Adanon who heard that roar cried out, crouching in trepidation and gnashing their teeth.

Flames. A giant wall of flames roared in front of Dayraven.

Small and fragile, he cowered before it. The heat from it would melt his eyes, scorch his flesh, and incinerate his bones. He could not tell what fueled this otherworldly fire, but it burned and raged without end. High above, at the top of the towering wall, the flames licked skyward and glowed against inky and eerie darkness. What was on the wall's other side? How could anything pass through it? It would make sense to turn away from this inferno and flee, but the strangest feeling nagged at him: He was supposed to walk through it somehow. With a terrible urgency, the importance of crossing the wall of flames throbbed in his mind. He had to do it. He could not remember why, but he had to.

Dayraven shielded his face with his hands and tried to peer through the roiling fire. The heat was unbearable. He winced as smoke began to curl from the skin on his hands.

Before he could cry out in agony, a shadow floated and moved inside the wall of flames. The shadow enlarged, and as it neared him it grew legs, arms, and a head. No longer floating, a man's outline became clearer as it paced toward him. Nearer still it approached. When the man emerged on the edge of the wall of fire, his features resolved into those of a Caergilese soldier, the one Dayraven had slain at the Battle of Iarfaen. His empty eyes stared at Dayraven as the flames licked all around him.

The sting on his hands intensifying, Dayraven feared he would burst into flames but could not back away from the wall of fire. He clutched his chest. "I'm . . . so sorry. I didn't know. Didn't know what I was taking. I never should have been there." He blinked his stinging eyes and wiped his brow. When he looked again, he gasped. The Caergilese soldier had become Imharr.

Surrounded by flames but somehow not consumed by them, Imharr's still and expressionless form gazed at Dayraven. It seemed to Dayraven that the flames trapped his friend. He could never leave them now. Imharr said nothing, but in his friend's eyes dwelled a terrible accusation. Dayraven wrung his hands and shook his head, but still Imharr's face did not change.

"I didn't mean for it to happen that way. I didn't know." He ran his hands through his hair and tugged it. He could not back away because he wanted to pull Imharr away from the fire, but it was too hot. His flesh was smoking, and the agony of the heat tore a cry from his parched throat.

Darkness and silence. The presence of the elf hissed around his mind like morning mist caressing and dripping from the bark of a tree. It was cold and full of shadows. Someone was touching his brow.

"Dayraven. Dayraven, lad. You were having a bad dream. Just a nightmare. You're alright now."

"Gnorn?" His voice croaked, and his throat still burned as it had in his dream. "Water."

"Here, lad." A thick hand grasped him at the back of his neck and tilted his head up. "Here." A flask nudged his hand, and he grasped it.

Dayraven put the flask to his mouth. Cool water slid down his throat and dribbled on his chin and jaw. He swallowed with difficulty at first, but a few more gulps of water soothed him. Once the pain in his throat subsided, his entire body announced its stiffness and weakness. His muscles and joints ached like he had become an old man, and only Gnorn's strong hand kept his head from falling. To add to his growing sense of bewilderment, the wooden floor beneath him groaned as it rose and fell, and a dull moan seemed to surround him.

"Where?"

"On a ship. Bound for Asdralad. To see Urd."

"Urd? Where . . . did you say?"

"The Isle of Asdralad. Rest now."

"Why's it so dark?"

"It's night, lad. We're in a tent. Lady Sequara ordered the sailors to rig it up for you. Lay still now and rest."

"Who?"

"I'll explain everything. Right now it's important you rest."

"But . . ." A memory descended on him: crimson scales gleaming in the firelight. Veined, leathery wings blotting out the stars. Dagger teeth and enormous curved claws flashing. Amber eyes with death lurking behind them. Beneath the dragon's monstrous bulk, Imharr crouched in agony. The terrible column of fire . . .

Dayraven shuddered. His weak body trembled as the unfathomable agony of loss clenched his heart and sank it down, down. "He's gone. He's gone. Isn't he?"

Gnorn shifted in the darkness. "Who?"

"Imharr. I saw . . ."

"No, lad . . ." The Dweorg's voice choked, and he swallowed. "Imharr is safe. But you *must* rest."

A flood of recollections possessed Dayraven: Imharr teasing him about Ebba, slapping him on the back after a jest, teaching him to care for his bow. "Imharr," he whispered. "I saw . . ."

"Please, Dayraven. There'll be time to tell you everything. But he was safe and alive when we left him. Sequara healed his hand. Just rest now, lad." Gnorn's voice was blurred as if far away.

Imharr telling him about his dead mother, wrestling him to the grass on the hills outside of Kinsford, working alongside him and Father in the fields. "Left him? Where?" Dayraven's voice quivered.

"Please. Lady Sequara told me to keep you calm. Just lie down, and I'll tell you what happened. Nice and slow, though. Alright?"

"But why? Why would he leave me, unless . . ." Imharr telling him of the murder of his family in Adanon, looking like a warrior with Wreaker at his side and Torrlond's ensign on his grey kirtle, smiling at him just before the end, when he rushed toward the dragon's gaping maw. Sobs shook his fragile body and sent needles of pain into his throat.

A slice of the darkness parted to reveal stars for a moment, then a shadowed figure rose before them. The darkness returned.

"Dayraven. You'll be alright. You must rest now."

It was a woman's voice. She spoke with a foreign accent, and now she chanted softly in a strange tongue. But why was her voice so familiar? It bothered Dayraven that he could not place her, but his wonder waned as a new feeling seeped into him. *Peace.* It was the woman again. Somehow the word soothed him from within his mind. He floated backwards and sank into something soft and inviting. *Rest.*

A slow breath eased out of him, and his weary body went slack. *Sweet rest. Heal.* The woman, so familiar and beautiful, whispered in his mind. Unlike the indifferent susurrations of the elf-shard, her whispers were warm and earthy. With them came a multitude of fragmented but vivid memories: a simple dwelling of tan stone under the bright sun, a mother's smile, a little brother's giggle, a fair city by a blue bay. Her calming presence brushed up against him, and he allowed her energy to caress his. He thought perhaps her hand was caressing his forehead as well, and he realized she had done this before. He could trust her. He would be alright. *Rest,* she whispered.

DAYRAVEN'S EYES OPENED AND GAZED UPWARD. SUNLIGHT BLED through tiny chinks in the weave of the canvas tent above him. The steady hush of the elf-shard cast its shade over his awareness. He was alone, but the ship still groaned and rocked beneath him. The tang of salty air lay beneath the smell of damp canvas. *Still at sea. How long have I been asleep?*

Piecemeal images of Imharr's dying act slammed into his mind again: his friend's smile, his leap toward the dragon's maw with Wreaker raised aloft, and a column of fire so hot that the illuminated night air seemed to bend and waver around it. *But Gnorn said . . . Was it a dream? I've been dreaming so long.* He winced until he remembered to breathe. Tremors convulsed his weak body for a while, and tension wracked his stiff muscles. But then he steadied his breathing and relaxed his tight fists until his open hands rested on his stomach. When he felt calm enough, he sat up. The act took more out of him than he had anticipated, and he splayed his hands on the deck to hold himself up as a wave of dizziness hit him. When it passed, he pushed a blanket off of him and leaned forward with a groan to get on his hands and knees. Breathing heavily with the effort, he shuffled forward until his head pierced the entrance to the tent.

The world went white when sunlight hit his face and then red as he clenched his eyes closed to ward them from the unaccustomed brightness. As he knelt and waited for his eyes to adjust, the salt-laden wind whipped his face and sent chills down his trembling body.

"Awake now?" said a deep voice above him.

"Captain Orvandil?" His voice was hoarse and rusty from disuse.

"Captain no more. Welcome back. Some sea air will do you good. Let me help."

Strong hands grasped him by the armpits and lifted him. Dayraven's body protested with knots of pain in his back and joints, but it felt good to rise. He opened his eyes and winced. The blurred form of the huge blond Thjoth stood before him and smiled in his grim way.

Dayraven squinted in the still bright sunlight, but his eyes were adjusting enough that he could see now. Orvandil's hands supported him as if he were a doll. He looked down at himself. He was emaciated. Strange clothes covered him: a sliver kirtle and dark breeches.

"Imharr?"

The tall Thjoth nodded. "He lives. With his uncle back in Adanon, fighting Torrlonders."

"His uncle? The Torrlonders?" Hope and fear together swelled in Dayraven's chest, and he trembled with the effort to contain his emotions.

"There is much to tell. First, get your legs under you."

"I can stand now." His body shivered like a dry leaf in the wind. He managed a brief, wry smile. "Perhaps with a little help . . ."

Orvandil grunted. "Mmm. Lean on me for now."

The Thjoth stooped and put Dayraven's left arm over his neck as he supported the younger man with his massive right arm. That gave Dayraven his first good view of the infinite grey-blue waters surrounding them in every direction. Waves glistened in the sun, and the small ship they were on murmured as it cut through them. Wind rippled the tight sail, which thrummed and, at the edges, snapped. In the ship's prow, three dark-haired and bronze-skinned sailors spoke together in loud words that sounded both jocular and foreign to Dayraven's ears. From behind came a familiar, gravelly voice.

"Well, now. Good to see you up."

A squat man with a scarred face appeared in front of Dayraven. He searched his memories. "The shaper? Abon?"

"Helped save your life," said Orvandil.

The shaper, who claimed he was the wizard Galdor's servant, had tried and failed to convince him to flee during the Battle of Iarfaen. Iarfaen: that's where it all went wrong. He was running to help Imharr when Brond tried to kill him. With the flash of memory, his free hand jerked to the right side of his neck, where it met a narrow, long ridge on the otherwise smooth skin. So, there was a scar where Brond had sliced him open, and since it itched, he guessed it was still healing. But what happened then? Dayraven shook his head. There were dark gaps in his memory.

"Easy," said Orvandil. "Take it slow."

Dayraven took a deep breath and closed his eyes. When he opened them, he felt calmer. "I'm alright. Just confused. And hungry."

"Good," said the Thjoth. "Hunger is good. Means you're alive."

He nodded and tried to smile. "Gnorn's here too, isn't he?"

"Aye," said Abon. "But sailing on the Great Sea doesn't agree with the poor fellow." He pointed somewhere behind Dayraven.

He turned around, but the ship's mast, sail, and rigging obscured his view. With Orvandil's help, he walked aft until he cleared the sail by ducking under it. Gnorn's broad back appeared. The Dweorg leaned over the ship's side as he groaned. Three more southern sailors were there tending to the rigging.

But the person who most caught Dayraven's eye was a woman of the south standing over Gnorn. Dressed in a long black tunic and trousers, she was patting the miserable Dweorg on the shoulder. Perhaps realizing the presence of someone new, she stood straighter. She turned and gazed at him. Nodding in greeting, she stepped toward him. As she approached, her eyes never left Dayraven's.

Myriad sensations flooded him, and he nearly staggered with the force of them. It was good that Orvandil was holding him up. The feeling of being watched from behind was strong, and he understood by it that this woman harbored the gift in great measure. He heard once again a frightened voice calling him away from the brightness and, later, a soothing influence that kept his tortured mind in one piece. With her dark eyes and raven hair, she was beautiful, but why should she have such a powerful effect on him? Most disorienting was the unavoidable conviction that he had always known this woman, though it was a clear impossibility. *Never seen her before. Have I?* He didn't even know her name, but it was almost as if their minds were somehow linked. Could she hear his thoughts now?

"You?"

"Hello, Dayraven. I am Sequara of Asdralad."

DAYRAVEN ATE AND RESTED FOR THE REMAINDER OF THE VOYAGE, though Orvandil coaxed him into a little exercise to help him regain some strength. With his returning vigor and the news that Imharr lived, his spirits lifted, though not without bouts of sorrow when he recalled the Caergilese soldier he had slain and Hlokk and all the death he had witnessed. During this time, he asked many questions of the Thjoth and Abon. They informed him of everything that had happened during and since the Battle of Iarfaen, including Brond's treachery, the arrival of Imharr's uncle and Sequara, the slow journey to Adanon, the Torrlonders' challenge to King Balch, and the coming of the dragons to Palahon and their narrow escape along with Imharr's heroism and survival.

Dayraven stayed silent as he listened. He nodded when the shaper finished, and he kept his silence for a long while afterwards as he gazed from the ship's stern in the direction of the mainland.

Somewhere over the vast waters in the kingdom of Adanon was his friend, who was in truth his brother. Imharr was home. While he had not found his sister, he had found family. A slight smile crossed Dayrave's face, and he shook his head. It left him melancholy and yet happy for his friend to think of it, knowing Imharr had gained his place.

But what is my *place now?* His body was healing, allowing his thoughts to dwell on the looming presence in his mind. He cursed the elf-shard, which stroked his mind like a feather raising goose-bumps on his skin. Had it not been for the elf, he never would have left the Mark, and he never would have needed to ask such a question.

A hand rested on his shoulder. Dayraven turned. With a sickly smile pasted across his pale face, Gnorn stood before him. The Dweorg's eyes crossed, and he nearly teetered over before righting himself.

Dayraven held his friend's arm to steady him. "You alright?"

Gnorn belched and groaned. "No. Dweorgs have never taken to sailing on ships or boats of any kind. Entrusting one's life to planks of wood on the surface of the vast, bottomless water is as unnatural as flying." He hugged his stomach and moaned.

"Perhaps you should . . ."

The Dweorg held up one hand. "No. I'm fine. It's nothing that'll keep me from having a word with you, lad." He pinched one eye closed, clasped his stomach, and groaned again.

"I . . . I'm so sorry about Hlokk."

Gnorn straightened and gazed at Dayraven with his sad, wrinkle-framed eyes for a moment and then forced another smile. "Mourn not for Hlokk. He died as he wished, and he dwells with our ancestors now. It's the living we must care for. Eh, lad? We must help one another muddle through it all."

Dayraven returned Gnorn's gaze. The Dweorg had lost his brother in truth. His frail bravery in the face of vast sorrow pushed Dayraven over the edge, his own sadness for Hlokk's loss becoming enmeshed with Gnorn's grief. It was too much. His throat tightened, and his eyes clouded over with unshed tears, so he only nodded in response and looked down at the ship's wake in the choppy water beneath them. Gnorn put his hand on Dayraven's shoulder and waited.

DAYRAVEN EXCHANGED FEW WORDS WITH THE QUIET SORCERESS during the voyage. It was a small enough ship, but they somehow managed to avoid each other most of the time. For his part, he could not shake the feeling that all his thoughts were open to her. Sequara had been in his mind, seen his deepest fears and desires. She must have beheld the elf-shard in there. The idea made him feel naked and vulnerable in her presence. Not to mention like a monstrous freak. The power of the gift in her tugged on his awareness the whole time. It was strong. She must have felt its far greater strength emanating from the thing lodged in his mind.

Still, the woman had saved his life, and he wanted her to know he was grateful. When the ship sailed within sight of Kiriath, chief city of the island kingdom of Asdralad, he mustered the courage to join the sorceress at the ship's prow. The sea wind whipped their hair as they gazed ahead at the tan-colored buildings nestled in a bay of Halion Sound. The domes and towers of the city seemed to hover above the water, which was the most beautiful and clear shade of blue Dayraven had ever seen. Dark green trees lined the cliffs looming above and around the city.

"Your city seems fair from afar," he said to fill the silence as he glanced at her.

She continued to gaze ahead as if contemplating something pleasant. A half smile formed on her lips. "It is even fairer once you're inside it."

"Did you grow up there?"

She turned to him as if weighing his question. "I came to Kiriath as a girl after the sorcerers of our island found the gift in me. Before that, I lived with my family further to the north, not far from the shore."

Vivid images sprang to life in Dayraven's mind. They were fragments of moments flooding him all at once: looking up into the face of a browned and rough but kindly man who held a staff as he walked. Wind kicking up dust in a dry field with rows of trees bearing some dark fruit. The warm embrace and kiss of a pretty woman with dark eyes much like Sequara's. A mischievous little boy who laughed as he ran away and hid behind a simple, squarish dwelling hewn from tan-colored stone. A grey-haired and wrinkled old woman sitting by a fireside and smiling as she sewed and told stories. Exuding feelings of calm, content, and deep-seated affection, the fragments dispersed and gave way to a more sustained narrative that unfolded before Dayraven's eyes.

As if inhabiting another's form in a dream, he saw from the eyes of a dark-haired little girl in a plain white frock. She arrived in a new place, a city with buildings larger than any she had ever seen. There was a big courtyard with stately columns and statues lined around its periphery. The girl stood in it with her hands clasped together, terrified and painfully alone. The other children in the courtyard wore much finer, more colorful clothes. They spared her hardly a glance as they spoke in their fine accents in small groups. Ashamed of her clothes and her manner of speaking, the little girl tried to disappear in the shadows as she locked her gaze on the cut and polished stones beneath her feet.

Dayraven stood with his mouth hanging open and stared at the sorceress. The images were Sequara's memories.

"You . . . you were alone. And afraid. You felt different from all the others."

Sequara betrayed no surprise, but her eyes narrowed as she gazed at Dayraven. "It seems some of my memories remain in your mind from when I healed you back in Caergilion. They should disappear soon."

"Oh." Dayraven wondered how many of *his* memories were knocking around in her head.

Still showing no emotion, the sorceress turned away from him and gazed back across Halion Sound. "Most children who enter training in the palace in Kiriath come from the noble families. These families have supplied nearly all of Asdralad's monarchs. The gift runs strong in them. My parents were simple farmers."

"And there was a boy . . . your little brother. And a grandmother. The memories of them are . . . comforting."

A brief smile escaped the grave sorceress. "Yes. My grandmother and parents have all gone back to Oruma. I don't often see my brother, who runs the farm with his family now." Her face turned as emotionless as stone. "They were good people. But they comfort me no more now than any other of my people. I serve all." She gave a brief glance at Dayraven. "As I said, these memories should fade from your mind. In the meantime, it would be best not to speak of them."

"Oh. I see." More silence followed. He pursed his lips until he could think of something to say that would not sound too stupid. "So, you came to Kiriath to train? To learn to use . . ."

"The gift? Yes." She looked him in the eye again. "It's important that one with the gift learn to use it. Especially one with the potential for great power."

It took some effort for Dayraven to keep looking at her face. *She means to make me a wizard. Do I have a choice now?* "Well . . . thank you. For saving my life."

"It was my duty."

Dayraven blinked at her. A keen intensity burned behind her beautiful eyes, and he felt his cheeks flush as he wondered if she read his thoughts. He turned his gaze back across the bay and said nothing else as they approached the city. What would he find in that foreign place?

At least the sorceress promised he would see Urd. Strange that this woman from so far away should know his great aunt. Then again, the old woman had always been gone for long periods from the Mark, and she kept her secrets well. He had always suspected there was far more to Urd than anyone in Kinsford could guess. What would she say when she saw him?

THE SAILORS WERE STILL SECURING THE SHIP TO THE DOCK WHEN Sequara urged Dayraven, Orvandil, Gnorn, and Abon ashore. A small contingent of palace guards dressed in white tunics and black leather armor awaited them at the bottom of the gangplank. Without the sea breeze and with all the bodies around beneath the bright sun, the southern heat grew almost uncomfortable to Dayraven. He snatched glimpses of the city as they hustled through — buildings of tan stone with spacious windows, a few tall towers in compounds tucked away from the main thoroughfare, two columned structures that were obviously temples with worshipers streaming in and out, and darkskinned folk in garb featuring vivid colors he had never imagined before who were talking, laughing, and haggling in a babble of what he presumed was Andumaic. Many of the people were bare-armed, and some of the women — old and young — wore long skirts along with a short, buttoned upper garment that left their bellies bare, something that would have been immodest in the Mark but here, in consideration of the heat, Dayraven supposed, was practical. In addition to the pervasive smell of fish, the air contained a smoky flavor with more than a hint of aromatic spices that awakened his appetite and curiosity.

He and his friends swiftly became the object of considerable curiosity themselves. Though folk paid obvious deference to Sequara with bows as she passed, their gazes lingered on Dayraven, Gnorn, Abon, and especially Orvandil. Though he thought little of it while on the ship with Sequara and the dark-skinned sailors, he suddenly grew conscious of how pale and strange he must have looked to the people of Asdralad.

Once through the city, Sequara and her guards escorted them up a long series of stairs straight to the palace of Queen Faldira atop a hill overlooking the colorful city of Kiriath. A small form waited just inside the shadow of the palace's main doors, and Dayraven recognized Urd even as he felt the familiar presence of the gift in her. As the two guards at each of the doors bowed to Sequara, the old woman stepped forward into the sunlight and gazed back at Dayraven. Her eyes narrowed, and she tilted her chin up as she frowned. New lines creased the skin of the old woman's delicate face.

Dayraven could not have said which was greater: his relief at seeing her or his guilt at the disaster that was his journey, his joy at her presence or his shame at his failures. Unable to keep looking at his great aunt, he stood with his hands folded before him and stared down at the colorful stones that were part of a mosaic beneath his feet.

No one else spoke or moved as Urd approached her grand-nephew and stopped in front of him. The old woman reached up to grasp Dayraven's chin and move his head until he looked her in the face. While appraising him with the frown still chiseled on her face, she seemed to read everything that had happened to him in his eyes, which grew misty. When a single tear spilled over and ran down his cheek, Urd broke her gaze and embraced him. He returned it, and they trembled as they wept together.

After a moment passed, Sequara spoke to Orvandil, Gnorn, and Abon. "I hope you'll not find our hospitality wanting if we wait for introductions until we come before Queen Faldira. She'll be anxious to meet you."

Urd let go of Dayraven and turned toward the Thjoth, the Dweorg, and the shaper. She wiped her eyes with her sleeve. "The queen awaits you all. After you've washed and changed, we'll dine together with her, provided you're not too tired."

"Tired?" said Gnorn. "Not in the least, but I'm famished after suffering aboard that rocking tub for so long. A meal would be most welcome."

Urd smiled. "Come, then. This way."

Not long later, white-garbed maids conducted Dayraven to a round table in a dining hall with generous windows, through which a pleasant sea breeze drifted. On the walls hung bright, multi-colored tapestries with hues and patterns leaping out at the viewer. Like his companions, Dayraven was now clean and dressed in new clothes, in his case a wine-red tunic of some fabric more soft than any he had felt before and a pair of white, baggy breeches. The clothes were comfortable in the heat and fit the guests well, with the exception of Gnorn, whose green tunic had sleeves that were too long for his stocky arms. The Dweorg also had to keep hiking up his breeches, which bunched up around his ankles, since none could be found to fit him properly. "Bloody breeches," he muttered under his breath as he gave them a tug before sitting down on the chair to Dayraven's left.

Dayraven smiled at his friend until Sequara walked into the room. The sorceress had changed into a crimson dress that left her lithe, muscle-lined arms exposed. The vivid color would have seemed outlandish in the Mark or Torrlond, but, as Dayraven had noticed in his hurried walk through Kiriath, folk in Asdralad favored such bright hues. Still, it wasn't the color that caught his attention. When the sorceress entered the room, a vivid image of another woman — regal and tall — imposed itself where Sequara stood. Accompanying the flash of the vision was a little girl's awe of the woman. Dayraven realized a heartbeat later, when the image had faded and he once again beheld Sequara, that it had been a memory belonging to the sorceress.

"Better close your mouth," whispered Orvandil, who sat next to Dayraven on his right. The Thjoth grinned. Abon, who sat on the other side of Orvandil, chuckled as well.

"No. It's not . . . That is, she's . . ." Dayraven flushed and looked down at the table, which only drew more mirth from his friends. He hoped his cheeks were not as red as Sequara's dress.

It was well for him that everyone's attention turned to Urd and another woman who walked through the doors. When they arrived, Abon rose from his seat, and so then did Orvandil and Gnorn. Realizing he was seeing in the flesh an older version of the woman from Sequara's memory, Dayraven followed suit.

Urd wore her usual brown robe. The tall woman conversing with her was clad in a gown that at first glance seemed golden but then appeared so iridescent that it was difficult to say what color it was. As she moved, it reflected hues of turquoise, blue, or red depending on the play of the light. A deep-blue sapphire ornamented the center of the golden band she wore around her brow, and on the index finger of her right hand she wore a ring with a similar gem. In the middle of her dark, long tresses streaked a band of silver hair, which framed a face that was fair to look on. Most impressive of all to Dayraven was the strength of the gift in this woman. Though Urd and Sequara were among the strongest he had encountered with the gift, this elegant woman was, if anything, slightly more powerful. Yet something in her bearing made her seem gentle at the same time. He decided it was her slight smile and her eyes. With a look he would have described as both kind and imposing, the woman turned toward the table and spoke.

"Welcome to Asdralad. I am Faldira, queen of this island, and I speak with the voice of my people when I say your arrival brings hope in troubled times. You may be seated, and while my servants bring out our meal, I ask that you allow me to greet each of you as our guests." The queen spoke the Northern Tongue with an accent similar to Sequara's. Her voice was placid like a deep, still lake, confirming Dayraven's impression of her.

When he and the others were seated, the queen sat at the table as well, and Urd and Sequara took seats on either side of her. Queen Faldira looked at the shaper and said, "Abon, it's good to see you on our shores again. How fares your master, our friend and ally Galdor?"

Abon inclined his head before answering. "Well, your Majesty, when last I saw him, though he's hard beset by the followers of the Way in Ellond. They grow in numbers and power."

"I see. And King Fullan?"

"The king protects Galdor as best he can, but more of the nobles under the Way's sway are calling for my master's removal and even death. Things have reached a boiling point, and his Majesty is in a difficult place. He must work hard to maintain control of Ellond, and even he will not find it easy to keep our kingdom from joining Torrlond when the time comes."

Faldira nodded but revealed no emotion in her countenance. "Let us hope he can." As servants clad in white began placing covered platters of aromatic food and glass pitchers of red wine on the table, she next faced Orvandil. The spicy fragrances were foreign to Dayraven, but they whetted his curiosity and his appetite.

"Orvandil. Sequara tells me you are a man with great military experience."

Like Abon, the big Thjoth bowed his head before speaking to Queen Faldira. "Some, your Majesty. Most Thjoths know how to fight."

Gnorn shifted in his seat next to Dayraven and grunted, but no one else seemed to notice.

The queen nodded, and her eyes narrowed and hardened as she continued to address Orvandil. "We in Asdralad have long enjoyed peace, but we must change. The time has come to prepare ourselves for war. We have need of warriors like you to help train an army to fight against the Torrlonders. Combat, organization, and strategy: We have little experience in such facets of warfare. We could pay you well for loyal service if you would help to remedy our lack."

Orvandil scratched the beard over his chin and frowned. "I'm here for Dayraven. If he stays, I stay, and then I'll see what I can do. You need good weapons too. For that, you might seek help from the Dweorg."

Gnorn's head jerked toward Orvandil, but Faldira kept her gaze on the Thjoth. "Whether or not Dayraven stays with us will be his decision to make, but we hope he will, at least for a time."

Turning to Gnorn as the white-clad servants finished setting the table with goblets for the wine and silver plates for the food, the queen spoke to the Dweorg. "Gnorn, you are a Dweorg of the Fyrnhowes. The weapons forged by your kind are indeed legendary for their strength and keenness. Am I to understand you have knowledge of the craft of making weapons?"

Gnorn smiled and bowed. "Aye, my lady. My brother and I were the finest weaponsmiths in Etinstone. I too am here for Dayraven, but if he stays, I'll try to be of use to you, I assure you. If your smiths are willing to learn, I can teach them a thing or two."

"Good," said the queen. "We'll need all the help that willing friends can lend us." She turned toward Dayraven. His heart beat faster as Queen Faldira, so strong in the gift and the nearest thing he had seen to ethereal in a woman of flesh, seemed to see into his soul by looking into the window of his eyes. What did the queen see there? Most certainly she sensed the monstrous power the elf had lodged in him. But she gave away nothing in her countenance as she addressed him.

"And Dayraven. Urd has told us much of you. It would seem many things depend on your decisions about your immediate future. We have much to speak about. But now our food is ready, and it would be unseemly to keep guests waiting."

Relieved that he would not have to answer questions for the present, Dayraven bowed to the queen and sighed.

The table was set. Gnorn rubbed his palms together in anticipation. But the eagerness in the Dweorg's eyes gave way to a puzzled expression when the servants removed the covers from the platters of food. His eyebrows lowered, and then one popped up as he pursed his lips.

When Dayraven took a look at the food, he understood Gnorn's reaction. On the platters steamed various vegetables he had never before seen in sauces of deep red and orange hues. One dish looked something like beans, but the stringy greens were much longer than any beans he had ever encountered. In vain he looked for some sort of meat, but there were numerous creatures of the sea Dayraven never had heard of, let alone contemplated eating.

Abon, having been to the island before, seemed more comfortable than the other guests, and the shaper reached for some of the seafood, some sort of hard-shelled thing with antennae, like a giant red insect. Orvandil followed suit.

Dayraven and Gnorn looked at each other and shrugged. They

each reached for some of the dish in front of them. Dayraven's appeared to be a leafy vegetable in one of the red sauces. There were squares of some white spongy thing in it as well. He glanced at Urd, who was smiling at him and Gnorn. The old woman pointed at one of several piles of flat bread that was doughy and baked in a round shape. "Use the bread to eat it. Like this." She tore off a wedge of the bread in her hand and scooped up some of her sauced vegetable in it before popping it in her mouth.

Gnorn handed the dish he had just taken a portion from to Dayraven and proceeded with eagerness to follow Urd's example. As he shoveled up a large helping of the food with his bread, the old woman said, "I'd be careful with that one, Gnorn. It bites back a little."

Gnorn smiled and said, "Not to worry. We Dweorgs are fond of good fare no matter where we are." Then he stuffed the lot into his mouth and began chewing with vigor.

Before long, his smile disappeared and his eyes bulged. Still holding the dish, Dayraven watched as the Dweorg, now red all over his full cheeks, chewed faster. Beads of sweat began to form on his brow, and he sniffed loudly. With trembling hands, Gnorn reached for a pitcher of wine and sloshed some in the goblet before him in such haste that drops spilled on the table. After swallowing his food, he downed the entire goblet in a few gulps.

With a slight frown on her face, Queen Faldira blinked at Gnorn. "Do you find it to your liking, friend Dweorg?"

Gnorn's cheeks puffed out and he blew through his mouth before answering, "Good, your Majesty. Hotter than a forge, but good!" He poured some more of the wine in his goblet.

Dayraven looked down at the dish he was still holding — some sort of long red vegetable floated in the sauce — and passed it to Orvandil, who gave an awkward smile and passed it on without taking any to Abon.

The shaper laughed aloud, and Urd followed suit. Soon the rest of them joined in, including Gnorn. Dayraven watched the others laughing, and he noticed even Sequara was smiling. *It would take some getting used to if I stayed here. I must think about it now. At least I know what they want of me.*

. . .

A FEW DAYS AFTER THEIR ARRIVAL IN ASDRALAD, ABON DECLARED his intention to depart on a ship bound for his native land. The shaper wished to return to Galdor in Ellond, where the wizard had need of all the support he could obtain to keep his kingdom from siding with Torrlond.

Dayraven said goodbye to Abon in Queen Faldira's palace. He was grateful to the fellow for the role he had played in saving his life, and he was certain he had never heard a finer shaper. He told Abon so at their parting.

"When you sing, the old stories come to life. It's been an honor to hear and to know you."

The shaper smiled and answered in his raspy voice, "That's the highest praise anyone could give me, Dayraven of the Mark." He grasped Dayraven by the hand. "The honor is mine. I hope we'll meet again."

"As do I."

Green bag slung over his shoulder, Abon turned to walk down the hall and disappear around the first corner.

A short while later, Dayraven walked alone in the cedar-lined garden behind the palace. Bright flowers surrounded him everywhere, and the hibiscus trees were a thing of wonder to his northern eyes. He found a shady spot by the wall, which he could see over as he leaned on it, and gazed between the cedars out at the view of the bay. Numerous fishing vessels skimmed the brilliant azure waters of Halion Sound, but one sail diminished and grew in distance from the others as it drifted northward.

He imagined Abon was aboard that ship. He found himself longing to be on such a vessel making its way north. *The Mark's so far away now. Ebba, Father, and everyone in Kinsford. If only I could join them.*

Footsteps crunched on one of the gravel paths that led to the pool in the garden's center, and awareness of the gift bloomed in him. Dayraven turned around and looked between the hibiscus trees. Queen Faldira and Urd were approaching. The latter wore her brown robe, whereas the queen was clad in a bright yellow gown. He walked toward them and met them at the pool, where they each sat down on one of the stone benches.

"Greetings, Dayraven," said Faldira.

He bowed as he stood at the other end of the pool. "Greetings, your Majesty."

"Will you join us, please?" The queen gestured at the bench nearest Dayraven, and so he sat and waited.

"Dayraven, my child," said Urd. "We must speak."

Except for the faint murmurings of the elf-shard in his mind, there was silence. Dayraven broke it with a sigh. "I know what you want of me." He looked at the two women without blinking.

"Please understand, Dayraven, we do not ask this for our own sakes only." Faldira's voice was soothing and calm, but he could hear the urgency behind it.

"I know."

"You must be trained now. There's no choice." Urd gazed at him. She frowned as she continued, "With so much power in you, you must learn to wield the gift. It could kill you otherwise. Or worse."

Dayraven remembered the irresistible violence when the elf-shard awakened in his mind, how it tore his spirit from him when he encountered the priest in Wolvendon, the aglak in Hasumere, and the dragon in Palahon. He had convinced himself he could master its power with his will alone, but he knew that had been a false and desperate hope.

"I know."

The women waited for him to say more.

He sighed again and looked at the patterns the colorful stones made in the pool as he ran his fingers through his hair. "I had thought I could return to the Mark one day. I wanted my life back. I wanted . . . to go back. To wed Ebba. To work our land outside Kinsford. To see Father play with his grandchildren. To grow old with my people. *My people.*"

He looked at the women again, and he kept his voice flat. "I will have no people. If I do as you wish, I will never have anyone. Should the Mark join Torrlond in its war of conquest, it may even be that I will fight against those who were my own."

Urd gazed at him and nodded. The old woman folded her hands in her lap and sighed. "There's a strong chance that could happen."

"That is true," said Faldira, "though we are not asking you now to join us in the coming war or to take a side. For the present, we only ask that you allow us to train you. What you will do consequently will be your decision. You will be free to choose as you will, but I fear you will be forced to decide one way or the other. With the power that is in you, you will find it difficult to remain apart from the coming conflict. It will consume all of Andumedan."

Urd straightened her back and looked hard at Dayraven. "And Bledla has made it clear how he feels about you."

Dayraven gave a wry smile and ran two fingers along the scar on his neck. The supreme priest of the Way wanted him dead. But why had he not just done the job himself when they met?

During his meeting with Bledla in King Earconwald's tent outside Hasumere, the power of the gift in the man had been shocking. Perhaps even more formidable was the man's steel conviction. Even Faldira seemed weak compared to him. There could be no more dangerous foe in Eormenlond.

"You want me to stop him. The supreme priest."

Queen Faldira nodded once, her face expressionless.

"You should know that this . . . thing, though it may seem like the gift, it's not *me*. What the elf put there . . . I know not what it is, but it is far greater than I am. The gods-cursed elf put it in my mind . . . It lives in my *mind*. I do not know if I can wield it."

As if to confirm his words, the elf-shard rustled like a chill autumn wind through dying leaves.

"We may be able to help you," said the queen. "If you agree to train here, we will do everything we can to help you come to terms with it."

He shook his head. "I still held on to the idea that I could win my life back. Foolish, perhaps. And now, everything is . . ." He tried to muster a smile, knowing how weak it must look. "I may prove useless to you as well."

Urd smiled sadly. "Nothing is certain. But you are here now."

He stared at his great aunt for a while. He nodded. "Very well. If you say I must train and learn to control this thing, this *curse*, then I will train. As for the rest, let's see. I can't promise you anything, except that I'll try to learn to use it. But I'll not hide from you the truth: One day I hope to be rid of it. If there is a way, I will have this thing out of me."

Urd opened her mouth as if to speak, but Queen Faldira raised her palm and said, "So be it. Your training will begin on the morrow."

2
UP IN FLAMES

"Curse those dung-eating Torrlonders. Curse their bloody ancestors and all their bloody kin. We'll stab those suckers of hairy goat teats and bleed the whoreson bastards until we wipe them from our land." King Balch unleashed a string of curses as the scout hurried away, and he scowled at Duke Anarad as if challenging him to disagree. The duke, of course, knew better, and he limited his response to a smile and a nod.

Balch was in a good mood. He and nearly three hundred of his loyal men waited in a patch of forest on the northern edge of the Briufaen Hills, which lay in the far east of Adanon, his kingdom. At least it ought it to be his kingdom. It *was* his kingdom. Just because the Torrlonders and their beasts had destroyed or occupied the four major cities of Palahon, Dwarioth, Harieth, and Galathon and controlled most of the countryside, that did not make Adanon theirs.

He and his followers clung to the hills and the wastes, living in hardship and scarcity while endeavoring to remain a thorn in the side of the Torrlonders. It was working. By Oruma and Anghara it was. They would drive out the invaders and their damned white-robed priests or die trying. *Rona was right. This is the way to go. Win or not, we'll gain glory. Never let it be said we gave in. And if those pig-licking Torrlonders win, we'll give them naught but ashes to rule over.*

Balch smiled as he thought of his queen. He had left her and their three sons safely tucked away deep in the Briufaen Hills, where the Torrlonders would never find them. He thought back on all the hardships. The first week had been the worst. The escape from Palahon had been a narrow thing. By the Father and Mother's luck, when the attack came on their chief city, he and Rona had already departed with the three princes to hide them from the approaching foe. When the dragons and Torrlond's army arrived, they were well away from Palahon. From afar they had watched their city burn in the night, but Queen Rona's determined eyes never looked away once until she said it was time to move.

Since then they had lived from the land, at times even reduced to begging from faithful villagers who pretended not to know whom they fed. Rona was a good woman, never complaining once about living a crude life in the wilderness when her true place was in a palace. In truth, she was the inspiration behind the Adanese resistance. *Woman's got more backbone and wits than all my barons and dukes put together.* But there were good men with him too. Men who bled and died for him. For Adanon.

Balch glanced at Duke Anarad crouching in the brush at his right side. Like the rest of them, Anarad was a bit worse for wear. He had been a strong and wise man all those years. Hard as steel, and twice as stubborn. Most of all, faithful. In their youth they had fought side by side many times, and more than once they had saved each other from their foes.

Balch could remember the time when the duke bested four well-trained Caergilese soldiers at once during a skirmish. Had it not been only a few years ago? But Anarad's losses had taken their toll. First his brother and his family. Then his sons, and finally his wife, dead from grief. At least he had found his nephew, young Imharr, who reminded Balch in so many ways of the younger version of Anarad.

In the present, the good duke appeared old and tired. When had grey taken over his beard like that? Living on the run from the Torrlonders had hollowed out the duke's cheeks and stolen some of his bulk. Come to think of it, Balch's own once large belly, which he patted out of habit as he sighed, was all but gone. But men like Anarad were brave and loyal, and that counted for much. He had lost many of them — good men like Duke Gwalor — to those thieving, horse-swiving Torrlonders. But he would avenge them. In fact, a taste of revenge was even now on its way, and that was what put him in a fine mood.

"You're sure about the scout's report?" Not wanting any of his men to overhear, he spoke in a near whisper to Duke Anarad.

With his jaw clenched in a concentrated frown, Anarad gazed out between the leaves in front of their hiding place. Like Balch and the rest of his soldiers, the man wore garments of a dark green hue and had smudged dirt on his face to blend in with the trees. "Yes, Sire. He's reliable. The bait will arrive soon." The man expected them at any moment. Balch well knew the look on his old friend's face. Anarad was tense with readiness, like a nocked arrow.

"Everyone in position, then?"

Anarad nodded. He looked up in the trees and squinted. Balch followed his gaze, and he could spot few enough of his men among the leaves and branches. A shadow here, an arm holding a bow there. They were well hidden. They had better be. Their only advantage against the Torrlonders was surprise.

It was the priests' beasts that did them in. Trolls, aglaks, pucas, and, most of all, those thrice-damned, bloody dragons. They were the reason he and his men had to strike and run. Strike and run before the foe overwhelmed them. Then hide until they could do it again. They could never take away the Torrlonders' advantage with the dragons. None of his sorcerers could match the supreme priest Bledla's feat of wielding the serpents of the air through the song of origin.

But they could take the other beasts. Balch's best sorcerers had succeeded in seizing control over a few of the trolls, aglaks, and pucas from the Way's priests, turning the monsters on their former masters. Small victories, but Balch would take any victory. He glanced over at Nalhad on his left.

"Ready?"

The sorcerer was already trembling, and his wide eyes looked haunted, but Balch paid no heed to that. Nalhad had proven his worth in several raids. Perhaps the most powerful of Balch's sorcerers, he was the most adept at taking over the trolls the white-robed priests commanded. The scout had reported a troll among the Torrlonders pursuing their men. Nalhad knew what he needed to do.

A bald man whose dark beard was just beginning to grey, the sorcerer exhaled as if he had been holding his breath for a minute. "Ready, Sire."

Nalhad was clad like the rest in woodsman's green clothes since his usual robes would have been conspicuous and a hindrance in the forest. He had also smudged dirt on his face, though Balch could not help but reflect that the fellow still looked as if he would be far happier locked up in his chambers back in Palahon with a candle and one of his precious books for company. Balch too missed the comfort and security of his castle walls. *Well, we've all found ourselves in a place we never wanted or expected. No point in dwelling on it. Just take back what's ours, and spit on the Torrlonders' stinking corpses.* Sweat beaded on Nalhad's forehead as he closed his eyes and began to chant under his breath in the ancient tongue of sorcerers.

King Balch grunted in approval and turned back toward Anarad. No fear was evident there, only determination. This raid had been the duke's plan. Balch was not sure it would work, but they had to try something. They were growing increasingly desperate as the Torrlonders tightened the noose. The plan was bold: They would use their weakness to entice their foes and then catch them by surprise.

Their enemy's supply trains going into occupied Galathon were most vulnerable where the road skirted the Briufaen Hills. The Torrlonders would expect a raid, so they would guard those supply trains well. Indeed, according to the scout, nearly five hundred soldiers accompanied by one white-robe and his enthralled troll guarded this particular large convoy. There was something of value there, of a certainty. Whatever it was, he aimed to take it from them.

Balch had sent a contingent of fifty mounted men to raid it, but it was only a feint. The fifty men, under the command of Baron Turnan, were to have made a half-hearted attack and flee from the Torrlonders. They were even now riding hard toward the forest, and, according to the scout, the Torrlonders had taken the bait. Nearly all the mounted soldiers, somewhere around half the escort, had broken from the convoy to chase the Adanese raiders.

Balch had known they would pursue his men since the Torrlonders were under orders to exterminate the resistance. *Let them think we're weak, and then we'll spring the trap.* His force of three hundred men was waiting in the trees for their prey to ride among them. Turnan and his men were to gallop along the forest path and then turn on their pursuers to make what would appear to be a last stand. That would cause the hemmed in Torrlonders to pause, and then his men would strike from all sides. *We'll fill them with arrows first, then surround them.*

It should work. If all went well, he and his men would wipe out the Torrlonders in the forest without suffering many losses. Then they would strike at the convoy with its weakened defenses and seize some much needed supplies and horses.

For it to work, Nalhad needed to wrest that troll from the priest. Such a monster could tip the balance in a skirmish. The scout said the troll was with the soldiers pursuing Turnan and his men. Unlike aglaks and pucas, trolls could keep up with horses. And they were fierce in battle. In one of the first raids, Balch and his men had filled one of the hairy monsters with spears before it went down. Prior to that, it killed more than a score of his followers.

Not this time. Once Nalhad took over the beast, the sorcerer would turn it on the bloody Torrlonders. Balch grinned in anticipation of the looks on their faces. Nalhad's whispered chanting grew more intense, and the sorcerer still clenched his eyes shut.

A faint rumbling rose in the distance. Duke Anarad shifted his stance and cracked his jaw. Nalhad continued chanting, and the strange words seemed to tumble out faster. Balch told himself he felt no fear. *Desperate men can't fear. They do what they must or die.*

Still, his damn hands were shaking, and he hoped no one heard his teeth chattering. Was it fear, or was it eagerness? *I'm quivering like a green boy with his trousers down before his first whore. Hell, it doesn't matter. Just look like a leader, and kill some of those swinish Torrlonders.*

A slight warm breeze caressed the leaves, and Balch reflected how strange it was to be on the verge of such violence on a pleasant late-summer day. *The land cares not. It'll drink all our blood. But it's* our *land, not theirs. Those sister-swiving beasts don't belong here.*

He growled, partly to stop his teeth from chattering, partly in anticipation of killing some Torrlonders. His hand stopped shaking when he grasped the hilt of his sword. He would draw it only when it was time. The smallest flash of steel could warn the Torrlonders. He and his men had even taken the precaution of wrapping their weapons in rags to avoid any clinking that could give them away. Everything depended on surprising the Torrlonders and springing the trap at just the right time.

The pounding of hooves grew louder, and the ground beneath Balch began to tremble. His pulse responded to the hooves. That would be Baron Turnan and his men. Oruma and Anghara grant that most of them were unharmed. Turnan was a good man. He had volunteered for the task, knowing full well he and his men would be the most exposed.

Horses charged by like a sudden thunderstorm, and King Balch crouched lower in his hiding place behind the trees. Through the leaves he caught flashes of the steeds' flesh and glints of steel from the weapons and byrnies of their riders. The ground shook under him. Most of them were still riding if he was any judge. *Good. We'll need every last man to drive out the bastards.*

A seeming earthquake of hooves followed. The enormous rumbling sent shivers through Balch's body. The Torrlonders had arrived hard on the heels of Balch's men. That would make it difficult for Turnan and his lads to swing around. No matter. He and his soldiers would tear the Torrlonders to bits.

He glanced at Duke Anarad, who was gazing at someone high above him in the trees and awaiting a signal. The duke's eyes widened, then he turned to Balch and nodded. Anarad's face seemed to hang there for an eternity, waiting for him to do something. He noted the intensity in the man's dark eyes, the lines on his brow, the frown on his fierce face. Strange how sharpened everything became in the instant before combat. Hell. It was time.

Balch unsheathed his blade and, as he brandished it high, yelled as loud as he could: "Archers! Loose!"

The air filled with the buzzing of arrows, and soon after followed a series of grunts and screams. Balch waited until several more volleys landed, then he shouted, "Charge! Kill the bastards! Kill them all!"

Sparing a glance behind him, he observed that Nalhad was still crouching down and chanting with his eyes closed. The sorcerer would do his job. Now it was time to fight.

Balch and Anarad emerged onto the wide forest path with dozens of their men swarming in front of them and behind from the trees. Ahead, beneath the canopy, the mounted Torrlonders wheeled their horses around in disarray. Many of the soldiers in their grey kirtles held shields over their heads to protect them from the falling arrows. But this left them open to the attacks from Balch's foot soldiers, many of whom wielded pikes and spears to stab the Torrlonders from their mounts. Already quite a few of the foe were unhorsed and writhing on the forest floor. On the other side, Turnan and his men would be engaging the Torrlonders. All was going according to plan. But where was the damn troll?

A deep, ear-splitting bellow seized Balch's attention even as he ran toward the melee. The bodies of a half dozen of his men flew in the air and splatted like fluid-filled sacks against tree trunks and branches. *There.* The huge troll loomed into view up ahead on the right.

Fifteen feet of muscle and hair, the monster roared again and displayed its yellow fangs. In its wild brown eyes was the threat of wrath and destruction. Its shaggy, matted hair waved as it wreaked havoc among Balch's men. Huge and gnarled muscles rippled under its bark-like, wrinkled hide, which showed on its upper arms, thighs, and buttocks. Wielding one man's limp body by the legs as a club, the troll swung into the Adanese ranks. Bones cracked, and three more bodies flew.

"Make haste, Nalhad!" screamed Balch. But the king's thoughts did not linger on the troll. A group of unhorsed Torrlonders rushed toward him with swords raised and snarls on their faces.

Six of the grey-kirtled soldiers ran toward Balch. Anarad and two Adanese soldiers stepped up beside the king. The duke yelled defiance and swung his sword at the closest attacker. The Torrlonder's upheld sword sparked as Anarad's blade ricocheted off it to crash into its bearer's helm. The foe crumpled.

The next Torrlonder lunged for Anarad, but Balch ran in and thrust his blade, piercing the man in the face. Sharp steel ruptured the jelly of his eye and sank in deep before scraping on the bone of its socket. Blood welled from the man's face, and he screamed for only a moment before falling and writhing with his hands clutching where his eye had been.

Anarad parried another man's sword thrust then kicked his opponent's feet from under him as he rushed in with his weapon extended in front. The Torrlonder hit the ground hard, and Anarad's blade pierced his unprotected face with a spray of blood and teeth.

Metal clanged as Balch's two other soldiers engaged with the other Torrlonders. Balch gritted his teeth and hamstrung one from behind, slicing his blade deep into the flesh of the man's thigh though his breeches, which flooded with red. When the grey-kirtled man gasped in agony, Balch's man shoved the tip of his sword through the Torrlonder's throat. Gore rushed out.

Balch turned around. The remaining Torrlonder stood over something. The man hacked at the prostrate body of the other Adanese soldier who had come to help the king. He moved toward him.

Anarad reached the Torrlonder first. His sword smashed into the side of the soldier's head with a blow that bit through his indented helm. The soldier flailed as his body jerked in the air and then dropped to the ground.

"Ha!" yelled Balch. That felt good. But things could go ill if Nalhad did not wrest the troll from the Way's priest. He looked back where he had last seen the monster.

A huge grin took over the king's face.

The troll was smashing grey-kirtled Torrlonders, tossing their carcasses like rags and crushing their flesh into pulp. Blood splattered and ran down the monster's arms, legs, and chest like the sweat of battle. Its eyes rolled insanely, and its cavernous roars promised death as it wheeled and swung in a macabre dance.

Balch's men stayed clear of the beast, and elsewhere it appeared they were gaining the upper hand. Few of the Torrlonders remained on their steeds, and they fought in small knots of men without any order or direction. More went down as arrows sprouted from their limbs and necks. The Adanese surrounded them and drew in for the kill. Most of the Torrlonders were already fleeing the battle when they could have saved themselves by forming ranks. *They've no stomach for the fight. No matter. We'll hunt them down like animals.*

"Press them! Close in! Kill every last one, and show no mercy!" screamed Balch as he ran toward a circle of his men closing in on three wounded Torrlonders. The king turned to Duke Anarad and laughed in triumph. "This is butcher's work! Sweep the scum from our land!"

Anarad nodded and lifted his reddened blade.

Balch turned back to look for Nalhad. The sorcerer approached him with a smile on his face. The king returned the smile. "Excellent!" he shouted. "Let's see how the Torrlonders like their beasts now!"

The sky darkened. A vast shadow winked across the forest floor, swallowing the little patches of sunlight in gloom as it passed, and the air rushed overhead in a gale so loud that Balch reached for his ears. Leaves hissed and trembled in the wake of the wind, and a moment later, a giant ball of fire hurled down and exploded on top of the troll.

"Shit! Bloody fuck!"

Chaos erupted. Nalhad went down on his knees shrieking, and the troll screamed in horrific agony as greedy flames roared and engulfed it in an instant. Eerily it clutched all around as if drowning. The tormented creature writhed and spun like a large shadow inside the raging conflagration. The sickening stench of burning flesh and hair invaded the air, and the monster's crazed, haunted bellowing filled the forest.

"Bloody, bleeding fuck!" cursed King Balch. "Dragon!" He turned to Anarad. "We must regroup. To the . . ." Arrows buzzed all around them. One punched into Anarad's shoulder, and the duke grunted. Balch stared at it with open mouth and bulging eyes. More arrows flew. A sudden, sharp pain lashed across the king's thigh, but there was no shaft embedded in it. Only a bloody rip in his breeches. An arrow had nicked him, giving him a scratch. But what was happening? Why were their men shooting at them?

The answer came in the form of newcomers in grey kirtles. They emerged from the forest behind them with bows, spears, and swords ready for the kill. Some were mounted, but others had alighted from their horses to shoot their bows. The trees were swarming with them. Hundreds of them.

Balch froze. He realized why the Torrlonders had withdrawn so easily. It was a trap. They had known the dragon was coming, and a lot more Torrlonders had followed from behind. Either the convoy was much larger than reported, or these soldiers had been lying in wait somewhere. Either way, they had known all about the Adanese ploy. "Oh fuck." A trap around a trap. "Treachery and villainy! Retreat! Retreat!"

Close to the Torrlonders, Nalhad staggered up, his hands pressed to his head as if in a drunken swoon.

"No!" screamed Balch. "Stay down, you fool!"

Nalhad jerked forward. A bloody spearhead jutted out of the sorcerer's chest, and an instant later an arrow tore out his throat in a spray of blood. The man went down on his face with shock-widened eyes.

Fire poured down from the sky. Missiles flew from everywhere at once. Men screamed. The Adanese began to run in every direction, but Duke Anarad shouted at Balch's side, "To me! To me! Stand fast! Stand here!"

Several men obeyed the command, and more followed. Soon Anarad had gathered three dozen, most led by his nephew Imharr, who was in charge of a company of soldiers. They hid behind trunks as arrows rained past them. More fire burned a huge swath of the trees, and shrieking men rolled on the forest floor aflame. Anarad and Balch crouched together behind one large elm. The duke grimaced with the arrow protruding from the back of his shoulder, but he gazed with a fierce grin at Balch. "Sire, it's time for you to leave. We'll be your rearguard."

"No. I won't leave you behind."

"Don't be a fool. Without you, there's no resistance. I beg you to bear witness, my king: Imharr is my heir. Now, go!" The man waved his sword as if he meant to use it on Balch. "Imharr! Hool!" he shouted at his nephew and the soldier next to him. "Flee with the king. Protect him with your lives."

Imharr opened his mouth to protest, but his uncle cut him off. "Do as I say! There's no time."

Gazing intently at Anarad, the young man trembled but nodded.

Balch stared at his faithful duke. "I will avenge you."

"Go!" Anarad stood at his full height and screamed, "Charge!" He held his sword aloft and dashed toward the Torrlonders. The men he had gathered followed him into the hail of arrows and spears.

Balch swallowed his grief and rage and said to the two young men, "Come. We live another day for Adanon." Imharr's pain was plain on his face, but he joined the other soldier and his king as they ran from the approaching Torrlonders deeper into the forest.

Clusters of Adanese and Torrlonders still fought all around them, many rolling on the ground, grunting and tearing at each other's faces in a desperate bid to live. Another enormous spray of roaring flames descended. Trees crackled. Bodies screamed. Several fires burned in the forest, casting dancing shadows amidst a ruddy glow. Even with the buffer Anarad and the others were providing, arrows rained down.

Balch charged through a wall of flames with his two men. They emerged on the other side and helped pat down the flames on each other before moving on. The stink of smoke and death was everywhere. At least the smoke would provide some cover. *Precious little good that'll do if the serpent of the air spots us. Oruma and Anghara grant that some of my men escape.* The king fought down a wave of despair. *Bloody disaster. Someone must've told the bloody, goat-swiving Torrlonders. That cursed troll was their bait for Nalhad. Damn them all.*

Balch and his two men ran. Soon he was sweating and breathing hard, but he kept running. He blinked and ducked as a branch swatted his face and scratched his cheek. The screams of battle were growing fainter, but he knew pursuit would come. The Torrlonders would round up and kill as many as they could. And with the dragon flying overhead, it would be difficult to evade them. *Run. Run harder.*

It would take two days to reach their camp on foot. He hoped someone would get there sooner to warn Rona and the others. If the Torrlonders knew about their ambush, what else did they know? Eyes stinging from the smoke, his heart pounded and his lungs burned as he gasped for breath and choked. He forced himself to keep running.

Balch and his two men, hardy young fellows both, kept up a good pace throughout the day. The one named Hool seemed a quiet, dependable sort, but of course there was no time for discourse as they fled. Imharr, whom everyone called "Silverhand" for the strange-hued scarring on his sword hand, had proved one of their most capable fighters. A good fellow to have around. His grief for his uncle was nearly palpable, but he never complained. Balch shared that grief, both for Anarad and for all his lost followers. The day was a disaster, but they would recover somehow and avenge their losses.

They found a spring to drink from, but Balch's belly felt like it was digesting itself for lack of food by the time night was falling. Fearing pursuit, they dared not hunt for game, but they found a rotten tree stump with grubs inside it. They used their swords to chop away layers of wood and expose the wriggling creatures, which they grabbed as fast as they could and popped into their mouths. Balch's fingers trembled while digging for his meal. Dread of the Torrlonders surrounding them competed with his hunger, and the waning light made it difficult to see his tiny prey. He fought the urge to vomit as the mucus-covered grubs squished between his teeth. All three men grunted and breathed loudly during their meal at the stump in the dim forest. *Like pigs at a trough. This is what the Torrlonders have reduced us to. We'll survive, damn them.*

It occurred to Balch that if survival was his greatest possible act of defiance against the Torrlonders, then he was in a desperate place indeed.

They rested beneath a thicket that night. Nightmares haunted the half-sleep that Balch drifted in and out of. The forest throbbed with the sounds of creatures of the dark, and the three men jumped at every new noise — each one could have been the Torrlonders catching up to them.

At one point, terrified screaming from somewhere in the forest pierced the night and jerked the king awake. Cackling, high-pitched shrieks resembling human laughter followed.

Pucas. They must have caught some poor bastard on the run from the battle. The cunning trackers were the real danger now. The Torrlonders often let loose the nasty nocturnal beasts, and they would be sure to sniff out the three weary men in time. Balch and his two soldiers would not know the nightgangers were upon them until their sharp teeth sank into their flesh and dagger nails sliced into their eyes. The king resolved to rest a little longer before moving on. He was sure he would not sleep anymore.

Somehow, Balch awoke with the morning light. Hool was yawning and stretching next to him. Imharr, who had the last watch, crouched nearby and leaned on a tree, his face fixed in a stony expression that conveyed grief, rage, and determination all at once.

"Your Majesty." Imharr nodded. His voice sounded gravelly from exhaustion. "If you're ready, we had best get going. Before the sun rose, there was yelling in the distance. Too far off to know who, but it didn't sound friendly. Our first task is to get you to safety."

Balch nodded. "Aye." This young fellow was a good man, like his uncle had been. The sort he he would want by his side in the wilds with all sorts of mad beasts and swiving Torrlonders on his tail.

Fighting through the haze in his mind, the king thought about rising and wrinkled his nose. He could hardly stand his own reek: he smelled of sweat, smoke, and blood. His body ached from lying on the damp ground, and when he moved the leg that the arrow had grazed, it burned with pain. The muscle in his thigh near the wound was stiff, and the flesh around it felt puffy and stretched.

He sat up with a groan and examined the wound through the tear in his breeches, poking it with his index finger. The flesh was red and angry, though it was hard to tell how infected it was due to the blood caked around the gash in his thigh. *Shit*.

They kept trudging in the direction of their camp deep in the Briufaen Hills. Due to Balch's wound, which burned more fiercely as the day progressed, he walked with a limp up and down the steep hills. They found little to eat that day — a few green acorns that upset their stomachs more than anything — and Balch began to sweat with a fever as the wound throbbed more and more.

Pain radiated all over his leg, and he grew so clumsy that he stumbled now and again. Soon his damn lungs seemed to contract, and he began to feel not enough air was entering them. His breathing grew hoarse, and he noticed Hool and Imharr exchanging concerned glances.

Trying to forget everything but the need to keep moving, Balch kept his weary eyes on the legs of Imharr, who took the lead. But the king's fever grew hotter until his tongue felt too large for his mouth and his whole body throbbed with pain. The bone beneath the rotten flesh of his thigh seemed aflame, and his breathing diminished to a gasping wheeze.

At length, while they rested beneath a fir, Imharr looked the king in the eye. "Your Majesty. Hool and I were talking. That wound of yours is bad. We need to have it cleaned properly."

Balch grunted. He glanced down through the tear in his breeches. The arrow wound was seeping white pus now, and his whole thigh was grotesquely swollen. It also stank like a week-old corpse. The king was finding it difficult to speak as his fever sent spikes of pain through his brain. Sweat dripped down his brow and soaked his clothes. "When we . . . get to camp."

Imharr looked uncomfortable for a moment, pursing his lips and gazing at the ground. "Begging your pardon, your Majesty, but it's unlikely the camp's there now. Someone must've gotten word to them. It was time to move on anyway."

Balch grunted with the effort it took to form words. "What are you trying to say? Out with it."

Imharr displayed no fear at the king's scowl, just that same determined look engraved on his face. "Hool says there's a village south of the brook we passed a mile back. Just outside the hills a spell. The brook will lead us to it." Hool was from around those parts. He knew the land well enough, but any village was a deathtrap.

Balch's eyelids fluttered. It was becoming so damn hard to think through the pain, let alone speak. "Torrlonders. They'll be . . . looking in the villages."

Imharr and Hool looked at each other with nervous frowns. The former answered, "That may be, your Majesty. We'll have to chance it. You might not make it otherwise."

"Damn you." The boy was right, but that did not mean Balch had to like it. The king choked and succumbed to a fit of coughing. He was not certain he could resume breathing after the fit, but the wheezing started again.

The two young men looked down at their hands. Balch was too tired to be angry with them. He just wanted to lie down somewhere comfortable and die. *Damn it all. Poor lads. They're just trying to keep my foolish old hide in one piece.* The king sighed. "Alright. Not sure I can get up from here, but we'll take a peek . . . at this village of yours. Perhaps we'll find it empty of Torrlonders . . . though I wouldn't bet . . . your old granny's dried up turd on it."

The two young men hoisted up the king. When he rose to his feet, the ground swam under him, and he would have collapsed without their arms holding him up. Leaning on Hool and Imharr, who half carried their king, Balch hobbled back toward the brook they had passed.

Though it was only a mile away, it felt like an eternity to reach it, and every step was agony as veins of pain shot up and down his leg. Sweat dripped from the king, and the trees swirled all around him. His head ached so hard he thought it might explode. By the time they reached the brook, Balch could go no further. The king dropped to the ground and gasped for breath. He never wanted to rise again. Voices bent and careened nearby, and sometime later — it seemed like a long time had passed — Imharr's face swam before him.

"Stay here with Hool, your Majesty," he thought it said. It was hard to tell since the voice sounded so warped and fuzzy in his ears. "I'll just go check to see if the village is safe."

As if I could bloody well go anywhere. The face disappeared, and Balch stared up at trees wavering above him. They swayed in a slight breeze, and the sky above them was a deep blue. One could disappear in that blue. *What if the Torrlonders are there? What if they kill him, or torture him to find me?* wondered some part of the king's mind with a little stab of panic. *Shit. I'm dead anyway.*

. . .

VAGUE IMPRESSIONS OF A JOURNEY SOMEWHERE BRUSHED THE periphery of Balch's senses. A group of shadowy people hovered near him, and hands grabbed him by the arms and legs to raise him onto something with a hairy back. A donkey? Yes. He knew that smell. He slumped on the back of a donkey, but he had no idea how long he was there.

Then there was darkness, punctuated by a terrible pain in his thigh. Squeezing and burning. Digging down into his bone, ripping apart fat and gristle and muscle. Had he screamed at that pain? Yes, he must have, for he remembered his throat being torn and raw. Something burned him. His flesh was afire. Of course: the fever. But what fever raged so intensely? And the burning found a focus in his throbbing thigh . . . Darkness took him again.

His senses came back when he awoke on a bed of straw in a dim hut.

Balch blinked and listened to the sound of his own breathing for a while. Light bled under the crooked door of the simple hut and spilled inside, allowing him to view his surroundings. There was not much to see: four soot covered walls, a thatched roof supported by bent rafters, some crude pots next to a fireplace, and a couple of stools. A look behind him revealed one open window, which did little to alleviate the smell of smoke and grease in the hut.

Sitting up with a groan and removing the blanket or patched up cloak that covered him, Balch found he was wearing only an old but clean tunic. He raised the tunic far enough to stare at his aching leg. A bandage made from a clean white rag was wound around the thigh, covering his wound. Fresh blood had soaked into the portion of the bandage over the wound, making a long red splotch on it. The swelling and burning in his leg had subsided somewhat, and it no longer throbbed quite so much.

The village. We made it. Must get out now. Must find Rona and the boys.

The door creaked open. Imharr stepped inside. He held the door, and an old woman in a patched up frock with a twine belt walked in.

"Good to see you awake . . . Gorlan." Standing behind the old woman, the young man gave King Balch a ridiculous conspiratorial wink.

Balch rolled his eyes. *At least he had enough sense not to tell them who I am. 'Gorlan' must be his horse's name or some such thing.*

"We owe much thanks to the villagers here. Mara here patched you up nicely." Imharr's momentary smile made the king want to curse and inform him just how "patched up" he felt.

The old woman too smiled at Balch, revealing not a tooth in her head. "Took some hot iron to that scrape of yours, I did. And not a moment too soon. But now it's best you're off. Torrlonders'll be looking for the likes of you. Already visited here once before you arrived."

Balch's eyes widened and looked at Imharr.

The young man nodded. "The villagers know about the battle, Gorlan. The Torrlonders ordered them not to help any of us soldiers, but they're faithful to Adanon. Still, we can't risk staying here long. Something else you should know: Mara's grandson said he knows the direction of King Balch's new camp. I sent the boy to see if he could find them. Might be a scout will pick him up. I gave the boy a message. Told him to say *we're* here. They'll know where to find us . . . Gorlan." Imharr's next wink preceded the most foolish grin Balch had ever seen.

King Balch didn't know whether to shout at the idiot to stop grinning or to jump up and hug the young man. *If he calls me 'Gorlan' one more time like that . . . Ah, but he's done well, keeping me alive. There's yet a bit of hope, then.* "Thank you." His voice was raw and grainy still. He cleared his throat and turned to the old woman, who was bent over with age but clearly happy to have helped Adanon's cause. "And thank you, Mara. I'm in your debt."

"Hmmm," said the old woman as she looked him in the eye. "Might be I'll remember that. *Gorlan.*"

Damn. She knew. Of course she did. A sliver of fear stabbed Balch, but pride in his stubborn people overwhelmed it. They knew who he was and the risk of helping him, but they did it anyway. He smiled and nodded at the old woman in understanding. As soon as he was well enough, he needed to leave.

The door burst open, and a breathless Hool stopped only to shut it behind him. "Torrlonders! They'll be here in a moment. We've got to run."

Imharr's eyes widened. Balch felt like a cornered deer. Only Mara remained calm. "Not on that leg, you won't. Not a chance they won't catch you."

Balch's fists tightened as he gazed at the old woman. It would only be right to spare her and the other villagers what was coming. He would go and meet these Torrlonders before they reached the village and die fighting them. At least the villagers might be saved that way. He reached to his side for his sword, but of course it wasn't there. *Caught in nothing but a tunic. Damnation!*

Mara's eyes hardened. "Strip. All three of you."

Imharr squinted and frowned. "What?"

"If you want to live, strip. And stay here. I'll return in a moment."

A DOZEN TORRLONDER SOLDIERS IN GREY KIRTLES DESCENDED ON the village. The men clinked in their byrnies, and they bore spears as well as swords. Three had bows. Even worse were the accompanying white-robed priest and the six pucas he wielded. The priest had a pinched, sour face and oily hair, but the beasts he controlled were the most frightening aspect of the invading party.

Dark green flesh covered their wiry, muscled little bodies. Sharp teeth exposed in a rictus, they hissed at the frightened villagers while herding them, crouching and running about in sudden, jerky movements, sometimes on their hind legs and sometimes on all fours. Their yellow eyes glowed with malice, and their pointed ears were set back on their heads. Everywhere they went, they snuffled at the ground and at a few of the Adanese villagers, who shivered and cried out as the beasts pawed them.

While the pucas crawled from hut to hut sniffing at each dwelling, the soldiers rounded up the remaining villagers, pounding open their doors, cursing them, and shoving them into a trembling circle at the village's center. There were only fifty or so of them: women, old men, and children — the men of fighting age were all gone. A woman screamed as a soldier wrung her by the arm and pushed her into the crowd. Children sobbed while their mothers tried in vain to soothe them. Some looked around as if in appeal for help that would not come. Others gazed down at the ground before them in an effort not to look the Torrlonders in the eyes.

Among the villagers hunched King Balch, Imharr, and Hool. In fact, they were huddled in the midst of the old women, each wearing a frock and a shawl, using the latter to cover their beards. Mara had improvised the disguises quite well, considering how little time there had been. She and a few other old women also wore shawls and covered their faces so that Balch and his men would not be the only ones. The disguise *might* work. Balch was short enough to pass for a woman, though he had to be sure to keep his thick beard under the shawl. At least he did not need to pretend to limp, and the effort of standing left him feeling dizzy and feeble. Imharr and Hool were tall for Adanese, but by Torrlonder standards they were at most average, and each stooped to look smaller. Still, those two were the tallest old ladies present by nearly a head. Balch rolled his eyes. *Mother's tits. We don't have a flea's fart of a chance.*

The broad-shouldered soldier who appeared to be in charge began yelling at the villagers in the Northern Tongue. Balch knew not one of them would understand the words.

"Right, you ragged bunch of shit-kickers! We know some of those Adanese soldiers came here. Our little trackers never lie. Tell us where they are, and we'll spare you. If not, it would be but a moment's work to gut the lot of you. Might be we'll give some of you to the pucas for sport."

Several of the other soldiers chuckled at this idea.

"Out with it, then, you sorry savages!"

The anvil-jawed Torrlonder approached an old man, who kept his eyes steadfastly on the ground. "You! Where are the soldiers?" He towered over the old man, whom he grabbed by the arm and shook. "Soldiers! Where. Are. They?" he yelled, as if screaming would make the villager understand. "Bloody idiot." A back-handed blow sent the old man sprawling on the ground.

At this the pucas grew excited and let loose a round of hideous cackling. Shuffling on all fours, they neared the old man, who staggered up and gazed with wide eyes and quivering lips at the approaching beasts.

The leader of the soldiers growled. "Let's try this another way, then. Might as well have a little fun out of it. Eh, lads?"

The other soldiers laughed.

Balch knew that laugh and what it meant. There was no mirth in it, only lust. Men were the cruelest of animals — especially those with swords at the throats of the helpless — and war had a way of bringing out the worst in them. Not that there was anything besides the worst in these filthy Torrlonders. *Damn them.* He began to shake under his frock — with fear and rage and weakness all at once, he supposed. He fought the urge to reach for his sword, which he had belted on just before Mara threw the frock over him.

"Your men are all gone," continued the leader. "You poor ladies no doubt need some pleasuring. Don't they, boys?"

"Aye!" said another soldier. "And we're just the men to do it!"

The rest laughed as if the fellow had just said the funniest thing in the world.

With sudden speed the lead soldier grabbed a woman who had two children clinging to her. The woman wailed, and her two waif-like children grasped her frock, but the soldier cuffed them both until they lay on the ground sobbing. The woman continued wailing and clutching for her children, but the lead soldier slapped her face hard and then held her up by the arm. Her eyes rolled up, and blood trickled from her nose.

No! screamed Balch in his mind. If he went for the Torrlonders, he might kill one or two before they laid him low. Nearby, Imharr was looking hard at the lead soldier and trembling, his breaths coming loud through his nose. The young man's eyes were enraged. Perhaps the three of them could . . . *No, we'll die first, then these villagers will die too after the beasts have their way with them. Damn them.*

"You look like you been lonely." The soldiers' commander grabbed the terrified woman's frock in his two hands and ripped it down the middle.

The woman trembled and tried to cover her body by clasping the rent garment. She cried out her daughter and son's names in a despairing, drawn out wail racked by sobs: "Naia! Teg!"

Seizing the woman by her neck with one hand and cupping her left breast with the other, the commanding soldier fleered and declared, "Skinny as a rail, but you'll do. And, until someone tells us where those bloody soldiers are, we'll keep taking another of your women — right down to the grannies."

A low growl escaped Balch's throat.

The Torrlonder turned to his men. "Who wants her first?"

"I volunteer, m'lord." One smiling soldier stepped forward and lifted his byrny in front to get at the belt holding up his breeches.

"Borulf. She's all yours." He shoved the bleeding woman toward his laughing soldier, a big man who threw her to the ground and sat on her as he tugged at the buckle on his belt. When the woman screamed and struggled under him, he slapped her face. Two other soldiers came and laughed as they pinned down the woman's arms and legs. The one at her legs spread them far, and she screamed. Perhaps smelling the blood and fear, the pucas sniffed and grew agitated as they circled around and chittered.

"Ooooh, I like 'em like that!" said Borulf. His leer revealed several gaps in his teeth.

Oruma take me. Him first, thought Balch as he glared at Borulf. His right hand drifted toward his sword while his left still held up the shawl over his face.

Just then a voice said in the Northern Tongue, "You must be the ugliest old woman I ever saw." It was the white-robed priest of the Way, who stood a few feet from Balch as he stared at the king's half covered face. Suspicion marked the oily-haired priest's narrowing eyes, and his mouth hung open as if he was about to say something.

Damnation. I'm to die in a fucking frock. Balch's leg ached like a demon was gnawing on it. He would probably go down before landing a blow, but he no longer cared. He growled as he dropped the shawl and went for his sword, hiking up the frock to get at it.

The priest's countenance changed, but it was not the look Balch expected. There was wide-eyed surprise for a moment, but something else followed: pain. The white-robed man winced, clutched at his head with both hands, and screamed as he crumpled into a heap on the ground.

Balch scowled at the man. "I'm not *that* ugly."

The commanding soldier turned toward the writhing, moaning priest with a puzzled frown. "What in Edan's name?"

Understanding widened his eyes. "There's a bloody sorcerer nearby! They've got the pucas!" He unsheathed his sword and jumped at one of the wiry beasts, severing its head in a spray of blood. The other five pucas leapt and attacked the Torrlonders, snarling and clawing with the razor nails on their three-fingered hands.

At the same time, arrows buzzed. Several sprouted from the Torrlonders, who grunted and screamed. One hit Borulf, who had managed to get his breeches down and was lifting his byrny, and burrowed deep in his bare ass. The large soldier shot up screaming as the woman beneath him scrambled backwards.

His shrieks grew even more desperate when a puca lunged at him and clamped down on his dangling genitals with its sharp teeth, shaking its head to rip loose its gory prize. Blood fountained from the mutilated, frantic man, who squealed like a stuck pig as the puca gnawed and clawed open his exposed belly. Shiny innards spilled out. When Borulf went down writhing, the nightganger lifted its bloody face to the sky and released a triumphant, throaty laugh.

Balch, Imharr, and Hool unsheathed their swords and advanced on the Torrlonders while the villagers fled in every direction. The grey-kirtled soldiers had turned their backs on the villagers, so it was an easy thing for Imharr and Hool to slay two of them by chopping at their necks, splashing blood and snapping bone.

When the two bodies collapsed, the Torrlonders' commander turned around and recoiled at the three bearded men in frocks with swords raised. "You!" he said with rage in his eyes. He shot toward Balch as others turned around to engage Imharr and Hool.

Damn! Too weak even to hold a sword. Knowing the end was nigh, Balch screamed and raised his weapon in defiance. Steel clanged, but it was not Balch's blade that parried the Torrlonder's sword.

Imharr stood before his king, holding off the Torrlonder. The bigger man struck at Balch's defender again, but Imharr Silverhand was quick, even in a bloody frock. Damn him, the lad was quick!

He dodged and parried, angering the Torrlonder further with a slash that left a red stripe on the man's cheek. Men yelled and steel clanged elsewhere, but Balch gasped and leaned over with his hands on his knees as he watched Anarad's nephew, whom he was too weak to aid.

The Torrlonder screamed and attacked, but Imharr leapt aside, pivoted, and swept his sword at the passing soldier. The Torrlonder turned and readied himself for another attack, but then he seemed to realize Imharr's blade had contacted his neck. His hand went to his throat, which squirted red from a long, deep cut. With widened eyes, the Torrlonder raised his sword again, but a metallic ping shook his head from behind. His face slackened, and his eyes rolled up. He teetered and fell forward, planting his face into the ground with a hard crunch as his armor clattered. An arrow stuck out of the back of the man's skull, having punched through the helm. He was the last Torrlonder to go down.

Balch looked around. A large party of his green-clad soldiers had approached from behind the huts of the village. Fifty or so of them stood around the scene of carnage. They must have snuck up while the Torrlonders distracted themselves with their "sport." Served the bastards right.

He checked to make sure Hool was alive. The young man stood over the body of the white-robed priest, from which Hool pulled his reddened sword. *Good. That one won't send any more beasts against us.* The foul pucas were all dead too.

The young mother the Torrlonders had been about to rape stood up shaking, weeping, and holding her hands to her bleeding face. Someone hobbled toward her offering a shawl to cover her ruined frock. It was Mara. The old woman covered her and held her by the shoulder as she led her back toward one of the huts, where Balch guessed her two children were hiding. He hoped to find a way to thank Mara someday. *Good woman.*

He turned toward his soldiers. Feeling ridiculous in his frock and leaning on his sword so that he would not fall, Balch gave up on appearing dignified when he addressed them. "Thanks be to Oruma and Anghara!" His voice was more wheezing than commanding, but it would have to do. "You men came not a moment too soon. Who leads you?"

A woman's voice declared, "I do."

He knew that voice better than any other. Queen Rona stepped forward from behind one of the huts. A village boy who had been standing next to her ran toward the hut in which Mara disappeared. *Her grandson*, thought Balch. *The one Imharr sent. Thank the Mother and Father.*

Rona walked thirty paces to Balch until she stood before him. Balch could have melted in her arms, except that she was eyeing him with a mischievous grin.

"You look terrible in a frock."

Balch growled. "Aye. And I feel worse than I look."

She smiled before she leapt forward and embraced him, and he leaned on her and kissed her, not caring who saw. "You're a gorgeous sight for my weary eyes, my love," he said when he released her. He looked her in the eyes. "And you're the reason I carry on."

She scoffed as if to dismiss her importance and then looked down at his leg. "You're wounded. There's someone here who can help."

Balch looked over Rona's shoulder and saw a strange man approaching. Clad in a green cloak and green and brown garb that was elegant though designed to blend into the forest, the man was slender and tall. He wore his dark hair long and kept his face shaved in the manner of the easterners of Eormenlond.

Balch released Rona and leaned on his sword again as the man drew up within a few feet. Now that he was near enough, Balch saw strands of grey in his hair, but he was still a handsome man.

According Balch as much dignity as he might have had the king worn his finest garments instead of an old village lady's dirty frock, he bowed and said in the Northern Tongue with an Andumaic accent, "King Balch. My name is Lord Vilyanad of Asdralad. Queen Faldira has sent me as a messenger and a harbinger of future aid. The queen is raising an army even now, and she intends to send a portion of it here to fight the Torrlonders."

This man was a sorcerer. The noble houses of Asdralad were full of them. And he was powerful in the gift, for he it must have been who seized the pucas from the priest of the Way. "My thanks to you, Lord

Vilyanad. I would fain discuss this future aid with you, but now I fear I am too weary even to stand much longer."

"Your Majesty is wounded, I see. I am a skilled healer and will be able to assist you."

"That would be welcome. Most bloody welcome."

3
THE LAST SURVIVOR

Deep in the Wildlands and south of the Ironwood, a lone man rode a grey stallion. With his fiery-red hair, fur cloak, long fur boots, long wool kirtle of a green hue, and thick leather belt, Munzil was the perfect image of an Ilarchae warrior. Like many of his brethren inhabiting the Wildlands, he wore no breeches and kept his hair tied behind his head with a strap of leather pierced by a bone needle. And, of course, he carried weapons: a knife in his left boot, an axe tucked into his belt, and a broad sword in a scabbard at his side. Of average size for an Ilarchae man, he knew from his travels that he would have impressed folk elsewhere as a large and intimidating figure. But Munzil was not like most other Ilarchae, a fact that presented itself to him every day in the waking world.

To begin with, he was alone.

Being alone meant he had to be wary. Munzil was long used to watching his own back. He had not survived this long by being a fool. Not that it made him feel any easier now. He was entering the territory of the Blood Spears, a tribe known for their ferocity and bravery. The Blood Spears were among the largest tribes of the Ilarchae in the Wildlands, and they had won great renown in battle over the years. Tales of their warriors' deeds reached the ears of the other tribes, and the cry of their war horns inspired fear and confusion in their foes. Yet, if what Munzil had heard proved true, none of these facts would save them.

He had come to see for himself. If the rumors did not err, this could be the time. The man they spoke of could be the one. Munzil had to see him first to know. He needed to see the man in action. The coming battle was an opportunity to do just that, and he had ridden many miles through many dangers to witness it.

In order to avoid capture by other tribes, he had stayed closer to the Ironwood than most would have dared. Any number of things on its fringes — wolves, nightgangers, trolls, aglaks, elves, or one of the forest's lonely, twisted monsters — could have killed him. But the gods had spared him. Most would have feared the dreaded Ironwood too much to undertake such a journey, but death could take nothing from Munzil. In whatever form it came, he would greet it like an old friend.

Several days ago, when he reckoned he rode nigh the territory of the Blood Spears, he had turned south toward the lands in which folk dwelled. Since then he had met not one living soul. Plenty of the dead, though.

Three villages of the Blood Spears he had ridden through, each like the others: burned to the ground and filled with corpses. The stench of war was familiar enough to Munzil — the smoke and the rotting bodies — as was the gathering of carrion crows and buzzing flies all over the slain. He did not mind the company of the dead. The lone god, Siedvar, would see to them all, as he had so many Munzil had known over the years. In fact, each village's charred ruins had brought a grim smile to his lips. *He might be the one. He just might.*

It had been easy to make his way toward the brewing conflict. The burned out villages were like an arrow pointing in the right direction, a trail of death leading to his destination. And now, on the horizon, Munzil could make out the gathering of crows and the four columns of smoke promising battle. *Not yet begun, perhaps. At least it's not over yet.* He dug his heels into the horse's side, and it sped into a gallop. *Time to see if the tales are true. Let's see what the man's made of.*

Munzil rode hard until he deemed it too risky to ride at a gallop.

He did not want to miss the proceedings, but he also did not wish to become wrapped up in the battle. *Need to find a good place to watch from.*

He rode toward one of the many bare, gentle hills inhabiting the landscape. Ever present on these rolling plains, the wind kicked up and howled as if it meant to claw him off his horse. The grass for miles around bowed in giant waves and ripples. Based on the nearness of the approaching crow-clouds and the drifting smoke, he guessed the battle would be taking place on the other side of this wall of swellings in the land. Swiveling in every direction, he kept a wary eye out for scouts as he prodded his horse up the hill.

Long before he crested the wind-swept hill, the roar of the multitudes on the other side reached his ears. Munzil had seen plenty of battles, and he had no intention of becoming entangled in this one, but the din still sent shivers through him. No way to be this close and not feel that thrill and fear. After alighting from his horse and hobbling it, he walked the rest of the way up the hill, crouching low as he neared its summit despite muscles sore and weary from all the riding. *No point in making my presence too obvious.* He had a good idea what he would see on the other side, but it still took his breath away when the view opened up beneath him.

In a vast, level valley surrounded on every side by hills like the bottom of a giant bowl, two armies faced one another so that the two ends of the plain were seething and boiling with bodies. Since both sides would have agreed on the location, it afforded no tactical advantage to either. Strength, courage, and the gods would decide the outcome. Two giant bonfires flanked each army. The air around the flames wavered with their heat, and their smoke rose to the realm of the gods. By common consent, the sacred fires designated where each army should stand at the battle's start. Each side would have performed animal and human sacrifices in those conflagrations, but in the end, the victor would put out the loser's two fires.

The assembled villages and clans of the Blood Spear tribe occupied the side of the valley closest to Munzil so that he stood nearly behind them as he gazed down. Above the sea of fighters jutted the usual sorts of totems of the clans affixed to long, wooden poles. There was a troll's skull, a warg skin, a bear skin, a boar's skull, and a cloak made of something black — perhaps raven feathers. Five clans, then.

In addition, hanging on another pole by a rope around his neck, the tortured and bleeding body of a naked man swayed in the wind. It was hard to tell for sure from such a distance, but Munzil guessed someone had performed the blood eagle on the man. This would have involved carving him open from the back, cracking open his ribs at the spine until they resembled gruesome wings, and pulling his lungs out through the wounds — all while he was alive. He must have been some captured scout or warrior from the other side.

Like other tribes of the Ilarchae, the Blood Spears performed the ritual to ask for the gods' favor in battle. They were going to need it. A large tribe, their warriors, including those women who chose to fight alongside the men, appeared to number more than three thousand. Impressive. But not enough.

The foes of the Blood Spears — those who had come to take their land and their wealth and make them thralls — swarmed on the other side of the valley. Far off to their right, in the folds of a hill, they had picketed their thousands of horses. The tribes of the Wildlands seldom fought on horseback. They preferred the solid ground beneath their feet and the personal valor of the foot soldier. The army was too far away for Munzil to make out much detail, but he knew one thing: There were more of them than there were of the Blood Spears. Mayhap as many as six thousand.

It was a huge force. Seldom had one war-leader among the Ilarchae been able to gather so many under his command. It was a good sign. One had to be a strong leader to sway so many. Munzil stroked his red beard as he took it all in. *He might be the one.* He would need to await the outcome of this battle to know for certain. It was one thing to gather a large force and another thing to lead it. His dealings with the outlanders had taught him that.

The two hordes chanted war songs in an effort to whip themselves into a battle fury. It would not be long now. Munzil could not hear the farther army, but the words of the Blood Spears' slow song floated up to him as thousands of voices raged, "Death! Death! Death to our foes! Death! We are coming! Death!" Between the roiling bonfires the sea of warriors stirred and shifted in no particular formation. The bravest and most eager would be at the front of the battle lines. As they banged their spears on their shields, some of them tore at their hair and wheeled around in a crazed dance. A few of the more animated ones even gnawed on their shields as they let forth feral screams.

Wolfhides. Those big warriors were working themselves into a frenzy so intense they would feel no pain for the duration of the battle. Neither bite of sword nor blow of axe would stop them until a mortal wound felled them. Many would fight on after losing a limb. Most of them would die. Munzil smiled at the Wolfhides. The soft, little folk huddled in their cities of stone in the kingdoms to the south and west of the Wildlands were right to fear such warriors devoted to death.

Crows, ravens, and eagles wheeled overhead. The chanting of the doomed throngs below swelled to the heavens along with the smoke from the sacred fires. The presence of the gods touched Munzil's awareness. In that valley was a great gathering of strength and courage. And though none of the glorious victors or slain knew it yet, Munzil was their brother. *I am alive. The gods have kept me so for a purpose.* The Ilarchae, as the outlanders called them all, were a mighty people. In their ignorance, the stone-dwellers thought of the many tribes of the Ilarchae as all the same, as one people. Mayhap it was time they thought of themselves that way too. *The time is approaching.*

The battle lust below reached a fever pitch. With goosebumps covering his flesh, Munzil could feel when it was ready to burst like floodwaters smashing a dam. He had to wait only a little longer until the war horns began cleaving the sky. Dozens of them wailed the call to death. To Munzil's ears their sound was seductive. The multitudes rumbled and roared as they surged forward in a wave of grim ecstasy. It vibrated all over his body — a divine, mad rush into death's embrace.

No volleys of arrows preceded the clash of armies. Unlike the cowardly stone-dwellers, the tribes of the Wildlands disdained the use of bows in battle since even a weakling could kill with one. It took no courage to kill a man from afar, and there was no glory in it. Only a fool would sing songs of a warrior who killed in such a way. Far better to face your foe and look in his eyes when one of you joined Siedvar on the last journey. That was a deed worthy of a song.

A big man at the forefront of the Blood Spears lifted a long spear as he ran toward his foes. Its steel tip glinted when the warrior cocked his arm back. With his cast it sailed high and far, well behind the foe's front lines. It was a gesture of defiance, a vow to dedicate the slain to Roknar, chief of the gods. All the warriors the spear passed over were potentially part of the sacrifice, but the man who threw it had to make good on his vow by killing them. Thus, it was a boast that the warrior now had to fulfill. That spear thrower must have been a great champion. Munzil would keep his eye on him.

The spear arced downward, and in the midst of the Blood Spears' foes the warriors parted to make room for its landing. One huge man, however, stayed firm. As other warriors moved away, he waited alone and dropped his shield to the ground. Adjusting his position so that he stood where the spear would land, he raised his hands before him as if preparing to wrestle with the oncoming projectile. The weapon sailed straight down toward his chest, but at the last moment he leapt aside and, with alarming speed and dexterity, snatched the spear's shaft before it landed. The warriors all around him broke out in deafening cheers.

Every warrior of the Blood Spears halted his or her advance and froze. All would have recognized the meaning of such a portent. It was nothing short of the gods' declaration. The Blood Spears were doomed.

The man who caught the spear bellowed and brandished the weapon in challenge to the entire army opposing him. Then he rushed onward, and his exultant warriors closed in and followed him toward the foe. The distance was still great, but Munzil could tell the man was a giant even among the Ilarchae. And he was clad in black: exactly as the tales described him. It was him. *He is the one. The gods have shown him to me. What clearer sign could there be?*

The meeting of the armies was as the jolt and long roll of echoing thunder. Steel clanged and grated on the iron rims and bosses of the round linden shields. Men and women screamed in rapture and terror and pain. The storm of swords and hail of spears had begun.

For a long while, all was anarchy as the front lines ground against each other and the warriors behind strove to come at the foe. Fresh corpses fell, and the living trampled them underfoot. Those in the thick of the press had little room to maneuver. They stabbed and tore at each other in a swarm of bodies. But Munzil began to discern the tide of the battle.

Wedges of warriors broke through the front line of the Blood Spears. Even more ominous for them was the fact that the larger army was beginning to outflank them on both sides. If their foes succeeded in surrounding them, the Blood Spears would not last long.

Munzil admired them. They gained much honor through their hopeless struggle — more than if they had really possessed a chance at victory. The catching of the spear had been the clearest possible sign, yet they fought on without flinching in the face of certain doom.

In the middle, where the largest wedge of warriors broke asunder the front line of the Blood Spears, the huge warrior in black wielded that spear as well as his great sword in a whirlwind of death. A ring of his warriors surrounded him, but they allowed a couple Blood Spears through at a time to encounter the black clad man, who chopped and slew them in quick succession.

On they fought. The din of battle assaulted Munzil's ears, and he watched without blinking as more of the combatants succumbed. Men and women raged and screamed and perished. The sun had not moved far in the sky when the battle's outcome grew clear. Broken bodies lay in skewed positions all over the battlefield. Except for the cloak of raven feathers, the totems Munzil had seen earlier hoisted atop their poles lay trampled in the mud and blood. One at a time, the other four had teetered and fallen when a group of the foe's warriors surrounded their bearers and left nothing living in their wake.

Engulfed by foes on every side save behind them, the Blood Spears refused to retreat. Instead, they died. Small pockets of them fought on back to back as their foes closed in. Their champion who had thrown the spear to dedicate the slain to Roknar was still alive. He had killed at least a score of warriors, and he made his way closer to the black clad man. The latter waved his arms and screamed orders to his followers, who left the champion of the Blood Spears unmolested and parted before him to give him a clear path.

Munzil smiled. *Yes. This will decide everything.*

Across the field they eyed each other. The two massive warriors paced forward. With a scream, the champion of the Blood Spears sprinted toward his foe.

The man in black waited for a moment, and then he planted the spear tip in the mud before charging forward. Now each had only a sword. The singers would be sure to mention how the two fought on equal terms. *More glory to the victor.*

The giant warriors careened at full speed toward each other. At the last moment, each swung his big blade in the air. They met with a shock of steel, and they grunted when their huge bodies slammed into each other. Both men kept their footing, but the champion of the Blood Spears stumbled back a few paces before planting his boots firmly. His foe advanced and slashed, but he sprang backwards. These men were not just big. They possessed deadly speed as well.

As word spread of the unfolding duel, the rest of the field ceased fighting to await the outcome of that clash. Silence seized the valley. Standing side by side with those who strove to kill them only moments before, the warriors of both armies stared, tense and eager to witness what would live forever when the singers passed it on.

The two warriors locked eyes and circled one another, each making sudden feints to test the other's reaction. Nothing decisive happened, but everyone seemed to be waiting for the moment. Rare was the day among the peoples of this world when two such champions met in deadly dance. Transfixed, Munzil stepped forward and forgot everything else while he watched. *They're waiting for the right time.* One could not plan for it, Munzil knew. It would come. They would know when it did.

Quick as a striking snake, the black clad man surged forward. In a blur of motion, their big blades rang out once, twice, thrice. Their swords flashed in the sunlight, and, from his distant perch, Munzil heard each knell moments after the blades met. The champion of the Blood Spears parried well, but with each blow he stepped back a pace. He was a fraction of a moment slower than his foe. Blood flew from his thigh with the next sweep of the blades, and he stumbled.

Another series of clangs, and the black clad warrior caught him in the shoulder. Though the byrny would have blunted the blow, the sword's edge could have bitten through or at the least bruised the flesh by crushing the mail into it. Either way, it slowed the champion.

The two men swung and wheeled and clashed, at one point locking swords. Like two giant bears, their massive frames leaned against each other, but the champion of the Blood Spears began to quiver and bend backward. He growled with the strain, and then he lost his balance.

His foe took advantage of the moment and shifted his weight to one leg, which he stomped down with sudden force on the champion's knee. The leg bent the wrong way. As far away as he was, Munzil heard the gristly pop a moment later, when the man fell to the ground. An agonized scream followed.

When the wounded warrior managed to rise on his one good leg, a white sliver of jagged bone jutted out of the other leg's calf above his boot. The limb hung and jiggled at an odd angle.

The black clad warrior waited for his opponent. The moment he was up and balanced on his one leg, he smashed his face with a fist. The wounded man tumbled back down like a felled tree.

Dazed and shaking his head, the champion of the Blood Spears struggled to rise again on one leg. He staggered up by leaning on his sword. He mostlike did not see his foe's blade coming. Munzil would have missed it had he blinked.

The blade disappeared in the man's chest, and he cried out as his body shuddered. He still managed to hold his sword in one hand. With his other hand, he grasped the blade jutting from his ruined body and held it. It must have sliced deep into the man's hand, but it did not matter. He had one goal: to hold his foe's blade so that he could strike him. Crying out in agony, the dying champion swung his weapon toward the other man's head.

The black clad warrior caught his arm before the sword fell. He held the arm where it was in mid-swing for a moment as it trembled. The two adversaries stared at one another, the one with his blade buried in the other's chest, and it struck Munzil as an oddly intimate moment.

The champion of the Blood Spears screamed once more, and in his cry Munzil heard defiance in the face of defeat. The champion's sword tilted over and dropped in the mud. His head sagged to one side. As he fell backward, his foe withdrew his sword from the ruined body. When the corpse hit the ground, the one still standing bellowed in triumph.

At the same time, the shoulders of the remaining warriors of the Blood Spears sagged. Many dropped their weapons where they stood. The battle was over. They and their kin were thralls now. Their tribe no more. At best, some of them might hope to buy their freedom someday, or perhaps earn it through some worthy deed. But this was the day when the Blood Spears would pass into memory. They were one of the many tribes in this world to have struggled for supremacy and lost. That struggle would go on until life ended in the last battle.

Munzil nodded. He knew what it meant. He well knew the sense of doom those warriors were feeling. Thralls they might be, but they had gained honor this day.

A few of the Blood Spears — most of them the remaining Wolfhides, no doubt — kept fighting. They would die soon.

Munzil stood from his crouch, turned around, and walked back to his horse. Shortly it would be time to meet the man he had ridden so far to see.

WITH ALL THE BUSTLE IN THE VICTORIOUS ARMY'S CAMP, MUNZIL was able to ride quite close before anyone took notice of him. Already sounding drunk, groups of warriors greeted their conquest with competing songs and cheers. The singers were offering impromptu accounts of the battle, embellishing them with the usual formulas. Campfires crackled and smoked, and the savory odor of roasted meat wafted in the air. Among the knots of carousing warriors were clusters of animal hide tents. There were thousands of the temporary dwellings on the plain, and they were mostlike laid out by village and clan. No doubt some of the warriors who had brought their mates or found new ones were celebrating inside those tents.

One of a group of three sentries spotted him. The one pointed toward him, and the others gazed in his direction as their bodies tensed and stood a little straighter. They did not look like they were about to welcome him.

As Munzil rode closer to the sentries at a trot, he began to wonder if he had thought this all through properly. The camp of an army fresh from the rush of victory could be a dangerous place.

As if to confirm this thought, voices rose in anger. Behind the sentries and near a campfire, a tussle had broken out over something, mostlike claims over spoils or thralls. Horns of mead splashed on the ground, swords flashed out, men shouted, and in a moment someone lay bleeding on the ground while someone else spat and shouted curses over him. Others restrained the man, but his victim, who coughed up gouts of blood, would never rise again. *Their blood's still hot,* thought Munzil. *Too late to turn back now.*

Those sentries did not appear friendly at all. Especially the hulking woman, who glared at him as if pondering the best way to kill him. He dismounted and held his hands up in the air, palms forward in token of peace.

The woman and the two men next to her advanced toward Munzil. She stood the tallest of the three and took up the middle position. Over her torso she wore mail and a long kirtle. Her blonde hair was braided and tied behind her head, and she had a nasty scar running across her left cheek. The intensity in her bright blue eyes told Munzil it would not do to trifle with her, and her big jaw seemed chiseled out of rock as she scowled at him. Wearing a mask of calm, he had to overcome the urge to back away from her.

She did not stop pounding towards Munzil until she stood looking down at him inches from his face. "Who are you?" she demanded as she unsheathed a big sword. She had just eaten some meat with roasted garlic and washed it down with mead, to judge by her breath. "Speak, little man."

The two men stood on either side of her with icy stares, and their hands grasped the shafts of their spears, so Munzil deemed it would do little good to appeal to them. He thought it best to keep his hands raised, but he did not cease staring her in the eyes, lest she guess how intimidated he felt. "I come with an honorable purpose. I seek your war-leader."

The wind rushed out of Munzil's stomach when her fist crushed it, and he could not help letting a grunt escape as he buckled over.

"I asked who you are, not why you're here," said her voice above him.

When he could stand straight again, he forced a smile. "Munzil is my name."

Her eyes narrowed, and her voice went cold with the threat of violence: "Of what tribe?"

Munzil swallowed before answering, but he stood tall and declared, "I am Munzil of the Grey Wolves."

Her eyes widened just a bit, and she smiled as if anticipating how much sport she could get from killing him. "The Grey Wolves are long dead, fool. The Bear Fangs killed them all twelve winters gone. And whoever you are, you'll be joining them for lying to me."

He did not flinch as she began to raise her sword. "Not *all*. They traded the survivors to the southerners. In Sildharan the rest died trying to win freedom. I alone escaped some ten winters ago. I am the last of us."

The woman lowered her sword a bit, but she wrinkled her nose and spat. "Pah! An escaped thrall? A man with no tribe? You must be telling the truth since no man would lie about something so pathetic. You can offer nothing to us. You are nothing." She shoved him, and he staggered back a few paces. "Begone, little beggar, or I'll add you and your withered manhood to my tally of today's slain."

He stood his ground. "You're wrong. I have something worthy to offer you all, and I must speak to your war-leader."

Her eyes took on an almost vacant look, and she smiled as she stepped toward Munzil with her sword up.

This one likes to kill, thought Munzil. He did not draw his weapon, but he raised his hands again in token of peace. *I must speak with him. I didn't ride all this way for nothing.* "I can't fight you, woman. I need to speak with your war-leader. If he's the man I think he is, he'll want to hear what I have to say." He backed up as she brandished her blade and clenched her teeth. "The gods have sent me, damn you!"

"What's this, Skuld?" The gravelly voice belonged to a huge man who approached from the campfire where the man had been killed in the earlier quarrel.

The big woman's sword froze in the air for a moment, then she lowered it. Her furious gaze never left Munzil as she answered, "A beggar. A flea that wants scratching. A little man who wants to die."

The man loomed over even the woman by a head, and he was broader in the shoulders than an ox. He too was blond, and he had braided his thick beard. Wearing a helm and a byrny, he walked up to the fierce woman with his hand on the pommel of his sword and an amused smile across his face. The two men with spears parted to make way for the newcomer. "He says the gods sent him. What's he want?"

"To meet Siedvar. I was about to grant his wish."

Munzil broke in, "I am Munzil of the Grey Wolves. I rode here from west of the Ironwood to speak with your war-leader. I have something important to say to him. The gods have given me a vision, and it concerns him."

The huge man regarded Munzil for a moment with his bright blue eyes and the same amused smile. "Very well, then, Munzil of the dead Grey Wolves. I am Gorm, chieftain of the Boar Clan of the Fire Dragon Tribe. I'll take you to our war-leader. But if you do not satisfy him that you're not wasting his time, you may wish I had let my little sister Skuld kill you."

MUNZIL WALKED BENEATH A VAST TENT MADE FROM ANIMAL HIDES stitched together with leather thongs and stretched on a network of long timber poles. Openings on all four sides allowed plenty of light to enter, but since the sun was setting, braziers added their glow and their smoke to the tent. Feasting men and a few women, all warriors who took part in the battle, occupied several rows of tables with benches. They ate, drank, laughed, sang, shouted, quarreled, and caroused as thralls weaved between the tables with pitchers of mead. A few of the feasters spared Munzil a curious glance as Gorm led him, and many more greeted his huge guide with loud cheers, but they returned to their celebrations shortly after.

Amidst the tumult, Munzil followed Gorm to the back of the tent, where thirty or so warriors stood around a man sitting on a large oak chair. The chair had to be large, for on it sat a man who mostlike outmatched even Gorm in height, though this man's muscular body was harder and leaner. Even as he lounged in the chair, he had an intensity about him that suggested great energy. He was made for glory, and Munzil judged that commanding loyalty was his natural right.

This could be none other than the man Munzil had felt compelled to ride so far to see: Surt. No longer clad in his battle gear, the legendary war-leader still wore a black kirtle, while his cloak and boots were made from the furs of black bears. His hair, which he had tied behind his head, was dark for a man of the tribes, a chestnut brown hue, and so was his beard. The descriptions Munzil had heard, though they seemed the exaggerations of tales, were true.

Holding a horn of ale in one hand, Surt laughed and conversed with the warriors standing around him. His deep voice and the force of his laugh hinted his anger was as quick as his mirth. In his eyes, though he was still a young man, Munzil saw wisdom. Even more important, the smiling faces of his followers showed their burning loyalty. This was not the slavish subservience the cowardly stone-dwellers displayed to their preening monarchs. The free among the Ilarchae were all noble, and leadership fell to those who proved themselves most worthy. Even the thralls among them had a dignity and courage seldom seen outside the Wildlands. Their faith grew out of the bonds their deeds formed, for their leader offered protection and rewards in return for valor and action.

Munzil did not need to hear the man speak. He could see it. *He is the one.* Still, he would need to explain himself.

Gorm paused when Surt called one of his warriors to approach him. Munzil waited behind his guide.

"Vitar. Come here, you rangy bastard." The war-leader spoke with a grim smile, and there was laughter in his keen eyes. The other warriors chuckled. One of them, a tall, thin fellow who could not have seen more than eighteen winters, stepped forward with a smile.

"At your command, War-leader."

"I saw what you did today." Surt nodded and grew serious as he gazed at the warrior before him. "Three. That's how many you slew in the span of as many breaths. It was well done, and while warding me."

"It was my honor to stand among your guard."

"And how many in all did you send to Siedvar this day?"

"Twelve at least."

"By the gods. Did they die well?"

"They all fought to the last."

"Did they now? And this was your third battle?"

"Fourth, War-leader."

"Fourth. Very good. You fought bravely. Come here."

As the young man approached and went down on one knee, Surt reached to his side, where a large wooden box with an open lid rested on the floor. The war-leader dug inside the box with his hand, and metallic objects jingled inside it. After a moment, he drew out a slim gold arm ring. "Your arm."

Vitar smiled and held out his arm, on which Surt slipped the ring. When he finished, he tousled the lad's straw-colored hair, slapped his shoulder, and laughed.

"Well done, Vitar. The Fire Dragons will remember your courage, and we will count on it in future battles."

"Yes, War-leader."

"A draught for Vitar!" Surt lifted his drinking horn.

The other warriors responded with a cheer and took a deep drink from their horns.

After the young man rose, he rejoined his companions, who thumped his back and stared with cheerful admiration at his glittering arm ring. Surt's gaze turned to Munzil's guide.

"Welcome, Gorm. You bring us a guest?"

Gorm stepped forward. "This man came riding to our camp from west of the Ironwood, he says. He says the gods sent him, and he wants to speak with you."

Surt's dark eyebrows rose. "The gods?" His eyes locked onto Munzil, who held his breath as he waited. "Who are you, and what do the gods want of me?"

Munzil did not blame Surt for the skepticism in his voice. He would need to be convincing now. Everything depended on this moment. For so long he had wondered if it could be accomplished. Now the answer was so close, sitting here before him in the form of this man, whose discerning eyes gazed at Munzil, weighing him.

Munzil knew. *It is him. He is the one.* His courage grew along with his conviction.

"Hail to you, Surt, War-leader of the Fire Dragons." With his fist Munzil pounded his chest over his heart in greeting. "I have ridden far to see you. I am Munzil, last of the Grey Wolves. My folk are all dead, and I am a man with no tribe, but the gods have kept me alive for a task. Today is the day I fulfill it."

The war-leader grunted. "Hmm. You have my interest. You were the man on the hill watching our battle today."

It was a statement, not a question. Munzil had not been sure anyone had seen him. Little escaped this man. It would be best to use great care in his answers. "I was, War-leader. Your victory was a great deed, and the singers will spread word of it over all the tribes."

Surt gave a wry half-smile. "And how do you deem the Blood Spears conducted themselves?"

The warriors gathered around their leader grew silent and gazed at Munzil. Everyone seemed to know the importance of his answer.

Munzil stood straight and declared, "With great honor. They fell in defense of their land and freedom, and I saw no cowards among them. The champion who faced you was one of the mightiest fighters I've seen. He died a true warrior's death. Great is the glory you gained in defeating him."

Several of the older warriors nodded in approval. Surt's dark eyes gazed at Munzil, and then he too nodded. "Gundar was a good warrior. The greatest of the Blood Spears. Very brave."

"I had not known his name, but it will live long."

"Aye, that it will." Surt's eyes narrowed as he appraised Munzil. "At least you know how to use fair words, Munzil of the Grey Wolves. I will hear you out. But before you speak of your purpose, I will know more of you to make a true deeming. To begin, you will tell me how you lived when the Bear Fangs slew your folk in battle."

Munzil blinked in response to the question and all it implied. Of course he would need to explain that. He drew a deep breath before beginning. "I did not survive through cowardice. In the battle that broke my people, I took three grave wounds. When I fainted through loss of blood, I thought myself dead. I awoke a thrall of the Bear Fangs. By the time they nursed me back to health, they had already traded the remnants of my people to the southerners in the kingdom of Sildharan."

Surt nodded. "Hmm. Go on."

"When I was fit enough, the Bear Fangs thought to keep me as a thrall. But I begged them to trade me to the Sildharae as well. My wife and children were among those they had traded earlier, and I wished to be with my people, even if it was in thralldom."

"Children, you say? How many had you?"

Munzil paused with the pain of memory. "Two. A daughter of eight winters and a son of five. They were the only ones who survived birth. They were dear to me." Images of his red-haired children came into Munzil's mind. Inga had been as beautiful and bright as her mother, and Erzil had been a clever little mischief. Some wounds never healed.

A few of the older warriors around Surt nodded with understanding. Most tribesmen were fond of their children. Those who had lost their own would know some of Munzil's pain.

He cleared his throat. The difficulty of telling his tale surprised him. It had been more than ten winters since it passed, and he had spoken of it to no one. Surt stared and waited for him to continue, so he obliged. "By the time I arrived in Sildharan, they were dead. It took me many months to discover the truth of what happened."

"And what did happen to the Grey Wolves in Sildharan?"

Munzil could tell Surt knew. The man guessed this was the heart of the matter. He might not know Munzil's exact purpose yet, but he was shrewd enough to suppose it had something to do with the demise of the Grey Wolves. *Now I must show them.*

"As you know, many that once belonged to the tribes of the Wildlands are now slaves in Sildharan. Some in the outlander kingdom of Golgar as well. The southerners do not treat our kind with honor. They are greedy for the fruit of our labor, but they regard us as the lowest of beasts. They use as thralls some of their own dark-skinned kind as well — those taken in war and those who fall into debt or poverty — but they give them the easier tasks and keep them separate from us. For the people of the tribes they keep the worst and most difficult toil, things none of them would do for themselves, and many of them are cruel masters. But the worst is there is no redemption from thralldom for us. They give us no opening to buy or win our freedom. They give us no chance to win back our honor. The people of the tribes who are slaves among them can own nothing, and they breed our kind like animals. Once a tribesman is traded as a thrall to their kingdoms, he will be a thrall until he dies from exhaustion or beatings. There is no hope. There are even some of our kin who have been born slaves there for generations, and they are truly beasts. Such wretches know nothing of the way of honor. They know only the meagerness of their short and brutal lives."

"This is common knowledge throughout the Wildlands," said one of the warriors standing near Surt, a big young man with reddish hair. "It's the price some pay for defeat." His sneer said he thought Munzil a weakling who deserved his fate.

"No," said Munzil, his voice trembling with passion. "*Thralldom* is the price of defeat. I do not blame the Bear Fangs for destroying my folk in open and fair battle. The gods spoke. But we tribesmen do a twisted thing when we trade our thralls to the southerners. In doing so, we condemn them to the worst dishonor. No brave foe deserves it. It is no thralldom of the sort we know. They would make us worse than beasts. The Sildharae despise us. To them we are not men, but tools. There is no release from such disgrace but death."

Surt gazed at Munzil with narrowing eyes. "And so the remnant of the Grey Wolves died."

Munzil nodded. "Yes. They were all traded to a great lord among the Sildharae, one of their holy men. The man held vast lands and had many soldiers under his command. He ordered his overseers to work our folk to the bone. Many died under his cruelty. The rest died when they fought for freedom. Even the children. Better than living as animals."

"And what of you? How did you escape?"

"The Bear Fangs traded me to a different master among the Sildharae, an officer of their army. When I heard of where the Grey Wolves were, I tried to escape him and join my family and my people thrice. The third time, my master decided to grant my wish and gave me to the holy man who owned the rest of the Grey Wolves. On that day he laughed at me, knowing full well my new owner was a far crueler man than he was. When I arrived, I learned what had befallen the rest of my folk. Other slaves from the Wildlands told me about the uprising of the Grey Wolves. My folk fell with courage."

"So you ran away with your wolf's tail between your legs and skulked back to the Wildlands," said one of the young warriors. He looked at Munzil with a contemptuous smirk.

Munzil gazed at the man and then gave him a teeth-baring smile until the warrior looked away. "No. I stayed. I toiled. I bled. And I feigned obedience until the Sildharae believed me broken. Then, after a summer and winter had passed, I did my duty. I, Munzil, avenged the Grey Wolves."

He paused to take in the looks Surt's warriors were giving him. Most wore curious frowns. A few lowered their brows with suspicion. Surt's blade-like gaze was impossible to read.

Munzil continued, "The Sildharae holy man had a weakness. Their greatest holy men and women often have no mates, but this one . . . He made a habit of ordering his soldiers to bring him one of our women for his pleasure."

Munzil swallowed. He would not tell them how he had heard the *sorcerer*, the outlander word for a holy man, had forced his own Uva to be one of those women he raped before she died with Inga and Erzil and the rest of the Grey Wolves. Some secrets he would keep. "After his soldiers beat the woman, they would leave her with him to do as he wished. He did this in the same place every time, a small dwelling on the outskirts of his lands. I found out where, and I escaped my quarters one night when I knew he would be there. I hid in the dwelling with a knife I had stolen and waited. The soldiers arrived first with the woman and did their work on her, stripping her and striking her until she bled. The holy man arrived and bade them go. Once the soldiers left and he began to take his pleasure, I crept behind him and slit open his throat before he could utter one of his spells. While he was still choking on his blood, I cut him open and stuffed his guts in his face. I escaped in the darkness of night and fled to the foothills of the Amlar Mountains. Alone, I crossed the mountains back into the Wildlands. Painful and slow was that journey, and I nearly died more than once."

"What of the woman?" asked Surt.

Munzil sighed. This part of the story he was not proud of, but Surt would know if he lied. "She . . . she told me she wanted to die. The shame of what he did to her . . . It wasn't the first time. She was one of his favorites. All her near kin despised her for it. None of them among the slaves would speak to her. She said I had done a great deed, and that I should escape. She said the soldiers would not follow me if they thought *she* had slain their master, and she was right. As soon as I left, she set the dwelling on fire. She burned inside with his corpse. Her name was Orsa, and she was of the White Fox tribe. She was a brave woman."

Surt shifted in his chair. "And then?"

Years of hardship. So many memories Munzil tried not to think about. He shook his head to banish them. "I survived. In the Wildlands it's a hard life without a tribe, but I found a way. The outlanders want few things from us other than thralls, but two other things we people of the tribes have that they desire: timber and furs. It took me years and much toil, but at length I won a living as a trader. I find the outlanders in the kingdoms of Ellond and Torrlond the timber and furs they want in exchange for goods the western tribes want. I have even learned to speak the stone-dwellers' tongue after a fashion since it helps in my dealings with them."

"A man can live doing such trade?"

Munzil smiled. "I have prospered enough to own two small ships now, and I am well known in the region to the east of Sirukinn's Wall. But that matters naught. My real purpose has to do with something I heard during my last voyage to Torrlond. And with you."

"You western tribes have let the stone-dwellers corrupt and weaken you," said a stocky young warrior with his arms crossed before his chest. "How do we even know you speak the truth? You could be lying about the whole thing."

Munzil looked at the youth and paused. "A fair question." He removed the pin on his cloak and dropped it on the ground. Then he slipped his arms through his kirtle and lowered it to expose his chest and back. He turned around twice so that they all could see by the light of the braziers how his back was a mass of taut, crisscrossing scars. Whips had left some of the marks, and hot iron the others. "That is what the Sildharae do to escaped thralls. And to any they deem too slow in their toil under the hot sun." He raised his kirtle and put his arms back in the sleeves.

Surt's face did not change. He gestured with one hand for Munzil to continue. "Let's hear about this task of yours, then."

Munzil nodded. "While I was in the Torrlonders' chief *city*, as they call the largest piles of stone wherein their people dwell, I spoke with a man I know, what they call a *merchant*, a trader and dealer in goods. He told me something that caught my ear at the time, but I knew nothing of its full weight until later. He told me of the Torrlonders' war of conquest."

"These are old tidings, tradesman," said the same red-haired warrior who had challenged him before. "We all know of Torrlond's war in the south."

"In the south, yes. But it's now an open secret that once Torrlond conquers Adanon, it will turn towards the east. The Torrlonders want more and more land. Their holy men want to rule all the kingdoms of the stone-dwellers so their god will grow mighty. King Earconwald means to conquer Sildharan. The time will come soon when his thousands and thousands of warriors will march east. And they say their chief holy man wields dragons."

"A tale for children. And so what?" said one of the younger warriors with scorn in his frown. "Even were it all true, why should we care what the outlanders do?"

Munzil gazed at his questioner and smiled for so long that the man frowned at him as if he had lost his wits. "Because it gives us something we have long needed. A chance we must seize."

"Speak plainly," growled Surt. "What is your purpose here?"

It was time. They might think him a madman. It did not matter. "Long after I returned to the Wildlands, a vision came to me as I slept one night. The gods sent it to me. It was no ordinary dream. In the vision, I saw a white dragon attacking a vast kingdom, the kingdom of Sildharan. The white dragon was Torrlond, whose white-robed chief holy man, it is said, wields the serpents of the air as weapons. From afar, all the tribes of the Wildlands beheld this dragon, and they waited until another dragon flew over them: a black dragon. Then, marching as one, the tribes followed the black dragon. Like the grasses of the plains were our warriors. And above us flew the black dragon breathing fire like a beacon to light the way. Following the great beast, we came to a vast wall stretching up to the sky. It was Sirukinn's Wall. I know it was, for behind that wall were our imprisoned kin in the kingdom of Sildharan. But the dragon laughed at the wall and roared. With its roar, the great wall crumbled, and we swarmed over it to slay its makers. Joining with the white dragon, we destroyed the Sildharae. Our kin on the other side greeted us, and as a free and glad folk we took the spoils of that land."

Several of the warriors now glanced at each other with raised eyebrows to confirm their opinions of Munzil's madness. Surt's fingers drummed the armrest of the oak chair he sat on.

Munzil needed to explain quickly. *He must understand. He is the one.* "The next day, I heard of you. The tales told of how you lead the Fire Dragons in victorious battle. They told of how you wear black, and of how your warriors follow you with great faith."

Surt's eyes widened just enough to betray his growing curiosity. His warriors began to grumble and murmur that Munzil was witless and should be cast out. Munzil ignored them and kept his gaze locked on the war-leader. "You see it, don't you? War-leader of the Fire Dragons. You *are* the black dragon. The tribes will unite. You will be not just the war-leader of this tribe, but of *all* of them."

The warriors' voices grew louder, and some clamored for someone to slay Munzil where he stood. "Shall I kill him now, my lord?" asked Gorm with a puzzled frown on his face. The big man's hand rested on the pommel of his sword.

"Stay," commanded Surt, and they all fell silent. Even some of the revelers at the other tables quieted and looked over. With his anger plain on his face, Surt could have daunted anyone. "Speak on, man."

Munzil swallowed. It was all rushing out at once, not the way he had imagined saying it, but he knew he was right. "Can't you all see it? No? Well, it took me time as well. I thought when I slew that Sildharae holy man I was finished. I had avenged my folk, I believed. I was wrong. For years it ate at me. Something was . . . missing. I could see it perhaps because I am alone. That is my purpose, I suppose. I am the messenger the gods chose. But you will see it as well."

"See what? What do you speak of?" demanded Surt.

"We folk of the tribes have dwelled in the Wildlands fighting and slaying each other for hundreds of winters."

"That is our way," said a grey-bearded warrior. "There's no greater glory than in battle. It is the ancient way of honor, and we will never change."

"We must change!" Munzil clenched one fist and shook it. "The tribes will cease slaying each other, but we will not cease gaining honor. A common foe will bring us together. The time has come. Think of it. We are *strong*. If all the tribes of the Wildlands fought as one, think of what we could do. But as long as we keep slaying each other in little raids and battles and trading our thralls to the southerners for trinkets, we will trap ourselves in these hard lands. The gods mean much more for us. The outlanders have armies with ten times as many warriors as the greatest tribes have. But think what we could do if we forge the tribes together."

The huge war-leader leaned forward in his seat as his hands gripped the armrests. He did not hide the fascination in his eager grin and in his widening eyes. "How?"

"The Torrlonders' war is our chance. We must not allow them to win the glory of conquering Sildharan for themselves. The vision from the gods was clear: we must ally with them. When they attack the Sildharae from the west, the eastern portion of Sildharan will be open to us. If we attack at the same time, we'll crack open Sildharan between us like a walnut. But first we must be as one. One war-leader must gather all the tribes behind him. We must send messengers to all of them. We'll tell them the time has come to break free of the Wildlands and take the riches of the soft southerners. We'll call for a moot of all the war-leaders, and from them we'll pick the most worthy to lead us all. But I know who it will be. All the tribes must ally with Torrlond under one war-leader: you. Surt of the Fire Dragons."

Surt gazed at Munzil for a long time, stroking his beard and frowning. All the nearby warriors watched their leader until he broke out in a smile and pointed at Munzil. "You're mad, Munzil of the Grey Wolves. You *are* mad, and so are your visions." He laughed.

Several of the younger warriors smirked and nodded in approval of those words.

Surt stood at his full height. "But they say those the gods touch *are* mad. Mayhap a little madness is what we need. Sit down at one of our tables and feast with us. We'll talk of your madness and your visions over a horn of mead or two, and let us see if they begin to make more sense."

The smirks of the younger warriors disappeared.

Munzil smiled at the tall war-leader. He *was* the one.

4
USING ONE'S GIFT

"Gone. All fears, all desires, all sorrow, all joy. Free your mind of all. You are the soil. The trees. The air. Everything. Nothing."

Queen Faldira's words echoed in Dayraven's mind as he slipped into an awareness of the energy surrounding him. For a moment his consciousness floated above him, then it expanded in all directions, exploding until he was no longer Dayraven but a presence in the wind. Above Kiriath he wandered, observing and taking in all the minds swirling and striving in the island's chief city.

More lives appeared even as each of them grew smaller and blurred into one another, as if they were both separate and one. From the smallest ants crawling in the corner of the room in which his body sat to the giant networks of energy contained in the island's forests, the uncountable array of life forms making up the island brushed against Dayraven's awareness. Taken together, they were part of the seamless fabric of the island's past, present, and future, which existed as one entity beyond the cycles of time.

Beyond Asdralad he soared until each life was a mote in the bones and flesh of the land. The island diminished until it was a streak of gold surrounded by blue. A far larger land mass lay across the water to the north of it, curving on the horizon and filled with browns and greens. Over Eormenlond he floated until the sharp stars grew closer, their light pulsing and bleeding into the surrounding darkness as the swarming world below receded to a blue and green and brown mass with swirls of vaporous white hovering above. Life teemed around and within him, part of something infinitely sublime and vast. The realm of origins they called it, though it was not a place in time but a state outside of place and time. It was nowhere and everywhere.

He had once thought of it as the elf-state. Then it had terrified him. He had been wise to fear it. Even now, his mind strained with the effort of not allowing the terror and the bliss to overwhelm him. It was necessary to keep some part of him aware of his individual existence, like a line connected to the little knot of energy he thought of as himself. Strange it was to observe himself in this way, as if he were at once both Dayraven and an infinite presence watching Dayraven.

Still contained in his mind, the elf-shard accompanied him on his journey to the realm of origins. It was both a shadow within him and a vastness that dwarfed him. The realm of origins was a state it knew well, and in most ways it seemed to be a creature of it.

But the presence of the elf also whispered of a state beyond all origins, a nothingness that both attracted and repulsed Dayraven. He ignored the susurrations and kept his wary truce with the elf-shard, which seemed content to escort him on his voyage in a segregated portion of his mind. For the moment, at least, it allowed him to remain in control as he drifted in the realm where all with the gift must go to exercise it.

Without any awareness of what he knew as the passage of time in the mundane world of forms, he nevertheless sensed it was the right moment to return. He allowed himself to make the journey, shedding the strangeness of perceiving all of life at once until he focused only on his own breathing. At first, it seemed someone else was keeping time with slow, deliberate breaths in the darkness. He made the leap to associate the breathing with his body.

Eyes flicked open, and light entered them. He awoke in his body with its bones and tissues and flesh, its coursing blood and steady intakes and expulsions of the surrounding air. Time returned, though he did not know how long it had been since the queen initiated him in the mind-calming exercise. Perhaps the sun had moved only a little, or perhaps it had set and risen again. The elf-shard's breath coiled around the corners of his mind, receding into shadows, but he felt clean and at peace, his senses sharp and crisp.

The meditation exercises came with such ease to Dayraven that it seemed he had performed them all his life. In fact, only a matter of weeks had passed since he arrived in Asdralad, but he made rapid progress as Queen Faldira's pupil once he recovered from his wound and his fatigue. The sense of despair too at what he had lost grew less overwhelming, though it stabbed through to his consciousness at times and throbbed like a dull ache. Urd and Sequara also helped in Dayraven's training, but it was the gentle yet intimidating queen of Asdralad who became his principal teacher, the one who opened his eyes to wielding the gift.

And Dayraven was eager to learn. Guilt over time lost, the destruction of Caergilion, the Caergilese man he had killed in the Battle of Iarfaen, Torrlond's ongoing war in Adanon, and Imharr's near death motivated him. For his first few days in Asdralad, Dayraven's grief and regret were heavy, but the queen helped him find calm. She gave him purpose by showing him first how to live with the gift. He was aware of how this was evolving into a desire to help those now facing Torrlond's War of the Way. Thus grief grew into quiet determination. Having made an unspoken pact with the elf-shard, Dayraven poured himself into training.

And yet, something still held him back. Day and night, the Mark was with him. In this strange, beautiful island kingdom surrounded by azure waters, his yearning for his rough northern home never departed. Like a stubborn, brooding watch dog, this yearning inhabited a hidden piece of his mind and guarded it from all else. He dreamed of Ebba and Father, of Kinsford's folk and its timber halls, of the hills like solid green waves and meadows separating their farmland and common pasture lands from the Southweald. One day he would return. He had to. Dayraven could not bear the thought of never seeing Kinsford again. Surely he could hold on to that guilty hope. What harm could it do, even if he knew he was fooling himself?

He looked around. The small room in Faldira's palace where he exercised contained only the plain rug he sat on. The light streaming through the lone window had dimmed to evening's golden-ruddy glow, indicating his meditation had lasted a long time. Behind him the door clicked and opened. Queen Faldira came in and sat facing him on the opposite side of the rug. Out of respect, he waited for her to speak.

"You just returned."

"Yes, your Majesty."

"Very good. When we weave the songs of origin, we travel where you were in an instant. Without thought we slip into the beginnings. There only can we wield power. Your mind readily goes there, but you must learn to control the journey. You make good progress. Soon you'll begin to learn the songs."

"Mai duinal han," said Dayraven in heavily accented High Andumaic, for he had begun to learn that tongue as part of his training since most lore was written in it. *I am ready.*

Faldira gazed at him a moment, her face unreadable. "You've progressed more than I dared hope," she responded in the Northern Tongue. "Yet grief still drives you. The wounds have healed on the surface, but beneath there's much pain. Because of our need, I've allowed you to learn what most take years to master. But I fear for you, Dayraven. We release power with great care, lest we lose control of it — lest we lose ourselves. In balance lies true mastery of the gift. Great power lies within you, but it will consume you if we're not careful. You'll burn bright and brief."

Dayraven kept his face calm, struggling to hide his eagerness. "As you wish, my lady. I'll follow the path you open to me. But I do feel ready. My grief is there still, as you say, but rather than running before it, I've made it my companion. I know it well now, and having made my peace, it helps me on my way."

Faldira hesitated again as she studied Dayraven, then she smiled. "I'll consider your request, then."

"Thank you, your Majesty." Trying to keep even a hint of impatience from his voice, Dayraven looked down at the floor and said, "The songs of origin . . ."

"Yes?"

"I've been wondering. How is it I wielded the gift without knowing them? I struck the dragon with lightning."

"Not lightning, exactly. In your tongue it is called wizard's fire. In High Andumaic it is *almakhti*, for it is the concentration of energy from the air around the sorcerer or sorceress. Few with the gift, fewer than a hundred in all of Andumedan, have enough power to summon it, let alone wield it. As for how you used it without first knowing the song of origin, in truth I do not know. That is one of the mysteries surrounding your . . . condition. I have been pondering the matter since Sequara spoke of it. Perhaps your unconscious mind heard Sequara utter the words since she attempted the spell just before you did."

Dayraven seized at the explanation. "It might be. When I cut the priest's control over our horses back in Wolvendon, something like it happened. I heard him sing a song of origin first." He frowned with a sudden realization. "But in Hasumere it was different. I never heard anyone utter the song of origin until after I took control of the aglak. The high priest chanted something, but it was after . . ."

Faldira smiled. "Then we must discard that theory. One thing I do know: It is unheard of to wield the gift without using the songs of origin. And, even if it were possible, I suspect it would also be dangerous. Perhaps your encounter with the elf somehow placed the songs in your mind without you knowing it. Rather like inserting memories in you."

Faldira's words were near the mark. The elf *had* inserted something in his mind. The shard of the elf's presence in him hissed its monotonous liturgy of darkness, the constant backdrop to his thoughts and dreams. Perhaps the queen was right, though it gave him little comfort to think of it that way. He decided not to share these thoughts with her for now. He needed to think it over.

"At any rate," she continued, "we will soon begin teaching the songs to you. You must be conscious and in control when you use the gift. Otherwise, the consequences could be disastrous. Traveling to the realm of origins is what allows us to access the gift, but the songs of origin are what bring us in communion with that which we seek to influence in the world of forms. At the same time, they remind us of our separation from that which we wield, thus preserving our awareness of our individuality. Without them, one could grow *lost*."

He nodded. "I understand."

"In the meantime, we are finished for today. Your next lesson will be in the garden at sunrise on the morrow."

"Thank you, your Majesty." Dayraven inclined his head as Queen Faldira stood and exited the room. He sighed and sat for a long while, staring at the door. He was tired. Thoughts of those he had left behind drifted in his mind. What would Imharr say if he could speak to him now? *I need some company.*

He rose and exited the room to emerge in a hallway of the palace. Making his way through the now familiar corridors past a few palace guards standing at their posts, Dayraven reached the front entrance. The guards there nodded in respect, a gesture he returned before walking around the palace over the colorful floor mosaics wrapping around the building's exterior.

At the rear of the palace, he glanced over at the wall of the garden and the cedars rising above it, but he did not linger. Instead, he kept walking until he left Queen Faldira's residence behind for an open, dusty field, whence voices shouted, metal clanged, and wood clacked as several hundred men stood in formations or sparred in small groups. Most of those who gave orders to the training soldiers wore the white of Faldira's palace guards. However, there were two in positions of authority standing out not only because they wore kirtles of blue and green over their byrnies, but also because of their lighter skin and respective heights. One was much bigger and taller than any other man on the field, whereas the other was much stouter and shorter.

For the last several weeks, Orvandil and Gnorn had been busy assisting the queen's guards in training an army for Asdralad. Both seemed content with their task, which bound the two together in a way that made Dayraven smile as he watched them. The Thjoth and the Dweorg were natural foes due to the history of bloodshed between their peoples, but Dayraven's two friends seemed to have made a truce.

They stood next to one another facing a score of new recruits in a line. Most of the trainees held staves, but a few gripped wooden practice swords. The bronze-skinned natives of Asdralad were clad in tunics displaying an array of vivid colors, many of which Dayraven had never seen or imagined before his arrival on the island. None of them wore armor of any sort.

Orvandil held a sword, and Gnorn clasped his axe in a casual posture as the Thjoth belted out instructions in the Northern Tongue. A bald, older man in a maroon robe stood by them translating Orvandil's words into Andumaic for the recruits. Since Orvandil's back was turned toward Dayraven, he walked closer to hear what the Thjoth was saying.

"The right distance matters in combat. Life or death." Orvandil paused often to allow his translator to catch up. "All depends on what type of weapon you wield. Those with pikes and spears want greater distance. Those with shorter weapons have the advantage in a tight space."

Even after the translator finished, Orvandil's audience gazed at him with nervous faces. "Understand?" asked the Thjoth in his deep voice.

They all stared and blinked at him, none seeming the wiser.

"Look here," said Orvandil as he sheathed his sword. He approached one of the men and pointed at the staff he was holding. "Hand it over."

After the translator spoke, the man smiled and held out the staff. Orvandil grasped it and strode back toward Gnorn. He pointed at the staff and said, "Long."

"Aglu," repeated the translator, and the solemn-faced men all nodded.

Satisfied with their response, Orvandil said to Gnorn, "Friend Dweorg. If you will, hold up your axe."

Once Gnorn complied, Orvandil pointed at the Dweorg's weapon and declared, "Short."

"Purcu," said the translator. The men stared in Gnorn's direction, and at once they broke out in smiles. Some pointed at the stout Dweorg and repeated the word with a nod and a laugh. "Purcu. Purcu."

Gnorn, who seemed to realize he was the object of some mirth, crossed his arms and rolled his eyes.

Orvandil plunged on without noticing the men's amusement.

"Right. Long and short," he said as he pointed at his staff and Gnorn's axe.

"Aglu ri Purcu," barked the translator.

The men seemed to be biting their tongues to contain their laughter. Gnorn let out a low growl and tugged on his thick beard.

Orvandil extended his staff from where he was standing and pointed it toward Gnorn. "At a distance, the *long* weapon holds the advantage over the *short* one."

Even the old translator was having difficulty keeping a straight face now, and when giggles disrupted his translation, the rest of the men burst out laughing.

Still pointing the staff at Gnorn's chest, Orvandil looked on with a puzzled frown and lowered brow. "By the gods' mead. What ails them?"

Gnorn roared and swung his axe, truncating the staff with a loud crack and sending most of its length clattering to the ground as the Thjoth held the stump. Orvandil's head snapped toward Gnorn. The laughter ceased, and the wide-eyed men gaped at the Dweorg.

"There," said Gnorn with a broad grin. "Advantage to the short!"

Orvandil's surprise vanished with a smile of comprehension. He chuckled. The nervous men joined in a moment later. Dayraven laughed with them.

Not long later, when the gloaming grew too dark to see well, the trainees dispersed for their homes in and around Kiriath. "Dayraven, lad," said Gnorn once he turned his back on his charges. "Good to see you out, though you're too late to join in the sparring today."

"It's good to be out. I've been locked up in the palace with Queen Faldira, Urd, and Sequara for so long, I'd forgotten the color of the sky." To help him gain his strength and endurance back, Dayraven had taken part in some of the training with Asdralad's new soldiers, reminding him at times of when Gnorn, Hlokk, Imharr, and he had served under Orvandil's command. Those days were a lifetime ago, though scant two months had passed. And Hlokk was gone, while Imharr was far away, likely in danger. Sometimes when he sparred, he saw images in his mind of the Battle of Iarfaen, the day when he took a life, searing into his mind the Caergilese man's final thoughts as the spark leaked from his ruined body. For these and other reasons, he found himself of two minds about taking part in the drills while wielding Sweothol, which still reminded him of his father and the Mark and everything he had wanted to be.

"Sounds a hard life, hanging about a palace with beautiful women." The Dweorg winked and nudged his elbow against Orvandil's leg. The Thjoth looked down and cracked a smile.

Dayraven shook his head and laughed. "Harder than you'd think."

Gnorn's face grew more serious. Though he still smiled, Dayraven recognized the sorrow in the Dweorg's brown eyes, which had grown even sadder since his brother's death. "We know, lad. We're all doing our bit. What you're doing is hardest of all, but it's most important too."

Dayraven nodded. Orvandil and Gnorn stepped up beside him, and the three began walking back toward the palace together.

Dayraven smiled at his friends. "How goes the training?"

"Well enough," said Gnorn. "Now half of them at least know which end of a sword to poke the Torrlonders with. That is, if they had any swords. I've been teaching the smiths, but it's slow work."

"Hmmm," grunted Orvandil. "They learn. Or they die."

"They're lucky to have you two. Keep working at it. They'll get better."

"And what of you?" asked Gnorn. "How goes *your* training?"

"The same. I'm working at it and getting better."

"All we can do," said Gnorn. "Keep working at it with the gifts we have."

Dayraven nodded. *The gifts we have. In my case,* the *gift.* Part of him still wished he did not have it. In truth, *much* of him. "Let's find some food. I'm starving."

"The second person has four forms in High Andumaic. Each expresses a different degree of familiarity or formality. Their nominative singular forms in ascending order from least to most formal are *tai*, *tumai*, *tunilai*, and *haldurai*."

Brow lowered and mouth hanging open in confusion, Dayraven

nodded as Sequara explained. In a small room furnished with four chairs and a table, upon which rested two manuscripts in an elegant script he had not yet mastered, they were having their daily lesson in High Andumaic.

They sat across from one another. A large window let in the sunlight that seemed to be always present during the bright days in Asdralad. It shone on Sequara's dress, a comfortable topaz-blue garment. Dayraven was growing accustomed to the garb on Asdralad, but he was less easy with the flashes of Sequara's memories he still saw, especially when in her presence. He tried to ignore the fragmented images and looked down at the dark breeches and white kirtle he wore, preferring them over the bright colors folk favored on the island.

He had asked her how to say "you." He knew about *tumai* and *tunilai*, but he had not learned all their forms, which changed depending on the grammatical situation. As for the other ways of saying "you," he had no idea what they were for.

"Repeat them," said Sequara. The aloof sorceress had proven a capable and patient teacher, and Dayraven was surprised at how much he enjoyed the time spent with her.

"*Tai, tumai, tunilai*, and . . . *hal* . . ."

"*Haldurai*."

"*Haldurai*. Thank you. What do they all mean?"

She smiled. "'You.'"

He could not help returning the smile. "Yes, I know. But what are they for? That is, when do I use one or the other?"

Sequara thought for a moment, tracing the curve of her chin with her index finger. "It's a bit complicated if you're not used to it, I suppose. *Tai* is for children or servants or the most intimate of friends. It can also be used to insult someone . . . or as a way to show affection. It all depends on how you say it."

"*How* you say it?"

"Well, yes. If I say to you, '*tai*'" — she snapped out the word and made her beautiful face supercilious by raising her eyebrows and frowning at him — "then clearly I am telling you how inferior you are."

He blinked. "I see."

PHILIP CHASE

"But if I say, '*tai*'" — this time she said the word softly and gave a warm smile — "then I am showing deep affection."

Dayraven looked down at the manuscripts on the table. *Affection? That's enough to turn a man's legs to jelly.* It was a good thing he was sitting. He cleared his throat. "That does sound nicer."

Her face grew serious again. "As for *tumai*, friends would use it for each other as well as siblings or relatives who are close in years. *Tunilai* is for addressing one's superiors, whether in years or status. Also for acquaintances and strangers when there is no clear distinction in years or status."

"I understand." *I think.*

"And *haldurai* is the most formal and respectful. One uses it during ceremonies, such as marriage, and for Oruma and Anghara, the Father and Mother . . . and, I suppose, for your gods as well. You should use it when you address Queen Faldira."

Dayraven cringed inwardly for a moment. He had been using *tunilai* with Faldira, but the queen had never reprimanded him or hinted at any displeasure. He would learn the correct forms for *haldurai* and use them the next time he saw her. "I see. Thank you." He stirred a little in his chair as he found the courage to ask his next question. For some reason, it seemed important to him. "How do the people of Asdralad address *you*?"

"*Haldurai*." Sequara's brief smile was almost regretful. "The moment I became heir to the throne. Even my own parents, before they returned to the Father and Mother. My brother addresses me as such on the rare occasions when he comes to Kiriath."

Dayraven knew from his glimpses of Sequara's memories that this did not sit easy with her. Some images he had seen — a certain stiffness in her brother's bearing, awe and even fear in the eyes of her nephews — suggested the distance and the gap of status between her and her brother caused her some pain no matter what she pretended, but he respected her wish to say nothing of such things. His last question was even more difficult to ask, but he needed the answer, at the least for practical reasons. "And how should *I* address you?" His voice was quieter than he had intended.

Sequara stared at him for a long moment, and he wondered if he should have kept his silence. For once she seemed uncertain how to reply. "I . . . I am your teacher. And I am older than you. But you are not of Asdralad. I will not be your queen. And the measure of the gift in you puts you on more than equal footing. *Tunilai* is the obvious choice."

Dayraven was not sure why, but the answer disappointed him. *Tunilai* seemed to assert a gap between them, a level of formality that meant pretending they had not shared so many of each other's dreams, fears, and desires when she entered his mind to save his life in Caergilion. But of course it was sensible. "*Tunilai*. Yes." *At least it's not haldurai.*

"Now, I think you should begin learning the vowels in the High Andumaic script. Once you're able to read, it will help you to learn the history of Andumedan. In that history you will learn how the greatest sorcerers have succeeded and failed to use the gift to better civilization. Our sages have recorded their stories in High Andumaic over the centuries. You will see how they have used the songs of origin."

"Are the songs of origin recorded in the High Andumaic script as well?"

Her eyes widened, and she shook her head. "The songs are *never* written. It would be a sacrilege to try to capture the ancient tongue Oruma gave to humankind when he endowed us with understanding."

Dayraven nodded. "I see."

"Good." She smiled and placed her hand on the manuscript. "This particular treatise is about evidence for the existence of an ancient dragon named Gorsarhad. If she's real and alive, she would be the eldest of living dragons. I thought it would be appropriate subject matter for you. But before you can read it, we must learn the letters."

"I'm ready to learn."

They dived into the lesson, with Dayraven repeating the names of the letters and tracing their flowing lines. But they had not progressed far when a knock sounded at the door.

"*Vaunos*," said Sequara in formal High Andumaic. It was the polite form of command. Dayraven translated in his mind. *Please come in.*

When the door opened, Urd entered with another woman behind her.

Dayraven's mouth hung open, and he stared at the newcomer. He knew this woman, though she belonged to another place, another life. *His* other life. Though she had the bronze skin of the south and dark strands in her grey hair, hers was a familiar face from the Mark. From Kinsford, in fact.

"Kulva?"

Kulva was the bondswoman of Thegn Baldred. His father Baldulf had bought her in Caergilion and brought her to Kinsford long before Dayraven was born. Like Imharr, she was born in Adanon. She was the only other southerner Dayraven had ever seen before his encounter with the elf changed his life and tore him from his home. Wearing a blue frock in the simple and sedate style of the Mark, Kulva appeared a little older than he remembered, more bent over and with more wrinkles and grey hair. But she smiled at him when she said, "Hello, Dayraven."

"May we join you?" Clad in her usual brown robe, Urd pointed at the two empty chairs at the table with her walking stick.

"Please do," said Sequara.

As the two newcomers sat, Urd turned to Sequara. "My dear, this is Kulva."

Sequara smiled. "Urd has told me about you. The aid you've given her and us over the years has been most important. Welcome to Asdralad."

"Thank you, my lady. I'm glad to have been of some small service."

"Aid?" Dayraven wrinkled his nose and frowned. To add to his confusion, his yearning for home returned with renewed strength at Kulva's presence. One familiar face could bring up so many unbidden memories. "I don't understand. I mean, it's good to see you, Kulva. Someone from home . . ."

Urd smiled. "Kulva has been my eyes and ears in Kinsford for many years. Someone to keep watch on things when I was away. The information she gave me often proved valuable."

Dayraven had never suspected old Kulva of spying for Urd. The two women had hidden their relationship well. Either that, or he was a witless fool who could not see what was under his nose. He shook his head and laughed. "Another of your secrets, Grandmother. I suppose even Baldred had no idea."

Urd gave a mischievous smile. "Most men are not hard to keep secrets from."

Kulva put a hand on Dayraven's arm. "It's good to see you too, Dayraven. I'm glad you're well, and that you're here."

Dayraven saw a depth in the woman's eyes he had not suspected before. He had never imagined she was anything other than a simple bondswoman. *Of course, she has a story too.* "Thank you. Well, it seems there are some things you learn about home only after you leave it."

Kulva kept her dark eyes on him as she nodded. He realized she, long exiled from her home, knew the truth of his words better than he.

Urd cleared her throat. "I asked Kulva to come to me here if something should happen in the Mark. It was needful for us to know as soon as possible."

"Know what? What's happened?"

Urd and Kulva both looked at Dayraven, and in their tight frowns he saw something was wrong.

"There's no gentle way to tell you this, my boy. King Ithamar sent messengers to Earl Stigand in Kinsford. In a fortnight, Ithamar will hold a moot of his earls and thegns in Wolvendon. They must decide how the Mark will answer King Earconwald of Torrlond."

Dayraven's chest tightened, and he clenched his fists as he swallowed. "You mean . . . the Torrlonders . . ."

Urd sighed. "Earconwald and Bledla have called on King Ithamar to renew the Mark's pledge to the old alliance. I expect the Torrlonders are demanding the same of King Fullan of Ellond."

"Then they will join the Torrlonders in war?"

"Not yet. The pledge is a first step. Earconwald and Bledla will mostlike finish their conquest of Adanon without aid from Ellond or the Mark. But when it comes time to march on the eastern kingdoms, Torrlond will want its allies to ensure the defeat of Sildharan, especially if Asdralad and Sundara help the Sildharae."

Dayraven had known this day would come, but he still did not wish to believe it. "How do you know all this?"

Kulva gave a wry smile. "Baldred talks. He repeats everything Earl Stigand tells him and the other thegns."

Dayraven sighed and sank in his chair. One of those thegns was his father. If only there was some way to tell them. He wanted to return to Kinsford and tell Father the truth. How Earconwald and Bledla were waging an unjust war stemming from greed and zeal. How the Torrlonders and the peoples of Eormenlond's other kingdoms were not what they seemed. How the world was more complex than they dreamed, and how there was good and evil everywhere and in everyone. He wanted his folk to know . . . *But they're not my folk. I'm an exile. A man with no people. They're more likely to kill me than to listen to me.*

He clenched his jaw as a new feeling took root in his heart: a quiet but firm determination. Even if they did not know him, he would not give up on his people. He would not give in to despair. *I must serve them as I can. I must stop Bledla before the Torrlonders draw everyone into their mad war.*

"Well," he said. "We knew the day would come. The sooner we stop Bledla and Earconwald, the better."

Urd gazed at him with a sad smile, but he saw pride in her eyes. The old woman nodded. "For now, these tidings change little for us. You must continue learning, my boy, and keep your resolution."

"I will."

He turned to Kulva. Even as they spoke of the Mark, there were certain things his heart ached to know. "If you would, please tell me news of Kinsford. How is my father?"

"Edgil was healthy in body when I left." Kulva's eyes narrowed. "But I'll not lie to you. He misses you. The man keeps busy with his fields, and he performs his duties as well as ever. But everyone sees it. They whisper about him after he passes by. Earl Stigand frowns at the whisperers, but he too worries for his old friend. When you left, your father's heart went with you."

Dayraven swallowed and cleared his throat to keep the tears from forming. He gazed down at the manuscripts on the table until he felt sure he could speak without choking. He looked up again. All three women waited with patient and gentle smiles.

"And Ebba?" He could say no more.

It was enough for Kulva, whose nod told of her understanding. But she glanced over at Sequara as if uncertain what she should say in front of the sorceress.

"It's alright," said Dayraven. "Nothing to hide." He did not care to explain that Sequara knew as much about his feelings for Ebba as he did since she had entered his mind and seen his memories. Sequara glanced at him, and in the subtle rise of the eyebrows over her dark eyes he saw a momentary acknowledgement of something shared between them. Urd watched the sorceress with a curious squint, and Dayraven wondered how much his great aunt suspected.

Kulva sighed. "Very well. After you left the Mark, we saw nothing of Ebba for many days. We heard her cries and her mourning, but she kept to her father's hall like a new-made widow. She was that upset. Her father . . . Guthere decided it would be best to marry her off. 'A clean break mends most swiftly,' he kept saying to everyone, as if he was trying to convince himself he was doing the right thing." Kulva shook her head and rolled her eyes. "Men and their foolish notions. He would listen to no one, not even Sigitha. As if the girl's own mother wouldn't know her daughter's mind. Once the idea entered his stubborn head . . . Well, he cast about and found out there was a thegn in Wolvendon seeking a wife, a widower with a girl and a boy nearly grown. They made swift arrangements, and the thegn came to fetch her. They wed in Stanflet, but there was little enough cheer. Ebba . . . she went quietly in the end, like something was broken in her. No one in Kinsford has seen her since." Kulva folded her hands and waited for Dayraven.

"The man . . . his name?"

"Leofwin. Son of Leofbald. One of King Ithamar's own thegns."

"And . . . what sort of man . . . How did he seem to you?"

"I don't mind saying I'm a fair enough judge of men. They said he was a fierce warrior, but people say lots of things. I watched him close, and though he's no doubt strong enough, I never saw anything but honor and kindness in him. He was that gentle with our Ebba. Like he was nursing a wounded bird. And his daughter and son were as well-mannered as anyone could expect. It was clear the man loved his children too. Leofwin's a patient, good man. Might be that's why Ebba went so quietlike."

Dayraven at first did not understand how he felt. These tidings tore something from him, leaving a vast hole. But there was no anger. No jealousy. No wild, keening pain. Stunned he was for certain. But he was also surprised to find he was glad. Glad for Ebba, for he did not believe Kulva would lie to him. *She might find happiness yet. Better that she find some peace with this man than always to feel grief for me. Yes.* He nodded at Kulva. "Then it's for the best. Thank you for telling me."

Urd and Sequara gazed at him. Both of them were so strong. Yet in both women's narrowing eyes he perceived a measure of sorrow for him, and he turned away from them.

"We'll leave you for now, my boy. You need time to take everything in."

Dayraven looked up and forced a smile. "No. I'm fine. Truly."

Urd was already leading Kulva out the door. "I'll look in on you in the evening." Their backs disappeared through the door.

Sequara too rose.

Dayraven looked up at her. "Please. Let's continue with the lesson now."

Her gaze was nearly too intense to bear. She smiled and put her hand on his shoulder, which she squeezed. "I must see Queen Faldira for a moment. We'll resume in a while."

As she left and closed the door behind her, Dayraven thanked her inwardly for the lie about seeing the queen. Now alone in the room, he put his head in his hands and sighed.

Sudden sobs shook his body. He wept freely.

"Khalosae ni tundil ar dagrodhan varthway. Mubhasae an gwandil ni faradhan brithway." As the energy inhabiting his form reached out, Dayraven chanted the song of origin several times. His awareness departed from his body and expanded, but the song of origin shifted his attention toward the goat he was staring at. Save for the whispering elf-shard that never left him, all things other than the small animal receded to a vast but less present background. A simple milking goat, the creature munched on the dry grass in the field behind Queen Faldira's palace.

Other goats bleated and stuttered and grazed nearby, and Dayraven could feel the presence of three people as well. One was the goatherder boy who looked on nervously but had given him permission to use one from his herd beforehand. Another was Queen Faldira, who observed him with calm patience. The third was the one he had to watch out for: Sequara. Today the younger sorceress was assisting the queen in training Dayraven. He ignored all other presences to concentrate on the goat.

When Dayraven's energy inhabited the creature, it stopped chewing and looked up with a blank expression. He knew the animal's mind, its fears and desires, and the story of its short existence. A goat was a creature of simple pleasures and large appetites: warmth, comfort, defecation, copulation, and, above all, food. Any food. Perhaps it was not so unlike most humans.

As the hairy creature with the horns stared with vacant brown eyes, Dayraven strengthened his hold on it. He could have directed it to do any number of things, and the goat would have obeyed as if it were heeding its own mind. But he did nothing of the sort. Instead, he calmed his thoughts. Disregarding the murmurs of the elf-shard and penning in its vast power behind a barrier in his mind, he stayed focused on the goat and waited for the attack. He would keep control over the song of origin. He would not break.

It came like a sudden storm. Sharp and strong was the energy lashing out at him and seeking to seize power over the goat. The creature stood staring as if unaware of the massive struggle taking place over its little mind. Invisible to the eye but palpable to his psyche, the energy assaulting Dayraven was a spear-like concentration of that which permeated all living things. In it he recognized Sequara's unique presence as something intimately familiar. He recognized her fierce strength in the gift as well. His eyes narrowed as he told himself to keep looking at the goat. *I will keep control over the song of origin. I wield the goat.*

But cracks began to form in his control. The energy slamming against him was too forceful and wild. Panic welled up in him as the cracks widened with swift violence. He hastened to pour his energy into the cracks, but to no avail. With a bright flash of pain that seemed to split his head, Sequara's relentless energy ripped open his power and flooded into the goat. Knowing the inevitable nausea that would come, Dayraven retreated and summoned the tatters of his energy back into his body.

The world resumed its normal colors. He tasted sour vomit in his mouth, which he forced down as he wavered on his feet. Clutching his stomach, Dayraven shook his head and forced his eyes to focus. Soon he was able to see and hold his body steady. He looked toward Queen Faldira. "I'm sorry, your Majesty," he said in High Andumaic. "She is strong."

The queen nodded and answered him in the same tongue. "And you were using only a fraction of your strength. Why?"

Dayraven could not lie to his teacher, who commanded deep respect even though she was the gentlest person he ever met. "I . . . fear. When it all comes . . . I lack . . ." He could not remember the word in High Andumaic, so he said in the Northern Tongue, "control."

"We've discussed this before, Dayraven. When you unleash the gift, you must find the balance between control and power. Particularly when you struggle against another with the gift. A trial between those with the gift for mastery over something is dangerous, which is why we must practice. You are right to fear your power, for it is immense. But let us see what happens when you allow a little more to emerge. Do not look inward so much. Let yourself free. Now, are you ready to try again?"

The goat-herder, who understood neither High Andumaic nor the Northern Tongue, looked on in amazement. *He'll have a story to tell his family tonight,* thought Dayraven. He glanced at Sequara, who gave him a quick smile and nod, perhaps half in challenge and half in encouragement. Looking back toward Queen Faldira, he bowed and tried to keep his face impassive. "Yes, your majesty. I will try."

He took a deep breath and closed his eyes. Almost as if mocking him, the presence of the elf oozed its shadow-breath in his mind. *I am far stronger than you, far greater than you can conceive,* it seemed to say. When he opened his eyes, he focused again on the goat and chanted the song of origin. "Khalosae ni tundil ar dagrodhan varthway. Mubhasae an gwandil ni faradhan brithway."

Again his energy left his body and sought out the goat. He repeated the song of origin in his mind as Queen Faldira had taught him in order to maintain his focus on the creature he wished to wield. As he did so, he was aware of a deep well in his mind, a vast sea of power contained in him straining to be free.

He had found that he could use songs of origin while stifling the thing the elf had put in him. It was like holding back a huge shadow, but it was less frightening to use the gift that way since it was far easier to keep control when he did not tap the reservoir the elf had inserted in him.

Afraid but eager to show the queen he could succeed, he thought about using a tiny portion of the elf-shard's power. If he could let just a little bit of the elf-shard seep through, a bare fraction of its strength, perhaps he could draw from its power and manipulate it.

His energy pulsed toward the goat and began to dwell in it. Still repeating the song of origin in his mind, he groped toward the vast foreign presence occupying him. There in his mind was the barrier he had erected to restrain the elf-shard. Breath held as he made the most delicate adjustment he could within his mind, he opened a fissure in it.

Hungry and aware, the elf-shard awakened with immediate violence and slammed against his defenses. He shuddered with the impact. But somehow, the barrier held, and he remained in control of his mind. Power leaked out of the fissure he had torn. He sensed the escape of energy from the shard of the elf, and it was both one with him and a presence foreign to him. As it mingled with the energy native to Dayraven, it increased his power over the goat, so he allowed it to continue to bleed out. His hold over the beast was much stronger than before. Ignoring the relief that flooded a part of his mind, he steadied himself.

Something changed. Once roused, the presence of the elf became more insistent. Greedy. It leaked out with greater and swifter force, like a sudden flood after a hard rain. Dayraven stopped repeating the song of origin as he struggled to keep it under control.

As an explosion of light, the shard of the elf leapt out of Dayraven and seized the tiny spark of life that was the goat with such ravenous might that Dayraven lost all sense of the world of forms. He was a vast light, and a tendril of energy connected him to this small creature, a mere speck in the infinite void, with such steel firmness that nothing else could ever seize it again.

It became a desperate struggle between Dayraven and the elf-shard over who was in control. Forgetting the song of origin of goats, Dayraven wrenched and lurched to find himself. The elf-shard opposed him not with malice but with indifference. He was a man clinging to a piece of wood that drifted according to the whims of a sea stretching in every direction beyond his paltry field of vision. Yet, somehow, Dayraven found the fragments of his energy amidst the enormous rush of power. Collecting the fragments, he formed the will to emerge. Inch by painful inch, he pulled his mind to the forefront.

And then, all at once, he was back. Perhaps it had allowed him to return, though he did not know why. But with his return, he was surprised to find he could once again contain the flow of the elf-shard's power. He asserted control over the enormous force gushing from him. It eased and lessened by degrees. It was a tremendous battle, but at length, he found he could check and direct the rush of energy, holding it back to a trickle that fed the gift in him.

When he knew he held sway, he brought his focus back to the goat. The little beast was still in his grip. The goat-herder, Queen Faldira, and Sequara were dim presences that he might have overlooked had he not known to seek them.

Something new entered Dayraven's awareness. Fear. It was not coming from him, but from the small presences that were Faldira and Sequara. Why should they be afraid?

He severed his connection with the gift and drifted back to his body and the world of forms. The vast power of the elf-shard receded to a cold whisper caressing the darkest folds of his mind. The field behind the palace returned, as did the goats and the goat-herder. The boy wore the same awestruck look as before, and the animals, including the one Dayraven had controlled, were nibbling at the grass.

Faldira and Sequara stared at Dayraven in wide-eyed horror. Sweat was running down their foreheads and made dark stains on the front of their gowns.

"What . . . what's wrong?" he said in the Northern Tongue, forgetting all his High Andumaic. "What happened?"

"Dayraven?" said Faldira. Was her voice trembling? "Do you know how long it's been?"

He looked up in the sky. A few wispy clouds amidst a field of blue. The sun did not hover where he expected it. It had moved quite a bit since he had woven his spell over the goat. He had not known so much time passed. "I . . . hadn't realized. I thought . . ."

One of the goats bleated.

"Did I succeed?"

"Succeed?" said Faldira. Her eyes were still wide. "Neither Sequara nor I could pry your energy from the creature, if that is what you mean."

Sequara's breaths came in ragged gasps. "We tried so hard . . . We feared for your life. For our lives too, to speak the truth. How could so much energy come from anyone?"

He stared back at the two women. Though they tried to mask it, the fear in their eyes was like a terrible accusation. He had never seen either of them so perturbed. "I don't know . . . I . . ."

"I felt it before, when I healed you," said Sequara. Her shoulders drooped, and her eyes were now less afraid, but in them he still saw something else. Was it sorrow? Pity? "And when you struck the dragon. But to try to oppose it . . . when it all comes rushing out . . . It's like swimming against a raging river."

Faldira regained her composure. "It's alright, Dayraven. You have returned. My greatest fear was that you would never come back. That we had lost you. But you are here. That is what matters. You will learn to control this. You must, or you will be lost. For now, perhaps it would be wiser to restrain yourself."

"Yes, your Majesty."

"I am sorry. It was I who bid you to release more of your energy." The queen half smiled and raised her eyebrows. "I did not mean quite so much."

"I'm sorry. I didn't know . . ." Dayraven wanted to plead with them, to tell them it was still he who was standing before them. The energy that frightened them was not his. It was the elf, the thing the elf put in his mind, the shard that even now rustled and stroked the edges of his awareness. His mouth opened, but no words would come.

It was Sequara who came to him first. She put her hand on his shoulder and looked in his eyes as she smiled. The fear was gone. "It's alright. You're back."

Dayraven stared at her for a long moment, and then he let out a sigh. He could never have put into words what Sequara's smile meant. Though neither would have acknowledged it aloud, with their shared memories, she would know better than anyone what he was feeling.

He returned the smile. "Thank you."

"Let us return to the palace," said Queen Faldira. "We're finished for now."

In honor of Orvandil and Gnorn, Dayraven wore a fine brown robe over his plain white kirtle and dark breeches. By Asdralad's standards the robe was simple, yet Dayraven was still not accustomed to its light, soft feel as it brushed his skin. Everything about Asdralad was gentler than the Mark. Even after several months, the place still felt foreign: older, tamer, and more elegant than his home kingdom.

In this season of the year, he was accustomed to the weather turning cold, but the days were still pleasant and warm on the island, making his stay there feel timeless. He admired Asdralad's many beauties, yet at times he also missed the simple ruggedness and the more dramatic cycles of his birthplace. If not for the presence of Urd, Gnorn, Orvandil, Sequara, and Faldira, he would have felt out of place in the island kingdom. But now the Dweorg and the Thjoth were about to leave, and only Urd and Kulva would remain as reminders of his former life.

Dayraven entered a small banqueting room with a graceful, round table at its center. Around the table sat Urd, Gnorn, Orvandil, Queen Faldira, and Sequara. As Dayraven took his place between Urd and Sequara, servants finished bringing out the food. There was rice, pheasant, lobster, spiced beans, yellow lentils, okra in a hot pepper sauce, oranges, pomegranates, and flat bread in silver serving dishes and red wine in their goblets. Candle flames reflected on their silver plates.

"Ah, you made it before we finished off the food," said Gnorn to Dayraven as he forked a roast pheasant with a gleam in his eyes.

"How could I not see you off properly?" Dayraven lifted his wine glass and smiled. Gnorn winked and took a draught from his own goblet. The Dweorg would no doubt feel the lack of that wine once he departed.

"In truth, I'll miss you two," said Dayraven as his face grew serious. "Though I know you leave for a good purpose."

The Dweorg smiled, though it did not touch his sad eyes. "You'll miss us no more than we'll miss you. I couldn't bear to leave if I didn't know you're in trusted hands here. And truth be told, perhaps we may do more good where we're going. We may be able to buy you a little more time, and that, my lad, may be the most important thing we can do. Besides," Gnorn jerked his fat thumb at Orvandil sitting next to him, "the big fellow here's getting itchy for action, you know. A Thjoth can't go more than a few months without a fight. As for me, Dweorgs weren't made for islands, though I've found the hospitality and the fare here most excellent." He finished with a bow toward Faldira.

The queen smiled. "A small price to pay for all you've given us. You and Orvandil have helped in many ways to ready our army, and we're grateful for the service you're about to embark on. Orvandil is the most able candidate to lead our forces, and his request to make you his second in command was wise. The two of you work well together. You'll need to. Your mission will be dangerous, and there will be little comfort along the way. I'll be relying on your reports."

"We'll serve you as best we can, your Majesty," said Orvandil. "Adanon is where we can do most. Good training ground for your soldiers too. Nothing like true combat to harden an army. Besides, the Dweorg's right. It's a bit quieter here than I'm used to."

"Let's pray to the Mother and Father it remains so," said Sequara.

Faldira gazed somewhere far away. "I fear Asdralad's long peace will end. Our time to enter the War of the Way is coming." Her eyes returned to the dinner table as she looked at her companions. "But now let us speak of gentler matters while there's light still to gather round. Urd, you were telling me earlier of the hills this time of year in the Mark. How the trees change color with winter's approach. I would like to see that someday."

The old woman smiled. "Yes, it's a sight worth the journey too, my lady. Like fire marching over the hills in bursts and flashes of red, orange, and yellow. But it lasts only a short while, like all things of beauty. An exquisite yielding before winter's long sleep."

As Urd continued to describe the foliage in the Mark, Dayraven remembered his home and its people. Her words brought keen memories to his mind. The landscape of hills and trees with their vibrant, dying leaves appeared to him, and so too did the hardy folk who dwelled in it. He thought of his father and Ebba most, but he recognized his feelings were changing. Though he still cared as deeply as ever for them, his life had taken a different turn. He was becoming someone they would not understand, and he would never be the same.

Just then he glanced at Sequara, who was listening to Urd and did not notice his look. In the last months she and Dayraven had become more comfortable in one another's presence. She was his teacher of High Andumaic, and he learned much of the gift from her as well. The esteem between them was heartfelt.

But they never discussed the moment when she entered his mind to save his life. There was something awkward about it, something intimate they felt safer not acknowledging. Dayraven thought about it, though, and he guessed from an occasional lingering look Sequara did too. He knew that his memories still bled into her awareness, even as he lived hers from time to time each day. *She sees the leaf-clad hills of the Mark even as I do. Feels the longing their memory awakens.*

The sorceress for the most part treated Dayraven with formal and respectful distance. He understood she always focused on the heavy task before her of one day ruling Asdralad. Part of that meant training Dayraven, which she did with efficient patience.

Dayraven reached for his wine goblet. As it happened, Sequara reached for hers at the same moment, and their hands brushed.

They looked at one another.

Her dark brown eyes seemed so serious and sad that Dayraven

feared she read his thoughts. He smiled and felt himself blushing. Unable to look at her any longer, he turned back to Urd, who finished her account of the Southweald's beauty during the changing seasons.

The conversation turned to other matters, and Dayraven spoke little to Sequara that night. Melancholy settled on him like the first morning frost on the hills of the Mark. He told himself it must have stemmed from the imminent departure of Gnorn and Orvandil.

5

A REASON TO FIGHT

The foamy-prowed ship cut through the waves, leaving the golden shores of Asdralad far behind. Orvandil stood in the bow and gazed out over the swells of the Great Sea. The wind tossed his blond hair back, and he closed his eyes as he breathed in the thick scent of salt. At sea all the complications of life seemed to lessen. With only wind and water all about him, a man could shed all the worries and pretensions weighing him down.

This was no Thjothic warship he was on, but still it was good to return to the sea, the only place he belonged other than a battlefield. And that was where he was heading. Once again, he was off to kill. Only this time, it was for a just cause, if such existed in the world. He shook his head and smiled grimly at the thought. *Just cause or not, I needed it. Gods curse me, I needed it.*

After months in Asdralad, the ever present itch had grown into a terrible urge. Orvandil never felt truly alive unless he was gritting his teeth at death and dealing it out. He wondered if Queen Faldira guessed the real reason he had volunteered to lead the troops into Adanon to fight the Torrlonders. He would let the others think it was out of a desire to help. And perhaps he *was* the most fit for the task.

But his true motive was simple. He needed to fight. He needed it like a shivering drunkard needed mead. Like a fish needed water. Like a man needed air. His hunger for it was taking on a sharp edge. Sometimes he believed he had entered this life for only one purpose: to take it away. Without this purpose, everything else went stale. Good food was a pleasure that lasted only so long before a man shat it out. Dice and gambling were mere distractions. A woman could satisfy him for a little while. But the ecstasy of combat . . . When he fought, he fulfilled his reason for being in the world. In battle, he could almost touch perfection. There was a grim exhilaration every time steel rang out, and when it carved through flesh and bone, there was the thrill that, one more time, it was not his life seeping into the soil.

Was he a murderer? He had never slain anyone outside of combat, but the distinction seemed less important to him the longer he lived. Killing was the only thing that made him feel alive. He had not asked for it, but the gods had made him thuswise, and he cursed them.

But there was *one* woman who, at one time at least, might have kept him from any battle had she wished to. Of course, it was far too late for that. He had been seeing her of late in his dreams. And when he made love to the woman at the tavern back in Kiriath, he saw *her* face. One night, he had whispered her name while spilling inside the woman. The last thing a woman wanted to hear while pumping her hips on top of a man was another woman's name on his lips. Dalriana deserved better.

A young widow of one of Asdralad's minor noble houses, she had married an old spice and silk merchant for his money at her parents' insistence. The merchant died and left Dalriana all his wealth, including several taverns in Kiriath. Orvandil had met her at one of them, and she had been a comfort to him during his stay in Asdralad. Being a noblewoman and a merchant, she spoke the Northern Tongue well, probably better than he did. She had the dark beauty of the southerners, and she was a clever, vibrant woman. He had no idea what she saw in him. Perhaps something different.

Anyway, on the night when the name escaped him in a whisper, he knew it was time to move on. Sooner or later, it always was. Dalriana had the grace to pretend not to have heard, but the strained silence after their passion told everything. Orvandil heard himself whisper again the name that never left him. "Osynia."

All the wandering, all the fighting, and all the killing had not lessened the power of that name, even with all the intervening years. And what had he become? He was no different from Bledla's dragons. The beasts' sole purpose was to slay. The ultimate predator. He still got shivers thinking about the one he got close to back in Palahon. Imharr had proven the monsters could bleed. Perhaps he would have a chance to fight one in Adanon. To slay a dragon or die in combat against one. Either way, the glory would be great. Was that why he was here? For glory?

Yes. And no. The answer would have been simpler once, but Dayraven had changed that. Dayraven. Hardly more man than boy, the lad from the Mark had a strange way about him. From the first day he had met him back in Etinstone, when he looked in Dayraven's eyes and saw . . . What? A reflection of himself?

He had no words for it. Words had never been his strength. In some way Dayraven had known him, had seen through him. He knew not how, but the lad saw something worthwhile there. And that made Orvandil feel a desire to live up to that image, as if he could be the thing Dayraven saw. Mayhap it was only the aura of the boy's own goodness. But no . . . he could see people, deep into them. Orvandil wanted to be what Dayraven saw.

It had not been easy to leave the young man back in Asdralad. At first, it felt like he was abandoning him, leaving behind a sacred charge. But the lad had convinced him otherwise. When they had spoken, he had understood right away. The lad needed to learn to use the gift, the wondrous power that was in him. Others had a different part to play. There was no need for Orvandil to go mad on the peaceful island when he could do more good elsewhere. "But make sure you come back," Dayraven had said in that strange way of his. "I'm going to need you." He had said it not out of sentiment, but as a hard fact, like a prophecy.

That was one reason why Orvandil had requested Gnorn as his second in command. To be sure, the Dweorg was stout in battle and had a good head for tactics. He had also become a friend, as impossible as that might have seemed at one time. But, most of all, he was a reminder. Gnorn saw Dayraven with sharper eyes than even Orvandil did. The Dweorg knew what the boy was, sensed it in his gut. Orvandil needed that clear-sightedness near him. He needed to remember Dayraven's goodness, to keep in mind he fought for more than just another chance to kill. Gnorn would keep him anchored to that.

The ship crashed through a large wave, and the misty spray pattering his face yanked Orvandil's thoughts back to the present. He wiped droplets from his beard and looked behind him. The sailors attended to the rigging and stepped between the rows of Asdralad's newly trained soldiers, who huddled together looking like lost lambs. Or lambs lined up for slaughter. Leaving behind their colorful garb on their island, the men crouched in the boat in their forest browns and greens. The messengers had reported most of the fighting in Adanon happened in the tree-covered Briufaen Hills and the foothills of the eastern Marar Mountains. The resistance to Torrlond was strongest in eastern Adanon, but it kept on the move and reinvented itself as the desperate circumstances demanded. These young men from Asdralad, until now the sons of farmers, merchants, sailors, and weavers, were to join that struggle. He hoped they would survive. Most would not.

In the distance, three ships like the one Orvandil rode in skimmed the waves with pregnant sails. They too carried a cargo of soldiers who were green in more than one sense of the word. In all, a dozen ships had set out from Asdralad carrying five hundred men under Orvandil's command. Two sorcerers also sailed with them, each assigned to a different ship. Not a large force, by any means. More symbolic than anything, but it was better than nothing, and more would follow – those even now training under the tutelage of Faldira's best palace guards, like Karad, whom Orvandil had given all the knowledge he could.

The plan was to make for the rugged peninsula where the Briufaen Hills marched into the sea. There they would separate and land miles from each other. They would time their approach for the evening hours. The setting sun would be sinking behind them, which would make it harder for the Torrlonders to spot them, but they would not make land until darkness fell.

Once on Adanese soil, they would divide into squads of ten and make for a rallying point in the hills, where Balch's forces were supposed to meet them. Orvandil reckoned they would be lucky if half of them made it there. Looking on their young faces, he almost felt guilt over their fates, but Asdralad needed men with experience in combat. Some would make it, and they would come out of it haunted but hardened. They needed calluses over their hands and their minds. Men numb with what they had seen and done. Who would do what they had to do to stay alive. That was the price. As it was, these poor fellows were raw and terrified. They huddled in the ship and clutched their spears and swords as if they might need them at any moment. The nervousness and fear was there to read on their faces, and so was the misery of those few who were seasick.

Among those who hung over the ship's side in order to share their breakfast with the sea was, of course, Gnorn. When they boarded, the Dweorg had looked wide-eyed at the ship and muttered to Orvandil, "I must be mad to go with you." He had responded with a teeth-baring smile.

Just a few feet away from Orvandil, the Dweorg wiped his beard as he clambered down from the boat's side and sank down. He groaned and rolled his eyes.

"Take cheer: This voyage is only three times as long as the last, and a tenth of it is already behind us."

Gnorn's stare was baleful. "Merely a tenth? Curse me for a fool for setting foot on a ship again."

"You were on an island. If ever you wanted to leave it, you needed to board a ship. Or swim."

"Then curse me for boarding one in the first place."

"Had to. We needed to make sure the lad was safe."

Gnorn gave a weak smile. "Aye. We did. We're doing right by leaving him, are we not?"

Orvandil hesitated. "Yes. We are. He needs time to learn. We can give it to him."

The Dweorg nodded, and his face hardened with a frown. "And so we shall. But I'll need a full account from him of everything that happens while we're gone. For the book, you know."

"Things should be quiet enough there. Where we're headed, though . . . You might see a thing or two for your book."

In the darkness of night, the sailors scurried to reef the ship's sail and drop the anchor. Some of the soldiers assisted in lowering the two rowboats lashed to the ship's side. The moon gave enough light to make out the thin white shoreline in the distance. Waves crashed and ground on rocks. When they had anchored the ship, the rowboats began ferrying the men to the shore. Orvandil heard Gnorn scrambling down a rope ladder to board the first boat. "By the ancestors' beards," the Dweorg muttered despite the order for silence, "I'll be first to plant my feet on dry land."

Orvandil smiled and waited his turn. A while after the first run had departed, the returning oars splashed over the moan of the waves breaking on the distant shore. The approaching rowboats appeared as pitching shadows on the surface of the dark sea. First one then another bumped into the ship's side, and more men laden with weapons and packs climbed down the rope ladders. They lowered further supplies as well as bundles of spears and bows tied up in canvas.

The Thjoth was the last aboard one of the boats. The men were packed tight, but they made room for their leader. Some shivered in the darkness, a couple with their teeth chattering. When Orvandil settled on his rocking seat, water splashed against his boots. A good couple inches of bilge sloshed around the bottom of the boat. To judge by the sharp stench, there was plenty of vomit down there as well. This would be a bit of a rough ride.

The sailors put their backs into it and guided the rowboat toward shore with good skill, but as they approached and the waves grew rougher, the boat bucked like an unbroken horse. Some of the men moaned, and several emptied their stomachs with choked grunts. "Keep it down," snapped Orvandil. The soldiers needed no translation. The moaning stopped. *Now if they could just puke more quietly*.

A big wave gave a moment's notice by roaring before it crashed down on the boat. Cold water soaked Orvandil to the bone, and he blinked and spat out the taste of salt. The sailors began bailing furiously. One soldier screamed something and pointed at the water. The dim moonlight outlined a hand sinking under the waves. The soldier screamed again. Orvandil lunged to slap his face, stinging his palm and snapping the man's head sideways. "Shut up!" Terror and incomprehension emanated from the soldier's wide eyes, his mouth still open as if preparing for another scream.

Orvandil looked at where the hand had disappeared. Only churning water. The poor bastard would sink fast with his pack and byrny on. He deemed they were not too far from shore. *Shame.*

He threw off his helm and unbuckled his scabbard. No time to remove his byrny. His pack slid off his back, then he took a deep breath and dove into the water.

A cold embrace met him. The waves' pounding and men's groaning of a moment before gave way to the eerie pulse of the currents under the water, which blurred and throbbed in his ears. It was dark under the waves at night, and Orvandil groped blindly. His palms squished into the sandy bottom.

With the slow, clumsy movements of a man underwater, he felt around with his hands until he could no longer hold his breath. One last frantic feel, then he launched up with his powerful legs. Orvandil was a skilled swimmer, but even he had difficulty breaking the surface with a byrny on. But after kicking and pushing with his strong limbs, his face splashed through to meet air. He gasped and sucked in to fill his lungs as the crash of breaking waves momentarily rushed back into his ears. Cold water closed over his face, and the noises fled again in the silence and darkness of the enveloping sea.

He reached the muddy bottom again and moved his hands in wild circles over the gritty sand. Nothing but stones. He would have to give up soon, and he doubted he had the strength to try another search. Cursing inwardly, he prepared to launch himself again when his left foot kicked something. Most likely a large stone, but he hunched over to feel for it anyway.

A soft limb fell into his grasp, and when he felt down it, he was able to clasp a hand. The hand did not clasp back, but Orvandil grabbed the body to remove the heavy pack. By the time he finished, he knew he needed more air, unless he wanted to keep this poor man company at the sea's bottom.

Leaving the body behind, he launched up again and broke the surface. Waves crashed, and sweet air filled his lungs. The water swallowed him again. He swam down and again found the body, which he grasped by the tunic and pulled behind him as he struggled in the direction in which he reckoned the shore lay. He hoped he guessed right.

Twice more he came up for air before he found he was able to stand with his head above water. Occasional waves surged over his head, but, tugging the limp body behind him, he trudged closer to the shore. When the water was down to his waist, some of the soldiers on the beach spotted him and ran out to help. Two of them reached him at once, and he let them carry the unmoving body to the shore.

Orvandil glanced at them and knew he had been dragging a corpse. They might try to pump his chest and revive him, but this one would stay dead. His breath coming in ragged gasps, the Thjoth made an effort to stand tall before the soldiers as he made his way to the shore, but he stumbled to his hands and knees when a wave punched his back and rolled over him. His fingers clutched silt as the salty wave pulled at him while retreating back to the sea.

When the water had receded, a hand grasped his arm and helped to pull him up. Orvandil rose and looked at Gnorn, whose face was hidden in shadows as he stood in the water.

"No helping him," said Orvandil between heavy breaths. "I take lives. Don't save them."

"His death was not your doing, my friend. And the deed was no wasted effort. The men all know what you did. They already fear you. Now they'll respect you too. Mayhap even love you."

Orvandil shook his head and barked a quick laugh. What if they knew that his first thought had been fear of their discovery by the Torrlonders when the body washed ashore? Did Gnorn guess? For a fleeting moment he had wondered if he might save the fellow, but the acceptance that he was retrieving a corpse had come easily. It would be good to deserve that love, to be the man Dayraven saw, but he knew himself too well. "Fear and respect will do. It's a cruel and senseless task, leading men to war. You try to keep them alive while you send them to their deaths."

They trudged through the waves toward the shore together.

"Few things in this life make sense. Least of all death's coming," said Gnorn after a moment. "But we carry on."

Orvandil grunted. "Aye. Death's coming is unknown, but it comes for us if we linger on this beach. As soon as we hide that body, we break into squads and make for the rallying point."

"Right. My nine men are ready. We'll be first off. Mostlike first to arrive too."

"Oh? What makes you so confident?"

"I'm a Dweorg, am I not?"

"So?"

"We Dweorgs are skilled rangers. We know these lands better than any other folk."

"Because your eyes are closer to the ground?"

"Ha! No, because we're cleverer than you big louts."

"Care to make a wager on it, then?"

"It would pain me to rob you, but since you offer . . . Let's say the one who reaches the rallying point later scrubs the other's byrny clean."

"Done."

"Just be sure you make it there. My byrny will be rusty from all this sea water and in much need of a good scrubbing."

"Fear not for me, friend Dweorg. I'll be there. And when you arrive, you can give your byrny its scrubbing after you finish mine."

"We shall see."

Orvandil smiled. He had made a good choice in Gnorn for his second in command. The Dweorg would not let him forget why they were there. This would be a grim struggle, but, for a change, perhaps he had a reason to fight.

Orvandil peered through the brush. He was sweating and breathing hard, but he would not have rested if it had not been for his panting men, who had collapsed onto the ground and were holding their stomachs in an attempt to subdue their heavy breaths. Due to the trees, he could see little, but he knew somewhere back there behind all the leaves and brush lurked their pursuers.

"Do you think we lost them?" whispered Unil, whose back leaned against a tree trunk as he sat on the forest floor. The man's chest heaved as he gasped for air. Unil was the only one among those following Orvandil who could speak the Northern Tongue, and as such he served as a translator between the Thjoth and his other eight men. Or at least there had been eight — until the villagers alerted the Torrlonders to their presence. The messages had emphasized the villages were loyal. Not all of them, apparently. The Adanese people must have grown desperate to betray those who had come to help them. Orvandil had lost two men in the initial scuffle. Adnun and Omal. Pierced by arrows and chopped to pieces. Both had been young men.

"No chance. We move on as soon as you catch your breath. Look for a good place to ambush them."

Unil winced but nodded in affirmation.

A trader in spices, Unil was among the oldest of the recruits, at least to judge by the lines around his eyes and the grey invading his dark hair. He made up for his age by being far cleverer than most. Orvandil had been able to guess from their conversations that he was a fairly wealthy man. He wondered why the trader had joined in the effort and volunteered to fight in Adanon. *Mostlike the only stupid thing he ever did.*

"Ready?"

Unil nodded again and whispered the order in Andumaic. *"Jaunos."* Using his spear as a staff, the trader groaned and rose. The other six men got up from where they hid in the brush and looked at Orvandil with eyes that pleaded for some kind of assurance.

"Let's go."

As they ran through the trees, Orvandil wondered about their strategy of breaking up into small units when they arrived in Adanon. *Had we landed and stuck together as one army, the Torrlonders and their dragons would have finished us fast.* This was not smart either, but it *was* the only way. In war, the weaker side had few attractive options.

He thought back to the ambush. The temptation to stay and fight had been strong, but he would have lost all his men. Probably his life too. He needed to lead first and fight when it made sense. At the moment, leading meant running. At least a score of Torrlonders with half a dozen pucas presented bad odds for him and his seven remaining men. The Torrlonders were using those pucas to track them. If they let the beasts get too far ahead, perhaps Orvandil could take them out first. Then it would be easier to lose the soldiers. Or, better yet, surprise them.

High-pitched buzzing filled the air. "Arrows!" yelled Orvandil as he ducked. Shafts thudded and quivered in the tree trunks nearby, and someone cried out in agony. Orvandil looked back. Unil was writhing on the forest floor. An arrow had buried itself deep in the spice trader's thigh. Around the shaft, blood seeped into his breeches and darkened them in a widening circle. Orvandil ran toward him.

"Leave me," hissed Unil between his teeth as he shooed Orvandil away with his hand.

"Can't. The men won't know what I'm saying." Clasping hands, he tugged up the trader, who screamed and hopped on his good leg. Orvandil threw down his pack, turned away from Unil, and crouched. "Get on my back." When he felt Unil's arm around his neck, the Thjoth put his hands back and lifted the man under his legs, drawing out a shriek of pain.

"This is going to hurt."

"Just leave me!" Unil pleaded, but he still held on.

Orvandil ran as fast as he could with his burden. Unil's sweaty arms clutched onto his neck and chest as the Asdralae trader breathed in loud gasps through his nose. Up ahead, he was surprised to see his other six men waiting for them. "Go! *Jaunos!*" He was sure he mispronounced the Andumaic word, but he figured they knew what he meant since they started sprinting.

Crashing and snapping through the brush and the branches, which clawed and scratched at his limbs, Orvandil realized they could not outrun their pursuers this way. As if in confirmation, another volley of arrows whizzed by and bit into the trees near them in a series of thwoks. At least there were no agonized cries. It was time to make a stand, but he needed a good place. A large boulder in the midst of the trees caught his attention, and he yelled to his men, "Over here!"

All six followed.

When he reached the boulder, Orvandil tried to put down Unil with care. "Stay here."

The limp body fell off him and collapsed to the ground with a final thud. It lay still.

"Unil?"

The arrow that had punctured the back of the spice trader's helm to nestle in his brain answered for him. With his head twisted at an odd angle, his vacant eyes stared to the side. He had been a gentle man with a fine sense of humor.

Orvandil bent down and picked up Unil's spear, which the man had somehow managed to hold on to in death. "We fight now," he growled.

The six young men seemed to need no translation. With their backs to the boulder, they readied their spears and bows and waited.

They did not need to wait for long. Six pucas thrashed out of the trees toward them, snarling and hissing as they leapt about on all fours. The twenty grey-kirtled Torrlonders followed, their eyes hidden under the shadow of their helms as they lifted their bows and spears.

Orvandil did not wait for them. Raising Unil's spear, he heaved it with all his strength. The weapon sliced the air and pierced a bowman through the chest with such force that it knocked him back and pinned him to a tree, where his lifeless limbs slumped. The Thjoth used the momentum of his cast to charge forward as he slipped his long dagger out of its sheath. He did not break his stride as he flipped the dagger into his throwing hand and hurled it. A moment later, another Torrlonder bowman cried out and grasped at the bloody mass that had been his eye, from which the dagger protruded, before he went down twitching.

Four arrows and two spears flew from behind Orvandil. Both spears missed any target but the ground, but two pucas shrieked and fell after arrows drilled into their bony chests. *At least they didn't hit me.* Orvandil had not known if his men would follow, but he smiled at their futile loyalty.

The Torrlonders nocked their arrows. Orvandil was sure he would not reach them before the first volley pincushioned him.

A hail of arrows filled the air, whistling and buzzing toward their mark. The Torrlonders groaned and cried out in shock as shafts sprouted from their bodies. For a fraction of a moment, Orvandil wondered how his six men had launched so many at once, but of course the missiles had come from another direction. The Torrlonders turned to face their new attackers, green clad men who swarmed from the trees off to Orvandil's left.

His sword unsheathed, the Thjoth never stopped running, and he reached the distracted Torrlonders before they could react. With a sweep of his blade, he sheared off the first one's head, from whose neck cords of blood flew and spattered the tree behind him. The next one he carved in half from shoulder to arse. The man's guts slopped out and spilled over the ground. Screaming in triumph and moving in a blur, Orvandil raged among his foes like a wolf among terrified sheep. Three more succumbed to the sharp edge of his blade before all the Torrlonders and their pucas lay dead. Arrows protruded from most of their corpses.

The forest was silent as he surveyed the carnage. Breathing hard and holding his blade poised before him to cleave the next thing that moved, the Thjoth found himself wishing for more foes to mow down. He ground his teeth as he stifled the ecstasy of the battle rage. *Plenty more later.*

Before facing their green clad rescuers, Orvandil glanced around to check on his men. All six were standing near him, gasping for breath but unharmed. Two held reddened blades. *Good.*

"Rawn daehi glinnath arbaeth!" shouted one of the newcomers in Ondunic. Orvandil had no idea what the man said, but he sounded angry. The dark, little man wore leather armor and had a long, scraggly beard. Like the rest of the thirty or so ragged Adanese fighters gathering around him, he looked like he had not eaten a good meal in a long time. They all kept their weapons ready and stared at Orvandil and his men with hungry eyes.

"We come from Asdralad," said Orvandil to the one who had shouted. "Queen Faldira has sent us to aid you against the Torrlonders.

My men speak only Andumaic, and I speak no Ondunic. Is there one among you who knows the Northern Tongue?"

"What are the words?" demanded the man who had shouted before. Clearly, he was in charge.

Orvandil nodded at him. "The eagle and the raven have come to join the wolf."

"Then let the feast begin," answered the man who led the Adanese. "Welcome to Adanon. Or what is left of it."

"Our thanks for the welcome, and for your timely appearance."

The man waved at his men, who began carving arrows from corpses and stripping them of anything useful. "We've been looking for you. You must be the Thjoth."

"I am Orvandil."

"I am Uwain. A few of your squads have arrived at our camp already. All are short a few men, but any help is a boon to us, so long as you can feed yourselves." Above his gaunt cheeks Uwain's wary eyes seemed like a cornered animal's — they never lost the threat of violence. Orvandil wondered if he had been a nobleman.

"Understood. We've brought some supplies for a start. Was there a Dweorg among those who arrived?"

"A Dweorg? No, not when last I left camp."

Despite the wager he had with Gnorn, the answer disappointed Orvandil. Things were worse here than he had believed. These desperate men were on their last legs. He wondered once again how many of the young volunteers from Asdralad would make it. *Mayhap none, in the end. This mission is doomed. A sentence of death. Well, we're here to stall the Torrlonders, and so we will.* "Lead the way back to camp then, Uwain."

THE CAMP CENTERED ON A PATCH OF THE FOREST FEATURING A rocky outcrop in the side of a hill. With no break in the trees, the thick canopy concealed all beneath it, one rise among many in the forested landscape. Runnels of erosion had formed plant-choked trenches and gullies deep enough to hide soldiers in and provide natural barriers should any foe attack. It was a defensible enough position, at least if no dragons swooped down from the air, and Orvandil reckoned there might be approaches to it on the other side of the hill, no doubt as well guarded as this path, not to mention lookouts atop the hill's crest. As he climbed the hill behind Uwain, he took a few casual glances around him. Numerous watchful sentries hid behind trees and perched in the branches above. They held their bows ready and had smeared their faces with mud to blend in with the forest. There were mostlike others that he missed, and he approved of the caution.

When they trudged higher, there was a bubbling, liquid sound. As the running water grew louder, more men came into view, and these made no effort to hide. More and more half-starved fighters appeared, all of them as shabby as Uwain's group, and though they all watched Orvandil with wary eyes, these appeared to be at rest. A few even gathered in groups to throw dice or chat in Ondunic.

A stream, the source of the bubbling, ran down from above the outcrop and spilled over its edge, producing a small cataract that splashed in a clear pool. The steady tapping of the water had hollowed a bowl out of the flat rock, whence the water continued its journey down the hill. Behind the cataract was the mouth of a small cave. A lance of sunlight stabbed through the forest canopy and produced a small, dim fragment of rainbow in the water's spray.

Not far from the mouth of the cave on two tree stumps sat a short, bearded southerner and a slight woman who wore fine robes beneath a green cloak. Three boys sat on some large rocks nearby, the eldest hardly a teen, though these southerners were so small, it was hard for Orvandil to judge. He recognized King Balch, though the monarch had lost almost all his extra flesh, and Queen Rona of Adanon. The boys must have been their three sons. With cups carved out of wood still in their hands, they appeared to have just finished a meal.

Standing behind Adanon's royal family as if guarding them was the familiar though somewhat battered form of Imharr. Orvandil's former soldier's face broke out in a huge grin as he strode forward. "Orvandil." He nodded. "You're a sight for sore eyes, my friend."

The two clasped forearms, and, after glancing at Imharr's scarred and strangely hued hand, Orvandil smiled. "It's good to see you too, Imharr."

Imharr's smile gave way to a concerned frown, and he swallowed before speaking again. "How is Day?"

"Learning and thriving when I left him. He'll make us proud."

Imharr nodded and then found his smile again. "Good. That is good. I knew he would."

Beside Orvandil, Uwain cleared his throat as if growing impatient. "Your Majesties," he said in the Northern Tongue, "I bring you Orvandil, captain of the forces Queen Faldira of Asdralad has sent."

King Balch rose. Like his followers, he was dressed in forest greens, and he walked with a limp as he approached Orvandil. "Captain Orvandil." At least he had not lost his loud voice. "Welcome to our court." Balch gestured with his hands as if pointing out a splendid palace. He laughed, but there was no mirth in it. "I fear you'll find our accommodations less comfortable than when you last stayed with us."

"I'm not here for comfort, your Majesty."

"Good. Very good. You'll find damned little of it. Your men have begun to arrive. That is well since we'll not be able to stay here much longer. The Torrlonders' beasts have our scent again. We'll need to move on soon. We have a day or two at most."

"How many of my men have arrived?"

"Your group is the sixth by my count. But most squads have lost men. I've left them all in the charge of the sorcerer Vilyanad until you arrived. He's proven a most able and useful man. Our thanks to Queen Faldira for the aid she's sent. It's too little and too late, but no other kingdom has lifted a finger on our behalf. But they will see, won't they? Once the Torrlonders have finished with us."

"You speak as if defeat is sure."

"It is. We have no room for hope in our empty bellies. Only revenge. We'll send as many troll-swiving Torrlonders as we can to their greedy god."

"Then I will help you do that. But now I would speak with Vilyanad. I must see to my men."

"Of course. But remember, we leave in two days at most. We may have to flee at a moment's notice. Any of your men who have not found us by then are on their own."

Orvandil thought of Gnorn and the many men of Asdralad who were struggling for survival in this foreign land. He nodded. "Understood."

Balch nodded at Imharr. "Duke Imharr will take you to Vilyanad. No doubt you two will wish to catch up on the way. I'll send someone to fetch you in the evening so that you may join me and my captains as we discuss our future strategy."

"Yes, your Majesty." Orvandil bowed toward Queen Rona. "Your Majesty."

The grave queen nodded back to him. She had said nothing, but she had observed him the whole time. In her eyes Orvandil saw a fierce determination. *That one at least is not yet broken.*

"This way." Imharr gestured with his scarred hand, and Orvandil fell in beside him, his men following.

"*Duke* Imharr?" Orvandil frowned. "That can only mean your uncle . . . I'm sorry. He was a good man."

Imharr looked down and nodded as they walked, his grief and care written on his face. He released a long sigh. "We've lost a lot of good people." He looked up. "But we struggle on. Now tell me of Asdralad, if you will, to lighten my heart for a moment."

Imharr and Orvandil exchanged a little more news on their way to Vilyanad and the other Asdralae on another part of the hill. When they reached the encampment, Imharr put his hand on Orvandil's shoulder. "I must return to the king. We'll speak again soon."

The survivors of Orvandil's squad called out and smiled for the first time since they had set out from Asdralad upon seeing more than thirty of their fellow Asdralae, who were busy setting up green canvas tents and fortifying their position on the tree-covered slope by digging trenches. Cries of greeting preceded embraces and chatter in Andumaic. Vilyanad, who had been overseeing the men, came over to greet Orvandil. The slender, handsome sorcerer had somehow managed to preserve his elegance in the midst of the forest, though his fine clothes were beginning to fray.

"Captain Orvandil. I relinquish command of these men to you."

"Lord Vilyanad. Queen Faldira sends her greetings. We have much to discuss."

"Yes. If you would follow me, I'll apprise you of our situation."

"Our situation is bloody bad. But our first order of business is to find as many of our men as we can. As soon as possible, we'll organize patrols to go out with the Adanese in search of them."

"Very well."

"Also, I want you to round up a third of each of our men's food provisions and make a gift of them to the Adanese."

"Is that wise?"

"We'll be depending on the Adanese for our lives. Best to make friends. Besides, the men will have to learn to hunt sooner or later."

The sorcerer nodded in agreement. "I will carry out your orders."

"You've done a fine job getting the men started on the ditches. More than likely we'll never use them, but it's good to keep them busy."

"I thought as much."

"I'd like you to stay in charge here while I'm gone."

"But you've only just arrived. Where will you go?"

"To lead one of the patrols. I've got a byrny that needs cleaning and a Dweorg to find."

OVER THE NEXT NIGHT AND DAY, THE SQUADS OF ASDRALAE trickled into the camp. Some of them had banded together in larger units, and some came in threes or pairs. Some came bandaged and limping from wounds. None came without losses. Along with the Adanese fighters led by Imharr, Orvandil and his patrols helped to save many of the Asdralae from further harm. The Torrlonders were thick on the ground and closing in.

On the second evening after Orvandil's arrival, King Balch insisted it was time to leave. They would break camp under the cover of night and depart for a new location. Death waited for them if they stayed. It was only a matter of time before the dragons arrived, and behind them the Torrlonders would swarm in overwhelming numbers.

Orvandil could not object. Two hundred and ninety-nine of his men had reported in. It was more than he had dared to hope for. The two sorcerers were among them. Gnorn was not. "Curse the Dweorg," he muttered as he left the meeting of Balch's captains. "Where is he?" He would tell Vilyanad to order the men to break camp. Gnorn would have to survive and find them somehow. *The Dweorg's stubborn. He might make it yet.*

By the time he reached the portion of the hill on which the Asdralae encamped, the sun was setting and leaving the forest to the grey of twilight. He found Vilyanad sitting on a boulder in conference with the other two sorcerers and asked them to spread the orders to the men.

Vilyanad looked grave at the news, his mouth set in a frown, but he nodded. "Yes, Captain Orvandil. Let us hope the rest will find us."

"We can hope so."

A deep, resounding bellow split the air from above. Orvandil flinched as the abrupt roar assaulted his ears. The leaves of the trees susurrated and vibrated in a gust, and branches swayed. A sudden glowing pulsed behind the Thjoth, and he jerked around in time to see flames roiling down on the portion of the camp he had just left, where Balch and his men were preparing to depart. Screams followed, and several trees crackled and hissed as a blaze engulfed them. They were too late. The dragons had come.

Most of the terror-struck Asdralae froze, their eyes bulging and mouths wide open. Some of them cried out and called on their god and goddess. Vilyanad grabbed Orvandil's arm. "I sense only one. Probably scouting on its own."

"Can you do anything?"

The sorcerer shook his head. "I've tried and failed to seize the beasts. I cannot wield the song of origin of dragons, but I can lessen the destruction from the flames."

"Do it. And have the men ready their bows and follow me."

"Where?"

"To fight the bloody dragon."

Orvandil did not wait for an answer. He grabbed a spear from one of his soldiers and sprinted toward the flames. Fiery chaos swept up the Adanese. Amidst trees burning eerie orange and red, some of the soldiers cowered and hid, coughing and holding their hands over their faces to ward them from the heat. Others ran for cover. A few bodies rolled on the ground in flames. Their raw shrieks clawed the night air. Orvandil stood and scanned the dark sky for any sign of the serpent of the air.

The howling gust was his only warning. Some instinct told the Thjoth to dive, and as his chest hit the ground, a surge of heat passed over him. He looked up. Churning flames engulfed a broad swath of the forest in front of him. Smoke rose to the sky, which was calm and dark. But death lurked in that darkness somewhere, waiting to descend. Rising to his feet, Orvandil brandished the spear and yelled, "Come back, beast! I'm still here!"

A large group of the Asdralae came running toward him out of the trees with their bows ready and arrows nocked. Quite a tempting target. Orvandil waved his arms. "Break up! Spread out!"

Vilyanad, who was at their head, looked straight at Orvandil, but the sorcerer's half closed eyes appeared in a trance as he mumbled something the Thjoth could not hear.

"Spread out, damn you all!"

Too late. The lingworm swooped down behind the men and opened its jaws to disgorge its deadly breath. Orvandil had one chance.

He screamed as he cast the spear into the sky over his doomed soldiers. The weapon sailed true, but it seemed so tiny before the gigantic beast plummeting toward its prey with outspread wings.

Fire erupted from the beast's maw and descended upon the hapless men, but before it hit, Vilyanad shouted something and waved his arms. Swerving away from the Asdralae, the ball of fire obeyed and jerked in the direction in which the sorcerer waved to smash into the trees, which exploded into flames. At the same moment, Orvandil's thrown spear pierced the dragon's left wing, and a spray of blood followed its flight out the other side. The serpent of the air shrieked and jerked its head toward its punctured wing.

"Fill it with arrows! Loose!" yelled Orvandil.

A storm of arrows rushed upward from the Asdralae as the dragon streaked by. Orvandil could not be sure, but he thought he heard some of the missiles bite. Many clattered off scales, and broken shafts spiraled back to the earth. With luck, some of them were now lodged in the beast's wings.

A long silence followed. When it seemed the lingworm would not return, a few timid cheers broke out among the tense Asdralae. In the glow of the burning trees, their smiles were relieved, and they clapped each other on their backs. Orvandil decided to let them enjoy the moment. They would have few such victories to celebrate. Many of the Adanese began trickling back through the trees, though their eyes never stopped glancing at the ominous night sky.

Surrounded by a ring of warriors under Imharr's command, King Balch emerged from the cave behind the cataract. The water still gurgled, but the rest of the outcrop had become blackened and withered. Flames sputtered on the remnants of the smoking brush, and steam rose from the polluted pool. The red light of the fires lit Balch's face, and his eyes had the crazed look of a man who knew his death was coming. The king approached Orvandil with a fey smile across his face. "A brave fight. You and your men fared better than any have thus far against the dragons, Captain Orvandil. I'd give my left testicle to have a chance at sticking one of those fucking monsters like that."

"The beasts are not unbeatable. They bleed," said Orvandil in a loud voice. He wanted the Asdralae and the Adanese to hear.

Balch nodded. "Yes, they do, and it gladdens my heart to witness it. But that bloody one will return. And it will have much more company. Those goat-swiving Torrlonders know exactly where we are now. The dragons are the eyes of their supreme priest. We must flee."

"I'll have my men finish breaking camp. We'll meet you at the appointed place within two days. Until then, farewell, your Majesty." Orvandil shouted orders at his men, and Vilyanad translated them into Andumaic. They rushed back to finish packing their gear while Vilyanad and the other two sorcerers tamed the flames with their spells.

The dwindling fires cast long, dancing shadows and provided light to see by as the Asdralae hurried to pack. When they were ready, Orvandil barked his orders. "Scouts first. You know what to do. The rest of you, form up. Spread out, and keep alert if you want to see the dawn."

"Already leaving?" asked a familiar gruff voice. "We've only just arrived."

Orvandil spun around. From the trees emerged a group of men. Gnorn trudged at their head. In the ruddy light, the Dweorg's teeth showed behind his broad smile. Orvandil sighed and cracked a smile back at his friend.

"You're late."

"We were detained. If it hadn't been for those flames, we'd still be bumping around in the dark. Looks like we missed something."

"I'll tell you about it on the march, and you can tell me what happened to you."

Gnorn scowled and took a look at Orvandil's chest, where his byrny lay under his kirtle. "I don't suppose you've scrubbed it yet?"

"No. Quite rusty, in fact."

"Hmmm. And I don't suppose there's time for a tired Dweorg and his men to get a drink and a quick nap?"

"A drink, yes. You'll have to wait for the nap, unless you care to greet Bledla's dragons and Torrlond's army when you wake up."

"I thought as much."

Orvandil glanced at Gnorn's group, which was large. There might have been as many as thirty men behind him. "Looks like you found some friends. How many of your squad did you lose?"

The Dweorg turned around to his men as if to count them, but when he looked back at Orvandil he smiled and said, "None. Not a scratch among us. I picked up the others along the way."

The Thjoth nodded. "In that case, the wager's settled. Yours is the only squad to make it whole. Now get that drink and fall in. We've got a long march ahead."

"U<small>RKHALION</small> <small>VARDUNAY</small> <small>NANDUINAE</small> <small>AR</small> <small>NIDANWY</small>. I<small>NTHULION</small> shovhanay silvuinae an gilvanwy." The supreme priest intoned the healing spell in his bass voice. The largest bloody gash in the leathery wing closed as the energy from Bledla flowed into the dragon. The beast purred with a deep, gravelly rumble in its throat, and he sensed its pleasure at the lessening of pain.

He removed his palm, on which hot dragon blood was smeared, from the sealed wound. This one would leave a scar on the wing. The eleven smaller wounds had been easier to close. Some of the arrows, which lay on the cobblestones near Bledla's feet, had lodged in the wing, and he had broken each shaft before removing them. He guessed a spear had made the larger hole, but whatever did it had punctured a major vein. Dried blood still covered the wing, which the dragon began licking with its rough, forked tongue as it coiled into a ball. It would need a day's rest and some fresh meat. He would send a live horse or cow for it.

The heathens would pay for daring to harm the instrument of Edan's will. Now Bledla knew the insurgents' exact location. Balch was there. He felt it in his bones. No doubt the vulgar man and his followers would flee, but Bledla's other dragons were in pursuit of them and would find them. Six thousand soldiers were also on their way to reinforce those already in the area, encircling the rebels in a constricting noose. This time the unbelievers would not escape. The insurgency would end as the righteous agents of the Way crushed it through Edan's guidance.

And yet, things were taking too long in the south. He had hoped the victory of the Way in Adanon would be as swift as it had been in Caergilion. But the Adanese were sneaking cowards who refused to fight in the open. Hiding in forests and caves, they struck unawares and slithered away. As long as Balch and his followers kept harassing King Earconwald's army with help from the local population, Adanon could not truly belong to the Eternal. It was an insufferable delay in the fulfillment of Edan's Kingdom – in the salvation of all. The supreme priest's fists clenched, but he suppressed a snarl. *I must be patient. Edan will accomplish His will when the time is right. For now we keep our faith and fight. All will go according to His plan.*

Bledla looked away from the dragon's red scales, which gleamed in the light of torches lining the perimeter of the empty courtyard, part of a complex of squat buildings and towers surrounded by thick stone walls. The castle, which had once belonged to an Adanese duke named Gwalor, served as the headquarters of the Torrlonders in Galathon. Its towers were shadows against the moonlit sky.

He was sick of the place. He was sick of the locals, who had all converted to the Way, else they would be dead. Priests initiated every convert into the path of salvation, but Bledla could still sense the simmering resentment from the Adanese. He sometimes caught a hint of it in their eyes on the streets. To his face they bowed and scraped, but if ever he glanced at one of them, there was the hard look of hatred before fear or a veneer of sycophancy replaced it. Once in a while a Torrlonder soldier would turn up murdered, his body stuffed away in an alley. The soldiers now had orders never to go out in groups of less than a dozen among the Adanese. *The fools ought to fall on their knees in gratitude. We've given them a chance at salvation. But time will separate the wheat from the chaff. We will unmask the false ones who aid their demon-worshiping former king, and they will burn for their treachery.*

Byrnies clinked at the other end of the courtyard, and a group of guards emerged into the torchlight. The guards usually stayed as far as possible from Bledla when he was with his dragons. These, however, were in the company of a white-robed man. As they neared him, Bledla sensed the gift in the High Priest Joruman. He had grown mistrustful of the man. Joruman was skilled at hiding his emotions, but the supreme priest sensed something behind the smooth façade. *He's a clever, ambitious one. I must be careful of him.*

In the midst of the eight guards walked two men, one large and the other enormous. Both were clad in the manner of the barbaric Ilarchae, wearing no breeches and covering their long kirtles with fur cloaks. *What are these two doing here?*

When they were close enough to speak to Bledla without shouting, Joruman raised his hand to halt the procession. The smaller of the Ilarchae had long red hair, whereas the huge one was blond and wore his beard braided. Both of them stared open-mouthed and wide-eyed at the dragon next to the supreme priest. The eight grey-kirtled guards kept their gazes on the cobblestones. Only the smiling high priest looked at Bledla.

"Blessed be the Eternal, my lord," said Joruman with a bow.

"And the kingdom of Edan. What brings you here at this hour?"

"My lord, these two are visitors from the Wildlands. They claim to represent one of the Ilarchae chieftains, who proposes an *alliance*." The high priest spoke with a grin that implied the Ilarchae were ignorant children playing at statecraft.

"Then why not take them to King Earconwald?"

"The king is . . . occupied at the moment, and so I thought you would be most fit to render a decision regarding how we are to receive these . . . men."

Earconwald's fornicating with some local whore again, no doubt. "They are heathens, are they not?"

The red-haired barbarian cleared his throat. "Your pardon, my lord. We can speak for ourselves."

Surprised to hear the Northern Tongue on the lips of a barbarian, Bledla stared at the man. "Very well. Answer my question."

"We worship the gods of our ancestors, but we are willing to listen to your priests talk about your god." He glanced up again at the dragon before continuing. "You must be the chief holy man of the Torrlonders. We have heard of your war, and we have ridden fast and far to offer our strength. We tribes of the Wildlands have a foe in common with you: the Sildharae. If it is true you will march on Sildharan after you subdue this kingdom, we are ready to swear an oath. When you attack the Sildharae from the west, we will attack them from the east, and they will fall between us."

"And will you convert to the Way and worship only Edan?"

"Our leader has said he will allow your priests amongst us, but we are free folk who worship what we please. Some may decide to follow your god."

"Who is your leader?"

"Surt, war-leader of the Fire Dragons. He will be the one to unite us. I have seen it."

"And who are you?"

"I am Munzil of the Grey Wolves. This is Gorm, a great chieftain of the Fire Dragons. He does not speak your tongue." Upon hearing his name, the larger man stopped staring at the dragon to grunt and nod at Bledla.

Bledla gazed at Munzil and stroked his beard. *Edan has sent them. This is the answer. The delay here in Adanon was only to give the barbarians time to come to us. The east will fall, and we will usher in the Kingdom. Your wisdom is manifest to your servant, mighty Edan.*

"Munzil of the Grey Wolves, you and Gorm of the Fire Dragons are welcome here. On the morrow, when King Earconwald is ready for an audience, I will introduce you to him. Then we will discuss our alliance. If the king approves, we will send one of our lords to accompany you back to the Wildlands to bear witness to the terms we agree on." *We'll need someone clever there to see to our interests, but someone I don't want too near me.*

Bledla looked at Joruman and smiled.

The high priest wore a puzzled frown until comprehension widened his eyes.

6

FINDING AN ADVANTAGE

*D*amn *the old man. He thinks to be rid of me. We'll see who's rid of whom. He knows less than he thinks...*

The High Priest Joruman cursed his spiritual superior, the Supreme Priest Bledla, for the thousandth time on his voyage. His back muscles twisted with knots of pain, and the flesh of his inner thighs was sore from rocking in the saddle for so long on the miserable brown nag beneath him. Hissing and moaning through the endless grasslands with no opposition to blunt its force, the fierce wind pried into the thick fur cloak Joruman wore and watered up his eyes. Though the sky was blue overhead, the same wind drove a few orphaned snowflakes past him in a nearly horizontal flight. They must have come from the grey clouds far off in the distance, making a long journey before landing on that desolate piece of earth.

Joruman's had been a long journey too, and the company had been less than stimulating. The group of Ilarchae warriors he was forced to travel with had been carousing, feasting, belching, jostling, brawling, farting, and yelling at all hours in their guttural, incomprehensible language. The high priest spent most of the voyage, whether in ship or on horse, huddled as far away as courtesy would allow from the barbarians. In addition to Munzil and Gorm, there were seven other warriors, all of the Fire Dragon tribe, and a dozen thralls who had manned the ships. Joruman could see little difference between the warriors and the thralls. One was as filthy as the other, and they all carried weapons.

The most hideous of them all was the monstrosity called Skuld. Joruman distanced himself from her as much and as often as he could. The scar-faced heathen was undoubtedly the most enormous woman he ever laid eyes on. Not only did she drink more and fart louder than the others, but the first time Skuld met Joruman, she had reached under the high priest's white robe and, to the merriment of the other Ilarchae, grabbed ahold of his manhood. Joruman had been too stunned to react.

With a grin on his face, Munzil had explained, "She thought all you priests must be . . . What is your word? *Eunuchs*. I told her you never lie with women. She said there was only one way that was possible. It seems she was wrong."

Joruman had fantasized a dozen ways to avenge himself upon the monstrosity, but following through would be bad for diplomacy. Allying with the barbarians, he had decided, could work to forward his plans, which were more important than his injured dignity, and anyway King Earconwald approved of the idea. The hideous creature seemed important according to whatever ranking the Ilarchae practiced. Most astonishing was how the men treated her as an equal. Apparently, Skuld was the sister of Gorm, who was some sort of lord among the savages. With arms twice the size of Joruman's, no doubt she was also a fierce warrior.

He watched Skuld riding ahead of him, speaking in her loud voice to the man ahorse next to her in words that sounded like rough grunts to Joruman's ears. Twisting the ring on the pinky finger of his right hand, he pictured her in the frilly gown of a Torrlonder noblewoman. He chuckled to himself at how ridiculous the freak would look, though he had to admit there was a handsome quality to her face, and he reckoned she would not be timid in bed.

"Quite a woman, isn't she?"

Joruman turned toward the voice. Lost in his fantasy about Skuld and wrapped in his fur, he had not heard Munzil ride up next to him. The barbarian was grinning at him as if he guessed Joruman's thoughts.

Joruman felt his face flush, but he supposed it mattered little since the wind had already chafed his cheeks red. He put on a casual smile that he hoped expressed both indifference and a measure of contempt, though it was hard to know if he was achieving the right effect since his face was frozen. "A bit rough for my taste."

Munzil pursed his lips and then nodded. "Life is rough here in the Wildlands. The rough survive."

"And the rest?"

The barbarian's face hardened. "Death awaits."

The high priest stared at his companion for a long moment. "So it does. Even for the strong."

"Aye. But they leave deeds behind. Deeds their kin will tell of with pride."

Joruman snorted. "And when the kin die? Where will such deeds go? To the same abyss. No, my friend. Strength alone is not enough. It merely delays the inevitable. The only real answer is . . . transcendence."

Munzil squinted in obvious ignorance of the word. "Even the gods will succumb one day."

Joruman shook his head and grinned. "I speak not of your gods, man."

Munzil stared ahead and was silent for a long enough time that Joruman thought he would not respond. At length, he looked at the high priest again. "I know little of what you speak, but I know this: A brave life rewards itself."

Joruman shrugged. "If you say so." He smiled again and gave Munzil a deep nod that bordered on a mocking bow.

The barbarian looked on with a stony face before riding ahead without another word.

The high priest chuckled at the man's back. For the moment, he would pretend to forget all the insults. He was a patient man, and these barbarians were potentially useful tools. But Bledla . . . *The old man will pay for this. Half-mad zealot with his head full of cobwebs and prophecies. He thinks to interrupt my ascent, but I will use this journey to my advantage as well.*

Despite the supreme priest's intentions, this journey would only strengthen Joruman's position. What was more, he now knew it was possible to grow more powerful than Bledla. That boy from the Mark had frightened the supreme priest. In truth, he had frightened Joruman too.

But Dayraven was most likely dead. It was a pity in a way, and a part of him regretted that circumstances had forced him to hasten the young man's demise. It would have been interesting to have had an opportunity to study him, and he might have even been an ally. But the boy was an obstacle to their immediate plans, and so Joruman had acted in the interest of all. Most importantly, he could have been a hindrance to Joruman's future plans, which far outweighed one life. In this matter, he had made the necessary calculation. Still, he would have to study the elves further. There was something unsettling and unstable about Dayraven, but there had been so much power in the boy. *If I could find a way to harness it . . .* But first this matter of the Ilarchae. The journey was nearly finished, and soon he would find what awaited him. *By Aldmund's blessed balls, these have been the most tedious weeks of my existence.*

One thing was certain: The Wildlands were as miserable and squalid a place as the stories told. There was nothing that could pass for civilization, and the few dismal villages they rode through were little more than mud holes for pigs. Worst of all was the complete ignorance among the Ilarchae of two things: letters and the gift. One of the thralls who had manned the ship had enough of the gift to make a decent priest, had the fellow been born in Torrlond. Instead, the poor bastard wallowed in stupidity. If Joruman succeeded in his ambitions, he would work toward eradicating such appalling witlessness.

The sharp wind gusted, and he drew close the fur cloak he wore over his white robe. Soon, Munzil had earlier assured him, a thick blanket of snow and ice would cover this plain. He hoped to have concluded his business here and departed before that happened. *Wretched place.*

He was saddle sore and ill-tempered after all the sailing and riding. But he was a patient man, and he would procure something useful from it all. Perhaps this Surt fellow would prove interesting. Munzil spoke of him with a crazed expression in his eyes, but no doubt these superstitious barbarians were easy to impress.

Joruman took in his first sight of their destination as he paused on his nag atop a slight rise in the monotonous grasslands. Squinting in the morning sunlight, he tried to ignore the sting on his wind-burned face and cracked lips. His breath misted and curled in front of him, and its moisture settled on his beard, which he had not trimmed in days.

Below them on the cold plain were more than two hundred small animal hide tents pitched around one large tent. Among the tents were more than a hundred tall poles standing upright in clusters of three to five. All the poles had some object affixed to their tops, but the objects were too far away to see distinctly. Smoke from many fires drifted upward until the wind yanked it all and dispersed it in Joruman's direction. The wind carried the smoke's scent, and to the high priest's mind it promised much needed warmth. But, in addition to the warmth, he would also find a couple hundred more of the Ilarchae for his only company.

According to Munzil, leaders from upwards of forty tribes would be present for their great moot. Each leader had sworn some sort of sacred oath to bring only six warriors with him. Thus, according to prior instructions, only Munzil and Gorm were to accompany Joruman down into the plain. The high priest would have celebrated parting ways with his other traveling companions, especially Skuld, but he did not expect those awaiting him below to be an improvement.

Nearby, the huge woman leaned to one side in her saddle and grunted as a loud, long fart erupted beneath her, starting as a deep rumble and petering out in a high whine.

His lip wrinkled in a disgusted sneer, Joruman stared at Skuld and asked, "Was that you or your horse?"

The hideous woman showed her teeth in a crazed grin.

On the other side of the high priest, Munzil chuckled. "Come, priest. Surt waits." He clucked his tongue, and his horse moved towards the encampment.

"Let's get this over with," Joruman said to no one in particular.

Following Gorm and Munzil, the high priest urged his nag toward the tents. He did not look back to see in which direction Skuld and the others rode, but their laughter carried far, and he could not help wondering if he was its object. The lot of them could go straight to their graves and rot there, for all he cared.

When they neared the encampment, Joruman began to make out some of the objects tied to the top of the wooden poles. One was a huge skull that belonged, he guessed, to a troll. Another was clearly a boar's skull. Yet others seemed to be the hides of wolves, bears, dogs, or other creatures. Some were cloaks made of feathers from eagles and ravens.

"They are the totems of the clans," said Munzil. "Each tribe holds at least three clans, some as many as five."

Joruman looked over at the red-haired savage, who had been watching him gaze up at the objects on their poles. He raised his eyebrows and nodded as if he found the information interesting.

"They are the strength of the tribes. We carry them into battle."

The high priest stifled the urge to roll his eyes. *Charming.*

"They are important," continued Munzil. "They remind us of who we are and where we belong. Like that ring you're always playing with." He nodded towards Joruman's right hand.

The high priest glanced at the ring his mother had given him. Then he looked back at his companion, one eyebrow rising in mild surprise. The barbarian, he had to admit, harbored his own sort of cleverness.

A cry from up ahead snatched his attention. A tall, lean, grey-whiskered man wrapped in a fur cloak approached them on foot. Something was wrong with the fellow's face, and when he drew close, Joruman saw a hollow, scar-covered socket where his left eye should have been. The man seemed to be addressing them.

"Oi! Gorm! Du aft kommzt. Tida izt."

Joruman's huge blond companion bellowed in answer, "Ach! Ond hezt du ollam dam motem gafrazen, shtek?" Each sharp word grated on the high priest's ears like a blade on a whetstone. Gorm alighted from his big, shaggy horse and laughed as he embraced the lean man. Each slapped the other's shoulder as if trying to knock the other man over.

As the two men exchanged words in their barbaric tongue, Munzil leaned over from his horse. "He is Valdur, chieftain of the Fire Dragons' Bear Clan."

Joruman pursed his lips as if he were impressed. "Ah. An important man, then."

"Every man is important, priest."

The high priest could not suppress a half smile. "Just so. But some more than others. Some men's greatness will cause them to influence the world more than others, to affect more lives. That makes them more important, more useful. Surt, for example. You cannot deny *he* is more useful than, say, one of your thralls."

The red-haired savage grunted in reluctant agreement.

"Speaking of the great man, when will we meet him?"

"Valdur will take us to him now. You will come before Surt, and I will accompany you to translate."

"Very *useful* of you."

Munzil stared at Joruman for a fraction longer than the high priest thought civil, but he turned away, seeming to leave something unsaid. He dismounted and led his horse on foot behind Valdur and Gorm. "Come."

Joruman alighted from his horse and, seeing no one offer to take the nag, led it himself. *The savages have little respect for rank, but they will fear power. I could show them real power. Perhaps a little display is in order.*

Valdur led them between the tents, which seemed arrayed in no order Joruman could discern. Though the ground was nearly frozen, the paths were muddy. A thin skin of ice covered some of the smaller puddles. At the moment the encampment was quiet, which was strange since the Ilarchae Joruman had traveled with had been almost never silent. A couple hundred of the savages ought to be producing a cacophony of inarticulate grunts and shouts. Only hushed voices emanated from some of the tents, and a few hard faces of bearded warriors peeked out from the shadows of their animal hide shelters as the high priest walked by. The air was still, even tense.

"Why are they all so quiet?"

Munzil turned to answer. "The oaths. They have all sworn to keep the peace until the great moot ends. That means no drinking mead, and they'll mostly keep to themselves. That way is best. There are blood feuds between many tribes."

"Ah. I see. That's polite of them." *I could find myself in the midst of a brawl here.*

They reached the open entrance of the large tent, which was made from numerous animal hides stitched together and stretched on a network of wooden poles. Since the hides did not reach the ground, plenty of pale light streamed in to reveal benches arrayed in a large circle. No one occupied the shelter, and Joruman found himself longing for the warmth and comfort of one of the smaller tents.

Valdur turned to the high priest. "Eoch har abidan. Surt komt." His voice was gruff, and his one-eyed gaze was as hard as steel.

"He wishes for you to stay here. The war-leader Surt will come soon," said Munzil.

Joruman smiled at the one-eyed brute. "Very well. I'll make myself comfortable here." With a wave of his hand, he gestured at the interior of the cold tent.

Irony was lost on the savages, who stared at the high priest with their stony, hostile faces. Munzil said something in the barbaric Ilarchae tongue, after which Valdur grunted and took the reins of all three horses, leaving them to the silence and shadows under the drafty shelter.

The high priest stepped inside and inspected the crude wooden benches. He turned his back on Munzil as he spoke in a quiet, precise tone that hinted at strained patience. "Is it the usual custom among you to keep a guest waiting in this way?"

"You must not enter the tent of any war-leader yet. It would make problems. After all the tribes' war-leaders have chosen one of their number to lead them all, there will be much to discuss. Until then, this tent belongs to all. It is . . ."

Joruman turned to face the savage. "Neutral ground?"

"Yes."

"I see."

"For now, the War-leader Surt wishes to greet you. It is an honor he wishes to give. After that, you will have a warm tent and a hot meal before rest." Munzil smirked in a way that suggested he read Joruman's thoughts.

Yes. A little too clever, this one. "Then I await the honor. And the warm tent."

He did not need to wait for long. Footsteps approached from one of the muddy paths outside, and a man taller than even Gorm ducked under the tent's entrance. Clad in black fur boots and a black fur cloak over a long black kirtle, the man lacked Gorm's bulk but was still thick with muscles. His hair and beard were dark brown, and he was younger than Joruman expected. Surt's eyes locked onto the high priest.

"Vel-coom." He drew out the word in his deep bass as if trying it for the first time. He glanced toward Munzil with a question in his eyes. The red-haired man nodded, confirming it was Surt's attempt to speak the Northern Tongue.

Joruman smiled. *A stab at being civilized. That counts as diplomacy, I suppose.*

The big man continued in his own rough tongue with more confidence. "Fyr-Vyrms hargtoch Surt eom ich."

"Welcome," translated Munzil. "I am Surt, War-leader of the Fire Dragons."

Joruman smiled and looked up at the huge Ilarchae. "Thank you, War-leader Surt. I am the High Priest Joruman. I come representing his Majesty King Earconwald of Torrlond and his most holy eminence, Bledla, Supreme Priest of the Way."

Munzil said a line or two in the Ilarchae tongue, and Joruman hoped he did not mangle the translation too much.

Surt smiled and nodded. More outlandish speech grated from his tongue, which Munzil rendered as, "We tribes of the Wildlands wish to do two new things. We wish to fight as one, under one war-leader. And we wish to join with you outlanders in war. The Sildharae have wronged the folk of the tribes by withholding honor from their thralls. If the Torrlonders want to fight the Sildharae, we folk of the tribes will come together and add our spears and swords to the battle. We will fight under our totems, and you under your banners, but together we will destroy Sildharan and divide the land and spoils. So tell us now in sooth: Will you Torrlonders make war on the Sildharae?"

Putting on a solemn face, Joruman nodded. "We *will* make war on Sildharan. When the time is right. The proposal to have the Ilarchae as allies in war pleases King Earconwald and the Supreme Priest Bledla. If the Ilarchae wish to join us in this war, then we must discuss the conditions and terms. King Earconwald has authorized me to negotiate those terms in good faith. I will spell them out before the leaders of your tribes. If the Ilarchae all join under one leader, no doubt it will be easier for us to come to an agreement."

After Munzil finished translating, Surt grinned like a bear about to rip open a fish. "On dan morgan urnam hargtocham vollu veh vindan."

Munzil's eyes kindled with a crazed smile as he interpreted the words, "We will choose our war-leader on the morrow."

THE NEXT DAY, AFTER A WARM AND LONG SLEEP UNDER A PILE OF musty furs inside a small tent, Joruman found himself in the large shelter again. This time, forty-three Ilarchae sat around the benches, each one the war-leader of his or her tribe.

Never had the high priest beheld such an unsightly gathering of savages. They ranged in age, but most were grey-haired and presented faces grooved with wrinkles. Only a few were young like Surt. At least four of them were women, though Joruman had a hard time telling since the women were so massive and, like the men, dressed as warriors. One he suspected of being female had a sparse but visible beard. They all wore fur boots and fur cloaks over their long kirtles, which broad leather belts encircled. Bone needles inserted in leather straps held their hair back. Most wore armor, some leather and some linked byrnies, and all carried grim weapons, such as large axes and broad swords. Most of them also sported scars on their faces, testaments to their participation in many battles. Some were missing an ear, a hand, or some other part of their anatomy. One had no nose. The only thing worse than their appearance was the sour, pungent reek of their body odor. Taken together, they were the ugliest collection of human beings Joruman had ever witnessed in one place.

He and Munzil completed the company. The six warriors each war-leader was allowed to bring were following orders to remain in their tents. This, Munzil had explained, was a necessary precaution against sudden passion turning the meeting into a bloodbath.

The war-leaders spoke in twos and threes in what sounded like loud arguments to the high priest. But Joruman had found such was the *only* way the Ilarchae spoke, so for all he knew, they were giving each other fond compliments or discussing the weather. He turned to his red-haired translator. "Do they represent all the tribes in the Wildlands?"

"No. A dozen have not come."

"So. Forty-three of fifty-five tribes here. How many warriors would they be able to muster?"

"One thousand a hundred times over."

"A hundred thousand?"

"Yes. And there are forty-four tribes here. I am the last of the Grey Wolves."

"A hundred thousand and *one* warriors, then."

Joruman smiled, but Munzil only stared back with a face like stone.

"Hargtochas!" boomed Surt above the din. The rest of the tent fell silent.

Once he got started, the war-leader of the Fire Dragons spoke for some time, and his words elicited an occasional murmur or nod from the others, which Joruman took to mean agreement on their part. Munzil whispered intermittent phrases in the Northern Tongue to him, by which he gathered Surt was reviewing the injustices the Sildharae had perpetrated on the Ilarchae. At one point, most of them shouted and raised their fists, some even leaping up from their benches with anger contorting their faces. The high priest flinched in the expectation they would commence brawling, but then he realized their sudden fit signified hearty accord with some point Surt had just made. Shortly after this, the war-leader of the Fire Dragons gestured toward Joruman.

Munzil leaned toward him. "It's your time, priest. Speak your king's wishes. I will tell them your words."

Joruman rose. He grinned at the forty-three savage faces gazing at him. "War-leaders of the Ilarchae. I am Joruman, high priest of the Way of Edan. I come from the kingdom of Torrlond representing King Earconwald and the Supreme Priest Bledla." He stopped to allow

Munzil to render his words into their barbaric tongue. The faces seemed unimpressed.

"Some of you have made the offer of an alliance in war with Torrlond. The offer pleases King Earconwald, who will invade Sildharan and crush those who have oppressed you." Again he paused for Munzil, and still they stared with dull-eyed contempt. Joruman waited for another reaction, but when none came, he decided to forge ahead.

"Hear now the terms and conditions for our alliance. If you wish to join Torrlond when it conquers the Sildharae, the first condition is that you will wait to attack Sildharan until an agreed upon time, which will come at King Earconwald's command. If we attack the enemy simultaneously from west and east, creating two fronts, the Sildharae will not withstand us for long."

This time, after Munzil translated, several grunts came. Joruman took them for concurrence, so he smiled and continued. "Second: Once we have destroyed the enemy, you will allow the priests of the Way to come among your tribes and tell your people of our god, Edan. You will not hinder those among you who wish to convert to the Way." Bledla had insisted on this bit of idiocy, so the Ilarchae would have to swallow it.

When Munzil finished explaining this condition, one of the war-leaders rose. Built like a bear, the man was nearly as hairy as one as well, except on the top of his bald head, which a deep scar crossed like jagged pink lightning. His shaggy grey and blond beard grew so far down his broad chest that he almost could have tucked its tip into his belt, next to the big axe hanging there. He grasped the top of the weapon as if he meant to use it, and his fierce blue eyes gazed at Joruman as he unleashed words that stabbed the air. "Ach, vee! Vaklingas gut wezan nocht shtork!" he began, and his words grew more vehement as he continued.

When the bear finished his tirade, Joruman looked toward Munzil, who gazed at the hairy war-leader with hard eyes, as if he were thinking of murdering the man. "What did he say?" asked the high priest.

"He doesn't like that condition."

"What did he say *exactly*?"

Munzil looked at Joruman and paused as if considering how much he should reveal. "He says the tribes should not allow you priests in white robes among us."

"So I gathered. Why not?"

Munzil sighed. "He says a little, smiling, weak man like you cannot have strong gods. He thinks if you priests walk among us, you will weaken us too."

Joruman grinned. This outburst was exactly what he needed. *I should thank the brute.* He stared at the war-leader and allowed his face to harden. Locking eyes with the hairy fellow, he asked Munzil, "Who is this man?"

"He is Rugnach, war-leader of the Strong Axe tribe."

Still Joruman kept his gaze on the bear. "Then tell Rugnach the priests of the Way are far mightier than he thinks. I am only one priest, but I could kill every man and woman in this tent in an instant."

Munzil hesitated. When Joruman glanced at him, he saw the disbelief in the red-haired barbarian's frown.

"Tell him," he growled as he turned his gaze back on Rugnach.

Munzil spoke. When he finished, silence filled the tent. The flat gazes of the Ilarchae all fell on the high priest.

At once, barks of laughter erupted among the war-leaders, and some of them slapped their knees as if Munzil had just told them the funniest jest they ever heard. Only Surt did not laugh as he cast a dark gaze on his fellow war-leaders and then glanced at Joruman.

The high priest allowed his mind to enter the realm of origins, filling him with the true perception of the world. This heightened awareness of the deeper reality — of all the fears and desires tugging at the mere mortals around him, in contrast with his serene grasp of the origins behind everything dwelling in the world of forms — intoxicated him with a sense of real power. He raised his arms, and when the air around him sparked with energy, the rest of the tent seemed to darken.

As open-mouthed astonishment replaced mirthful smiles on the dull faces of the barbarians, Joruman's grin expressed the bliss of his power as well as his imminent triumph. The gift was strong in him, and he never felt more alive than when demonstrating this fact to others. *Now they will see what it means to be strong.*

"Alakathon indomiel ar galathon anrhuniae! Vortalion marduniel im paradon khalghoniae!"

When Joruman unleashed the song of origin, writhing currents of energy sprang to life around his hands, and his face glowed blue in the otherworldly light. In a sharp explosion of sound and brightness, an intense blue-white flash split the air and streaked upward from his extended arms. After the violent, jagged light of the wizard's fire was gone and its after-image faded, a gaping hole half a foot in diameter appeared in the top of the tent, and around its edges smoke still curled. Dust motes swirled in the column of sunlight now streaming into the middle of the tent. The stench of burnt hide filled the air.

The sunlight revealed the wide-eyed, gape-mouthed expressions on the war-leaders' faces. Five of them had fallen backwards off their benches, and a dozen covered their ears. Even Munzil appeared shocked, and he stared at Joruman as if seeing him for the first time.

Deep satisfaction and pleasure suffused the high priest until his glance chanced on Surt. The war-leader of the Fire Dragons stood with arms folded and gazed at the high priest with a wolfish grin. *That one knows little of fear*, thought Joruman. *He's glad to see the others cowed. He'll make a smart leader.*

Continuing to gaze at the high priest, the Fire Dragons' war-leader broke the silence with his deep voice. "Olla halichas mannas dus machu?"

Munzil spoke, and the red-haired barbarian's voice wavered. "He wants to know if all priests make lightning like that."

"Few have such power," answered Joruman. "But Edan gives us priests many other abilities. The stronger ones can control fire and the other elements. We can take over the minds of living creatures, including any one of you. If I wished to, I could seize your mind and command you to slay yourself." He did not tell them how difficult and dangerous such a thing would be, nor that he could wield the minds of only a few men or women at a time. The war-leaders' fear grew more visible in their bulging eyes as Munzil rendered the words into the Ilarchae tongue.

Surt grunted and nodded. He still grinned. "Ond halichas mannas Sildharans? Machu deh zich dingas?"

"What of the sorcerers among the Sildharae?" said Munzil. "Can they not do these things as well?"

"Some can. But among all those with the gift in Eormenlond and the kingdoms beyond the seas, only his Eminence, the Supreme Priest Bledla, has the power to wield dragons. So Edan has shown his strength over all other gods. If you don't believe it, ask this man and the one called Gorm." Joruman pointed at Munzil. "They have seen one of the twelve dragons Bledla commands."

When Munzil finished translating, he nodded solemnly to confirm the high priest's claim.

"With these dragons at our head, Torrlond's army is unstoppable. When we finish conquering Adanon, we will come east and subdue Sildharan. If you wish to be on the side of the victors, you should join us now. King Earconwald is a generous monarch, and he will allow you to inhabit a portion of the conquered lands as lords if you submit to his rule." The high priest paused to allow Munzil time to translate. "The cities of Sildharan, including Thulhan, Shohan, Nahan, Shinan, and Kelgaon, will belong to King Earconwald. You and your kin who are now thralls in Sildharan may choose to inhabit that land as subjects of Torrlond or remain in the Wildlands. Either way, you will be free."

Surt spoke again, and Munzil rendered his words as, "What of plunder and thralls we take in war?"

"Those you may keep."

The war-leader of the Fire Dragons nodded. "Sva! Eochas gahyrdu, hargtochas. Hu sagu eochas?"

A thick-set, red-haired woman rose from her bench. A web of wrinkles lined her leathery face. Gaps stood between her blackened teeth, and a scar crossed her chin. Two fingers were lacking from the fist she raised. "Aich! Aich, sag ich!" Her rough voice reminded Joruman of boar bristles.

As the hag faced the other war-leaders and continued, Munzil leaned toward the high priest and explained, "She is Gunburcha of the Stone Fists, one of the tribes in the west, nearest to the border with Sildharan. She favors allying with Torrlond."

Joruman nodded to acknowledge the information. He waited as

many of the leaders grunted and nodded in agreement with Gunburcha.

When she finished, several others had their say. Each time, Munzil informed the high priest that the war-leaders were disposed to join the Torrlonders. The dominant sentiment was they had much to gain from the alliance, and nothing to lose. A few who said nothing appeared thoughtful, including Rugnach of the Strong Axes, but none said anything in opposition. Joruman grew more pleased.

Surt spoke again. "Sva! Hu machu veh? Hva eochas vid Torrlondas vochtan vollu?"

"Aich!" came in a loud chorus from the war-leaders' lips.

"Ond hva nocht sagt?"

Silence. Surt gazed around at them all.

Munzil smiled and said to Joruman, "They have spoken in favor of the alliance with Torrlond. They will each swear an oath to abide by your conditions. Now they must agree on who will lead us all."

"Nu veh dam hargtocham ollas vylkas vindan muzu," declared Surt. "Hva vollu eochas vylgan? Hva voldt dam deodam?"

"Surt!" cried one.

"Surt!" shouted another.

"Surt! Surt!"

Even Munzil joined in, shouting "Surt!" and clenching his fist.

Joruman glanced at the war-leader of the Fire Dragons. The big man took in the cries of his name with no display of emotion, only a slight frown carved in his stone face. He raised his palm to silence the others.

The tent went quiet.

Surt looked upon the other war-leaders. "Hva ellar? Volt onig odor dam deodam voldan?"

"Vol ich!" shouted one of the war-leaders who had remained silent, one of the younger ones. A huge man, he rose to his full height. With light brown hair and braided beard, he was not quite as tall as Surt, but he was broader. Clad in a byrny and clutching the pommel of his broad sword, the man gazed with brow lowered over his aggressive blue eyes at Surt, who met the gaze and nodded once with a grim smile.

"What's happening?" Joruman asked Munzil.

The red-haired savage stared at the man who had stood up. "He is Hochna of the Boar Tusks. He challenges Surt to be war-leader of all the tribes." Munzil swallowed. "They will fight to the death for the right."

"Well, then. May the best man win." Joruman despised such brutality, but it was not his place to stop it. *Besides, this should be interesting. Let's see what Surt's made of.*

With no further words spoken, Hochna took off his fur cloak and discarded it. Surt followed suit. Both men unsheathed their giant blades. The two walked toward the empty center of the tent, beneath where the wizard's fire from Joruman's spell had rent a hole in the hide. The column of sunlight separated them as they faced each other.

Hochna swung his weapon, but Surt parried the blow so that their blades flashed and clanged in the sunlight. Again and again Hochna wheeled his sword, but each time Surt blocked it without backing up a pace. The war-leader of the Fire Dragons seemed to be waiting, perhaps testing his foe, perhaps toying with him. Then, rushing forward, he went on the offensive.

Swift and strong was the attack Surt launched. Hochna parried two strikes before the third tore into his right thigh. Blade sliced through muscle and flesh, and droplets of blood sprayed over some of the other war-leaders, who took no other notice than to smile. Surt did not let up. Twice more steel rang against steel, and the next blur of his blade took Hochna in the face.

The war-leader of the Boar Tusks fell backwards and landed hard on his back with a grunt. When he sat up, he wiped at the blood pulsing and streaming down his cheek and forehead from a long, deep gash. He looked like a man who just realized the bite he took was too big to swallow.

Surt drove his blade into the ground and gestured for Hochna to rise. The latter complied and stabbed the ground with his blade as well. He roared and rushed at Surt.

With his burly arms, Hochna tried to grab Surt and crush him. The war-leader of the Fire Dragons was too quick. He leapt and brought his left knee into Hochna's gut. The big man grunted and buckled over, and Surt's fist cracked into his face. Hochna staggered backwards, his nose askew and bleeding. The man blinked and shook his head, but his eyes did not focus.

Striding forward for the kill, Surt lunged and grasped Hochna's braided beard. At the same time he put one foot behind the big man's leg. Pulling his opponent backwards and tripping him, he slammed Hochna's head into the ground. Surt sat on top of Hochna's stomach and pounded the man's face with his fists. With each blow, bone cracked and blood spattered.

Hochna yelled and managed to turn over onto his belly to shield his face, but Surt stayed on top of him and pulled one of the big man's arms behind him. Grasping the arm by the wrist and elbow, Surt bent it and forced it up into an impossible position as he sat on Hochna's back. Hochna growled and tried to no avail to resist. With veins popping out on his forehead, Surt's muscled arms trembled, and he gritted his teeth as he jerked the arm up higher. A loud pop preceded a tearing sound, ripping a scream from the war-leader of the Boar Tusks.

Crying out in agony, Hochna was helpless as Surt rolled him over on his back again and sat on him. The dislocated arm flopped to his side. The man on top grasped Hochna's face. Groaning and gasping in panicked breaths, the war-leader of the Boar Tusks tried to fend his foe away with his one remaining hand.

Surt grabbed the good hand and bent a finger back until it snapped, drawing a cry from Hochna. Surt growled and bent. Another finger popped. When his foe cried out again, Surt grasped his face with both hands. The war-leader of the Fire Dragons shoved his thumbs in each of Hochna's eyes. Like a vise, the remaining fingers stilled the trembling head. Surt clenched his teeth in a feral grin as he dug down with his thumbs. Hochna shrieked in helpless terror, his legs quivering and drumming the soil. Blood welled from the gaps Surt's thumbs forced in the eyes. A moment later, the orbs burst, with slick jelly slurping out along with the blood.

Gore oozing from the dark, hollow sockets in his face, Hochna let loose a long wail. Surt choked off the wail by clenching his opponent's throat. Squeezing harder, his fingers sank into the man's flesh. The war-leader of the Boar Tusks wheezed, and his good arm and legs twitched until something crunched under Surt's grip. The limbs grew still.

Digging deeper with his fingers and bearing down with all his weight, Surt bellowed in triumph as more gristly cracks and pops came. Flesh gave way. Blood gushed from the neck. The war-leader of the Fire Dragons twisted his hand, and something snapped when he pulled. Surt roared and raised his sticky, crimsoned fist. It held the crushed and dripping remains of Hochna's throat.

The war-leaders of the Ilarchae shouted their approval. "Surt! Surt!" they chanted.

Splattered in gore, Surt rose to his full height and looked on them all as if daring another to rise up and challenge him.

"Surt! Surt!" they cried.

Appalled and fascinated, Joruman smiled at the man. Here was a tool the high priest could exploit. *Well, my barbarian friend. It seems we both sent an effective message today. A* useful *man, indeed.*

7
AN ANNOUNCEMENT

On what passed for a winter morning in Asdralad, Dayraven awoke in his small chamber in Queen Faldira's palace. Just as they had done in his dreams, the elf-shard's whispers slithered in his waking mind. In the relative cold of sunrise, he huddled beneath thick blankets and peered at the walls, which were grey save for where white lines of light seeped in through cracks in the window's shutters. Other than his small but comfortable sleeping mat, there was little to occupy the room: a chamber pot, a wooden chest for spare clothes, a stool, and a plain desk on which rested two manuscripts in High Andumaic, a half-melted candle with a pool of hardened wax around it, and a basin of clean water. His head turned toward the corner nearest the sleeping mat.

Sweothol leaned in its baldric on the wall. He had not touched the sword since Orvandil and Gnorn left. In the shadows its red gem was a blotch of darkness on the hilt. An image from his boyhood came to him: the sword in its baldric strapped on his father, the gem on the pommel visible above the scabbard. Edgil's rugged, bearded face turned, revealing the keenness in his eyes before his habitual frown turned into a smile. Even the man's smiles had always seemed sad, never touching his eyes. His father had worn the sword only on rare occasions. But whenever he did, it was a reminder of the great deeds the man had performed in service to Torrlond. Anyone in the Mark who saw the gem on that sword and heard it named would have recalled the story of Edgil's glory.

Dayraven sighed. There would be deep snow in the Mark now, and folk in Kinsford would be huddled around the fires in their halls. One could not truly speak of winter in Asdralad, he mused. The nights were cool enough, but only the old spoke of the last time it snowed on the island. He found himself wishing for a thick blanket of white on the ground, the crunch of his boots on it and the piercing air entering his lungs and worming its way through the thickest furs.

But he had little time to indulge in such memories. Messages came every month from Orvandil and Gnorn in Adanon, sometimes with word from Imharr. The tidings were mercilessly ill. Torrlond's army swept away all opposition. They overwhelmed the resistance among the Adanese with superior numbers, and those who fought them paid a heavy price. Worst of all were the dragons. The beasts, or "Bledla's pets," as Gnorn called them in his reports, not only fought on Torrlond's behalf, but they also hunted down all organized resistance. Though many sorcerers tried, none could wield the song of origin or hope to wrest the serpents of the air from the Supreme Priest Bledla's control, and more than a few had died in the process.

The only good news was a lull in the fighting during the winter months, but this was mainly because the Adanese and Asdralae fighters were licking their wounds and hiding from the Torrlonders, who never ceased pursuing them. War and death spread throughout Adanon, and as yet no aid came from the east. Somehow, with the help Asdralad sent under Orvandil and Gnorn's command, the Adanese held on. All of this increased Dayraven's sense of urgency, and he worked ever harder to master the songs of origin.

He made good progress. As Faldira, Urd, and Sequara taught him the words, Dayraven took them in and mastered them. In the realm of origins he repeated the words, making what they signified part of himself. Of beasts, plants, and elements he saw the beginnings, and he understood them for what they were. With this understanding came the ability to mold and move them. In the realm of origins, those who knew how to use the gift kept some will of their own to change the world of forms. If they failed to retain this will, they would never return. But such risk decreased as Dayraven grew confident in his abilities. His focus and the degree of his power made him like no other apprentice the queen of Asdralad had ever taught, even Sequara. Faldira recognized Dayraven's uniqueness, and she and Urd took hope from it. As for Dayraven, he sometimes awoke in the middle of night feeling crushed under a heavy burden, but he remembered Imharr, Gnorn, Orvandil, and all those fighting against Torrlond, and he trained harder.

All the while, he crafted an understanding with the shard of the elf within him. In the realm of origins, Dayraven learned to draw from the power of the elf without allowing it to take over his being. It was like knowing how much rein to give a muscled and spirited wild horse. Give it too much room, and it would run away with him helplessly bouncing atop it. Too little, and it would fight him so that he would go nowhere. Just the right amount, and he could race like the wind with it.

But he always had to respect the fact that it was a creature far more powerful than he was. Indeed, in the case of the elf, infinitely more powerful. When he succeeded in achieving the right balance and tapping into the elf's power, which was most of the time now, his ability in the gift was like no other's. He became adept at letting just enough of it seep through the barrier in his mind to keep it in his control. Still, it was a dangerous dance, for its vastness threatened to submerge him until he disappeared in it. In addition, he felt an unnerving sense that his unspoken truce with the elf-shard could be fleeting. Always there was the nagging worry that an enormous will was sleeping and waiting to awaken at the right, or wrong, time.

Still, his ability to use the spells grew stronger. He could sing hundreds of songs of origin, and they all came easily to him. So great was his mastery that it often seemed creatures were ready to obey his will before he sang the song of origin and focused his energy, though that feeling was no doubt a product of the strange influence the realm of origins had on his perception of time. And, of course, he learned the song of origin of dragons, though he had no opportunity to test his power over the beasts as yet. That day would come, and he would do everything he could to be ready. He had no doubt he would succeed in wielding them with the elf-shard's power. *If* it cooperated.

Dayraven's mastery of High Andumaic also grew. He was proficient enough that he found his lessons with Sequara a pleasant diversion from the rigors of meditation and spell-weaving. In fact, he rather looked forward to their daily conversations. This morning, after he breakfasted, he would meet her in the room where she instructed him. With this thought, he flipped the blankets off and rose to dress.

The stone floor chilled his bare feet. When he splashed cold water on his face from the basin, goose bumps broke out all over his flesh. Puffing air from his cheeks, he pulled on his black breeches and white kirtle. Next he wore his boots and brown robe. Though he was still a bit chilly, the day would warm up to the point where the robe would provide more than enough warmth. Turning back to his sleeping mat, he picked up the blankets and shook them, sending motes of dust chasing each other in the slits of sunlight around the small room. He laid the blankets down and tucked them under the mat, and then, with a smile on his face, he smoothed every wrinkle he could find.

Just as he finished ironing out the blankets, the door to his chamber clicked open. Dayraven pivoted around to see a tiny, grey-haired woman bent with age standing before him. Her white dress declared her one of Faldira's servants. She was armed with a bundle of straw tied together at one end, which Dayraven had seen her wield with great efficiency as a short broom.

"Good morning, Jhaia," he said in High Andumaic. He moved to give the old woman a better view of the sleeping mat. Then he smiled at her.

Jhaia's eyebrows arched up. The old woman seemed unimpressed. Without a word, she tottered over to the window and opened the shutters, allowing the morning sunlight to spill in and brighten the chamber. A slight, cool breeze with a scent of the sea caressed Dayraven's skin and fingered his robe.

Hands on her hips, Jhaia peered down at the sleeping mat. "Only the donkey's tail got stuck in the door," she muttered as she shook her head.

Dayraven's smile disappeared. "I beg your pardon?" The old woman spoke the local form of Andumaic, which Dayraven still found difficult to understand. It didn't help that Jhaia was missing most of her teeth. On top of that, she insisted on speaking almost exclusively in idioms that never made any sense to him. Her head was filled with pithy sayings no doubt inherited from her grandmother's grandmother, and she seemed to take a perverse pleasure in unleashing them all on Dayraven. "'The donkey's tail'?"

Jhaia picked up Dayraven's pillow, which lay in a crumpled heap to the side of the sleeping mat. She placed it in the dead center at the head of the mat and smoothed it out before fixing a couple small wrinkles in the blanket. She did not turn to meet Dayraven's gaze, but the old woman smiled wickedly.

"Oh." His shoulders drooped. "You win again."

For the last fortnight, Dayraven had waged an undeclared battle against the old woman, who was the maid in charge of his wing of the palace. It had started when he tried to make his bed in an effort to make her job easier. That first time Jhaia had snorted with contempt at his attempt and shaken out the blankets before arranging them crisply in a series of swift, competent moves. It was the first of many failures, and he had not yet succeeded in meeting her standards. At least he was getting better: Today she did not undo his efforts, which was in itself a great compliment.

"We'll see again tomorrow," said Dayraven with a nod.

The old woman smiled and shook her head. Then she stared at Dayraven's chest and tsked. "Why not wear something besides that white tunic?" she asked. "You look like a servant."

"But . . ." He was not sure how to answer the white clad servant, so he stared down and gestured at his kirtle. "It's comfortable."

She shook her head again as if he were a hopeless student, and no amount of explaining would get through to him. Then she tottered over to the chest of clothes and opened the lid. A moment later, her hand came out grasping a bright red kirtle. She held it out and nodded with a smile. "Fit for a lordling like you."

Dayraven's eyes widened. "I'm not a . . . It's nice, but too . . . red?"

Her eyes rolled up, and she turned her back to him to fold the

PHILIP CHASE

garment and place it back in the chest. "The crow cares not if the pomegranate's ripe. Off with you, then."

Thus dismissed, Dayraven breathed a sigh as he walked out of the room and down the hall. The swift, confident whisks of Jhaia's broom sounded behind him. Relieved to have escaped without the bright red kirtle, he scratched his head as he wondered what a crow and a pomegranate had to do with anything.

After breaking his fast with fruit, flat bread, and fresh goat milk, Dayraven walked through the palace to the small room with the table and four chairs, where Sequara would give him his lesson in High Andumaic. The room was unoccupied, but the sun streamed in through the open window and warmed it. He took a seat, gazed at the chair where Sequara always sat, and smiled.

WHILE RUNNING THROUGH A SERIES OF CONJUGATIONS OF THE pluperfect tense for strong verbs that he knew he would get right, Dayraven reminded himself to stay focused and keep the triumphant, silly grin off his face. Sequara sat across the table from him, her arms crossed before her chest and her beautiful face fixed in a look of perfect calm. This was his favorite part of the day, perhaps because the pressure of learning to wield the gift did not enter into his study of High Andumaic, which came to him with little perceived effort. He sometimes wondered if Sequara's still vivid memories in his mind helped his comprehension of the language, but he never dared to ask about it.

He admitted to himself that he enjoyed Sequara's company. The fact that they shared each other's memories created an unspoken bond, but he also respected her discipline and the compassion dwelling beneath her devotion to duty. The depth behind her dark eyes captivated him, and her quick, understated wit lifted his spirits. Of course, he did not wish to make her – or himself – uncomfortable with even the slightest admission of his admiration, and so he ended up staring down at the table half the time. He looked up when he finished the conjugation.

"Excellent," said Sequara. "Though your accent's not perfect, you're quite fluent now in High Andumaic."

More pleased by the praise than he could account for, Dayraven smiled. "Thank you. I have a good teacher."

"Any teacher can be good with an eager pupil."

He blushed a little. "Not so. You've been patient and understanding."

"I'm glad you think so. Do you have any questions about the conjugations before we move on?"

"Actually, I was wondering about something Jhaia said."

"Jhaia?"

"Yes. Something about a crow and an unripe pomegranate."

A smile bloomed on Sequara's face, and her light laughter was pleasant music. "Other than humor, idioms are the most difficult aspect of a language for an outsider to understand. Jhaia contains a wealth of them."

"So what does this one mean?"

"'The crow doesn't care whether the pomegranate is ripe.' It sounds to me as if Jhaia is questioning someone's judgement on some matter. It implies one doesn't know what's good and what's not." Sequara raised a questioning eyebrow, and her mouth curved in an amused grin.

"Oh. I see." Dayraven looked down at his white kirtle and smiled. "It would seem she doesn't approve of my choice in garments."

"You mustn't mind our Jhaia. She thinks her age entitles her to mother everyone."

"Not to worry. We have an understanding, Jhaia and I." The smile eased off his face. "Does she have children?"

"Three. And eight grandchildren, the last I heard."

"I'm sure she's a formidable mother."

"Yes. And a kind, patient one. She once nursed me through a bad flu when I was twelve." The sorceress glanced about the room. "I used to stay in this wing of the palace. *Jhaia's* wing. She was always so tidy and particular about things."

"That hasn't changed."

Sequara's smile broadened. "Once, when I was a girl, I returned to my room after breakfast and ruffled the blankets on my bed to see if she would notice."

Dayraven laughed. "Did she?"

"When I checked in the afternoon, the blankets were as smooth as glass. Not a wrinkle. She never said a word about it, though."

"I have a hard time believing you committed such a mischievous act."

She laughed and waved a dismissive hand. "That's nothing. One time I locked a rival in an outhouse."

"You did what?"

"The truth is he was a bully and a snob, and he tried to make my life as horrible as he could. He was a couple years older than I and from one of the most distinguished families in Asdralad. He hated me for being stronger in the gift than he was."

"So you locked him in an outhouse?"

Her face looked contrite as she peered down at the table and winced a little. "It was poor judgement on my part, though I planned his humiliation carefully. The door opened out, and I hid a piece of wood nearby for the purpose of trapping him. I followed him from a discreet distance, and when he went inside, I jammed the piece of wood in place. He was stuck in there for quite a while before someone found him, crying and pounding on the door from the inside. He never knew who did it. But Jhaia figured it out."

"What did she do?"

Sequara sighed. "She didn't yell. She didn't even scold me. Instead, she used the most effective thing she could have: guilt. She made me understand how much pressure the boy was under from his family. They expected him to be Faldira's heir. Their honor and name were at stake. She told me how disappointed she was in me, and she made me see how I let down Queen Faldira. That was what I needed to hear. I couldn't bear the thought of the queen thinking less of me. From then on I behaved no matter what he did. Well, mostly."

"And no trouble came of it?"

"Jhaia told no one. She was always looking out for me. Like a mother."

There was a long pause. Dayraven and Sequara stared at one

another, their smiles fading as they gazed longer at each other's faces. Locking eyes with her was at once blissful and nerve-wracking, and it seemed she was trying to find a way to say something. A surge of emotion blazed to life between them as fragments of memories from Sequara's girlhood flashed in Dayraven's mind. He shared the complex array of emotions she experienced as a girl in the palace. The emotions were as real as if he had experienced them himself, for so many of her memories swirled in his mind. Did she know he was remembering along with her now?

To end the silence, he said the first thing he thought of. "I never knew my mother."

The moment it was out, he knew he had just made things worse, and he broke his gaze by turning to the table. He should have brought the conversation back to grammar. Or the weather. Instead, he crossed a line that, by silent agreement, the two of them had avoided all these months.

Since they shared so many of each other's memories on the day she entered his mind to save his life, Sequara almost certainly knew Dayraven's mother had died giving birth to him. But they stayed away from deep personal subjects to avoid the awkwardness of acknowledging the bond between them. It was rather like they had stumbled upon each other naked and implicitly agreed to keep quiet about it. Only this was worse. Their minds had been naked. There had been nowhere to hide their memories, secrets, fears, and desires. Bringing up a deeply personal part of his past was an open acknowledgement of their shared memories and bond.

He glanced up at Sequara to see if he had offended her. There was no anger or coldness in her face — only a sad smile. "It must have been hard to grow up without her. To always wonder what she was like."

Tension eased out of him. They had crossed a boundary, and nothing had happened. Perhaps he had been too cautious all this time. Perhaps she was not as worried about it as he thought. "Yes. Sometimes. Mostly I didn't think about her. I couldn't grieve for her since I never knew her. I wanted to. But can you feel sorrow for someone you've never met? It was her absence that I thought about. I wondered about her at times. Like when I saw other children with their mothers. But I was happy enough. I had Father. And Imharr."

She shut her eyes for a moment. "Imharr. Yes."

"You met him . . . You came to know him when you brought me from Caergilion."

"Yes." She paused with her mouth half open, as if a thought were waiting for the right words to deliver it. "He cares very much for you. Like a brother."

He nodded. The connection between them swelled like a billowing thunderhead threatening to unleash a hard rain. Even the elf-shard's murmurs seemed to diminish to a gentle hush as his bond with Sequara intensified. His heart raced and seemed to expand in his chest while his body shivered in the charged room. In his mind images from his memories and hers alternated in rapid succession. Father and Imharr working the fields outside of Kinsford. Father, Mother, and Grandmother tending the olive grove. Hiding from Ebba behind a tree and surprising her when they were six. Racing her little brother Elur on the beach and laughing when the noisy waves splashed them. Entering the dimness of the Southweald for the first time when Father taught him to hunt and, after wandering off, worrying for a panicked moment he was lost. Arriving with her hand in Father's hand at the palace in Kiriath only to endure the stares of the noble children. *Father let go of me that day.* It was impossible to separate them, as if their pasts had merged and belonged equally to both of them. Sequara was seeing all these memories too. He knew it.

Her wet eyes gazed past him with a blank expression. A tear rolled down her cheek. "I miss my family," she said. The words rushed out like a confession. "My mother. My father. Grandmother. All gone. My little brother. We were so close once. He's a stranger now. His wife and children fear me. There's no one to . . ."

She looked at him, and her eyes were pleading.

But it was gone the next moment. At once her expression hardened with narrowed eyes and set jaw. The sorrow disappeared. The emotion hanging in the air dissipated, and an invisible knife severed the bond between them. Looking at the floor, she seemed to search for words. She wiped her eye with a finger and looked up, her face a controlled mask. "I have something to tell you." A brief pause. A line formed on each of her cheeks as her jaw muscles tightened. "Today has been our last lesson."

With a fragile grin Dayraven tried to hide his sudden disappointment, not fully understanding why it was so strong. "But surely we can still meet . . . to speak . . ."

As his face reddened, Sequara saved him from having to finish. "Yes, of course. We'll speak again. But not for some time. I have a journey to make. I leave on the morrow."

"What?" This time he failed altogether to hide the alarm in his voice, and he blinked at her. "Where?"

She sighed before answering, "To the mainland."

"You mean Adanon?"

"Yes."

Though he dreaded the answer, he could not help asking, "Why?"

"I'm the heir to Asdralad's throne. Many sorcerers have risked their lives trying to break Bledla's power over the dragons. It's my duty to share that risk, even if I fail."

Too many thoughts raced through Dayraven's mind for him to restrain them all. "But many have died. You can't . . . It's too dangerous."

"I must."

"Then I'll go with you." The words were out before Dayraven thought of stopping them. Sequara stared at him, and he stared back for several awkward heartbeats, feeling the blood rush to his warming face. His outburst had been a clear announcement, a confession better left unsaid. The force of it surprised even him, and as his mouth hung open, he wished he could have stuffed the words back into it.

"Don't be a fool, Dayraven." Her face with its lowered brow was as stern as her voice. "You have a purpose. You've grown powerful, but your training's unfinished. Never forget you may be our best hope. That must be your sole focus. I too have a duty, and I'll perform it."

As Dayraven realized what feelings had broken through, he struggled to suppress them. It was foolish. Childish. Impossible. "I . . . I'm sorry. You're right. Forgive me."

Sequara's face softened into a half smile as she gazed at him.

"There's nothing to forgive. Keep up your training. You have the best of teachers in Queen Faldira and Urd. Farewell, Dayraven. May Oruma and Anghara guide you."

Too bewildered to speak, he sat on the chair with his mouth stuck open as Sequara rose, turned her back, and exited the door.

He was alone. Strange silence pervaded the room. Emptiness gripped his chest. He sat for a long time thinking of what he should have said before she left.

Dayraven watched Sequara depart from the palace the next morning. He stood behind Queen Faldira and Urd at the front entrance. Glancing at Dayraven, Sequara gave him a brief nod, which he was careful to return with the same emotionless expression. After the sorceress embraced his great aunt and then the queen, she turned away in silence and descended the steps leading down to the city. She was clad in the black tunic and baggy trousers she preferred to travel in. Six of the palace guards went with her, including old Karad, who watched over her like a faithful hound, and more soldiers would be waiting at the ship.

Seagulls hovering in the air above cried as a cool breeze tossed back Dayraven's hair. The morning sun promised to warm the island as it glistened off the domes and towers of the city and shimmered in the blue water beyond. He chewed his lip as he waited for Faldira and Urd, who kept their gaze on the young sorceress as she progressed down the hill and into the city. In vain he tried to suppress the anxiety that spiked when Sequara's small form vanished behind one of the buildings below. He frowned at her green clad guards, who also disappeared as they kept close behind her. Those men would accompany her to Adanon and remain with her there. He pictured himself running down the steps and through the city to leap aboard her ship and journey with her. It was a ridiculous notion, he knew. Perhaps it was for the best they would be apart. *That should give me time to grow some sense. I just hope she'll be safe.*

The queen and his aunt turned around. He stepped aside to let them pass and then fell in with them. As he walked back into the palace at Urd's side, the old woman looked up at him. "You look pale, my boy. Are you well?"

He forced a smile. "Well enough. A little tired."

"You've been training hard. Progress is good, but you mustn't burn yourself out."

"Yes, Grandmother."

Queen Faldira turned toward him. "Would you like to rest before we begin today's lesson?"

"No, your Majesty. I'm fine. It will be good to clear my mind. We have much to do. I have much to learn."

The queen stared at him for a moment. "Very well. Let us go to the garden, then. You must practice dividing your mind so that you may maintain several songs of origin at once."

As it turned out, by tapping into the power of the elf-shard, Dayraven was able to hold six songs of origin simultaneously on his first try that morning. They were simple spells — he wielded a snake, a seagull, a cat, a hibiscus tree, a ferret, and a housefly — and Faldira did not hide how impressed she was at his ability.

"Is it not normal to wield more than one creature or one spell at a time?" he asked.

The queen smiled at his question. "Within limits according to one's power, it is possible to control many creatures of the same species with one spell since they all share the same song of origin. Using more than one song of origin at a time, however, is a different matter. Also, the more disparate the creatures, the harder it is to wield them. Controlling several types of bird is easier than a bird and a cat. Most of those with the gift would struggle to hold even one of the spells you just used. A small minority have enough power to maintain two, perhaps three, songs of origin. Few can manage more than that."

"Why?"

"It's a matter of strength in the gift. Each of us has a certain amount of strength, and every spell requires some of it. When you wield one thing by singing a song of origin, you may devote all of your strength in the gift to it. But if you seek to control two things of different origin, you divide your strength in half, rather like lifting two objects instead of one. Three becomes that much more difficult."

"So the more power in the gift you have, the more songs of origin you can weave at once."

"Correct." She smiled. "Now I think it's time to push you a little harder."

Queen Faldira put Dayraven through a series of exercises in which he divided his mind. With a controlled trickle of energy from the elf-shard, he was able to hold power over as many as nine different creatures at once. She surprised him during some of the exercises by attacking his power over one or more of the creatures he wielded. With his mind divided, it was much harder to resist her attempts to break his spell. He succeeded in maintaining control, but he also knew she was holding back, perhaps testing him for weaknesses.

After they ceased, she issued a challenge. "Weave a song of origin over as many creatures as you can. I will attempt to break your power over them one at a time. Maintain your control for as long as possible."

In an instant, Dayraven's energy expanded to the realm of origins, and he sang the required songs one after another until he wielded nine creatures. He drew a steady dribble of energy from the elf-shard, focusing on holding back the vast majority of the power that threatened to burst through.

The assault of the queen's energy was sudden and strong, like a mighty gust. Spread thin and vulnerable, he could do little to resist as her energy prodded and stabbed at his hold over the housefly. She severed the cords of his energy with a snap, and he lurched with dizziness.

He could have drawn more power from the elf-shard, but that would have been dangerous. From experience, he knew tapping too much from it could unleash it all at once, with consequences that would be far worse than just losing control. When the elf-shard escaped, it shredded and scattered him, and he could never be sure of his return to his body.

One by one, Faldira peeled and snatched the creatures away from his influence, each time producing a prick of pain in his mind and a disorienting wave of nausea he struggled to suppress. But each time, as he maintained power over fewer creatures, it took her longer to break his control over the next one.

When he wielded only three creatures, she could make no more headway against him. Her power crashed and scattered against him, probing for some weakness and stabbing with controlled force. Drawing a constant stream of energy from the elf-shard, Dayraven held firm and steady control over the seagull, the cat, and the ferret.

Faldira hid her emotions better than anyone Dayraven had ever met, but after she had been frowning in concentration for many unfruitful heartbeats in an attempt to break his power over the seagull, her eyes widened and a line appeared on her brow. With the exception of the time when the elf-shard escaped his mind while he was resisting Sequara's attempt to wrest the goat from him, it was the closest thing to shock he had ever seen on the queen's face. The assault of her energy ceased. All was calm as Dayraven breathed in the realm of origins.

"You may release them now." Her voice seemed to come from far away.

Dayraven complied. The ferret and the cat looked around for a moment as if dazed, then they ran off. The seagull cried once and flew away from the garden. The realm of origins dissipated. Dayraven snapped back to the present, where the presence of the elf still brushed against his awareness. Faldira stared at him with intensity in her eyes. Fearing he had given offense, he bowed his head slightly and waited for the queen to speak.

"Unheard of. No one with a mind divided in three should be able to resist such an attack."

The tone of her voice made him wonder if she regarded him with some kind of horror. He remembered the day the people of Kinsford exiled him, the looks on their terrified faces as they stared at him in the Doomring. They thought he was a monster. "I'm . . . It's the elf. Its . . . presence is with me." He did not dare to tell her he was extracting only a tiny portion of its energy.

"Wherever it comes from . . ." She hesitated. "What's more important is that you are learning to control it."

When Dayraven looked up, he saw no fear in her face. Her smile was gentle. He let a sigh escape, and he realized how much he wanted to please the queen. No, it went beyond that. She was one of the few who could understand him. She was an anchor that kept him tied to the world. If she thought him a dangerous force beyond control or redemption, then there was nowhere else to go.

"You *must* be cautious and circumspect," she continued. "It's not enough to be good in your intentions. You must also be wise."

"Yes, your Majesty."

"This afternoon we will have a discussion on this matter. I think it best to have Urd with us for that. In the meantime, your time is your own. Perhaps you would like to rest before the noon meal?"

"Yes, your Majesty. Thank you."

In fact, Dayraven was close to exhausted. The exercises with Faldira were grueling and always drained him both mentally and physically. They were without doubt more demanding than any training he had done under his father or Orvandil, and this morning was especially tough. The most difficult part was keeping the elf-shard in check. In addition, he had slept little the previous night, spending the whole time turning from side to side as he thought back on his conversation with Sequara and imagined himself saying the right words. Only he couldn't decide what the right words were.

He returned to his room with images of Sequara running through his head. The training had occupied him for a few hours, but now that he was idle, thoughts of the beautiful sorceress flooded him. Where was she now? Somewhere in the middle of the Great Sea, far from shore. What was she thinking about? Was she thinking of him? *More likely she's thinking about her mission.*

Still, it must have occurred to her how strange it was to have their shared memories leap out like that. Was such a thing normal after being healed through sorcery? Did it happen to others with such intensity? Was it supposed to last so long? He resolved to ask Urd and Queen Faldira. It would not be a betrayal of Sequara to tell them of the shared memories. Perhaps they would be able to help. At the least, it would be good to know if others with the gift suffered from similar effects after their minds touched.

Dayraven reached his room and, after opening the door, smiled at his perfectly made sleeping mat. Jhaia knew her work well. Sequara's story of attempting to confound the old woman by ruffling her bed came to his mind. He peeled up the blankets with care. After taking off his boots and brown robe, he lay down, covered his body with the blankets, and closed his eyes.

Sequara invaded his mind. Even the voyage to Adanon was dangerous, but her mission was a doomed one. At best, failure awaited her. At worst . . .

No. His eyes opened, and his fists clenched. *I can't dwell on it. She's strong and can fend for herself. Worrying won't help her.*

But he could not stop. A thousand things could happen to her. Worst of all, in the end, she would seek out Bledla's dragons. He had met the cold supreme priest. He knew the old man's power. Sequara was strong — stronger than almost anyone — but not that strong. She should not have gone. He should have persuaded her. Their parting conversation began to replay in his mind again. *'Don't be a fool, Dayraven.'*

But I am a fool.

He yawned and closed his eyes again. After taking three deep breaths, he willed his body to relax. *I need to rest. Let go.* His body drifted, and he floated toward sleep.

At once, the elf-shard awakened on its own. Before Dayraven had a chance to think of curtailing it or even to panic, the power the elf had inserted in him blasted his mental barriers to shreds and ripped free. In a vast explosion of energy, the elf beamed in all directions from his mind like a celestial beacon. Dayraven gasped as minute pieces of him spun outwards and scattered in the realm of origins. Bright light enveloped him.

With profound disorientation and gut-wrenching nausea, Dayraven awoke. The sharp hiss of the elf-shard grated on his mind like fingernails raking the flesh of his back. A fuzzy pulse filled his ears, and colors swirled and blurred before him. It took several moments for him to understand where he was, and he could only lie on his sleeping mat for a long time groaning, his stomach roiling. The terrible sensation of the elf-shard shattering him to pieces with such sudden violence returned for a moment, and, with a surge of nausea, he rolled to the side and vomited on the floor.

The sharp stench of his stomach acid mixed with the half-digested fruit and now curdled milk he had consumed that morning permeated the little chamber. At least he felt a little better, though his throat burned. His eyes focused, and his ears cleared with a pair of pops. A shudder shook his shoulders and head. The presence of the elf diminished to its usual whisper, emitting its shadows that glided over his awareness like vapor.

He moaned. "Trying to send me a message?"

The elf-shard did not answer him.

Still feeling strangely displaced, he lay for a while longer and worried about cleaning up the mess before Jhaia or anyone else found him. When he found the strength to sit up, the room spun for a moment, but after he shook his head, his eyes regained their focus.

Using a rag he stole from a storage closet down the hallway and the basin of water on his desk, he cleaned up the vomit, after which he tossed the dirty water out the window. To judge by the sun overhead, it was about midday. With a sense of relief, he guessed no one would have missed him. Putting on his boots and robe, he left the shutters of his window open to air out the room and made his way toward the kitchens, where he washed his hands. From there he walked to the small dining room where he usually ate with Faldira, Urd, and Sequara. Short of breath and stooping, he felt as wrung out as the rag he had just used.

When he arrived in the dining room, he straightened his shoulders. The queen and his great aunt were already sitting at the round table. The sight of the empty seat where Sequara always sat jarred him. Various fruits, flatbread, vegetables in sauces, and a large platter of fried fish covered the table along with glasses for the wine. He had no desire to touch any of it. Faldira and Urd appeared to be halfway through their meal. Dayraven took his usual seat.

Urd looked up from her food. "Welcome, child. We were about to send for you. No use sleeping away . . . Gods, boy. What happened to you?"

Dayraven forced a weak smile. "I'm fine."

"You look like all the blood's been drained from you."

"That bad?"

Urd and Faldira glanced at each other, their concern written in the former's frown and the latter's raised eyebrows.

The queen looked at Dayraven. "If something is amiss, I hope you would feel free to tell us."

He looked down at the empty plate in front of him and sighed. "There *is* something I wanted to discuss with you both. Two things, in fact."

Urd put down her wine glass. "We're listening."

It took some time for him to gather his thoughts. "When someone with the gift heals someone else, is it normal for the two to share each other's memories?"

"Yes," answered the queen. "Since their minds touch, they experience each other's emotions. This often includes the transfer of memories. This is one of the things that make using the gift on another human being so difficult."

So there was nothing unusual in what Dayraven and Sequara were experiencing. That at least was a relief. "In that case, both the healer and the one healed would feel what it was like to be the other."

"Yes."

His next question was equally important. "Do the effects last forever?"

Faldira's eyes narrowed. "No. Usually they fade the same day. In serious cases, they can last two or three days. It depends on how much of the gift the healer needed to use."

The relief disappeared. "Oh."

Urd leaned forward in her chair. "Why do you ask of this?"

"I . . . After Sequara saved my life in Caergilion, we had glimpses of each other's memories. Fragments of images, really."

"Though it can feel strange, there's nothing uncommon in that," assured the queen.

"The last time it happened was yesterday. And it was rather . . . vivid."

Faldira and Urd glanced at each other again. "That *is* uncommon," said his great aunt. "It's been many months."

"I was nearly dead. In fact, I think I was well on my way. Perhaps because she needed to use so much of the gift to call me back . . ."

"That would not explain everything," said the queen. Her face was calm, but one eyebrow arched up as she continued. "It might also have something to do with the strength of the gift in you. Are you certain she is also still seeing your memories?"

"I . . . think so."

"I will speak to Sequara of it when she returns. Perhaps it will resolve itself before then. The sheer amount of the gift in you might be explanation enough if it is only you experiencing the flashes of memory. With such unprecedented power, the effects are bound to be unprecedented as well."

"Perhaps." Dayraven cleared his throat. "That brings me to the second issue. I just had . . . The reason I . . . The elf. It put *something* in me. In my mind. I can feel it there. Like a piece of glass buried in my mind. It's the source of the power. Sometimes I can use it. I can keep it down and draw from it. But other times . . . It's alive. It has its own will. I can't always control it. When I lay down to rest today, it burst forth from me, tearing me to pieces. I was gone. I wasn't sure I would ever wake up. But I did, and I felt so . . . broken. It's happened before. Not for a long time, but . . . I had hoped it was under my sway, but I see how foolish the thought is. I don't know when it will happen again. But it will."

The room went silent. Faldira and Urd were both masters at hiding their emotions, but Dayraven's training had taught him to be more aware of subtle manifestations of people's feelings. No doubt his strength in the gift also made him more perceptive. Their slightly widened eyes betrayed a measure of alarm as well as pity and sorrow as they gazed on him.

It was the queen who spoke. "A terrible burden has fallen on you, Dayraven. But that is the first reason why you must train. Only by learning to use the gift do you have a hope of containing this power in you. You have made great progress towards mastering the songs of origin."

"But I don't know how reliable I'll be. It could break free. If the elf awakens at the wrong time, if I lose control . . ."

"Then we will deal with such an event when it comes." Faldira reached across the table and rested her hand on his. "We are with you, and we will do what we can to help. For now, the important thing is that you train, and keep telling us whenever the power of the elf emerges without your bidding. Perhaps we can learn what spurs it."

"If I come back, I will tell you."

"My boy," said Urd. "You are wise to tell us of this, and you are also wise to fear this thing. But do not allow such fear to keep you from doing what you can now. You returned to us. You found your way back, and you will be able to do so again. And the Queen is right. Your training has progressed far. The power of the elf may have broken free, and it may do so again. But, unless I miss my guess, you are learning to find some balance with it. You may or may not come to wholly wield this power in you, but we will do everything we can to help you. You're not alone."

Dayraven looked back at the two women, and though the fear was not gone, he found resolve by its side. He nodded to them and smiled. "Thank you. And now, I believe my hunger is returning."

"That's as good a sign as any," said Urd as she handed the platter of fish to him.

"Eat and gather your strength. We have much to discuss."

8

PLOTS BENEATH PLOTS

The man standing under the huge oak tree fidgeted and flicked his fingers in a series of odd gestures. His pacing had left a confusion of footprints in the thin layer of snow beneath the tree. He pulled the hood of the worn and patched brown robe he wore further down over his head, not quite concealing his long white beard. His breath misted in front of him as his head moved from side to side, scanning the shadows of the nearby manicured shrubs as if he was expecting someone or something to leap out of them.

"Damn and blast, they're getting nearer. He'd best show up soon," he said to himself.

When he squinted up at the sun through the bare branches, his hood tipped back, revealing a pair of green eyes on an old and lined but still lean face. His smile belied the worry in his voice.

He leaned over and patted the grooved bark of the oak. "Well, sleepy old friend. I shall miss you, you know. And your brethren. You're the best company I've had here." His bony, veined hand caressed the tree. Its lichen-covered, rough skin rubbing against the pads of his fingers resembled his spotted, old flesh.

The green-eyed man sighed. "I'll come back if I'm able." He nodded as if expecting the oak to reply, then he chuckled. "I recall when you were mere seedlings." His smile turned into a confused frown, and his eyes narrowed. "But how could I? You're more than three hundred winters older than I am . . . I suppose I've been talking with you too much." Shaking his head in sudden mirth, he laughed aloud. "It matters naught. You're still the best company I've had here." With both arms he surrounded the oak in a tender embrace and put his ear up to the bark. There he stood with his eyes closed.

"Ahem." Somewhere behind him a man cleared his throat.

Still embracing the tree and shutting his eyes, the old man spoke. "Ah, your Majesty. You've arrived." He opened his eyes and turned around to give a slight bow to the newcomer.

The man facing him in the large lane in between the manicured shrubs was in his middle years. Of average build, he had a blond beard and blue eyes, and he wore an embroidered, fur-lined cloak of a dark green hue, which he kept tight around his body as if trying to stay warm or hide something. His hood too was up, but anyone on the palace grounds would have recognized King Fullan of Ellond. A curious smile crossed his handsome face, and one eyebrow was raised. "How did you know it was me?"

The green-eyed old man smiled and pointed behind him. "The tree told me."

The king pursed his lips and nodded.

"And," added the old man, "anyone else would have tried to kill me."

A somber frown took over Fullan's face. "In that you're quite correct, old friend. There's a pretty price on your head now. I should know. I'm to pay it should anyone bring your head to me."

"You flatter me, your Majesty."

Fullan shook his head. "No. I'm merely trying to impress on you that your life is in danger here. It's time for you to leave, Galdor."

The wizard Galdor let loose a rich, mirthful laugh. "My life's in danger no matter where I go. I'm an old man, your Majesty. A little thing can bring an old man to his rest, you know. But fear not. I'm rather attached to my head, and I plan on keeping it a while longer."

"Good. I'm depending on it. But why this meeting? I thought you would be gone by now. Has anything changed?"

"My apologies, your Majesty. There is some risk in this, but there are two things I thought worth telling you before I leave. The first is that our suspicions were correct." The wizard reached inside his robe and then held out a folded piece of vellum. The wax seal on it was broken.

The king reached for the paper and took it. "What's this?"

"A letter in Earl Freomar's own hand, with his seal. It's addressed to none other than King Earconwald of Torrlond."

The king frowned down at the paper. "And how did you come by it?"

"In fact, it did not reach Torrlond since my dear friend Abon happened upon the man carrying it."

"And how did he convince the man to hand over the letter?"

"Alas, he could not convince him to give it willingly. I'm afraid he resorted to sticking a dagger in the fellow, and now Freomar is short one messenger, though he does not know it yet."

"I take it when you say, 'happened upon him,' you mean you sent Abon to intercept the letter."

"I might have had something to do with it."

"And did the shaper have justification for killing the man?"

"You must judge for yourself when you read the letter, your Majesty, but, since we are pressed for time, I will summarize its contents for you."

"Very well."

"Earl Freomar intends to betray you to the Torrlonders in return for the title of Duke of Ellond. He is to wait until after we follow the Torrlonders to their war in the east since they know the common folk will more willingly follow you to battle. Earl Roric is of his party. They and their most loyal thegns will seek to slay you in battle at an opportune time."

Fullan sighed. "This is grave news."

"Grave enough to bring you to yours." The wizard bared his teeth in a ridiculous grin.

The king rolled his eyes and shook his head, but he could not keep a slight smile from his lips. "Really, Galdor. Is this the time?"

Galdor inclined his head in a slight bow. "My apologies, your

Majesty. I know they were once your friends, and I too remember the promise of their youth. But you must find a way to weaken them before they act. Expose them to the other nobles. That letter should help. It's what we've needed all along. Even those favorably disposed toward Torrlond will side with you when they see Freomar and Roric's betrayal. Once you've done this, you'll weaken support for Torrlond enough to assert your power once again. The people will follow you, and you know which nobles to trust."

King Fullan nodded. His jaw was clenched shut, and his face revealed little emotion at the wizard's news, but Galdor well knew what the determined look behind his bright eyes meant. "And what's the second thing you wanted to tell me?"

Galdor bent forward and lowered his voice to a near whisper. "A vision, your Majesty."

The king's eyes widened, and he leaned in closer as the wizard continued.

"We will meet again. Ere that, when you are somewhere far from here, strange ships will come. I know not whence, but when they come, that will be the moment to unveil yourself."

"You're certain? Strange ships?"

"Yes. Strange and strong. Whether they are foes or friends I know not. It was rather vague, I'm afraid."

Fullan frowned and stroked his beard. "Not much to go on, is it?"

"I'm sorry, your Majesty. It's the best I can do. The visions tell me what they want to, and no more. They also have a way of being perfectly apparent long after they're useful. In the meantime, you should proceed as we've planned."

"Alright. I've learned to trust you and your dreams. Is that everything?"

"Yes. I'll be depriving you of my company now."

The king smiled. "I'll feel deprived too. And surrounded by wolves. If it weren't so dangerous for you, I'd keep you by my side."

"Nonsense, your Majesty. You need me gone to carry on your little mummery for the Torrlonders and their lickspittles here. But the time will come. Remember the ships."

"I will. Farewell, old friend."

"We'll see each other again on a distant shore." The old wizard nodded to underscore the certainty in his voice.

King Fullan returned the nod and, with a flourish of his cloak, he turned to depart down the shrub-lined lane behind him.

"Not that way, your Majesty."

Fullan looked back at the wizard with his eyebrows raised in question.

Galdor grinned. "I'm expecting company from that direction, and it wouldn't do for you to be seen so near a heretic and traitor for whose head you must pay so dearly." The wizard winked. "I should take the eastern path if I were you."

"Very well. Just make sure you stay alive."

"Not to worry, your Majesty. I plan to."

The king nodded and turned to walk down a smaller lane leading in the direction of the eastern cloister. He disappeared behind the shrubs, and, with a sigh, Galdor imagined him making his way out of the maze back into the royal palace, Stithfast, in the heart of Ellordor, City of Spires.

A few moments after Fullan was gone, the wizard spoke aloud, "You may come out now, Abon."

A nearby shrub stirred, and from behind it emerged the scar-faced shaper, who walked toward Galdor. The squat man wore a sword at his side, and slung over his grey cloak was the green bag in which he kept his harp. He gripped a throwing knife.

"Did you hear everything?"

"Yes, my lord. All of it. That true about the vision? The ships and all?"

The wizard looked somewhere far away. "Yes, the ships. I could not be sure where they're from. But when they come, that will be the time for him to become king in more than name once again."

"And what about him seeing you again?"

Galdor shrugged. "I made up that part."

"I thought as much."

"He'll feel better that way."

The shaper smirked. "I reckon so."

The old man laughed. "Ah, dear Abon. I can't fool you, can I? I'll miss you as well."

"Oh? And where am I going?"

"To the island kingdom of Asdralad."

"You've a message for Queen Faldira?"

"Yes. I want her to know everything that's transpired here, including the fact that King Fullan is waiting for the right time to spring our little trap on the Torrlonders. You must tell her it's time to muster our armies. We must all come together to defend the east. We cannot repeat the mistake of allowing Caergilion to fall alone. And it appears there's little we can do now in Adanon but delay the Torrlonders until the spring. They will strike soon at Sildharan. I'll prepare things in Sundara and Golgar. King Tirgalan is sympathetic toward our cause, so I believe we may count on the Sundarae to come to our aid. But the Golgae are unlikely to help. Still, I must try to make them see the common threat. Since I cannot be in Asdralad, I need you to be my eyes, ears, and voice there. Also, you'll need to help look after the lad."

"Dayraven? Another vision?"

"Just a hunch. But for now, we're about to have company. Two priests of the Way are approaching, and if my guess is correct, they'll have soldiers with them. There's no time to run, and we are surrounded anyway."

"Surrounded?"

"Yes, my friend. There's a tightening noose around us. Soldiers loyal to Freomar are combing over the palace. They're closing in."

"What of the king?"

"Quite right. I can't have them discovering King Fullan was here, especially with the letter he now carries, so we'll be creating a little distraction in a moment. It would be best for you to disappear again. Watch my back for me."

The shaper flipped the knife and caught it. "It'll be my pleasure, my lord." He hurried back over to the shrub and squatted down behind it without a noise.

Galdor waited beneath the oak, humming the melody to a common drinking song and compensating for his lack of intonation with his enthusiasm. At length, the sounds of clinking byrnies and hurried footsteps arose from somewhere in the maze of shrubs. The old wizard hummed more loudly.

When six breathless soldiers and two white-robed priests emerged at the end of the lane, Galdor smiled and opened his arms in welcome. "Greetings! Kind of you to join me. Do you come in peace?"

Steel rang out as the soldiers all unsheathed their swords.

"Ah. Perhaps not."

Galdor felt a surge of energy and the presence of the gift when one of the two priests began singing a song of origin. It was Aldhelm, one of the most powerful among Ellond's priests of the Way and a fervent ally of Torrlond. He would not have come to chat.

The green-eyed old man grinned as, without a thought, he entered the realm of origins and intoned his own spell. "Alakathon gilathae ar voludar khuldar. Vortalion inkhathae ni manukhar bholdar."

With a loud crack and a flash of light, a glowing wheel with spokes of writhing blue bolts of energy sprang to life before Galdor's upheld hands and buzzed as it hung in the air before him. The jagged current of wizard's fire that surged from the priest Aldhelm's hands crashed into the wheel with an explosive burst and a loud bang. The impact shattered Galdor's shield of energy in a violent fracturing of blue-white tendrils that streaked in sundry directions, leaving smoking scars on the ground and the shrubs. The old wizard's ears rang, but he was otherwise unhurt.

Galdor could sense even from a distance that the second priest, a man he recognized as a Torrlonder, was weaker in the gift than his comrade. He was not strong enough to wield wizard's fire, but the Torrlonder carried a lit torch with him, and even then he began to weave the song of origin of fire. "Agadatha ar hurolin . . ."

The Torrlonder priest choked off when a bright object flew from between the shrubs to his left and smacked into his neck. The handle of Abon's throwing knife protruded from the man's throat. Instead of the remaining words of the spell, blood gushed from his mouth and spattered the snow beneath him as his eyes widened in shock. The torch fell onto the snow with a hiss. While the priest went to his knees and collapsed on his face, Aldhelm and the soldiers pivoted toward the shrubs.

"Orduno im broghyu ar vardha grondin. Unwarno an daghdu im durna hradin," chanted Galdor before they could harm the shaper. Strong was the bond he had cultivated over the years with with the life in this garden, and it leapt to obey his will.

Aldhelm and the soldiers with him jerked to a halt and gawked down at their feet, where the roots of shrubs and trees had broken through the cold soil to coil around their ankles. Their eyes widened in horror as the tough roots snaked up their legs. The soldiers shouted and hacked at the roots with their blades, but for every one they chopped, three more slithered around them, gripping them tight as they curled upward. A panicked song of origin spilled from Aldhelm's lips, but it was too little to counteract the strength of the gift in Galdor, who kept chanting his spell.

One by one, the soldiers and the priest of the Way toppled over as the thickening roots constricted around their bodies. More roots broke through the soil to worm their way over the men's faces, muffling and choking off their screams as they tightened around throats and slunk into noses and mouths. Even as they ceased trembling in their struggles, the bodies disappeared beneath the tangle of swarming vegetation. A few heartbeats later, humps of writhing roots and soil concealed them. When Galdor ceased chanting, the roots grew still. The old wizard stared at the mounds as he took a few deep breaths.

Abon emerged from the shrubs and plucked his knife from the dead priest's neck. After he wiped it on a patch of snow-covered grass, he walked toward the wizard.

Galdor was still gazing at the mounds with a blank expression. "Regrettable. Aldhelm could have been a great man. All of them had mothers. Families. Loved ones. Someone will mourn each of them. Ellonders slaying one another. People killing people. Such a waste. What are we coming to, Abon?"

The shaper stroked the scar on his face. "They would not have regretted slaying you, my lord."

The wizard sighed. "I suppose you're right."

"And we have a more pressing worry. Those screams and Aldhelm's wizard's fire will tell every priest in Ellordor your location."

Galdor nodded and grinned. "Yes. You're as observant as ever, dear Abon. This garden will be swarming with priests and soldiers in a few moments."

"In which case, mayhap we should be somewhere else."

"Eh?"

"Leave. We need to leave. Right now."

"Ah. You have the right of it again, my friend." The old wizard walked back to the oak. He put his hands on his hips for a moment, then he scratched his beard as he gazed up at the tree.

"What? Are we going to climb it and hide up there like squirrels?" said Abon's voice behind him.

Galdor chuckled, but he did not answer the shaper. Instead, he opened his arms wide and embraced the tree again, caressing its bark with his fingers.

"My lord? I know you're fond of them, but is this the time?"

"Hush, Abon." The wizard's hands circled in search of something, and, when they reached the level of his thighs, they paused on two gnarled knobs in the bark on opposite sides of the tree. He pressed them, and something clicked. "Ah."

A crack outlining a narrow panel one quarter of a man's height appeared on the bark at the base of the tree trunk. Galdor kneeled down and put the tips of his fingers to the crack, but he was unable to gain a hold. "Help me pull it."

Abon joined the wizard, and by jamming his knife in the crack, the shaper was able to widen the gap enough for his fingers to grasp and pry loose the panel. When he pulled, the panel came free like a little wooden door. It proved to be two inches thick and had a handle attached to it on the inside. What the small door disguised was a naturally hollowed out portion of the tree's wide, convoluted trunk. The clever maker of the door had shaped it and layered it with oak bark to hide the hollow in the tree. A groove on the door's bottom and the two lock mechanisms that Galdor had triggered fastened the door in place, perfecting the illusion that it was a natural part of the tree.

The wizard grinned as he watched Abon's eyes go wide at what lay hidden behind the little door. Below the hollow in the oak trunk gaped a hole in the ground just large enough for a man to slip down. It was hard to tell how far the hole went since it was pitch dark down it.

Galdor stood up and scratched his beard again. "It's smaller than I remembered. I suppose we'll have to fit."

"What?"

"Do you like it? I had it made years ago. One never knows when a secret exit will come in handy. Ha! Only the king knows about it. Well, and the fellows who dug the tunnel. But they're trustworthy, especially since they're dead now. May their souls rest in peace."

"Where's it go?"

The wizard raised his bushy eyebrows and smiled like a naughty child stealing a sweet. "Out." He looked behind him at the garden path. "The snow's sparse, and I've been pacing here for too long for them to make sense of our footprints. They'll be puzzling over our whereabouts for quite a while. Let's go."

Galdor put his hand on the tree and looked up at it. "I always liked you best." He put his index finger to his lips and whispered, "But don't tell the others." With a wink at Abon, he knelt and began to lower himself feet first down the hole. When his legs had disappeared up to his hips, he paused and began to wince. With a sudden drop and a yelp, he fell in so that only his shoulders, arms, and head peeked out of the hole. He grasped tree roots to keep himself from plunging further. His eyes bulged and his red cheeks puffed out as he groaned and sputtered with the effort of holding his body's weight. It was a tight fit, and, as his legs dangled beneath him, he imagined various ways he might injure himself by plummeting too far. He looked up at Abon and forced a toothy smile. "Help me down, will you?"

Abon knelt down and grasped the wizard's arms. With a few grunts and murmured curses, the shaper lowered him a couple more feet until the soles of Galdor's boots touched firm dirt.

The wizard blinked and smiled. "Oh. Not so bad." The hole smelled of the earth, and darkness surrounded him, but it was deepest to his left, where there seemed to be an open space. He looked up at the circle of light above him. "Don't forget the door, now. There's a good man."

"You'll have to hold me up, my lord."

"Very well." The wizard moved forward and held up his arms. Abon's feet then his backside formed a silhouette against the circle of light above him, darkening the hole further. Pieces of dirt and pebbles bounced off the old man's face as the shaper wiggled his hips in. "Yuck." He closed his eyes and spat out some grit. When Galdor felt Abon's legs swinging down, he grasped the calves and guided the shaper's boots onto his shoulders.

"Right. Stand on my shoulders while you put the door in place." He grunted and winced when the feet pressed down. His shoulders sagged and his spine compressed with the shaper's full weight bearing down on him. "Ugh! You're on the heavy side these days, aren't you?"

"I'm sure not made for squeezing down rabbit holes."

"It seemed a clever idea when I was planning it." The old wizard spoke between clenched teeth.

Abon struggled above him, and the shaper's weight shifted, causing the wizard almost to lose his balance and topple over. "Damn! How's the cursed thing supposed to fit?"

Galdor groaned. "Bottom first. In the groove. Then pull it shut . . . with the handle. Aargh! Hurry up! Old men aren't meant to be footstools for fat shapers!"

There was a sound of wood knocking on wood, then a click as the hole went black. "Got it!" said Abon above the wizard. "I'll let myself down now."

The shaper's left leg stepped off the wizard's shoulder, which caused most of his weight to shift to the right leg, shoving Galdor into the earthen wall.

"Ooof!"

"Look out!" Abon's right boot scrambled into the side of the hole, sending a shower of small rocks and dirt on the wizard's head.

"Ouch! Damn and blast!" He leapt to the left just before Abon's body came crashing down amidst a small avalanche of dirt.

The shaper coughed and choked.

"Everything alright?"

"Wonderful, my lord," came Abon's flat voice from the blackness.

"Well, we're alive."

"For now."

"I'd love to see the looks on the faces of those priests when they can't find us in the garden."

"If it's all the same to you, my lord, I'd rather be far away. And someplace where I can see the light of day."

"I suppose you're right. Just a moment." The wizard murmured the same spell he had used moments earlier to call upon the roots. Through it, he joined with the oak above him and prodded its bark to grow until it sealed the secret panel for good. "No chance they'll find their way down here."

"Very good, my lord," replied the shaper's voice from the darkness. "So, where do we go now? It's blacker than my arsehole down here. I can't see my hand before my face. What if we get lost?"

"We can't. There's only one way to go. We follow the tunnel."

"To where?"

"To freedom, of course."

"I meant something a little more particular, my lord."

"Oh. In that case, northward. Out of the palace, and closer to the docks, where we'll each find a ship awaiting us. Follow me."

The wizard took a few tentative steps with his hands out before him. His gentle footsteps grating on dirt and stone sounded strangely loud in the dark silence beneath the earth. Emptiness waited in front of him, giving him the sensation that he was about to step into a void. But moist soil and roots met his hands to his left and right. When he reached up, the roof of the tunnel proved only a few inches higher than his head. "Rabbit hole, indeed." He chuckled.

Abon mumbled behind him, "More like a grave."

TIME AND SPACE LOST THEIR MEANING IN THE COOL, DARK TUNNEL, which led the two men on for a long way. Their path seemed to go neither up nor down, but it was difficult to judge how level it was with no vision to guide them and nothing to give them a sense of direction. Even the old wizard had to suppress the occasional pang of fear in the narrow blackness, and the illogical idea that they were going in circles proved stubborn. But he kept his calm and his wits. Since they had slowed their pace to avoid bumping into the walls of the tunnel, their journey was not as far as it might have seemed. As for Abon, the shaper kept up a steady string of curses behind the wizard, for which Galdor was grateful since it was a reminder that he was not alone in the dark.

At length, the wizard's hands met a dirt wall in front of him, and with a little more feeling around, he discovered the wooden rungs of what he presumed to be a ladder. "Ah. We've arrived."

"Arrived where, my lord?" Abon's breathing behind him was loud.

"A friend's place. We're expected. We need to climb up now. Perhaps you should go first."

"*I* should go first?"

"There's a ladder just here. You'll meet a trap door above you. Just give it a little push."

"Alright, my lord."

Abon's boots clopped on the rungs as he climbed up. A moment later, he began grunting from above. "'A little push'? It won't budge."

"Push harder."

A succession of louder grunts came. "Damnation! Damn! Damn! Damn!" A banging noise accompanied each curse.

Galdor winced. "I hope you're not using your head."

The shaper growled, and a dim bar of light penetrated the darkness from above.

"Excellent work. Keep at it," said the wizard.

Abon grunted again, and the bar of light expanded to a bright square as wood grated on dirt. Abon's form blocked the light as he climbed up, but it returned when he clambered out. The shaper was no longer visible, but he breathed in loud gasps. "I'm up, my lord."

"I'm right behind you." Galdor blinked up at the light and climbed the rungs until his head popped up in a room most would have called dark. But, compared to the complete blackness whence the two men just emerged, the dim and grey room was beautifully bright.

"A cellar?" Abon's heavy breaths misted in front of him as he sat on the floor.

"Yes." The wizard finished climbing out of the hole and, after he stood up, he brushed particles of dirt off his robe.

"Whoever it belongs to put a fucking crate on top of the fucking trap door." The shaper rose to his feet and jerked his thumb at a nearby wooden crate full of large squash.

"Oh, dear. No wonder you had such a hard time. At least it was only one crate, eh?" Galdor grinned.

A long, pregnant silence accompanied the shaper's glare.

Galdor blinked in mock innocence, shrugged, and then looked around. They were in a small dirt cellar filled with grain sacks, barrels, and crates laden with fruits, vegetables, and dried foodstuffs. Sealed jars also covered much of the floor, but a path in the middle of all the clutter led to a flight of wooden stairs that provided access to a slightly open door. Dim light seeping through the crack in the door allowed them to see their surroundings. "Well, up we go. We need to clean up before we take our ride."

"Ride?"

The wizard provided no further explanation as he moved forward, pausing to pluck an apple from a crate before climbing the creaky stairs. When he reached the top, he pushed the door and stuck his head out, swiveling it to the right and left as if on the lookout for danger. He turned around, faced Abon, and put a conspiratorial finger to his lips. "Shhhhh." Then he took a large bite of the apple he was holding, and, as he chomped noisily, his eyes grew big with pleasure. "Hmmm. Delicious," he said while still chewing.

Abon rolled his eyes.

Galdor turned around and exited the door, with Abon following and staying on the alert. They walked down a long hallway with several doors on the right and left. Wooden panels carved with figures and patterns covered the length of the hallway and bespoke the luxury and opulence of the house they found themselves in. Natural light spilled from two open doorways on the right, and it was much warmer in the hallway than in the cellar. There was a heavy scent of perfume in the air. A woman's giggle came from behind one of the closed doors, and another woman moaned behind a different door.

"Wait . . ." Abon froze where he stood. "Is this . . . ?"

From one of the open doorways on the right, a beautiful young woman with dark brown hair stepped into the hall. The tiny, lacy article of clothing she wore – some sort of nightdress – did little to conceal her curves. She covered her initial surprise at seeing the two men in the hallway with a seductive smile. "You naughty boys lost? You're meant to check in at the front first."

Galdor gave a courteous bow and a warm, grandfatherly smile to the woman as he looked her in the eyes. "Hello, my dear. We came in the back way." He took another bite of the apple.

"There's no . . ."

"We're in fact here on important business concerning your mistress." The mouthful of apple he spoke around undercut the notion of 'importance' to any 'business' they might be on, but the young woman, a practiced professional, betrayed no sign of doubt in her demeanor. Galdor swallowed. "Would you kindly do me the favor of fetching her for me?"

The young woman's eyes narrowed, and her pretty lips made a slight frown. "She might be busy now, but I can go ask."

The wizard reached inside his patched robe with his free hand and brought out a fat leather purse that he jingled. "She has nothing to fear from us, I assure you." He put the apple in his mouth and, biting down, held it there while he stuck his index finger and thumb into the purse and brought out a thick silver coin, which he held out to the young woman. "Eesh ish . . ." he began, but then he put away the purse and plucked the apple from his mouth, handing off the half eaten fruit to Abon, who looked down at it as the wizard continued. "This is for your trouble and your silence. No one but your mistress is to know we're here. She'll thank you for your cooperation."

The young woman looked at the silver with a blank expression then reached out for it. After she took it, the wizard tugged at a ring on the middle finger of his left hand. "And give this to your mistress. She'll know me by it." He dropped the ring into her open palm. It was gold with a rectangle of ruby set in it. "Now make haste, my dear. And remember . . ." He held his index finger to his mouth and shushed.

The young woman smiled and nodded, then she turned to walk with a practiced saunter down the hallway, the smooth curves of her buttocks peeking below the garment she wore until she disappeared around a corner. The creaking of stairs came a moment later as she ascended them.

"Lady Hildegarth's brothel?" Abon's shock was plain on his face. He was still gawking with his mouth open at where the young woman had turned the corner.

"Don't say 'brothel.' She hates the word more than any other, save for 'whore.' It's a *house of pleasure*, and the young ladies are *courtesans*. Those are the words you use when the clientele pay a thousand times more than they do on the streets. And the ladies here are highly skilled. Or, so I'm told."

"Yes, but why are *we* here?"

"There are few I could trust as much as I do Lady Hildegarth. She owes me a bit of a debt, you see."

Abon nodded. "Many of us owe you a debt, my lord."

"Well, dear friend, you've paid yours many times over."

"No, my lord. Not until I breathe my last."

"Well, I don't know . . . For now, you can give me back my apple."

THE WIZARD WAS NEARLY FINISHED WITH THE FRUIT WHEN THE stairs groaned again with footsteps. A moment later, a woman with a confident and proprietary air strode toward them down the hallway. Middle-aged and strikingly beautiful, she had long strawberry blonde hair pinned up in a circular nest atop her head — the latest fashion among the wealthy ladies — and wore an elegant pink gown that revealed a generous amount of cleavage. A diamond necklace adorned her neck, and jeweled rings flashed on the majority of her fingers.

Lady Hildegarth favored the wizard with a silky smile. "Galdor. How good to see you." She held out his ruby ring between the index finger and thumb of her right hand.

"Lady Hildegarth." Galdor gave a slight bow and clasped her hand, which he kissed before taking his ring and putting it back on his finger. "The pleasure is mine."

"I've been expecting you. I hope your journey here went smoothly."

The wizard glanced at Abon, who was covered in smudges of dirt. He supposed he looked much the same. "For the most part, yes. We had to get a little dirty. And we did encounter a small crate on top of the trap door."

"Not *that small*," mumbled Abon.

Lady Hildegarth pursed her lips in displeasure. "Really? I told Eofor to keep the trap door clear. I'm so sorry. I'll have a word with him. Strong as an ox he is, but about as bright as one too."

"No need to trouble him, my lady. We managed."

"Well, I suppose you're in a hurry now. There was quite a disturbance here not so long ago. Two booms like thunder toward the palace, and then priests scurrying like white cockroaches from everywhere as fast as they could go in that direction."

"Imagine that. I suppose that means we'll encounter fewer priests where we're going."

Her smooth smile returned. "I suppose you're right. You two had better clean up in Edith's room. I'll have Eofor prepare the carriage."

After Galdor and Abon washed up, Lady Hildegarth insisted on feeding them and fussed over them like a doting mother. When all was ready, they left her large and elegant house in one of the most upscale neighborhoods of Ellordor inside a covered carriage driven by Eofor, a huge but simple and friendly fellow who smiled endearingly at everyone he met. The carriage had Lady Hildegarth's ensign painted on its door, so it was certain no one would disturb them during their ride. Most of the noble and powerful men in Ellordor had too many secrets in Lady Hildegarth's hands to risk interfering with her business. They knew the carriage usually carried her skilled courtesans to the private dwellings of those who did not wish to visit the house of pleasure in person. The noblewomen did not deign to acknowledge the carriage's existence with a glance. And so, when it passed, nearly everyone looked the other way.

Inside the carriage rode Galdor, Abon, Lady Hildegarth, and a now fully clothed Edith, the young woman Galdor and Abon met in the hallway. The women accompanied them in case they encountered any obstacles and the need for an explanation arose. Galdor and Abon sat inside the enclosed carriage with their hoods concealing their faces.

The carriage rolled northward, bumping over the cobbled streets of Ellordor without ever needing to stop, though in many places the traffic of folk, horses, carts, and other carriages slowed it. If people thought it strange to see Lady Hildegarth's carriage in the poorer neighborhoods near the docks, no one dwelled on it for long.

At length, the cries of seagulls and the shouts of the dockworkers announced their arrival. Before Galdor stepped out of the carriage, he kissed Lady Hildegarth and Edith on the hand. "I thank you both for your charming company. May Edan bless you and keep you."

Edith smiled, and Lady Hildegarth replied, "And you, my dear friend. I shall miss you. Be careful."

When they exited, a cold breeze met them. Red-faced Eofor smiled in his fur cloak atop the carriage and waved before he flicked the reins and the carriage rolled away. The wizard and the shaper took a quick look around. Sparse patches of snow covered the out-of-the-way corners where no folk walked along the busy docks, but only large, dirty puddles lay in the cobbled pathways. A thin, cold mist hovered above the wide Theodamar. On the eastern bank of the river where they stood, a long row of ships waited, most unloading or taking on cargo as sailors and dockworkers yelled, laughed, cursed, spat, and went about their tasks. A few ships rowed up or down the river.

Galdor led Abon into a small alley in between two warehouses. There were no priests or enemies in sight, but it was best to remain cautious. He pointed down the docks at a large ship tied up. "There lies your vessel. When you meet the captain, say to him, 'The sun shines bright in Asdralad year round.' He's expecting you, and you may trust him. He'll take you all the way to the island kingdom. Don't forget everything you're to tell Queen Faldira. And keep an eye on the lad."

"Yes, my lord. Where's your ship?"

"Two down from yours. I'm sailing for Sildharan first. I'll disembark in Thulhan and meet with King Naitaran briefly. From there I'll make my way by land to Golgar and then Sundara. There's much work to do. We'll meet again in the east, my friend."

"You telling me that to make me feel better?"

"Of course."

Abon grinned. "I thought so."

9

HANGING BY A THREAD

Spring arrived later in the Marar Mountains than it did in the fertile lowlands of Adanon. After surviving for several months by hiding in caves tucked among the cold mountains, Sequara was impatient for warmer weather. In the nooks and shadows of the bare rocks around her lay patches of snow. The far off plains, however, were green again, and the soft pastels of the early leaves cloaked the trees of the foothills. To the west lay the River Maranant, and on the other side of that natural boundary lay the erstwhile kingdom of Caergilion's chief city of Iarfaen.

Now the Caergilese city was a stronghold of the Torrlonders. It was also an important point in the Torrlonders' supply chain. The Adanese, the Asdralae under Sequara's command, and some refugee fighters from Caergilion had spent the last few weeks in futile attempts to disrupt that supply chain. Even more than about fighting, war was about supplies. If you could starve an enemy, you could defeat them. The problem was that her side was the one starving.

Had it not been for Adanon's people, the fighters would have perished. The simple but resourceful villagers, who pretended obedience to King Earconwald and the Way, ran the risk of providing food and sometimes shelter for those who fought under King Balch. It was a terrible risk. When the Torrlonders caught them, they exacted severe and often grotesque punishments, taking out their wrath by inventing new ways of torture.

Sequara shivered, half from cold and half from the memory of the village of sixty or so inhabitants she had seen a fortnight earlier. The Torrlonder soldiers had stripped every man, woman, and child naked and then tied them to stakes, blinded them, mutilated them, and left them to die. This was punishment for succoring Balch's forces and refusing to reveal their location, which they had not known anyway.

Worse yet, she too had killed many. Most of Sequara's victims had been Torrlond's grey-kirtled soldiers, but some had also been Caergilese or Adanese in the forced service of their conqueror. The majority she had slain using almakhti, or what the barbarians called wizard's fire. There were times when she loathed herself for it. Always she had seen herself as a healer, but now she was becoming a killer. It sickened her to use her energy to produce the jagged blue currents that left death in their wake. She feared she would never be able to wash herself of the horrible smell of burnt hair and flesh, and her nightmares meant that death haunted her nights as well as her days.

Sequara suppressed the urge to vomit. She wished she could shed the stinking fur cloak wrapped around her and fly to somewhere warm. Life in the cold, harsh mountains did not suit her, and this war was going ill indeed. Twice she had attempted to use the song of origin of dragons. Twice she had failed.

The first time had been only a month after she arrived. The dragon had been scouting far away then, increasing the difficulty. The second time, about six weeks ago, she had been much closer. They had ambushed a company of Torrlonders, and the dragon turned up moments later. As soon as it arrived, she crouched behind a tree and attempted to use the song of origin, trembling and sweating while fires raged and soldiers screamed and died all around her. It had not gone as she wished. She could not wield the song, let alone seize the serpents of the air from Bledla's control, though she had begun to feel some connection to the beast forming in the realm of origins. In the end, sensing her attempt to seize it from its master, the dragon had come for her, and she had fled. Their ambush turned into a rout.

Her failure ate at her. People were suffering and dying, and she could not stop it. Not only that, but Asdralad too would someday face the threat of Torrlond's aggression. And that day was not far away. How would the small island kingdom withstand so much power and hate? When she thought about it, it seemed hopeless.

But she would not break. She would try again. During the last attempt, she had felt like she *could* have mastered the song of origin. Perhaps she could do it. It *must* be possible. She had been too nervous, too eager. Calm and focus were needed.

That was why she had come to this place. It was away from the camp, and it afforded a view of Adanon's plains to the south. She had come to gather her strength, to find the steadiness required of her to wield the spell. She needed to be strong, so she would make herself strong.

But it was not easy. Morale among the forces fighting against the Torrlonders reflected their despair. They were sick of the harsh life in the mountains, sick of each other, and sick of death. Only hatred of the Torrlonders kept them going. *If I must, I will use hate.*

With memories of all the atrocities the Torrlonders had committed running through her mind, Sequara clenched her fists. Thousands upon thousands of innocents dead, all for the greed of a few and the madness inspired by a religion that rewarded its crazed followers for despising those who differed from them. King Earconwald and the Supreme Priest Bledla drove their followers, but they could have perpetrated none of their evils without the consent of those who obeyed them. For a moment, she indulged her despair, giving vent to what she knew to be her worst thoughts. *I hate the barbarians. I hate them for what they've made me do. For what I've become. I hate them all.* She would destroy as many as she could. She would visit wrath and revenge upon them. She would surely die, but before that she would . . .

An image of Dayraven came to her unbidden. He sat at the table in the small room where she had always instructed him in Queen Faldira's palace. Wearing his brown robe, white tunic, and dark trousers, he gazed at her with his serious blue eyes before looking down at the table, as if he knew how his eyes saw through her, saw too much of her. How was it that he experienced her memories for so long after she had healed him, just as she did his? Why was he lodged in her mind so strongly? It was strange how often she thought of the young man, even so far away. Sweet, foolish, innocent, powerful, dangerous, beautiful . . . *I don't want to die.*

She shook her head to rid herself of the selfish thought, but Dayraven would not leave her mind. *My whole life, I have devoted myself to duty. I knew what I was bound to do. It was never easy, but I always knew. Now . . .* She swallowed the lump in her throat and suppressed the tears brimming in her eyes. *I must seek detachment. I will hear the Mother and Father in the realm of origins.*

She sat on a rock and closed her eyes. To the realm of origins she journeyed, and as she meditated in that place, her will found its focus and hardened. Calm seeped into her as she grew aware of the land's strength. The roots of the mountains reached deep into the earth. Ancient rock and stone whispered of the passing centuries, during which the land witnessed the coming and passing of countless lives. A life was a fleeting thought, an offering of a mote of dust into the vast flame of existence. *Her* life was an offering. Purpose must be firm. Courage must be keen to make the most of one's brief time.

"My lady?" said a man's voice in High Andumaic.

Sequara's eyes snapped open. She returned to the world of forms amidst the grey rock of the mountain and the view of the green plains beyond the foothills. The sharp wind buffeted the mountain and toyed with strands of her hair.

Without looking behind her, she sensed the gift in great measure in the one who had addressed her. She stood and turned around to find Vilyanad waiting some twenty feet behind her on the path. He had been in this hell longer than she had, and though he looked worn and weary, perhaps thinner as well, he was as gracious as ever. A good example. A good man. He had been one of the few members of Asdralad's nobility to act with genuine kindness toward her after Faldira chose her as heir. She was glad to have him here. "Lord Vilyanad. Is it time for the council?"

The sorcerer drew his fur cloak closer around him and nodded. "Yes, my lady. Would you like me to walk back with you?"

"Your company is welcome."

When she drew near him on the rocky path, he gave a slight bow and began walking beside her. She turned to him. "May I speak frankly with you, Lord Vilyanad?"

"Of course, my lady."

"You were once Queen Faldira's closest rival. You nearly occupied Asdralad's throne."

Vilyanad gave a wry smile. "That is true. But King Nayarid made the right choice. Queen Faldira was most worthy to succeed him. Just as *you* are most worthy to succeed her."

Sequara stopped walking and looked him in the eyes. "Am I?" She smiled. "I thank you for saying so. But had you been king, would you have chosen me?"

He hesitated. "I don't know. The choice was not mine to make. But I do believe the queen chose well."

"Fair enough. And what about where we find ourselves now? Had you been king, what would you have done about Torrlond?"

This time his hesitation was longer, and he sighed. "I don't know. Sometimes there are no good choices. When aggression and violence threaten, one must do one of three things: flee, fight, or die."

"It seems we're doing all three."

"We have little room to maneuver. We're doing what we can. Within such limitations, we use what strength and wisdom we have. It may not be enough. We may lose. But is that a reason not to try?"

She gazed at him for a moment. "Of course you're right. Let's see how long we hold up here. I don't know how much longer our allies will last. I don't know how long we'll last. But we must try."

Vilyanad's eyes narrowed, and he looked at her with new intensity. "My lady . . . The truth is we here in Adanon are doomed. Our purpose is not to win, but to delay the Torrlonders until others are ready to fight them. You . . . Forgive me for saying so, but there's no need for you to stay here. You've done your duty. You tried. You must not blame yourself for failing where none of us has succeeded. Five times I've tried to wrest the dragons from Bledla. It's not my fate to stop him, and I'm lucky to be alive. Nearly a dozen of our strongest sorcerers have died here. That must not be your fate. Asdralad has need of you. Go back. Leave this place and return to your people."

Did he know how tempting his counsel was? How she yearned to return to the island kingdom? And it was not only for the sake of her people . . . No. *I still have a duty here. I was close the last time. I can wield the song of origin.* "There's nothing to forgive. It was I who wished to speak frankly, and I thank you for your words. But I can't return yet. There's still a chance. I must try at least once more."

The elder sorcerer gave her a slight bow. "As you wish, my lady. I do not question your judgement, but I urge you to consider what you'll do should you not succeed the next time."

"Thank you. Now, since I suppose there's no way out of it, we had best proceed to the council."

"WE ARE MET TO DECIDE OUR FUTURE COURSE. ONE THING IS certain: We must move damn soon. The goat-swiving Torrlonders are on our scent. Baron Trabon and his party caught some of their shit-licking scouts only a few miles from here." Speaking in the Northern Tongue for the benefit of those at the council who did not know Ondunic, Balch sat across from Sequara with the ruddy glow of flames reflected on his face. Adanon's rightful king was much thinner than he had been when she first met him not even a year before. It seemed an eternity had passed, and Balch appeared the worse for it. Dark circles occupied the spaces under his eyes, and he hunched in his seat as if the effort of sitting up was nearly too much for him. In truth, she worried about his sanity even more than his health.

Around a fire in a shallow cave they all sat, using large rocks as makeshift seats. They waited for Baron Aevor to translate Balch's words into Ondunic for Daen and Goel. The latter were the leaders of the Caergilese refugees, as starved as the Adanese and even poorer in the way of weapons. Though the two bearded and ragged leaders wore swords stolen from the Torrlonder dead, most of their followers used bows, hunting knives, small axes, slings, and an assortment of farming implements. Few had armor. In fact, they had hardly enough rags to clothe themselves. Sequara reflected that the first alliance between Caergilese and Adanese in all of their bloody history – fragile and born of desperate necessity – would likely be short lived. *Better late than never.*

"Six soldiers with as many pucas," said Baron Trabon. "There was a company of twenty Torrlonders not far behind them. We lost eleven men when we ambushed them, though we took care to keep downwind of the pucas." He nearly spat the last word.

"They know where we are." On Balch's left sat Duke Uwain, the gaunt, little man who, along with Imharr, was the highest ranking member of Adanon's nobility still alive. Uwain's eyes were even more haunted than Balch's, and his dark grey beard was long and unkempt. The distant look on his grinning face was that of a man who had lost touch with reality. "The time is coming. Prepare yourselves."

"For what?"

Orvandil's bass voice seemed to tug the duke back to the present, and his scowl was sullen as he stared at the Thjoth and answered, "For battle. For death, man. The Torrlonders won't stop until we're all rotting corpses."

Sequara glanced to her right, where sat Orvandil, with Gnorn occupying the place to his right. The Thjoth and the Dweorg were the true military commanders of the Asdralae forces, but, as long as she had been in Adanon, they consulted Sequara in their decisions and gave her the final say. She was glad of their presence and their loyalty, and she was certain the war would have been over without them.

"You speak with the voice of despair, Duke Uwain." On Balch and Rona's right sat Imharr, whom everyone called Silverhand. It was no accident that the king and queen had separated the two dukes, for Uwain made no secret of his contempt for Imharr, even going as far as once calling him an escaped slave and questioning his legitimacy. Balch had forced the older duke to apologize for that, but there was no love lost between the two noblemen. Jaw clenched tight, Imharr regarded Uwain with the same determined defiance he showed in battle again and again.

To the smaller man's credit, he did not flinch from Imharr's steel gaze. "Where there is no hope, despair is all that remains." Uwain's words came in a snarl. "Only a fool . . ."

"Whether or not there is hope," interrupted Queen Rona, "The

Torrlonders will buy our lives dearly. Never let it be said we Adanese prize our lives more than our freedom." She looked around as if to challenge anyone to contradict her. She was thinner than she had been mere months ago as well, and her cheekbones protruded from her face, but she somehow kept on looking like a queen, even now sitting erect and wearing a dress beneath her fur cloak. Sequara well knew – as did everyone else present – that the small woman was the true strength behind Adanon's resistance to the Torrlonders.

Avoiding the queen's eyes, Duke Uwain winced and appeared chastised for a moment. He stared at the fire with his jaw clenched tight.

Balch smiled and nodded. "The Queen is right. But now we must make a decision. Spring is come. War will resume in full force. Our first decision is where to go from here. Do we all stay together, or do we split up again? Where and how will we strike next?"

Daen spoke next in Ondunic, and Baron Aevor rendered his words in the Northern Tongue. "He says we should stay together. Our strength is greatest when we're all combined. If we're divided, the Torrlonders will pick us off one by one."

Sequara nodded. Naturally, the Caergilese would want them all to stay together. They had the fewest supplies and the most to gain. Also, she suspected they did not trust the Adanese and wanted to keep close to them.

Balch looked at Daen with his dark eyes. "If we're to remain as one army, where do we go? We need a position we can defend as well as supplies."

There was a long silence. Everyone seemed to be waiting for someone else to speak.

"There is nowhere to go." Duke Uwain still stared at the flames as he spoke. "The Caergilese is right. We should stay as one army. But there is no reasonable position of defense, is there? So, what do we do?" He looked up and sneered as he pounded his fist into his open palm. "We should *attack* as one army. An all-out assault. Let's end this starvation, this cowering. An end to it all."

"You speak of suicide," said Gnorn.

"There's nothing else left, fool!" Uwain trembled where he sat. He appeared coiled to leap across the fire and assail Gnorn.

"There are other ways," said Vilyanad, who sat to Sequara's left. To his left was the Asdralae sorceress Namila. Only they remained of those with the gift that Queen Faldira had sent to Adanon, and, though she had a talent for healing, Namila was far weaker in power than Vilyanad. The two of them had become lovers, but Sequara pretended not to know as long as they performed their duties. The monarch was forbidden relationships or family, but others with the gift in Asdralad could do as they pleased, and it was rumored that Vilyanad had fathered a child with at least one of his lovers. "Incursions. Raids. Sabotage," continued the sorcerer. "We must use stealth as our ally since we have not enough strength to confront the Torrlonders head on."

"We've tried all those things, and look at us!" spat Uwain. "Keep skulking like a coward if you like, but I'll have no more of this cringing in caves."

Namila pointed at Uwain. "Watch your tongue! How dare you insult those who come to your aid?"

Goel yelled something in Ondunic, and before Aevor could translate, Uwain, Balch, Trabon, Daen, Namila, Vilyanad, and Gnorn all shouted or spoke at once in an excited babble of languages. It went on as each tried harder to raise his or her voice over the din. Uwain and Goel even stood up and began pointing and shaking their fists at each other.

Looking around at them with narrowed eyes, Sequara smothered her anger and slipped into the realm of origins. No one would hear her chanting above the shouting. "Agadatha indurol ar feniar imbrithway. Khalavatha ardunol in shoniar targonway."

The fire roared and leapt up to the roof of the cave. Several of those present gasped, and their startled, gape-mouthed faces glowed bright in the flash of heat. Vilyanad and Namila were less surprised than the others since they would have felt Sequara drawing upon the gift. Orvandil gave a grim smile. Perhaps the Thjoth had heard her chanting since he sat next to her and had not been shouting. After the moment of brightness, the cave seemed dimmer than before, though the fire returned to its normal size. Amidst the stunned silence, Sequara rose from her seat.

She gazed around at them all. "Look at you. If the Torrlonders could see you now, they would laugh. We *must* stay united in purpose, or we will die. As it is, we are still alive, and with every breath we will defy the Torrlonders. We may not agree on the best way forward, but we must agree to hear each other's counsel without quarreling like frightened children. Since this is the kingdom of Adanon, we will all defer to its rightful rulers. King Balch and Queen Rona will come to a decision after hearing our counsel. Then, having had our say, we *all* must obey their decision, whether we agree with it or not." She looked at Baron Aevor. "Translate."

Aevor closed his mouth and swallowed before he began rendering her words into Ondunic. When he finished, everyone was silent for a moment.

Queen Rona stood up. "Thank you, Lady Sequara." She exchanged nods with the sorceress, who sat again. "While you were all speaking, an idea occurred to me. It may be desperate, but *we* are desperate. It will require some volunteers . . ."

ON A RUGGED SLOPE OVERLOOKING IARFAEN, SEQUARA CROUCHED behind a boulder and peered down at the occupied city. They were not far from where the Battle of Iarfaen happened so many months ago — not far from where Sequara first saw Dayraven and plunged into his mind as he lay dying. The most frightening thing about that day filled with blood and sweaty fear had been the vastness of the gift in him. Nevertheless, on that day she had saved his life. She shivered at the memory and then focused on the city below her. She was here for a different reason now.

"Not a bad view, my lady."

Sequara glanced at Karad, who crouched next to her. The veteran managed a smile, but she perceived his worry for her behind his eyes. She wished she could have convinced him and the eleven other Asdralae soldiers accompanying her to stay behind, but Karad would not hear of it, and Gnorn and Orvandil had backed him. She was taking a terrible risk, and if she failed, there was little or nothing her soldiers could do. She knew they would die for her, but she did not want their deaths added to the tally on her conscience.

She managed to return Karad's smile and gave him a nod. "We'll be able to see the Torrlonders leave the city in pursuit of the Caergilese."

"And their beasts."

"Yes. Those too." But only one of those beasts concerned Sequara at the moment. *The one that truly matters.* She looked back at the view beneath her.

The rising sun glistened off the surface of the River Maranant as it skirted Iarfaen and snaked off into the distance. Since it was early morning, there seemed to be little activity in and around the walled city, but it was hard to tell at such a distance. The breeze toyed with tiny banners flapping atop the towers, and though it was too far to see them, Sequara knew they displayed King Earconwald's ensign.

Somewhere down there was one of Bledla's dragons, which he had posted in various locations throughout Caergilion and Adanon to protect the Torrlonder forces, making nearly impossible any significant rebel attacks on the occupying army. In addition to wreaking havoc among the rebels, the monsters had slain a handful of Asdralae sorcerers while they tried to seize the serpents of the air from the supreme priest's control. It was an incalculably tragic loss for Asdralad, and though not all the sorcerers had been friendly to her, Sequara mourned them. No one could match Bledla's power, and in any case, no one but he could wield the song of origin, though Sequara believed she had begun to sense the beasts' true inner nature while trying.

Despite their lack of success, it was apparent that Bledla had instructed the beasts to seek out and slay anyone with the gift who tried to use the song of origin of dragons. Though no sorcerers succeeded in using the spell to master them, the beasts could sense when someone was attempting it. Thus, the sorcerers became traceable targets for the fiery lingworms, and more often than not, they had died. This made the beasts even more dangerous, but also predictable in at least one way.

This time, Sequara *wanted* the dragon to come after her. Her task was to draw it away to make possible the real attack. What no one else knew, save perhaps Vilyanad, was that she hoped to succeed in wresting the dragon from Bledla. *I've come so close before.*

The sorceress let out a long sigh and turned to Karad. "You secured the rope?"

He nodded. "Aye, my lady, and I sent Unan in to leave some stores deep in the cave. We'll be safe in there. That is, if we need it."

A couple minutes' walk from their current position, they had spotted a perfect place to hide from the dragon should that prove necessary. It was a small cave in the side of a cliff, accessible only from above by tying a rope to a boulder at the top of the cliff. Its entrance was far too small for the dragon to fit through, but it was also deep, and it twisted so that they could hide from any flames the beast might disgorge into the mouth. At least it gave them the illusion of safety.

The sun rose higher while the chill wind tossed Sequara's cloak and brought tears to her eyes. She rubbed her hands against each other. The palms were sweaty despite the cold. "Waiting is the worst part," she said loud enough for Karad to hear.

"Aye, my lady. That it is." The veteran looked at her and swallowed.

"Look. On the road," said one of the younger men.

Sequara peeked above the boulder she was crouching behind. After scanning the horizon for a moment, she spotted a small cloud of dust hovering over the road leading to the city.

"Horses and riders. In a hurry," said Unan. "Looks like the Caergilese have done their bit."

The muscular young guard could see further than Sequara could, and she trusted his judgement. The plan was in motion, and it would run its course. She must focus on her part.

Karad nodded. "The caravan scouts. Now we wait for them to enter the city."

"The Torrlonders'll rush out soon after," said Unan.

"And the dragon," said one of the other soldiers in a voice that he tried without success to keep flat.

Sequara locked her eyes onto the dust cloud. The moment was coming. She steadied her breathing.

. . .

When horns blared in the distance from the direction of Iarfaen, Imharr turned to Orvandil. "The Torrlonders have taken the bait."

The Thjoth nodded. "Aye."

"Daen and Goel and their lot should be here soon." Gnorn tugged on his beard. "If they didn't get mixed up with the Torrlonder caravan, that is."

"They know their part. They'll be here." Imharr clenched his jaw as he tugged on the hilt of Wreaker, unsheathing the blade a few inches before letting it drop and then repeating the same motion again. It had become a habit of his, a ritual even, before battle. He peered down into the narrow valley below them, at the bottom of which several rills running down from the rocky slopes converged in a stream.

"Aye," said Orvandil. "Soon enough."

Turning back to his two friends, Imharr glimpsed the sorcerer Vilyanad and some of the few hundred remaining Asdralae soldiers behind them on the slope. Most were well hidden behind boulders. "I'd best see to my soldiers now." He grasped Orvandil's forearm and then Gnorn's. "Luck to you, my friends."

Gnorn nodded. "We'll see you after the battle, lad."

Imharr returned the nod and headed toward another part of the slope, where the Adanese soldiers under his command were even then taking their positions behind the cover of rocks and the scraggly pines clinging to the hillsides.

Hundreds of soldiers on steeds poured out of Iarfaen's front gate until Sequara estimated they reached a thousand. Their helms, spear points, and byrnies glittered in the sun. Among them lumbered a score of hairy trolls, and she thought she could pick out a few white robes on the horses. So many soldiers to deal with a ragged band of farmers. The Torrlonders meant to wipe them all out.

It was time for Sequara to enter the realm of origins. Just as her mind slipped away and embraced the peace that only one with the gift could know, a blur of red shot up from somewhere in the city. Even from as far away as she was, she heard the mighty clap of its wings as it flapped to gain altitude. The beast surged higher. Riding the currents, it pierced the air like an arrow and streaked away from the city, growing smaller every moment.

Calm. She would keep her control. The Father and Mother were with her. In creation time, she was one with the beginnings of things. In a steady voice, she sang the song of origin:

Urkhalion an dwinathon ni partholan varlas,
Valdarion ar hiraethon im rhegolan wirdas!
Gholgoniae sheerdalu di vorway maghona,
Dardhuniae sintalu ar donway bildhona!

She repeated the song again and again. At first, it seemed to have no effect. Like water sliding off a rock, she could gain no hold. But after a while, her energy bumped into something vast. It was nothing she could wrap around, let alone master, but she had gained a tentative hold on it. Or rather, she had gained its attention.

She felt a change in the vastness, an itch of awareness as it turned its mind in her direction. A fraction of a moment later, her eyes saw the creature abruptly bank and pivot around in the world of forms. Its response was automatic, a bending to an undeniable command from a will not its own. It was still a speck in the sky, but it hurled toward her with speed no other creature in Andumedan could match.

Sequara kept her focus, and she dug deeper as she repeated the song of origin over and over. Still the vastness of the creature was like an impenetrable wall, and there was almost nothing for her to clutch onto. Too big, too ancient it was. So huge and yet so foreign, like nothing else she had encountered in the realm of origins. Her strength in the gift, so uncommonly powerful among humankind, felt small and inadequate next to it. She crashed against the dragon's energy, but she was like a child assaulting a castle with a stick. She threw herself with more force against it, and this time she recoiled with such violence that it nearly broke her connection to the world of forms. Her sweating body swayed, but she righted herself as she fought to stay in the realm of origins. She gritted her teeth and rushed forward again.

. . .

His silver-hued hand gripping Wreaker's hilt, Imharr crouched behind a group of pines, peering between their needles down at the far end of the valley, where the Caergilese under Daen and Goel's command were filing along in a quick but orderly march. Most of their numbers were still with them, meaning they had withdrawn from the Torrlonder caravan before engaging for too long. Of course, the Caergilese had needed to make the attack convincing enough, else the Torrlonders would suspect the trap they were about to rush into. Most of the time, they would be relying on a dragon to spy such a trap from the air. This time, if all went well, they would be rushing in blind.

"They don't seem in much of a hurry, my lord." Nayan crouched next to Imharr. "Do you think the Torrlonders are following?"

"They'll come." Imharr turned to his soldier. "Remind Gilad to wait for my signal, and tell him to pass the word along. We must not move until Lord Vilyanad has finished."

Nayan nodded. "Yes, my lord." The soldier scurried over to where Gilad and his men were hiding.

Imharr watched him for a moment and then returned his gaze to where the Caergilese were marching along the valley floor. *Let's just hope they come without their dragon.* He spared a thought for Sequara and hoped the sorceress would escape unscathed.

Again she sang the song of origin, and again she crashed into the vast energy that was growing nearer and so should have been easier to master. Still she could not grasp it. She heaved everything at it, holding back not even the smallest fraction of her energy. The impact was terrible. Sequara recoiled and shattered into a thousand pieces.

Without Queen Faldira's training, she would have died then. As it was, she fought back panic as she struggled to maintain enough control to draw the fragments of her energy back to her body. It was like spiraling outward while trying to grasp pieces of mist blowing further and further from her. At last, however, her scattered energy began to coalesce, and at once it snapped back into her crouching body.

At first, it was like looking through fractured glass that was spinning. The world of forms felt fragmented, and a horrible nausea ripped at her stomach. She fell over and kept her eyes shut for a few moments. When she opened them, Karad, Unan, and the others stood over her with deep frowns on their grave faces. She could see again, and her body was hers.

"It's coming," she said in a strained voice. "It knows we're here, and I can't stop it. Head for the cave. Now."

"To the cave!" yelled Karad.

They all turned and sprinted. Sequara rolled over and tried to get up. She took two steps before the dizziness knocked her over, and she scraped her elbows, knees, and palms on the rock. Hands grabbed her up, and when she stood again, there were Karad and Unan, one on each side of her. The other soldiers waited ahead. Most of them gazed out over the city with terror plain on their wide-eyed faces at the approaching monster.

"We'll carry you, my lady," said Karad.

She looked behind them over the city. Now close enough to appear distinctly, the dragon streaked toward them in the sky. They did not have much time. "No. Too slow. I'm fine. It's wearing off. I'll be able to keep up, but I can't use spells anytime soon. You others run ahead, get into the cave. Let's go."

At first her legs were wobbly, but fear of a horrible death was a strong motivation, and soon enough Sequara was running alongside Karad and Unan. The others were just ahead, scrambling on the rocks and turning the corner that led toward the cliff. They would need to start descending the rope as soon as they reached it to give everyone time to clamber in the cave. She glanced back again.

The crimson serpent of the air was a rocketing mass that took up a greater portion of the sky than any creature should. She could almost discern its features: the veins in its wings, its amber eyes, its spiked back, and its white teeth and claws. Sequara picked up her pace. The top of the cliff was around the next corner. They would make it. With a little luck, they would all make it.

As she rounded an outcrop of rock to gain her first view of the cliff, screams broke out ahead. At first, she feared the dragon was already upon them, but then she jerked to a sudden halt when the cause of the commotion appeared before her.

A patrol of Torrlonders stood between her men and the boulder to which they had tied the rope. The grey-kirtled soldiers outnumbered her men two to one. With death behind and before them, the Asdralae yelled and rushed at their foes.

A DULL RUMBLE CRESCENDOED INTO THE THUNDER OF HOOVES AND stomping trolls when the Torrlonders and their beasts of battle flooded the combe that the Caergilese had marched through moments before. The last of Daen and Goel's men were still visible at the valley's other end, and, sensing their prey within reach, the Torrlonders surged forward.

Imharr's grim smile came a moment before another trembling shook the earth, and he felt its vibrations beneath his feet. Vilyanad was doing his work. *Time to help out.* "Alright, lads! Now! Put your backs into it!" He rushed forward to the nearest boulder and began pushing. Nayan joined him a moment later, and they grunted as they heaved. The boulder moved with shocking ease, and Imharr reckoned that, in obedience to Vilyanad's spell, it would have plummeted down the slope even without encouragement from him and Nayan. Elsewhere below him and on the opposite slope, hundreds of rocks and boulders crashed toward the Torrlonders, who, strung out along the valley, were caught between the two avalanches.

The vast and terrible din sounded as if the very earth was groaning in agony, but most horrifying was when the surging flood of boulders reached the cowering Torrlonders. Flesh and bone exploded with every impact, and sprays of blood and guts erupted where shrieking men, screaming horses, and bellowing trolls had stood a moment before.

The twin avalanches ended as suddenly as they had begun, leaving an eerie silence for a couple heartbeats. From within the cloud of dust settling over the valley floor came moans and the agonized screams of the wounded. A few small rocks cracked as they bounced down the slopes, but Imharr knew that Vilyanad would now be holding back further avalanches. *Time to clean up what's left.* He unsheathed Wreaker and brandished it. "Adanon!"

SEQUARA'S MEN HAD THE INITIAL ADVANTAGE AS THE FIERCENESS OF the Asdralae surprised the Torrlonders. Two of them dropped with bloody gashes in the initial onslaught, and the others fell back. But their commander barked orders, and the greater numbers began to tell. First one, then two, then three of Sequara's men went down with bleeding wounds. The Torrlonders hacked their fallen bodies.

By instinct, Sequara reached for the gift. But when she tried to enter the realm of origins, the nausea returned with renewed force. The world spun, and she lurched as she nearly fell. Karad held her up. She pressed her fingertips to her forehead and said, "If we don't get in the cave, we're all dead. Go."

Unan and Karad unsheathed their blades and rushed toward the fray. Sequara reached inside her cloak and grasped the hilt of her curved blade. As dizzy as she was, she would be of little use, but she would not stand back while her men died. She ran close behind the two faithful guards.

By now the close melee was a chaos of blurring and chopping steel. Swords rang out, and men screamed like feral animals in fear and pain. Droplets of blood flew and spattered as the edges of blades ripped through flesh. A Torrlonder snarled and swung at Sequara, but she dodged the blade and thrust her sword forward. She was unbalanced, but somehow the tip found the man's face beneath his helm, and he cried out as he flinched.

She was trying to maneuver closer to the boulder they had tied the rope to. At the same time, the Torrlonders were pressing her and her men closer to the cliff's edge. To her right, Unan was yelling as he wheeled his sword around with his strong arms. A Torrlonder fell when he cleaved the man through his helm down to his teeth, sending blood squirting from the ruin of his face. Karad kept two grey-kirtled men away from Sequara. He wounded one in the shoulder, but the other nicked the veteran's thigh at the same time.

The inevitable took only a few moments. One by one, Sequara's men died as they succumbed to the blades of their foes. Unan struggled against three, but they surrounded him and hacked at him until he fell to his knees. The next blow sliced through half his neck in a spray of blood, and he slumped to the ground.

Even as Sequara's heart lurched with Unan's death, the man who had wounded Karad rushed at him and tackled him. Karad stumbled back and lost his footing, the two of them disappearing when they tumbled over the cliff's edge in an embrace. A long moment later, their bodies cracked on the rocks below.

A woman's scream sounded in Sequara's ears, and it took her a moment to realize it was tearing through her own throat.

Stabbing and twisting their blades, the Torrlonders finished off her wounded and hapless men. The impaled, helpless Asdralae — most of them little more than boys — bled and twitched and cried out in anguish before going silent. Tears of sorrow and rage clouded Sequara's eyes. She was close to the rope now, but it was too late.

With her heels only inches from the cliff's edge, she glanced behind at the rock-littered ground waiting far below. Dizzy with the aftereffects of her failure with the dragon, she swayed in the strong wind. She stood alone and faced the ten Torrlonders remaining on their feet. Some were wounded, but all of the pale-skinned barbarians gazed at her with hate and lust-twisted sneers as they breathed in heavy gasps. One licked his lips and wiggled the tip of his tongue at her. Other than the groans of the dying, the place was quiet. The grey-kirtled soldiers formed a line. They advanced toward Sequara with snarls and leering grins across their faces.

"You're dead, bitch! But we'll have some fun with you first!"

"Come 'ere, cunt! We'll show you how to use a blade."

Sequara held her sword ready. When she reached for the gift, the nausea still assaulted her, and she wobbled as she almost fell backwards. But she also sensed something else. Something huge. Like a gigantic storm front, the presence of the enormous serpent of the air hurled toward her from behind and below. It was coming with stealth and terrible swiftness.

A deep, loud rush of howling wind assaulted the cliff. Wide-eyed shock seized the Torrlonders' faces as a giant shadow swallowed them.

Sequara threw her sword and leaped for the rope. Blistering heat surged over the flesh of her back. Though it seemed out of reach as she plummeted toward the far away base of the cliff, her hands somehow grasped the rope hanging out beneath the cliff's lip. But as she half slid and half fell, swinging wildly on the rope, it burned into her palms with a sharp pain. She cried out when the pain forced her to release the rope. As her body spun and dropped, it was Dayraven's beautiful face she saw. Something smashed into her back just before a skull-jarring flash erupted in her head.

Behind Imharr ran his men, and off to his right he caught a glimpse of the Asdralae under Orvandil and Gnorn's command scrambling downslope. He could hear the battle cries of the descending Adanese soldiers on the combe's other side, though he could not see the opposite slope through the dust cloud choking the valley floor. He also knew that the Caergilese would have turned around by now to complete the ambush. Approaching the dust cloud, he caught a glimpse of movement within it, a looming shadow that emerged with a snarl as a huge troll with blood sheeting its face lunged toward him.

Covered with dust, the troll appeared like a huge ghost. Imharr ducked, and a massive, hairy arm swept over his head even as he flicked Wreaker into the beast's thigh, slicing through hair and bark-like flesh. Several of his soldiers engaged the troll at once, but, with a piercing roar, it careened into them, sending bodies flying with the bone-cracking impact. In the next heartbeat, Imharr caught a glimpse of a ruddy glow from further within the dust cloud.

"Down!" he screamed even as he dived for the ground, grunting when he hit.

A stream of flames coursed above him, washing his body with its heat. Shrieks of agony sounded behind him. "Damn them!" screamed Imharr as he leapt up and sprinted toward the source of the flames. Coughing and choking on dust, he caught a glimpse of white that resolved into the form of a robed priest of the Way holding a torch. With dust caking his beard and face, the priest seemed like an apparition. The man was even then chanting to prepare another burst of flames.

Imharr switched Wreaker to his left hand as he sprang toward the priest, who thrust his torch straight at him. Flames roiled from the torch just as Imharr reached the man and grasped the torch's head with his right hand. The priest's smirk gave way to wide-eyed shock when the flames sizzled out, smothered beneath Imharr's grip. A moment later, the white-robed man gasped and lurched when Wreaker passed through his chest. A crimson gout coughed from his mouth, spattering his beard and chin in sharp contrast to the white dust on his face.

A moment later, the troll bellowed, and Imharr pivoted to face it. But, instead of attacking, the massive beast shook its head and ran in the other direction. "Let it go!" yelled Imharr. "Do *not* engage that troll!"

Though he could hear the clashing of weapons from elsewhere within the dust cloud, he could not see any other living Torrlonders nearby. Their corpses littered the ground, their grey kirtles whitened beneath a layer of dust with spatters of dark blood standing out in contrast. Many gaped with blank stares, while others were so badly pulped as to be barely recognizable as human. *We've got to get out of here. Sequara won't be able to keep the dragon away for much longer.* He bent down to wipe soot from his unharmed hand on the dead priest's robe, leaving a black smear on it. With a grim smile, he flexed the scarred and silvered hand that, while not impervious to flame, resisted it much longer than normal flesh. *Dragon blood's good for something, at least.* He shook his head and transferred Wreaker back to his sword hand.

Someone arrived through the dust to stand next to him. "Duke Silverhand. The Torrlonders are all dead or dying."

Imharr faced Nayan, breathing a sigh of relief that the young man was unharmed. "Time to leave, then. Spread the word to the men to disengage and begin our withdrawal." Looking away from the grotesque forms of the Torrlonder dead, he spat dust and grit from his mouth. "This day is ours."

"Sequara! My lady!"

Gently touching her fingers to her throbbing head, at first Sequara thought she must have been dreaming in her half-dazed state. But then the voice came again, yelling her name. With a leap of her heart, she recognized it. *But it can't be. I saw him fall.* "Karad!" She winced as the effort of yelling sent a stab of pain through her skull. "Karad!" This time his name came out like a sob, and she cursed her weakness. She sat up, groaning with the ache in her head and the nauseating dizziness that the effort caused. She splayed her arms out to steady herself and then, jerking up her hands, cried out like she had touched hot iron when her palms contacted rock and grit. *The rope. I must have lost a lot of skin on my hands.* She opened her eyes.

It made little difference. Deep in the cave, there was almost no light, but she could make out the faint glow at its entrance. She did not know how long she had been lying within it, but she recalled crawling on hands and knees into the cave after landing right in its entrance. Before that, falling. Twisting in desperation, she had swung on the rope with enough momentum to sway her back toward the cliff before her stinging hands let go. It was all a blur, but it came back to her in fragmented images.

Desperate crawling deeper into the cave. The dragon returning and vomiting flames into the cave's entrance, roaring its frustration. Lurching for the gift, which eluded her in her nearly unconscious state, and curling up into a ball in a corner of the cave while the intense heat nearly baked her. She lost count of how many times the dragon returned, needing time to fly around and come at the cave high up in the cliff face. But its flames never reached her.

In the end, with a final wrathful bellow, the dragon had wheeled round for its last pass at the cave, and Sequara let the darkness take her.

"Lady Sequara! Are you in the cave?" Karad's panicked voice seemed to come from above her.

She crawled toward the light. "Yes! I'm here, Karad!" Neary crying with relief at the sound of his voice, she winced again and fought through the nausea.

"My lady! The rope's gone! Give me a moment to tie together these cloaks, and I'll haul you up!"

"Alright. I'm coming."

A LONG WHILE LATER, SHE STOOD AT THE TOP OF THE CLIFF AGAIN, breathing hard and placing the back of her wounded hand against Karad's shoulder to steady herself. She stared at the gruesome absurdity of the remains of the Torrlonders who had been facing her when the dragon arrived. Other than ashes and pieces of metal and bone, only their lower legs remained. Ten pairs of boots with feet still in them, all laid out in a row. Other bodies lay strewn all over the top of the cliff, including those of her loyal soldiers, all lifeless now.

"My lady. I thought I'd lost you." Tears wet Karad's cheeks, and he beamed a smile at her.

Sequara nodded. "And I you."

Still grinning, the veteran nodded in return. "I landed on top of the other fellow. Got banged up, but not so bad as he did. Broke his back. I had to play dead until the dragon left. That part wasn't hard, but thinking about you . . ." A sob choked off whatever else he was going to say.

"It's alright. We're alright now." *But poor Unan, and all the others . . .*

Karad swallowed before mastering himself. "Aye, my lady. We are. And, your pardon for saying so, but I reckon it's time to head back to Asdralad. You've done your bit here."

Sequara thought of the dead, those she had led and those she had slain. Amidst all that swirling pain, one clear thought emerged like the light at the end of that cave: She would never master the song of origin of dragons. This encounter had taught her that bitter lesson. And even if their ploy of drawing away the dragon succeeded on this day, she did not believe she would survive a second attempt, much less keep her sanity amidst all this death. "Yes, Karad. I think you're right. It's time to go home." She sighed in utter exhaustion, still leaning on the veteran for support. "Let's head back to camp. Find out what happened. But first, we bury our fallen."

. . .

ON A DAY WHEN SPRING WAS IN FULL SWING, DAYRAVEN SAT ON ONE of the benches near the pool at the center of the palace garden in Kiriath. A riot of colors surrounded him as the flowers and hibiscus trees gloried in the bright new life coursing through them. He wished he could partake in the mood, but Sequara's long absence and the lack of tidings from Adanon chilled everything.

Queen Faldira sat on the bench opposite his, making a good show of instructing him on the subtle differences between mastering one's emotions as a source of power and allowing them to master one. Dayraven in turn made a good show of listening, but he could not keep his mind off Sequara. For the thousandth time, he was on the verge of telling the queen he would go to Adanon. His mastery of the gift was near enough to complete, and his truce with the elf-shard was holding. If he could go to Adanon and seize the dragons from Bledla, that would end everything, and Sequara could return to Asdralad. The words were about to form and tumble from his lips, and he could not stop them.

And then, as if the vision in his mind had called forth her spirit, she appeared.

Wearing travel-worn clothes and looking thinner, she stepped out of the palace and into the garden in the middle of Dayraven's lesson. She kept her face emotionless, but there was a keen intensity in her beautiful, tired eyes. Not just tired, but haunted. Her feet crunched on the gravel walkway, so she had to be real. He also felt the distinct presence of the gift in her.

No doubt sensing the same presence, Faldira stood up and turned around. With tears blurring his vision, Dayraven watched the queen and her heir approach and embrace one another without saying a word. Yearning to do the same, he checked his feelings and merely smiled when the two women shook with sobs of release.

Sequara looked his way over Faldira's shoulder as she leaned on the queen. In her tearful eyes he saw deep sorrow and fatigue, perhaps defeat. She could not wield the song of origin of dragons. She had witnessed death and horrors, and Dayraven longed to comfort her. Even as his heart raced, he forced his breaths to a deep, steady rhythm

PHILIP CHASE

and closed his eyes. He did not yet trust his legs to rise from the bench.

Just when he opened his eyes and worked up the courage to say something, Urd appeared in the garden's entrance. "Ah! It's true then. You've returned, my dear." The old woman's voice shook with emotion.

Sequara turned to face Dayraven's great aunt. They walked toward each other and embraced. "I failed, Urd. I could do nothing. The song's beyond me." Even her voice was tired and strained.

Urd held the young woman by the shoulders and looked up into her eyes. "Never mind. There'll be other trials ahead. For now, you're home and safe. I expect you're wanting a wash and a long sleep."

"Yes. I could sleep for days, I think. Only there's so little time. Torrlond advances every day. Its troops are everywhere, and many in the southwest have allied themselves with the enemy. Some are even eager to please the Torrlonders, so they betray us. I don't blame them. What the Torrlonders do to those who resist is unspeakable." Sequara shuddered as she finished.

"So how long? How much longer can we hold out in Adanon?" asked Urd.

Sequara's face was grim, her mouth a tight line across her face and her eyes narrowed. "Orvandil thinks the rebel forces can last another month or two. Three at most. He and Gnorn have stayed to command our soldiers there. Vilyanad and Namila are assisting them as well. They are all brave and have done much for us. But before midsummer, there will be nothing left to resist the Torrlonders in Caergilion and Adanon."

"And then? Where they turn next is our gravest concern." Urd clenched her small right hand into a fist. "We must not fail to unite before Torrlond makes its next move. What do our spies tell us of Earconwald and Bledla's intentions?"

"All our sources agree on this matter. The east. Sildharan. Once they control the southwest, Earconwald and Bledla plan to strike against Andumedan's only remaining kingdom that can hope to match their strength. With the greatest of the eastern kingdoms out of their way, the others will fall."

Queen Faldira's face was calm yet determined. "Then we must not let them defeat Sildharan. There will we unite. Sundara is with us, and we must try to convince Golgar. Our troops are nearly ready. Our ships grow in number every day. Asdralad's time to enter the war on a large scale is coming. When it arrives, we'll sail east to aid Sildharan. We must all be ready soon." She glanced at Dayraven, and the other two women's eyes followed hers.

Dayraven blinked at the three women. For the first time, he understood the terrible weight of their hopes.

"Well," said Queen Faldira, breaking the silence, "Let's discuss these matters when you've eaten and rested, Sequara."

After the two older women enfolded the younger, the three of them disappeared into the palace, leaving Dayraven alone in the garden. A mess of emotions, he smiled and sighed. "Welcome back," he whispered.

10

THE TRIUMPH OF THE WAY

"Out of my way! I'll brook no more delay!"

The Supreme Priest Bledla shouted over the din of battle and shoved aside two of the white-kirtled temple guards assigned to guard him. Another explosion of wizard's fire flashed ahead, its boom drowning out his bass voice so that he could hardly hear his own words. In the blue sky overhead, his dragons disgorged fire onto the screaming heathens. Trolls and aglaks bellowed as they ripped apart bodies, and pucas shrieked with laughter as they swarmed over the foe. The Torrlonder soldiers also were overwhelming the Adanese, Asdralae, and Caergilese insurgents, who were making their last stand in stubborn knots amidst the caves of the Marar Mountains. *Let them skulk. Balch and his men are in a corner now.* If they tried to hide, Bledla's dragons would smoke every one of the vermin out of their holes. Edan's wrath was at last thundering down upon the vile unbelievers. They would taste despair before they died.

But who was this heathenish sorcerer that dared to defy Edan's will for so long? Morcar and Heremod ought to have taken him out by now, but still the man was making a fool out of his two high priests. That would not do. The Eternal and the pagans alike must witness Edan's strength. Bledla would deal with the sorcerer himself.

As the supreme priest strode closer to the combat, the score of temple guards fell in behind him. A few hundred yards in front of him, Morcar and Heremod in their white robes struggled in the duel of wizard's fire with the sorcerer. They held their own, but two high priests ought to have defeated a lone heathen sorcerer without a great amount of effort. Instead, they were unable to subdue the man, who fought with fury and power. The gift emanated from him even at a distance, and he was strong. But he was also cunning, and that was how he kept eluding Morcar and Heremod.

The chaos of battle swarmed all over the rocks of the mountain peaks. Men screamed. Steel clanged. Arrows filled the sky, and three of Bledla's guards rushed to cover him with shields. They need not have, for a dragon swooped down and breathed fire over the missiles. The burning shafts withered, twisting downward and falling nowhere near the supreme priest.

The detritus of battle covered the mountain rocks. Corpses lay everywhere. Troll, aglak, and puca carcasses littered the crags. Flames born in the dragons' bellies still licked some of the charred heathen bodies. Others felled by arrows and steel's edge wore the grey kirtles of the Torrlonders, and Bledla gritted his teeth at the loss of life among the Eternal. *Enough good men have perished fighting these vile pagans. I will end this. Now.*

Up ahead, the unknown sorcerer defended himself against Morcar and Heremod with the crackling blue wheel of an energy shield. The two high priests pounded it with wizard's fire. Explosions of energy erupted from the shield, but it held for a while. When it shattered in blue sparks, the wily sorcerer dove behind an outcrop, narrowly avoiding Heremod's jagged stream of energy, which slammed into the rock and sent hundreds of stone splinters ricocheting amidst stench and smoke.

In the distance, one of Bledla's dragons swooped down on three insurgents who had been sneaking away. They tried to flee towards cover, but too late. The mighty wyrm flew in low and snapped its huge jaws over one. Blood sprayed, and when the dragon veered upward, a pair of legs fell from its teeth with ropes of crimson spiraling from them. In the claws of its hind legs it grasped the other two men, who screamed as the lingworm flew away from the peak and dropped their flailing bodies into a deep, green valley far below, where their deaths awaited them.

In his mind, Bledla made his commands known to the dragon. It was not speech, but a series of mental images conveying his desire. The beast obeyed at once, turning in its flight and streaking toward the outcrop where the heathen sorcerer hid from Morcar and Heremod. It made a wide arc and flew behind the sorcerer. Then, with a giant clap of its wings, it shot in for the kill.

The sorcerer must have sensed it coming, for he bolted from behind the outcrop. Heremod and Morcar began shouting their spells, but the dragon was faster. Fire erupted from its giant maw and roiled toward the fleeing sorcerer. The man had his spell ready. He dove for the ground and swept his hands toward Heremod and Morcar as the dragon whooshed by in a gust of wind. Obeying the sorcerer's spell, the fire coalesced and abruptly shifted direction, streaking toward the two high priests as an enormous flaming ball.

With a brief moment to respond, Morcar and Heremod had time only to redirect their wizard's fire at the fireball speeding towards them. Two jagged blue currents collided with bright flames, and the resulting explosion split the air with a huge boom. Tongues of fire and shafts of energy spiraled outward, and the two high priests flew backward several feet, each landing and rolling in a tangle of limbs. The largest portion of the flames collided with one of Bledla's guards, hurling him down with a scream, wreathed in fire.

Bledla murmured a song of origin and flicked his wrist, dousing the flames, but still the scorched man moaned and writhed on the ground. "Enough!" The supreme priest thrust his hands out in front of him and cried out, "Alakathon gorghothae ar galathon khuldar, Vortalion bhurudonae im paradon bholdar!"

The enemy sorcerer saw him coming, and the wheel of a bright blue energy shield sprang to life before his hands. Feeling the difference in their strengths and bathing in the aura of the writhing blue currents buzzing and snaking around him, Bledla smiled. Had the heathen known what was coming, he would have tried a different tactic.

A gigantic column of energy flashed and forked from the supreme priest's hands, bleaching all color from the mountainscape and hurtling at the sorcerer amidst a detonation that rent the sky. With a blinding flare and an ear-splitting crack, the man's shield burst asunder, sending him reeling backwards. From his hands Bledla kept emitting the droning and writhing wizard's fire, which seized the sorcerer's body and shook him like a wolf snapping a snake around in its teeth. The man screamed in agony ere the current released him and knocked him on his back. The wizard's fire ceased, leaving a red afterglow that lingered for a moment. As Bledla approached the smoking corpse, all was silence.

When the supreme priest reached the dead sorcerer, he had his first close look at the man. With bronze skin and long dark hair just beginning to grey, the man was clean shaven. He wore elegant but worn garments beneath a green cloak. When he was alive, many would have called him handsome. But now dark scorch marks marred his face and body, and steaming blood oozed out of a large hole in his chest. Death glazed the eyes with which he stared at the sky, and the stench of burnt flesh was thick around him. Bledla did not recognize him.

"Go fetch the Adanese," he said to one of the temple guards who followed him. Most of them were still blinking, shaking their heads, and poking at their ears in an attempt to slough off the after effects of the wizard's fire. "I want to know who this was."

The guard bowed. "Yes, my lord." He took off running.

The supreme priest surveyed the mountain peaks around him. The battle was over. His dragons coasted and veered in the sky, and the grey-kirtled Torrlonders were rounding up small pockets of surviving rebels, who stood with heads hung low and clutched their wounds. A soldier ran towards him.

"My lord!" cried the grey-kirtled man before he stopped running. When he reached Bledla, he bowed low and then looked up with a smile. "King Earconwald has sent me to tell you: We've captured Balch wounded but alive. The battle's over. We've won, my lord. Adanon is ours."

"Very good. And what of Rona?"

"My lord?"

"The Adanese false queen. Is she also captured?"

"No, my lord. But she's only a woman."

Bledla narrowed his eyes and paused before he spoke with a lowered voice. "Is that what King Earconwald said?"

"My lord? Uh . . . perhaps . . ." The man's smile disappeared.

"It would be foolish to underestimate the *woman* who led the Adanese resistance and delayed our conquest of this land so many months. Would it not?"

The messenger's mouth hung open for a while before he could gather his wits to reply, "Forgive me please, my lord. It's not my place to . . . If you say so, my lord." He looked at the ground.

"And the three princes?"

The man continued staring at his feet. "Yes, my lord. They were with her. But one was wounded." He looked up hopefully, a tentative smile returning to his face.

"Then we will send out search parties to find them as soon as possible. See that my orders are carried out, and report to me afterwards."

The man stood with his eyes wide, and he paled as he stammered, "My lord . . . That might be . . . difficult."

Bledla scowled as he lowered his eyebrows and intoned in his deep voice, "Why?"

The soldier flinched and shrank. "She escaped, we think. A report came in from a soldier whose advance patrol was ambushed as we were setting up the perimeter. I was there when he arrived. He was the only survivor. He said he saw the Adanese queen, or at least a woman matching her description."

"Why am I hearing of this only now?"

"Uh . . . I . . ."

"Never mind. For now, tell me the rest. A woman and three boys did not slaughter one of our patrols on their own. Did they?"

"No, my lord. Not just them. There were others. Adanese and Asdralae soldiers. There was a Thjoth leading them. And a Dweorg."

"*The* Thjoth, I presume you mean. He has also escaped with the queen and her three whelps?"

"I-I . . . I think so, my lord."

"And no one had enough wit to inform me until now, or at least to send troops after them?"

The man's mouth opened and his chin quivered, but no sounds came out as he stared at Bledla.

"Enough. See that my orders are carried out. I will send dragons as well. Queen Rona and Orvandil can still make a great deal of trouble if we don't capture or kill them. We do *not* want any further delays in the accomplishment of Edan's will. Do we?"

"No, my lord."

"Good. Now go."

The soldier turned and fled back the way he came, crossing paths with the temple guard Bledla had sent away. With the white-kirtled guard walked a small, wiry man with a long, scraggly beard and leather armor. His eyes darted everywhere, never resting for long on anything, and he shrank in on himself as if expecting a blow to strike him at any moment. When he reached the supreme priest, the dark little man bowed. "My lord, you sent for me?"

"Uwain. Your king is captured."

The Adanese duke's eyes looked aside, and his scowl could not hide his shame. "My lord knows the traitor Balch is no king of mine."

Bledla smiled. "Yes. And I will not forget your service to Edan in leading us here. But you promised you would reveal the rebels' location in stealth. You were confident we would take them by surprise."

"And so you did. You . . . We've won, my lord."

"The battle, yes. But it seems your queen has escaped us. There must have been some advance warning."

"My lord, one cannot lead an entire army into the mountains without being noticed. The day is ours. The rebellion is over. Even Rona can make little difference now."

Bledla gazed at the little man, who cringed and looked away. "Edan grant that your words prove correct. But I have not asked you here for your advice." He moved aside and gestured at the corpse of the sorcerer. "I am hoping you will tell me the identity of that man."

Uwain's eyes narrowed, and his face contorted into a sneer. "Vilyanad. An Asdralae sorcerer. He's killed a lot of your men." He turned and pointed at another corpse a hundred yards away. It was a woman. Two arrows protruded from her chest. "That one there was his whore. Another Asdralae. A sorceress named Namila."

Bledla stroked his long, white beard. "I've heard of Vilyanad. He nearly became king of Asdralad, I believe. But Faldira won out. She it is who rules the island kingdom, and she it was who sent him to meddle here. The Asdralae have indeed been a thorn in our side, have they not?"

With a puzzled frown on his face, Uwain seemed unsure if Bledla was addressing him, but he answered. "My lord, the war here would have ended long ago had it not been for the Asdralae."

The supreme priest narrowed his eyes and stroked his beard. He inhaled a deep breath and released it slowly. *Edan has revealed what I must do. 'His purpose is ever the path of wisdom,' saith the Prophet.* The one true god had given him great power, and the gift surged in him as the bliss of certainty permeated his being. It must have shown on his face, for the little Adanese man cowered before him. "Yes. You speak soothly. Thus, we must find a suitable way to punish them. Mustn't we?"

FLANKED BY THE HIGH PRIESTS HEREMOD AND MORCAR AND standing behind King Earconwald on a shelf high up on a rocky outcrop not far from the city of Iarfaen, Bledla smiled. A torrent of shouts, the cries of the Eternal, broke from Torrlond's unrivalled army assembled like a swollen flood beneath the outcrop and before the city. Soldiers in grey kirtles greeted their sovereign as one body with overflowing joy and enthusiasm in spite of just emerging from the toil of grim battle the previous day. Most hailed from Torrlond, but some were recruits from Caergilion and Adanon who had the wisdom and humility to take Edan's blessing and ally themselves to their conquerors. Their submission to the Way allowed them to share Edan's grace with the Torrlonders, who had fought for a year from one end of southwestern Eormenlond to another to bring about Edan's will. These were conquerors, Edan's chosen Eternal, and even the losses they suffered could not check their righteous jubilation, for their many victories proved their cause's rightness and Edan's blessing.

On one side of the army hunched hundreds of tall trolls and aglaks. Most of the hairy giants and their slimy cousins of the fens appeared mournful with their sagging frowns, while others stared ahead with vacant eyes. Scores had bleeding wounds, some with broken weapons still protruding from their flesh. Gangs of small pucas skulked among the larger creatures. Many of the wiry, little beasts rocked back and forth where they sat, and terror dwelled in their wide eyes. But none ventured to flee, for they were thralls of the Way.

Bledla wondered how much longer these beasts would be of use. There were far fewer of them now, and enemy sorcerers had been able to turn them against the Torrlonders at times. Not only that, but there was a toll among the priests of the Way who controlled the trolls, aglaks, and pucas. Some had become unbalanced with the deaths of the creatures they wielded. A few were no longer in their right minds. He needed to keep in mind that not all of Edan's tools were of equal strength. There might come a time to discard the lesser beasts of battle. They had served their purpose, and their bondage had fulfilled the prophecies.

Equally forlorn were the rebel captives. The exultant Torrlonder army hemmed in a couple hundred chained men, former soldiers of Adanon and a few rebel bandits from Caergilion, who stood beneath the outcrop. Stripped of their armor, their arms, and their dignity, many were wounded or scorched and could not easily stand. The worst off leaned on others, who did their best to help their comrades. In stark contrast to their captors' joy, hope had abandoned these filthy, wretched men. Some beheld the ground, but others gazed up at the spectacle above them on the outcrop. Of the latter, some had tears in their eyes, while others looked up with defiance even in their final defeat.

Bledla smiled at what the captors and captives alike beheld. Next to King Earconwald stood a desolate figure whom two large soldiers of Torrlond held by the arms. The short man had long, unkempt hair of a dark hue and a greying beard. Dark spots like bruises encircled the tired eyes on his battered and bleeding face. His shirt and breeches were once fine garments, but now mud stained them. Two stripes of dried blood streaked down the torn white shirt from his wounded left shoulder. He also seemed to favor one leg, though Bledla could see no sign of a wound there. The false king's face contorted as the two guards pulled his arms behind him with deliberate force. Balch did not seem so proud and defiant now that his end approached.

Earconwald sneered at the groaning man and then shouted to his army, "Soldiers of Torrlond and the Way!"

Cheers broke out as the Torrlonders waved their fists high. The Caergilese and Adanese who fought for Torrlond seemed less enthusiastic. None of them punched the air, and their faces displayed little emotion. Among them stood Duke Uwain, who gazed at Balch with haunted eyes as if some horror transfixed him. Since none of his countrymen stood near him, there was an empty circle around the duke, as if he were a pariah. But the rest of the Adanese and Caergilese were careful at least to cheer until Earconwald held up his palm to signal he would continue.

"With the fall of this last bastion of heathens, Torrlond rules the southwest. In the dukedoms of Caergilion and Adanon, Edan holds sway. In just over one year from Caergilion's fall, our triumph is complete, brethren. Edan's blessed us with swift victory!"

A deafening flood of shouts erupted from the army while their captives despaired and gazed at the ground with blank, exhausted faces.

"And, though we've toiled, we'll not rest. Our mission is not yet over. But Edan will see us through the struggle, just as He has brought us thus far. Edan will give His servants courage. No, the Eternal will never rest until all of Eormenlond lives under the Way. For then, it's as the Prophet Aldmund spoke. We'll usher in the kingdom of our Lord, the kingdom of the Eternal, the kingdom of Edan!"

With more thunderous cheers Torrlond's soldiers declared their will to follow their leader wherever he might take them. Bledla smiled. Their outpouring was a pleasing offering to Edan, even if the man who addressed them was a hollow shell.

"I know, brethren, you'll see it through. You'll never give up until we've accomplished Edan's will. For by your willingness to fight, you show you're indeed among the Eternal. Your reward will be great, for

Edan will call you at the end of times to dwell in His kingdom in everlasting bliss."

More wild shouts flowed from Torrlond's army. But the shouts subsided as King Earconwald looked out over his forces with a stern countenance.

"But now, there's one here before us who, though we extended Edan's grace and mercy, heeded not the way of righteousness."

Silence followed as all eyes gazed up at the wounded man standing in the grip of the two soldiers. Bledla nodded with approval as Earconwald gestured with an open hand at Balch and continued.

"This man, once a ruler, proved himself unworthy of kingship by his refusal of Edan's call."

Now jeers and taunts came from the multitude of Torrlonders. Many spat as they glared with disdainful scowls at the false king. The prisoners looked on without a noise.

"For it's always the way of the proud and unrighteous to cling to their wickedness. Instead of avoiding bloodshed; instead of receiving Edan's grace; instead of embracing his salvation, this man chose death. Edan sent us as His scourge, and we'll make the way clear for the Kingdom that will be our inheritance."

Confident cheers and shouts of "Blessed be the Eternal!" rang out. Amidst the exaltation, Bledla could almost forget that Earconwald believed not one word of what he was uttering about Edan. He had tried to save the king from his arrogance. He had tried to correct him since his childhood and set him on the right path. Edan was his witness that he tried. It was a failure that itched at him, but Edan's will would be done. The supreme priest listened as the man who wore the title of Torrlond's sovereign continued.

"But Edan is also merciful." Silence again. The Torrlonders and their captives awaited the king's next words. Earconwald let the silence draw out a little longer, then he turned to the wounded man who was once the ruler of Adanon. The supreme priest had to admit the king was a practiced showman, but the hypocrite's usefulness as Edan's tool would one day come to an abrupt end.

Earconwald extended his arm and pointed at the false king. "You, Balch, proved yourself unworthy of the title of king, and by your stubbornness in the ways of darkness unfit to be one of my dukes. Nevertheless, I extend to you Edan's mercy. If you'll repent and become a true follower of the Way, I'll spare your life. This is your final chance to serve as an example for your people." Earconwald pointed his sword at the fettered prisoners lined up some thirty feet below him. He walked closer to the defeated man. "What's your answer? Do you submit to salvation?" he demanded with an air of offended righteousness, his mouth scowling and his chin cocked high.

Balch raised his head and looked through his tangled hair toward Earconwald. In his wounded and filthy state, he resembled one taken over by madness or demons. His dark brown eyes were expressionless for a moment, but they narrowed as his mouth curved downward in a frown.

The wretch spat a mixture of blood and spittle at Earconwald, hitting his shiny corselet. As it oozed down the gleaming metal, a few cheers came from some of the more defiant prisoners, but there was no other noise until Balch spoke in a loud voice. "I do *not* submit. I defy you. My sons live, and one of them will rule from Adanon's throne someday. So go fuck your mother's rotten corpse, you childless coward!"

Earconwald's eyes widened, and his jaw clenched as his nostrils flared. "So be it!" declared the trembling King of Torrlond, who did not move his gaze from Balch. Bledla recognized the look of rage on Earconwald, like a red-faced boy about to explode in a tantrum. Balch was a vulgar fool, but all the same the supreme priest could not help but smile at the public allusion to Earconwald's impotence. Edan was ending the line of Torrlond's kings, for only He could rule the Kingdom of the Eternal.

Torrlond's last king bared his teeth in a grin and then lifted his blade to strike. The two guards forced Balch to kneel. Expecting the blow to sever his neck, Balch lowered his head. But Earconwald shifted the blade and stabbed through his right thigh instead. A gasp of agony escaped the wide-eyed wretch as blood poured forth, and then he trembled and grimaced. The two large soldiers pulled him up at Earconwald's gesture.

Torrlond's king cried out, "I give you no king's death, for you're unworthy of one!"

Earconwald turned around to face Bledla. "Send some pucas to the cliff's bottom."

Arrogant fool, thought Bledla. *Edan's servants are not yours to command for your sport.* But the supreme priest held his tongue and nodded at Heremod, who grinned and waved a hand. In response, a dozen of the gangly little beasts let loose shrill cries and scampered to the cliff's base.

"Throw him down," said Earconwald in a cold voice to the two soldiers.

Balch's eyes widened just before the two men heaved him off the edge. He landed with a squishy thud and the cracking of bones. A weak groan came from his ruined body just as the pucas leapt on him. He cried out when the beasts began tearing his flesh and sinking their sharp teeth into him. His cry changed to a wet, gurgling sound and then subsided as the pucas ripped and flung away gobbets of flesh and organs. Balch's former soldiers turned away and hung their heads in desolation.

"That's *your* end as well if you refuse to submit!" declared Earconwald from atop the cliff to the prisoners. "Mercy to the obedient, destruction to unbelievers!"

Cheers once again poured from Torrlond's ranks. King Earconwald waved in response, then he turned around to give orders to the two high priests. "Do the same to any who refuse to submit to the Way and my rule. Draw it out a bit so our soldiers can enjoy the spectacle. Line them up one by one, and initiate any converts right away. Make a good show of granting their salvation. We'll need some collaborators out here. I'm sure you'll be able to persuade some. When you've finished, give me a list of any nobles who come over." He made as if to depart, but then he turned back and added with a wink, "Try not to enjoy yourselves too much."

"Yes, Sire," answered Heremod, revealing his crooked teeth in another wide grin.

In contrast, Morcar appeared pale, and Bledla recognized the haunted look in the man's eyes. *His power in the gift rivals Heremod's, but he's one of the haunted. The suffering and deaths of the beasts he has wielded weigh on him.* Heremod, on the other hand, was enjoying all the death rather too much. *Another sort of madness. They both bear watching.*

The king turned to the supreme priest with a smirk and glanced at the row of twelve dragons perched above and behind them on the outcrop, their claws scratching and digging into the stone, their amber eyes darting here and there as if seeking prey. Looming over everyone and casting shadows that covered swaths of the soldiers, the beasts were the greatest part of the entire spectacle. Such a sight was unheard of in Eormenlond, for dragons were solitary beasts that brooked no rival's company. It was all through the power Edan granted Bledla. When Earconwald' eyes took in the beasts, his smile faltered. "I'm sure if you leave them up there, they'll aid in the persuasion."

"No doubt, Sire, you're correct." Without a word, Bledla glanced at the twelve dragons, and at once the beasts directed their vast reptilian gazes at him. He imparted a simple mental image to them, instructing them to stay put until he gave further orders. Several snorted in acknowledgement of the unspoken command. The supreme priest turned back to his king. "They'll remain until I give them leave to depart."

"Very good," remarked the king. Yet a careful observer might have noted behind his forced smile he was not entirely pleased at the ease with which his chief advisor controlled the beasts. Bledla was a very careful observer.

Nevertheless, the secular leader feigned pleasure with the spiritual one as they descended the hill together with twenty guards marching under Captain Nothelm's command. With the Torrlonders' interspersed cheers sounding behind them, Earconwald chatted about the ease of their last victory in the southwest, comparing it to Caergilion's fall, before they first unleashed the dragons. Their superior numbers and the beasts decided all subsequent battles.

As he spoke, Bledla recalled how the king had kept well behind the front lines in every battle. Sometimes he had not even bothered to show up, leaving his dukes to command the soldiers while he whored and drank. The man never reddened his sword unless he used it on a helpless prisoner like Balch.

Earconwald blathered on about how easy defeating Caergilion had been. "Adanon was a tougher nut to crack, I'll grant. But even when the cowards ran away and hid, they couldn't hold out for long. One year. *One year* to conquer the southwest."

So long, thought Bledla. *I had thought to have brought all of Eormenlond under the Way by now. A year of trials it was. Edan has tested me. I must trust in His wisdom that it was not wasted. All will happen according to His plan.*

"One year," laughed Earconwald as they walked toward their tents. "Beyond even our wildest hopes. How easy it's been. Had I known, I would have begun sooner."

"Yes, Sire," answered the Supreme Priest. "Edan has blessed us."

"If that's how you like to see it," said Earconwald in a voice so low only Bledla heard. "No doubt Edan will continue to bless us and sanction all we do as we conquer the rest of Eormenlond. Right, old friend?" He flashed a disingenuous smile.

"Edan is always on the side of the righteous, Sire."

Too elated for caution, Earconwald replied with a ridiculous wink, "Well, we know one thing: Edan's certainly on the side of the victorious."

The supreme priest managed a reluctant smile. Just as he began to feel the strain on his patience was growing too large, King Earconwald made a fortunate change in subject. "By the way, I've decided to take your advice. At tonight's meeting, I'll announce the change of plans and give orders to the dukes to ready the ships. Our fleet's already awaiting us in Deriol Sound. We can take what supplies we need from Iarfaen, leaving behind a garrison of our soldiers under Duke Athelgar and posting one of the more pliant locals nominally in charge. Perhaps that Uwain fellow will do. He deserves a little reward, don't you think? The rest's a simple change of course."

"Very well, Sire. Uwain has tied himself firmly to us, so he'll make a fine figurehead, so long as it's clear Athelgar is in command. But, if you'll pardon me for venturing to reiterate an important point, it would be wisest to keep our new course known to as few as possible. Once we're underway, it will be safe to inform the soldiers."

"As you like, Bledla, though we needn't skulk about at this point. Who could possibly challenge us?"

The supreme priest gave no answer, for at that moment, someone he had long been expecting emerged from a white tent they approached. Four temple guards in their white kirtles escorted his dearest brother in the Way, the High Priest Arna. *At last. I've needed someone I can trust nearby.*

When he saw Bledla and Earconwald, Arna dismissed the guards and walked toward his two masters.

Ignoring the irksome monarch at his side, Bledla gave a genuine smile. "Arna. It's good to see you after so long. Blessed be the Eternal."

"And the Kingdom of Edan," replied the High Priest Arna, who gathered his white robe as he bowed to his sovereign and his spiritual lord in turn.

Another loud chorus of cheers erupted in the background from the soldiers.

"Ah, Arna," said Earconwald lazily. "You missed a good performance. What a shame. Balch refused your blessed faith, so we had to dispose of the poor fellow. As you can hear, there's more to watch if you care to see it. Heremod and Morcar are hard at work on the Adanese prisoners."

The elderly high priest blinked and wore a confused frown for a moment, but he regained his composure with a smile. "Your Majesty, it's good to see you well."

"The High Priest Arna has had a long journey, Sire," said Bledla. "No doubt he requires rest."

The king shrugged and yawned. "Of course. Well, I'll leave you two to discuss the coming of your Kingdom, or praise Edan, or whatever you like. I'll be celebrating our victory in my own manner."

"Yes, Sire," replied the supreme priest as he and Arna bowed.

After the king and his guards left the two white-robed wizards standing together, Bledla gazed after the monarch and shook his head. "He means he'll be fornicating with some wretched local women. The beast prefers the unwilling ones. But it matters little. Let the damned wallow in their filth." He smiled as he faced Arna. "Come, old friend. My tent's nearby. We have much to discuss, though you must be weary from your journey."

"My lord, after I arrived, the temple guards provided refreshments and bath water. I feel well enough to do some catching up."

"Good. Then come this way. We have urgent matters to discuss. You must be wondering why I called you from Torrhelm."

The two servants of Edan reached Bledla's unadorned tent in little time. Inside were eight fully armed temple guards standing at attention. Bledla dismissed them, ordering them to keep watch at the entrance and let no one pass without obtaining permission. When they were gone, the two old men sat across from each other in plain wooden chairs.

"So, my old friend," began the Supreme Priest, "how were your charges when you left Torrhelm? I refer to the priests we have sent back to you."

Arna swallowed and licked his lips. "Colburga and I are doing what we can. She is a gifted healer. We make progress among those priests in whom the madness is not too far gone. In those whose minds have snapped . . ." He shook his head. "Even Colburga cannot reach them. They gibber like the beasts they wielded, flinching from every touch, as if reliving the deaths of the pucas, aglaks, or trolls. I fear, my lord, that they may never return."

Bledla nodded solemnly. "Many are the sacrifices the Eternal make in service to Edan. We will continue to care for those priests until the end. They have earned our reverence, and they are no less martyrs than those slain in battle. When the Kingdom of the Eternal comes, Edan will return their minds to them and give them peace."

"Yes, my lord."

"And how fares the High Priest Joruman? I take it you left him in charge in Torrhelm with the appropriate instructions?"

"Yes, my lord. He has assisted me ably since he returned from his successful negotiations with the Ilarchae in the Wildlands."

"Ah, yes. Joruman was right for the task. He's a clever one, a true diplomat. I'm certain he knew how to entice the Ilarchae. And with that, the last piece falls into place. The barbarians will be hardy allies in the coming conquest of the east. They're keen to avenge old wrongs

PHILIP CHASE

the people of Sildharan committed against them. We may even wean them from their brute superstitions and bring them over to the Eternal."

"One hopes, my lord."

"And did you watch him as I asked? Did Joruman show any signs of scheming?"

Arna bowed his head. "None that I could discern, my lord."

The supreme priest stroked his white beard. "Still, I do not trust the man. He's hiding something. Even when he's obeying my will, he's scheming. I sense it in him."

"Is it wise, then, to leave him in charge in Torrhelm?"

"For now, he can do little harm there. He'll not dare to defy my orders openly, and he works well enough for our cause."

"Who would defy Edan's representative when the consequences are so clear to behold? Caergilion and Adanon now kneel before Edan. Praise Him."

Bledla smiled at his friend. "Yes. The southwest belongs to Edan now."

"And our kindred kingdoms are with us as well."

"Indeed. As we expected, the Mark and Ellond will come to our aid. It's a good sign they recognize the old alliance. Many of the Ellonder nobles are among the faithful, and in the coming days our cousins to the northwest will no doubt grow more zealous in the way of truth. We must guide them away from the demons many of them still follow in their blindness. Edan will reveal His truth to them."

The high priest folded his hands in reverence. "I believe in my heart He intends to bring them into His fold."

"Yes. By enlisting them as allies, we give them the opportunity to join the ranks of the Eternal." The supreme priest narrowed his eyes. "And perhaps best of all is we defeated the blasphemer in Ellond. With Galdor fled, King Fullan has no choice but to side with us. Fullan's commitment is doubtful, however. After he's led his troops east, we'll replace him with a true believer. When the time is right. For now, Edan has blessed us. We've won over the mother kingdom."

"That is excellent, my lord," Arna hastened to say. "Ellond will be an important ally in the coming war. It's fitting our kin across the

Theodamar should fight by our side. It seems our old foe has lost his last battle against you."

"Yes. Galdor's been spreading his diseased heresies longer than any remember save the two of us. Had you not exposed him all those years ago, who knows what damage he would have done?"

Arna nodded and swallowed.

Bledla continued. "If only our priests had managed to slay him. It seems he fled east, most likely to his heathen friends in Sundara. There he'll no doubt attempt to convince the kingdoms of the east to band together to oppose us. Let them. Galdor works in our favor, for it will only bring the end sooner. A final and complete triumph. At all costs we must avoid a protracted chase like the one we've had here. It has taken a great deal of time, but our victories here in the southwest have shown us our true strength. Nothing can oppose Edan's will. One final, glorious battle for Edan and the Way, and Eormenlond will be ready. The time's coming, my old friend. And the traitor's days will end soon, with the coming of the Kingdom. All his efforts to pervert our true faith were in vain. No one can prevail over the faithful, for Edan is our guide."

"Yes, my lord. Edan be praised."

Bledla's eyes gleamed as he leaned closer to his friend. "But before that final battle, there's one important matter we must discuss. It's why I called you."

Arna wore a puzzled frown. "My lord, you know I'm ready to serve you. Tell me what you would have me do."

Bledla nodded. "Good. I've found the days tedious without your company. Communicating through the seeing crystal is not the same as having you here in the flesh." He leaned still closer as he said in a low tone, "I must reveal my heart to you alone: There is a traitor among us."

Arna froze with his mouth open for a moment. "My lord?"

"Someone privy to knowledge best kept hidden from our enemies."

"Joruman?"

"No. One reason I sent him away was to test whether it could be him. The leaks of information continued in his absence."

"Then who?"

"It may be one of Earconwald's dukes or earls. It cannot be Earconwald himself. The fool has nothing to gain from impeding our progress. As for Heremod and Morcar, they have ambitions outside their duty to the Way. I must rule out no one. That's why I need you now. You and I alone have given everything for our cause. 'They will be rewarded according to their purity,' saith the blessed Prophet Aldmund."

Arna fidgeted in his chair and looked around. "My lord, what makes you believe this? Who could gain from betraying us?"

"There must be a traitor. Among our foes here, agents from outside the southwest anticipated some of our tactics and moves. They knew things discussed only in our inner circle, among Torrlond's highest lords."

"No one else was privy to this knowledge?"

"Outside of those lords, I spoke of such matters only to you through the seeing crystal. Whoever their source is, the foreign agents came to incite the people here against us. Sorcerers from outside the southwest used spells to wrest the trolls, aglaks, and pucas away from our priests, making the beasts less reliable during battle. Some even tried to take the dragons. How they learned the song of origin I do not know."

"None of them succeeded, of course?"

"Of course. Our priests had difficulties controlling the lesser beasts, but our enemies could never stop us in the end. Edan has blessed me with complete power over the dragons, and no one can challenge His might."

Arna bowed. "All will learn the truth of this, my lord."

"Indeed. Are you certain you've no need for rest? You look weary, my friend."

The high priest blinked. "I'm fine, my lord. Perhaps . . . after our discussion, I may rest. But these are important matters that should come first."

Bledla nodded and resumed, "Fortunately, we killed nearly all the outsiders who came to interfere. And we know whence the majority of them came: Asdralad. Queen Faldira's been busy opposing us, sending heathen sorcerers and soldiers to support the Adanese. She may be their source for the song of origin of dragons. Perhaps they kept that lore in Asdralad after all. However, none but I can wield it."

"Praise Edan. Faldira could not deny His will."

"She could not defeat us, but she has delayed us, and for that there must be a price."

"Ah, Galdor's conspiracy. But they failed, my lord. Galdor has fled Ellond, and the Asdralae could not stop you."

Bledla looked with stern eyes and lowered brow at his friend. "Yes, they failed. But we must punish them. They'll serve as an example to anyone who opposes Edan. Galdor's time will wait until our conquest of the east. But the Asdralae are nearer at hand."

"My lord? But preparations are underway for the march east."

The supreme priest nodded. "Exactly what we want them to think. By now, everyone expects us to attack the eastern kingdoms. We let everyone know this. And we *will* conquer them. But first, Edan has ordained we should punish Faldira's insolence."

"But, my lord, won't that give the eastern kingdoms more time to prepare their defense? Might they even attack our borders?"

"Let them prepare. They're weak and disorganized, and even Sildharan lacks strength to attack us. They can't send their army outside their own kingdom because of all their Ilarchae slaves. The moment their soldiers leave, the slaves will revolt, and they know this. They're rotten from within. And now the Ilarchae are our allies. Besides, half our army guards our borders, enough to defend Torrlond. Our foes know their only chance is to defend their lands, but they won't stand against our strength. They'll learn this after we make an example of Asdralad. They will fear and quake when they learn of the island's fate."

Arna nodded in understanding. "I see, my lord. But will the delay be worth it? After all, Asdralad has little tactical significance."

"True, it has no military power. However, it has ideological significance. First, we must eliminate Faldira for daring to oppose us. But Asdralad's also a center of the heathen cult of Oruma and Anghara. Many sorcerers of the southwest and the east have trained there. Edan has commanded me to destroy it before moving to the east. Once the eastern kingdoms see the Way prevail over their cult, they'll understand the true power of Edan. It took little to persuade Earconwald of this wisdom."

Arna cleared his throat. "My lord, it is the wisest course. Edan will guide us."

"Yes, my friend. He has guided our every move. Now you see why I require your presence. I have much to do, and the contest with Faldira will occupy me when we invade Asdralad. I want you to be my eyes and find our traitor. It's possible he'll reveal himself when we conquer Faldira, his true mistress. You'll need to watch closely. Your power will be of great service in the coming battle as well. The witch Urd may still be in Asdralad, and there will be other sorcerers."

The high priest bowed. "My lord, I'll do my best to serve you."

"I know you will. Soon it will be over, my friend. After we've destroyed Asdralad, we'll sail back to Torrhelm through Mikla Sound and there gather our armies for the final battle. Then we will behold what we've long awaited."

"The Kingdom of the Eternal," whispered Arna as he stared ahead. "And we'll rest with Edan."

Bledla smiled. "Yes, it's coming. Soon we who toil for Edan will gain our rest."

11

THE COUNCIL OF KIRIATH

Alakathon galdunial im targon var brimmil,
    Haldonon inghonial ar burnon in valil.
    Bhondin dal vorar dwinnor an dannin,
Dorwin ni khalar valnor di ghalnin.

Dayraven stared forward in concentration as he chanted the song of origin. Between two rows of hibiscus trees he stood. Their heavy red flowers drooped low and swayed in a light breeze. Elsewhere in the garden, flowers of sundry hues bloomed on bushes in a glory of color.

But he paid little heed to the beauty surrounding him. Or rather, so deep was he in the realm of origins, he perceived that beauty as inseparable from him. Even the elf-shard, the constant companion whose shadow-whispers curled around his awareness, seemed to acknowledge its bond with him by keeping their long held truce. At the same time, when he was in the realm of origins, he perceived the thing in his mind as a vast presence looming all around him. He retained a healthy wariness of it even as he drew forth a trickle of its power.

Repeating the song of origin, he held his hands apart with the palms facing each other. Wrinkles of concentration around his eyes and mouth disappeared as his face relaxed. At once, a writhing current of blue wizard's fire, or *almakhti*, sparked to life between his palms. At first thin, the current grew thicker and emitted more light, whitening his countenance as he chanted on. The current's hum grew louder than Dayraven's voice until, with a bright flash and a loud buzz, it erupted into a large sphere composed of dancing shafts of energy that droned and pulsed as they surrounded his standing form. While the sphere coruscated and vibrated around him, his look betrayed no emotion. Then he began a new chant:

Larathil ghaldoniae im varothan hirithiel,
Bharadil omduniae ar bregilan gildoniel.
Vishway imdhara ni lommin inkhatha,
Turway valmara di sarwin sholatha.

In response, the garden's many flowers unfolded and opened wide as if time sped up for them alone. The process of a long sunny morning evolved in mere moments. And then, the petals grew visibly larger and their colors more vivid. Those that had been drooping stood erect as if seeking the bright sun above. The trees' branches swayed and yearned upward, sprouting new offshoots that curled into life. Even the air teemed with an intense concentration of the energy underlying the world of forms.

Dayraven maintained the sphere of energy around him even as he stared ahead, seeming empty of any thoughts.

But something changed. A hint of emotion passed over his blinking eyes as an image flickered before him: Sequara lying still – wounded or dead – with scorch marks on her beautiful face. The sphere of electricity brightened and hummed louder. At once, a jagged current burst from the sphere, faster than eye could follow. The current's main trunk cracked and shot into the nearby pool, which glowed blue-bright for a moment, while a small offshoot lashed the garden's wall, blasting a chunk of rock away with a loud snap. The sphere crackled and disintegrated while the now duller flowers and trees shrank and sagged back to their former positions. The water of the pool was steaming. Dayraven returned to the waking world with a frown on his face. The elf-shard hissed in his mind as if in mockery of his failure.

"What's the matter with you, boy? You nearly roasted me!" Clutching her walking stick, Urd sat on one of the stone benches around the pool.

He sighed and put his hands on his head. "Sorry, Grandmother. When the energy grew too great for the sphere, I could think of no better place to direct it than the pool." Dayraven glanced at the black scar on the stone wall. A burnt odor invaded his nose.

"Hmmph," snorted the old woman, who wore her brown robe and had her white hair bound behind her. "You should apologize to the queen, not me, for knocking holes in her garden wall. You're lucky you didn't split open a tree. And why did the energy grow too great? You were thinking of something, or someone, that put your mind off balance. Few have ever had enough power in the gift to do what you were doing. It's nothing to trifle with." She wagged her finger at him. "But strength alone is not enough. Maintaining a sphere of wizard's fire requires perfect balance."

Dayraven peered at the gravel path beneath him. "I was thinking of . . . what's at stake."

Urd froze for a moment, and then the edges of her mouth curved in a sad smile. "Well, you mustn't dwell on it, my boy. You will either succeed or you won't. Thinking about it won't help you in the least. Be in the now, and don't become lost in what comes after it."

Dayraven released a long sigh. "I will try."

Urd nodded. "I know how difficult it is, how impossible it sounds, but you must learn to let go. It's a great burden we've put on you. But if you're to help, you must shed your attachments, let yourself spread out. Rise beyond the body you think of as you. Even as you're of the world, you must go beyond *your* world. Let go, child. Let go of Imharr, your father, me, and . . . anyone else you love, all your ties. Most of all, let go of yourself. When you lose differentiation between yourself and others, between yourself and the world around you, you become a wizard. Don't worry. We'll all still be part of you, and you'll then understand us."

Dayraven took a deep breath. "Balance and detachment. Queen Faldira's always saying the same. Detachment leads to insight of oneself as a manifestation of the Mother and Father, Anghara and Oruma, who are in all things. The sorcerer unites with the balance in empathy with all that is. Imbalance results from wanting too much, wanting to hold on. Those with the gift who achieve detachment and balance wield the songs of origin. When we sing them, we unite with the Mother and Father in what we seek to control. We go back to its creation."

Urd nodded. "Yes, that's how Queen Faldira understands it. Anghara and Oruma. The Mother and Father. Life and Death. She is the sun, he the moon. She's warmth and light and birth. He's cold and darkness and deliverance. That's how the Andumae understand things."

"But don't the priests of the Way also wield magic? They use the songs of origin as well. How do they understand these things?"

Urd's bright eyes narrowed as she smiled. "Different paths. Our ancestors, the Ilarchae who left the Wildlands, learned many things from the Andumae, including the songs of origin. There was a time when our people brought Oruma and Anghara into the company of our ancestral gods with their sacred groves. But the Prophet Aldmund changed all that. He it was who proclaimed the Way. He it was who first understood Oruma and Anghara were eternity and time, the sundering of the first energy into the world of things we dwell in. That first energy he called Edan, which the priests of the Way worship as their god. They also detach from the world, but they join themselves to Edan. That is the well of their power. That is what the Supreme Priest Bledla lives and destroys for."

"Then, if anything is worthy of worship, we all should bow to Edan since he's the ultimate source."

"Not *he*, really. *It*. Men always seem to want to put power in the hands of a male god, don't they? Do you imagine Edan has a cock?"

Dayraven smiled and held up his palms in surrender. "*It*, then. But my point is that the worshipers of Edan understand some things aright. The first energy, as you said. Is it not most worthy of worship?"

"Yes, they do understand some things, yet we all understand imperfectly. The failing of those like the supreme priest is, while they sacrifice everything for communion with Edan, they don't see Edan in anyone who's not of their mind. Nor do they grasp that Oruma and Anghara are different faces of Edan, or even that our ancestors' gods are aspects of Edan. Or, my boy, that even you and I are parts of their god. Those like Bledla have indeed learned to give themselves over to their Way, but they haven't learned how to go beyond the Way, which is only an extended sense of themselves. Thus, instead of purifying their hearts, they seek to purify the world. It's possible even Bledla doesn't truly grasp what the Prophet Aldmund meant by Edan. Do you? Do you know Edan enough to impose your vision on all others? To force those who see elsewise to see what you do, or slay them?"

Dayraven swallowed before he said quietly, "No. Of course not. It's not even possible to make others see what you see. To try is madness. It's a sickness that comes from fear. Yet it would seem this fear gives Bledla great conviction and power."

"Yes, but even the supreme priest of the Way has his limits, as we hope to find out."

Urd's smile warmed Dayraven's heart, but at the same time it reminded him of home. *Will I ever forget?* he wondered. *Still so much to learn. Will there be time?* The elf-shard's dark murmurs slid over his thoughts.

"Grandmother," he said, "what if I fail? What if, when the time comes, I can't destroy Bledla's control over the dragons? What if the elf-shard betrays me?"

"If those events come, we'll have to deal with them as best we can. But why borrow so many worries? You've failed nothing thus far."

"I just don't know if I was meant for this. I can't forget the Mark and the life I left behind, even though home was so long ago, like many years, not just one. In some way it's a different life, someone else's, yet still mine. Part of me doesn't wish to let go. When I think of my task, I doubt myself."

Urd half smiled. "It will be as it will be, my boy. Your only task is to meet fate with courage. As for the rest, time will tell what will happen when you encounter Bledla. But look at your progress. You read and speak High Andumaic nearly as well as I do, and your control over your power surpasses our expectations — and this all in a year. Even the greatest sorcerers need twenty years for the course of study you've completed here in Kiriath. It's as if you were born with the songs of origin on your tongue. I've never seen the like."

"But what will happen in the moment when I must call upon the power of the elf-shard? When it's not a mere exercise in which I face someone I trust?"

"It's true you are untested. But your control over the power the elf put in you is strong. Queen Faldira's exercises and time have done much good. There's no question: Within you is the gift in greater measure than in any other in all of Eormenlond. Perhaps you are the strongest ever to wield the songs of origin. Soon enough your test will come. For now, remember your past is part of you, but you're part of all. The wizard has no attachments. He loves all, yet hoards no desires."

"I understand, Grandmother. I'll do my best. But it's hard. Love of the Mark runs deep in me." Dayraven looked around the garden as a breeze fingered a loose strand of his hair and wafted the flowers' sweet fragrance past him, though they could not cover the stench of the scarred wall. "I confess, though, I've grown to love much in this place too."

"What's that foul smell?" broke in a woman's voice.

Dayraven tensed at the voice, but he calmed as he turned toward Sequara, who entered the garden through the open doors to Queen Faldira's palace. The sorceress wore a dark green gown of silk over her slender figure. Keeping his face free of emotion, Dayraven suppressed a stupid, nervous grin at the beauty and depth behind her dark eyes.

In the months since her return, they had resumed a cordial friendship. Yet there was an unspoken strain between them. It seemed to him Sequara avoided being alone with him. Out of wariness and a desire to please her, he kept a respectful distance from her. And still fragments of her memories surfaced at times in his mind. From an occasional lingering look from her, he guessed she continued to see images of his past as well. No one, including Queen Faldira and Urd, could explain why the memories so persisted, so he reckoned the best course was to keep silent about them.

Urd grinned at Sequara and gestured toward the blackened portion of the wall. "Dayraven's been trying to topple Queen Faldira's wall with *almakhti*."

She smiled. "I wondered what the noise was. I doubt the queen will appreciate you rearranging her garden."

Dayraven felt his face turn red, but Sequara's smile gladdened his heart. *Pity she seldom smiles. She also feels a burden.* "You don't think I've improved it? The good news is I spared Grandmother, who thinks I nearly roasted her."

She nodded. "That is good news. And, in return, I have news for you. Some old friends have turned up, and we'll see them shortly. In fact, Queen Faldira's called a council."

"There must be tidings from abroad," said Urd. She turned to Dayraven. "This is what we've been waiting for. Come, child."

IN A PALACE CHAMBER WITH WIDE WINDOWS, COLORFUL TAPESTRIES adorning the walls, and a large round table at its center, Dayraven recognized a dozen nobles of Asdralad standing and speaking with Queen Faldira on one side, all wearing their elegant robes and gowns of various bright hues. In most of them he sensed the presence of the gift, though none were nearly as powerful as the queen. No doubt feeling the vast amount of the gift in him, a few of them glanced at him and did a poor job of concealing their curiosity. On the room's other side stood Abon. After a rough voyage, he had arrived more than a fortnight before with ominous messages from the wizard Galdor. The squat shaper tugged at the tuft of hair on his chin as his scarred face looked up at the towering man he addressed.

"Orvandil!"

The giant Thjoth turned at Dayraven's voice, and a broad smile crossed his face. He was dressed for battle, with a mud-stained dark blue kirtle over his byrny and his long sword in the scabbard by his side.

"Dayraven," boomed his deep voice. They clasped hands and shoulders.

"Good to see you."

"Look at you, with a proper beard now." Orvandil stroked his own much thicker beard as he continued to grin.

"And have you forgotten me?" said a gruff voice from behind the Thjoth. Its owner, a broad-shouldered and thick-bearded man less than five feet high, stepped forward and scowled with his arms crossed before his chest. With his large axe tucked into his belt, he wore a byrny under his travel-worn green kirtle. A twinkle in his large brown eyes belied the sorrow that Dayraven had often perceived behind them.

"Gnorn. Never." Dayraven embraced the Dweorg, whose frown changed to a bright smile as he laughed and clapped his friend on the back. "Forgive me. I didn't see you behind Orvandil."

"No matter! I've grown used to being overlooked in the company of longshanks. Even if I weren't a Dweorg, he'd tower over me. At least he provides good shade."

The four men laughed together, after which Gnorn said, "It's been too long, lad. But I see we left you in good hands here."

Dayraven looked toward Faldira, but his glance fell on Sequara, who had just joined the queen and the nobles. Her presence always seemed to tug at him. "Asdralad's been good to me." He turned back to his friends. "But what of you two? What news do you bring from Adanon?"

The smiles disappeared as Orvandil and Gnorn grew serious at once. The Dweorg spoke up. "Ill news, I fear. But you'll hear all shortly."

Just then everyone's heads turned as two more newcomers arrived in the room. One was a woman Daryaven could not place. Clad in a blue dress that was conservative by the standards of Asdralad, she was petite and thin. Though her somber countenance bespoke some sorrow, she stood erect and bore herself as one in authority. When her eyes met Dayraven's, she smiled as if she recognized him. He returned the smile and nodded, feeling as if he had met her before.

But he forgot everything else when he saw who was walking next to the woman. "Imharr!"

Imharr's somber face broke out in his familiar smile, bringing to Dayraven's mind a flood of memories. "Day!" He looked to the woman, who nodded permission to him with a subtle grin, and then he was striding toward Dayraven.

The two friends embraced and clapped each other on the back.

Imharr was the first to speak. "Ah, but it's good to see you." He grasped Dayraven by the shoulders and looked him in the eyes. "My brother." His smile collapsed, and he shuddered as he suppressed a sob. He sniffed and wiped at his eyes, which had grown moist, before he took a deep breath and composed himself. "Been that worried about you, I suppose."

Dayraven swallowed the lump in his throat as he fought back his own tears. "You were worried about *me*?" He managed a weak smile. "You're the one who's been at war." He glanced at his friend's hand, scarred with silver-hued flesh. "I heard about your hand."

Imharr grinned and held up the hand, wiggling the fingers. "Works better than ever."

Dayraven cleared his throat and took a deep breath. "I'm glad. And I'm glad you're here, though I see there's a tale of sorrow behind your arrival."

Imharr nodded, his face solemn. "Yes. Many tales of sorrow, I fear. You'll hear some of them soon." He smiled again. "But I would hear of you as well."

Dayraven returned the smile. "There's little to tell. Most of the time I spend reading, meditating, and worrying."

A soft yet commanding voice rose above the chatter in the room. "We're all assembled now. Let us gather around the table." Queen Faldira led the way to the table and took a seat at one of the elegantly carved wooden chairs. Sequara sat on her right, while the nobles of Asdralad ranged themselves around the table.

Imharr nodded at Dayraven and spoke in a quieter voice. "After the council, then. I must take my place next to Queen Rona." He squeezed Dayraven's shoulder and went to sit beside the woman he had entered the room with.

Dayraven found a seat across from Queen Faldira with Gnorn, Orvandil, and Abon on his left. Urd was on his right.

Faldira looked toward Imharr's companion as she began. "First, we welcome Queen Rona of Adanon, whom it is our honor to host. In her company is Duke Imharr, captain of her guard. Since our newly arrived friends do not speak Andumaic, we'll use the Northern Tongue at this meeting."

Queen Rona stood, and everyone waited for her to speak. "I thank you, Queen Faldira, and the people of Asdralad for all you have done for Adanon in our time of need. If it ever comes in my power, I swear by the Mother and Father I will do all I can to repay you for the sacrifices you have made and the refuge you have provided. We Adanese are a proud people, but not so proud that we cannot show proper gratitude towards those who earn it through their friendship and their blood."

Rona moved from her seat and went to her knees on the floor before inclining her head in a bow towards Faldira. A murmur arose among the Asdralae nobles, and Imharr joined the queen, kneeling a few feet behind her with his head held low.

Like everyone else, Dayraven stared at the woman, whose gesture touched him deeply. He studied Adanon's queen with renewed interest. Here was a proud woman who had endured much, and he reckoned that humbling herself was not a thing she was accustomed to. It must have required great courage and strength.

Faldira stood up from her seat and walked to Rona. The tall Asdralae queen bent and took the Adanese queen's hand. "Arise. You fought valiantly against the most terrible of foes. We are friends and equals who have come to counsel one another as to how we might defeat that common enemy."

Rona stood and, with a tear running down her cheek, retook her seat. Imharr followed suit. When they were seated once more, Faldira returned to her place and spoke again.

"We're all friends here, but grim news and dire circumstances bring us together today. The southwest has fallen. War comes soon to the east. Captain Orvandil and Captain Gnorn, who just came from leading our forces in Adanon, bring us the latest tidings." She nodded toward the Thjoth and the Dweorg, after which Orvandil stood and bowed. "Thank you, your Majesty."

He took his seat and spoke with a heavy voice. "The queen speaks truth. Torrlond's conquered the southwest. The last pocket of resistance is gone. For long we hid in mountain caves and harassed Earconwald's troops when we could. Yet, wherever we gathered, the foe's beasts found us. Dragons can spot a hare from miles in the sky, and pucas outwit the best woodsmen. As long as they control the beasts, there's no hiding from Torrlond's army.

"Yet our greatest risk was always betrayal. Some help Torrlond and the Way for their own gain. Some out of despair and fear. The southwest's folk are afraid. They should be. Torrlond's army has ravaged their lands, and only those who convert to their damned faith live. I know not what the motive was, but in the end, I deem betrayal led to our ruin. There is no other way the Torrlonders could have come upon us with such swiftness. I cannot say with certainty who it was that betrayed us, so I will name no one."

"Uwain," said Rona with a face like stone.

"Mostlike," said Gnorn with a nod. "Duke Uwain went missing a few days before Earconwald's forces attacked us. Before that he was slipping into madness."

Orvandil watched Queen Rona as if waiting for her to say more, but she only clenched her jaw, so the Thjoth continued. "In our last refuge in the caves of the Marar Mountains, the Torrlonders took us unawares. King Balch fought well, but he had no chance. He knew the end was come. When the Torrlonder army was upon us, he took us aside and bade us to find a way out with Queen Rona and the three princes. He wanted us to save them while he kept back the Torrlonders. He was a brave king.

"Lord Vilyanad too chose to remain. He said the dragons would come to him. Lady Namila would not leave him. They won great honor for your island kingdom during their time in Adanon, but that was their greatest deed."

Queen Faldira bowed her head, and several of the Asdralae nobles murmured and nodded. When they quieted, Orvandil resumed.

"We fled, and for long we were able to avoid the Torrlonders. But they had laid their trap with cunning. Before the attack, they surrounded our position, and we met one of their patrols. They outnumbered us, and we lost many good men. Most grievous was the loss of Prince Lelwyn."

At this word, Queen Rona's eyes tightened and hardened, and she cleared her throat. "What Captain Orvandil does not tell you is how long he carried my son's body through the mountains before the arrow wound in his chest took his life. For that, and for everything else they did, I can never thank him and Captain Gnorn enough. And by my dead son's name, I swear that one of his younger brothers will sit Adanon's throne someday."

There was a long silence before Orvandil nodded at Rona and took up the tale again. "We struggled for long in the mountains, at times hiding from the dragons that flew overhead. But at last we emerged from them where the Torrlonders least expected us: in Torrlond. There we headed west until we reached the Sundering Sea. In a village we stole a tradesman's boat, which brought us here." The Thjoth pointed down at the table.

"It's a grim story you tell, Captain Orvandil," said Urd. "But in it are deeds worthy of remembrance, and we must take hope from them."

"And what will the Torrlonders' next move be?" asked one of the noblemen.

The Thjoth answered in his deep, steady voice, "All signs say Torrlond gathers for a great push to the east. There are rumors the Mark and Ellond will join Torrlond, but others here may know more of that than I."

When Orvandil finished, silence followed. Dayraven's heart sank. *Folk of the Mark among our foes. Father. Earl Stigand, Guthere, Ebba's husband. All of them. If only they knew the truth about Torrlond. They think as I once thought. They'll follow Torrlond to war.*

Asdralad's frowning nobles glanced at each other, their intense stares betraying the fear beneath the calm veneer on their faces. Tension hovered thick in the room, but Queen Faldira's voice broke the silence like a warm breeze dispelling a chill. "Thank you, Captain Orvandil. As you say, we have news of Torrlond's alliances. Our old friend Abon comes with messages from Galdor of Ellond. Abon, if you please."

The shaper stood to bow to the queen and sat again. "Your Majesty. Nobles of Asdralad. Friends. First I must apologize for my late arrival. I had hoped to reach Asdralad much sooner. Alas, it was not to be. The ship I took from Ellordor fell into the hands of Thjothic raiders." The shaper looked toward Orvandil with a wry smile. "Your kin are not gentle, but they at least have the wisdom to honor shapers."

Orvandil's only response was to raise his eyebrows in a curt acknowledgement.

Abon continued. "The Thjoths did not demand ransom from me or enthrall me as they did the rest of those aboard the ship. But they bade me to sing. So I wove nearly every tale I know for them for several days at sea and for over two months in Grimrik. I was almost out of songs when their king, a fierce fellow called Vols, agreed to let me go."

At the mention of the Thjothic king, one side of Orvandil's mouth curled up in what might have been a smile. Abon watched his reaction, then he continued. "After feasting me well and bidding me to sing for so long, King Vols put me on another ship and left me on a remote shore of Torrlond, near the North Downs. It took me days to find a village, days more to reach Norfast, and much longer to find a ship that would bring me here. But here at last I find myself, and I will fulfill my errand.

"The wizard Galdor sends you his greetings from exile. My master fled Ellond after the danger to his life grew too great. Nobles allied to Earconwald and Bledla have taken control of Ellond. They act in the Way's name, murdering anyone who opposes them. Strengthened by priests from Torrlond, these nobles forced King Fullan's hand. He has declared he'll uphold our kingdom's ancient alliance with Torrlond." Abon paused, and his mouth formed a cunning smile. "However, unknown to our foes, the king and those nobles faithful to him await the right moment to come over to your side. In the hour of battle, King Earconwald will know Ellond's folk are not his servants."

"Will the Ellonders fight against the Torrlonders?" asked one of the Asdralae nobles. "Are not many of them followers of the Way? Will they raise arms against their kin to help us?"

"Not all Ellonders worship Edan," said the shaper. "Many of us honor the old gods. And even most of those who follow the Way do not wish to follow the Torrlonders' orders. Some of the ambitious nobles have cast their lot with Earconwald for their own benefit. Almost all the soldiers will follow King Fullan."

"And what of the Markmen?" asked a noblewoman.

"As Orvandil said," the shaper answered with a glance at Dayraven, "in addition to Ellond, the kingdom of the Mark will march with Torrlond in the coming days. Even though most of his people do not follow the Way, King Ithamar will honor the old alliance his ancestors swore to. His folk are few, but they're hardy, and we'll find it hard work to fight them."

Again Dayraven thought of home and his people. *If only I could tell them. No time. And who'd listen? I'm an exile, without a people. They could even slay me. No. I must do my duty. Defeat Torrlond, then they'll understand. They must.*

Abon continued, "Galdor bids me to tell you all the signs are in place. War soon comes to the east, most likely to Sildharan. It's the most powerful kingdom of Eormenlond after Torrlond. If Earconwald and Bledla break Sildharan, the others have no chance. We must be sure this doesn't happen. We can't repeat the mistakes of the southwest, where Caergilion fell alone and only Asdralad came to the aid of Adanon. Unite behind Sildharan or perish."

Urd spoke up. "We also have heard rumors that the Ilarchae of the Wildlands are allying with Torrlond. If it's true, then those who would conquer Eormenlond will attack the east from two fronts: Torrlond and its allies from the west, and the Ilarchae from the east. The Ilarchae are eager for revenge against Sildharan, for that kingdom has enslaved many folk of the Wildlands."

Queen Faldira nodded. "Sildharan is where we decide Eormenlond's future. Among those banded together against the coming tide are Asdralad, the troops King Fullan of Ellond will bring over, Sildharan, and Sundara. This means well-nigh all of Eormenlond will join in the war."

Abon said, "My master is attempting to persuade Golgar to aid us as well. He deems it unlikely, but the Golgae at least wouldn't help Torrlond, for they have small love of the Way. Among Eormenlond's kingdoms, that leaves only Grimrik. King Vols listened to everything I had to say about Torrlond's war, but I do not know his mind. The Thjoths are an unknown. It appears they're biding their time, present company excluded, of course." Abon bowed to Orvandil, who nodded in return, then the shaper concluded. "My master bids you gird yourselves for war. Now's the time to sail east."

One of the noblemen spoke up, a silver-haired man. "There's one potential ally you've not named, though one sits here among us. What of the Dweorgs? Can they give no aid? Surely they must know they can't long hide from Torrlond."

Gnorn looked at the man. "Speak not of the Dweorgs, friend. There are so few, and they'll never march forth again from their hills. The rival tribes sealed their doom long ago. They'll have naught to do with your peoples' wars."

Queen Faldira said, "Gnorn is correct. We sent emissaries to the Dweorghlithes and other Dweorg fastnesses. Their response was firm. There'll be no help from that quarter. The board's all but set now. As you heard, Torrlond will strike in the east. Our sources confirm this, and Earconwald and Bledla have made no secret of their intentions. They'll first try to crush Sildharan, their greatest threat. We must do our part to hold up that ancient kingdom, the east's greatest bastion. King Naitaran of Sildharan is proud, but he'll not refuse our aid. Together, we'll hold off our enemies. Torrlond has but one real advantage: the dragons."

The frowns deepened on the faces around the table, and now, knowing what others expected of him in the coming days, Dayraven swallowed. *Why has this burden come to me? I asked for none of this.*

The queen continued, "The great lingworms turn the tide of every battle. No army has withstood their fires, and Bledla alone controls the serpents of the air. Long ago, when we Andumae first set foot on these shores as refugees from a faraway land, a few of the wisest and strongest in the gift among us knew and wielded the song of origin of dragons. In those earliest days, among human races, only the Dweorgs dwelt in Andumedan, but the dragons ruled most of the land. A great war followed between the Andumae and the serpents of the air, but our people prevailed and settled the plains. Years passed. The Andumae built great kingdoms, but we fell to fighting one another. War and disease ruined our splendor. When the remaining dragons returned, they found none left who were powerful enough to use the song of origin. But the secret of the song remained. Here in Asdralad we passed on the song of origin of dragons for a time, though none could wield it. That is, until the Prophet Aldmund came.

"Aldmund visited these shores before he proclaimed the Way in his native Torrlond, and mostlike he learned the song of origin of dragons here, even though the priests of the Way claim he received it in a revelation from Edan. What's certain is Aldmund was the first to master the spell to control dragons in more than a thousand years. We thought the song had died with him, but it seems he passed it down to his successors, the supreme priests of the Way. None could use it, however, until now. In the meantime, even here in Asdralad we forgot the long unused song.

"Then, a few months more than a year ago, we learned from a source in Torrlond that Bledla had awakened the old spell. For years the supreme priest had been hunting dragons and enthralling them in secrecy. What's more, our source informed us the supreme priest intended to use his power over the dragons in a great war that would envelop all of Andumedan and hasten the coming of the Kingdom of the Eternal. We find ourselves in the midst of that war."

Dayraven thought of the vast history he was part of. *So many lives and deaths bound in this old spell. And now me. How did I wander into it all?*

Faldira looked around the room. Her glance fell at last on Dayraven, who swallowed again in his dry throat. She continued. "At great risk, our source in Torrlond passed on to us the song of origin of dragons. I'm unable to wield it. Many have tried and failed. Even Galdor. We sought long and gave up hope of finding anyone to wield the spell. You see, the key to defeating Torrlond is to destroy their one advantage we can't match. If we take away Bledla's power over the dragons, we eliminate their greatest weapon. What's more, we show the Way is not invincible, and this may break the Torrlonders' resolve."

The Queen ceased speaking. Silence followed until a nobleman, one with no trace of the gift, asked, "But, your Majesty, you said no one other than Bledla can wield the song of origin. What can we do, other than surrender or perish?"

Faldira answered, "I did not say no other can wield the song." Dayraven sensed the eyes of the queen, Sequara, Urd, Imharr, Orvandil, Gnorn, and Abon all resting on him. The others in the room followed their glances until everyone stared at him. Their fears and hopes pressed down. *I'm only Dayraven of the Mark.*

"Some of you know Dayraven, our friend Urd's grandnephew," said Faldira. "For those who don't, I will tell you he came to us through great peril. Twice he eluded death, once at an elf's hands, and we hope he'll help us. For the last year we have taught him everything we know about using the gift, and he's learned the song of origin of dragons. We believe he'll be able to challenge Bledla's control of the great serpents."

Dayraven returned their stares, scanning the faces and seeing the nobles' disbelief in their narrowing eyes. The elf-shard's cold breath skimmed his mind and wrapped it in mist-shadows. But in Urd, Imharr, Gnorn, Orvandil, Abon, and Sequara's gazes he sensed their faith in him. And in the queen's gentle smile he saw hope, which kindled a spark of determination inside him. The spark caught fire until he knew what he must do. *No good asking why. I must only try to do what's before me.*

Now addressing Dayraven, Queen Faldira asked, "Are you willing to take on this task? Will you go with us to wrest away the supreme priest's power over the dragons?"

All waited for his answer. Even the elf-shard's hiss seemed to lessen for a moment. He inhaled deeply and closed his eyes until he released his breath. *This could be the end of me. If it is, so be it.*

"I've not used the song yet. I don't know if I'll succeed. It's possible I won't. But, yes, I'm willing. 'Meet your fate with courage,' someone wise once told me. It's my fate to go with you, and I'll either fall with you or share victory."

"Well said, lad!" shouted Gnorn as he thumped the table with his fat fist, causing several nobles to flinch.

"Indeed," said Faldira, "it is well said. And you'll not face this burden alone." The queen looked at everyone around the table. "For the time has come for us all to ready ourselves. We've long had peace here in Asdralad, and we may achieve peace yet. But first comes a great test. We must stand and face those who would take our freedom or our lives. In two days, we leave our shores and sail east. We'll make land in Sundara, where King Tirgalan will receive us. Then, with the troops of Sundara, we'll march north. Prepare all your ships and able-bodied soldiers. We muster here in the Bay of Kiriath on the morning of the second day from this. On the third bell after the sun's rising we'll depart. Go now and ready your soldiers and your hearts for the coming trial."

Everyone rose from their seats and, after bowing to the queen, went away to make preparations. Imharr caught Dayraven's eye, nodded, and smiled. "I'll see to Queen Rona and find you afterwards."

Dayraven smiled and nodded back. Feeling at peace with his resolution, he stood while Orvandil and Gnorn clasped him on the shoulders. He began to follow them toward the door, but as he was exiting, Sequara approached. Their eyes met. Dayraven looked to his two friends and said, "You two go and wash up, then wait for me. I know where to find some excellent wine we can share with Imharr and Abon."

"That'll be a good start," answered Gnorn. "Best thing to go with good wine's a good story. We've got plenty of catching up to do."

As the Dweorg and Thjoth receded down the hall, Dayraven turned to Sequara. She stood at a distance. No one else remained in the room. They had not been alone together in a long time.

"Dayraven," she began, "I want to tell you I . . . We . . . have faith in you." She swallowed and took a deep breath. "Ever since we brought you from Caergilion, I've known you are . . . unique. It's not what the elf did to you. There's something else. Urd knows what I speak of, as does Queen Faldira. Even Imharr understands in his own way."

He recalled the Battle of Iarfaen, when Bledla's servant nearly slew him. He remembered little after save Sequara entering his mind and calling him with such urgency. They had never spoken at length of that moment of ineffable intimacy, not even mentioned it in a long while. Especially after her return from Adanon, Dayraven had felt some awkwardness between him and the formal sorceress, the heir to Asdralad's throne. But now that awkwardness seemed to slide away, and in its place he found affection and a deep connection to her. He guessed by her subtle smile and the look in her eyes she felt it too. He yearned to acknowledge their bond, so he said, "Thank you. I'll never forget what you did for me in Caergilion."

Sequara looked down at the floor. "I was doing my duty, as you are now."

Silence followed. In that silence their two minds danced, nearly touching one another but holding back at the last moment.

"Yes. There'll be great tests ahead for us."

They stood a moment gazing at each other until she spoke. "I have preparations to make, and you better find that wine you promised for your friends."

Dayraven smiled. "You're right. Shouldn't keep them waiting."

He gestured toward the door then followed her until they came to the hall that led down to the wine cellar. "Goodbye for now, then."

She turned and gave him a brief smile. Dayraven once again saw in her eyes the knowledge of their bond. He watched her disappear down the hall before he went on his way.

12

FIRE AND RUIN

The forewarning that woke Dayraven before dawn evoked a sudden, gut-wrenching fear. The vision's after-image still burned in his mind after it tore him out of sleep: a wall of flames rising up to envelop Faldira's palace and everything inside it. Had it been a dream? It seemed too clear, too real. Tightness seized his muscles and his insides, and he sat up with his hand over his galloping heart. Staring into the darkness, he listened to the deeper darkness of the elf-shard in his mind. Its shadow-whispers seemed to prophesy the destruction he had witnessed in his nightmare. Dayraven shivered, but his hands were clammy with sweat.

Unable to shake away the foreboding, he stood up from his bed and shuffled to the window, where he opened the shutters. Pale moonlight invaded his room. A fresh breeze caressed his face, but the night was otherwise still. In the dark he dressed himself in his breeches, cordwain shoes, and kirtle and put his brown robe over all. He groped toward his chamber's door and swung it open. Shadows and silence awaited him. He stepped into the hallway with care.

Creeping toward the front doors of the palace, he found his way by sliding his hand on the smooth, cool wall. It was not long before the orange glow of torchlight painted the walls and floor of a larger hallway ahead of him. But before he reached it, the presence of the gift spiked somewhere in the darkness near him. Dayraven nearly bumped into her before Sequara's outline grew visible. Something had woken her as well.

"Did you feel it?"

From the darkness answered Sequara's voice, and he sensed the strain in it. "Yes." There was a pause before she said, "Come with me. Quickly."

Dayraven trailed Sequara around a corner down the larger corridor, along which torches in sconces lit the way. The ruddy light revealed Sequara's dark-colored long tunic and loose trousers. He frowned at the curved blade she bore in the scabbard at her side.

They emerged in the palace's large central hall, where eight of the queen's guards stood by pillars with torches mounted on them. The fully armed guards bowed as Sequara passed into the hallway leading to the palace's front doors. The doors were open. Dayraven followed Sequara outside into the night, where they met eight more guards holding torches and two robed figures who were strong in the gift.

From the palace's height, Urd and Queen Faldira looked out over the quiet city into the Bay of Kiriath. The silvered seascape glistened under the moonlight while the breaking waves moaned in the distance. Fixing her gaze into the darkness beyond, Faldira spoke in a voice that betrayed no fear but suggested reconciliation to the fate awaiting her. "They're coming."

Dayraven knew what she meant, but he did not wish to believe it. Perhaps there was some other explanation for the forewarning they all felt. He looked out into the stillness over the waters. Nothing but night. The queen, however, left no doubt with her next words. "Torrlond's not striking in the east. They've come for us first."

Queen Faldira turned toward Dayraven and Sequara. "We face our trial sooner than we thought. Torrlond's ships even now enter Halion Sound to seal us off. We'll prepare what defenses we have and contest their landing on the shoreline. That will at least provide my people a chance to flee inland." Deep in her gentle eyes, Dayraven discerned some untold sorrow. He wondered what she foresaw. But she only smiled at him and said, "Do your best."

He turned to Urd, who put her hand on his arm and said, "You'll know when, child. Prepare yourself."

Too soon, thought Dayraven. The elf-shard hissed in mockery. *No one knows when darkness comes*, its whispers seemed to say, *but it comes*. He nodded to Urd and tried to appear resolute, clenching his jaw.

"Sound the call to arms. Rouse the nobles and captains. Send swift messengers to summon them to the bay," the queen commanded her guards. "There we'll take our stand. Send messengers into the city to order all non-combatants to evacuate. We'll give the Torrlonders no easy landing."

As one guard sounded the conch that signaled warning to Kiriath's citizens, the others scurried off to find the troops' leaders. Soon the palace swarmed with hurried activity and shouts. Servants bearing torches ran in sundry directions. Soldiers scrambled to find their companies. Panic palpable under the skin strained their discipline, threatening to tear everything loose.

For a moment, Dayraven wanted to go back to sleep and dismiss it all as a nightmare. Too stunned to comprehend fully what was happening, he let the current sweep him. He drifted almost heedless of where he went. At length, he found himself stumbling back towards his room. He was not certain why, but something in the back of his mind was waiting for him there.

Before he reached the hallway leading to his small chamber, he encountered Queen Rona in the company of Imharr and her six other surviving guards. The two remaining princes, her sons of eight and ten years, were also there, as was old Kulva, who had happily attached herself to her native kingdom's queen. The alarm at all the commotion was evident in their frowns and alert gazes. The queen looked him in the eyes, and he could see the fear in hers, though she hid it well.

"Please, tell me. What is happening?" She managed to keep her voice steady, but the urgency was there. It seemed she was looking to *him* for help and assurance. For hope.

The gods help us. Dayraven looked at the Adanese queen, and he tried to smile as sorrow for her arose in him. To the Torrlonders she had lost a kingdom, a husband, and a son. She had run from them, and now they had come again to sack her place of refuge. His refuge too.

"The Torrlonders have come to Asdralad. You should not stay in the palace. It . . . may not be safe."

The solemn queen did not ask him how he knew this. She only nodded at his words and said, "Where should I go?"

Just then the old housemaid Jhaia hobbled toward them down the hallway. Dayraven could think of nothing else.

"Jhaia! Please come here," he said in Andumaic.

The old woman approached them. "When the drought comes, then follow the locusts. Disturbing an old woman in the night. How will I do my chores on the morrow?" she asked Dayraven, frowning at him as if he were the source of her woes.

"Jhaia. I need your help."

"Of course you do, boy. You still haven't learned to make a proper bed. When the cow sat on the nest, it broke the eggs."

"I'm sure you're right. But now I need you to take care of someone else. Make sure they're safe. This is Queen Rona. These are her two sons, and the others her followers. He is my friend Imharr." He gestured at the queen and the others, who stared with incomprehension since he spoke to Jhaia in Andumaic. "They do not speak your tongue, but they are friends. They fled from Adanon to escape the Torrlonders, who will want to kill them. You must take them somewhere safe. You must leave the palace now."

Confusion took over Jhaia's frown as she squinted. "But who will tend to the palace?"

Dayraven grasped her shoulders and looked deep in her eyes. "Please, Jhaia. The palace is about to become a dangerous place. You must leave. Go somewhere safe. Somewhere inland. Hide these good people from the Torrlonders."

The old woman grinned. "I know a place. Back to my forest."

Dayraven nodded. "Good. Very good. You must leave now. Take a few things. Some food and water. Then flee to the forest. Go far from here. You will know when it's safe to return. Someone will come for you."

"Alright, alright. Don't rush an old woman. The tortoise won't flit like the hummingbird, but she'll nest all the same when it's time."

He bent and kissed the old woman on the brow. "Thank you. Stay safe."

"Now, now. Get along with you." She brushed him away as if swatting a fly, but she smiled too.

Dayraven faced Rona and switched back to the Northern Tongue. "Her name is Jhaia. She's a good woman and knows the island well." He glanced at Imharr. "She'll take you somewhere safe."

Imharr took a step toward Dayraven, who could see the conflict on his friend's face. Before he spoke, Dayraven held up his palm. "You must stay with Queen Rona. You know this, so there's no point in arguing. Protect her, and keep youself from harm. We'll come for you when it's safe."

Imharr wavered for a moment, but then he nodded before releasing a sigh. "Alright. But you'd better come out of this in one piece. You hear me? Show that white-robe and his dragons what power is." He leaned forward and embraced Dayraven, who returned the gesture while trying to suppress a spike of fear for his friend's life.

Dayraven released Imharr and attempted a reassuring smile before facing Rona again. "Jhaia's from Asdralad's inland forest. She has family there, and it's mostlike the safest place to hide. She will guide you."

The queen looked with eyes narrowed in doubt at the old woman, but then she nodded. "Alright. There may be nowhere safe from those bloodthirsty beasts, but we'll go with her."

"Queen Faldira, Urd, and Dayraven will keep us all safe, your Majesty," said Kulva. She nodded at Dayraven with her mouth set tight in conviction.

He wished he felt half as sure as she looked. "We'll do everything we can. Gather your things and flee. Follow Jhaia to safety." He looked one last time at Imharr.

As if understanding Dayraven's need for assurance, Imharr smiled, evoking memories of Kinsford and the Mark. "I'll see you again, my brother."

Too choked to speak, Dayraven settled for a nod and a weak smile. "Go," he managed to say. He turned from them and proceeded towards his chamber. The palace echoed with more cries, and Dayraven thought he could hear screams coming from the city now. When he reached the darkened hallway leading to his room, he walked down it carefully. He opened the door and peered in. Though the moonlight spilled in through the open window, it was still dark and shadowy within. Why had he come there? To say goodbye?

His gaze chanced on the back wall, and he understood. Making his way back to the shadowed corner where his sleeping mat lay, he felt along the wall. When his hand bumped against a scabbard, he seized it. He stood next to the window and removed his robe. Then he looped the baldric attached to the scabbard around his shoulder and buckled it on. Moonlight reflected on the jeweled pommel of Sweothol, the sword his father gave him. Thus armed, Dayraven put his robe back on and exited his chamber. He felt his way back down the pitch-black hall toward the torchlight.

Chaos still gripped the palace as people ran in every direction. Where was he supposed to go? He walked through the palace halls seeking calm, and he let his feet take him where they would. Without thinking about it, he reached the front doors and walked past the guards, nodding to them but not stopping. Down the steps he descended, and soon enough he found himself entering the city.

He wandered down Kiriath's main street toward the bay, hardly remembering how he made his way down from the palace. Soldiers clinking in battle gear rushed by him in the direction of the strand while frantic citizens lit torches outside their homes and shops. As word of the imminent invasion spread, many raised their frightened voices and fled past him, outside the city and toward the hills. At the moment, there was no evidence of the threat approaching over the water, but Asdralad's people placed great trust in their queen's prescience. They also had heard a great deal about the destructive power of Torrlond's army and its dragons.

Toward the beach Dayraven walked as if in a dream. Soldiers dug trenches by torchlight, stabbing the sand with desperate, frenzied strokes. Men shouted through the darkness. Ignoring the wild preparations, he walked past them all toward the waves lapping the shore. Under the moonlight, the white foam of the breaking and churning water seemed to glow. Beyond the shore lay the vast blackness of the water and the night sky. He found the gentle moan of Halion Sound's ebb and flow incongruously soothing. *How could destruction come over these waves?*

A hand grasped Dayraven's shoulder. "No need to swim out for 'em, lad. They'll be here soon enough."

Gnorn's voice pulled Dayraven back to the present. He turned around. The torchlight framed Orvandil and Abon's silhouettes behind the Dweorg's. All three were dressed for battle.

"Urd told us you'd be here," said Gnorn. "We're to make sure you don't get into mischief."

Dayraven smiled. They would protect him from the misadventures of battle while he tried to master the dragons with the song of origin. He would need to be as close as possible to the great lingworms without endangering himself. "You've played that role before. I entrust my safety to your hands. I only hope I prove worth the bother."

"Already have," said Orvandil.

"If Queen Faldira and Urd think you have a chance, I'll risk my neck for you again," said Abon.

"Then let's do what we can."

"We're behind you, lad," said Gnorn, who handed Dayraven some bread and cheese then held up a flask. "Have a bite. No good fighting on an empty belly."

After the friends breakfasted, the pre-dawn passed in a frenzy of preparations. The queen ordered her soldiers to torch the docks so Torrlond's fleet would have to beach their large ships and fight their way to shore. As darkness swallowed the billowing smoke from the conflagrations, soldiers dug defensive lines up the beach by the eerie, shifting firelight. The nobles and captains arrayed their men in ranks with bowmen in the rear and spearmen in front.

Things calmed somewhat as dawn approached, and for a moment Dayraven hoped they had all been wrong about the warning. Standing apart with Gnorn, Orvandil, and Abon, he looked upon the rows of soldiers. They wore the same white and black uniforms that the queen's personal guard wore. They were the soldiers of Asdralad's first proper army. Thanks to Gnorn's training, the island's blacksmiths had equipped them well enough for battle. Outside of the palace guards, most had learned what they knew of warfare only in the last year. Some had combat experience in Adanon, but most were untested. Dayraven admired and pitied them.

He turned his gaze out over the waters. As dawn's red and orange and pink seeped across the heavens, the last of the stars receded. But then a yellow light flickered in the sky and winked out. For a moment, he wondered if some new bright star had burst into life, but it did not take long to realize what the flame was. Gasps and murmurs among the soldiers revealed that some of them had seen it too. A voice cried, "Dragon fire! They're coming!" Three, four, then five more bursts appeared from afar. The soldiers' murmuring grew to a cacophony of shouts until Dayraven wondered if they would all turn and flee. Just then, stepping away from a gathering of her most powerful remaining sorcerers, Asdralad's queen strode forward with her hand raised.

Silence spread in a wave throughout the troops. Faldira walked to the front line and faced her subjects. She wore her sapphire crown and a long tunic of bright turquoise with loose trousers. At her side hung a curved scabbard with the bright gold hilt of a sword visible at its top. The sun rose and the sky burned behind her.

"Soldiers of Asdralad! Today the sun rises on our island. No matter what happens in the coming battle, it will rise again tomorrow, and for many more tomorrows. We fight for that future, and for our people. For your families, your children, and the children to come. Torrlond's army hastens here to take away something more precious than our land or wealth, or even our lives: They would have our minds and our souls. These things we deny them if we don't give in. Weapons can't cut them. Fire can't burn them. Don't give in this day, my people, and we'll defeat Torrlond, for they'll never have our minds or souls. They think to make all of Andumedan like them, but they'll fail. The final victory belongs to those who stand against them. For the destroyers will one day find they're not strong enough to quell the human spirit. Those who resist them in the future will take heart from us, my people. They'll remember us, and in the hour when they break the oppressor's shackles, they'll honor the glorious dead of Asdralad. Fight now, my people. Fight! For the future!"

Unshed tears blurred Dayraven's vision and his throat tightened as the queen's words emboldened Asdralad's soldiers. While she spoke, a spark of determination quickened in their faces, their jaws clenching and eyes narrowing as they stood in ordered rows with set shoulders. When she finished, they erupted in cheers and brandished their weapons in defiance of Torrlond's army and its serpents of fire. *Even in the face of doom, who wouldn't fight for such a queen?* thought Dayraven. *I must help. I must defeat Bledla. Perhaps they could even win . . .*

He waited. They all waited for heart-pounding moments as the early morning sun tinged Halion Sound red. At length, a few masts emerged in the distance, then more and more joined them. They kept coming until a forest of masts sprouted over the water, so many that some of Asdralad's soldiers began murmuring again.

"Must be nine hundred ships in that fleet," said Orvandil. "Means thirty thousand soldiers, maybe more, plus their beasts."

Dayraven trusted the Thjoth's judgment. No sign came of the dragons again for a long while, but then tiny specks wheeled in the sky above Torrlond's vast fleet. While running his finger along the scar on his neck, he counted them. *Nine, ten, eleven . . . Yes, twelve of them. When do I begin? Not yet. Urd said I'd know.*

The elf-shard soughed in his mind like a cold breeze on a bare tree branch. Long had it held the truce with him. Its vast power trembled behind the barrier in his mind. It was waiting for him to tap it, to siphon off a portion of energy small enough for him to control and large enough to wield the song of origin of dragons. *This is it. Don't break it now*, he said to it. Its monotonous whisper continued.

The sun rose higher in the sky. Asdralad's anxious soldiers looked on as the invading ships grew bigger. Some stared into the sky at the approaching dragons, whose wings and trailing tails became visible to the keen-sighted as they wheeled over the ships. Dayraven fixed his attention on the serpents of the air. *I must prepare myself. Soon. The time will come soon.*

He felt a stirring of power. Queen Faldira, Urd, Sequara, and the rest of the remaining sorcerers were chanting beneath their breath, all facing the coming fleet. Dayraven understood what they were doing, but he could not take part since he needed to conserve his strength for his sole purpose: the dragons. He watched as they continued to sing the song of origin, and all the while the Torrlonder ships grew closer, cutting the waves in their eagerness to gain the shore.

At once, a grey mound broke the surface of the water near one of the ships, and Dayraven blinked in awe as it bulged upward, foamy water cascading down its sides. Breaching the sound, a leviathan of the deep loomed upward and twisted in the air, its two flat arms spinning as it flipped over, exposing its white, striped belly to the sky. As if cowering beneath the vast beast's shadow, the tilting ship suddenly appeared much smaller. And then came the impact. So great was the distance, the sounds of screaming men, the snapping of the mast, and the splintering of the ship amidst the roar of water came a moment after Dayraven witnessed the leviathan's enormous back smash into the hapless vessel. Water splashed upward in an explosion, tossing within it the dark forms of shattered wood and bodies, as Halion Sound sucked the wondrous beast down again. Once the surface settled, where there had been a ship, there was nothing but choppy water and detritus.

Several more of the huge creatures breached the sound, attacking and smashing half a dozen more ships into splinters and wreckage while their passengers shrieked their terror. But at the same time, plummeting from the sky, the dragons were streaking toward them.

"Release the whales!" commanded Queen Faldira.

The sorcerers ceased chanting, and the leviathans disappeared beneath the water, save for one that seemed to be sliding closer to a ship. Dayraven noticed one of the sorcerers still intoning, his eyes closed in concentration. Perhaps, lost in the realm of origins, he had not heard the queen. Perhaps he wished to inflict more damage before the dragons arrived. A moment later, the leviathan he wielded surged upward, looming over the ship.

Before the leviathan could land, several streams of dragon fire enveloped it. Behind the avalanche of flames surged three of the lingworms, which slammed into the creature of the depths and fastened their jaws around it. The vast leviathan writhed as it crashed back into the sound with a plume of water, but the frenzied dragons continued rending it with their claws and ripping away huge chunks of it with their teeth, flinging away gobbets as they whipped their necks.

The sorcerer who had been wielding the leviathan shrieked in agony and clutched his head as he spun and fell on his face.

Dayraven turned his gaze away from the motionless body of the sorcerer back to the sky, where the three dragons were even then rejoining the others. *It's time.* He took deep, long breaths. Letting the sense of himself spread out, he started to detach from the palpable fear around and within him. For several heartbeats he adjusted his breaths to the greater rhythm all around. At last, he drifted away from the confines of the illusion of himself into the crisper, truer reality of the realm of origins.

The elf-shard was an immeasurable force within him and all around him. Allowing a trickle of its power to escape into him, he became the conduit for an enormous rush of energy. For a moment he paused to make sure he was in control of the flow. It remained steady and stable. Balance and detachment. Taking one more deep breath, Dayraven expanded ever outward.

He became an observer, part of all that surrounded him yet unaffected by any of it. As his mind journeyed away from his body inhabiting the world of forms, he remained aware of Gnorn, Orvandil, and Abon standing nearby to defend it. To them, time was passing, perhaps a little, perhaps a lot. Not far away he felt Sequara, who stood protectively next to her queen and Urd. He sensed each of the five thousand or so Asdralae soldiers waiting for their individual deaths. Dayraven, however, perceived them all not as separate and distinct, but as many faces of the same life.

And dim but growing was the presence of the Torrlonders approaching in their ships. These men were also faces of the same life animating Asdralad's soldiers. *All one,* a voice said — perhaps his own, perhaps the elf-shard's. Also part of that life were the dragons, on which Dayraven fixed his thoughts. Closer they rushed, monstrous manifestations on high, teeming with the energy focused within them. Dayraven's energy clutched toward them. The nearer he advanced, the larger their presence grew.

Soon they blocked out all else until their vastness dwarfed him. He was near them now. Only a little further, and he would make contact. After checking again to make sure the flow of the elf-shard's power from his mind was steady, he lunged toward the beasts.

He touched them. The life that dwelt in Dayraven felt the presence of the dragons as palpably as if his flesh brushed their scales. He grasped the dragons' place in the world and saw the span of their creation. Powerful and terrible they were, wondrous and beautiful, awesome to behold. Deep were their memories, much deeper than humankind's. They were hard scales and hot fire, sleek and sharp, cunning and fierce, jealous and, most surprising, tender. His voice chanted their song of origin:

Urkhalion an dwinathon ni partholan varlas,
Valdarion ar hiraethon im rhegolan wirdas.
Gholgoniae sheerdalu di vorway maghona,
Dardhuniae sintalu ar donway bildhona.

Again and again he sang the words as ancient as time. With each repetition, the dragons' presence grew stronger in him, and his in them. First in the more pliable, younger dragons his connection grew, then even in the larger ones he had a hold. Dayraven was almost startled to find how easily he succeeded in gaining a link with the great lingworms. Only one other had achieved this feat since the Prophet Aldmund's time. He stifled his growing elation. *Balance. This is not about Dayraven of the Mark.*

He continued to chant as he focused on regulating the flow of power from the elf-shard, which pricked and tingled in his mind like a sliver of glass and at the same time loomed all around him. He was building his connection to the dragons. Stronger it grew until Dayraven felt soon he could use his will to break another's hold over the beasts. High over Torrlond's fleet, he saw from the dragons' eyes: nearly a thousand ships speckled the shimmering water while the brown island kingdom loomed closer, smoke rising near the lines of breaking waves where the docks had been. Wind and wisps of cloud rushed by as giant wings clove the air.

But their enthralled state muted the joy of the flight. Strong bonds surrounded their spirits. He perceived the fear and hatred their captivity produced. More than anything, Dayraven recognized how these great serpents chafed to obey no one's will but their own. Only the dim hope for freedom — fragile like a candle's flame in the wind — kept the proud beasts from descending into screaming madness. Soon he would offer them that freedom, and he knew they would leap for it. His grip was nearly strong enough now. Yes, almost there. It was almost too easy.

With the suddenness and wrath of thunder, it came. Pain, terrible pain seized Dayraven's spirit from all around. Something enormous beat his mind down, shred his energy that he tried in vain to extend to the dragons. Dayraven recognized the reckless power and zeal raging against him. The Supreme Priest Bledla had awakened to his presence and now bent his formidable will toward destroying whatever threatened his hold over the dragons.

Dayraven realized Bledla's greater experience in this realm, and the supreme priest had the advantage of a long held connection with the lingworms. Having expected this, he was not unprepared for the onslaught. But its magnitude and ferocity drove him back reeling. *So strong. But he won't win easily. I have at least one advantage.* Steadying himself, he allowed the flow of power from the elf-shard to increase ever so slightly and prepared to wrestle for control of the dragons with Bledla.

The supreme priest was ready. In vain Dayraven tried to break through to the beasts, for now Bledla's giant will stood in his way. With no way around, Dayraven rushed forward at him. The collision of their wills nearly sent him cringing down, but he held on.

It was a dangerous contest. If Bledla prevailed, the energy constituting Dayraven's spirit might never make its way back to his body, in which case it would dissipate into the void whence all emerge and whither all return. Tapping yet more into the elf-shard's power, Dayraven teetered with its sudden surge. For a moment, he feared it would explode outward and shatter him, but he kept a firm grip on it and reined it in. Then, turning his attention to Bledla's mighty energy, he renewed his attack.

Again they clashed. This time, he felt Bledla stagger back at the power of his onslaught, and in the realm of origins he sensed the supreme priest's alarm. Though it was impossible to exchange words in that realm, as their energy wrestled for supremacy over the dragons, Dayraven and Bledla perceived each other's thoughts as clearly as if they stood together and conversed. While Dayraven struggled, the sameness he shared with Bledla came to him with a shock. Indeed, it seemed he had known the supreme priest all his life, even beyond his life. *I felt this kinship before,* thought Dayraven as he strained against Bledla. *Yet your path is wrong. You don't understand Edan. Edan is life. In the blindness of your zeal, you chose death.*

Bledla's mighty presence scoffed at Dayraven, who heard all his thoughts at once. *Fool! I am what you could have been. I am Edan's Prophet! He allowed us both great power. But I returned it all to Him, while you strive for His foes. Thus, I will prevail. Thus, I smite you down!*

Agony stabbed throughout Dayraven's spirit, extracting his scream before he knew what happened. Bledla focused all his energy into a mighty force that tore at him from a thousand different directions. As the supreme priest ripped away shreds of his energy that fell into the void, Dayraven began to lose the sense of himself. Bledla was breaking him down over the field of the world, thus ending his individual existence. This thought elicited a stab of panic. Lurching back, he tried to retrieve the fragments of his consciousness. Outward they spread, slipping from his grasp like vapor through his hands. The fight to wrest control of the dragons from Bledla was becoming a dire struggle for his survival.

One recourse remained. Dayraven reached into his mind and opened a space wider than he had ever before dared to unleash the power of the elf-shard. At the same time, he braced himself for the struggle to contain and control it.

As if awakening from a long sleep and seeking its freedom in infinite directions at once, the elf-shard exploded from him and smashed Dayraven's will into thousands of splinters spiraling outward. His cry of agony disappeared in its bottomless roar. It was far more violent and painful than anything Bledla had done to him.

Leaving the supreme priest far behind, he fled in pursuit of himself, reaching out in blind terror. Whether for a moment or for days or years, Dayraven lost all sense of anything but raw, fearful pain at losing himself this way. Wildly retreating, his last conscious thought was that

Bledla had won. The elf-shard's deafening howl came from a vast hole of infinite shadow and depth that sucked in the scattered fragments of his being. Darkness enfolded him as he plummeted.

With a sickening jolt, Dayraven awoke in the world of light and sound to screams and the sharp clashing of weapons. The pointed hiss of the elf-shard's breath seemed to scold and mock him. Compared to the unbounded roar when it exploded far beyond his control, it was almost welcome.

Opening his eyes, he found he was lying face down in sand. He tried to rise, but he was too dizzy and weak. The world blurred. He was unsteadily contained in his body still and lacked control over it. Blinking his eyes to focus them, he tried to concentrate enough to see, but nausea took hold of him and he retched. Vomit choked him then stung his throat and nose.

"He's waking!" said Abon's fuzzy voice amidst the tumult of battle.

Not sure where the voice came from, Dayraven tried to lift his head and see where the shaper stood.

"Stay down!" said Abon.

Colors shifted. Several blurry forms in front of Dayraven moved fast. Weapons rang. A man screamed.

"Need to move him soon. Can't stay much longer," said Orvandil nearby.

Shaking himself, Dayraven made a desperate effort to bring his mind back to the waking world. His hands trembled as he willed them to touch his face, on which grains of sand stuck. Brushing the flesh of his cheeks, he knew he was real and alive, and he knew where his body waited for him. When he focused on his breathing as Queen Faldira taught him, it became more regular and calm. At once the world sharpened, and his energy snapped back into place. The elf shard's hiss diminished to a cool susurration that toyed with the edges of his awareness. Though he felt drained and weak, his vision returned as the disorienting feeling receded. When he could see again, he almost wished he could not.

Only a few hundred yards down the beach, three dragons swooped down from the sky and vomited flames onto Asdralad's fleeing soldiers, who stumbled and flailed in the fires. One great worm held a writhing body in a huge foreclaw. Another dove low and plucked a fleeing man from the ground with gaping jaws. When the beast's jaw muscles tightened, its teeth sheared the screaming man in half. A pair of legs fell and twisted in the air with ropes of blood trailing behind. Burning corpses littered the sands. Hundreds of beached ships clogged the bay, each a hundred feet long with giant trolls and aglaks standing guard near them. In the reddened waves tumbled hundreds of bloody bodies, ghastly signs that Torrlond's army had found its landing contested. But now soldiers in grey kirtles and battle gear advanced with lustful eyes and fierce, victorious grins on their faces. Only a few pockets of resistance remained as the badly outnumbered soldiers of Asdralad lived out their last few moments.

I failed, thought Dayraven as despair gripped him. The elf-shard's whispers darkened. A shadow clutched his mind.

Strong hands took hold of his chest and sat him up.

"Leave me!" he screamed at Orvandil. "I failed."

"You'll try again," returned the Thjoth. "But only if you live."

Dayraven looked up at Orvandil's blond beard and fierce blue eyes. He nodded.

"Here come some more!" yelled Gnorn, who appeared next to Orvandil.

"Stay here," said the Thjoth as he laid Dayraven back in the sand. Too weak and dizzy to stand on his own, he had no other choice than to obey his friend.

Nine Torrlonders rushed at them. Orvandil, Gnorn, and Abon waited gripping their weapons. The foremost attacker yelled and ran at Orvandil with sword aloft. Spotting the opening, the Thjoth blurred forward in a fluid motion and thrust his blade with deadly precision, tearing open the man's neck in a blossom of red. Before any could react, Orvandil swung his blade up then down through the helm of the next with a crimson splash, shearing the man's head in half down to the neck and crumpling the body. A third tried to bring his blade down on the Thjoth, but Orvandil caught his assailant's hand in mid-swing and plunged his large sword through the man's byrny. The Thjoth used the dead man's sword to deflect the next soldier's blow then carved through the shocked man's neck with his big blade, sending the head spinning to the ground amidst a mist of blood before the body toppled.

In the meantime, Abon ducked under an attacker's sword and sank his blade into the man's belly from under his byrny, slicing a wide arc from which slick intestines spilled like squirming eels. His next opponent fared no better as the shaper deflected the man's blow then swept his blade across his face. The man screamed and crumpled. Gnorn was no less busy with his axe as it bit through an attacker's collarbone and shoulder. The man shrieked as his limp arm dangled away from his bleeding torso. Diving low under a wild stroke from the next Torrlonder, the Dweorg swung his axe and swept a leg off the man, who crashed to the sand screaming and clutching the spurting stump.

One last soldier of Torrlond ran by the three defenders toward Dayraven with sword raised. Too weak for magic, Dayraven feebly struggled to unsheathe Sweothol. By the time the soldier stood over him, he had it out, but his shaking hands fumbled the blade into the sand. The soldier smirked as he brought down his sword for an easy kill. Dayraven slumped over, shielding his face with his trembling hands.

A loud crunch changed the soldier's smile into wide-eyed shock in mid-swing. He collapsed with his full weight on top of Dayraven, who grunted when the impact drove the air from his lungs. His bulging eyes staring into Dayraven's, the Torrlonder gasped and twitched before lying still. Gnorn's axe blade jutted from his back. The hurled weapon had shattered the man's byrny and cloven his spine in half. Orvandil and Abon pulled Dayraven out from under the limp, sweaty body and helped him to rise to his unsteady feet. A splotch of wet blood stained Dayraven's robe, and he suppressed the urge to throw up again. The shaper returned Sweothol to its scabbard. With his foot planted on the corpse, Gnorn plucked out his axe.

At that moment, a giant flash preceded a loud crack and boom that exploded the air, and their four heads jerked in the blast's direction.

Two hundred yards to their left, Queen Faldira and the Supreme Priest Bledla faced one another. The queen in her turquoise tunic and the priest in his white robe stood some fifty feet apart and held out their palms. Between them writhed an enormous bolt of wizard's fire that lashed to and fro, instantly scorching the few hapless soldiers in its path. The middle of the flow of energy was thicker and white-hot and blindingly bright. This portion of the bolt heaved closer to Faldira as she and Bledla strained for mastery. The queen's face was tight with concentration, her eyes squinting at the brightness and her teeth clenched, and her arms shook with the effort. From Bledla's wide eyes leaped triumph. His illuminated smile was crazed.

Others joined the contest. Urd and Sequara rushed to Faldira's side, chanting spells to aid her. *Almakhti* shot forth and buzzed from their extended hands to merge with the queen's. That halted the progression of Bledla's energy toward the queen of the Asdralae for a moment. But three white-robed priests — one huge and red-haired, another small and dark-haired, and the third an old man — stepped forward in a line to help their master. Wizard's fire erupted from their hands, swelling the crackling and writhing column to the girth of a large tree. The bolt's thick central portion jerked closer to the three women. Its intensity was blinding, and thin tendrils of energy sparked and flew from it in every direction, scorching the fleeing and screaming soldiers.

Shielding his eyes with his hands, Dayraven bitterly cursed his weakness. He reached for the realm of origins and lurched back when nausea assaulted him. "No!" He clenched his fists, but his wounded spirit was far too fragile to call upon the gift. The elf-shard taunted him with its steady hush, as if it wished to remind him he was only a helpless and fleeting witness to the inevitable darkness. "Help me!" he screamed. It ignored him. With his tenuous hold on his body, its vast power was indifferent and inaccessible to him.

Unable even to walk unaided, he lunged forward in an attempt to reach the women. The ground rushed up at his collapsing body, and grains of sand dug into his cheek and the palms of his hands as he grunted with the impact. Orvandil and Gnorn picked him up by the arms, and he screamed in helpless fury and desperation. Then a giant shadow descended from above.

Out of the sky swooped a great lingworm, veering toward the three women. Just as the serpent of the air disgorged a burst of flames at them, Dayraven tried to scream, but no sound would come.

The almakhti from Urd's hands winked out, and the central, white-hot portion of the column of wizard's fire wrenched toward the women. The old witch shouted a spell and waved her hands towards the dragon's flames, exploding the burst of fire into flickering tongues that dispersed in myriad directions.

The supreme priest snarled and pitched his body forward, thrusting his arms even further before him. The white heat of the energy bolt rushed toward the women. Faldira stumbled backwards then shouted something at Sequara, who shook her head in protest. With her shoulder, the queen shoved her heir out of the way just before her power shattered in a cascade of sparks.

With a giant crack and a blinding flash, the priests' bolt of wizard's fire struck Faldira and sent her seared body flying backward, twisting her like a rag in the wind before she landed face down in the sand. Smoke rose from the beloved queen's broken form. Dayraven stood in wide-eyed and gape-mouthed disbelief, trembling all over his body.

He screamed in inarticulate animal rage, but he was still helpless to do anything except watch as Sequara climbed to her hands and knees. She arose amidst smoke and destruction. The demoralized soldiers of Asdralad flung themselves to their deaths, wildly attempting to cut down the priests of the Way, whom Torrlond's troops encased in a semi-circle.

Urd struggled up and grabbed Sequara's arm while screaming at her. The old witch pointed toward Dayraven and shouted until Sequara nodded. As the four priests of the Way closed in through the smoke, the young sorceress looked at Urd with wild eyes then ran toward Dayraven. One of the priests, the old one, broke off from the others in pursuit of Sequara, while Bledla and the two others strode closer to Urd. The old woman awaited them.

Urd gazed through the smoke in Dayraven's direction. Her beautiful eyes fixed on him, and then she turned toward her three attackers. White-haired and fragile, the small woman faced the men down like a mother bear defending her cubs. She folded her hands in front of her chest, and she sang a spell. Dayraven could not hear it, but he sensed a vast release of power from her. After the old woman finished her song, she held her arms outward as if preparing for an embrace. An invisible force pulsed from her body as an expanding ring of wind, brushing back the smoke in a quick gust. Urd's body crumpled backward into the sand. For a moment there was strange silence.

Even the Supreme Priest Bledla wore a puzzled frown at the energy that radiated from Urd. As the ring of energy struck the priests, they stumbled backwards with eyes widened in surprise. They stared at their hands and then all around them. By the time the wind reached Dayraven, it had weakened, but he understood what his great aunt had done. In the wind he felt her spirit, and he knew then she had somehow sent all the energy of her being forth with her last effort. Like a distant echo he heard Urd telling him to run now and face the aggressors of Torrlond later. *Live for another day*, she told him. Then her voice faded away forever.

To judge by their still bewildered faces, Bledla and his priests did not comprehend what just happened, but the effects were visible on the battleground. The beasts of battle and even the dragons ceased to fight. With thuds that vibrated the earth, the serpents of fire landed one by one on the beach and shook their massive heads as if dazed. Standing guard next to the ships, the trolls and aglaks looked around them in a stupor as if waking from a nightmare. Somehow, by pouring forth her energy and melding it with theirs, Urd had taken away the power of the priests of the Way, at least for a moment. In the echo of her dying spirit she had told Dayraven all this. As the dispersed fragments of her energy mingled with the priests', she disoriented them and shut off their access to the gift.

Sequara sprinted toward Dayraven and the others, leaving the white-robed old man further behind. He waved his hands and shouted, "Stop!"

Dayraven sensed that, as the old man had run further from Urd, her final spell had achieved less of an effect on him. He still had power, and now he stood behind Sequara singing a spell. She did not notice him.

Dayraven reacted without thinking. Grasping for the gift and gritting his teeth through the nausea, he forgot everything else and thundered out the words, "Alakathon indomiel ar galathon anrhuniae, Vortalion marduniel im paradon khalghoniae!" From his hands erupted a bolt of wizard's fire that streaked towards the old priest.

The old man had seen Dayraven chanting, however, and he held up his palms while singing a quick counterspell. His shield of wizard's fire sprang to life just as Dayraven's bolt struck with a bright, shattering flash and knocked the priest ten feet backward. He landed in a cloud of dust and smoke.

Dayraven's knees gave out, and he collapsed into Orvandil's arms with that last effort, clinging on to consciousness. He shook his head as the ground swam under him.

Sequara reached them a moment later. "Run!" she yelled with tear tracks streaking through soot smudged across her face. "Urd bought us a little time only. The priests' power will return."

"They may not need it," said Abon as he pointed. "Look." Behind them swarmed hundreds of Torrlonders closing in on them. "Can't fight them all."

"Then we'll fight till we fall!" yelled Gnorn, who gripped his axe. Orvandil raised his blade, as did Abon.

But as they abode their doom, someone nearby shouted, "To Queen Sequara! Save the queen!"

Dayraven recognized the man waving his sword. It was Karad, the veteran and Sequara's personal guard. Some of Asdralad's soldiers gathered around him and rallied to aid their new queen. With the dragons no longer chasing them across the strand, more soon joined them. Screaming battle cries, they rushed headlong into the sea of grey kirtles, cutting the attackers off from Sequara and the others, at least for a short while.

Sequara watched her soldiers engage the foe. Her eyes were narrowed, and her fists were clenched. She reached a trembling hand toward Karad as if she would scream at him to retreat, but then she lowered it. She turned to Orvandil, swallowing before making the effort to speak. "We must save Dayraven. Get us out of here."

The tall Thjoth sheathed his sword and hoisted Dayraven onto his shoulder like a sack. "The enemy's cut off the city. Find a boat. This way."

They hastened away from the melee along the beach. Orvandil carried Dayraven while Abon and Gnorn guarded the rear. Once again cursing his weakness, Dayraven tried to catch his breath as he bounced on the Thjoth's hard shoulder. Orvandil's byrny dug into his gut, and the ground rushed by beneath him. There was no choice but to endure the ride since his legs were too weak still to carry him. He tried to see what was happening up ahead.

Sequara ran in front, turning her head as she sought a likely vessel. With the raging battle receding behind them, they ran past Torrlond's beached fleet, hoping to hide behind the large ships. Sequara stopped near one's bow for a moment and then turned around as she pointed to smoke rising from the remains of the docks. "I see one! There, near the . . ."

A huge, clawed hand swept out from behind the bow and slammed into Sequara's back. She landed face down in the sand with a muffled grunt. In the next instant, an aglak emerged, dripping with seaweed and baring its mucus-covered teeth as it roared and rushed toward the stricken sorceress.

"Go!" shrieked Dayraven. Orvandil dropped him and he landed hard. The Thjoth ran toward the beast, screaming to distract it from Sequara. Drawing his blade, the tall warrior ducked under the enraged aglak's blow, which could have toppled a tree. He wheeled around and, before the aglak turned, brought his sword's edge down on its wrist, severing the hand. Holding up its bleeding limb, the beast screamed and lunged its head with mouth wide open at Orvandil. The Thjoth dodged the sharp teeth and arced his sword up. With a mighty swing, he brought it down on the beast's huge neck. Bone cracked and blood spurted, and the creature's body crashed hard into the grit. The sword bit more than halfway through the neck, but when Orvandil raised it, the blade was shortened, having snapped in half. The aglak gurgled and twitched before it went still in the wet sand.

Abon ran to Sequara while Gnorn picked up Dayraven. The sorceress gasped and, after a moment, said weakly, "Thank you . . . I'm alright . . . just need to catch my breath . . . It was frightened. The trolls and aglaks are free of the priests. They don't know where to turn or hide now. But it gives me an idea. Bring Dayraven to that vessel and prepare to leave. I'll be right behind you."

"No," groaned Dayraven.

"No arguing. Now!"

Too weak to do anything about it, Dayraven could only watch as Orvandil picked him up and ran towards the boat, which was half in the water and somehow, perhaps due to the wind's direction, had not burned with the dock it had been tied to. Abon and Gnorn were behind them. When Orvandil laid Dayraven in the elegant and slender boat, a clinker-built vessel about twenty-five feet long, he rested his back against the side and gazed out toward Sequara. The huge forms of aglaks and trolls came toward her from behind the ships. She was a small black figure that disappeared behind dozens of the giants.

Dayraven almost cried out, but he realized what she was doing just as Gnorn said, "The beasts are coming for her! Go back!"

"No," said Dayraven. "She's casting a spell over them. Wait for her."

Moments later, the throng of trolls and aglaks dispersed, each beast heading back for a ship in Torrlond's beached fleet. Sequara ran toward Dayraven and the others. By the time she reached them, they were nearly ready to shove off. "Go!" she yelled as she leapt into the boat. Orvandil pulled a rope taut and tied it to prepare the sail.

Panting hard, Sequara told them between breaths, "I managed to control most of the remaining trolls and aglaks. Don't know how long it'll last, but I ordered them to knock holes in the bottoms of the ships. It won't be long before the priests regain control, but it might slow down pursuit."

"What of the dragons?" asked Abon. "Can't they spot us from the air?"

"Seems they have something else in mind," said Gnorn, who pointed up in the sky. The twelve great lingworms flew over the waves in the direction of the mainland, becoming specks streaking northward in the sky.

"Bledla will have his hands full bringing them back," said Sequara. "Urd saved us." She swallowed and seemed to choke back tears as she looked down at her lap.

"For now," mumbled Abon.

He and Orvandil leaped into the water to shove the boat into the foaming waves. After they climbed back on board, the shaper rowed out while the Thjoth finished readying the small sail. Once underway, Orvandil steered the tiller so the vessel sailed south.

"Have you been turned upside down?" asked Gnorn. "The only way out of Halion Sound is north."

"No way out there, friend. The Torrlonders will have vessels at the sound's mouth to waylay anyone seeking escape."

"And what do we do once we reach the sound's end and Torrlond's ships have us cornered like rats?" asked Gnorn.

Orvandil smiled grimly at the Dweorg. "Stay alive."

With no sign of pursuit yet, everyone in the party sagged in exhaustion. As they sailed on, the full grief of their losses overtook them. They wept or held their heads in silence. Too depleted to think ahead, Dayraven let sorrow envelop him as the wind bore them south over the waters. The only voice he heard was the elf-shard's. Like a shadow-mist, its whispers enclosed his mind in darkness.

THE SUPREME PRIEST BLEDLA STOOD NEAR THE SMOKING RUINS OF Kiriath with eyes closed in concentration, chanting beneath his breath. On the strand, eleven dragons stood tamely in a row where the waves lapped the sands. Hundreds of bloated corpses bobbed in the water. Thousands more of the dead lay all over the beach. Seagulls screamed and milled among mangled and burned bodies. Soldiers in grey kirtles tended to Torrlond's wounded and put to death any of the enemy still breathing. They shrieked for mercy, but the Torrlonders gave none.

Even as the supreme priest chanted in communion with Edan, a thought ate away at a corner of his mind. *Alive. How? The boy lives.*

As Bledla continued his spell, a huge shadow winked over him. The twelfth dragon whooshed overhead. Wheeling around, the last and largest of the dragons landed by its fellow captives with a loud thud and a roar. Even though they had fled many miles by the time Bledla regained control over his powers, the long shackles that bound the great serpents to the supreme priest were too strong to dissipate under the witch's pernicious influence. But he was far from celebrating.

Dayraven lives. What does it mean? I have defeated him, but if he had wielded all that power in him . . . Edan, tell your servant what it means!

Bledla opened his eyes and made an effort to slow his breaths. The High Priests Arna, Heremod, and Morcar stood nearby and listened as the supreme priest declared, "There. The last of them. It was a near thing and a clever ploy, but at least we're rid of the witch and the false queen." He gazed up at two large, wooden poles some soldiers had erected on the beach. From a rope attached to one's top hung Queen Faldira's charred body, and from the other Urd's corpse dangled in the breeze. A measure of satisfaction gave Bledla an angry smile, but the women's deaths brought him no peace. They had trained the boy.

A soldier ran up to the supreme priest. "My lord," he said as he bowed and caught his breath. "King Earconwald sent me to inform you the shipwrights have repaired six vessels, which he ordered to sail south in pursuit of the fugitives. As you requested, our best trackers are aboard. Twelve more ships will be ready in short time. Also, we've destroyed the last pockets of resistance in the city. The king is even now making his way to the palace, and he bids me to tell you he awaits you there. Kiriath is ours, my lord."

"And with it, Asdralad," answered Bledla. "Good. Edan's justice will be done. The palace will burn with the rest of the city. When more ships are ready, we'll send them to every corner of the island. We must send our finest soldiers into the Forest of Yalawyn, where the fugitives will no doubt seek refuge. The high priests and I will board the next ready ships. You may go."

After the messenger left, Bledla turned to the three high priests and hissed through his teeth, "This is the *last* time we use the trolls, aglaks, or pucas in battle. The lesser beasts come too easily under our enemies' sway, and the delay with the ships is proving costly. It's only the dragons they cannot reach, though that boy nearly had them. We *must* find Dayraven and kill him."

"My lord," asked Heremod in a tentative voice, "Why not send the dragons? They'll find him in no time."

"Fool!" snapped Bledla. "Did I not just say the boy nearly brought them under his spell? Had I not intervened, had I not been close enough, he would have succeeded! Do you want me to send them so he can master them and bid them return to roast your stupid hide?"

The three priests looked down at their feet. "No," continued their master, "we cannot send out the dragons for *him*. We must capture and slay him ourselves. Some of our soldiers spotted him and the others sailing south, so they must have realized the blockade to the north would prevent their escape. Our ships will outpace their boat and catch them soon enough. It's a matter of time. And if our foes make it to land, our trackers will find them in Yalawyn. They have nowhere to go. Edan will deliver them."

"Yes, my lord," said the High Priest Arna, whose blackened face and frizzled beard bore witness to his encounter with Dayraven. "Edan will prevail. All will happen according to His wisdom."

Bledla looked at his old friend and shook his head. "You know, Arna, don't you? You're no fool like the others. You realize what this means. Did you not feel that boy's power? He wielded the song of origin of dragons. How? So much power. If you had felt it when it exploded from him . . . Treachery and deceit! Fire and ruin to all unbelievers and traitors! How did that boy elude us?"

None of them dared answer. Bledla's wild eyes had widened as he asked the questions, but they narrowed when he said to himself. "Ah, but Edan did not allow him to control it. It was too much for him. He couldn't contain it. I see it now: a lesson in humility. Edan sent him as a test. Yes, that's it. Edan tests our fortitude and piety, brethren. And we will *not* fail. We will not fail you, mighty Edan."

"No, my lord," answered Arna, "and we'll move on to new triumphs."

Bledla nodded. "Yes, my friend. As is your wont, you remind me of the right path. We must have faith. Though the boy has escaped for now, we gained a great victory this day. Behold." He gestured at the two hanging and swaying bodies. The ropes they dangled from creaked in the breeze. "Edan has handed over two of our most wicked foes. Never again will they interfere with the Way's progress."

Heremod looked up and grinned. Morcar's smile was more tentative and nervous. Arna nodded at his leader, who continued to speak. "Just so, all enemies will perish. That boy Dayraven, the heretic

Galdor, the so-called rulers of the eastern kingdoms: All will soon know there's only one Edan, and He rewards only the faithful who follow Him. Though we may be weary, we will triumph. Let us regain our strength and prepare to smite the foe. And then, on to the east. Edan will bless us."

"Blessed be the Eternal!" declared the three high priests.

"But come now," said Bledla, "before we depart, our debauched king calls for us. He'll want to celebrate in his fashion, but we must move. When we slay Dayraven, we'll sail back to Torrhelm and there gather all our forces for the final push. Our moment draws near, brethren. Soon, we'll behold the Kingdom of the Eternal."

13

CAPTIVES

"With the wind behind us, we reach Halion Sound's end at nightfall," said Orvandil, who still steered the boat southward.

It was the first time any of the party had spoken in a long while, for they could find no language for their sorrow. Giving voice to words was an act of defiance, a reminder amidst the thick silence that there was more to life than the all-consuming grief. None of the others replied. The silence asserted itself again.

The small square sail rippled and cracked as the breeze pushed them along. The sun had moved in the clear sky above them as they sailed on a peaceful, cloudless day that belied the horror they fled. Dayraven listened to the gurgle of water sliding by against the boat's side, and, though he knew better, he indulged the thought of no pursuit. Perhaps he was just too numb to imagine anything beyond the wave of grief besieging him. Along with the rush of the water, the elf-shard's dark murmur hushed in the crevices of his waking mind, where it clung like a stubborn mist.

He and Sequara had said nothing since they escaped Kiriath, and the others had spoken little enough. Though his strength was returning, he sat with his back against the boat's side in guilt and despair over his failure's enormous cost. He ran his fingers through his hair. Bledla had won. All that time spent training, all the sacrifices that others made for him. And he failed. Asdralad's people would bear the brunt of the Torrlonders' wrath and wanton destruction. Nothing tore at his heart more than the loss of Urd and Queen Faldira. And Imharr — was he alive? The thought of his friend trapped on the island gnawed at him. The idea of Jhaia leading them to safety had seemed the best course at the time, the only option in the midst of the chaos, but looking back now, it seemed desperate and foolish. If the Torrlonders found him . . . He could not bear the idea of Imharr's death resulting from his failure. *How can we carry on? I must find a way to gather hope. But how? Faldira and Urd are gone. There's no hope. But I'll honor them. Carry on until I join them.*

Abon squinted as he gazed north. "This same wind will push our enemies' sails. We can't let down our guard."

Orvandil did not allow the conversation to die this time. "They'll need to sail fast to catch us."

Looking pale and hanging dejectedly over the boat's side, Gnorn groaned. But he turned to look at Orvandil and nodded, as if he understood the need to break the silence. "I'd rather face Torrlond's entire army single-handedly on land than go another mile in this tub. As if it weren't enough I only just arrived on this island. Curse every boat, ship, raft, or manner of device that floats. It's simply unnatural for a Dweorg to bob about with nothing between his feet and the watery depths but a few planks of wood."

Orvandil chuckled. "Your pardon, friend. But we sail till nightfall. Abon is right. The Torrlonders will send search parties. And though a Dweorg on land is formidable, we'd best put some miles between us and them."

"What do we do tonight?" asked Abon.

Orvandil thought a moment. "Seek shelter in Yalawyn. In the dark, they'll have a hard time tracking us. We also need to eat. The forest will provide."

"Pray, don't mention food just now," pleaded Gnorn, who clung to the boat's side and moaned.

"Then what?" said Abon. "Wait in the forest till they catch us?"

"If you have ideas, share them," said Orvandil.

"What's that back there?" asked Sequara, speaking for the first time since they set sail. They all looked northward, where she pointed to six distant white objects shimmering on the horizon.

"Sails," said Orvandil. "They're following."

"Have they seen us yet?" asked Abon.

"If we see them, they see us," said the Thjoth.

The shaper pointed west, where trees lined the distant shoreline. "Let's land over there and disappear in the forest. Our best chance is hiding now."

Orvandil gazed toward the trees and shook his head. "They'd know where we landed. Wouldn't be hard to track us after that. Only a matter of time before we'd have to turn and fight."

"Then let's land and wait for 'em," said Gnorn. "Better than dying out here, like a cork in a bathtub. Let me out of the tub at least."

Gnorn's words brought an image to Dayraven's mind. Sitting up, he awoke from his stupor. "Gnorn, you have it." Everyone turned toward him, no one with a more puzzled frown than the Dweorg's.

"Surely you don't think we should stand and fight?" said Abon.

Dayraven shook his head. "No. Not that. The cork and the bathtub."

The shaper squinted. "What about them?"

"We're the cork. Halion Sound is the tub. All we need to do is find a way out of it."

"And where might that be?"

"At Halion Sound's southern end there's only a narrow strip of land, beyond which lies the Great Sea."

"The Isthmus of Lod," said Sequara.

"Yes." Dayraven nodded. He was not certain the idea would work, but something had kindled the fight in him again. He needed to survive to honor Urd and Faldira's sacrifice. "How high and wide is it?"

Sequara's eyes narrowed. "At the eastern end of the isthmus the land's low and narrow, but even there it never quite succumbs to water, unless there's a strong storm."

"How wide is it, then?"

Sequara thought for a moment. "At high tide, perhaps a little over a thousand feet, and not much higher than sea level. Dayraven, what are you thinking?"

"The moon's full tonight, isn't it?" asked Dayraven.

"Yes," said Abon, "and there's a high tide coming. But you heard Lady Sequara. We can't sail over the strip of land, and this boat's too heavy to drag to sea before the Torrlonders make land. They'd be upon us before we moved out. That is, *if* we reach the Isthmus of Lod before their ships catch us."

Dayraven turned to Orvandil. "Make sure they don't catch us before the isthmus, and I'll take care of getting over it."

Sequara's eyes widened with comprehension. "Dayraven, is it possible? Do you have enough strength now to produce such a surge in the water?"

"One big wave's all we need to put us over the isthmus and into the Great Sea. We would leave the Torrlonders' large ships trapped behind in the sound. I can do it."

"What in damnation are you talking about?" Gnorn's eyes nearly popped out of his head. "If you mean to catch up this floating death-trap in some huge wave and deposit it into the Great Sea that never ends and has no bottom, then you can leave me on shore right over there!" He pointed his fat finger at the forested shoreline. "I'll be sure to greet the Torrlonders on your behalf as they sail by."

"No time for that," said Orvandil with a grim smile. "You'll have to stay on board with us." He turned to Dayraven. "Good plan. Boat might fall to pieces, but it's worth a try. They won't overtake us."

"Fall to pieces? Save me from these madmen!" said Gnorn as he gripped the boat's side even harder.

"Lady Sequara, please take the tiller," said Orvandil. Sequara moved to the stern while the Thjoth moved up and grasped one of two oars in the boat's bottom. "Keep us pointed south and slightly east, and hold that course," he bade her.

"Here." He handed the oar to Gnorn. "This'll keep you busy. Abon, give him a hand, and put your backs into it."

Fitting their oar into the oarlock, Abon and Gnorn sat next to each other on a bench on the port side while Orvandil and Dayraven took the other oar and rowed on the starboard side. Though Orvandil at times had to adjust the sail with ropes attached to the yard, they soon established a rhythm to their rowing that helped move the boat along.

But Torrlond's ships were still catching up. Dayraven centered his thoughts on the rowing to keep calm. He looked back once in a while, and every time he turned his head, the Torrlonders' sails had grown a little bigger. *We need to last till nightfall. Just a little longer.*

Time went by to the rhythm of the rowing. The oars creaked in their locks, splashed when they broke the plane of the water, and dripped as they rose. Creak, splash, drip. Creak, splash, drip. No one spoke as they focused their energy into their arms and backs. The four men were breathing hard. Unaccustomed to the oar's wood, Dayraven's hands stung with the chafing. He strained harder to keep their boat ahead, but the ships gained on them as the shoreline glided by. He glanced back. "Shit." Their large bows grew closer as they clove the water.

Sweat ran down his body. His arms and back burned and ached, but he and his companions did not slacken their pace. The sun began its descent to the west, which spurred him on. But the ships loomed so near that, when he looked back, he discerned human forms standing at the bows. *They think they'll have us soon. Not if I can help it.* He ignored painful blisters on his hands and clenched his jaw as he kept time with Orvandil. His breathing grew ragged, and he closed his eyes to focus on the rowing.

"Well," said Gnorn between heavy breaths, "at least this is good medicine for sea-sickness. I'd rather grip my axe than an oar any day, but it helps to give a fellow something to do."

"You may get to use your axe soon enough at the rate they're catching up," said Abon between grunts.

"Take heart," said Sequara. "We'll outlast them until night falls."

Dayraven perceived uncertainty, even fear, beneath her voice. *She disciplines herself well, better than I do, but I know her. I hope the spell works. Mustn't fail again.*

The sky darkened as the gloaming descended around them. Save for Orvandil, the men were gasping for breath. Dayraven's back was so stiff and his arms so sore he longed to change positions, but he could not stop for anything. He looked once more through the twilight. The ships were so near they would soon be within bowshot. *Just a little more. We need just a little more time.*

"How far's the southern shore now?" he asked Sequara in a hoarse voice.

"It's growing difficult to see, but I think we'll be there in little time," she answered from the stern. "You better begin soon."

Just as she finished speaking, whistling noises preceded several splashes not far behind them.

"Arrows!" cried Abon.

Dayraven looked at Orvandil. The Thjoth caught his glance and said, "I'll handle this side. Begin your spell."

Dayraven's cramped and blistered hands let go of the oar, and he moved to the boat's bow, where he sat on a bench. He calmed himself with deep, steady breaths and focused on the water. He tried to shut out everything else, but it was not easy to keep out awareness of the ships closing in behind. The cold breath of the elf-shard caressed his mind. He would need to draw from its power again. He told himself not to think about what happened the last time he siphoned more than a trickle of its energy. *This has to work.*

Sequara said, "It's not far ahead. The Isthmus of Lod."

More whishing sounds filled the air. At least fifty small splashes broke the water's surface a few feet behind them, and a pair of wooden thuds heralded two arrows biting into their boat.

"Everyone all right?" asked Sequara.

"For the time being," answered Abon.

"Give it everything," said Orvandil. "We're nearly there."

Furiously they rowed while Dayraven let go of himself. *Now. It must be now.*

Cutting his mind adrift into the realm of origins, he perceived only the water and brought himself below its surface. Deep, deep down went the waters of Halion Sound. Untold depths awaited him, a secret realm where the sun's light never reached. A cosmos unto itself, the great water made Dayraven see his own energy as a tiny speck amidst enormous splendor. Teeming with wonders it was, playful and strong, and more ancient than life that breathed on land. Its energy was far vaster than any waking creature's, and Dayraven realized he could influence this great water for only the briefest moment. A moment was all he needed.

The infinite presence of the elf-shard pervaded the water. It seemed at home there. Suppressing all the grief and guilt and fear of his earlier failure, Dayraven kept the impassive calm of one who walked in the realm of origins. He braced himself and called upon the energy the elf had inserted in him. It stirred and rushed outward from the sliver of glass in his mind, and he grasped ahold of it like a man leaping on a charging bull. He rode its power and felt it submit to his will. Drawing an even trickle of energy from the elf-shard, he sang one of the eldest of the songs of origin:

Shorunai parishwu ar ghanyon durgon,
Volunai ombharu mi khardyon rhandon.
Vuishway randillon di borhar haldunom,
Uronay angwillon im ghalnar dulardom.

How many times he repeated the song he did not know, but his connection to the water increased until it nearly absorbed his being. Then, with the flow of power from the elf-shard, he knew he could move it. A quick but strong stirring from the deepest depths of the sound. Far down Dayraven moved with the current as it lurched and swung up. Rushing upward, the water seemed eager to answer his call, as if it desired to reveal its power. Rising further, the enormous current grew in strength until it reached the swelling surface as a monstrous wave and rolled southward, gathering momentum like a lumbering giant.

Almost exhausted by the effort, Dayraven sensed the energy of the wave approaching. He severed the stream of power from the elf-shard, more than a little relieved that he had been able to contain it, and departed from the realm of origins. The elf-shard diminished to its customary whisper, brushing his mind with its dark tendrils. His eyes snapped open, and sweat ran down his brow. He released a long sigh. "I've unleashed the water's power."

When he shook away the remnants of his trance, Dayraven took his bearings. Their boat drew near the sound's end. The water was peaceful and even as it lapped the beach's sand. Though night had fallen, the white shoreline glowed just ahead under the moonlight.

Orvandil, Gnorn, and Abon splashed their oars in the water, but soon they could go no further.

Dayraven turned around and sought Sequara. A dozen arrow shafts protruded from various points in the boat. The sorceress's dark form crouched at the stern. Behind her, two huge ships loomed like great shadows about to swallow them. Four others came just behind them. They had slackened their sails and were rowing in for the kill, their oars smiting the water. The shouts and laughter of the men on board were full of confidence. They gloried and boasted as they cornered their prey.

A small wave hit the boat, rocking them slightly. Gnorn, Abon, and Orvandil stopped rowing.

Another small wave bumped them. Gnorn asked, "Is that it?"

"Ready bows!" came the command from Torrlond's ships. The creaking of yew followed. Dayraven prepared to unleash wizard's fire. He believed he had enough strength left for it. He sensed Sequara reaching for the gift as well.

A dull rumble arose. It grew louder.

A moment later, a mighty wall of water thundered, and the confident shouts of Torrlond's soldiers became screams of terror. Dayraven wondered if his plan was in fact as wise as it first seemed.

"Oh fuck," said Abon. "Fucking bloody fuck."

"It's a watery grave I'll have!" shouted Gnorn.

"Hold on!" Dayraven gripped the boat's side with one hand and the bench with the other.

A bellowing gust of wind tore at them just before the giant wave snatched their boat and tossed it into the air. The water's roar drowned out everything save Gnorn's long wail as their vessel pitched upward for what seemed far too long. Water sprayed Dayraven from all sides, and the wind threatened to tear him to pieces. In the darkness, only his hands clutching desperately to wood told him he was still in the boat.

Then they plummeted, and his stomach lurched upward. An image flashed in his mind of what would happen if the wave did not carry them far enough: the boat shattering and splintering to bloodied pieces on rocky land.

With a loud splash, water stung his face and soaked his body, and he tasted salt as he swallowed a mouthful. The impact jarred his body and sent him tumbling. Something hard jabbed into his back.

So much water surrounded him that, at first, he thought he had fallen into the sea. But the wooden strakes beneath him told him the boat had merely taken on water. It was still afloat, however, and in one piece. With salty, cold water sloshing around him, he got up on his hands and knees with a groan and looked about. Orvandil sat in front of him, still upright on the bench.

"Hoi!" shouted the Thjoth with uncustomary exuberance. "That was a wave such as I've not ridden in many a year. I die a happy man."

"Please don't just yet," said Dayraven. "Is everyone all right?"

"I'm fine," said Sequara as she sat up in the back of the boat with a hand on one hip. "A bit bruised."

"A thousand curses on all boats and those foolish enough to risk life and limb in them!" A pair of stout legs waved in the air. The rest of Gnorn's body flailed beneath his bench, and his face poked just above the water, some of which he spat out of his mouth. "Aaak! Put me on land at once!"

Dayraven realized with a start that Gnorn's bench was otherwise empty. The shaper was gone. "Abon!"

The others looked about the boat before scanning the dark water for any sign of the shaper. A moment later, something splashed only five yards or so behind them. A raspy voice gasped for air.

"Over here," said Orvandil, who grabbed the one oar remaining in the boat. He extended it into the darkness in the direction of the splashing. Abon swam towards them. The oar jerked, and the Thjoth pulled it back toward the boat. The vessel rocked when Orvandil reached over the side and pulled up the choking and dripping shaper. "My fucking harp! If it's damaged," he said to Dayraven between gasps, "I'll knock your fucking head off after I kiss it for saving our skins."

"Look," said Sequara. She pointed northward back at the Isthmus of Lod. The pale light of the rising full moon revealed the hulking ruins of all six ships that had chased them. Too large for the wave to carry them as far, the ships had knocked into one another and crashed on the isthmus, buckling and shattering a couple hundred feet from where Dayraven and the others floated in safety. A few faint groans and screams emanated from the wrecks.

"Let them gloat over us now," said Gnorn as he shook his fist at the wreckage. "Hey! Come get us!"

"Not too loud," said Orvandil. "More must be on the way. Let's sail north a bit before we make land on Yalawyn's eastern side. We stick close to shore tonight. The boat's damaged, and it's made for Halion Sound, not the Great Sea. I say we sail through the night, land for food in the morning. Then figure out how to leave Asdralad."

"Agreed," said Abon, "though, with the chase over, I'm feeling the hunger pinching."

"Let's take the tiller in shifts," said Dayraven. "The others can sleep while one of us steers."

"Sleep?" said Gnorn. "In this? I'm not a fish." The Dweorg pointed at the shin-deep bilge in the boat.

"Best start bailing," said Orvandil. "Use what you can find." He plucked Gnorn's helm from his head and put it in the Dweorg's hands. "This'll do."

At length, the five of them managed to remove most of the water, and Orvandil took the first watch at the tiller. The others lay down and tried to sleep, wet and shivering in the cooler night. Dayraven and Sequara lay next to one another with their heads toward the bow, while Abon and Gnorn lay with their heads pointed toward Orvandil, who sat at the stern.

Dayraven kept a respectful gap between him and the sorceress. But her shivering grew in intensity, and her teeth began to chatter. Gathering courage, he pondered how to propose coming together to preserve their body heat.

"Lie closer to keep warm," she whispered before he could get out a word.

"Yes. Alright."

They shuffled closer, and, lying on their sides, they faced each other. She was mere inches from him, and his breath caught at being so close to her. She closed the gap. A thrill ran through Dayraven when her body pressed against his, a response of his flesh that he observed even as it passed. She put her arm around his torso, and he rested his arm on top of her waist before covering them both with his brown robe. Since he was taller, she nestled her face against his chest. Breathing in her dark hair's scent, his throat tightened as he thought of how wounded and grief-stricken the formidable sorceress now seemed. The toll of the day's losses was beyond his mind's capacity to grasp, and the throbbing pain at his core threatened to steal his breath away, but he told himself that, for Sequara's sake, he must remain calm.

After a moment, using Faldira's training, he succeeded in relaxing his mind, and his body followed. Releasing his pent up breath, he let go of himself and embraced the comfort of Sequara's closeness. A girlhood memory of a late morning in bed with her mother flickered in his mind, and he smiled. The glimpses into her past were as fresh and vivid as ever, and at that moment he was grateful for them. Her warmth soothed him, and soon they ceased shivering. With her face beneath his, he stole a glance at her dark eyes. They were closed and peaceful. But even as he listened to her even breaths, he knew she held great sorrow within her. It was a sorrow he shared.

With a long sigh, he allowed his thoughts to linger on Urd, Faldira, and the many who perished that day. What if he had been able to control the elf-shard? He could have defeated Bledla and wrested the dragons from him. It would have changed the whole battle. So many lives spared. But it was too late. He had not controlled it. He had failed. And now, here he was with Sequara, like two orphans clinging to each other, adrift on the Great Sea. The distant waves breaking and moaning on shore seemed to speak of their isolation and loneliness.

Tears gathering in his eyes, Dayraven gazed up at the stars in the firmament above. The darkness between the stars brought to mind the elf-shard, whose cold breaths slithered and skimmed over his awareness.

But there were so many points of light up there. In the arc of brightness streaking across the middle, he recognized what his folk called Brynea, the River of Fire guarding the realm of the gods. As one vast field of life and energy he saw the flickering lights. *The same stars glow above the Mark.*

"Sublime," he murmured. "It's sublime."

"Yes," whispered Sequara.

They drifted to sleep in each other's arms.

THE HOLLOW PAIN IN DAYRAVEN'S BELLY PRODDED HIM AWAKE. Even more than usual, the elf-shard's whispers had cast a pall over his dreams. He willed away the lingering echoes of despair. Then he remembered. Worry for Imharr. The loss of Urd and Faldira hit him in the gut far harder than his nightmares could. It was a weight he could not shed. For a long while he lay still, but at last he summoned the courage to open his eyes.

In the greyness just before dawn, Sequara's beautiful face lay inches from his. Her eyes were closed and her breaths steady and slow. She still slept with one arm wrapped around him, prompting a sad and gentle smile from him.

The comfort of her presence pulled him away from the overwhelming despair. For a brief moment, he wished the morning could last longer to prolong their embrace, but he remembered his grief and his duty. Trying not to waken Sequara, he extricated himself with slow movements, leaving his brown robe covering her. Moving made him realize how sore and stiff he was, especially in his back and arms from the rowing, and from sleeping on the boat's hard planks. His hands still stung from the blisters.

As he got to his knees, Sequara stirred and groaned with a troubled frown on her face. He had never seen her looking so vulnerable save in her childhood memories, and for some reason he found this glimpse into her almost overwhelming. He swallowed and, stopping his hand as it reached out, repressed the desire to stroke her cheek to comfort her. Only with difficulty did he tug his gaze away from her. *We have great trials ahead. Keep focused. Balance and detachment.*

He looked up. Orvandil sat at the tiller. The Thjoth must have steered the boat through the night without waking anyone. He made his way aft, ducking under the sail and avoiding Gnorn and Abon's sleeping forms, until he reached the Thjoth. "You should have wakened one of us," he said quietly as he sat on a bench.

The Dweorg and the shaper snored.

"Look at those two sleeping babes." Orvandil smiled and nodded

THE PROPHET OF EDAN

toward Gnorn and Abon. "I've no heart to wake them. Besides, does me good to be at the tiller again. Reminds me of my roaming days."

"We're in for some roaming now. Where are we?"

"We sailed northward through the night along Asdralad's eastern shoreline. Soon we should make land and enter the forest of Yalawyn. In the light we'll find food and fresh water to fill our flasks. None of us has had anything to eat since yesterday morning, and there's been little enough to drink. We've had some hard labor since then."

Realizing how weak he felt, Dayraven agreed. "Sounds good. No need to wake the others yet, I suppose."

They approached a forested spur of land, behind which Dayraven guessed there lay a small bay.

Orvandil steered for it. "Looks good enough. We'll land after we pass this clump of trees."

The air was still, and the sun began its ascent above the horizon of the endless sea as they approached the spur of land. Bars of red, orange, and pink painted distant clouds. Dayraven looked out in awe at the reddish-orange sliver cresting the vast, grey body of water beneath it. Some said unknown lands waited out there. According to their lore, the Andumae came from one of them nigh two thousand years ago. The Ilarchae too came from other lands, cold and rough islands far in the north of the world. Only the Dweorgs had dwelled so long in Eormenlond that no one could say if they ever had any other home.

Dayraven turned forward as they passed the spur. As he had guessed, they approached a small bay with a narrow beach, behind which the forest formed a shadowy wall. A welcome haven for weary travelers.

But then his eyes followed the shoreline's curve to the other end, beyond which something made his heart fall. Three large ships sailing southward approached the bay's other side, and those on board had a clear view of their boat. He sat straighter as a chill clutched his spine.

"By the gods' mead," said Orvandil. "Torrlonders. How did they know?"

"Bledla's a wary foe. He foresees much." Dayraven knew it too well.

Orvandil frowned. "They likely sent ships around the island, and soldiers into the forest. They want to find us badly. Seems you made an impression."

"Now what?"

"Don't know. They've seen us. We could flee into the forest, but it may be filled with soldiers already. The open sea's a risk for us in this boat even if their ships weren't swifter. Either way, they'll corner us, and we'll have to fight."

In desperation, Dayraven gazed out at the endless body of water, wondering if it presented better odds than the forest. As if to crush any such hope, three more sails appeared on the horizon to the east. "More of them," he said to Orvandil as he pointed toward the sun. "Looks like we take our chances in Yalawyn." If it came to taking a stand, he had no doubt he and Sequara could kill many soldiers with wizard's fire. Recalling the Caergilese soldier he had slain in the Battle of Iarfaen, he had no desire to take more lives. But he would defend himself. They would be no easy prey. Still, with their numbers, it was only a matter of time before the Torrlonders would overcome them, and, though he did not feel the presence of the gift on those ships, Bledla was out there somewhere.

Orvandil held his hand over his brow as he looked toward the ships to the east. His expression changed to a grim smile. "Those are no ships of Torrlond." He looked at Dayraven. "This boat's done well enough thus far. Let's see how she handles the Great Sea."

"What do my ears hear?" demanded Gnorn as he shot up from sleep. "The Great Sea? Instead of, 'How about some nice breakfast on land that doesn't sway to and fro beneath us,' I waken to 'Let's float out on this piece of wood to our deaths'."

"We have company," said Orvandil, pointing to Torrlond's ships.

Gnorn squinted one eye and wrinkled his fat nose. "Can't we just head for land and have Dayraven produce another of those waves to greet the Torrlonders?"

"I'm afraid not," answered Dayraven. "Stirring a wave in the confines of Halion Sound is one thing, but the Great Sea's quite another. It's far too large for anyone to influence. Besides, Orvandil seems to know whoever's aboard those ships out there." He looked at the Thjoth. "Old friends?"

Orvandil shrugged. "Perhaps. Perhaps not."

By now Sequara and Abon had risen. The shaper peered out at Torrlond's approaching ships. "They don't give up easily, do they? Shall we row again?"

"Not with only one oar," answered Orvandil. "Rest your backs."

The Thjoth adjusted the sail then steered their boat to the open sea. Torrlond's three ships changed course toward them. Thus began another chase.

Fortunately for the small company, the Great Sea was relatively calm as the sun warmed the morning. Exhausted and weak, Dayraven put his hope in the ships Orvandil steered them towards. Every now and again, he glanced at the ships behind them, which grew larger while the land receded. Those in front began to diminish as they sailed further out to sea.

After a short time of pitching on the waves, Orvandil said to Dayraven, "Tie your kirtle to the oar and wave it."

Dayraven removed Sweothol's baldric then stripped bare to the waist. The morning sea breeze was cool on his flesh. After he fixed his white kirtle to the oar by the sleeves, he stood in the bow and twirled it on the end of the oar as high as he could. His sore arms grew tired, but he held it up as it rippled in the wind. At first, he wondered if those in the ships they pursued would even notice. But then, to his delight, it had the desired effect. "They're turning around."

Orvandil nodded. "Don't celebrate yet. Let me speak when we reach them."

"Wonderful," said Gnorn. "We're to rely on a Thjoth for diplomacy."

"Diplomacy?" said Orvandil with a frown, as if he had never heard the word. He followed with a wicked smile.

Gnorn rolled his eyes.

Dayraven untied his kirtle and dressed after collecting his robe from Sequara, and then he looked out once again. Tacking with great deftness, the ships skimmed toward them at a good pace. As the sun rose higher, he saw they were indeed different from those of Torrlond. Not quite as large, they were sleeker and more nimble. He guessed each of the clinker-built vessels with square sails was about ninety feet long and held at least fifty men. They rode the waves closer. The rudders near the sterns on the starboard sides grew visible, and a score of oars jutted out each side of the ships from oar ports. Just above the oar ports, on the outer side of the uppermost strakes, shield-battens held rows of round shields. Atop each vessel's prow was a carved dragon's head with mouth agape. When they came within shouting distance of the lead ship, Dayraven glanced behind. Torrlond's three ships still gave chase and would approach within little time.

The oars of the lead ship ceased rowing while men reefed its sail. The other two ships followed suit as an anchor dropped from the lead ship. Orvandil steered for the waiting vessel. A score of bowmen appeared over its side with arrows nocked and pointed toward the small boat. With the sun behind them, it was difficult to see their faces, but it seemed to Dayraven these men were of greater stature than most. He wondered if he and his friends had fled from something bad to something worse.

A tall man with blond hair and a long beard leaped up to the ship's bow. As he stood on the dragon's head, he shouted in a bass voice, "Most seamen flee my ships, yet you follow. Who are you that fly from the Torrlonders, and what do you want? Speak quickly."

"Not again," mumbled Abon, who put his hand on his bald head.

The man addressing them spoke in the Northern Tongue, but with an accent Dayraven recognized at once. *He sounds like Orvandil. These men are Thjoths.*

"Let me board and I'll tell you who I am," answered Orvandil. "Hyrstan vorra hvi tusan fjoran."

"Looks like a reunion," muttered Gnorn. "Hope it's a happy one."

"Thu?" answered the man on board, then he laughed deeply. "Kari thur hjallan, Orvandil!"

"Did he sound happy?" asked Gnorn.

"I couldn't quite make it out," whispered Dayraven.

Orvandil reefed their sail and steered their boat alongside the larger vessel with the remaining oar. When their boat bumped alongside the ship, two ropes and a rope ladder fell down to them. Upon securing their boat, Orvandil went up first, followed by Sequara, Abon, and Gnorn, who nearly fell in the water when grasping for the ladder and collapsed onto the deck of the Thjoths' ship with a crash and a grunt. As Dayraven climbed up last, he looked behind him. The Torrlonders' ships had almost reached them and had slackened their sails to come up close to the Thjoths.

A strong pair of arms attached to a bear of a man hauled Dayraven onto the ship. The men standing on deck were hardened warriors, the smallest of them a large man. Some had bright red hair and some brown, but most were blond and wore it long with full beards. Beneath their kirtles they wore byrnies, and their helms displayed images of boars, bears, and wolves. They held their weapons ready.

Orvandil spoke in Thjothic to the man who first addressed them, and Dayraven got a better look at him now. Not quite as tall as Orvandil, he was nevertheless a daunting spectacle. Dressed in war gear and wearing a long sword at his side, he appeared to have seen around forty winters. His eyebrows lowered over fierce blue eyes as Orvandil spoke. A moment later, the Torrlonders' ships dropped anchor.

"Men of Grimrik!" shouted a man with a red-crested helm from the Torrlonders' lead ship. "You have on board your ship fugitives from Torrlond and enemies of the Way. They are *our* captives. Surrender them to us, and no harm will come to you."

A chorus of laughter erupted from the Thjoths. The man Orvandil had spoken to gave a wolfish, teeth-baring smile. "Captives belong to those who capture them. If you want them, come and take them. *If* you think you can, little man!"

Bowmen on both sides nocked arrows while the Thjoths raised their axes, spears, and swords.

The captain of the Torrlonder ship glanced back toward Asdralad as if awaiting something. "Beware!" he shouted. "If you defy our orders, King Earconwald may conquer Grimrik next. Surrender the captives, and you keep our friendship."

"Torrlond has no friends," answered the Thjoths' leader. "Only lackeys. If you're too craven to fight, be off with you, or I'll board your ships and take them in payment for your arrogance after I feed your corpses to the fish. I give you to the count of ten."

The Thjoths' chieftain took a spear from a warrior next to him.

Heaving it back with his muscled arm, he leapt forward three steps, grunted, and cast it toward the captain's ship. The captain and his men ducked. The spear sailed over their heads and thumped into the ship's mast, in which it lodged and quivered. Dayraven awed at the distance of the cast. The Torrlonders murmured among themselves.

With one last look toward the island and then back toward the Thjothic ships, the captain ordered his men to weigh anchor and make taut the sail while the oarsmen turned the ship around. The other two ships of Torrlond followed suit, and the captain disappeared below deck.

When the Torrlonders began their retreat toward Asdralad, Orvandil said, "They'll come back once they've found more of their ships."

"Let them come," said the Thjoths' chieftain. "We'll be long gone, and those sluggards could never catch my girls." He slapped the neck of the dragon's head on the prow and took a good look at Sequara, winking at her as he smiled broadly. "But now, what should I do with my *captives?*" The Thjoths laughed.

Sequara was composed as she stared back, but Dayraven saw the anger in her eyes.

Gnorn looked at Dayraven and said, "Not sure I like his tone."

"Neither am I," answered Dayraven, who gritted his teeth as the Thjoths gazed at Sequara. He thought of reaching for the gift, but Orvandil turned and shook his head as he looked in Dayraven's eyes. Dayraven understood and nodded.

Orvandil stepped forward. "As a free Thjoth, I stand as pledge of safety to my companions. Anyone who wants to claim them must fight me first, unless he's a coward."

The Thjoths went silent, but their leader smiled and stepped closer to Orvandil. "Very well. But what will you fight with?" He glanced at Orvandil's empty scabbard. "You have no sword."

Orvandil smiled in return. "I broke it splitting open an aglak's neck. I won't need a sword to do the same to you."

"An idle boast. Let's see." Steel whispered when the leader unsheathed his sword and leapt toward Orvandil, who backed up a pace. The rest of the men cleared a space on deck for the two now squaring off. Even those on the other two Thjothic ships gazed at the unfolding spectacle.

Gnorn reached for his axe, but Dayraven put his hand on the Dweorg's arm. "No. He knows what he's about." At the same time, he glanced at his sword in its scabbard. Without a second thought, he unsheathed Sweothol and shouted, "Orvandil! Here's a blade fit for you!"

He tossed Sweothol to Orvandil, who turned to catch the sword by the hilt with his left hand. The Thjoths' leader took advantage of the moment Orvandil looked away and swung his sword. But Orvandil anticipated the move. He ducked under the blow and hurled his right fist into his opponent's stomach. Such a blow would have leveled most men. But this was not most men, and his byrny took much of the impact even as he grunted.

"You're old and slow," said Orvandil as they separated and faced off again.

"And you're as weak as a little girl. My youngest daughter's hit me harder."

They rushed at each other again, exchanging sword blows and parrying with rapid clangs. The leader came down hard with his blade, but Orvandil caught his wrist. At the same time, the chieftain grasped Orvandil's sword hand. They struggled for a moment as they growled at each other. Orvandil pushed his opponent backward, but then the man let go and thrust his helm into Orvandil's face with a crack. They separated. Blood trickled from Orvandil's nose.

"Now you look prettier," said the chieftain.

Orvandil smiled fiercely and rushed forward, raining sword blows on his opponent, who parried deftly but stepped backward. Sweothol flashed in Orvandil's hand as the blades rang out. The Thjoth's skill with the weapon took Dayraven's breath away, though his opponent's skill was not much less. Notwithstanding the man's prowess, Orvandil had him in retreat. When the chieftain's back was almost to the ship's side, he grabbed a shield and heaved it at Orvandil like a discus. Orvandil backed a pace and swung Sweothol, which, with a loud crack, split the linden shield in halves that thudded and rocked on the deck.

"Not bad," said the leader.

"Quit running away, and you'll see more."

The leader leapt forward and struck a series of blows at Orvandil, who parried and backed away in turn.

"Enough play," said Orvandil. He returned even harder blows, and Sweothol sang. The dueling Thjoths' movements became a blur that Dayraven could not follow. Steel rang. The two sweating men grunted. Dayraven's mouth hung open. He was not certain if it was more frightening or beautiful.

The chieftain appeared hard set as he backed off. Orvandil maneuvered him back against the ship's side to the gap where he had taken the shield from. The bigger man yelled as he swung down. The leader's sword came up to deflect the blow, but Sweothol shattered it in pieces that clinked on the deck. In a flash, Orvandil's free fist delivered a punch that snapped the chieftain's head back. Before his dazed opponent recovered, Orvandil dropped Sweothol and grabbed the man's ankles in one swift motion. Growling and swinging the feet up, Orvandil toppled the wide-eyed chieftain head first over the ship's side. A moment later came a splash. The Thjoths broke out in laughter.

One threw a rope over the side. When it went taut, several of them hauled their leader up. Not much later, the bedraggled chieftain came up dripping but laughing. His nose bled like Orvandil's. As he wiped it with a cloth one of his men handed him, he said, "You broke my last spare sword, but I think that was the longest I've lasted against you since you were a lad."

"Only because I've not eaten in more than a day," answered Orvandil.

"Ah, and I thought you were being gentle. But we'll soon remedy your hunger," said the leader as the two men laughed and embraced each other. "Byran mota, nu hjolan skaft utord!" At his command, men aboard all three ships scrambled to weigh anchor and set sail. After the tension of the fight, Dayraven breathed a sigh and smiled at the strange greeting between old friends he had witnessed.

With his arm around the man's shoulders, Orvandil brought the dripping wet chieftain to Dayraven and the others while the three ships tacked to sail eastward.

"Friends," said Orvandil. He handed Sweothol back to Dayraven, who sheathed the sword knowing he would never be able to make it sing as Orvandil had. "Here is my kinsman: Vols, King of Grimrik."

"King?" said Dayraven. "But..."

King Vols grinned at his surprise. "We Thjoths are not given to such ceremony as you outlanders are. Among us, a king is one of the folk. He works and fights as all other warriors do, or he's no true leader."

"It's so among my people too," answered Dayraven. Against all probability, he felt he could grow to like this man. He sensed beneath the laughter a shrewd mind. "But we didn't know Orvandil was kinsman to Grimrik's king."

Vols looked sidelong at Orvandil. "Cousin Orvandil keeps his secrets."

Dayraven smiled at his tall friend. "A man of few words is oft a man of great deeds. I'm Dayraven of the Mark, your Majesty."

"Hardy folk dwell in that kingdom, as I hear," returned Vols. "If they're as strong as the blade you loaned my cousin, they're hardy folk indeed."

"This," said Orvandil, "is Abon of Ellond, greatest of shapers. But I hear you've had the good fortune to host him before."

"Indeed," said the Thjoths' king as he gazed on Abon with a grin. "It seems the gods do not wish you to part from our company, friend shaper."

Abon winced. "It seems so, your Majesty."

"You'll lighten our journey with a new tale or two, then." It was not a question.

"It will be my pleasure to play for you again," said Abon with a forced smile and a nod.

"And I," said Gnorn, who stepped forward with his arms crossed in front of him and a frown on his face, "am Gnorn, Dweorg of the Fyrnhowes."

King Vols' eyes widened as he beheld Gnorn. "One of our ancient foes. You declare yourself boldly, Gnorn of the Fyrnhowes, but I marvel that you travel with my cousin, who should be your rightful foe."

The Dweorg cleared his throat and cocked his bearded chin up, doing his best to look dignified before the descendant of the man who ruined his people. "Though your ancestors slew us and drove us from our homes, I've learned some of your folk's virtues through your kinsman. Perhaps I'll come to learn more."

"Well said," answered Vols as he inclined his head. "I see wisdom is a virtue of the Dweorgs."

"And," said Orvandil, "this is Lady Sequara, Asdralad's rightful queen since Faldira has perished." He bowed his head.

King Vols looked over Sequara before he smiled roguishly and bowed in turn. "Queen Sequara, I beg your pardon for any offense."

"None taken," she answered proudly. "But I ask you not to address me with such title. Not until I've freed my kingdom from Torrlond will anyone call me queen."

Vols bowed again. "As you wish. You bring heavy news, though I already guessed about Asdralad's fall. We were sailing off Adanon's coast when we spotted Torrlond's fleet on its way west. We followed to discover their doings."

"What brought you near Adanon? Were you raiding?" asked Orvandil.

The king of the Thjoths grinned. "It was no simple raid. In truth, it was the shaper who convinced me to voyage there." He nodded at Abon.

Abon put his hand on his chest. "Me?"

Vols turned to him. "In addition to gracing us with your tales, you told us many things during your time with us. Enough things to start me thinking. I wanted to see for myself what the Torrlonders were doing. We Thjoths might want to take an interest in Torrlond's war."

"Will you fight them? Will the Thjoths join in the war?" asked Dayraven.

Vols looked at him, and his eyes narrowed. "That is not my decision to make alone. For now, we watch. We didn't approach the blockade Earconwald set before Halion Sound, but it was easy to see their purpose. Just now we're on our way east to resupply our ships on Firdal. You must tell me how you passed the blockade without being captured."

At that moment one of Vols' men approached with food and drink for the companions. "Ah, but speaking comes later," said the king. "Now, you must eat. I fear I have nothing more comfortable to sit on than our benches."

"That'll do just fine," said Gnorn. "Never thought I'd want to dine while pitching to and fro on the waves, but starvation has a way changing one's point of view."

"Truer words were never spoken. Are you content to sail east with us, then?"

"In fact," answered Sequara, "we must journey east to Glirdan, Sundara's chief city. There we'll join those who oppose Torrlond's conquest of Eormenlond. You would do a great service in conveying us. You may also learn more to help you decide the best course for Grimrik in the coming war, which will consume all of Andumedan. The Thjoths would be valiant allies, and Torrlond's rulers will leave no kingdom unthreatened. We of Asdralad have learned the terrible truth of this."

King Vols nodded. "We'll take you to Glirdan. As for the rest, I make no promises. Later. We'll discuss such things at the right time. Now, eat and thank whatever gods you pray to that you breathe fresh air and feel sunlight on your skin."

The friends sat down to their meal. Such simple fare as mead, dry bread, and salted meat never tasted so good. Afterwards, Vols brought them below deck, where they slept in hammocks. Even Gnorn fell asleep without a word. As he lay down, Dayraven looked at Sequara, who closed her eyes. *We're tired, not least from our grief. But now we may rest. Orvandil's people would be strong allies. We must win the Thjoths' aid. Vols is cautious, though he may seem reckless. For now, we're safe.* With such thoughts Dayraven too succumbed to a deep, long sleep that he shared only with the murmuring elf-shard.

14

ORIGINS

Evening approached when Vols bade his three ships to land and resupply on the island of Firdal, the southernmost of the Isles of Yaladir. The Thjoths sent out men for fresh water and game, seeking the beautiful but flightless birds inhabiting the island. Dayraven knew the birds with iridescent feathers and long, graceful necks were sacred to Asdralad's people, but he and Sequara said nothing. He looked at her when the Thjoths presented the smoking carcasses on spits to their guests first. Her nod said everything: *Take and eat — we need these people.* As they sat around a crackling fire on the beach and ate with Gnorn, Abon, and Orvandil, he gazed at Sequara and realized she would sacrifice almost anything for her duty, and for Asdralad's welfare.

With a smile far too charming for a barbarian, King Vols approached the five companions while they finished their meal. "Friends. I hope you feel rested and well fed. Orvandil has told me of your ordeal. We'll finish our business here then depart before dark. We mustn't tarry. From what Orvandil said, I deem the Torrlonders will be looking hard for you."

As Vols glanced at him, Dayraven saw wariness behind the leader's eyes. *This one's no fool*, thought Dayraven.

THE PROPHET OF EDAN

"But for now," continued the king of the Thjoths, "eat and enjoy." He looked at Abon, who had finished his meat and was cleaning his harp. "Our feast lacks only one thing: Master shaper, sing a tale for us, if you will. Most of my men with us today understand the Northern Tongue well enough to follow."

Abon bowed. "My lord, as you wish."

The shaper began tuning his harp. The Thjoths, who were eating or picking their teeth with their daggers, gathered around as soon as they heard Abon plucking and tightening the strings. By the time he looked up, Abon had an audience of nearly one hundred fifty burly Thjoths talking and laughing as they sat around him on the sandy beach. When he finished tuning, the shaper looked up and grinned.

His hands leapt to the strings, his fingers flitting faster than anyone could follow. Sweet was the harp's trembling. Silence spread over the throng as the shaper warmed up his voice with a chant that featured a snaking and flowing rhythm. The music's rapture flooded Dayraven as he peered around at the Thjoths. They had all stopped eating. Many of them stared with jaws agape and eyes wide. One sat open-mouthed with the point of his forgotten dagger still stuck in his teeth. Abon looked around, and Dayraven knew he and the rest would follow where the shaper took them.

Plucking the strings with one hand, Abon kept the rhythm alive. A cunning smile crossed his face. He pointed at his jagged scar with his free hand and said, "I'll play the song that earned me this pretty face." The Thjoths chuckled and then quieted down when he continued.

"It's a song of ancient things, of the old gods all the folk of Ellond and Torrlond and the Mark once worshipped, the gods you Thjoths worship still under names not so different. I sang it once in Ellond, and followers of the Way heard me. They found me afterwards and cut me to pieces, leaving me for dead. And dead I would have been, had someone not saved my life. You see, the followers of the Way hate the old gods and seek to destroy the old lore. They'll stop at nothing until all of Eormenlond's kingdoms fall under their mastery and worship only Edan. But our ancestors passed down sacred wisdom in their stories of the gods. We'll never forget, or allow others to erase our memories."

As the shaper again chanted the rhythm, Dayraven thought, *clever, Abon. Make them see the Way threatens them as well.*

Then Abon launched into song:
Deep was the darkness ere the dawn of all things,
Vacant was the void, without voice, without form,
Silent and still, without sorrow, without joy,
Ere the frost, ere the fire, ere the firmament was made.
But in the gap there grew the ground of all worlds,
Tallest of trees, towering forever,
Oldest of oaks, the origin of life,
Long are its limbs, Laeroth is it hight.
Know we that nine is the number of its branches,
One for each world, whose waters are its dew.
Where reach its roots none reckon among men,
The living may not learn their length nor their end.
A bud then bulged on a branch of the tree,
A monstrous mass, a mound it became,
Wondrous was its weight as the winters passed,
Five hundred followed by four hundred more.
Inside of it slept the serpent of the air,
The worm awaited 'til her wakening should come,
The dragon dreamed 'til she drove her way out,
Then the lingworm leapt from Laeroth at once!
Hringvolnir was she hight, huge and cunning,
Fierce was the fire that flamed from her jaws,
The winds of the worlds her wings set forth,
Her clutching claws clove to the tree.
Hungry was Hringvolnir, in her heart greed gnawed,
Eager to eat, she eyed the old oak,
The branch that birthed her she broke with her teeth,
She fed on the first-born, the fount of life.
Her yearning never yielded, for years she devoured,
And her belly grew big, like a barrow it swelled
With the murderers of mortals, all monsters are her kin,
Until burst forth her brood, the bane of mankind.
From her sides they slithered, bringing sickness and disease,

With their dame they delved and dug in the tree,
Greedily grasping and gulping it down,
They shattered away shards. Then shook the oak.
It creaked and cracked. A crevice formed
In the trunk of the tree, where the tribe of the gods
Abode 'til their birth. From the bole they came forth,
Nine was their number, from the gnarled one they broke.
Arose then Regnor, the ruler and first-born,
The husband of Hruga beheld the great dragon
And the myriad monsters that marred the tree,
The wielder of wisdom, he wist the cure.
The lofty one asked Logan, the lord of fire,
To work a weapon to wield against the beast,
He bade him bring the bolt of heaven
To fling at the fierce one, with flames destroy her.
Ready was Regnor, his rede he made known:
He bade the bold one, Bolthar the strong,
To stand before the serpent and summon her to battle,
To drive the dragon to a dreadful wrath.
The bane of the bull, Bolthar the mighty,
He leapt toward the lingworm, laughing in his heart,
His message was not meek, nor his manner timid
When he defied the fiend to fight for her life.
In her rage she roared and reached for the god,
In mind to maul him with her monstrous teeth
And set fire to his flesh. She flung wide her mouth,
The gigantic jaws jarred the nine worlds.
But ready was Regnor, the ruler of the gods,
He was fain to let fly the fiery bolt,
With his thews he threw the thunderous weapon,
It streaked in the serpent, straight down the throat.
The greedy one gulped, grim was her end,
When the bolt reached her belly, it burst in the worm,
The flesh of the fire-drake flew into pieces,
Little did the ling-worm her last meal enjoy . . .
The shaper continued the song of creation, telling how the brood

of creatures the dragon Hringvolnir spawned had fled from the gods and hid in dark, secret places, whence they haunt humankind. They await their vengeance that will come with the nine worlds' dissolution and the gods' end.

He sang of how the gods built the nine worlds on the oak tree Laeroth with the primal dragon's flesh and bones, from which they wrought the lands, and her blood, which became the seas. With his great strength, Bolthar lifted up the mountains and high places of the worlds, whereas the goddess Dyna created all trees, plants, and growing things. With the worlds established, the gods fashioned creatures to inhabit them. Halmar made the sea's creatures, and Regnor and Hruga made those that dwell on land. The goddess Glora infused in all creatures the desire to procreate, thus ensuring their continuation. Then they assigned realms to themselves. Regnor ruled the skies, Halmar the seas, Dyna the forests, Bolthar the mountains. Syn, goddess of ice and cold, took to herself the frozen netherworld of hell, whereas Logan, the god of fire, kept to the flames beneath the earth, where he forges weapons for the gods.

Last of all, the gods made humankind, women and men. The god Regnor shaped them from clay, and the goddess Hruga breathed life into them. But it was the lone god, Sithfar, who brought the gods' children to their world, designating places and kingdoms and teaching wisdom, songs, and runes. And Sithfar will lead each individual on their final journey, back to the void that was before the oak tree Laeroth, a place of which the ancient songs speak little.

Such was the story of creation Abon sang. The Thjoths knew it from childhood, but every one of the big warriors sat entranced until the shaper finished, after which they roared in approval.

To judge by his smile, the tale pleased King Vols. The leader rose and slipped a large, ornate arm-ring of silver with gilded knot patterns off his arm, after which he unsheathed his sword. Placing the arm-ring around the blade, he extended the weapon over the fire and gazed at the shaper.

Knowing the correct response to complete the ancient ritual, Abon set his harp down and rose to his feet. Facing the king from the other side of the fire, the shaper drew his weapon and positioned the point opposite Vols' sword tip. The king raised his hilt to slide the arm-ring onto Abon's blade. It whined as it skimmed along the steel and rang when it hit the sword's cross-guard.

Having presented this gift, Vols declared, "Such a song's worthy of more, yet I give what I have at the moment. Let this ring be the sign of my oath: No one may harm this man without bringing down my vengeance. We are bound. You have honored us with your lore, shaper."

Abon bowed to the king as he accepted the gift by slipping it off his sword and onto his arm. "The honor's mine, my lord. I accept this gift. We are bound."

The Thjoths cheered again, and then King Vols gave orders to sail. It was nearly dark when the five companions found themselves waiting on the beach around the fire as the Thjoths readied their ships.

"Well, the song pleased them," said Gnorn. The Dweorg looked across the fire at Orvandil and asked, "You suppose King Vols will agree to fight against Torrlond?"

Orvandil took a deep breath. "Hard to say. Vols wants to join us. He's a wise man. But a king among the Thjoths is not the same as a king among other folk. He must win them over. Grimrik's folk are keen in warfare, but they stand on their own. They've never allied themselves to anyone. One thing's certain: The Thjoths must fight Torrlond at some time. Vols must show them this."

"How?" asked Abon. "There's little time before the war reaches the east."

Orvandil answered, "It will take time. But once the Thjoths act, no one is swifter to reach a battle. Vols will call a folkmoot. He has asked me to help make our case. I don't know if I'll be of any use. It's been long since I left."

Dayraven wondered why Orvandil had departed from Grimrik, drifting as a mercenary and fighting for others when he was an honored kinsman of the king. He sensed some hidden pain. Sharing a story among friends was one way to ease old wounds. So, as the world beyond their little fire darkened, he asked, "Why did you leave? Your cousin loves you, as do the other men."

Orvandil hesitated. "Not all in Grimrik love me." He sighed before continuing. "I left of my own will . . . It was long ago, another life."

"We're all living other lives now," said Sequara.

The Thjoth nodded and scratched his blond beard, gazing at the sputtering flames with his keen eyes. "When I was not much older than you, Dayraven, I loved a certain woman. A noblewoman among our people. My foster-brother, Thioldolf, loved her too. Since childhood we three had been companions. One day we two realized the other loved her, and that poisoned our friendship. We quarreled, and she made peace between us for a time. Then, at a feast, Thioldolf and I both grew drunk. We made challenges and swore oaths. According to our people's custom, we agreed to duel. *Holmgang*, we call it. We swore to meet on the island of Vargholm and fight to the death. She forbade us, saying she'd never wed the victor, but we'd made our oaths.

"What more is there to say? You see me here now, and Thioldolf's no more. Neither of us wanted to fight when the time came, but we had spoken the oaths, and we were fools, full of pride. I slew my foster-brother on Vargholm. Afterwards, I burned his body on a pyre and built a mound around it. Then I returned home. For a long time I thought him the luckier, for she kept her word and wedded another. I had nothing but his blood on my hands. Since we had followed the customs, it was not murder and his family could do nothing to avenge him. My life was not in danger, but it was bitter. I had no wish to stay near reminders of happiness that fled from me."

The companions were silent. The Thjoth looked up. "That's why I left."

"Perhaps," said Sequara, "it's time for you to return."

"Yes," answered Orvandil. He glanced at Sequara. "It's been too long. I'll go back to Valfoss and the Mjothelf that runs nigh it. I might do some good there now."

"Long ago, my people had a different name for that river and the hills you call the Fyrnhowes," said Gnorn. The fire crackled. Its shadows flickered across his face.

Orvandil looked across the fire at the Dweorg. "Sorry, my friend. That's another wrong I can't put right."

Gnorn smiled and his large eyes glittered. "No matter. In our own small way, you and I will put it right as we fight side by side. We have much to do. But for the moment, let's see if your friends need a hand loading their ships. I feel myself warming up to sea travel now."

"Now, there's something new," said Abon with raised eyebrows.

Gnorn, Orvandil, and Abon rose and strode toward the three beached ships. Dayraven was about to follow, but Sequara stayed seated next to the fire with a pensive frown across her face. He sat down again and waited.

She looked absently at the fire's last, sputtering tongues of flame. "It's strange. The tale he told of his love for the woman . . . what passion does when it rules us. It can even make us betray those dearest to us." She looked in Dayraven's eyes, and he gazed back at her beautiful face glowing in the ruddy light.

He cleared his throat, trying to answer calmly. "That sort of love lies behind many of the greatest tales. It creates and destroys. In Abon's song, it's the gift and curse of the goddess Glora. You and I wouldn't be here without it. Nothing would."

Sequara's eyes widened as she stared at Dayraven. She looked down abruptly at the glowing embers. "You're right. But it's an invitation to loss and sorrow."

"Yes, of course."

He too stared at the dying embers as they went black and smoked. At length, he said, "Perhaps we should join the others. They must be nearly ready to sail." Though he managed to control his voice, he was glad she could no longer see his face in the twilight.

THEY JOURNEYED OVER THE GREAT SEA BY NIGHT, TRUSTING IN THE Thjoths' seamanship. Morning came, and Dayraven grew to respect the courage of the men who sailed the foamy-necked dragon ships over the waves. No other folk of Eormenlond dared venture out as far as the Thjoths did into the Great Sea. They sailed night and day and manned the ships in shifts. Two days passed, fair and sunny, but the sky turned iron grey on the third. That night, a storm hammered down on them.

If Dayraven had admired the tall warriors' courage before, their reaction to the lashing rain and huge waves tossing the ships convinced him they were in fact all fey. The ships pitched up and down mountainous swells. The wind roared through darkness and drove stinging sea-spray. Flashes of jagged lightning illuminated the night, unveiling intermittent images of the ghastly, turbulent seascape. And the laughing Thjoths shouted and rejoiced at staring death and chaos in the face. Tiny and frail their ships seemed on the vast, angry waters. Dayraven feared they would not hold together while cresting the waves' dizzying heights and plummeting into their cavernous valleys. The elf-shard's cold shadow-whisper grew more insistent, as if it yearned toward the dark depths of the sea.

Dayraven was not the only one who worried. Gnorn grew more miserable than ever, shouting his regret that he was foolish enough to forget the evils of all ships and swearing over the howling wind he would never budge from the first rock he might cling to.

But the harsh weather passed. When daylight returned, Dayraven was astonished to see the three ships had not only weathered the storm, but also had stayed not far from one another and on course. On the fifth day, Orvandil assured Gnorn he would by eventide find his legs on steady land. "The greater part of the Gulf of Bahan lies behind us. We'll make Glirdan before dark falls, my friend."

"Not a moment too soon," said Gnorn. "Though I've no idea how you know where we are or where we're heading. All I see is endless water in every direction. It's enough to drive anyone to madness. For all I know, you and your barmy friends have taken us to the world's outlands, where demons and monsters rule."

It was not long before they spotted land in the distance: Sundara's shoreline rising above blue waters and glistening in late afternoon sunlight. A rocky, golden-brown landscape tinged with clusters of green pastures and trees took form. This, reflected Dayraven, was the coast the Andumae had seen from their ships when they first approached Eormenlond seventeen hundred years before, when only the Dweorgs dwelt in the hills and dragons ruled the lands. At length, the city's domes and spires took shape, glistening atop a large ness jutting out into the sea. As they sailed closer, the buildings largely wrought of white marble beneath red-tiled roofs grew more distinct in their details. He sighed at how much the place put him in mind of Asdralad's chief city of Kiriath, yet Glirdan was larger and twice as old.

The Thjoths reefed their sails and rowed nigh the docks at the city's feet. Dayraven looked up at the stately columns of ancient buildings, some more than a thousand years old. To him, the antique city exuded splendor and decay, like a hoar old man whose youthful deeds lent him the air of greatness. He sensed the footsteps of countless generations that had lived and died in this storied place. Of all the cities of Eormenlond, only Sundara's second city of Tinubor could claim a similar age. With awe and reverence Dayraven beheld Glirdan, chief city of Sundara.

But he also sensed the indifference in the elf-shard's dark murmurs. Mortals' little attempts to change the world around them were fleeting scars on the landscape. Nothing more. They might dignify their efforts with the names of cities and kingdoms and record their histories as if they mattered, but their names and the very stones they built them of would all disappear as if they never were. He shuddered and returned to the present, trying to recapture his awe for the old city.

As the three Thjothic ships docked with white flags aloft in token of peace, the stares of Glirdan's dark-haired citizens and dockworkers showed their astonishment. The merchants and other citizens wore long, colorful garments like those among Asdralad's wealthier people, while the workers wore shorter, plainer clothes of white and grey. More stopped what they were doing to view the spectacle of the dragon ships and the burly northern warriors aboard them. They murmured amongst themselves in the local form of Andumaic. Dayraven found he could understand most of what he heard, though the accent was strange to his ears. Many of the comments were not flattering toward the feared Thjoths, so he deemed it best not to translate.

One figure stood out among the crowd: an old man with a long white beard, long white hair, and fair skin. At first, the old man reminded Dayraven of Bledla, and he nearly recoiled at the vision of the supreme priest. But the vision changed and softened, and he realized the old man rather seemed in some way like Urd. Clad in a tattered brown robe with worn patches of sundry colors sewn on the elbows and other frayed places, he was not so tall and imposing as

PHILIP CHASE

Bledla. Beneath the brown robe, he wore a long garment of white that nearly came down to his leather sandals. The old man's kind eyes and his smile erased the last of Dayraven's fears even as he sensed the gift dwelling in him in greater measure than in any he had ever met save Bledla. He needed no one to tell him this man who waited for them at Glirdan's docks was none other than Galdor of Ellond, the wizard that Urd had wanted him to journey to when he was exiled from the Mark, another life ago.

"My lord!" called out Abon as seamen leapt out of the ships to tie hawsers to the dock and secure the gangplanks. "It's good beyond words to see you."

Realizing the Thjoths were no threat, Glirdan's citizens dispersed and returned to their business, though many continued to cast wary looks toward the foreign ships and their sailors.

The wizard Galdor approached. "Ah, Abon. You've arrived. I thought you might be on one of these ships. Though Asdralad's fleet comes not in your wake, you seem to have made friends along the way."

Abon walked down the gangplank with King Vols striding close behind. "Alas, my lord, that fleet will never come." The shaper gestured toward the Thjoths' ruler. "But these are friends, indeed. I present Vols, King of the Thjoths. We owe our lives to him and his men." The shaper turned to Vols. "Your Majesty, I present my master, the wizard Galdor of Ellond."

Galdor raised one eyebrow as he looked at Abon. "You bring grave news, though I confess I feared it already. But let greetings come first, as is fitting." He turned to the Thjoths' leader. "King Vols," said the old man with a smile, "it's an honor to meet you. Many are the tales that mention the prowess of your warriors and ships." The wizard glanced at the three Thjothic vessels, stroking his beard and narrowing his eyes as he examined them with more than passing curiosity.

Vols laughed. "Not all the tales are good, I'd wager. But it's an equal honor to meet the great wizard Galdor. I too have heard a tale or two of you. Yet a wise man heeds tales little when he has the man before him to take his measure."

"Spoken like a true king. I serve a good king, so I may know another when I see him."

"Yet, if what I hear is sooth, King Fullan of Ellond will soon march with your foes among Torrlond's troops."

Galdor's brow furrowed and he nodded. "We'll speak of that this evening if you'll join us in council with King Tirgalan after we dine."

Vols smiled. "It will be my pleasure."

Abon next introduced Orvandil and Gnorn to Galdor, who thanked the Thjoth and the Dweorg for their service to Asdralad and to their cause. "Queen Faldira's messengers have oft spoken your praise. You've done much for us."

"And we hope to do more," said Gnorn. "But, alas, that queen of whom you speak is no longer with us." The Dweorg's head bowed.

The wizard Galdor sighed. "From afar I saw glimmerings of these tidings. Asdralad's ruin reached my dreams. Yes, I have feared for these last few days as I waited for you. Yet do not despair, friends."

Then came Sequara, who smiled sadly at the old wizard. She tried to speak, but the words stuck in her throat.

Galdor lifted his arms. "Come, my child." Tears welled in the old man's eyes. The sorceress embraced him and shook with grief, her sorrow pouring out.

Gnorn, Orvandil, Abon, and even Vols looked down. The Thjoths all looked away or pretended to busy themselves in other conversations.

Dayraven watched as he held back his own tears. *Had I not failed . . . Had I defeated Bledla, maintained control over the elf-shard's power, this grief never would have been.*

With Sequara still in his arms, Galdor turned towards Dayraven. Tears trickled down the old man's wrinkled cheeks, but he kept his gentle smile. "Come here, Dayraven."

At first, Dayraven looked down as his legs froze in place. He forced them to walk to the old man and Sequara. Once again he looked at Galdor, who winked at him as if he were about to play a prank.

Something strange about the old man struck Dayraven, but he could not put words to it. The wizard seemed of the earth and yet unbound, as if he came from nowhere in particular and could call anywhere home. He said to Dayraven, "You and I might have met long ago. But that was not meant to be. Others undertook the task of training you, and they've done well. Perhaps I'm meant to teach you something else. Let's see."

Dayraven blinked as he looked into the old man's intense green eyes beneath his bushy white eyebrows. He was able to breathe more deeply as peace gathered inside him. Even the shadow of the elf-shard's whisper lifted a little. He was surprised to realize he was smiling back at Galdor, who put one hand on Dayraven's shoulder as he held Sequara with his other arm like a grandfather. The connection he felt with the old wizard was immediate and deep. Galdor was one who imbibed the beauty and sorrow all around him. The old man understood him. His presence was a comfort.

"Don't torture your mind with what might have been," said the old wizard. "What has happened will bear fruit you know nothing of yet, and may never know. Fate ever goes as it must."

Dayraven nodded.

"But now," declared Galdor as he turned toward the others, "it's time to bring weary guests to dinner, and then we may discuss our losses and what we'll do."

Vols bade his men to find their meal and supplies for a long voyage. Their leader followed the wizard Galdor through Glirdan's cobbled streets along with Abon, Sequara, Orvandil, Gnorn, and Dayraven to the palace of King Tirgalan of Sundara.

GALDOR CHATTED WITH VOLS AT THE FRONT OF THE PARTY, occasionally pointing out landmarks and speaking of the excellent quality of last year's grapes. While he followed and soaked in the living history all around him, Dayraven wished destiny had brought him to stay longer in Glirdan. It was a city with much to teach him, the very stones whispering of elder days. Its dark-complexioned citizens in their colorful garb gave nervous glances or stared openly at the strange party on its way to King Tirgalan's palace, which waited on a hill near the top of the ness.

As they proceeded, Sequara fell in next to Dayraven. She managed a fragile smile, behind which he sensed her raw grief. "Long ago, the people who came to dwell in Asdralad sailed from Sundara. Were it not for my longing to restore my island, I could wish to settle here and forget about all wars."

Dayraven smiled in return. "It puts me in mind of Kiriath. It's a fair place with old memories. But it's also in terrible danger if we don't stop Torrlond, and I fear we won't rest here long. Perhaps on some happier day we'll return."

"Perhaps." Her gaze lingered on him a little longer.

Galdor pointed ahead at their first clear view of the columned palace. "We'll arrive shortly. King Tirgalan's expecting us."

The palace of white marble loomed high against the sky. So bright was the weathered stone in the sunlight that it seemed the long centuries had bleached all color from it. Its façade was of a rectangular construction and featured thick, fluted columns supporting the triangular roof of a large portico. Outside the tall front doors of bronze stood a row of guards clad in shining corselets over wine red tunics. Their graceful helms sported high golden crests that curved behind their heads. Each held a spear and wore a sword at his side, standing motionless as Galdor led the party. The two central guards parted to make way for the wizard and the rest when they ascended the large marble stairs leading to the doors. As the wizard walked by, the guards bowed, and two who stood close to the doors opened them by pulling on thick bronze rings.

When they passed inside, Dayraven admired the rows of large columns supporting the vast central hall's roof. Spacious and graceful it was. Light poured in high, open windows that reached nearly from floor to ceiling at the sides of the hall. It felt like being inside and outside at the same time, or like standing in a grove of giant trees with perfectly formed trunks. Galdor led them to the hall's end, after which they passed down a smaller corridor until they came to a pair of ornate doors. Two guards bowed and opened the doors, letting the party pass inside.

On the far side of the spacious chamber, a throne formed of smooth white marble sat in front of a wine red and gold tapestry hanging from the ceiling. Statues of women and men lined the walls,

PHILIP CHASE

and Dayraven guessed they represented former queens and kings. So well executed were the statues that he half expected them to descend from their pedestals and greet the visitors. Galdor led them across the stone floor until they approached the throne, at which point the wizard bowed to its occupant. The others followed suit. Dayraven took a good look at King Tirgalan of Sundara.

Slightly older than middle-aged, Tirgalan was clean-shaven, as were most men in the Andumaic kingdoms. His once-dark hair had silvered, according well with the slim golden crown on his brow and the purple robe gracing his slender form. His dark eyes spoke of keen intelligence, and Dayraven sensed the large amount of the gift in him. Yet this man's face lacked the severity and ambition Dayraven associated with royalty. If anything, Tirgalan seemed almost too gentle for a king as he smiled at his newly arrived guests.

"Welcome," he said in the Northern Tongue. "It appears Galdor was right about the arrival of friends. Perhaps you're hungry? After introductions, we'll dine and discuss what has brought you all here."

Galdor introduced everyone to King Tirgalan, who thanked King Vols especially for his presence. Sundara's king then called servants to conduct the travelers to private chambers where they washed. When they were ready, they joined Tirgalan at his board in a small but elegant dining hall.

Torches and candles supplemented the waning sunlight streaming through open windows on the room's western wall. Dayraven peered out one window and admired the view: Beyond the city's domes and spires, the westering sun gilded the Great Sea. A few birds hung as black specks in the crimson sky, while scattered sails flecked the waters.

He broke his gaze and left the window. They took their places at a rectangular table, with King Tirgalan at one end and King Vols at the other. Galdor, Abon, and Gnorn sat on one side, while Sequara, Dayraven, and Orvandil occupied the other. Accustomed to spicier food after his stay in Asdralad, Dayraven found the excellence of the fare matched the quality of the wine. Their host's geniality complemented the feast, and by its end Dayraven felt a moment of peace. But this could not last, for they had dire matters to discuss.

The sunlight had dwindled away by the time servants cleared the board. The darkness surrounding the candle-lit room made Dayraven feel as if they were the lonely survivors of Eormenlond's destruction, according well with the elf-shard's slithering murmurs. But they were here to speak of whether they could avert that destruction, so he listened as King Tirgalan opened the discussion.

"A day will come when we properly lament the affliction of Asdralad's people and the deaths of Queen Faldira and Urd. Their loss is grievous to us all, not least to me. I reckoned them among my dearest friends, and the queen was my distant kinswoman. But today, we must keep their deaths in our hearts as we carry on and discuss how to stop those who took them from us. For Asdralad's fall makes our situation more dire. We've come to the brink of destruction. The Way has become a plague that will cover all of Andumedan unless we act together to stop it. Torrlond will soon attack Sildharan, the last impediment to the Way's domination of Andumedan. Alone, Sildharan will fall. But if we band together, we can stop Torrlond.

"My kingdom is even now preparing troops to march north to Sildharan. Though Galdor and others have tried to persuade him, King Veduir of Golgar refuses to help his kingdom's old foe, preferring to fall alone as Caergilion did. Asdralad cannot aid us now, while the enslaved peoples of Caergilion and Adanon and the kingdoms of the Mark and Ellond will march with Earconwald and Bledla. The Ilarchae too, it seems, will side with Torrlond. Thus the lines are drawn."

"The odds seem to be against you," observed Vols with a wry smile. "And, from what I hear, it's not only Torrlond's army you need fear. The beasts the priests have enslaved win Torrlond's battles. Bledla's fire-worms — these stand between you and victory."

Tirgalan sank in his chair and steepled his fingers as he sighed. "True. There were once those among the Andumae who wielded dragons. There were mighty sorcerers when our ancestors first came to Andumedan and fought the War of the Dragons. The last to use the song of origin of dragons before the Prophet Aldmund did was Ogmos the Great, the sorcerer who fathered Sildhar, Golg, and Rioda."

"The namesakes of three Andumaic kingdoms," said Gnorn. "One of which is no more."

Tirgalan nodded. "Yes. In the sixth century after our coming to these lands, Ogmos led many Andumae from Sundara northward to the Sea of Morthul. There he founded a great kingdom. But when he died, his three children quarreled over his realm. Sildhar, the eldest, was nearest to his father's power, and he determined to seize the kingship. But Golg and Rioda were proud and not without ambition."

"And so they went to war, and countless people suffered and died," said Sequara. Dayraven glanced at her and remembered reading about these events during his training in Asdralad.

Sundara's king shook his head and frowned. "In the northern war of the seventh century that followed, there were many sorrowful events. To the furthest north lay Rioda and her people, and to the south were Golg and his. In the middle, around the Sea of Morthul, Sildhar tightened his power. At length, he drove his brother Golg to the Osham Mountains, where Golg's people put up one of the greatest defenses in the annals. But, after Sildhar slew his brother, he left his nephew and Golg's remaining followers to cling to the mountains, where they founded the kingdom of Golgar. Said to be the most stubborn and hardy of the Andumae, Golgar's people to this day remember this slaughter. That's why they'll not aid us even now."

"That's a long time to hold a grudge," said Vols.

"Ill deeds often live longest in our memories, and more tragedy followed to solidify the hatred," answered Tirgalan. "Sildhar then turned towards his sister, whose city on the River Nurgleth awaited its fate. Though they resisted long, in the year 631, Rioda and her people fled west as their last defenses fell. Sildhar then claimed dominion over all the land between the Osham Mountains and the Amlar Mountains as far south as the Forest of Orudwyn and as far east as the coast of Andumedan, where the cities of Shinan and Kelgaon lie. After her defeat, Rioda led her people over Quinara Sound and beyond the Osham Mountains into western Andumedan. That region the Andumae had not yet ventured into, but there she carved out the kingdom of Riodara, a name that lives only in lore. The lands we call Ellond and Torrlond were once a great kingdom of the Andumae, but Riodara's destruction began with the Great War of the Four Kingdoms."

"That's the war that ended with the coming of the Ilarchae," said Dayraven. *My ancestors.*

"Yes," said Tirgalan. "But it began before their arrival. By the year 876, the Riodarae felt strong enough to avenge their ancestors' expulsion. There were many skirmishes between the old foes over the years, but the war that began between Riodara and Sildharan was on a new scale. Golgar joined forces with Riodara to avenge old wrongs against Sildharan. Sundara strove to stay neutral. But the enslavement of our settlers in the southwest of Andumedan aboard the ships of the Riodarae angered the ruler of Sundara, who protested to the king of the Riodarae. The Riodarae responded with flame and sword: They came and burned this city and Tinubor. Thus, we entered the war, which raged for more than a hundred years. Our wisest perished in that terrible time and in the disease that followed. The plague we call the Red Death took what little lore we had left, and we found our power over the dragons had disappeared forever."

Tirgalan looked up and shook his head. He folded his hands before him.

Galdor took up the tale. "But that lore did not perish. Asdralad's rulers long preserved the song of origin of dragons, though even they lost it in later years. But before they did, the Prophet Aldmund, founder of the Way, learned it on that island. After hundreds of years, it was he who wielded the song. He gave it to his successors, though more hundreds of years passed until another could use it. The Supreme Priest Bledla, unlike Aldmund, chose to exploit this power. However, we are witnessing something that hasn't happened in more than a thousand years. More than one walking in Eormenlond can wield the song of origin of dragons."

Galdor looked at Dayraven, who swallowed in his tightening throat. Once again he found himself the center of everyone's hopes, and once again he wished he had never met the elf in the Southweald.

King Vols tugged at his beard as he looked at Dayraven. "But the lad's already tested his power. He couldn't defeat Bledla. That's why we're sitting here, isn't it?"

King Tirgalan too inspected Dayraven. "Perhaps we should hear from Dayraven what occurred back in Asdralad. I for one have only heard what Sequara reported to me. What happened when you tried to wrest the dragons from Bledla's control?"

Dayraven shuddered at the memory of his encounter with the supreme priest. But he looked at Galdor, whose eyes reassured him. He remembered Urd's words in Asdralad before he lost her: *"Meet your fate with courage," she said. I must struggle on to whatever end awaits. Alright, then.*

Looking at Tirgalan, Dayraven began, "For a moment, I was with them. The song of origin brought me to the core of the dragons' energy. I saw from their eyes, knew their thoughts. Yes, the spell worked — so well I nearly lost them when I took heart at my success. But the real trial was yet to come. Bitter was the struggle I fought with Bledla, and I don't recall it willingly. His presence awoke to mine, and we fought only briefly for control. His power over them was like iron bands — long had he mastered them. What's more, he knew my fear. He knew I feared to lose myself, and he tried to tear my spirit in shreds. He was so strong. I needed more power to fight him."

Dayraven sighed. He was coming to the worst part. "The truth is I lost the struggle because I lost control over the power the elf put in me. I tried to explain it to Urd and Queen Faldira. Since I encountered the elf in the Southweald, a thing has dwelled in my mind. It is the power those of you with the gift sense. The gift was in me before that, but not like . . . It feels like a broken piece of glass lodged inside me. It's . . . alive. It has its own will. Sometimes I can control it and use it. But other times it betrays me. It awakens and shatters me with such force that I don't know if I'll come back. That's what happened when I sought more power to fight against Bledla." Cold shadows coiled around his mind. The elf-shard hissed.

"Well, well," said Galdor with a smile. "So it was not Bledla who defeated you. No, something in *you* defeated you. What's important is you came back. And your account reveals the supreme priest has one certain advantage: He has long established his control over the dragons. You were new to them, and therefore in a weaker position. We must think of two things: how you might make peace with your power, and how to overcome his advantage."

"Why not find other dragons Dayraven could wield?" suggested

Vols. "Those would destroy Torrlond's army or at least fight the dragons that harry you. You'd be in the same place then."

King Tirgalan leaned back in his chair. "That *would* put us in the same place as Torrlond and the Way. Would we then be any different? Slay one another or enslave beasts to do it for us until all are dead. Far better to find a way to take away Torrlond's one real advantage. If we can do this, we may avert the war altogether and spare many lives."

"Spare lives?" scoffed Vols with a lowered brow and a frown. "Why spare your foes? If we're to die at their hands, let's take them with us." He pounded the table with his fist and looked around as if challenging anyone to disagree.

Galdor smiled once again as he addressed the king of the Thjoths. "There's one practical consideration, your Majesty. We simply don't have time to find dragons. They dwell far in the mountains. Bledla spent years sending trackers to seek them so he could put the lingworms under his sway. By the time Torrlond's army is on our doorstep, we'd be lucky to have even one. The only way now is for Dayraven to wrest the dragons from Bledla. If we're fortunate, peace will follow. If not, then we'll all need courage in battle like the Thjoths'. But I note that you said, 'If *we* are to die, let *us* take them with us.' Does this mean you intend to join us against Torrlond?"

Vols grinned like a wolf. "King Fullan of Ellond is fortunate to have such a shrewd counselor. I'll not hide my intentions. We Thjoths must face Torrlond sooner or later, and it might as well be sooner. I'm inclined to join you, but this decision is not mine alone. On the morrow, I'll sail for Grimrik, where I'll call a moot. There all our warriors will decide our course. I've asked Orvandil to help make our case, for he's most familiar with both Torrlond's doings and your own. If we persuade them, Grimrik's warriors will fight by your side. If not, they'll one day avenge many of you when Torrlond comes to our kingdom."

Tirgalan nodded. "So be it. We'd be fortunate indeed to have the Thjoths by our side. And though we're loth to lose such a warrior as Captain Orvandil, perhaps he may do greater service in helping to bring his people to our aid."

"It will be my honor, your Majesty," said Orvandil with a slight bow to Tirgalan. "But there's one other warrior we must bring to Grimrik." He turned to his cousin Vols. "I ask that Gnorn accompany us."

Gnorn's head snapped toward Orvandil. "But that would mean . . . the first Dweorg to set foot on those lands in nearly two hundred years. The lands of my ancestors." The Dweorg's widened eyes flamed with yearning. "If I could once see them, I'd come back to face any death."

"Then it shall be so," said Vols.

Galdor looked at Orvandil with a thoughtful smile and said, "A wise choice, Orvandil. Yes, Gnorn of the Fyrnhowes shall sail with you to Grimrik. And I'll travel by land north to Sildharan. King Naitaran may need counsel, and, though he's a powerful sorcerer, he could use more who wield magic at his side. Therefore, Sequara and Dayraven, I hope you'll agree to accompany Abon and me. Perhaps we can devise a way around Bledla's power over the dragons as we journey. In the meantime, King Tirgalan will gather his forces here in Sundara. They'll all march north to join Sildharan's army. We've secured permission from King Veduir of Golgar to travel through his realm, though he'll commit none of his own troops. Your Majesty," he said to Tirgalan, "I counsel you to hasten: Earconwald and Bledla will strike soon. We must be at full strength before they do."

"We've begun to muster our soldiers," answered Tirgalan. "We'll set out close on your heels."

"Good," said the wizard. "That leaves one other matter: Torrlond's not as strong as its leaders think. We have a nasty surprise waiting for Earconwald and Bledla, something I don't mind saying I had a hand in. King Fullan is marching Ellond's forces to battle for Torrlond. However, at the right moment, Fullan will bring those loyal to him over to our side. Most of Ellond's soldiers will follow him, and they'll turn on our enemies when they least expect it." He faced King Vols. "I hope you'll forgive me for not mentioning it earlier in front of your men. We must keep this secret safe."

"A shrewd counselor indeed," said Vols. "So our foes have their weaknesses. And if Dayraven succeeds against Bledla, some of us might even come out alive."

Dayraven tried to appear resolute as he nodded. "I'll do what I can.

And whether we live or not, we'll stand together."

"Excellent," said Galdor. "Then it appears all's ready. Is anything needing?"

No one spoke for a moment until Orvandil cleared his throat and addressed King Tirgalan. "One small thing. I broke my sword in battle in Asdralad. If you'd give me one, your Majesty, I'd use it well."

King Tirgalan made to reply, but an impulse took Dayraven, and he spoke first. "If I may, your Majesty." Once he began to speak, the sudden idea seemed right to him, the only logical thing to do. He unbuckled his leather baldric then held out Sweothol in its scabbard to Orvandil. "This, I think, should suffice."

Orvandil's frown showed his surprise. "The sword your father gave you . . . I can't accept."

"You already did," said Dayraven, "when you dueled with King Vols. In truth, I knew then I had no more need of Sweothol. As I watched, I beheld the only warrior I ever saw worthy of it, save my father. The sword never belonged with me. And anyway, I don't think I'll ever need to fight with a blade again." He saw once more the terrible moment when he pierced the Caergilese soldier's heart with Sweothol at the Battle of Iarfaen. The man's dying memories were still with him.

Orvandil hesitated, but then he nodded and grasped the blade's hilt. "It's a kingly gift. But it leaves me even more beholden to you."

Dayraven smiled. "Not at all. I'm only putting it where it belongs. Sweothol will be of more use in your hands than in mine."

"Then all's ready," declared King Tirgalan. "I suggest we retire now. It may be our last chance for a secure rest. On the morrow, our great test begins."

Servants led the companions to their sleeping quarters. When Dayraven blew out his candle, he lay awake in darkness. The slithering breath of the elf-shard accompanied his thoughts. At last he saw the path he must take, and he steeled himself for it. In Sildharan he would again attempt to fight Bledla for control of the dragons. He did not know how, and he did not know if the elf-shard would allow him, but he would challenge Bledla again. The only question left was whether he would succeed or fail, whether he would live or die. But the latter no longer mattered so much.

15
TO BE A GOD

Wearing only his kirtle and breeches, Earconwald reclined on the generous bed in Queen Moda's chamber in Sigseld with a smirk on his face. His wine glass was nearly empty, and he was nursing the remainder of its contents. He was early. Moda would not arrive for some time since she was busy entertaining the noblewomen who came with their husbands for the celebration in Torrhelm. As he waited for his queen to arrive, he reflected on all the pleasure and satisfaction the last days had brought him.

When the Torrlonders conquered Caergilion and Adanon, Bledla had asked him to keep the troops disciplined, permitting them to destroy only where there was resistance. Though he offered no clemency to those who refused to obey Edan's calling, the pious old man wished to convert the populace to the Way. Pillaging and ravaging would have cowed the southwest's natives, but Bledla wanted true followers to swell the ranks of his believers. Mercy to the faithful, annihilation to unbelievers. For the supreme priest, destruction was a means, not an end.

Earconwald scoffed. For all the power he had at his command, the foolish old man had no idea how to enjoy it. His obsessive dependence on Edan limited his vision and made him weak. Allowing his superstitions to constrain him, Bledla wasted his days in self-flagellating misery. What good was his power if that was how he lived?

Earconwald had discovered the real meaning of power. Only one who exercised his might with no obligation to anyone or anything could experience true pleasure. He had ascertained this during their conquests, but most especially in the sacking of Asdralad. A king destroyed because he could. He needed no reason. With a wave of his finger, he could command the deaths of thousands. And *he* was the greatest king ever to dwell in Eormenlond. He would unite all the kingdoms under his sway. He would destroy all his foes, and his rule would be absolute. All would fear his wrath, and they would do anything to prove their love for him. Most of all, he would bow to no god. Instead, his people would bow to him, for was he not their god?

On Asdralad, he had tasted divinity. Such was Bledla's anger at the escape of the boy Dayraven and his comrades that he coldly told the king his army could have its way with the island kingdom. When the supreme priest thus abandoned any claim to Asdralad's people, Earconwald's lips had curved in a predatory smile, and he had laughed. Half his laughter was directed at Bledla for his stupid sullenness, and the other half was in anticipation of the coming pleasure.

The result was the most ecstatic orgy of murder, rape, and wanton devastation any group of beings had inflicted on another. Even now it fascinated and excited him to think of the helpless screams.

They had slain people and beasts of every kind, poisoned the wells with corpses and filth, and set fire to Kiriath. The slaughter was greatest inside the temples of Oruma and Anghara, where pathetic, shivering women, children, and elderly had taken refuge. After they covered the floors and walls in blood, Earconwald ordered his soldiers to burn down the temples with the rest of city, leaving nothing alive. With simple commands, he had rendered the once beautiful city into a hellish ruin over which only the wind wailed for unburied and mutilated corpses. Such was his power. It would be an eternal testament to the consequences of defying Eormenlond's rightful ruler. Only a few soldiers with weak stomachs had refused to participate in the bloodshed. They found themselves the object of ridicule and lost their comrades' trust. But they were few, and Earconwald would give orders to cull them in time.

When Kiriath was no more, he had designated a small force to stay behind and subdue the rest of the island, on which there were now only insignificant, scattered villages. The majority of the soldiers sailed away to rejoin Torrlond's vast army, which had already made its way back to Torrhelm in preparation for welcoming their allies from the Mark and Ellond. The moment for the final, glorious push east was coming. Sated with blood for the time being, Earconwald's lads would feel the hunger rise again soon. The king was pleased he had given his men some sport. They had earned it. And soon they would have more.

First, Sildharan, the east's major power, would fall. Rotten from within, the old kingdom depended on the Ilarchae slaves who despised it. It was so frail with decadence and corruption, he was confident it would not withstand Torrlond's mighty forces for more than a few days. The rest would be easy. All of Eormenlond would fall under his rule. Then would come celebrations that would dwarf even the one the Torrlonders were in the midst of now.

Still, this was not bad. Earconwald had to admit it was a sweet moment. He had already far outdone his stupid, pious father, who had defeated Caergilion and left with only a worthless treaty to show for it. Earconwald's triumph would last. The glory of his reign would live forever. Even now it was beginning, a foreshadowing of the successes to come. Torrhelm had hailed its returning king with jubilation. The soldiers marched through the streets covered in glory. Revelries and feasts in Sigseld and all over Torrhelm marked their victories. When the allies from the Mark and Ellond arrived, Torrlond's people had greeted their guests generously. To the believers, it was obvious Edan had blessed them. Earconwald cared not one jot for such superstitions, but he found them useful. *Convince them of their righteousness, give them something to fear and hate, and then they'll do anything.* His triumph and his rule would be absolute.

Of course, he had not been the least enthusiastic reveler. But now he was waiting on the bed of his queen. It had been a long time. He had enjoyed the spoils of war in the year he was away, so he was surprised at his anticipation while waiting for Moda. Though she had never provided him with an heir, and though she disgraced herself on numerous occasions with drunkenness, in one way she always pleased him. Perhaps that was why he kept her around.

A knock sounded. The door clicked open and closed. He stretched and took a deep breath, then he swung his legs around to sit up and put the wine glass on the floor next to his boots, mantle, sword, and crown. When he looked up, he frowned at what he saw.

A bearded man in a white robe stood inside the doorway. Why would those damned priests never leave him alone? Earconwald scowled, ready to unleash his wrath.

"Your Majesty? I've come as you bade me to." The High Priest Joruman's face wore a confused frown for a moment. It flipped over into one of his greasy smiles.

The king remembered. Of course. That was why he had come to Moda's chamber early. "Ah, Joruman. Yes." He returned the smile, and the high priest's shoulders relaxed. Earconwald looked down at his shirt and breeches and explained, "I thought you were the queen. I'm waiting for her. It's been a while."

"Then I can understand your disappointment."

Earconwald stared at Joruman for a moment, then he broke out in laughter. The high priest joined in.

The king slapped his knee and, after releasing a long sigh, ceased chuckling. The high priest too went silent.

"I called you here since there's so little opportunity for privacy. I wanted to tell you something before we set out for the east."

"I'm at your command, your Majesty."

"Good. You did well in your negotiations with the barbarians. They agreed to all our terms without argument?"

One of the high priest's eyebrows arched up. "It took a small amount of persuading, but I managed it."

"Very good. I'll be relying much on your skills of persuasion. Now, the real reason I called you: Our agreement stands. After we've won the war, we must find the first opportunity to remove Bledla. I'll expect your full support when the time comes."

"You already have it."

"And the new doctrines we discussed?"

"Once I'm supreme priest, I'll declare in no uncertain terms your power over the Way. The other doctrines will take some time, but I'm confident in their eventual passage. The Way already recognizes that Edan has sanctified your authority. It's not much of a leap from there to decree that his divinity resides in you."

"You have the support you need?"

"I've spent my time here in Torrhelm wisely. My network of priests has been expanding. They'll be ready when the time comes. The only significant opposition may come from the other high priests. Arna and Colburga must go. Heremod and Morcar can be bought."

"Excellent. I'll rely on you to accomplish it. And in the meantime, Bledla must not suspect anything."

"Bledla has no reason to question my loyalty to him. Everything shall be done according to your will. Is there any other way in which I might serve you, your Majesty?"

"No. You may go now. I only wished to reiterate our understanding and be sure of your resolve."

"My resolve is as firm as ever, your Majesty. Until the conclave, then?"

"Yes. I'll see you there."

Joruman bowed before he turned and walked toward the door. When he opened it, Queen Moda stood outside with one arm raised as if she were on the verge of knocking. Her eyes widened, and she released a small but startled gasp.

Joruman bowed to her. "Your Majesty. What a pleasure to see you. I've just finished my conference with the king. He awaits you." He gestured with one hand toward Earconwald and grinned.

Moda returned the smile. "Thank you, your Eminence."

The high priest walked out and disappeared.

Moda wore a crimson gown that showed her curves advantageously. Still sitting on the bed, Earconwald watched her backside as she closed and locked the door behind her. When she turned around, he grinned at the ample breasts nestling behind the tight gown. She was a beautiful specimen, and her sensuality aroused him.

She glanced back at the door. "What did *he* want?"

"Matters of the kingdom. Nothing to concern yourself with."

"Oh." Moda inclined her head in a slight bow. "I hope I've not kept you waiting long, my lord."

He leered at her. "Not to worry, my pet. I'm pleased to see you."

Her lips curved in a seductive smile. "And I you, my conquering king." She did know how to please him.

"Damn!" Sitting on the edge of the bed, Earconwald clutched his head in his hands, still trying to erase the persistent memories of women and children screaming as his soldiers raped and slaughtered them. Blood and suffering filled his mind. The images both aroused and repulsed him. His breeches were tangled around his ankles, his manhood dangling limp between his legs.

"My king?" Moda's voice trembled behind him. "I'm sorry. I can try to . . ."

"No." His raised fist silenced her. Tension filled the room. But then he seized control of his distracted thoughts, and his fingers relaxed. "We'll wait until tonight. I have much on my mind now. The meeting with the kings and my dukes. Tonight, my dear." The memories let go of him, and he could see the queen's chamber again. He turned to Moda and favored her with a smile. "Tonight, you may please me."

He stood and pulled up his breeches, and then, fumbling twice before succeeding, he tied them on. Leaning down to pick up the wine glass, he held it out to her. "I'll expect you here after the feast."

The fear left her eyes, and she smiled back at him as she took the glass. "Yes, my lord. It will be my pleasure."

Earconwald took ahold of his boots and, after nearly falling over and then steadying himself on the bed, pulled them on his feet. Then he straightened out his kirtle and picked up his red mantle. As he dressed, his queen lay on her large bed, her gown that she had pulled back down ruffled and her hair disheveled. She gave him a flirtatious smile and batted her eyelashes. "My love, are you certain you won't want me at your side during the meeting?"

"My dear Moda," he replied as he slipped the mantle around his shoulders, "I know you're eager to show off for the kings of the Mark and Ellond, but I assure you your presence is not required at this meeting. You'll have your chance later." His tone was only slightly mocking, but he included a warning in it.

She ventured to press the matter in a playful, silky voice. "Could it be you fear too much admiration will fall on the queen by your side?"

In the earlier years of their marriage, they had teased each other in this way, feigning to point out one another's jealousy. But that was long ago. Now, a convulsion altered Earconwald's face, his eyebrows lowering and nostrils flaring as his patience snapped. On this day, *nothing* should challenge his authority.

"Listen, slut," he hissed as he stormed to the bed. Her smile melted into a pout. She remained lying, but her body tensed and her eyes widened as he shouted. "You're never sober enough to realize when you're presentable. I'll be the judge of that. *I'll* tell you when to come before my nobles and subject kings. *I'll* tell you when to leave this room!" He jabbed his finger at the floor.

Normally, Moda would have lowered her head and mumbled something submissive to her husband. Perhaps it was the suddenness of his change, or his long absence had emboldened her, or something long building up in her at last gave way. Whatever it was, she ignored years of painful lessons and boldly said, "Am I your prisoner, then?"

Earconwald regarded her as if his dog had bitten his hand. His face reddened. His mouth twisted into a snarl. "How dare you speak back, whore!" The back of his hand cracked across her face, snapping her head back. The wine glass shattered on the floor.

Moda slowly turned toward him. As blood trickled from her nose, she looked up with enraging defiance in her eyes.

Towering over her, he shook his stinging hand and spat, "Worthless bag of bones. Sack of wine. You better know your place, or you'll find someone more useful in it. Bah! You couldn't even provide me an heir. Worse than useless, a mere burden on my wine cellars."

Moda touched her nose then looked down at the blood on her shaking hand. Her voice trembled, but she gazed straight at Earconwald's face. "As for your heir, you've tried to produce one on any number of women. It's *you* who are impotent, your Majesty."

King Earconwald's face went dark, his eyes blank of rational thought. In return, fear showed in Moda's widening eyes and open mouth, as if she could not believe the words had escaped her — fear that fed his sense of power.

A heartbeat after she uttered the words, his hands shot to her neck, the fingers digging into her white flesh. She could not speak, but her terrified eyes pleaded for mercy. There was none. Looking down at her, he tasted the seductive power to grant life or dispense death. Her slender hands pulled at his arms to no avail. A gasping whimper emitted from her throat.

He liked her this way. His fingers sank deeper, and he leaned over her on the bed. As he shook her, her breasts beneath her gown quivered and her head bumped against the backboard. His mastery of her was intoxicating, and he made her quiver more. Her fingers clawed uselessly at the arms pressing down on her. His smile was fierce. A wet gasp passed from her mouth, and her eyes widened further in terror. Her eyelids fluttered. He sensed the life leaving her against her will, and his heartbeat raced, throbbing all the way from his chest into his skull.

Build or destroy what I wish . . . Earconwald kept shaking her after her slender arms slumped to the bed and her eyes stared blankly. *What it means to be a god* . . . He pressed on her neck for some time, but his face began to twitch and tremble, and his eyes filled with moisture.

He released her. No breath. No pulse. Now shivering, he bent down and brought his face nearer to Moda's with its frozen look of terror. He lurched forward and kissed the gaping mouth, surrounding it with his lips. His tear dropped on her cheek.

A knock sounded on the door. Earconwald started, and his body jerked away from the corpse under him. He composed himself and wiped his eyes. Taking deep breaths, he paced to the door of the queen's chamber. By the time he reached it, his face was like stone. When he opened the door, he flinched and his mouth opened in shock. His dead father stood in front of him, a severe frown across his pale face.

Earconwald blinked, and the face resolved into the Supreme Priest Bledla. The old man stood in his white robe between two guards. Earconwald shook his head and closed his mouth, which had been hanging open.

"Your Majesty," began Bledla with a bow. "Forgive the intrusion. I thought it best we arrive at the conclave together. The kings and nobles await you, and Captain Nothelm told me I'd find you . . ." The supreme priest's deep voice stopped short. "What's happened here?"

Earconwald spoke in a flat monotone. "The queen's dead."

The two guards shifted and glanced at one another. Bledla entered the chamber and closed the door in their faces. He approached the lifeless body on the bed. Angry bruises already discolored the slender neck, and a trickle of blood leaked out her nose.

Showing little emotion or surprise, Bledla cocked one eyebrow. "I see. It's a mercy her father, Earl Stithmod, passed away last year, or he might have been distressed at her death. As it is, this is an unfortunate *accident*," he said as he covered the body and the face — and its horrified stare — with a red silk sheet. "We'll make the arrangements for the queen's funeral. Perhaps, however, it would be best to wait until after our triumphant return from the east to give her the proper ceremonies. For now, we'll dispose of the body, ah . . . in a respectful manner befitting her rank. The guards outside will be induced to keep silent." The supreme priest gazed at Earconwald with his hard eyes. "Your Majesty, you'll forgive me, I hope, but the kings and nobles are all in attendance. They await your commands in the council room. Our armies must depart for the east soon."

Earconwald gave a chilly smile. "I'm nearly ready, Bledla. Let me finish dressing, then I'll come with you. Today, we make a new beginning."

"Indeed, your Majesty." Bledla bowed and left the chamber, closing the door behind him.

Earconwald buckled on his scabbard and donned his crown, then he took a moment to smooth out his clothes. When he finished, he turned to ask Moda if anything was out of place, but then he remembered she would not answer.

Sneering at the body beneath the sheet for its uselessness, he turned and made for the door. The king emerged from the room in his full splendor, red mantle lined with fur flowing behind his fine garments and bejeweled crown resting on his brow. The two guards stood at attention but glanced with nervous eyes toward him.

Bledla whispered, "These two have careful directions to relocate the body. They'll meet me later for further instructions. This is a time for triumph, not funerals."

Earconwald smirked at his chief advisor. "Very good, Bledla. Proceed."

Leaving behind the unfortunate queen's corpse, Earconwald accompanied Bledla to the conclave with great sense of purpose.

TRAILED BY BLEDLA, CAPTAIN NOTHELM, AND A SCORE OF GUARDS, Earconwald beamed a magnanimous smile when he walked through the ornate doors into the circular chamber with sixty stately chairs ranged around the outer wall. Each oak chair was fit for a king, but a larger one rested directly opposite the entrance on a small dais. Windows at the top of the room gave plenty of light, and a large chandelier with a hundred burning candles hung by a thick chain from the ceiling. Over the stone floor lay a dazzling rug of red, black, purple, and white with various knotted patterns. Upon the rug milled men in a gathering like no other before in Eormenlond. Their conversations ceased, and Earconwald basked in the silence that accompanied his entrance as all eyes turned toward him.

The high priests in their white robes bowed as the king walked by and acknowledged them with a languid wave. Among them, Joruman's smile was knowing.

Duke Guthfrid, a big man with a scowling face beneath thick, dark eyebrows, stood next to Duke Ethelred. The king stopped before him. "Guthfrid, my good duke. The day is auspicious, is it not?"

The duke attempted a smile that better suited a bull than a man and then bowed. "It is as Edan wills it, your Majesty." Guthfrid was a pious, stupid ox, and Earconwald feared he was firmly in Ethelred's camp.

Earconwald turned to that particular duke next. "Cousin."

Ethelred answered with a bow. "Your Majesty." The most powerful noble in Torrlond other than the king, Duke Ethelred of Etinstone was Earconwald's cousin and heir. The stout man with beady eyes and grey-blond beard was a devout, uninteresting man who had five healthy sons with his fat wife. In their youth, Ethelred had gained distinction as a warrior, always outdoing Earconwald in feats of arms. The king hated him.

Earconwald moved on. Duke Durathror of Norfast smiled, his laughing eyes showing no fear of his sovereign. Earconwald smiled back and clasped Durathror's shoulders like an old friend. "Durathror. Ready as ever, I see."

"Always, my king." Tall and broad-chested was Duke Durathror of Norfast. His bearing and greying fair hair bespoke his half-Thjothic ancestry, which also made him untrustworthy in Earconwald's eyes.

Red-bearded Duke Weohstan and white-haired Heahmund, the eldest of Torrlond's dukes, smiled at Earconwald. "Your Majesty," they said in unison as they bowed.

"My good dukes. It gives me great joy to see you here." Both were connivers who would stab each other in the back just as soon as they would stab him.

Two figures stood out from everyone else in the chamber. These were large, outlandish men with pale skin, their long hair bound behind their heads with leather straps and bone pins. Earconwald had met them once before, when they came to him in Adanon to propose the alliance. The red-haired brute could speak the Northern Tongue, he recalled. Dressed in an ancient style, both barbarians were clad in long wool kirtles with bright colors in alternating stripes designating their clans and tribes. Thick leather belts cinched the kirtles at their broad waists. They had no breeches, but their furry boots reached their knees. Wearing long fur cloaks to complete their attire, they looked around like caged animals. They were emissaries from their leader Surt, who remained among the Ilarchae in the Wildlands.

Bledla escorted Earconwald towards the two savages while everyone else, seeing the king would be occupied for a moment, resumed their conversations.

Bledla gestured toward the red-haired barbarian. "This, your Majesty may remember, is Munzil, a nobleman among the Ilarchae and a trader of furs, which gives him familiarity with the Northern Tongue. He serves as translator for his companion." Bledla gestured toward the hulking, blond Ilarchae. "You may also recall Gorm, a great lord among the Ilarchae and lieutenant of their chosen war-leader, whom he represents."

King Earconwald hid his distaste behind a practiced smile. "Welcome to Torrlond. What message do you bear from your lands? You may speak."

The two Ilarchae bowed stiffly to Earconwald. They stank of horse and sweat. The one called Munzil nodded toward his huge companion, who startled the king by unsheathing a dagger from his side and sweeping it across his bare palm. When Gorm clenched the cut hand in a tight fist, blood dripped from it and pattered onto the rug. His rough voice and harsh tongue grated in the chamber, "Grazen eowdur fon hargtochi Surti. Urnam fochtam vollen veh fetzammen grondu."

In a somewhat smoother voice but with a strange accent, Munzil translated the words: "Greetings to you from the war-leader Surt. Together, we will crush our foe."

When Munzil finished translating, Gorm held out his bloody palm to Torrlond's king and glared at him like a giant boar contemplating a charge.

Earconwald glanced at the large, crimsoned hand hanging in front of him, then he grinned broadly. Surely the savages did not expect him to perform any such dramatic gestures? Reaching up to give Gorm's massive shoulder a manly slap, he declared, "We receive you as friends. Let us be united and destroy those who have harmed your people. Sildharan will pay for its evils, and I'll grant your kinsmen their freedom." Turning to Munzil, Earconwald nodded and said, "Tell him that."

The two barbarians looked at each other. A puzzled frown crossed the huge one's face as he waited with his bleeding hand still extended before him. The red-haired one began speaking to his companion.

Even as Munzil translated the words into the rude tongue of the Ilarchae, Earconwald followed Bledla with a measure of relief to greet Siric, Duke of Rimdale, a short and portly man with dark, receding hair, a greying beard, and cunning eyes like a merchant's. Other than Earconwald, Siric wore more costly garments and jewels than anyone in the room. As he bowed and kissed the large ring on Earconwald's right hand with a sycophantic grin, Siric did not hide his eagerness to please.

"Siric," said the king, his voice calm and well oiled. "It's good to see you. I hope you and your men have rested well here in Torrhelm."

"Your Majesty," beamed the duke. "We of Rimdale are pleased we may be of service. I hope Queen Moda's well."

Earconwald paused and stared. Then he remembered to smile. "She's better than ever, my friend."

When he approached King Fullan of Ellond, standing apart from the others but still close enough within the demands of courtesy, Earconwald gave a nod that could have conveyed respect, or perhaps a warning. "Cousin," he said somewhat coolly, "It's a special honor to have our mother kingdom's ruler present."

Fullan nodded. "The honor's mine, cousin. We recognize the bonds of kinship."

"As our kingdoms always have. Long may such loyalty endure." Earconwald glanced at the two Ellonder earls flanking Fullan, Freomar and Roric, both known supporters of the Way in Ellond. The former believed he was the leading candidate to become Duke of Ellond once Earconwald seized the mother kingdom. *Let him think so*. Earconwald's quick look to both earls said everything: *Keep a close watch on your king*.

Last he came to King Ithamar of the Mark, who had six warriors standing with him, all older than he. At around thirty winters, the tall, slender man was the youngest of the three kings present and, as far as Earconwald could tell, an unimaginative fool. He welcomed Ithamar with open arms and a bright smile. "I hope your journey from the Mark was not overlong, Ithamar."

"However long it might have been, we in the Mark will answer the call our forefathers swore to heed."

"Excellent. You're men of honor, indeed, and doughty warriors, I warrant. These are your earls, then?"

"Four are among my earls." Ithamar gestured toward those in front. "Earl Ranulf of Mere's End, Earl Stigand of Kinsford, Earl Haereth of Farwick, and Earl Hadulac of the Hemeldowns." The first was a leathery greybeard, the second a big, rough-looking man, the third tanned as the seafarers of Farwick were wont to be, and the fourth a gruff-looking, red-bearded fellow who reminded Earconwald of a troll. The earls bowed, and Ithamar introduced the other two. "These two are thegns who served Torrlond in your father's time. Athelgar is of my own hall in Wolvendon, and Edgil comes from Kinsford."

King Earconwald paused a moment, and he glanced aside at Bledla, whose widened eyes also betrayed sudden interest. Earconwald recovered and said to the tall, muscled warrior in front of him, "Edgil of the Mark? Yes, I recognize you now, though the years show on us both. You saved my father in Balnor Pass."

The warrior bowed. "Your Majesty, it was a great honor to serve in King Ermenred's personal guard. We all would have given our lives for such a leader."

You might have saved me some trouble if you hadn't saved him. Earconwald measured the rough warrior standing before him. *Father of the troublesome Dayraven. The fool doesn't seem to know about his son. Let's see what Bledla says later.* "We remember the service you Markmen rendered in the past, just as we'll honor the sacrifices you'll make in the days ahead."

He turned and, spreading his arms wide, raised his voice to address the entire room. "For a great moment has come, my friends. The moment that decides Eormenlond's future. The time has come to ask ourselves: Where will we be when that future comes?"

Earconwald gestured toward the chairs along the circular wall before he strode towards the throne waiting for him on the dais. The other kings, nobles, and priests took the signal to find their seats and stood before them. After Earconwald sat, the others followed suit, clustered together in their various parties. Filling nearly all the chairs, they waited for Earconwald's next word.

"Friends. So I name you, for I called you here knowing your good will and the bonds that unite us against our foes. As you're aware, we have for the last year fought in Edan's name in the southwest, and Edan granted us victory. When the heathens slew our own, we came in righteous anger, and Edan showed us the way. Now is the time to join us in our struggle. Now is the time when all who care for what's good and right band together against the darkness lingering in Eormenlond. Now is the time to declare not in words but in deeds you are on Edan's side. For the enemy even now gathers against us in the east. They know Edan is bringing His own unto him, and they'll oppose us as we bring the Way's light to Eormenlond. In their stubbornness and wickedness, they refuse the call, but we'll not relent until we perform Edan's will.

"The kingdoms of the east are banding together, sending their soldiers to Sildharan. Why? Why are the heathens swarming in the kingdom that enslaved hundreds of thousands of our friends, the Ilarchae? Why are the enemies of Edan sending their legions to that pit of wickedness? I'll tell you. They see the Way's progress. They're blinded as Edan's light covers Eormenlond and exposes all evil, and they fear it. They wish to stop us. They hope to keep the light away. Fools! One cannot oppose Edan, for He brings everything to His purpose. And now Edan has commanded us to defend His will and crush the enemy of light.

"The path before us is clear, my friends. Now is the time to declare yourselves. What say you? Will you honor the alliance our forefathers made? Will you join hands with us and take your rightful place among the Eternal? You may speak freely."

Silence followed, and most looked to see who would speak first. Duke Siric rose from his chair and bowed to Earconwald. "Your Majesty. Never will we let the heathens harm our own. As always, we march behind you proudly. Rimdale is with you."

Earconwald smiled at his subject. *Good, Siric. Faithful dog. But I know of your schemes.*

Before Siric sat, Duke Walstod of Woodburg was up as well. "Woodburg is no less proud to go to war with our brothers. Blessed be the Eternal." Long-nosed and thin with peppered chestnut hair and beard, Walstod was among the weakest of Torrlond's dukes. He looked about for confirmation that he had said the right thing.

Earconwald put the idiot out of his misery with a benevolent nod. *Virtuous, stupid Walstod. A true believer.*

Soon after rose Duke Durathror, who declared, "Never let it be said the men of Norfast came last to any fight. We're proud to march for you, my king."

Young King Ithamar stood up next, and though a hint of worry touched the frown on his handsome face, he spoke with conviction.

"Your Majesty. As I said, we in the Mark honor our obligations, and we defend our own. We've not forgotten where we came from."

A smile spread across Earconwald's face. "Excellent. Your soldiers and your ships will prove their value in the days ahead, I'm sure."

Earl Haereth of Farwick rose from his chair. "Since it pleases King Ithamar, the Mark's ships are at your service, your Majesty."

Regarding the seafarer earl with a pleasant air, Earconwald stroked his beard. *They better be, after the bribe I gave you to make sure your king made the right decision. But now, let's see what my cousin of Ellond has to say.* He turned his gaze on King Fullan, and all the other faces in the room followed.

Fullan of Ellond stood up from his chair while the two Ellonder earls on either side of him watched. "Your Majesty. We too in Ellond remember our kinship. By my faith in Edan, I'll lead my soldiers east with you."

Placing his hands on his chair's arms, Earconwald looked regally down at Fullan and nodded.

Hadulac of the Hemeldowns stood. The large earl looked at his fellow Markmen first, then he gazed around the room with a frown. He stroked his red beard before he spoke. "We in the Hemeldowns are no cowards, and we ever keep in mind our kinship to all of you. But I'll speak my mind now. Long have my folk thriven in our mountain homes, and long have we had peace. When the Way came from Torrlond to our ancestors, its followers lived among those who worshipped the old gods. Now, though many love only Edan, many more in the Mark still follow the old ways. Such folk live together. They trade, they toil in the same fields, and they even wed. Why can't this be so in Eormenlond? Why can't Edan's worshippers live with those who worship Regnor and Hruga or Orm and Angra? I don't know if one day there'll be only the Way. A time may come when some other god claims allegiance in Eormenlond. What then?

"Ages come and go. Friends and family perish. Kingdoms crumble. Spear and sword turn to rust, and shields rot into the earth. As our lives begin and end, do the gods want us to slay for them, or do we slay merely in the name of gods? I know not. One thing I do know: In this life that darkness enfolds, we must cling to friends. We must hold fast to kin. Thus, we of the Hemeldowns will keep our faith with King Ithamar. We will march with you all. We'll honor the old alliance. And I pray Edan truly goes with us, or we'll all be damned together. Let the future judge us by our deeds."

Hadulac sat down. Grim silence followed.

Earconwald forced a smile. He glanced toward Bledla, whose knuckles were white as they gripped the arms of his chair. Hadulac's speech was a surprise. They would have to wait to punish the earl of the Hemeldowns for his impudence, and it was clear they could not trust him. But they had won the day, had they not? All would march to war.

Yet Earconwald felt less triumphant than he should have. *Damn you, Hadulac. You'll suffer for this.* He pondered how best to rekindle the fervor he felt only moments before.

Bledla cleared his throat, and the king noticed the supreme priest looking at him. It was time for Earconwald to speak again. After he rose from his seat, all others stood and waited. As he scanned the faces in the room, Earconwald chose the right moment to begin.

"Then it's decided. This is the moment of destiny. Together, we'll march for the east. In Edan's name, we'll liberate Eormenlond for the Way. Even as we do, our allies, the Ilarchae, will attack Sildharan from the Wildlands, and at the appointed hour their kin will rise up against those who enslaved them. Thus, we'll smite our foes between the hammer and anvil, bringing light to all of Eormenlond. My friends. My brothers. In this blessed hour, let us resolve with bonds stronger than death to uphold one another in battle. We'll not cease until Edan grants victory. For He has called us forth, and He'll guide our every step."

"Blessed be the Eternal!" shouted the supreme priest.

"Blessed be the Eternal!" came the cry from the priests and nobles.

Yet Earconwald could not help but note that not all called out with the same enthusiasm, and the two Ilarchae stood in stony silence. *No matter*, he thought. *Whether they pretend to worship Edan or not is of no consequence in the end. The strong bring others to follow. Sooner or later, they'll all come to know my power. They'll follow whether they wish to or not, and I'll dispose of them when I wish. That is what it means to be a god.*

16

THE EMBRACE

Soon after Orvandil and Gnorn sailed with King Vols and his men for Grimrik, Dayraven set out with Sequara, Galdor, and Abon on horses King Tirgalan of Sundara gave them. They headed north from Glirdan and passed through a pleasant country of rolling hills and rocky outcrops. Sundara's climate was much like Asdralad's, and the hot summer sun burned overhead. But as they journeyed north, the hills grew higher and the breeze cooler. The villages they stopped in for food and water became smaller and simpler as the landscape grew more rugged. The local people cultivated grains and vegetables on terraced hillsides, and Dayraven admired the soft greens and light browns of their summer crops. By the end of the second day of riding, Galdor informed them they would see no more villages for some time. To their west lay the southern end of the Osham Mountains, while to the east the Forest of Orudwyn was not far off. Their path lay between mountains and forest.

"After one more day, we'll reach the River Lannad, Sundara's border with Golgar," declared the wizard as they made camp. "There begins a great plain, where the riding will be swifter. When we cross the Lannad, we'll be in Golgar's territory for two days. Though its people are Sildharan's foes, they'll not hinder our journey as long as we stay far east of their chief city, Holurad. Folk call it the Hidden City, and with good reason. Few outside Golgar have seen that mountain fastness, and its people closely guard the path to it. Once Golgar's lands give way, we'll find the southern end of the West Road, one of the great roads that mark Sildharan's southern boundary. The way is easy from there, though not short."

"And every mile brings us closer to Torrlond and its allies," remarked Abon.

Among them the Mark's folk, thought Dayraven. There had to be a way to deprive Bledla of the dragons. He pondered the task often as they progressed on their journey. The elf-shard offered no help in its ceaseless whispers of shadows and darkness, prying at his mind like a cold breeze soughing over withered grass. There had to be a way to defeat the supreme priest. He needed to honor Urd and Faldira, and he yearned to ease Sequara's anguish by helping to restore Asdralad.

As they rode, he often glanced at the sorceress. Vivid memories of the night they spent holding and consoling each other in the boat would not leave his mind. He held and examined those memories the way a child might clutch a favorite toy. At times, Sequara returned his gaze, and in the sad smiles they mustered for each other lay recognition of their common grief. But they spoke little along the way.

Just as the old wizard had said, the third day's end brought them to the River Lannad. It was nearly evening when its rushing water murmured somewhere ahead of them. Not much later, when they crested a hill, the river shimmered below in the setting sun, its smooth surface frothy in a few places where it battered rocks. In clefts between hills the Lannad cut its way through the rocky landscape, and clusters of willows and brush grew on its green banks. They unloaded their horses and staked out a campsite in the lee of a large boulder a few hundred feet from the river.

"The ford's not far," said Galdor, "but we'd best not risk crossing until daylight."

"Shall I get a fire going, then?" asked Abon.

"Yes, thank you, Abon. On the bank you'll find sufficient wood. Perhaps a warm meal is in order tonight."

The shaper headed for the river while Sequara, Dayraven, and

Galdor made the camp ready. When he finished laying out his blanket and spare cloak as a sleeping mat, Dayraven ventured closer to the river to gather grass for the horses. He carried it back to where they had tied up the steeds and caressed his mount's neck as he fed her.

He looked up and realized how quiet it was. The others were away from the camp on errands. Even the elf-shard's respiration was a dim hiss. In the moment of solitude, he found his thoughts lingering on his great aunt. He had lost so much with her death. *Not sure I'm worthy of her sacrifice. One thing I do know: I miss her.*

"Urd told me you handle horses well."

Dayraven spun around toward the wizard's voice. At the same time, he became aware of the strong presence of the gift, which he had grown used to in the old man's company and thus ignored most of the time. Galdor stood smiling with arms crossed, as if reading Dayraven's thoughts like an open book. Yet Dayraven did not find this idea alarming. It was a comfort to be with someone who knew his burdens. He smiled at the old man. "I always found it easy to understand beasts. As a child, I fancied they spoke to me. Even the trees and hills whispered their old secrets in a tongue I could almost understand. I suppose Urd recognized this as a sign of the gift."

"She did. She spoke of you to me long before you met the elf. Yet she wished to spare you a wizard's life. Do you understand why?"

Dayraven hesitated. "Yes. Even now I sometimes wish this lot had fallen to someone else. The most difficult part is I can't separate myself from the Mark. I can't escape who I am, what I love. I fear I'll fail."

Galdor's brow furrowed and he nodded as he stepped closer. He put his hand on Dayraven's shoulder. "Using the gift means leaving behind our individuality. Yet, at the same time, it comes from our love of life in the world of forms. You see, we can't wield the songs of origin unless we become one with the world around us. When we perceive we're one with what we seek to control — that we *are* what we seek to control — then we cease to exist as individuals. We tear the veil and face the numinous. Terrifying and sublime it is."

Dayraven nodded.

Galdor continued. "But don't despair because you can't forget what you love. Are any of us capable of this? We'd have no power if we did

— no life. Even Bledla loves with devotion matched by few, for he's given everything to Edan and the Way, though he fails to see beyond his narrow view of Edan. But know this: There's a difference between selfish attachment and love for life. Real love means you're capable of sacrificing for something or someone, as Urd did for you. This is the source of your power."

Dayraven puzzled over the wizard's words. "If this is so, then why are those who wield magic discouraged from having lovers or children? King Tirgalan spoke of Ogmos, one of the greatest sorcerers in the annals. He fathered Sildhar, Rioda, and Golg, didn't he?"

Galdor smiled. "Yes, Ogmos was perhaps the greatest sorcerer in the annals of the Andumae here in Eormenlond. According to the tales, he loved the woman with whom he fathered his three children. That's why he went north to found his own kingdom. As the most powerful sorcerer of his day, he could have been king of Sundara. But the ancient custom of the Andumae was that only the unwed could rule. When he married, he gave up kingship. But those among the Andumae who would have him as king followed him north. Many say Ogmos' decision to wed and father children led to the war that followed when his offspring quarreled over the kingdom, and over the span of history, their quarrel brought much ruin. They say it's an example of why a ruler or great sorcerer should never indulge in such attachments."

"What do you say?"

The old wizard thought before answering, wearing a slight smile and staring as if lost in his own memories. "I'm not sure. *I* loved someone — so much that it gave me almost unbearable joy and pain. But long ago we parted ways, and our fates have sundered us."

"Did she . . . Is she still . . ."

"Alive? Yes. But not *she*. He. *He* is still alive."

Dayraven tried to think of something to say as his mouth hung open. "Oh . . . I'm sorry."

"For what?"

"I mean . . . I shouldn't have pried."

Galdor smiled. "I invited you to, so there's no need to be sorry. But perhaps I've made you uncomfortable."

"No. It's just, I've never . . . Well, I've heard of . . ." He winced. "Sorry."

"There you go being sorry again. Whatever for this time?"

"I . . . I'm not sure."

"Dayraven. I don't need to tell you that people love. Sometimes we love someone that others say we aren't supposed to love. In my case, it was a man. In your case, it's a beautiful sorceress who happens to be the heir to Asdralad's throne."

Dayraven felt the blood rush to his face. "Is it that obvious?"

"Yes." Galdor chuckled. "But my point is this: Who is to say why we love or whom we may love? And what's the end of it all? Some loves seem to end in tragedy, as did mine. But I cannot regret it. I would never have understood half the things I know about life without that wonderful, painful experience."

"So, something happened to separate you?"

The old wizard bowed his head. "In fact, Bledla had a hand in breaking us apart. It's one of the reasons he hates me so much."

"Bledla?"

"Yes. You see, the supreme priest and I have known each other since our youth. We trained together in Torrhelm, back when I was a priest of the Way, before they kicked me out."

"Because of your love?"

"That, and some of my other unusual views." The wizard smiled and winked. "It's an old story best told another time, but it wasn't so long ago that this old man can't see when someone's in love. I know it can be difficult for those who use the gift. The greater the attachment, the greater the hardship when we leave. In the end, we lose all such attachments whether we will it or not. Death is the final breaking of the illusion, but those who wield magic must learn to transcend themselves before their final day. We who knowingly remove our masks must always hold dear ones close to our hearts, for through them we connect to the world, and through them we learn to see the world in ourselves. All the while, we prepare to let go of ourselves when we must."

The elf-shard's susurrations glided along the surface of Dayraven's mind and chilled it. Its whispers were cold and lonely. A vast, dark emptiness lay behind them.

The wizard looked hard at Dayraven. "But you must decide for yourself what you'll do. You have great power in your possession, so you must make difficult decisions. This you can't avoid. But I'll tell you this: Your love for the world around you and those in it gives you your true power, not the elf, or whatever it was the elf put in you. Without it, you could never challenge Bledla."

Dayraven took in Galdor's words with a sigh. "And we still haven't thought of a way to overcome Bledla's control over the dragons. This is the question I must answer."

Galdor grinned. "It may be the same question we were discussing just now. But an answer will come. We have many miles before we reach Sildharan."

"Yes, though those miles will pass. For now, I'll wash off the day's dust and sweat in the river while there's a bit of sunlight left."

"A good idea. I'll wait for Abon to make the fire."

Dayraven turned and headed for the river, but then he paused and looked back at the wizard, who was stroking one of the horse's noses. "Galdor?"

The old man turned toward him and raised an eyebrow. "Yes?"

"Thank you."

Galdor's green eyes seemed to sparkle as he smiled and nodded.

Deep in thought, Dayraven left the old wizard and headed for the river. Galdor had given him much to think about, and he sighed as he looked about him and listened to the gurgle of the river.

Slivers of bright red and orange in the west occupied the darkening sky, and he reckoned he had just enough time to bathe before it grew dark. He saw no one as he headed out of the camp and wondered where Sequara had gone. As was often the case, he found his thoughts lingering on her. *She must be thinking of home. Imharr is still there. Gods, keep him safe.* It was almost unbearable to think of what might be happening on Asdralad.

Looking for a shallow pool, he approached the river and headed upstream. The river's current drowned out all other sounds save the hush of the elf-shard, which seemed to meld with it. He thought about

Urd and the Mark, and he wondered if his father marched with Torrlond's army. *They'll come. Stigand, Guthere, Father. All. They'll consider it their duty. For kinsmen they lay down their lives. A sacrifice, though misguided. Yet I once thought like them. Now, they would see me as an outsider. A foe, even. Who am I now? Who is my family?*

His mind conjured an image of Sequara's beautiful face, and he grinned like a fool. *Gods, Galdor was right.* He broke from his thoughts when he spotted a promising spot for his bath. Just beyond a clump of brush, the river had carved a calm pool into the bank, and it looked deep enough.

Dayraven approached the pool but did not undress. He stood watching the water's flow, and he allowed his mind to dwell on Sequara. Soon, he was seeing her memories in fragmented images, from girlhood up to the day she saved his life in Caergilion. Some of the scenes drew a wistful smile from him, while others were a weight on his heart. Sequara's loneliness was a thread that wove its way through almost all. Longing to console her, to ease the pain of her daily sacrifice and self-denial, he focused on the memories until they became even more vivid in his mind. Embracing Sequara's humanity, even reliving her pain and her noble desire to heal and live up to her calling as Faldira's heir, he felt a welling of emotions. Fear of inadequacy. Sorrow at the loss of loved ones. Guilt for that sorrow. Determination to do right. Love for her home and her people. A desperate hope that she would not let them down. He released a long sigh.

I love her, he admitted to himself. *Just as Galdor said. I love her, and I will use that love to give me strength. To do what I must. To make the needed sacrifices, just as she would do.* A tear trickled down his cheek, and his view of the river grew blurry. Sequara's presence permeated him, and he even felt the familiar feeling of the gift in her.

"Dayraven."

He turned at the sound of her voice. Wiping the tear tracks from his cheeks, he managed a weak smile, almost laughing at himself. *Of course, it was no memory.* He had been sensing the actual presence of the gift in her. There she stood, the setting sun casting a red sheen on her raven hair. More beautiful than anyone he had ever known, and, with her memories dwelling in him, he felt he knew her as completely as one human can another.

Sequara approached him until she stood close. Her moist eyes revealed that she too had been weeping. Gazing at him, she shook her head. "You're seeing them too, aren't you?"

Not trusting his voice, he nodded.

As if expecting his response, she nodded in return, opened her mouth, and then paused. She shook her head again. "Your memories are . . ." She shuddered. "They call me. I can no longer . . ."

"Perhaps it doesn't matter. Just now. Perhaps we can . . ."

She nodded.

They reached out for one another at the same time. Her hands grasped his shoulders, and he found his arms around her waist. He leaned down as her face tilted up toward him, and her soft lips pressing on his sent of shiver of ecstasy through him. Slow and tender their kisses began, but they grew more eager until Dayraven lost himself in her. They broke away and smiled at each other. Sadness and joy dwelled together in those smiles.

"Whatever happens, at least we can give each other this." Sequara began to undress.

THEY LAY TOGETHER FOR A WHILE IN EACH OTHER'S ARMS AS THE echoes of their passion ebbed. Dayraven had never felt such bliss in his life, such contentedness as all else save the warmth of her body and the gift of her spirit fled from his awareness. Once her breaths slowed to normal, Sequara released a long sigh and stood from the pile of their clothes on the riverbank. She smiled and extended her hand. "Come. Let's have that bath you came here for."

He grasped her hand and followed her to the river. When they waded in, the cool, soothing water raised goosebumps on their skin. They found that the pool came up to their waists, and there they stood face to face. In the gloaming they held and caressed each other. Sweet and cool was the water on their flesh, and tender was their embrace as it flowed around them. After a few slow kisses, Sequara scooped up water in her hands and poured it over Dayraven's head.

When she repeated this enough times, she massaged his scalp, and then he did likewise for her. Between more kisses they massaged and rubbed each other's bodies clean with lavender they found on the riverbank.

Dayraven wished the world could remain thus. At the same time, he knew he bought more pain with each blissful moment. Realizing his union with Sequara had brought everything to a decision point, he envisioned two possible paths. One ended with his own happiness, but at a terrible price that he could never forget. The other led to uncertainty. The way he would take was obvious but not easy. A resolution formed in his mind even as he poured water over Sequara's chest and kissed her. He looked in her eyes and saw it there: Sequara had understood it even before he had. *Can't keep all this for myself. My task calls. I must lose myself, but this moment will remain with me. As Galdor said: loved ones allow us to connect with the world and see the world in us. This love will be my fuel. Only now, it's my time to let go.*

"I must leave. I understand now. I must walk my path alone." It was as if someone else were saying the words with his voice, but he knew they were right.

As she gazed at him, tears filled her eyes, but her voice did not waver when she said, "I know." Then she smiled. "You see? Already the pain begins. Always we pay for love with grief."

"And I would pay that price again and again."

She gazed at him before a gentle smile bloomed on her face. "As would I. It's a worthy price."

"When this is finished, I will find you."

She nodded, and they kissed once more before they left the river to put on their clothes. It was nearly dark as they walked to the camp. In silence they held each other's hands. When they reached the boulder their sleeping mats lay near, they found only the horses and a small pile of wood.

"Galdor and Abon must have gone to fetch more wood, or perhaps they're fishing or bathing," said Sequara.

"Just as well. Tell them for me."

"You mean to leave now?"

"I'll not have the strength to leave you tomorrow. If I don't do it now, I never will. Bledla's sacrificed everything for his cause. So must I. For you, and for everyone I hold dear, I do this."

"I understand. I want you to."

Dayraven packed his few things and loaded his horse. As it was dark and the ground rocky, he decided to lead his steed on foot. He turned to Sequara. "Your strength will guide me on the road ahead. Stay with Galdor and Abon. Be safe. I'll come to you."

"Where will you go?"

In Sequara's voice he heard her struggling to hold back tears, and he choked back his own. He hesitated, but somehow he knew where his journey would take him. "East. To the Forest of Orudwyn."

They kissed one last time, and he lingered over the kiss until he could almost not bear to leave. He broke away. "Stay safe. I'll find you."

"In Sildharan we'll meet. Follow your path, Dayraven. Don't swerve from it."

He looked back at Sequara as he pulled his horse. After a moment, darkness swallowed her. The murmuring elf-shard was his only companion.

He followed the Lannad on its journey east. Alone in the darkness he walked, hardly mindful even of the horse he led. Trusting the river to guide him to the forest, he listened to its babble. With no awareness of time and heedless of the ache in his limbs, he stopped only to slake his thirst and let his horse drink from the river. The beast also chewed grass on its bank. But even while he rested, Dayraven never ceased to ponder his destination. His thoughts centered on the sense of purpose building in him. It seemed to emanate from the presence the elf had inserted in his mind.

Gradually but inexorably, the elf-shard slithered and bled from within him into the darkness around him. His perception of it expanded until it was a vast force surrounding him. It was cosmic and playful, like a dance, yet at the same time terrible and tragic, like a solemn ritual. Its hugeness produced a sense of his individual insignificance, but at the same time he fathomed his purpose as he looked at the stars above and heard the river's rushing. As this purpose grew, he saw in it both death and birth. In his mind he said farewell to Dayraven of the Mark and to any claim on those he loved, both living and dead. Lingering over each in turn, he released his memories of them to the wind. To Urd, Faldira, and Hlokk, to Ebba, Imharr, and his father and the mother he never knew, to Kinsford's folk, to Orvandil and Gnorn, to Abon and Galdor, and last to Sequara of Asdralad he said goodbye.

When he finished, he took little notice of the tears running down his cheeks. He dwelled only on the clear calling urging him toward Orudwyn. What he would find there he did not know, but he knew he would lose himself. Time passed, and though his tired feet faltered in the darkness, he kept on his way. It seemed now to him his fate drove him, that he was fey, and he heeded neither hunger nor pain when he stumbled on the rocks. When dawn's red and orange broke into the morning sky and pierced the darkness, he took no notice other than to mount his horse and continue east.

On horseback in the morning's growing light his pace quickened, and it was not long before the brush and trees along the riverbanks thickened in larger clusters. Tall cedars and firs appeared, and soon enough a line of trees took form, Orudwyn's outlying sentries. The river disappeared inside the forest of broadleaf evergreens, oaks, ashes, acacias, and firs, all of which kept green even in Sundara's dry summer. Further in loomed giant trees with reddish bark that towered higher than any others he had ever seen or imagined. Dayraven thought, *They reach the gods' realm.*

As the sun shone down, he reflected on how this southern forest was more open, more airy and lighter than the Southweald, and its beauty of a different sort. Yet, if they were not as threatening and gloomy, Orudwyn's proud trees were no less ancient. They swayed in the breeze as if hearkening to the elf-shard that was rustling within him and stirring without him. Here was the place to meet his fate. He alighted from his horse and led it beneath the canopy, through which beams of sunlight stabbed to spot the forest floor.

At once Dayraven felt he had come to a place ordained for him. The events of his life, especially in the last year, led to this forest. He sensed something conscious observing him, perhaps some creature, perhaps the trees. Or rather, as he understood with a sudden insight, it was the presence of the elf watching him through the trees. He did not understand how it could see him at once from within his mind and from without, yet he was certain it was doing that.

Other than a few birds flitting from branch to branch, nothing from the world of forms stirred. He ventured further in, making sure to keep the river within hearing distance. Not sure what to expect, he walked his horse deeper into Orudwyn, and the steed followed. Their progress was easy, for the trees were spaced far apart. Indeed, it seemed the forest accepted his presence, even made his path clearer, as if it somehow sensed his purpose. Each step grew surer. Each movement forward increased his conviction.

The sun rose higher as he made his way beneath Orudwyn's leaves, all the while focusing on what called him. *This is where I'll find what I seek. I'm on the verge of it. It's all around me. It's within me.*

At length, his hunger and lack of sleep broke through to his consciousness. He looked around as one startled out of a dream. Before him stood a gnarled, ancient oak whose twisting roots webbed out over the forest floor and thick branches loomed high overhead. Bulges and folds covered its hoary hide along with scabs of lichen and moss. A few faded green and brown tatters hung from the oldest convoluted branches sagging to the ground, but most of the tree exulted in its enormous vivid-green crown. Its sunlit, almost translucent leaves trembled as the wind soughed through them, echoing the elf-shard's hiss. It seemed to Dayraven this thick oak was one of Orudwyn's eldest trees, that its memory extended long before the founding of Eormenlond's kingdoms, before even the coming of the Andumae. *Enough*, he thought as he gazed on it.

He tied his horse to another tree and sat on the earth beneath the oak, nestling between two large roots. Remembering his training from Urd and Queen Faldira, he allowed his body to loosen and his inner turmoil to fade. All fears and desires softened to a whisper, and soon they died out, surrendering to the elf-shard's steady hush. Thus prepared, he closed his eyes and opened himself to the vast energy of the forest thriving all around him. Behind the barrier in his mind, the elf-shard quickened as if recognizing something akin to it and yearning towards it. But he remained calm and in control. Soon he breathed in time with the forest's pulse — slow and deep. His breaths grew more and more slow, then almost impossibly dim, until he would have seemed to anyone stumbling upon him a sylvan statue sitting for eternity beneath the oak.

In the realm of origins he saw the forest's ancient cycle of birth and decay, and next to it the span of Eormenlond's kingdoms was the blink of an eye. Dayraven forgot the fleeting time of men and women, and instead he perceived himself as part of a moment in the many thousands of years during which the forest lived and died over and over. Interwoven threads of life and death bound together those thousands of years, and he was woven into them. Had he reflected on his minuteness in the face of such things, he might have gone mad with wonder or despair and never awakened. But Dayraven knew what he was doing, for he perceived no distinction between his energy and the forest's. In the realm of origins, he was part of its life. Only the illusion of existence differentiated him from its trees and beasts. Thus time passed as the sun continued its journey in the sky, but time meant nothing in the realm where Dayraven wandered.

And then the shard of the elf stirred, prodding at the membrane that segregated it from the rest of his mind. It wanted release.

He readied himself to seize the exit point of his mind and narrow the vast energy to a controlled stream. It was like grasping ahold of a wild horse as it streaked by, but he was determined never again to allow the elf-shard to destroy his chances of defeating Bledla. He had to learn to wield it without any risk of failure. Somehow, he needed to learn to draw upon its power without allowing it to shatter him in pieces. So he braced himself.

But then a memory flashed in his mind from the day when all the simplicity and certainty had fled from his life. When he encountered the sublime, celestial elf in the Southweald, before he succumbed to it, there had been a moment when he let go. During that moment, he had seen with clarity, and he had stopped feeling like he was drowning for a brief while.

The idea that came to him was terrifying, and he recoiled from it. What if he let go? What if, without any resistance or attempt at control, he allowed the elf-shard to explode from his mind and have its will? What if he let all of its vast power rush outward at once?

He was not certain he would ever come back. But then, why else had he come here? Why else had he said goodbye to everyone he loved?

It was like diving off a cliff in the dark.

Dayraven let go and dove.

I release you. Take me with you.

The barrier in his mind disappeared. He not only gave the elf-shard free rein, but he also embraced it as it emanated from him. The measureless outpouring of energy should have fragmented him into particles scattering across the infinite realm of origins until they lost distinction from the all-encompassing force animating all things. He exhaled a long breath.

Nothing happened.

Silence.

Darkness.

He could not have told how long he sat waiting with his eyes closed beneath the oak. At length, something stirred nearby, as if a presence had come close to his body. Somehow it seemed important to return to meet this presence, so he grew aware of his material being. In the body that sat in the world of forms, his physical senses returned. His legs were stiff with sitting atop the hard ground. The scents of earth and trees wafted by with a breeze that brushed and lingered over his face.

When he was ready, his eyes snapped open, and he beheld bright splinters of late afternoon sun amidst trees. He squinted as his eyes grew accustomed to the light. Soon he regained focus. Not more than twenty feet in front of him stood someone intimately familiar. Sequara.

When the strange flash of recognition came over Dayraven, he wondered how she had found him. *Did she follow me? Has she changed her mind?* He waited for her to speak.

However, instead of speaking, Sequara gazed at him with a look of desperate sorrow, her eyes pleading and her mouth open as if in pain. She extended her hand to bid him to come, to return to her and follow where she would go.

Dayraven began to rise from his spot beneath the oak, and he saw himself rushing to her. But he hesitated, and then his face's expression changed to impassive stone. "No," he said. He did not stir.

Sequara again gestured for him to approach, this time with more force, but still he sat beneath the oak, his countenance unmoved. When her third appeal produced no effect, her eyes winced with pain at his betrayal. Her gestures grew frantic as tears flowed from her eyes, but still Dayraven refused to move. She took out the curved sword from the scabbard at her side. Her eyes widened as madness took over her face, and her breast heaved while her breaths came hard and fast. Pointing the blade's tip at her heart, she appealed one last time to Dayraven with her eyes.

He stared at her.

She cried out and plunged the sword into her chest.

Dayraven remained where he sat.

She crumpled over in agony.

Yet she did not fall. Sequara pulled the blade out of her chest and stood erect. Instead of blood, light seeped then flowed from her wound, and the light grew until it covered her in a bright glow. After it grew nearly blinding in intensity, the glow subsided. The light became a garment clothing a new figure before Dayraven.

He recognized the elf he had met in the Southweald. The same deep, sky-blue eyes beckoned to him, and again she knew all his desires. The elf was as ethereal and sublime as the stars, and the temptation she embodied transcended the world of forms. As if she were an expression of his mind, within her eyes Dayraven saw all his memories from before the terrible day he had encountered her, before his exile.

The pools of her eyes reflected scenes of the Mark, Imharr, Ebba, Urd, and his father. She projected a return to an innocent, simple life if he would come with her. But Dayraven did not stir when her bright eyes commanded him to rise, for he knew this life she held out had never truly existed. She beckoned to him again, promising bliss everlasting, but Dayraven moved not an inch. The last time she called to him, she held her hands outward as if to embrace him, but he did not meet her.

Though she showed no other emotion, the elf-wife's seductive lips curved in a cunning smile that threatened annihilation. She extended her arms upward, and the elf grew. It was like watching a tree's growth over hundreds of years compressed into moments, for the elf kept towering until she reached the forest's top. Even then she did not stop, and at the same time her beautiful features transformed into the horrifying spectacle of a goddess of death.

Huge like the night sky was the woman looming over Dayraven, so large she shut out the sun. Lank strands of hair stuck to her head, and wounds festered with puss all over her gigantic body. Squirming lumps — maggots that were people — crawled beneath the putrid, grey flesh hanging in loose folds from her enormous bones. Hideous was her wrinkled visage, and her tongue as red as blood lolled between sharp, yellow teeth. Her face sagged so low that her red-veined eyeballs protruded until they almost fell out as they rolled around. The reek of decaying corpses nearly drove Dayraven to bury his face in his brown robe, but he sat firm and faced her.

A cackling, gurgling noise emanated from her mouth. She fixed her eyes on him, and huge clots of blood oozed over her lips. With the sound of popping bones and ligaments, her limbs inverted like a giant insect's to stoop on all fours. Her flat, veined dugs dangled low, and her horrible visage neared Dayraven. Her mouth gaped open. It seemed her intent was to devour him, but he did not move. Her huge maw overshadowed him, but he did not blink. Noisome saliva dropped on him, and the tip of her slick tongue came within inches of his face. Foul teeth surrounded him, yet Dayraven's face showed only equanimity. With a snap, utter darkness swallowed him.

For aeons, Dayraven sat in darkness. But time's passage meant nothing in this place, so he waited. While he abode in darkness, a voice spoke to him. It said not in words but in thought, *Life is the soul's sleep, death its awakening.*

As he pondered this, a glow sprang into existence and hovered in front of him. At length, the glow grew more definite and bright, and he realized it was much further away than he first thought. As it grew, it took on a long shape, but Dayraven could not yet say what it was. Higher it expanded until it seemed to go on infinitely. At the same time, nine branches grew out from it, and the branches also extended forever. Now Dayraven knew the glow was an immortal tree that gave its own light.

He sat before the all-encompassing oak Laeroth. Its majesty enveloped all the individual joys and tragedies of existence. On each of its nine branches, giant clouds exploded with cosmic violence, and within them bright stars leapt into existence. Whole worlds came to life then disappeared in wrath and chaos. Kingdoms arose and crumbled into dust. Individual beings were born into love and pain before they succumbed. All that ever was or would be took form on the tree, lingering for shorter or longer whiles, pulsing with beauty and splendor, but always ending in darkness while some new bright thing came into being.

It was all of life. For ages upon ages Dayraven watched, entranced as the eternal dance unfolded. In Laeroth's presence, he was beyond yet within the bliss and pain of the worlds. He accepted life as the breakage of eternity into time, and death as the return to eternity. Once he embraced life and death, he teetered on an abyss. Somehow, it was right he should fall toward the tree. So he let go.

He experienced the falling as if flying, and more aeons passed as he plummeted toward one of the nine branches. The branch grew until it took over his field of vision. He fell towards one of its innumerable stars. After some time, however, he saw it was no star, but a swirling glow containing uncountable stars of its own. Toward one he tumbled until that star became the largest thing he saw, a giant ball of gaseous, roiling brightness.

Still more aeons passed. He flew near the star toward a speck that enlarged until it became a blue orb with streaks of green, brown, and white. The orb grew until it became all that was. Dayraven awed at its immensity and at the vast water surrounding many lands. The swirls of white surrounded the orb, and he plummeted into one of them, its vapors enfolding him for a long while.

When he emerged from the vapors, a vision took form far below. At first blurry, the vision gradually sharpened. Like a bird, he looked down on a jagged, snow-clad mountain. Below the snow and the bare grey rock, an army of ragged pines blanketed the mountain's base. Though no one dwelled near it, he knew the mountain was in Eormenlond. It lay in the heart of the Osham Mountains, and folk as far away as the Mark had heard this mountain's name: the Wyrmberg.

Thus folk had named the craggy peak for more than a thousand years, for it was said to be home of the eldest dragon in Eormenlond. Most considered her a legend, but some swore by tales passed down over generations about her existence. Gorsarhad was she called, eldest of dragons. It seemed to him the elf-shard whispered her name, for the first time forming a distinct word from its susurration.

As he thought on all this, Dayraven continued to fall. He plummeted toward the snowy peak, which grew larger by the moment. He dropped faster and faster. He focused on the white snow, which grew bright. The brightness grew closer and larger until it began to push all other forms out of his vision. Soon all he could see was this brilliance, and he was sure the impact must come. Not long now. In moments he would hit.

Here it comes, he thought just before his body collided with the brightness.

17

THE HOMECOMING

Gnorn set sail with Orvandil, King Vols, and the rest of the Thjoths with a mixture of anticipation and dread. Much of the dread stemmed from the sea voyage, for they needed to sail to Eormenlond's other side to reach Grimrik. There were fleeting moments when he half suspected Orvandil had insisted on his presence as a diversion during the journey, for the Thjoths took an almost cruel delight in the Dweorg's seasickness. But, in truth, he was grateful beyond words for his friend's request that he accompany them to Grimrik. He would be the first Dweorg of the Fyrnhowes to see his ancestors' land in nigh two hundred years. Besides, Orvandil boasted the Thjoths' swift ships would complete the voyage in only ten days, though anyone else would need a fortnight. Orvandil made no idle boasts, so there was some consolation at least. *If only Hlokk was here*, was his chief thought as they clove through the waves and left behind Glirdan.

Along the way, Gnorn grew better acquainted with some of the warriors aboard King Vols' ship. The friendliest was Duneyr, a red-haired man with wrinkles around his eyes, probably from all the smiling he did, one of the things that set him apart from most of the others. He was small and wiry for a Thjoth, though large enough among men in most kingdoms. Vols put great faith in Duneyr, who took command when the king was abed. The Dweorg approved of the choice, for Duneyr was older and showed more wisdom and circumspection than most of his hasty and headstrong comrades. But Gnorn found much to admire in the tall sailors and warriors with whom he found himself. They were strong, fearless, and free, and the more he understood the old foes of his people, the more he respected them.

Across the Great Sea they journeyed, and as they sailed, Orvandil informed Gnorn of their bearings. First they went by the southern coast of Sundara. Past Sundara's second city of Tinubor they sailed. Clinging to a rocky peninsula that overlooked the churning water beneath it, Tinubor was smaller than Glirdan but just as old. Gnorn would have gladly stopped for a look at the ancient scrolls and books said to inhabit the many libraries of Tinubor, but he doubted the Thjoths held much interest in such things, and they were in haste.

Soon enough they left behind Sundara, and past Sildharan's rocky eastern coast with its gleaming cities of Kelgaon and Shinan they sailed. On a small, uninhabited island just past Shinan, the three ships made land to resupply, and Gnorn was glad to feel the earth beneath his feet after days at sea.

While they were waiting for King Vols and others to return with the supplies, most of the men drank mead and idled on the beach. Some of them diced, others gambled on friendly wrestling bouts between their fellows, and still others sat on the sandy beach telling stories. Gnorn and Orvandil were among the last. With the waves crashing against the sand and the seagulls' cries as a background, they listened to Duneyr, who recounted the tale of how he wed his wife. He spoke in the Northern Tongue for the benefit of the Dweorg, who had the impression that everyone else had heard the story many times but enjoyed listening to it again.

"With all the shrieking going on, the other women rushed into the hall, thinking I must have been too forward with poor Sivora. Well, when they arrived, they saw the real cause, and instead of helping, they broke out in laughter. For it was I who was in need of aid, and Sivora was clinging to my leg. I was dragging the woman on her belly behind me in my attempt to escape her advances."

The other Thjoths chuckled, and a warrior called Ekil One-Eye said, "It's a wonder you could drag her at all. Sivora must be twice your size." He winked his one eye.

More laughter followed, and Duneyr replied with a smile, "Desperation lends great strength to any man," which prompted yet more laughs.

"But not enough strength for you to get away," said Kialar, a blond fellow and a wily veteran with several battle scars across his face.

Duneyr nodded. "Indeed no. Twice my size and twice as stubborn she is. Sivora would have chased me down and sat on me until I consented to wed her. And besides, the women spread word of my . . . predicament. I was cornered. So we wed the next summer. Four sons and three daughters later, I remain the happiest man in Grimrik."

"To Sivora, and all stubborn wives!" said Asgrim, a muscled, lean fellow with hair that was dark for a Thjoth but grey at the temples. He raised his horn of mead.

"Sivora!" shouted the others, and they took a deep draft from their horns and cups.

Gnorn drank and chuckled along with the others.

"And what of you, friend Gnorn: Are you a married man?" asked Duneyr.

He glanced around at the faces awaiting his answer and tried to smile as he lowered his cup. "I? No. I've not had the privilege to settle down with a wife."

Orvandil clapped him on the shoulder. "Gnorn's a warrior, not a lover."

"Aye," said the Dweorg with a smile. "I'm wed to my axe." He patted the weapon, which hung in his belt.

The others chuckled. But one of the Thjoths, a young but large fellow called Halvard, scowled at Gnorn. "How can half a man be a warrior of any account?"

Orvandil's smile disappeared. "Take care, Halvard." The fierce gleam in his eyes belied his mild voice. It was a look Gnorn recognized as one he would never wish directed at him.

The young fellow's eyes expanded just long enough to show his fear of Orvandil, but he put on a brave face and frowned with contempt.

"Well, if the Dweorg's such a mighty warrior, why does he hide behind you?"

Orvandil began to rise, but Gnorn put his hand on his friend's knee. "It's alright. I don't blame the lad for doubting."

"If their kind are so tough," scoffed Halvard, "how was it our forefathers packed off the little grubbers without a fight?"

Gnorn stiffened. "There was much bloodshed. It took Dragvendil and all his warriors a score of years to defeat us."

"Bah! Wouldn't take me twenty winks to thrash you."

"Let's put a wager on it," said Bodvar, a bear of a man who carried an axe rather than a sword.

"Five silver pieces say the Dweorg lasts longer than the count of twenty," said Hakon, a blond warrior who had been friendly to Gnorn.

"What if he runs away?" asked Emund Grey-Tooth, a veteran whose remaining teeth were the same color as his hair.

"He won't," said Orvandil. He took out his purse and threw it on the ground. It jingled, and two of the fat coins spilled out. "I'll wager everything in there that Gnorn brings down Halvard first. Any takers?"

There was silence for a moment, and the Thjoths looked at one another as if waiting for someone to make a move. All at once, shouts broke out, and it took a while for them to settle all their bets. While they were sorting it out, Gnorn turned to Orvandil.

"Are you mad?" whispered the Dweorg between his teeth as he forced a smile. "That young fellow's twice my size!"

"But only half as smart. All you need do is put him on the ground before he gets ahold of you."

"Any suggestions?"

"Use your head. And don't let him get ahold of you."

Gnorn's eyes widened.

"Right, then!" Duneyr's voice rose above the throng, and the rest quieted. "I'll review the rules for Gnorn. No weapons. First one on the ground loses. In case of death, the winner pays wergild to the loser's kin."

Gnorn turned to Orvandil with his eyebrows raised. "Death?"

Orvandil plucked the cup out of his friend's hand and pointed at the axe in the Dweorg's belt. "Your weapon. I'll hold it."

"Did he say 'death'?" Gnorn got up and tugged out his axe.

Orvandil grasped the weapon and shrugged. "It seldom happens. At least when we're sober."

"How often is 'seldom'?"

Before Orvandil could answer, Halvard yelled and ran for the Dweorg, and all the others arose to make a wide ring around the two combatants.

Gnorn spun around to face the big man rushing at him like a wild boar. He stood his ground and narrowed his eyes as he assessed his situation. "By the ancestors' beards. Here's a hasty one."

A moment before Halvard reached him with his arms outstretched to maul him, Gnorn crouched down and then launched himself head foremost, avoiding the long arms and colliding into the young man's stomach with his helm.

On impact, Halvard wheezed and buckled over with the air knocked out of him on top of Gnorn. The Dweorg spread his stout legs and managed to keep his footing. He grasped his assailant by the torso, heaved him up, and bellowed, "Hzaatarku Kheendwunok!" With a loud grunt, he toppled over the young man, who landed on his back in the sand with a thump.

The wide-eyed Thjoths broke out in loud cheers and laughter, though most of them had lost silver.

Gnorn left Halvard gasping and clutching his belly in a fetal tuck. Trying not to show how his head rang and his back ached, he swaggered back toward Orvandil, who held out the Dweorg's axe and said, "Not even to the count of twenty."

He tucked his axe back into his belt. "Aye. As you advised, I used my head. And you owe me half your winnings."

Orvandil chuckled. "No. You earned them all. And a fair bit of respect on top."

The Dweorg grunted. "Not to mention a sore back."

After supplying on the small island, they left behind the gentler lands of the south for the rugged north. To their west they spotted the Edwend Downs, beyond which lay Slith, greatest of fens, and even Gnorn was happy not to make land there. Around the vast Wildlands they sailed, and he was equally content not to venture near the Ironwood. This seemed to the Dweorg the longest part of their journey, and though the tales he knew of those lands gave them a menacing air, he was not blind to the strange beauty they harbored, at least in the mild summer. He was relieved when Orvandil let him know they had entered the Savage Sea, and his anticipation grew when they reached the Gulf of Olfi.

They sailed by Vargholm early on the morning of the tenth day. Gnorn noted the melancholy settling on Orvandil, who stared blank-faced over the waters at the island where long ago he slew his foster-brother Thioldolf in a duel over the woman they loved. At the same time, the Dweorg's excitement grew when Grimrik's hilly coastline appeared in the distance behind tears in the veil of morning mist.

A deep-green, craggy landscape emerged behind the thinning fog. Gnorn awed at the hills his ancestors had dwelled on, hills the Thjoths mistook for the ancient Dweorgs' haunted barrows and hence named the Fyrnhowes. As he gazed without blinking on the coastal fells with fjords etched deep into them, a friendly hand rested on Gnorn's shoulder. He looked up at Orvandil, who said, "Welcome home, friend."

"Shouldn't I be saying that to you?"

"We'll see how welcome I am."

After sailing into one of the fjords, the three ships rowed toward a beach settlement at its end, where a long wooden hall waited. The ships crunched onto the shingle, and several warriors emerged from the hall to greet them.

"Skifu koniges er cuman!" shouted one on shore, and the Thjoths hollered greetings. Gnorn did not need to know Thjothic to understand they were glad to see each other. Within moments those on shore secured the ships. Byrnies clinked as those on board leapt onto the shingle. The large warriors on both sides embraced one another amidst loud laughter. Some with whom Gnorn had sailed pointed at him and Orvandil, and those from the shore stopped their laughter to stare and murmur questions to their comrades.

As they became the object of everyone's attention, Orvandil said to

Gnorn, "I wondered who'd make the bigger impression. At the moment, you're winning."

"Thanks. That's a comfort."

King Vols stopped for a brief but hearty meal in the hall, during which the men exchanged stories as they sat on benches and quaffed large horns of ale. But no story captured their attention so much as Orvandil's, who told them of the great war brewing. Gnorn surmised from their responses they were happy with Orvandil's homecoming and despised Torrlond's ambitions. The latter he concluded from the frowns of contempt every time the Thjoths uttered "Earconwald" and "Way" in their thick accents.

"It seems things are going well thus far," the Dweorg said to his friend when he had a chance.

"Hard part hasn't come."

After their meal, King Vols called a dozen men. To each he gave a black arrow, and they departed in haste.

Orvandil leaned closer to Gnorn. "Vols is summoning the moot. The black arrow's a war token. They'll ride hard to spread the word, and others will take up the arrows when their horses grow weary. Grimrik's warriors will assemble on the Thingvang, the plain outside Valfoss, in two days. There they'll decide whether or not to follow Vols to war."

"How many warriors does Grimrik hold?"

"Eight thousand. Each accounts for two of Torrlond's best," said Orvandil with a confident nod. Soon Vols gave orders, and the two friends set out with one hundred fifty Thjoths on foot for Valfoss.

OVER ROUGH HILLS THEY MARCHED, AND THEIR PACE WAS NOT feeble. The sun shone down on them from a clean sky. The only other beings in sight were sheep grazing on the green-clad fells and large hawks circling overhead. Orvandil walked next to Gnorn. "Vols likes stretching his legs on these hills, especially after a sea journey. How do you find it?"

Gnorn took a deep breath and exhaled. "Though a Dweorg's legs are half as long as a Thjoth's, I could walk over these lands for days on end."

"Good," said Orvandil with a quick smile. "But our journey ends today in Valfoss."

"Valfoss." Gnorn repeated the name with slow precision. "'Slaughter by the falls' it means in your tongue, does it not?"

A thoughtful frown crossed Orvandil's face. "Yes. Where Dragvendil slew your people by the thousands. We preserve our deeds in our names."

"You Thjoths are not unique in that. Might be it's best to have such reminders, so deeds both good and ill live on in our memories."

"Might be."

The fells gradually softened over their march until, when the sun was right overhead, Gnorn got his first glimpse of Valfoss. As they ascended the last height, he looked down on a broad, green plain that hills surrounded on three sides. The plain, the Thingvang, was flat save one bulging hill in its center. A mighty river, the Mjothelf, cut the plain in half, disappearing for a moment on the farther side of the lone hill, after which it wound out of sight towards the west, the only direction in which no hills stopped its course. The river entered the Thingvang from hills on the northern side, where it rushed down foamy white from sharp cliffs a hundred feet above the plain, forming a broad waterfall whose roar echoed around the fells. Hard by the fall's base stood a town of some three thousand souls: Valfoss, Grimrik's chief city. For Gnorn, Dweorg of the Fyrnhowes, the sight was bittersweet, but he nodded in acknowledgement of the fulfillment it brought to his long troubled heart.

Valfoss was a town of modest wooden structures with turf or thatch roofs. Standing out among these dwellings was the king's hall, a long, high-gabled building with a thatched roof and large wooden columns before its great doors. Skjold was it called, and since Dragvendil's days it had housed Grimrik's kings. To Skjold Vols led his men, and the large party covered the distance with good speed, anticipating reunions with their families and a homecoming feast. Riders had preceded them with news of the king's arrival, so Orvandil promised Gnorn the fare would be well worth the day's march.

After hailing lookouts atop the town's wooden wall, the large party followed Vols through the main gates. The welcome was warm, and Gnorn saw from their cheers the people loved their king. Most did not hide their curiosity about the Dweorg's presence. Some stared and others pointed while some children laughed. For his part, Gnorn muttered under his breath but smiled and waved to the children.

The party made its way on the town's muddy central street toward Skjold. Along the way, most of the returning warriors broke off to embrace their wives and families, thus diminishing the party until only Vols and his unwed warriors arrived at his hall. Since there were fewer legs to hide behind, this also made it more difficult for Gnorn to blend in. Trying to ignore the unwanted attention, he focused on the hall looming before him. Four tall guards waited at Skjold's large wooden doors, which they opened as King Vols ascended the flight of stairs leading to the entrance. At the top of the stairs, Vols turned around and, with a great smile, hailed his people, who cheered and whooped.

Amidst stares and whispers, Gnorn made his way behind Orvandil through the press towards the steps. One little boy with light blond hair stood in front of Gnorn and smirked as he measured his height with his hand in comparison to the Dweorg's. Evidently, he found it amusing to be an inch taller than a bearded man, and the laughing crowd found the spectacle occasion for mirth.

Orvandil smiled. "They like you already."

"Hmmph," grunted Gnorn through a frown, but he smiled and chuckled afterwards.

He entered the hall with Vols, Orvandil, and a score of warriors. Two rows of blackened wooden columns supported the lofty roof. Already a fire crackled in the central fire pit, and over it roasted several boars, whose scent roused Gnorn's appetite. Men were lighting torches fixed on the columns to gladden the hall. Preparations were well underway for a great feast. Servants scurried about putting up tapestries, hauling baskets of food or barrels of ale, and setting up tables behind the columns.

Opposite the fire pit on one side waited the high seat, near which a small group of women gathered. One pointed towards the tables as she spoke, giving directions and guiding the preparations. She was the center from which all the activity radiated. The women looked toward Vols, after which they smiled, except the one in charge. A tall, slender woman in a white and blue dress with golden brooches, she made her way toward them with such elegance that she almost seemed to glide. As she came closer, Gnorn noted her auburn hair was thick and curly and her eyes bright green. She was strikingly beautiful. Confessing to himself he had never met a woman with such grace save Faldira, Gnorn surmised she must be the queen.

His guess proved correct when Vols broke away from his warriors to sweep the woman off her feet in a tight embrace. He laughed and kissed her cheeks while she pretended to scold him and smiled. After he put her down, Vols led her by the hand to Gnorn and Orvandil, saying in the Northern Tongue, "We have guests, my dear. Let me introduce you. This," he said with a gesture, "is Gnorn, Dweorg of the Fyrnhowes, who honors us as the first of his kind to return to these lands in many a year."

"Gnorn, Dweorg of the Fyrnhowes," she repeated, "it's a pleasure to meet you."

"Your Majesty," said Gnorn as he bowed and took off his helm. "Now that I see you, I wonder how the man fortunate enough to call himself your husband could ever leave this fair hall. May I have the pleasure of hearing your name from your own lips?"

The queen smiled at King Vols. "Perhaps you should bring more Dweorgs back to teach our men to speak so fairly." She turned her smile on Gnorn. "I'm called Osynia, and you are welcome to this hall."

"And here," said Vols as he clasped Orvandil's shoulder, "is our other guest, though perhaps you recognize him."

Queen Osynia beheld Orvandil with a slight frown and narrowed eyes. For a moment there was an awkward silence. King Vols' grin disappeared. Orvandil's mouth crept into an apologetic half smile. It seemed to the Dweorg his friend's face clouded over as he gazed on the woman.

The queen ended the silence. "He who returns home, even after many years, is no guest, but one of us. You are welcome in this hall, Orvandil."

Orvandil broke his gaze and bowed his head. "Thank you, my lady."

As he looked on, Gnorn reckoned he knew who Osynia was: the woman Orvandil slew his foster-brother for. Orvandil had said she wed another, but he did not say whom. *So here's the cause of his departure,* thought Gnorn. *She's indeed a woman many would live or die for.*

"Good," said King Vols with the mirth in his face returning. "Then let this homecoming feast be like no other, for my cousin and champion has returned. Thes notta vil ol fljotan!"

The king put his arm around the queen, resting his hand on her shoulder. Having kept the same frown as she continued to stare at Orvandil, the queen turned away. Gnorn was relieved not to have been the recipient of that look. After Vols left with Osynia to see to the preparations, the two friends stood apart watching their hosts disappear arm in arm. The Dweorg looked up at the Thjoth. "Was that the hard part, then?"

Orvandil gave a wry smile. "Aye."

That night the feast was merry and plentiful. Ale flowed, and there was an abundance of roast meat with fresh bread and summer produce. Orvandil and Gnorn sat in places of honor nigh the king and queen, and during the festivities Vols introduced his three daughters to them with a proud smile lighting up his face.

The eldest was on the verge of womanhood, whereas the youngest had seen eight winters. All three were fair like their mother, and it touched Gnorn to see the immediate affection Orvandil bore them, like a slightly shy but doting uncle. As he watched his friend speak with them in a tone gentler than he thought the man capable of, he recalled his cousin Ilm's two girls back in Etinstone. For their part, Vols' girls had obviously heard many stories of their father's cousin and, with eager eyes and nervous smiles, regarded him as something of a hero.

"I hear you pack a hard punch," said Orvandil to the youngest, who was named Yrsa.

She nodded and stuck her chin out. "Father says I might be a shield-maiden someday."

"Father said that, did he?" asked Osynia with one eyebrow cocked.

Vols looked down sheepishly. "I might have told the lass a story or two . . ."

Osynia's eyes narrowed in a threatening stare, and he returned it with a shrug and a charming smile.

Yrsa ignored them and asked Orvandil, "Is it true you slew an aglak with one sword blow?"

"Two, truth be told," said Gnorn. "He cut its hand off with the first, and the second nearly took its head off. Broke the blade too."

A wide-eyed and delighted grin broke out across Yrsa's face. "Tell me more!"

"Later," said Osynia with a firm nod. "It's well past your bedtime."

Yrsa protested, but in vain, and soon servants escorted the three sisters away.

When the girls had left, Orvandil said to Vols and Osynia, "They're beautiful. You've been fortunate in my absence."

Vols slapped his cousin's shoulder. "Now that you're back, we'll be more fortunate."

Orvandil looked down at his trencher. "How long I stay remains to be seen. There are matters to discuss at the moot."

"But tonight, at least," said Osynia, "let there be merriment." She filled a large horn with ale and presented it to her husband. He took a draught and handed it to Orvandil, who followed suit and passed it to Gnorn, who drank and gave it to Duneyr, who moved it along in turn. Thus passed the horn of peace among the company. There was joy as they spoke and gathered round the fire to hearken to the king's shaper sing of former days.

But such nights do not last forever. The next day brought a different atmosphere to Skjold. Everyone prepared for the moot, and Orvandil spent hours closeted with Vols' council to discuss their strategy.

Gnorn was left to wander the hills around Valfoss for the day, where he listened for his ancestors' voices. As he looked down from the hill he sat on, hundreds of Thjoths arrived from their scattered farmsteads and put up tents around the Thingvang's periphery. *No denying they're strong folk,* he mused to himself. *To my old eyes, they're a young people, full of vigor. Their aid would be a boon in the struggle ahead. Let's see what tomorrow brings.*

. . .

When Gnorn stood on the Thingvang at noon the next day, it was crowded with armed warriors eagerly discussing tidings of war outside their kingdom. They congregated around the Thingvang's lone hill. Having nowhere else to go, Gnorn tagged along with Orvandil, who followed Vols and a few of the king's trusted advisors, such as Duneyr, Asgrim, and Kialar. No one spoke to the Dweorg or even paid much heed to him, which suited him fine. It was a relief to find today he was not the primary object of attention, though curious stares came his way, and he felt painfully out of place. *What use I am here I don't know.*

Men parted before King Vols, who made his way toward the Thingvang's hill with his advisors trailing behind. The King's Mound it was called, for from its height the king of Grimrik addressed the assembled Thjoths during the moot. When Vols and his six followers, including Orvandil, ascended the path winding up the hill, Gnorn debated whether or not to follow. With everything else on his mind, it seemed Orvandil had forgotten he was even there.

Having no instructions, the Dweorg decided to pretend he belonged with them rather than twiddle at the bottom of the hill and see nothing past the tall warriors standing in front of him. Besides, he reckoned the hill would afford a fine view of the plain, and it must have been a place of importance to his ancestors. So he followed along, nearly jogging to keep up with the seven tall Thjoths. When they reached a point halfway up the King's Mound, they made their way to a flat ledge that gave a commanding view of the assembly below. There was enough space for more than a dozen men on the ledge, which rose about thirty feet above the ground.

Thus Gnorn found himself gazing down from the King's Mound on eight thousand warriors of Grimrik. He did his best to look important and not feel ridiculous, though he found the latter impossible. At the same time, he marveled at the sea of tall, grim warriors, and he knew such a body would be formidable in battle. Asgrim held a large horn to his lips and winded it thrice, thus signaling the moot's beginning. When the third note's echo died, there was silence. King Vols held his right hand aloft to greet the assembly.

Since he spoke in Thjothic, Gnorn had little idea what Vols said, but he could tell the king was a practiced speaker, and he approved of his sure tone. More than ever Vols seemed a king as the warriors devoted full attention to his words, and respect showed in their eyes. Occasionally, the Dweorg heard words he recognized, such as "Way," "Earconwald," and "Torrlond," but he could not piece together the gist of anything. At length, Vols gestured toward Orvandil and said his name, then he ceased talking. Murmurs broke out among the crowd, and Gnorn understood the import of Orvandil's return. Orvandil stepped forward on the ledge and raised his hand. The murmuring died.

Though he could not understand, Gnorn surmised Orvandil spoke of Earconwald's ambitions and the threat Torrlond and the Way posed to Grimrik. His friend went on for some time. The warriors below listened with attentive gazes. Gnorn, however, found his thoughts wandering as he pondered how his ancestors would have viewed this hill he stood on. He imagined they used the King's Mound for similar purposes: for assemblies or important rituals. It would have been a sacred site to Dweorgs, and leaders of his people might be buried on the hill's top. He would investigate as soon as he had a chance. Perhaps there were still clues up there.

These thoughts ceased when Gnorn realized Orvandil had finished speaking. A new voice broke the air, coming from below. It sounded loud and angry. Gnorn searched for its source among the many faces. His gaze rested on a large warrior with long brown hair at the front of the crowd directly below the ledge. He seemed by his dress and golden arm rings, not to mention his forceful speech, to be important. Gnorn did not know the meaning of his words, but they weren't friendly. The man turned his back to the King's Mound to address the assembly, and he stood on a large boulder at the hill's base to be better heard and seen. Many nodded in agreement with his words, particularly those close to him.

Gnorn glanced at Orvandil and King Vols, who wore a concerned frown. Guessing the proceedings were not going smoothly, Gnorn looked up at Orvandil and whispered, "What's going on? What's he saying?"

Orvandil did not seem to hear him, so Gnorn whispered more loudly, "What's he saying?"

Still no response. The Dweorg elbowed Orvandil's arm and hissed, "Confound it! What's he saying?"

Orvandil looked down, eyebrows raised in surprise. "Gnorn? Sorry. Didn't realize you were here."

"I noticed."

"He says we shouldn't go to war," whispered the Thjoth. "Wait here to see what Earconwald does. He never threatened us, nor should we mind if he kills outlanders."

"Who's this coward?"

"No coward. He's Eyolf. A chieftain, and the elder brother of Thioldolf, my foster-brother. I warned Vols of this. My presence may doom our cause."

Gnorn's eyes widened. "But they can't be heeding him."

"Many agree Torrlond has nothing to do with us."

"Don't they know what's happening out there?"

"They will, one way or the other."

"You must convince them."

"I'll try."

When Eyolf finished speaking, the warriors around him broke out in loud cheers that spread to a great part of the assembly. Once the cheers died down, Orvandil declaimed from the ledge again. He spoke well and without hesitation. Gnorn thought, *surely they'll listen.*

Indeed, many of Vols' warriors shouted in approval once he ceased. Yet it seemed to Gnorn's ears the voices for Orvandil were fewer than those for the chieftain who stood against him.

The chieftain Eyolf, who never climbed down from the boulder, orated again in reaction to Orvandil. When he finished this time, the cheers were even louder. The man had scored a point. Though the majority of warriors listened to the debate in silence, each side had its supporters. But as Gnorn perceived Eyolf's side was stronger, he began to clench his fists and fidget.

Just as Orvandil was about to speak again, Gnorn stepped forward and said to King Vols, "Your Majesty, with your permission, might I say a word?"

Vols hesitated. "It's not the custom for outlanders to speak at our assembly."

"Yet my ancestors once spoke from this mound. Through them I claim the right."

The king smiled. "Very well. But many of my warriors don't know the Northern Tongue. How will they understand you?"

"Orvandil will tell them what I say." Gnorn turned to his friend. "Ready?"

Orvandil nodded, so Gnorn stepped forward to the ledge to address the eight thousand Thjoths below. Many murmured at the sight of the Dweorg there. But when Gnorn raised his right arm as he had seen King Vols and Orvandil do, they all fell silent.

"Warriors of Grimrik! I am Gnorn, Dweorg of the Fyrnhowes. I stand before you today as one whose ancestors dwelled in these lands before your people." Gnorn waited for Orvandil to translate before he continued.

"I am one of those whom your folk slew and pushed out of these lands in an ancient war that both sides fought with courage. So I come here today to challenge you all!" At this point, Gnorn took his axe from his belt and brandished it.

In response, thousands of Thjoths shouted with angry dismay in their voices and eyes.

"Gnorn," said Orvandil while shaking his head. "No weapons out on the mound."

Gnorn shrugged and smiled awkwardly. "Oh." He turned toward the assembly. "A thousand pardons! Or eight thousand, as it were."

When the Dweorg put away his axe, the warriors below began to calm, and their murmurs died once again when Gnorn raised his right hand to resume his speech.

"I see you're a brave and honorable people!"

That pacified them, and they listened once again. Gnorn continued, pausing often to let Orvandil translate.

"My folk are also brave and honorable. But I've seen what conquest does to a people. We Dweorgs of the Fyrnhowes are a dying race. We have no land of our own, and we've dwindled to a few. Soon, we'll all be gone. You can't know what this means, for you're prospering, and you call these lands your own. Ours is a fate few can speak of, though it's happened to many, and one day will happen to all, even the bravest.

"Kingdoms don't endure forever. Our lives are brief, and darkness enfolds them. In the hall's light we gather, and the fire warms us. We sit and listen to the shaper weave tales of our past, bringing to life, if only for a while, those who came before us by reciting their deeds. But outside there waits the vast, cold night. One day the darkness calls each of us from the hall, and we in truth know not what awaits us. What, then, are we to do in our brief moment?

"My friends, you know the answer! I see it written on your brave faces, in the light of your eyes! We leave our *deeds* behind for those who come after to weave into tales. And they'll remember us as they gather round the fire.

"Now ask yourselves: What deeds will you leave behind for them to pass on to their children? What will the shaper sing of *you*? When your kin remember this day, would you have them say their people stood by and waited for their foes to come conquer them? For be assured, Torrlond's army will come here if we allow it to conquer the east. They've said it themselves: There's no stopping until all of Eormenlond bows to their Edan. And though you're strong, you'll fall before their numbers. They'll surround you as crows surround a hawk, and you'll perish with your ways.

"Or, will the shaper sing of how you rose up and joined others to *fight* those who would conquer you? Will your kin raise their heads in pride as they tell how the Thjoths were foremost in battle? Will they boast of how Grimrik's folk went on to victory or glorious defeat with courage in their hearts? This is the choice before you now. Today you decide how the future deems you. Choose well, brave warriors of Grimrik!

"I am Gnorn, Dweorg of the Fyrnhowes. Though my people suffered at the hands of yours, I'd call it a great honor to fight by your side. What will you have, Thjoths? Will you join me?"

After Orvandil translated Gnorn's last sentence, silence settled over the Thingvang. Gnorn looked down, not knowing what to expect. No one moved. The distant waterfall rumbled and pounded the rocks. Eight thousand Thjoths stared at him.

A great shout came from below. Gnorn's eyes widened at young Halvard, who had called him half a man, waving his fist and belting out something like a war cry. At once, a few others that the Dweorg recognized from Vols' ship broke out in cheers and raised their fists. Soon others joined them. The cheers spread like fire to the entire assembly, and even many who formerly supported Eyolf against Orvandil yelled out their agreement at the top of their lungs.

The roar of eight thousand warriors tore asunder the sky and crashed against the King's Mound until it seemed its rocks would crack and tumble down. Orvandil and Vols looked at Gnorn. The king smiled as he bowed his head to the Dweorg. Gnorn bowed in return and stepped back.

King Vols moved forward and raised his hand. The assembly quieted. As he spoke to the thousands of warriors, Orvandil whispered to Gnorn, "Vols will tell them his own mind. He'll then put the question to them of whether or not to set out. The side with the most voices will decide our course."

Gnorn listened a while until King Vols paused in his speech. Though he could not understand the words, the Dweorg perceived the king was posing a question to his assembled warriors. Wondering if he was asking those in favor of going to war or those against to cry out, Gnorn braced himself for the response. *Well, whether alone or with eight thousand Thjoths and their ships, I'll soon make my way east. Of course, if they don't come, at least I wouldn't have to sail again. I wonder if I could make it on foot in time?*

18
SILDHARAN'S PRIDE

Early morning sunlight splintered and shimmered on the River Lannad's fluid surface. A lone figure sat on a large, flat rock on the riverbank looking down at the water and listening to the current's fractured music. As she gazed at the river, Sequara could not keep out memories of her meeting with Dayraven on its bank the evening before. Vivid images of their passion came to her mind, and in the midst of it all there was still that endearing gentleness in his face. Nor could she forget how they bathed together, how tenderly he said farewell, and how she sat and wept after he left until Galdor and Abon returned to camp.

She had not needed to explain anything to Galdor. Somehow the old wizard knew. He nodded and smiled gently as he covered Sequara with a spare cloak. Abon prepared their meal, and they passed the evening in silence.

Sequara had lain down but had not slept, and she had risen before the sun. Now she sat near the river not far from their camp and wondered where Dayraven was. *He said Orudwyn. Has he reached it yet? No. Not if he walked all night. But soon. What will he meet there? He seemed certain. The gift leads him.*

Footsteps approached along with a strong sense of the gift, and when she turned Galdor stood behind her. His eyes and gentle smile told of his worry.

"You didn't sleep much."

She shrugged and shook her head. "Not much, or not at all."

"Your thoughts are with him."

"Yes."

The old wizard hesitated and then nodded. Putting his hands on his knees, he bent and eased his way down until he sat beside Sequara. They gazed at the river, watching and listening to the passage of the water.

He broke the silence. "There was no other way."

"You knew?"

"I merely guess, and we're all at fate's mercy. Much is unknown, but we proceed as best we can. At the moment, I see Dayraven's departure was meant to be, and I hope it turns to our advantage."

"But is he ready?"

The wrinkles around Galdor's eyes deepened as he squinted and gazed over the river, as if he was trying to see something far away. He nodded. "It was time for him to take his path alone. What's left for us is to do our part."

She sighed. "I'm not certain I know my part any longer. My whole life I thought I knew. Since I was a child. Queen Faldira picked me out of thirty children with the gift in Asdralad to train as her successor. I was not from one of the noble families — not from one of the lines that usually supply Asdralad's rulers. But she seemed so certain when she chose me. I drew strength from her. Since I was from a family of simple farmers, I worked harder to prove I was worthy of her choice. And I never doubted. But now she's gone. I don't know who I am. Now Asdralad's no more . . ."

After she broke off, Galdor laid his hand on her shoulder. "Faldira knew what she was doing. She chose you for this time. Her choice was wise. Few would have the strength to come this far." The wizard smiled at Sequara, who managed to smile back, then he resumed.

"I too have found myself in unexpected places. When I left Ellond as a young man to train in Torrhelm and become a priest, the last place I saw myself was here."

"Why did you leave the Way?"

"I haven't left it. At least, not the Way *I* understand. Unfortunately for me, others preferred a slightly different interpretation."

"You mean Bledla?"

"Yes." Galdor chuckled, and then he paused as he pursed his lips, seeming to recall something far off. "We were friends once. The three of us: Bledla, Arna, and I. Young men, and headstrong. And talented. Especially Bledla. From the beginning he stood out. If you can believe it, he was not so different from Dayraven, at least in those early days. I had great hopes in him, like everyone. We all knew he would be the supreme priest one day. But his power was his undoing. He became too sure. He took the strength of the gift in him as a sign Edan had consecrated him for something tremendous, and he assumed *his* will was Edan's. Our falling out was inevitable. When he came into authority, he banned me from the priesthood and charged me with heresy. I had to flee for my life. He became the supreme priest, and Arna one of the high priests."

"So Arna took his side."

There was a long pause as the old wizard stared at the river. Sequara began to wonder if he had heard her.

But then he replied. "Yes. At least, until recently." Galdor turned to her with a grin, and his green eyes glinted.

"What do you mean?" Sequara's eyebrows lowered in thought until she realized what should have been so obvious. "The High Priest Arna . . . He's been helping us? He's our source in Torrhelm. *He* gave me the song of origin of dragons."

"Faldira, Urd, and I agreed it would be too dangerous to tell you about Arna. Had you been detained, his life too would have been in grave danger. The fewer who knew his identity, the better. I suppose Faldira never had the chance to tell you."

"No. And he almost died trying to tell me, I think."

"When?"

"I don't willingly recall that day. In Asdralad, when Torrlond invaded. Arna broke away from the others and followed me. Dayraven thought the worst . . . He nearly killed him with almakhti. Arna put up a shield in time, but he took a hard fall."

"Mostlike he was trying to help you. I hope Bledla hasn't discovered him."

"No, I think not. Dayraven took care of that. But how long has he been helping us?"

"Since Bledla's war became an inevitability. Arna contacted me in secret when he couldn't convince Bledla to spread the Way by peaceful means. For years, while Bledla gathered the dragons and forced the beasts under his sway, Arna pleaded with him. He argued the Prophet Aldmund had never meant for the Way to spread by violence. He lost the argument, so he risked everything for his belief."

"Will he help us in battle, then?"

Galdor's frown was pensive. "I don't know. His devotion to Bledla runs deep. I would imagine it tore him apart to play his role. We'll see what Arna does in the days ahead." The old wizard smiled again at Sequara. "In the meantime, I suppose Abon must be waiting for us at the camp. He'll have something ready to eat, and we must depart soon. We have many miles to cover."

AFTER THEY BREAKFASTED, GALDOR LED SEQUARA AND ABON downstream a short way to the ford across the Lannad. As the old wizard had said before, they soon found themselves riding on a great plain that was part of the kingdom of Golgar, though they were far from its chief city of Holurad. There were small villages along the way as well as fields with wheat and other grains basking in the summer sun. At times, the travelers saw slaves toiling in the fields under the supervision of guards and taskmasters. Some were no doubt captives from skirmishes with Sildharan or unfortunate natives who fell into debt to rich landowners, but most were Ilarchae. In spite of the animosity between the two kingdoms, the wealthy of Golgar bought large numbers of the barbarians from Sildharan, which obtained great wealth from such dealings and had become the locus for selling and trading in Ilarchae slaves.

It was one of the ironies of history that the Ilarchae had introduced the practice of slavery to the Andumae. Sequara had studied that history and knew it too well. Over hundreds of years, Sildharan

THE PROPHET OF EDAN

grew to depend on slaves bought from the tribes of the Wildlands. Since the northern barbarians were never united, it was easy to use one tribe to enslave members of another or to benefit from the savages' constant warfare. Sildharan's rulers made a handsome profit from selling some of the Ilarchae to other kingdoms, even to Sildharan's rivals, such as Torrlond, and its foes, such as Golgar. Sundara refused to buy the slaves, for its rulers regarded thralldom as a moral disease that brought low a kingdom and its people.

The only other kingdom in Eormenlond that possessed no slaves had been Asdralad. Thus, Sequara found the toilers under their masters' watchful eyes a disturbing sight. She frowned and narrowed her eyes in both shame and anger that Andumaic kingdoms would participate in the evil practice of claiming ownership over fellow human beings and exploiting them for profit.

The three companions rode past such scenes on their way north, heading for the border with Sildharan and the West Road, which would take them to Sildharan's cities further north. First they would reach Shohan, but their final destination was Thulhan, the largest of the three northern cities and the pride of Sildharan. Bordering Ellond at the end of Quinara Sound, it was the gateway into Sildharan from the west. Torrlond's army and its allies would almost certainly attempt to enter Sildharan through Thulhan, and that was where the kingdoms of the east would take their stand.

For two days of riding they would be in Golgar. Though Galdor did not expect trouble, he wished to keep quiet. He had negotiated with King Veduir of Golgar to allow Sundara's army to march north through his kingdom. Though he refused to help Sildharan, Veduir knew it was in his interest to stop Torrlond. He grudgingly granted the permission Galdor sought, but Golgar's people were ancient foes of Sildharan, and they would not take kindly to anyone seeking to help their northern neighbor. The wizard deemed it best they camp in the open rather than stay in a village inn, where folk might inquire about their journey. Thus, after the first day of riding in Golgar, they led their horses off the road as darkness descended and made a camp with no fire near a long row of brush at a wheat field's edge.

Having gone without sleep the night before, Sequara succumbed to exhaustion and drifted into deep slumber as soon as she lay her stiff body down on her spare cloak. It seemed only moments later when a hand shook her shoulder.

Her eyes blinked open.

"Lady Sequara," whispered Abon, whose dark silhouette blocked some of the stars from her view.

"Time to set out already, Abon?"

"Shhh. We have company."

Sequara sat up alert at once. "Does Galdor know?"

"He told me to wake you. Follow me."

Abon ducked low as he silently made his way from the brush. Sequara followed as quietly as she could. They had not gone far when they met Galdor, who was squatting low and peering over the wheat field. The wizard said nothing as Sequara and Abon shuffled up next to him, but he put his finger over his lips and then pointed out over the field.

When Sequara raised herself, she saw what had alarmed the wizard and the shaper. Under the moonlight were scores, perhaps hundreds, of dark forms walking through the field toward the northeast. Here and there moonlight glinted on metal tools or weapons among the large, silent figures. At once she realized who they were.

"Ilarchae," she whispered.

"Yes," said Galdor. "It seems they all have somewhere to go, and I doubt their masters sent them."

"But where?"

"To war. Something has happened, and I fear it's not good for Sildharan."

"You think the Ilarchae slaves are preparing for war?" asked Abon.

"Yes. We know of Torrlond's alliance with the Ilarchae of the Wildlands, who want revenge against Sildharan for enslaving their kin. It seems they've also organized their captive brethren here in the south. If the Ilarchae here in Golgar are on the move, those in Sildharan must be as well. They'll attack Sildharan from within."

"Look," hissed Abon. "Over there. Some are coming this way."

Galdor peered in the direction the shaper pointed. "They haven't seen us yet. But there are too many, and they've surrounded us on every side. If we try to ride away, we might have to fight, and some have bows. We must first try to hide."

"What about the horses?" asked Sequara.

Galdor thought a moment. "We'll conceal ourselves, but we can't afford to lose the horses. We don't have time to reach Sildharan without them, and these tidings make our journey all the more urgent. Sequara, listen closely. Establish a connection with the horses as soon as we hide. Keep them quiet. If the Ilarchae find them and take them, do nothing until they ride away and the field is clear. Once they're far enough, bring the horses back to us — without the riders."

"What if the Ilarchae discover us?"

"I'll take care of that."

The three hastened back for the brush, trying with incomplete success to step without noise. Sequara prayed to the Mother and Father that none of the Ilarchae heard. They picked up and packed their sleeping mats and hid any traces of their presence. Knowing she would soon need to sing a spell, Sequara kept calm and thanked Anghara and Oruma they had made no fire. By the time everything was in her pack, footsteps rustling in wheat approached through the darkness.

Following Galdor and Abon, Sequara scurried away, ducking to stay out of view. They hid in a part of the brush away from where they had tied up the horses. The sorceress winced every time one of them snapped a twig as they nestled into the brush and lay down. But soon enough they settled into their places, and the only sound she heard was her own breathing.

From her hiding place, she could not see the horses without moving and making noise. But Sequara did not need to see them as long as she felt their presence. She chanted softly: "Hrondin ar dwinnor, hurulas ni randuin. Khulyin im vardor, danulas an barduin."

As she repeated the spell, her awareness of the three horses' energy grew, and she let her energy mingle with theirs. Within moments, the bond was so complete she perceived what the horses were seeing: several large forms creeping toward them through the murk. *No need to keep them quiet now*, she thought. *At least it won't be hard to call them back. I only hope Galdor keeps the Ilarchae away from us.*

When the horses neighed, she already knew the Ilarchae had taken hold of them. The runaway slaves spoke in hushed voices. Through her connection to the horses, she heard them distinctly. Though she could not understand their harsh tongue, it seemed one was giving directions to the others. *They'll be looking for us now.*

"They're coming," she whispered to Galdor.

"I know. Whatever happens, be still until the last possible moment."

Galdor mumbled a song of origin beneath his breath. Sequara could not hear the words, but she sensed the rush of power in the wizard as he accessed the gift. He chanted for some time, and as he did, footsteps crunched closer to where they hid. For a moment, she worried they would hear him. The footsteps grew louder, and she held her breath. Galdor stopped. Had he finished the spell? Or had he heard them coming? Another step sounded next to her. Someone was upon them.

A huge man's dark form appeared ten feet from where she lay. Tall and broad-shouldered, he carried something gleaming in the moonlight: a large, curved sickle. Sequara remained motionless as he approached her. His breaths sounded heavy, and he gazed into the brush. Then he stepped near where she hid. Though his eyes remained shadowed, she marked his bearded face. He was bigger than she had thought, not much smaller than Orvandil. A few thin, scraggly branches stood between her and the man, and it seemed a desperate notion that their shade would keep him from seeing her. As he leaned in closer, she smelled his sweat's sharp odor. Her heart was pounding on her ribs, and she tried to calm herself. *I must keep him from yelling if he sees me.*

She reached for the sword at her side, wishing she had taken it out of its scabbard earlier. She extended her arm backward, all the while keeping her eyes on the man. Shifting her body, she hoped no twigs would break and give her away before she had the curved blade out. Her hand was moist and slippery. She must not drop the sword. No room for error. *If he attacks, I must defend myself. The throat. A quick thrust upward. If he makes noise, I'll have to call upon almakhti.* She grimaced at the idea of killing scores of Ilarchae slaves, and there was always the chance one's arrow or blade could find her. But she would do her duty.

The big man turned his face, and moonlight struck his eyes. He stared straight at her.

Sequara froze for a fraction of a breath, and her instincts screamed at her to draw the sword, leap out, and pierce his throat before he made a noise.

Yet something held her back, something in the man's eyes. Her hand relaxed its grip on the hilt of her sword. As a sorceress, Sequara recognized the glazed eyes of a man in a trance. She realized then what Galdor's spell was. A moment later, the man turned and spoke to someone nearby in a gravelly whisper. "Nachta. Hora vezan vendan."

A response came from the darkness, and the man in the trance stepped toward it. Two more nervous voices joined in. They seemed to argue over something, and the Ilarchae grew louder and more agitated. She understood they were fearful of discovery, and they were probably debating what to do about the horses and the missing owners. At length, however, one of the horses neighed as the Ilarchae mounted them. A moment later, their hoofs cantered away. There was nothing to do but wait.

It seemed an eternity to Sequara as they lay in the brush amidst the scent of dirt and decaying leaves. After a long silence, Galdor stirred. "This is an uncomfortable bed. Let's see if our friends have all departed."

Abon said, "I'll go first."

With little noise, the shaper crept out of the brush and took a few cautious paces forward. He disappeared into darkness. It seemed another eternity before Abon emerged back into view. "All gone. Safe to come out now."

Sequara lifted herself out of her hiding place with a relieved sigh. As she brushed a few small twigs and dry leaves off her clothes, she said to Galdor, "I nearly killed him. I realized just in time you had cast your spell on him. It was a risk."

The old wizard raised his eyebrows and smiled. "Yes, indeed. The poor fellow's even now waking up on one of our horses and wondering how he got there. But I learned a few things from him too. As we guessed, the Ilarchae are gathering for war, and they're organized. These are heading north to fight in Sildharan, but others will hide in Orudwyn to waylay Sundara's forces as they march north."

"Dayraven," said Sequara. "He went to Orudwyn. What if the Ilarchae come across him?"

Galdor shook his head. "If my guess is right, the Ilarchae won't disturb Dayraven. He'll take care of himself. But the Ilarchae will delay our friends. A costly delay, and there's little we can do now other than send a message to King Tirgalan. We must head north to warn King Naitaran of Sildharan he'll soon face foes outside and within his kingdom. It's time for our visitors to return our horses. While you take care of that, I'll find a suitable messenger to send to Tirgalan."

Sequara focused on the horses again, calling upon the connection she had made with them. From three miles away, she felt the weight of the Ilarchae on their backs, saw the dim nightscape the steeds were trotting through. Since the horses were calm, the riders must have had no expectation they would spook. Thus, it was easy for Sequara to prompt the steeds to rear and throw off all three yelping riders. The Ilarchae would never know why the horses panicked and galloped away. She also felt sure they would not risk coming back to find out since they were so afraid of discovery.

Time went by, and Sequara concentrated on her bond with the beasts so they could find her. It was not long before the distant pounding of hooves intruded on the night's stillness. She guided the beasts until their hooves grew louder. When their shadowy forms emerged from the darkness at a trot, she relinquished her connection to them. They snorted, seeming glad to be back with their previous riders. She petted them on their somewhat lathered flanks and necks to soothe them, and she caressed her brown steed's nose.

By the time she finished, Galdor had summoned a barn owl. The ghostly-white bird had slightly darker feathers on top of its head and black tips on its wings. Its head swiveled and its large, dark eyes stared up at the wizard as he knelt and whispered with open palms extended toward it. Galdor stood up. "Fly away now, to Tirgalan. Let him see in your eyes the memories I've put there. Bid him to be wary of the ambush he and his troops will meet on their way north."

After the three watched the bird flap its wings and flit into the darkness towards the south, they put their packs on their horses and prepared to leave the field. They agreed it would not be safe to stay there, so they rode for an hour until they came across another place with shrubs to rest near. They met no more Ilarchae that night, and Sequara slept peacefully.

BEFORE DAWN THEY SET OUT AGAIN. THEY REACHED THE WEST Road without incident by day's end, but it brought little relief. Once in Sildharan, they saw plenty of evidence war was brewing. During their journey north, they shared the road with troops King Naitaran had called to defend Thulhan from the imminent invasion.

Clad in gold colored tunics, Sildharan's soldiers had helms with graceful cheek guards curving forward and a neck guard arcing backward. They wore corselets of leather and bronze and carried curved blades at their sides. Greaves covered their otherwise bare shins, and sturdy leather shoes completed their gear. Some companies were foot soldiers, and a few were cavalry, while others consisted of bowmen and spearmen as well. All marched in disciplined order for the north.

The road led them through fertile country, the breadbasket of Sildharan. In two days they reached the city of Shohan, and Sequara regretted they had no time to linger in Sildharan's second largest city. Instead, they bypassed Shohan, from which many soldiers issued toward Thulhan, the city known as Sildharan's pride. In two and a half more days they would reach it.

As they closed in on Thulhan, their road converged with the River Nurgleth, at which point they left behind their tired horses in a village for some silver and a place on a large ferry laden with soldiers. Thus, it was from the river that Sequara first saw Thulhan, and she understood why Sildharan's people considered it their jewel.

They approached it from the south on the Nurgleth, which passed beneath a huge stone bridge that was part of the high wall surrounding the city. A gatehouse loomed on top of the bridge, and Sequara guessed it housed a portcullis that could be lowered into the water to cut off the city from a river attack. She noted guards atop the bridge with gleaming spears, and then the ferry passed under its shade for a while until it emerged to a view of the city spreading out on the western and eastern banks.

Second in size to Torrhelm among Eormenlond's cities, Thulhan sheltered some forty thousand people. But it was far older than Torrhelm, as the most ancient of its white, columned buildings testified. Some of the structures dated from the city's foundation, and they congregated near the river's banks. Most venerable were the Temples of Oruma and Anghara.

Identical in appearance, the places of worship stood facing each other on opposite sides of the river. The Temple of Oruma, god of death, loomed on the western bank, while that dedicated to Anghara, goddess of life, welcomed her devotees from the east. A long and wide row of steps led up to each temple from the river, and each of their façades boasted a row of thick, fluted columns with flowering capitals. Scores of tiny forms moved up and down the steps. At the top of the steps, huge bronze doors waited to let worshipers pass into the inner mysteries. Over the doors in the flowing letters of High Andumaic but on an immense scale were sacred scriptures identifying each temple's deity. Also, next to each temple was a public bathhouse, from which worshipers streamed toward the temples after performing their ablutions. Most commanding of all, upon both temples rested a vast white dome soaring up three hundred feet.

Beyond the oldest buildings by the river, newer constructions leapt high in the air. Dozens of tall towers identified the homes of ancient noble families, those in which sorcery ran deep. As in every Andumaic kingdom, the nobles who owned these towers vied to send individuals from their families to Sildharan's throne. But there were also buildings of Thulhan's commercial classes: busy shops of merchants who dealt in textiles, wine, fish, spices, and every other commodity necessary for a thriving urban center. And further out from these, though they were invisible from the river, Sequara did not doubt there were thousands of more humble and plain structures, the homes of the working classes.

When their ferry docked, Galdor leapt off in such haste that Sequara had difficulty keeping up with the old man through the press of soldiers. But Abon looked back and made sure she followed, and soon enough the three made their way on busy cobbled streets toward King Naitaran's palace. The streets were teeming with people, but there was nothing to suggest panic among the citizens. There was tension, to be sure, but the Sildharae seemed to have great faith that their rulers and army would deal with the imminent invasion, for they conducted their affairs as if nothing were out of the ordinary. Along the way, Sequara noted many shop owners used Ilarchae slaves to perform the most difficult labor. The blond and red-haired slaves seemed an ominous sight to her, and she wondered how many dwelled in the city.

When they arrived at Naitaran's palace, she noticed how much larger and more splendid it was than the modest structure she grew up in back in Kiriath. They approached it from a wide, cobbled courtyard that led to the main gate with iron doors looming twenty feet high. Intricate and gilded knot patterns outlined the gate, which stood in a huge, crenellated stone wall with a tower at each end. The two towers were cylindrical and tapered toward their crenellated tops. Regal and life-like statues lined each level of the two towers, and Sequara guessed the statues represented Sildharan's former kings and queens. Behind the entrance, the palace's vast central tower rose into view. One cylindrical tier rose upon another until it tapered to its top some four hundred feet above in a graceful, gilded onion dome. Many windows looked out of the tower, and Sequara reflected that its occupants could see far from them. Then, with a wry smile, she realized Dayraven would have dwelled on the same idea, imagining the view and gazing up at the tower with his naïve, open, sweet stare.

The captain of the guards at the gate recognized Galdor, and he sent one of his men to conduct the three travelers inside. The palace's interior was no less impressive, but Sequara had no time to reflect on the fine statues or delicate carvings on columns spiraling up to the lofty ceiling. Through several echoing corridors the guard led them until they came to a pair of sumptuous gilded doors.

When their guide told the guards at the doors the identities of the persons he was conducting, one went inside. He emerged shortly after, and several persons who appeared by their garb and jewelry to be noblemen or wealthy merchants followed him out, all of them ignoring the newcomers. After the dignitaries left, the guard gestured for Galdor, Sequara, and Abon to follow him in.

Sequara found herself inside the palace's dazzling throne room. Two rows of spiraled columns supported the high ceiling, and between the columns a long crimson rug with intricate floral patterns led from the door to the throne at the chamber's opposite end. Matching the rug, jewels gleamed in floral patterns in the walls. High windows at the sides of the wide chamber let in abundant light that stretched toward the room's center. The room's layout drew a visitor's gaze straight toward the magnificent throne. Hewn from white and grey marble, the throne sat beneath a stone canopy that four twisting columns supported. Stone it was, but the jeweled canopy was so delicately carved it appeared as light as air. On each side of the throne was a beautiful door, and Sequara guessed these doors led to the palace's central tower.

Occupying the throne was King Naitaran, a tall, thin man affecting a dignified pose with his back erect and his hands resting on his seat's marble armrests. Long-faced and clean-shaven in the manner of the east, his countenance was handsome but stern, and his long dark hair was beginning to grey. He wore a slender crown with an enormous ruby set in its center, and he was clad in flowing robes of black, gold, and purple. Sensing the gift in him, Sequara knew by reputation he was a powerful sorcerer, yet he was not as strong as Faldira had been, nor indeed as powerful as Galdor. He remained on his throne and regarded his three visitors with eyebrows lowered and mouth in a frown, as if debating whether they were truly worth his time.

"Welcome to you, Galdor." His voice was deep and pleasant, though guarded, and he spoke in formal High Andumaic, not Sildharan's local Andumaic. "And to your servant, Abon, the bard. But who is this you've brought with you? I recognize the gift in you, my lady, and if I'm not mistaken, someone has trained you well."

Galdor bowed and answered in High Andumaic. "Your Majesty, she is Lady Sequara of Asdralad, and with Faldira's passing, she is now queen of that kingdom."

King Naitaran raised one eyebrow as a look of mild curiosity passed over his face. "I see. Then you honor us with your visit, Queen Sequara."

Knowing the role she had to play, Sequara answered boldly. "The honor is mine, your Majesty. Long have I wished to visit your kingdom. Now that I'm here, I see it's fairer than tales make it. But I ask that you not name me queen until I've restored my kingdom. That, as you know, is why we come. We wish to aid you against Torrlond. Our common heritage and common enemy bind us in such times."

King Naitaran stroked his chin as he peered down at Sequara, revealing no emotion. "I sorrow at the grave tidings of Faldira's passing. Asdralad's reputation for learning and sorcery is high here, and we grieve to learn the Torrlonders profaned your sacred island. As for your offer of alliance, with all due respect for you and your station, it seems you have little to give. Therefore, I wish to make it clear I won't commit my kingdom to any future endeavors regarding Asdralad. Forgive me for speaking frankly, but there should be no misunderstanding. Of course, you are free to remain here as long as you like."

"Your Majesty," interrupted Galdor, "Lady Sequara is not here to ask for aid. She came to help, and you'll find her help of great use. It's in her interest, just as it's in the interest of us all, to stop Torrlond. That's why King Tirgalan is even now on his way with his troops, and at great risk I might add. We all understand we must stop Torrlond together."

King Naitaran made an attempt at a smile, or perhaps he meant it to be the patronizing smirk it appeared. "I remind you, Galdor, what I told you in the past: Sildharan is more than capable of caring for itself. For well over a thousand years we have kept civilization's light burning in the face of these barbarians from the north, and they're not about to defeat us during *my* reign. As I have made clear to you, if our friends from the south wish to come and share in our victory, then I'll honor our ancient alliance by permitting them. But their aid is no more than a diplomatic formality."

Galdor's eyebrows bristled. "A diplomatic formality? Your Majesty, I take it you're aware you're facing not only Torrlond's as yet undefeated army along with the power of the dragons the Supreme Priest Bledla wields, but also the soldiers of the Mark and Ellond, not to mention the Ilarchae to your northeast?"

"I assure you we're informed about these matters." Even Naitaran's voice was smug, giving Sequara the urge to punch his arrogant nose and make it bleed all over his precious throne. Unfortunately, he seemed to like hearing himself talk. "We're well protected, and I've fortified Sirukinn's Wall to the northeast. It's kept out the barbarians of the Wildlands for hundreds of years. It won't fail us now."

"Indeed? And what about the *barbarians* already in Sildharan?"

As he frowned, Naitaran appeared less than sure for the first time. His eyes narrowed as he asked Galdor, "What do you mean by this?"

"The Ilarchae you've enslaved within your kingdom are organizing into armed bands. They'll aid their brethren when the time comes. We know this because we ran across some on our way here."

"Impossible. The vast majority of our slaves are loyal and content. Their lives here are far better than in the untamed wilderness of the northeast. A few might cause trouble, but they pose no real threat. Even if this were not so, the Ilarchae don't have the skill or intelligence to organize an effective military operation, nor are they capable of keeping an alliance beyond their petty tribal ties. It's more than likely those coming from the Wildlands will squabble among themselves before they even reach our border. You'll see. They'll never breach Sirukinn's Wall. And we'll have no difficulty stopping any rebellion a ragtag group of slaves might attempt within this kingdom."

"I hope you're right, your Majesty. Nevertheless, I urge you to take steps to defend your kingdom from any internal threat."

"You worry yourself for naught, Galdor. Sildharan has kept out invaders from the west and north many times. We have preserved our ways over the centuries in the face of every threat, and we've prospered. As for the Ilarchae, let's not waste much thought on them. The only real threat comes from the west. However, Torrlond's rulers will find it impossible to bring their army beyond Quinara Sound. I'll grant that the fight with Earconwald and Bledla won't be easy, but we'll hold out. As the attackers, they'll be at a disadvantage."

"Alas, the peoples of Caergilion, Adanon, and Asdralad did not find the Torrlonders at a significant disadvantage."

"Conquering the southwest's petty kingdoms doesn't make Torrlond invincible. Here, they'll find their losses too great, and they'll go home in shame. And do not fear. Sildharan will gladly serve as the bulwark to prevent Torrlond from mastering our smaller neighbors. We all agree it's time to check Torrlond's pride."

'Torrlond's pride'? thought Sequara. She could not suppress an angry smile at the irony.

Galdor nodded, though she saw his frustration in his tight mouth. "Yes, your Majesty. Perhaps it's best to keep to what we agree on. I'm glad to hear you've made the preparations. The test will come soon."

"Our scouts inform me Torrlond and its allies will arrive within a week. We'll see how long it takes them to give up. Oruma and Anghara will grant us victory."

"May your words prove prophetic," said Galdor with a smile and a bow. The old wizard murmured under his breath, "Proud fool."

They parted in courtesy, but Sequara gritted her teeth at the king's arrogance. *I don't fight for him*, she thought to herself, *but for Asdralad. All that matters now is that we stop Torrlond.*

19

SEEING THE HIDDEN

With a jolt, Dayraven opened his eyes just as he returned to his body from the vision of the Wyrmberg. So absorbing was the sensation of falling and the enveloping brightness, he at first did not understand where he was. Weak and disoriented, he had difficulty remaining upright as a wave of dizziness threatened to push him over. His arms splayed out, and he steadied himself by grasping tree roots. The rough, snaking roots conveyed an earthiness that grounded him back in the world of forms. Sensing by the light it was late afternoon, he looked around and recalled the old oak in Orudwyn. A gentle wind hushed in the leaves and swayed the gnarled branches above and around him. But now, after the revelation of the life-tree Laeroth, the oak sheltering his body seemed more ephemeral and small. The horse remained where he had tied it. Nothing else was nearby but the other trees and a few birds flitting in them.

But, of course, his usual companion remained with him. The elf-shard murmured and coiled in his mind. After his complete surrender to it, it seemed less threatening, though it was still a thing of terrible wonder and power. It was more a part of him now, or perhaps he was more a part of it. Like a feather brushing the hairs on his flesh, it nudged him and conjured half-remembered fragments of his encounter with the elf, the death goddess, and the universal tree Laeroth. It all had been so real — so real that the world his body clung to now had seemed only a fleeting memory of a dream. The most potent moment of his vision was the Wyrmberg. Its white peak loomed in his imagination. Like a ghostly echo, the word the elf-shard had whispered came to the forefront of his thoughts: *Gorsarhad*. Eldest of living dragons.

Dayraven rose and made his way to the horse. After untying it, he led it through the trees to the river, where he and the steed drank deeply. He gathered grass from the riverbank and fed it to the beast as he stroked its nose. When he was satisfied the horse had enough, he cut a slender branch from a sapling and whittled its forked end to two sharp points with his hunting knife. With this small spear and much patience, he caught two fish, after which he gathered a few stones, tinder and twigs, and wood. Soon enough he had a fire crackling, over which he roasted the skewered fish. After eating the fish and some dry bread from his pack, he washed in the river then prepared his sleeping mat. That night Dayraven slept in the forest.

On the morrow he woke with the sun. He ate more of the dry bread and filled his water skin at the river. After he readied his horse, he began to make his way back out of the forest, keeping to the river as he walked and led his steed west. Orudwyn's trees imparted a sense of fulfillment and peace, though he knew his most difficult task lay ahead. But this did not matter. The difficulty did not daunt him. All that mattered was he knew where he must go, and he moved under the shade of the leaves and branches with that single purpose in mind. Even the elf-shard's murky whispers seemed to assure him.

In the time it took him to reach Orudwyn's outskirts, Dayraven thought of little other than the destination in his vision. Somewhere in his mind, he took note of the thinning trees and the brighter sun overhead. But he was so focused on what lay at the end of his journey, he did not see the line of Ilarchae thralls hiding at the forest's edge until he nearly bumped into them. Fortunately, they also did not see him. They were talking among themselves and all had their backs turned to him as they gazed out of the forest. It seemed they were waiting for something.

At once Dayraven understood. In his mind a vision unfolded of the men and women before him, slaves and toilers of the soil who had known little other than hardship during their brief lives, attacking a column of soldiers from Sundara on its way north. But the Ilarchae failed to take the soldiers by surprise, for other warriors of the southern kingdom who had hidden set upon the Ilarchae from behind, dropping them with arrows as a scythe slices through wheat. Steel flashed as rows of soldiers unsheathed swords and surrounded the Ilarchae.

Soon enough the ambushers became the ambushed. The slaves fought fiercely, but even as he admired their bravery and strength while the glimpse of their future unfolded, Dayraven understood doom hung over the men and women before him. Every one would soon end the story of his or her individual tragedy. Their lives had been hard. Their deaths would be too.

He stood a moment and looked upon them, for they had not yet noted his presence. They were ill prepared for battle. Some wore little more than rags, and many carried sharpened sticks or clubs as weapons, though others had managed to get ahold of swords and spears. None had armor of any sort, but they were willing to fight to end the grievances and burdened lives they suffered. Thus, it was with no fear but a sense of pity and sorrow that Dayraven approached the Ilarchae line from behind.

The Ilarchae did not notice him until he was among them. When Dayraven led his horse beside them, several turned then cried out in astonishment:

"Aelfurar er cuman!"

"Gutu Siedvar!"

Their eyes bulged as they gaped and scrambled over each other to get away from him. Though he did not understand their tongue, he knew from their cries that some took him for the god Sithfar, while others proclaimed him an elf. Perhaps they were not so far off. Sithfar would come for them soon.

Some ran away while others rushed toward the commotion. Dayraven looked upon the Ilarchae and calmly moved out of the forest. He wondered what they saw in him that frightened them so. He felt different, almost disembodied, after the revelation in the forest, but he could not see himself. Did he appear like an elf? He decided it must be the presence of the elf within him. Perhaps they sensed it. It was somehow more part of him now, and perhaps that had changed him. If they could hear its dark, cold whispers as he did, they would be truly afraid. Once clear of the trees, he mounted his horse and urged it to canter away.

All the while, the Ilarchae shouted behind him. It seemed from their cries a few had gathered courage and determined to stop him. Some had brought horses into the forest, for soon many hooves galloped toward him. So keenly did Dayraven sense the beasts behind him, he did not even turn back to command them to halt.

In fact, he did not even sing a song of origin. His response was quicker than instinct. Within the realm of origins, he recalled his connection to the beasts, a connection that had existed since the beginning of creation. Swift and strong, glorying in his speed, he *was* the horses, and he always had been. But now, it was their will to cease running after the lone man astride one of their brothers.

And so they did.

The horses of the Ilarchae first slowed then stopped even as their riders urged them forward with kicks and yells. Dayraven stopped his own horse and looked back. About twenty bewildered Ilarchae scurried off their steeds and cried out as they gawked at him. They fled back to the forest on their own legs, a couple of them tripping and rolling on their way, while their horses stood motionless.

A glint of steel here and there among the trees told him the Ilarchae line extended far. There were hundreds or even thousands waiting to ambush the Sundarae. It was best not to linger, for the Ilarchae would not let their fear conquer them for long. His destination called him, and there was little time. Having seen their fate, he knew he could do nothing for those unfortunate souls, and he frowned at the sorrow and the futility of knowing the future. Even if he tried to reason with them, which would be difficult since he did not know their tongue, he knew they would not listen. More likely, they would try to slay him. They wanted freedom and vengeance, and the Sundarae, allies of their foe, were in the way. Dayraven shook his head. He could not save them, but he could save others.

In addition, he had another matter to occupy his mind. As he turned his horse and rode away, he pondered the momentous revelation that had just come to him regarding the songs of origin: He did not need them. They were nothing more than a crutch. Indeed, they were a screen between him and true communion with the gift. There could be no doubt: No word had escaped his lips. The horses had fallen under his command without anything more than a thought while he inhabited the realm of origins. He had possessed no previous idea that he would respond that way. It was as if the command came from some will much larger than his. *The elf-shard.*

Memories came crashing back to him, and everything made sense. When he broke the priest's power over his horse and Imharr's horse, Rudumanu and Hraedflyht, back in Wolvendon; when he seized control of the aglak in the fens of Hasumere; when he used wizard's fire on the dragon breathing flames down on Imharr: On none of these occasions had he used a song of origin.

At last he understood. The songs of origin were in the way. To access the power the elf had put in him, they were at best unnecessary, and at worst an impediment. Trying to control the elf-shard while using the song of origin led to his defeat when he vied with Bledla to wield the dragons. He knew it in his bones. There could be no medium between him and the elf-shard if he wanted to call upon its power. He had to surrender. He must embrace it, not seek to control it, just as he had done in Orudwyn, and just as he had done now with the horses of the Ilarchae.

Queen Faldira and Urd had warned him of the danger of using the gift without the songs of origin, but how could they know? Nothing like his encounter with the elf had ever happened before. He wondered if his situation was unique, or if all those with the gift could dispense with the songs of origin if only they knew. Always the songs of origin had been at the heart of sorcery. Since the Andumae brought their knowledge of the gift with them to Eormenlond, and most likely for centuries before in their ancient homeland, the songs of origin had been the means by which those with the gift exercised their power. He suspected it would be difficult, if not impossible, for those with the gift to learn to use it without them. Perhaps there really was no one like him. Of course, his teachers could have been correct. It was possible he was doing something dangerous by dispensing with the songs of origin, for they were the means by which those with the gift focused their power and stayed anchored in the world of forms.

No matter. If he was going to defeat Bledla, he could no longer seek to control the elf-shard. Surrender was the path to victory. *If I must lose myself, then so be it.* Now he knew where he was going, and he knew what he would do when he reached there.

Once he found a ford to cross the Lannad, Dayraven rode his horse through the river into the kingdom of Golgar. He headed not north towards Sildharan, however, but northwest, towards the Osham Mountains. He knew from Galdor's descriptions this was roughly the direction of Golgar's chief city: Holurad, the Hidden City. *That's my path now. They'll guide me. No one else could find it.*

He did not know where to find Holurad, so he simply journeyed northwest. For two days and nights he rode through the fertile Plain of Golgar, passing many fields empty of laborers. The few slaves who remained were southerners, Andumae who had fallen into debt or become victims of raids. These laborers stared at him with frowns and narrow-eyed suspicion, as did the occasional taskmaster or landowner he saw along the way. Feeling their hostility, he kept his distance from them.

Dayraven stopped only to feed and water his horse and to nourish himself with the dried bread and salted meat left in his pack. He slept out in the open with no company other than his horse, the glimmering stars, and the looming presence of the elf-shard within and without him. Cold were its caressing whispers, which partook of the darkness between the stars. He stared up at it with equanimity and acceptance.

Speaking to no one, he kept his sense of purpose and his final goal before him.

On the third morning of riding from Orudwyn, when wind and sun had shredded distant clouds, white-peaked mountains loomed up before him. He stared for a long while atop his horse, for never before had he beheld the mightiest mountain range in Eormenlond save in his vision. Threatening to tear the azure sky with their sharp peaks, the Osham Mountains commanded his gaze and told him he was a creature of insignificance, a mere insect clinging to the earth's surface.

The lower parts of the mountains were clad in green pines, which gave way when they could no longer cling to the soaring grey surface. Unthinkably huge masses of rock seeking upward told the story of the earth's ancient agony. And from the shoulders to the zeniths of the mighty mountains, a blanket of bright snow and ice endured even in the hot summer. Somewhere among those jagged peaks waited his destination. He took a deep breath and urged his horse forward.

Dayraven continued to approach the growing mountains for a while, waiting for the right opportunity to find a clue as to Holurad's location. Not far into the morning, it came.

Small black dots appeared on the horizon. After some time, they grew clearer: mounted figures rushing toward him from the west. *At last*, he thought. They rode at a fast pace, heading straight for him. He directed his steed toward them. When they were close enough, he observed that the thirty or so horsemen wore black tunics under shining silver corselets. Their silver helms gleamed in the sun, and they each carried a spear. *Soldiers of Golgar. Perfect.*

Dayraven stopped his horse and waited for the soldiers to catch him. It did not take long. At first, the hooves sounded dim, but soon their din rose to a thunder, then they were upon him in a cloud of dust. As the dust settled, the mounted soldiers appeared around Dayraven in a ring, some with spears poised for casting. The men talked among themselves, and the talk centered on one of the riders, whose helm displayed a white plume on top. The soldiers spoke in the local form of Andumaic, but Dayraven understood most of it.

"Just as I said. Must be one of the escaped slaves, sir," said one. "He's an Ilarchae."

"Doesn't look like one," said another. "Slaves don't wear such garb."

"Maybe he slew his master and stole the garb and horse. Look at the fellow's hair. Has to be one of 'em. We should make him talk, sir. He'll tell us what they're about."

It was time to intervene.

Speaking in High Andumaic, Dayraven said, "I'm not one of the Ilarchae. But I've seen them. Your slaves have gathered into a war band in Orudwyn, from which they may even now be waylaying Sundara's army."

Several men started in surprise when Dayraven spoke in High Andumaic. Though he knew the common soldiers would mostlike not speak that ancient tongue, he hoped they would recognize it. Their white-plumed officer might even understand him. His hope proved well founded.

"Who are you, and where did you learn to speak our ancestors' tongue? Answer quickly," demanded the captain in High Andumaic, which he spoke haltingly but well enough. He looked at Dayraven with his brow lowered over his dark eyes.

"I am Dayraven of the Mark. I learned High Andumaic in Asdralad, where Queen Faldira trained me to use the gift."

The captain's eyes widened. "What are you doing here then, and how do you know the whereabouts of the Ilarchae slaves?"

"I saw them on the morning of the day before yesterday in Orudwyn. I rode from there seeking Holurad. I would speak to King Veduir."

"Not so easily done. But tell me this: Why would the Ilarchae let you pass unhindered?"

"They were afraid."

"Of what? One unarmed man on a horse?"

Dayraven smiled. "Are you certain I'm unarmed? Not only hands wield weapons."

The captain did not answer. He paused as he measured Dayraven, then he said, "Since you're so well traveled, Dayraven of the Mark, you must know not all are welcome in Holurad. Few outlanders have ever seen it. What makes you think you'll reach the Hidden City?"

Again Dayraven smiled. "Because *you* will take me there. Much more than you can know depends on my reaching it. Even the Hidden City won't remain safe if you don't help me."

"What do you mean? What could threaten Holurad? Who would dare raise a hand against Golgar? Be assured, we know how to defend our own. We've endured the strongest foes many times."

"Golgar's people are hardy. Yet if Torrlond conquers Sildharan, even the Osham Mountains won't protect you from its army and its dragons. There's something I must do to avert this. But I need your help. If you're willing, take me to Holurad so I may speak to your king."

The captain paused again, jaw set tight and eyes darting between Dayraven and some point behind him. At last they settled on Dayraven. "We were sent to gather news of the missing Ilarchae. Perhaps King Veduir would hear the tidings you bring of them. But I warn you, if anything you say proves untrue, I'll hunt you down myself."

"Do I seem untrue to you?"

The captain frowned. "No. I believe your claims, for now. You have the air of one with the gift. Had you wished to harm us, I deem you would have before now. It's possible you have something of value to say to King Veduir. I will take you to him, but only on the condition that you abide by Golgar's laws while we travel. In exchange, upon my honor, I will guarantee your safety. I must have your oath on this."

"Agreed. I swear to abide by your laws."

The captain ordered his men to lower their spears and break up the ring around Dayraven. He fell in with them, and they rode straight for the wall of mountains, which grew more breathtaking as they drew nearer. Dayraven could imagine nothing living among those rough rocks and craggy peaks save eagles or dragons. He recalled the story of how Golg and his people took refuge when his brother Sildhar drove them to the Osham Mountains, how they clung to life there after their defeat in that ancient war. *They threw themselves at the mercy of the mountains. They were strong indeed to survive in such a place.*

Just after the sun reached the height of midday, the captain stopped the company. They had come to the bottom of a large foothill. Turning their horses loose to graze, they ate dried bread from their packs. The captain broke off a piece of his and gave it to Dayraven, and then he ordered several men to share theirs with him as well. He accepted since he was nearly out of food.

"You'll need it for the trail ahead," said the captain.

"Won't the horses be doing most of the work?"

"For a time. But beyond a certain point, they'll not be able to carry us. The trails grow too steep."

When they finished eating, the captain approached Dayraven with a piece of black cloth in his hands. "Now you must fulfill our agreement. By the command of Golgar's rulers, no outsider is permitted to see the path to the Hidden City. I'm afraid you'll need to wear this over your eyes until we reach Holurad."

Dayraven looked at the captain and knew him for a decent man. Still, allowing strangers in a foreign land to blindfold him was unnerving. *Well, it won't be the greatest risk I'm taking.* He nodded. "Very well. Bind it over my eyes, then."

When the captain tied the cloth over Dayraven's face, his world went dark. He heard the captain say, "We'll lead your horse for now. When it's time to dismount, I'll guide you on foot. Don't fear. We know the paths better than most folk know their own beds. I'll not let you stumble, and we'll reach the city before the sun sets."

"I'm in your hands."

The captain assisted Dayraven onto his horse, and he held on to the beast once they were underway. The breeze caressed his face, and the sun warmed his skin. At times it seemed to burn less keenly, by which he guessed that clouds were passing overhead or they were riding beneath trees. When it warmed his flesh again, red tinged the darkness behind his eyelids and blindfold.

He could have merged his energy with his horse's had he wanted to see through its eyes, but he did not wish to betray the captain's trust. So, as he felt his steed climb upwards and leaned forward in his saddle, he was content to remain in darkness and listen to the elf-shard's murmur. He meditated on the vision he had seen in Orudwyn. High and bright was the peak of the Wyrmberg. He almost heard it calling him from afar, in accordance with the elf-shard's shadowy whispers.

As time passed, the air grew crisper and cooler. The clopping of the horses' hooves grew slower, and Dayraven tilted his torso even further forward on his steed, nearly standing in the stirrups at times as it labored up ever steeper paths. His thighs and lower back ached a bit. A few times he worried about losing his balance and falling off the horse, but he evened his breaths and grew a little more used to riding blind.

When they stopped, it seemed the sun must have moved about one quarter of its course through the sky since his blindfolding. New voices greeted the captain and his men, by which Dayraven guessed they must have reached some sort of resting station. Footsteps drew close.

"We'll proceed on foot. Let me help you down." The captain's voice came from below, on his right. A hand grasped Dayraven's hand. Standing in his right stirrup, he swung his left leg over the saddle, and another hand gently pressed on his back. He alighted from his horse with great care since he could not tell how far he was from the ground.

"Here. Eat and drink a bit more before we set out."

Dayraven felt more of the dry bread placed in his hand, and with the other hand he grasped the flask that bumped it. He ate and drank where he stood. When he finished, the captain said, "One of my men will take your pack. Put your hand on my shoulder, and keep to my right."

In darkness Dayraven stepped forward. He reckoned the unyielding surface beneath his feet was rock with a thin layer of dirt in places. They set out on a path that was at first nearly flat. But soon enough Dayraven's legs felt the trail steepen, and for much of the way it seemed they were laboring straight up a mountain. His breaths came a bit harder, and the muscles in his calves and thighs complained a little. Soon enough there was no more soil or soft mud beneath him, only bare rock. The air thinned, and the wind strengthened. In spite of the coolness, sweat began to soak into his blindfold.

Realizing his lack of vision was making him tense, he relaxed his body and let go, trusting in his other senses and the captain's guidance. He found the going easier. From the voices and footsteps accompanying them, Dayraven reckoned about ten of the captain's men walked with them, and he guessed the others had stayed behind at the rest station.

After many turns, Dayraven was no longer certain what direction they walked in. But he did not fear. The whispering of the elf-shard blended with the wind and, oddly enough, assured him. His legs and lungs had found their rhythm. Releasing his mind to dwell in the energy of the larger world surrounding him, he told himself only one direction mattered: that which led to his final destination. Each blind step brought him closer.

True to his word, the captain made sure Dayraven did not stumble, giving careful directions when they came to difficult spots. At one point, more voices ahead on the trail saluted them. A little further, something creaked back and forth, back and forth. Rope on wood. The wind picked up.

"We've come to a bridge. There's room for only one at a time," said the captain's voice a little in front of him. "I'll go first. Hold on to my shoulder with one hand. Keep your other hand on the rope, and don't let go, especially if it grows breezy. We might sway a bit, but don't fear. The bridge will hold."

The captain placed Dayraven's right hand on a thick, taut rope at chest level. It was rough on his palm. Dayraven felt the air with his left hand and, after touching the captain's back, grasped his shoulder. He squeezed more tightly than he had first meant to. The captain moved forward, and he followed, making little shuffling steps. The soles of his boots scuffed rock and then wood.

They trod onto what he perceived to be wooden planks of a footbridge, which protested each step and rocked so much in the wind that he was never sure when his feet would touch down. After a strong gust gave him the sensation he was tipping over, he gripped the captain's shoulder even harder. His other hand clenched the rope meant to keep those who would cross the bridge from falling.

"How far down is it?" asked Dayraven.

"Far enough to say as many goodbyes as you like on the way," said the captain with a laugh.

Dayraven smiled. "Perhaps it's better to be blindfolded for this."

The captain led him carefully. It seemed their progress was slow, and that the bridge was long. The wind howled, and the wooden planks groaned under the weight of their steps. But finally one of his steps did not produce a creak or bend a plank beneath him. Grit scraped under his boot. He sighed and relaxed his grip on the captain's shoulder. Dayraven was glad enough to feel solid rock under his feet again.

After the bridge, they continued for an indistinct length of time. There were stretches when the trail seemed fairly level, but for the most part his legs felt the steady climb upward. There was a pleasant enough strain in his muscles, and his breaths came in deeper gulps. He kept going without complaint and ceased to think within the limitations of his body.

In his darkness time grew irrelevant. Along with the elf-shard and its susurrations, Dayraven floated in the darkness. He perceived the contained energy of the sleeping mountain beneath his feet as well as the chaotic force of the wind. Without sight leading him, he drew from his ability to sense life in the realm of origins. Thus, he perceived that place in a manner he otherwise would not have. The subtlest expressions of its energy seeped into his consciousness, and he understood that even this inhospitable and rugged terrain bore teeming life hidden within it.

At the same time, the rhythm of their pace aided his meditation, and he said little along the way. Step followed step, but Dayraven almost felt as if he were gliding toward his destination. Gradually, he grew aware of a presence. At first dim, the presence grew in his mind with each pace forward until it loomed before him as something vast and indescribable. He examined the presence more closely, and at once he perceived what it was: one organism made of thousands of smaller ones. It was people he sensed, thousands of people together in one place.

Something was pulling him out of the dark world. He realized the captain was speaking to him. "We've reached Holurad. Behold the Hidden City."

Hands untied and pulled away the black cloth, leaving his face feeling strangely bare. It took a moment for Dayraven's eyes to adjust. He nearly gasped at what he beheld.

In the early evening light, Holurad spread out beneath him. On the slopes of three mountains and the shadowed vales between them congregated enough dwellings for ten thousand souls. A thick wall of stone snaked up and down the slopes and surrounded the city, and squat towers were interspersed along the wall. Outside the wall, green terraces covered the lower slopes, but the upper slopes were grey rock.

Wrought of the stone surrounding them, the dwellings appeared to grow out of the mountains. Undulating paths and streets ran along the slopes, connecting the buildings in a well organized web. Two score or so tall towers identified the abodes of the noble houses, and the venerable temples of Oruma and Anghara stood side by side on the western slope. Dayraven did not need to ask which structure was the king's palace. At the city's highest point on the northernmost of the three slopes, the largest structure in Holurad rested between tall towers at each of its four corners. Columns surrounded the building, and its shingled roof peaked high as it perched and guarded the Hidden City. Even though he knew its history, it seemed beyond strange to Dayraven to witness this thriving urban center in such a remote place.

The captain led him and the soldiers accompanying them down the slope until they arrived at a gate. The gate was open, but should the need have arisen, its thick iron bands would have kept out any but the most determined and strong invader. The gatekeepers recognized the captain and hailed him, but as they passed in, several guards took a good look at Dayraven.

One of the first things he noticed when he entered was the horses. They were much like the mounts he had seen Gnorn and Hlokk riding when he first met them. Unlike the swift, tall horses the captain and his men rode in the plain, the stocky and shaggy beasts in the city were well suited for the rugged terrain. Some pulled carts while others supported riders, though a tall man's feet were not far from the ground when riding one. It was obvious how the people of the mountain city depended on the sturdy animals.

The other marvel he could not take his eyes from was the elaborate carvings on every building. Even the humblest dwelling boasted an array of vine-like carvings twisting in intricate, patterned knots. Numerous statues stood life-like in the city's courtyards and cobbled streets, silently observing the citizens milling around and going about their business. Dayraven had never seen such skill in stonemasonry or stonecutting. "Your people must be the greatest carvers of stone in Eormenlond," he said to the captain.

PHILIP CHASE

"Some even say we're made of stone," he answered with a laugh.

Dayraven smiled. "Such labor makes your city fair. I'm glad for a sight of it."

"I'd show you more, but I surmise you wish to see King Veduir soon."

"Yes, I fear I must. Even before I eat, I would speak to him, if possible."

"Very well. This way."

The palace appeared even larger from close up. Dayraven bent over and clutched his thighs for a moment as he gathered his breath. A walk through Holurad was no easy stroll, and the Hidden City's folk must have had strong legs. While he rested, he marveled at the profusion of carvings on the walls behind the columns and the statues standing guard around the building. The captain waited for him, and when he nodded, they continued toward the doors. Living guards opened the great iron doors at the palace's front. Dayraven followed the captain inside while his men waited without.

The captain led him down several stone corridors until he found a well-dressed man and hailed him. From their conversation, Dayraven gathered the man was a close advisor to King Veduir, but he had no trace of the gift. The nobleman, who looked askance at Dayraven, informed the captain he would find the monarch instructing his young successor in the royal courtyard.

They continued through more hallways until they came to a doorway leading to an open courtyard with cloisters surrounding it. Mounted in alcoves in the cloisters were dozens of statues. So lifelike were they, Dayraven almost took them for real persons frozen in expressions of ecstasy, sorrow, joy, and contemplation. Down to the lines of their faces they appeared living beings, and he kept expecting them to move at any moment.

"How could anyone hew such beauty from stone?" he wondered aloud.

"Some say beauty lies hidden in the stone, and the true craftsman reveals it," said the captain. "King Veduir is a great patron of sculptors. There he is now. Follow me, if you please."

Long before they reached them, Dayraven sensed the gift in the two individuals at the courtyard's other end. The captain led him in their direction on a path that wove between rose bushes and other flowers. When they reached them, Dayraven beheld a man speaking to a girl whom he stood over.

Thin and childlike yet seeming to possess solemnity beyond her years, the girl was somewhere around twelve years of age. Clad in an elegant blue gown, the chosen heir to Golgar's throne stood and closed her eyes in meditation while the sorcerer-king instructed her. With a sad smile creasing his face, Dayraven thought of Sequara and how she had trained this way for years under Queen Faldira's tutelage. The memory of Asdralad and Sequara was like a ray of sunshine breaking through clouds, but then Dayraven recalled with a pang that Asdralad was no more, and Queen Faldira dead. He brought himself back to his present purpose.

As they neared the pair, Dayraven assessed King Veduir. Somewhat shorter than average even among the Andumae, Veduir was a bit past his prime but not yet old. Handsome and stocky, he had long, curly hair and a clean-shaven face with a strong, broad nose. His royal robes were silver and purple, but he wore no crown at the moment. He instructed his young successor in a deep, strong voice, but he ceased speaking when he looked toward the approaching captain. His young apprentice opened her eyes when the king addressed the captain in High Andumaic.

"Ah, Captain Uthron. You returned sooner than I thought you would, and with company."

"Your Majesty, soon after we departed for tidings of the Ilarchae, I found this man. He names himself Dayraven of the Mark, and he says he trained with Queen Faldira in Asdralad. He speaks High Andumaic, and he brings news of the Ilarchae. What's more, he set out seeking Holurad to speak with you concerning the war that begins to our north."

"I see."

King Veduir took a long look at Dayraven, then he turned his glance on his apprentice. "What do you make of this man?" he asked her.

The serious-faced girl stared at Dayraven intently before she answered. "I sense the gift in him in great measure, Sire. Greater by far than in any I have ever met." She blinked, and though she controlled her emotions well, the fear was evident on her face.

At the girl's words, Captain Uthron stirred. He looked at Dayraven with a frown, perhaps regretting having escorted such a dangerous person to his king.

Dayraven smiled to try to put them at ease.

Veduir nodded. He did not appear concerned. "As do I. But why should we trust him?"

He turned to Dayraven and repeated, "Why should we trust you? And what news do you bring of the Ilarchae?"

"As for the Ilarchae, I deem you already guess their purpose. But I can report what I saw: They formed a war band in Orudwyn to waylay the army of Sundara on its way north. As for why you should trust me, I'll tell you in plain words. I come to stop Torrlond from conquering Sildharan. Though that kingdom is your ancient foe, you know well the consequences should the Way triumph."

"Do I? Tell me: What do you imagine the consequences would be?"

"In time, the Torrlonders would march south and take the Plain of Golgar. Then, one of two things will happen: They will seize your crops and force you to starvation, or they will find Holurad with their dragons and conquer it. I would bet on the latter. The supreme priest is impatient to conquer all of Andumedan for the Way so that the Kingdom of the Eternal may begin. Or so he believes. Regardless, with dragons, it will be an easy matter for them to locate the Hidden City, and even your valiant people couldn't stand before the Torrlonders. You've discussed these possibilities with the wizard Galdor, I think."

"Galdor sent you? I already gave permission to Tirgalan to lead Sundara's troops through my lands. What more does he want? If the Ilarchae slaves get involved in the war, there's nothing I can do, though they should never expect to find a home in these lands again."

"Galdor did not send me. I parted from him a few days ago as he journeyed north to Sildharan. And I haven't come to ask you for troops."

"What, then, do you want?"

"I must journey to the Wyrmberg. Your people know the Osham Mountains better than any. I ask that you send rangers to guide me."

Veduir barked a laugh. "What sort of madness is this? It takes many days to reach the Wyrmberg, and it's no easy path. Why would you risk it? And why would *I* risk sending my men to guide you?"

"The Supreme Priest Bledla wields dragons for the Torrlonders. As a result, their army is undefeatable. The key to defeating Torrlond is to break Bledla's control over them. It would be a tactical victory, but even more importantly, it would also destroy Torrlond's pride and its army's confidence that Edan favors it. It could turn the tide of the war or even end it."

As Veduir listened, his brown eyes lit up with understanding. But he frowned when Dayraven finished. "You're right about the effect defeating Bledla would have. Break him, and you destroy their arrogance." His thick eyebrows lowered as he gazed at Dayraven. "I know why you wish to go to the Wyrmberg. Gorsarhad. You believe she'll help you contend with Bledla. But I must tell you no one's seen the great dragon in generations. Even if she's still alive, what makes you think you could wield her? In hundreds of years, only Bledla has mastered a dragon. And you wish to control the greatest dragon in Andumedan? Perhaps even Bledla couldn't. What if she simply devours you?"

"Gorsarhad lives. As for wielding her, I have exercised power over dragons before. I won't fail."

"Really?" Veduir scoffed. "Let's say you do find Gorsarhad, and you somehow manage to control her. What then? Can *you* defeat the Supreme Priest Bledla? Can *you*, a stripling from the forest of the Mark, defeat the greatest wizard of this age? I sense the gift in you. I know not how, but you have more power than any I have ever met. More than even Bledla has, I am certain. But can you control it? I have my doubts, for I sense one other thing: You are fey, Dayraven of the Mark. I see it in you, and I've never been wrong about such a thing. If you attempt this, death will come for you, most likely before you even reach Gorsarhad's lair."

Unmoved, Dayraven gazed back at King Veduir. "I will defeat Bledla."

Veduir's eyes widened, and he stared at Dayraven as if seeing something new. But his eyes hardened again before he spoke. "Very well. If you wish to die in your madness, that's your business. But I'll not burden my conscience by commanding any of my men to guide you, lest they be lost as well."

Dayraven swallowed and tried not to let his frustration show. "Your majesty, please reconsider. I will go alone if I must, but time is precious now. With your men leading me, I will find the Wyrmberg far more swiftly."

The young apprentice turned toward King Veduir, but she did not say anything. From the look in her dark eyes, Dayraven sensed she would have given a different answer, but she was too young to contradict her teacher and sovereign.

A moment later, Captain Uthron, who stood by during the conversation, cleared his throat. "Your Majesty, may I speak?"

King Veduir frowned as he looked on the captain. "You may."

"Sire, though you don't command it, I wish to volunteer to guide Dayraven to the Wyrmberg. If there's any chance he can safeguard our realm, then I'm willing to help, if it doesn't displease you."

King Veduir looked with stern eyes at Dayraven and the captain. But then he sighed and said, "Very well, Uthron. You may bring two of your rangers with you if they follow you willingly. But you may only guide this man to the mountain. I forbid you to set foot on it. Once he reaches the Wyrmberg, he's on his own."

King Veduir turned to Dayraven. "Do you understand? It will take my men nine days to guide you to the Wyrmberg, and this only because we know paths no one else has set foot on. Once you reach the mountain, *you* must find the way up. According to our lore, it takes three days to climb to Gorsarhad's lair, though no one has been foolish enough to try in generations. Don't risk my men's lives, though they may lead you willingly."

Dayraven nodded. "Sire, I'll do everything in my power to keep them from harm. And I thank you."

"Save your thanks for Captain Uthron, if you come out alive. But I wish you good fortune. I never laid eyes on a man of the Mark ere now, but it seems to me a young wizard with power like yours could have been a great leader among your people with time."

Dayraven bowed to acknowledge King Veduir's words. *A wizard like me has no people*, he thought to himself.

20

THE FURY OF THE ILARCHAE

"They say it's quiet in Thulhan, at least." In the plain beneath Keevan's gaze waited a massive and deafening army of Ilarchae outnumbering the Sildharae troops ten to one. Like locusts, they had appeared in the morning where there was empty landscape the day before. The barbarians clustered toward the eastern end of Sirukinn's Wall, so a great number of Sildharan's troops from further west, including Keevan's company of archers, had moved in to reinforce the portion of the wall nearest the Amlar Mountains.

Dressed in furs and the bright colors of their clans, the tall, pale savages kept to loose gatherings according, Keevan supposed, to tribe and kinship. Here and there they bore strange and grisly talismans fixed atop long poles. The half-rotted head of a bull, wolf, bear, or horse. A dog's flayed body. A troll skull pierced by an arrow. A cluster of dangling, bloody hands bound together. A cape of raven feathers. And many others. Beneath the hideous tokens, the savages hooted, bellowed, roared, cursed, and screamed in the most unholy din known to humanity.

"Not so quiet here, eh Captain?" Keevan winced as he realized the idiocy of his observation, but he had always been a talker when he got nervous, like when his mother had found out he had done something stupid. Again.

The captain's only answer was to spit over the wall, with the wind carrying the spittle before it hit the ground thirty feet below.

That was not the answer Keevan wanted, but he realized reassurance was in short supply both in the Sildharan's chief city and here at Sirukinn's wall, where they faced the enemy head on. If it was quiet in Thulhan, he imagined it was no peaceful silence. More like paralyzing dread of impending doom, and it had spread throughout the realm.

From great cities to small villages, the east's mightiest kingdom knew mass fear for the first time in hundreds of years. Torrlond's army was on its way, and with it came not only the troops of the Mark and Ellond, but also dragons. From the northeast descended the Ilarchae, united for the first time as a mighty force and massed right under Keevan's nose. But one thing more than any other had shaken the faith of the Sildharae in their kingdom's power: Most of the Ilarchae slaves within Sildharan had disappeared in the last two days after murdering many of their masters and gathering into large war bands.

The slayings of the Sildharae masters and their families down to the smallest children inspired naked terror. The Ilarchae thralls slaughtered whole farmsteads, not even sparing the animals, though they took horses whenever they could. Some fixed their former masters' heads on stakes as grisly signposts. There was even talk that the Ilarchae sacrificed some of their captives to their ruthless gods by burning the victims alive. Such was their fierce revenge for their long enslavement.

Word had come to the wall that King Naitaran had dispatched troops to destroy the slave war bands, though he dared not send many from Thulhan with Torrlond's army about to arrive. But the soldiers found only the blood-soaked aftermath of the barbarians' revenge. The war bands had melted into Sildharan's vast countryside without a trace.

With such dire threats and devastation abounding, not the least afraid were the soldiers guarding Sirukinn's Wall, and Keevan counted himself among the most afraid of them. Not that the wall gave him no confidence at all. From the end of the Amlar Mountains to the Gulf of Olfi, the massive, thirty foot high structure of grey stone snaked for twenty miles. Every half mile along the structure stood a huge tower housing the wall's guardians. On the northern side, two deep ditches paralleled the wall for its entire length. With their steep banks, these would slow down even the most determined assault.

But it was the great wall itself that presented the most formidable barrier. Its cut stones were impossible to scale, and its crenellations mocked any foolish enough to try to reach them. Never had it failed to keep out the barbarians from the north since King Sirukinn ordered it built hundreds of years before. Even so, King Naitaran had fortified it with ten thousand troops, a number most thought more than adequate to defend it from any attack.

Keevan's cheeks puffed out, and, realizing he had been holding his breath, he exhaled. He rubbed his sweaty palm on his golden tunic, his gaze locked on the massive army seething just out of bowshot from the wall. The Ilarchae had come by horse, but they had put their steeds aside. The barbarians, it was said, fought poorly on horseback. They were also weak in archery, according to Keevan's captain, who seemed to know about these things, but even he admitted their foot soldiers yielded to none in wielding throwing spears, large swords, and battleaxes. Keevan was glad none of those sharp edges could reach him at the moment, but he was not sure how long that state of affairs would last. The great horde below stood facing the defenders, jeering and roaring at the wall with increasing volume and passion. Never had Sirukinn's Wall failed, but never had the Ilarchae come as one hundred thousand warriors.

"They do seem keen, don't they, Captain?"

The captain snorted. "Savages are always eager for battle."

The Ilarchae began thumping their spears on the earth while chanting some primitive song in their harsh tongue. As they echoed off the wall, their thousands of voices merged into a reverberating force that threatened destruction. Keevan attempted to swallow in his suddenly dry throat, and his bladder prodded him with an urgent need for relief.

Whipping themselves into a frenzy, some of the larger Ilarchae stepped forward and screamed curses or threats, or perhaps oaths to perform some deed. They bit their shields, tore at their clothes, and raged at the wall as if their growls could bring it down. "Uh. I think they're coming, Captain." Keevan gawped as the Ilarchae warriors handed forward numerous crude but tall ladders and poles to the front of their ranks. His teeth began chattering, and he clamped his mouth shut, glad that the savage din of the Ilarchae at least masked the sound of his teeth. He glanced at his captain. "Shouldn't we send for reinforcements, m'lord?"

"No need, Keevan. Besides, the king's called every last soldier to defend Thulhan. Our duty is to protect this front. The brutes will never breach this wall while we're here."

Keevan blinked and tightened his white-knuckled grip on his bow. "But so many have come. They said the savages would never make it here." He should have listened to his mother and never left farming to join the king's forces. He had told her he would be an archer and thus was sure to stay out of harm's way. Some idea that turned out to be. And now his mother was not even around to slap him on the side of the head and tell him how stupid he was, just like his father.

The captain hawked up some more loose phlegm and spat again over the wall. "They have some leader, a fellow with one of their ugly names. 'Surt,' I think they call him. Whoever he is, he won't be able to keep this rabble in order. Look at them. They're ready to dash their brains out on the wall."

A moment later, Keevan started and almost dropped his bow when war horns broke the air. The Ilarchae tore open the heavens with screams that promised blood as they surged forward.

FACING SIRUKINN'S WALL FROM THE NORTH AMIDST A HUNDRED thousand proud Ilarchae warriors, Munzil stood with his sword in his hand and his shield on his arm. He gazed at the formidable defensive work before him. That wall was high. It was strong. But it would not hold back his people, for they were stronger. Flesh, blood, and bone would prevail over stone. He had seen it in the vision the gods bestowed on him. The wall stood between his brave people and their fate, and it would fail. Holding his head high among the warriors of the Fire Dragons, Munzil knew he was where he belonged.

Nearby were Gorm and Skuld as well as other members of the Boar Clan of the Fire Dragon Tribe. Since their journeys together, Gorm had begun treating Munzil as a brother, and even Skuld cracked the occasional smile his way. The big chieftain made no secret of the fact that he now shared Munzil's dream for the Ilarchae. And Munzil had inspired many others. His vision of uniting the free tribes into one military unit also had brought great honor to the Fire Dragons, for it was their war-leader who commanded all the tribes. Munzil looked toward Surt, who stood only a few feet away next to one-eyed Valdur and the other chieftains of the Fire Dragons.

The great man had planned every detail of the day's attack. With patience and foresight remarkable in one so young, he had sent secret messengers into Sildharan to organize the Ilarchae slaves there. The war-leader of the Fire Dragons, and now of all the folk of the tribes, had thought of everything, right down to the timing of the slave revolt. They would play a crucial part in their release from bondage. Munzil beamed with pride to think of it. Surt was not only the most formidable warrior ever born, but he also possessed a strong head for strategy and battle tactics. Clearly the gods had touched him. Dressed in his usual black garb, he was shaking his fist and leading the death chant, in which the warriors vowed to fight with honor and protect their brothers and sisters in battle.

"Death before dishonor! Death the mighty! We warriors embrace you! Death! Come where you will!"

Tears running down his cheeks, Munzil gazed at Surt even as he shouted with all the others in the chant that rose to the heavens and shook the foundations of the earth. He loved his people, the folk of the tribes. He loved the Fire Dragons. And he loved Surt, the man the gods chose to unite the Ilarchae and forge them into what fate meant for them: a people of greatness, freedom, and strength. But, as much as they had made Munzil one of their own, he was not there as a man of the Fire Dragons.

The Grey Wolves lived in him. He remembered his parents, his brothers and sisters, his wife, and, most of all, Inga and Erzil, his daughter and son. He was there for them and for all the members of his lost tribe. The Bear Fangs had defeated them, but it was the Sildharae that had disgraced his people and denied them their honor. It was the Sildharae that had wiped them from existence. Never again would the outlanders thus shame the folk of the tribes. They were here in all their strength: the Fire Dragons, Strong Axes, White Foxes, Stone Fists, Snow Bears, Bright Shields, Boar Tusks, Raven Eyes, Bear Fangs, Hawk Claws, Night Trolls, Red Swords, Cleft Skulls, Black Elks, and many more.

And the Grey Wolves.

Munzil gazed around at the multitude of warriors. Pride in his people surged within him. Their brave faces showed the sense of purpose now awakened in them. Tempered by the rugged lands of the cold north and the harsh sea, the folk of the tribes would at last realize how strong they were. Together, they could withstand any of the soft outlanders' kingdoms.

At the forefront of the war gathering, the Wolfhides began screaming more loudly, gnawing on their shields and rending their garments as the battle rage swept them up. One rapturous desire occupied them: to kill. No pain or wound short of a mortal blow would stop them. Those big warriors from every tribe would rush headlong into the most furious storm of steel, only thinking to satisfy their burning lust to slay. It went beyond courage. It was a god-inspired ecstasy that drove them.

Others passed forward ladders and poles with hooked ends. There were hundreds of them, but Munzil knew many would perish in the attempt to scale the wall. Live or die, it would be a great honor to be the first up one of the ladders.

War horns rent the sky and bellowed the signal to charge. Knowing he was fighting for the freedom and honor of his folk, Munzil screamed and ran forward in the glorious onslaught along with his hundred thousand brothers and sisters.

"Archers! Fit your bows!" ordered the captain.

Nocking an arrow, Keevan obeyed along with his comrades. His fingers were slippery with sweat. He hoped the arrow would not escape his grasp before the order came to loose.

"Look at the fools," the captain said as the Ilarchae rushed toward the ditches. "No line of attack. No chain of command. Not a shred of discipline. We'll mow 'em down."

The Ilarchae dashed into the first ditch, some falling on top of others. A horn sounded from the nearest tower.

The captain cried out, "Loose!"

Keevan released. A swarm of arrows droned and sped towards the attackers. Shafts sprouted from hundreds of the barbarians, who filled the ditch with their corpses. Still they came. When those carrying ladders or poles fell, others rushed to take their places.

"Fit your bows!" came the command.

With his hand shaking, Keevan reached behind and grabbed another arrow from his quiver. He nocked it, thanking Oruma and Anghara he had not dropped it.

"Loose!"

He let it fly. A buzz filled the air as thousands of shafts sped towards their targets of flesh.

More savages fell. Yet they still came. Some reached the second ditch only to crumple with shafts protruding from their bodies.

"Loose!" came the command two, three, four more times. Keevan was shaking all over now, but he obeyed each time. He did not know if any of his arrows had found a human target. He stifled the powerful urge to retch.

"Ha!" laughed the captain amidst the battle's din at the quagmire of corpses piling up before the wall. "Let 'em come all day like this, and we'll send the lot to Oruma!"

But then he lurched forward. His smile changed to a look of wide-eyed alarm as he collapsed to his knees and gasped for air. Keevan dropped his bow to catch the captain in his arms. Something wet oozed all over his hand. A spear shaft stuck out of his commander's back, the sharp tip having sheared through his bronze corselet. *His back? But that means...*

Crouching to hold his leader, the bowman looked behind the wall to the south just in time to see a volley of missiles fly from a second army of Ilarchae. The sky turned black for a moment, and then the storm of arrows and spears clanged on the wall and tore into flesh. A spear sailed into the soldier next to Keevan, spraying blood and hurling the body over the northern side of the wall. It was just stupid luck that nothing pierced the squatting bowman.

After the first hail of weapons, Keevan was too stunned to do anything more than gawk at his comrades lying dead or writhing and screaming in pools of blood. Just before the next wave came, the bowman realized with a shock where all the runaway Ilarchae slaves had gone.

Perhaps the barbarians were not as stupid and unorganized as everyone supposed. No one on the wall had thought to look behind.

The captain gasped in agony with a grimace creasing his face. He forced out words between ragged breaths. "Must bring word . . . to king if they take . . . wall." Blood crimsoned his teeth and burbled between his lips.

The tops of crude ladders and poles appeared with loud clacks above the northern side of the wall, and large metal hooks attached to them held them in place. Great numbers of Ilarchae slaves overwhelmed the few soldiers on the ground on the unprotected southern side as they hastened up stairs leading to the top. The Ilarchae *would* take the wall. They were enveloping the badly outnumbered Sildharae. Keevan crouched with his mouth hanging open. Missiles flew all around him. He wondered what he was supposed to do.

A dozen different thoughts skittered around in his head, and he could not settle on one of them. But he had to do something, so he rested the dying captain on his side and took up a dead man's halberd, though his hands shook so much he nearly dropped it. While arrows whistled by him, he hacked away at one ladder, shredding splinters off it until he chopped off its hooks. Stabbing the top of the ladder with the halberd, he pushed and grunted and managed to shift it off the wall, and then it teetered the other way, building its own momentum with the weight of several bodies on it. He winced when the yelping and wide-eyed foes climbing on the rungs plunged to their probable deaths, smacking the soil and a few other bodies with a crunching and splintering of wood and bones. He had no time to think on it, though, since a huge Ilarchae warrior emerged at the top of another ladder nearby, growling like a ravenous beast.

A soldier of Keevan's company ran toward the savage and brought down his sword. The Ilarchae caught the blade with his bare hand, and blood splattered from the wound. Yet the Ilarchae held on. Keevan's jaw dropped, and some part of his mind was aware that the wet warmth spreading all over his leg was his own piss. The snarling brute must have been one of the legendary Wolfhides, warriors from the Wildlands who felt no pain in battle.

The dismayed soldier jerked at his blade with both hands, but the Wolfhide held it firm as he roared. With his other hand, the Ilarchae warrior grasped his opponent's head and brought his teeth to the man's neck. The soldier struggled as the Wolfhide bit and tore into his windpipe, shaking his head and spraying blood everywhere.

"Oh shit." Keevan was in it now for sure. He could not avert his bulging eyes as his comrade shuddered then fell as if boneless. He had barely enough presence of mind to raise the halberd in defense. More Ilarchae scrambled up the ladder behind the Wolfhide.

Everywhere the bowman looked, barbarians had gained access to the wall. Up ladders and poles on the north side they climbed. On the southern side, they poured up the stairs and into the towers. Glancing behind, Keevan saw another Wolfhide had found his wounded captain. Two arrows had already pierced the Wolfhide — one in his left upper arm, one in his right side — but the wounds affected him no more than scratches might. Less, in fact. The giant warrior had cut off one of the commander's arms, and he held the helpless man by the hair with one hand. Swinging the reddened sword in his other hand, the barbarian lopped off the captain's head in one bloody sweep then bellowed in triumph as he raised his dripping prize by the hair.

A raw and inhuman cry escaped Keevan's throat as something propelled his legs to avenge his leader. Surprising the Ilarchae almost as much as himself, he sank his halberd into the savage's belly. The Wolfhide dropped the head and roared as he swung his giant sword at the halberd's shaft, shattering the wood. With the halberd's blade still planted in his guts and blood spattering his beard from his mouth, the Wolfhide growled and advanced on Keevan. The man's bright blue eyes were not human, but seemed rather to exude the chill and feral blankness of a predatory beast.

Keevan held up the broken shaft to defend himself, but he could not keep it steady. With terrible speed, the fierce Wolfhide slashed at the bowman, whose shaft deflected the blade just enough that the sword hit him flatling on his helm. The blow sent Keevan reeling over the wall's southern edge. He screamed as he fell.

As Munzil scaled the ladder, a warrior's body plummeted by, narrowly missing him before it smashed into the pile of corpses below. There it lay, its limbs askew and its head a disfigured, pulpy mess. Only one other warrior climbed above him now on the ladder. The man screamed as he reached the edge of the crenellated wall, where two arrows thumped into his torso before his arms twitched and he fell backwards. Hugging the ladder, Munzil avoided the falling corpse. He needed to move before those bowmen nocked fresh arrows.

He scrambled up the rest of the way and shoved his linden shield in front of his body. A pair of thuds knocked into the wood, and the heads of two arrows bit through, just missing his arm. Without knowing what was in front of him, he threw all his weight forward and slammed into something. Whatever it was, it cracked when he grunted and landed hard on it.

Munzil raised himself. Beneath his shield lay a bloodied and unconscious face, nose all askew with a sharp edge of white bone poking out of it. Standing at his full height, he reached toward his hip for his sheathed sword, but then a blur of movement to his side warned him. He raised his shield out of instinct.

A sword's edge crunched and bit through the metal rim and deep into the linden wood, spinning off a few splinters. The Sildharae warrior who wielded it tugged, but the blade was lodged in Munzil's shield. He twisted and jerked it, ripping the sword from his surprised attacker's grip.

But the man was no coward. Before Munzil could unsheathe his own sword, the Sildharae warrior punched him in the face. White flashed, and he staggered back. The man tackled him, and they both fell.

In a clatter of wood, metal, and grunting flesh, Munzil landed hard on his back with the man on top of him. His shield was pinned under him, so he slipped his arm out and raised it to deflect the man's next blow, which jarred the bone of his forearm. With his other hand, he reached toward his boot and slipped out the dagger sheathed in it.

Before Munzil could stab him, the warrior jerked toward the weapon and grabbed his wrist in a strong grip. That gave him the chance to punch his adversary in the temple, knocking him off balance and allowing Munzil to roll on top, straddling the man.

Now each man grasped the dagger with both hands and grunted as they struggled to push the weapon towards their foe. But Munzil was sitting on top, and the dagger was pointed at the hollow in the bottom of the Sildharae's neck. As if transfixed, he watched the slow but inexorable inching of the dagger's shiny tip toward the soldier's flesh. Both men breathed in ragged gasps. The wide-eyed foe's face trembled with his exertion. Veins protruded on his forehead, and he hissed through his teeth as he strained to keep the dagger from piercing his skin with its sheen of sweat.

Fearing an attack from behind, Munzil grunted and thrust down with all his strength. The blade moved to within a hair's breadth of the soldier's throat, and his desperate face reddened. Both men's arms shook with the effort.

Munzil looked into the soldier's brown eyes. The man returned his gaze. He was not sure what the man's expression was saying. Was he enraged? Afraid? Defiant? Perhaps all of them, but the Sildharae did not cry out in fear or beg for mercy. He just gasped and pushed with all his remaining strength.

It was not enough. Munzil shoved down harder. The blade's tip broke the man's dark skin in the hollow of his neck. A trickle of blood seeped in a line down his neck, and his arms shook more violently even as he weakened. His face contorted in a teeth-baring grimace, but his dark eyes stared into Munzil's as the dagger sank in deeper.

The blade slipped in and disappeared in the man's parting flesh. Blood welled out in gentle pulses as his heart pumped it out of the wound. A shiver passed through his body. His mouth opened as if he would speak. A gurgle of blood coughed out and spattered Munzil's face.

He pushed the weapon down until the tip touched the stone of the wall. The soldier's arms slumped to his sides. The vacant eyes in his slack face still stared into Munzil's. The last of the Grey Wolves whispered, "You died with honor."

THE WORLD SPUN, AND KEEVAN THE ARCHER PLUMMETED UNTIL HIS back slammed into something hard, but whatever it was gave way under him as he bounced and grunted. When he sat up, blinked his eyes, and shook his head, he first found he was not only alive but in awfully good shape for someone who should have fallen to his death. He next found he was sitting on top of a large Ilarchae's back, which he must have landed on.

The Ilarchae beneath him was lying on the stairs leading up the south side of the wall, and several other Ilarchae below were squirming in a tangle of limbs. He must have knocked them over as well. When he stood up from his unmoving cushion with nothing worse than a ringing head, Keevan realized he was halfway down the wall. Beneath him on the ground raged a chaotic melee as a few of Sildharan's soldiers rallied. The Ilarchae on the stairs below him recovered and lurched toward him with fury in their eyes and axes in their hands.

The bowman jumped the rest of the way to the ground. When the earth rushed up to meet him, he landed on his feet and rolled. He sprang up before anyone could cut or trample him. And then the real miracle happened. A neigh somewhere up ahead grabbed his attention. Through the press of bodies, a whinnying and riderless horse stamped and lashed out in circles. He remembered the captain's last words and determined to bear news to the king.

Amidst close fighting, he dodged bodies and edged closer to the horse. An Ilarchae challenged him with sword aloft, but an arrow pierced the barbarian through the neck with a splatter of blood, sending him down groveling.

Keevan picked up the man's crude sword, which was too heavy for him. Just when he looked up, another Ilarchae ran at him with a battle-axe. Screaming with terror or fury or both, the bowman lunged toward his attacker. But he tripped over a fallen soldier just before they met, which probably saved him. The axe sailed over his head as he fell and dropped his sword.

Now weaponless but much closer to the horse, Keevan scrambled up and left behind the sword as his attacker engaged with another man. Sprinting toward the beast, he hoped it would allow him to ride it. He was relieved to find it was one of the wall garrison's battle-trained horses, which meant the chaos would less likely spook it.

The archer danced in little steps as he reached for the reins, clicking his tongue to soothe the pacing beast. The horse fidgeted and gave a few nervous snorts, but it let him approach and grasp the reins. He petted the quieting steed in gratitude and, once he was sure it would not spook, leaped on its back. For the first day in his life, his luck was holding. Just as he urged the horse to gallop south, a sharp pain stung his left arm.

MUNZIL WIPED HIS REDDENED SWORD ON THE GOLDEN TUNIC OF THE fourth and last soldier he killed. Sweat dripped from him, mixing with the blood spattered all over his body. Most of the blood had belonged to the foe. Breathing hard and wincing when he leaned on his cut leg, he stood atop the wall and looked around. Only Ilarchae were standing as far as he could see. The battle was over. The folk of the tribes had won.

He did not know where Gorm and the others were. He could not see Surt. In the heat of battle, he had lost track of anything but the foe in front of him and the urge to stay alive. No thoughts of freedom or vengeance or the glory of the Ilarchae had come to him during the fighting. He had even forgotten his vision. In battle, there were only two motivations: to stay alive, and to do nothing to dishonor himself. He had accomplished both.

But now the struggle for Sirukinn's Wall was finished. Now, even as he gazed upon the carnage around him, the piles of bodies at the base of the wall, and the blood spattered upon the stones, he could reflect on what it meant. Even as the wounded and dying lay groaning and screaming, sounds that usually made him want to retch, triumph quickened in his chest and grew until it threatened to burst him asunder. He had to release it.

"Folk of the Wildlands!" he screamed in the middle of his labored breaths. "This wall will never hold us back again! We have won! We have won!"

As many of his brother and sister warriors turned toward him, he continued. "This is the beginning. We have come to this land to free our kin and find our fate. Surt and the gods will lead us to ever greater victories."

Though they were weary and hurt, they beamed at him with smiles of triumph. Some of them had been slaves only a few days ago. But now they had broken the chains. They had conquered the wall. They were strong. They were free.

The black dragon of Munzil's vision returned to his mind, lighting up the darkness with the roiling flames pouring out of its maw. He had been right. The gods had chosen Surt to lead them to their destiny. The war-leader's plan had worked. The coordinated attack on the wall had been god-inspired. Surt was the one.

"Hail, Surt!" came the hoarse cry from Munzil's parched throat as his fist beat the air.

"Hail, Surt!" answered his brothers and sisters from every tribe.

"Hail, Surt!" he screamed again.

"Hail, Surt!" they echoed even louder as more took up the cry.

"Hail, Surt!"

"Hail, Surt!" answered the mightiest army in Eormenlond, and the wall trembled at their voices.

As he rode the war horse at a canter to conserve its strength, blood continued to ooze from the gash where an arrow had torn open Keevan's forearm. Fortunately, it had been only a glancing shot.

Images from the battle's end still haunted him. After galloping far enough away to feel out of danger, he had stopped the horse and turned to look back. Few soldiers in gold tunics remained on the wall, whereas the Ilarchae swarmed everywhere. Dread sank in the pit of his stomach. Knowing that Sildharan had lost the wall to the barbarians for the first time in its glorious history, he had fled from the screams and clanging of weapons. Only when he had ridden far had Keevan noticed the blood on his head and face, and his back and left forearm ached terribly. He stank of piss and sweat and blood. But he was alive. For the moment.

Keevan rode the whole day. In great haste, he found food and drink at a farm, where he told the frightened farmers to flee, to hide if they would preserve their lives. He rode on in pain and despair, but he determined to keep going until he brought word to Thulhan of the terrible defeat. For all he knew, he was the wall's only survivor.

Towards evening, a cloud of dust appeared on the horizon, and he recognized a column of Sildharan's cavalry. No doubt they were some of the soldiers King Naitaran had sent to hunt down the runaway Ilarchae slaves. He could tell them where to find them.

Keevan rode hard toward the cavalry. Several horsemen broke off from the main column and rode toward him. When he reached them, he shouted, "Take me to your captain at once!"

Before long, Keevan stood before the captain of the one hundred horsemen. They spoke apart from the rest of the soldiers, and the captain offered the bowman his own water flask. Keevan took a deep draft before delivering the dire tidings.

When he informed the captain the Ilarchae slaves had joined forces with their brethren from the north, the officer's eyes went wide. When he told him the barbarians had overwhelmed the wall and most likely slain every one of the ten thousand soldiers posted there save himself, the captain's eyes bulged as he gaped, his lower lip trembling on his open mouth.

The man managed to stammer, "But . . . how could they? What . . . Where are they headed now?"

"I imagine if we wait here, we'll find out soon enough," answered Keevan, too exhausted to observe formalities.

The captain decided not to wait. Keevan's state and the prospect of more than a hundred thousand Ilarchae warriors marching toward them seemed more than enough to convince him a hasty retreat to

Thulhan was in order. He sent riders to enlighten other companies searching for the slaves and then gave orders to ride hard.

Keevan fell in with the horsemen. Three days after he fled from the wall, they reached Thulhan. Just before they entered the city, the messengers the captain had sent out returned to the company. They reported the Ilarchae army was indeed heading south. They also bore the ominous tidings that several of the companies King Naitaran dispatched in search of the Ilarchae slaves had disappeared.

Deeming it best to let someone else tell King Naitaran at least some of the disastrous news, the captain conducted the bowman, who was a firsthand witness after all, to the palace.

Thus, Keevan the archer appeared with his hands folded and head bowed low before King Naitaran in the palace's throne room in the late morning. Standing around the throne with solemn frowns directed at the bowman were a score of advisors and nobles in their colorful robes of costly fabrics, for the king had called a council that morning, and it was just underway. Keevan had heard of most of the illustrious members of the council, but there were three strangers present as well.

Talking over Keevan's head, King Naitaran told all the others that the strangers were the wizard Galdor of Ellond, his servant Abon, and the sorceress Sequara of Asdralad, which did little to alleviate the bowman's nerves. When Sildharan's ruler turned to Keevan with his indignant eyes, the archer felt like he was interrupting the royal dinner. The grave monarch spoke right at him. "Soldier, you may speak freely before this council and our guests." He made a slight gesture of command with one hand.

Keevan swallowed the spit in his mouth to try to loosen his throat. Sitting on his beautiful throne beneath its stone canopy, Sildharan's ruler looked as proud and strong as all the stories made him. The king wore a scowl as he wrinkled his nose and gazed down at Keevan the way he might stare at a great big turd plopped into the middle of his splendid throne room. In fact, Keevan was having a hard time finding his voice before the monarch and most powerful sorcerer of Sildharan. But when he managed to stutter to a start, his tale took on its own momentum and tumbled out of him. And as he told it, he could not help but notice by the monarch's widening eyes that it took even King Naitaran by surprise.

"They fought like beasts, your Majesty. Demons, I should say. Those Wolfhides can't be human. I've never seen lust for blood possess men like that. Pressed from both sides, we had no chance. I don't know how I survived, but I chose to honor my commander's last words in coming to you. I hope I've done right." He finished with a low bow, though he was not sure it was the proper thing to do. Still, it was better to be safe than sorry.

King Naitaran stared at the bowman with anger — or perhaps incomprehension — on his face. His eyebrows were raised halfway up his forehead, and his mouth hung open while a little twitch animated one side of the upper lip. No one dared to move, least of all Keevan.

Perhaps to fill the silence, the captain of the cavalry cleared his throat and said, "Your Majesty. My scouts reported the Ilarchae are riding not far behind us. They're coming here, your Majesty. They could arrive as soon as tomorrow."

Still Naitaran did not speak. He only kept staring at Keevan with something like madness in his eyes. The bowman took a couple steps back and wished he could have been anywhere else.

A member of the council, a thin old man named Vishwan, the master of the powerful spice guild, stuttered, "Sirukinn's Wall . . . taken? An army of barbarians? Here? Tomorrow? And Torrlond has arrived from the west. Perhaps, your Majesty, we should sue for peace?"

The monarch snapped his gaze toward the spice trader with such haste that the old man shrank back and looked at the floor, chastened into silence. Keevan was glad the attention was no longer focused on him, but a feeling of helplessness seized him as he watched the insanity of Sildharan's king unfold.

Naitaran turned to the wizard Galdor with the sort of constipated grin he might have worn while fishing his favorite ring from a latrine. Shrinking back, Keevan knew he did not want to be on the other end of that smile. But the old man just stood there waiting with a thoughtful frown.

The king broke his long silence. "Well, Galdor, it appears you were right. Perhaps that gives you some satisfaction?"

"None, your Majesty. The only satisfaction I can have now is in defeating Torrlond."

"Defeating Torrlond?" Naitaran rose from his throne, his eyes bulging and jaw trembling. "Don't talk to me of victory! I tell you, I don't fear death. I welcome it! What I *fear* is the infamy of losing what generations of kings and queens of Sildharan have held in sacred trust since the foundation of *this kingdom*. It will be King Naitaran's name that bears the stain of defeat. They'll say *I* lost the greatest realm in Eormenlond. Civilization's light will go out. Generations of lore will perish. And who will bear the blame? Only death will save me from shame, and I embrace it. Torrlond will buy its conquest with blood. But do not speak of victory. Only a fool could hope for victory now."

Galdor smiled sadly. "No one doubts your courage, your Majesty. Yet hope may prove wiser than despair."

Keevan had a hard time following the king and the wizard's words since they spoke in formal High Andumaic. Yet he could catch the gist of the conversation, and he hoped it was an argument Galdor would win. There was something about the white-bearded old man that made him want to trust him.

King Naitaran, however, did not hide his scorn. His hands moved in wild gestures as he leaned forward and spoke with increasing volume. "Hope? Have you not heard the reports? Torrlond is on our doorstep! They're even now within a short march to Thulhan. Earconwald's ships block Quinara Sound, sealing off escape. They'll form a tight ring around us, a strangling noose, and they'll begin their assault *this very day*. By even modest estimates, Torrlond brings one hundred and fifty thousand troops. The army of the Mark comes as well, raising their numbers further. And now, more than one hundred thousand bloodthirsty Ilarchae are burning my villages and slaughtering my people like sheep. And let's not forget the dragons. Isn't that right, Galdor? You're always reminding us of them. I have at most one hundred and ten thousand soldiers left to defend us. And where are our allies? We're alone."

"Not alone, your Majesty," said Galdor with stern eyes and voice. "Do not forget what I told you of King Fullan and the loyal Ellonders. And the troops of Sundara are on their way."

"But where are they? Torrlond is here!"

"You know as well as I the Ilarchae slaves in the south delayed them. They've fought their way through at a cost, and they'll arrive on the morrow."

The king slumped back into his throne, his lips twisting into a smirk. "On the morrow? Tomorrow they may come in time to bury us after Torrlond's dragons burn my city to the ground. Then they'll die in turn over our ruins. Torrlond is here! Earconwald and Bledla won't wait for the Sundarae to come help us. And even then, the Ilarchae will also come tomorrow. No, Galdor, tomorrow brings no hope. They'll still more than double our numbers, and we have no way to fight the dragons."

"We have a way," said the sorceress from Asdralad, the one called Sequara. "Dayraven will come."

Keevan had no idea who or what 'Dayraven' was, but he wanted the beautiful sorceress to be right. Once again, his monarch's response disappointed him.

"The boy you spoke of?" scoffed Naitaran. "This is your hope? This is the best you can do? No, my lady, you'd best stop deluding yourself. He'll never stop Bledla. He'll most likely never arrive. It's folly to hope now. My realm will join yours in ashes and dust. It's the will of Oruma and Anghara. It was meant to be. Destruction must follow creation. Death follows life. In some distant time of the great cycle, life may return, but now . . . We can't fight fate. We must embrace it."

Sequara looked Naitaran in the eye and calmly said, "You're wrong about Dayraven. And you're wrong to give up hope when your people need you."

Naitaran looked as if she had slapped him. Madness clouded the king's eyes, and Keevan dreaded what would next come out of his mouth — perhaps some wrathful spell. Not wanting to be even within a mile of a fight between great sorcerers, he cringed and shuffled back a couple more steps, as if that would do any good.

Sildharan's king was about to unleash his words when someone burst in the throne room and hurried towards them. The dignitaries parted to let through the newcomer.

A messenger in soldier's golden garb approached Naitaran's throne and bowed. Out of breath, the messenger struggled for a moment to speak.

"I beg you to forgive the intrusion, your Majesty. We thought it best to inform you right away."

Naitaran's brow lowered. "Inform me of what?"

"Your pardon, your Majesty, but I ran as fast as I could. Some of your scouts have returned with tidings. There are more ships coming down Quinara Sound. At least a hundred and fifty."

Keevan's heart sank into the floor. It was true, then. They were all doomed.

King Naitaran turned to Galdor and Sequara, raising his eyebrows as he looked down. "You see? More arrive every minute. Just when we thought Torrlond could bring no more."

The messenger cleared his throat. "Your pardon, your Majesty, but these aren't Torrlond's ships. These are different."

"What? Then who are they?"

The wizard Galdor stepped forward with a smile brightening his face. "The Thjoths, your Majesty. King Vols has come with Grimrik's warriors."

21

TAKEN BY SURPRISE

Gnorn's respect for the Thjoths' seamanship grew to awe as Grimrik's fleet made for Quinara Sound across the Gulf of Olfi. The foamy-necked sea dragons almost seemed to fly, such skill did the burly warriors show in harnessing the wind for their vessels. Scores of eager sails snapped as clinker-built bows carved through the waves. The Dweorg stood in the prow of the king's ship near Orvandil and Vols as they sailed toward death. While the salty wind toyed with their blond hair, the cousins gazed southeast and smiled. Never had Orvandil looked so happy. *I too am ready*, thought Gnorn. *I've seen the Fyrnhowes, my ancestors' hills. It's enough.*

The Thjoths showed no trace of fear. Instead, if Gnorn had judged by their singing and laughter, he might have supposed they were journeying toward a feast with unlimited quantities of mead. Each passing swell brought them closer to their fate, and they rushed into it.

At length, a slender strip of blue-green hovered on the horizon. It would not be long before they entered Quinara Sound. The Thjoths' eyes grew more eager and their singing louder as they neared land. More time passed until the sound's mouth came into view. With a sigh, Gnorn noted no ships of Torrlond awaiting them. But they would meet the enemy soon enough.

When they entered the sound in rows of twelve to twenty, the sails slackened and oars emerged from the ships. The warriors rowed in perfect time to drums as they cut through the water. King Vols's ship led the way at the front row's center, the rest following in disciplined formation. They skimmed on the water without rest. A little more than a day after they set out from Grimrik, they approached the long body of water's end.

Gnorn peered out. In the distance, where the River Nurgleth entered Quinara Sound, Thulhan's tall towers rose above the horizon. Another sight greeted him as well. In front of them waited two hundred ships' sails. And on the western shore of the sound massed a portion of Torrlond's army, even ranks of soldiers who appeared little more than insects from that distance.

King Vols smiled at Orvandil. "See those longships between us and the city?"

Orvandil nodded. "Aye."

"Whose sails do you reckon they are?"

"More than half Torrlond's. The others from the Mark. Farwick mostlike."

"By my tally, they outnumber us by fifty."

"Sixty."

The king raised his eyebrows. "Really? How long to clear them?"

"Not long."

Vols laughed. "Those from Farwick might jump overboard rather than fight the Torrlonders' war for them. At least the Torrlonders are too stupid to run." He grinned like a wolf. "Perhaps we'll find better sport on land. What say you, friend Gnorn?"

Gnorn patted his axe. "I confess my axe would be of more use with solid earth beneath my feet, though I'll swing it wherever need be."

"Good. Let's see what awaits us there, then." The king pointed at the western shore. They were close enough to see two separate armies there. "Can you make out their banners?" he asked.

Orvandil squinted as he held his hand to his brow to shade his eyes. "The first is Duke Guthfrid's of North Torrlond. Black and red banner."

"Tell me of the good duke."

"Arrogant, foolish, and a great lover of the Way. The second, the one closer to the city, is not one of Torrlond's. Golden sun on a blue background. King Fullan's. The soldiers wear Ellond's blue kirtles."

"King Fullan of Ellond. Now this grows interesting. From what Galdor's told us, no doubt the loyal duke is meant to keep an eye on the Ellonders." Vols stroked his beard. "How many follow Guthfrid?"

"He commands more soldiers than most other Torrlonder dukes — a little more than twenty thousand. Fullan brings fewer with him."

"And there are no other troops in sight?"

Orvandil gazed again across the water. "None I see. The bulk of Torrlond's forces are likely inland. They haven't begun their assault."

"Good. Earl Guthfrid's devoted to the Way, is he? Then I suppose he might like his very own victory in the name of Edan?"

Gnorn laughed. "I'd wager he would."

Vols grinned again, looking more than ever like a wolf about to pounce on its prey. "Let's give him his chance, then. Prepare to signal the other ships. Where's Duneyr's? He'll lead the attack on the fleet."

On Quinara Sound's western shore, King Fullan of Ellond stood in conference with Duke Guthfrid of North Torrlond between their two waiting armies. Tall and large bellied, Guthfrid scowled with thick, dark eyebrows lowered over his eyes as he towered over King Fullan. Known as a foul-tempered bully, Guthfrid was King Earconwald's choice to keep Ellond's king in line. The duke had made no effort to conceal his opinion that he outranked Fullan. His disdain had trickled down to his soldiers, who had already picked several fights with some of the Ellonders to whom they were supposedly allied. Fullan was sick of the idiot, but he kept a stoic face for the moment. Four of his own earls and several of Guthfrid's earls and lords stood nearby, all clad in war gear. Among Fullan's earls, Freomar and Roric, the Way's keenest supporters, watched him closely.

Earl Freomar believed he would be Ellond's next ruler, a duke under Earconwald's sway. It mattered little. Freomar did not know, could never know, the true burden of ruling a kingdom. He and Roric were both traitors, little more than King Earconwald's lackeys. Their betrayal saddened Fullan and grieved him far more than Guthfrid's stupidity. They had been friends in their youth, trusted comrades. But painful as it was, he would see justice done. It was his duty to Ellond, and he would never shirk it. Ruling had always meant making hard decisions, and never in his reign had there been a harder time than this.

Fullan pretended to focus on Guthfrid as the large duke spoke. They were discussing their latest orders, but one of Guthfrid's soldiers interrupted them to report ships were coming down the sound.

"More supply ships, no doubt," said Guthfrid, turning away in dismissal of the messenger.

The man licked his lips and cleared his throat. "They don't appear to be, my lord."

Guthfrid turned again, a big scowl pasted across his face. "No? Let's have a look."

The party moved closer to shore, where gentle waves lapped the sandy beach. Their position provided a perfect view of the incoming ships, which grew larger as their oars stroked the water. They were unlike any ships of Torrlond, Ellond, or the Mark. They were unlike the ships of Sildharan and the eastern kingdoms as well.

Recognition dawned on Fullan. He remembered something important the wizard Galdor had told him. As if a heavy burden had fallen from him, a lightness permeated his chest, and he knew beyond doubt the moment had come. *Strange ships, he said. No more pretending.*

"In the name of Edan," said one of Guthfrid's noblemen. "Thjoths! What are those devils doing here?"

"Perhaps they come to offer allegiance," suggested King Fullan with a hint of a smile.

Guthfrid's sneer made his contempt plain. "We don't need the allegiance of those heathens. Nor do they come with peaceful intentions. Earl Redwald, signal our ships to come ashore, and send a message to King Earconwald. The pagans love a sea battle, so we won't give them one. We want the ships closer before the Thjoths reach them so our bows can aid them."

Another nobleman pointed out to the sound. "Look! Half of them are breaking off and heading towards us."

"What are the fools doing?" demanded Guthfrid. "We have five times their number, and splitting up will weaken them." The big duke stroked his beard as he stared out at the approaching ships. "Redwald, wait. This will be easier than I thought. Signal the ships to come closer to us, but not to shore, and give out orders to prepare the archers. Then bring the message to King Earconwald and the Supreme Priest Bledla." He chuckled. "There won't be much left, though. The Thjoths won't even make it to land, and the dragons can take care of the rest."

Fullan said nothing, but he smiled grimly as he steeled himself for what must come.

Redwald departed, and Duke Guthfrid turned to King Fullan, whose two watchful earls still flanked him. Guthfrid spoke through his frown. "This is an opportunity to show our devotion to the Way." He glanced at Freomar and Roric, making no attempt at subtlety in what his face communicated: *Watch your king. Make sure he cooperates, and look for an opportunity.* He faced Fullan again with a scowl. "Prepare your bowmen and put your ranks in battle formation. We'll fill them with arrows first. If the Thjoths make it to land, my soldiers will take the brunt of the attack, but I want you to bring in your men where needed. Try flanking the heathens. Is that clear?"

Fullan glanced at his four earls then nodded. "Yes, Guthfrid. We'll be there. My men are ready."

"Blessed be the Eternal!" exclaimed Guthfrid.

King Fullan did not reply but turned and strode away with his earls to prepare his troops. At last the time had come. Just as Galdor had foretold.

Aboard King Vols' ship, Gnorn watched half the Thjothic longships, under Duneyr's command, head straight for Torrlond and Farwick's fleets. His ship and the other half of the Thjoths veered for the western shore. Through a series of signals sent from ship to ship, the Thjoths coordinated the synchronized maneuvers with remarkable speed.

"If we've timed it right," said Vols, "Duneyr and the others should begin to attack their fleets just before we reach shore."

"What if it doesn't work?" asked Gnorn. "Then it'll be our four thousand against their forty thousand on land, and the others sail against greater numbers as well."

"Then," winked Vols, "it'll be a fair fight."

Gnorn stared in slack-jawed disbelief, but then he let loose a deep laugh. These Thjoths were fey. In spite of his height and the dark history between their peoples, he almost felt like one of them. *It's a fine way to go.* He had time for only one regret: If he died, he did not know who would write Dayraven's story. *Someone will. Someone must. Might be I'll make it.*

He looked over at the other ships. Duneyr's lead ship would soon make contact with the first of Torrlond's vessels. Arrows began to fly both ways. Now outnumbered three to one, the Thjoths' ships led by Duneyr's did not slow down. The vessels of Torrlond and Farwick bunched up behind one another in disarray since they had been heading toward shore. Evidently, the Thjoths reached them sooner than they had anticipated, and they scrambled to fan out to a more advantageous formation.

But the Thjoths were too quick. They thundered into their foes. More arrows flew, and the Thjoths cast spears and grappling hooks. Ships collided amidst the storm of battle. Arrows and spears filled the air. Within moments, the Thjoths began pouring onto their foes' vessels. Bodies splashed into the water and disappeared. Gnorn watched as the tall warriors, in the rapture of their battle rage, leaped at their enemies.

Just then, the warriors around him raised their round shields over their heads. Gnorn turned around and stepped under the shield wall between Orvandil and Asgrim just before a hail of arrows moaned overhead. A moment later, the missiles bit into wooden shields with hundreds of loud thuds. A few groans and cries revealed some arrows had hit their mark. One arrow protruded from the deck where he had stood.

Gnorn gazed ahead. King Vols' ship would soon make land. In front of them on the beach stood Duke Guthfrid's twenty thousand troops in neat rows, the archers in front. Further off to the left were Ellond's blue-kirtled ranks.

"Attack the right flank!" cried King Vols, "and stay on the right! Warriors of Grimrik! We feast with the gods!"

Gnorn gripped his battle-axe. More arrows whistled from above.

AFTER KING FULLAN OF ELLOND HAD REACHED HIS TROOPS, HE AND his four earls commanded them into formation. He posted his archers in front, and when all was in order, he stood before them with his four earls at his side. Fullan turned to one, the youngest, and smiled. "Elfwy, the time has come. Go help Redwald deliver his message to King Earconwald."

The young earl called Elfwy smiled back and nodded before he ran to gather some of his men. Torrlond's two watchdogs exchanged puzzled glances with their brows lowered as King Fullan unsheathed his sword and spoke. "Freomar and Roric . . . We were friends in our youth, were we not?"

The two earls frowned in confusion. Freomar summoned a strained smile. "Of course, your Majesty."

Fullan nodded. "For that friendship's sake I mourn, but I do my duty nonetheless. I sentence you to death for treason against your king and Ellond."

By the time the two traitors understood what was happening and began to pull out their blades, Fullan had swung. He guided the sharp edge into the bit of neck exposed under Freomar's gilded helm. Blood splashed and bone crunched when sharp steel sheared through flesh and sinews. With wide-eyed shock frozen on his face, Freomar's head crooked at an odd angle and flapped to the side as his body teetered over and hit the reddened sand.

Roric had his blade out, but before he moved toward Fullan, he gasped and stumbled as the reddened tip of a spear jutted from his chest. Grasping the spear's shaft, large, burly Earl Ashere grimaced as he yanked the weapon out of Roric's back, sending a gout of blood spewing from the wound. The stricken man looked down at his ruined chest and then collapsed on the sand, leaving Ashere standing over him with a grim smile.

Fullan gazed at his faithful earl. "Thank you, Ashere."

Earl Ashere knelt on one knee. "As you command. To you, my lord and king, I swear faith unto death."

Fullan nodded, then he turned and strode over to address his soldiers. They were murmuring among themselves and staring with disbelief written in their widened eyes. Ellond's king held up his hand to silence them.

"Soldiers of Ellond. Brothers. Hear your king! Freomar and Roric betrayed us all — followers of the Way, and followers of the old gods alike. All Ellonders. There was a time when our kinship with Torrlond commanded our loyalty, for ours are sister kingdoms. But we came here not as the Torrlonders' brothers and allies, but as their *slaves*. That's what the Torrlonders seek, using the Way as a mask for conquest. King Earconwald lusts to rule all of Eormenlond, and once we serve his purpose, he'll claim it, including Ellond, for his own. Under Earconwald's orders, Earl Freomar and Earl Roric were set to slay me so that Earconwald could claim Ellond as his dukedom." At this, an angry murmur arose among the soldiers.

Fullan held up a palm again to quiet them, nodding before he continued. "The two of them would have murdered me and betrayed you all. But Ellond's kings are Folcwalda's descendants no less than Torrlond's. And Ellond's people are one, whether they bow to Edan or Regnor and Hruga. We of Ellond will bow to what gods we choose, but we'll bow to no men. I say Ellonders, worshippers of old gods and new, will never bow to Torrlonders, but will face them as equals. I say we're free, and we'll fight anyone who would enslave us. I say rather than be Torrlond's slaves, we'll fight them here and now for our freedom! Men of Ellond, we are no one's slaves! Brothers, will you fight with your king?"

Earl Ashere brandished his spear. "For King Fullan and Ellond!"

Loud cheers erupted from three quarters of Fullan's troops, while some looked about in confusion.

Fullan did not wait. "Good. Then prepare to battle for your freedom and for Ellond. Rotate your formations to the left! Archers, stay in front!"

Captains repeated the orders while Earl Ashere waved them on. Most of the blue-kirtled troops scurried to reform their lines so they faced the Torrlonders' left flank. Many wore grim smiles. A few were slower, but all obeyed. When they were ready, Fullan pointed his sword and commanded, "Archers! Fit your bows!"

Longbows groaned as men aimed them towards Duke Guthfrid's unsuspecting troops, who were already shooting arrows at the approaching Thjoths.

"Loose!"

With a high-pitched gust, thousands of arrows sped from Ellond's bows. Guthfrid's left flank withered. Men dropped to the sand with cries of agony, clutching shafts that sprouted from their bodies. Before the Torrlonders knew what hit them, Fullan's archers loosed again. Hundreds more cringed to the earth.

The shocked North Torrlonders scrambled to turn and answer Ellond's bows. Standing near his left flank, Duke Guthfrid turned red with rage and tried to reorganize his archers. "Turn about, fools! Loose at them! Loose!" He shook his fist and railed in Fullan's direction, "Traitor! Heathenish wretch! Edan will scourge you! Curse your vile blood! You'll . . ."

An arrow slapped straight into his left eye, abruptly halting his curses. Guthfrid wobbled a moment with the shaft protruding from his blood-spattered face, his other eye frozen in bafflement. He fell back, and when his body thudded on the sand, his limbs flopped up once with the impact. He did not stir again.

As soon as the ship ground onto the strand, Gnorn leapt out with his battle-axe ready. He splashed into waves above his knees as arrows zinged by. Cool water soaked his breeches and sloshed into his boots. Dozens of wooden thuds sounded as the Thjoths' shields filled with the missiles. A warrior next to him, big Bodvar, took an arrow in his shoulder but kept running. Another stumbled when an arrowhead ripped through his thigh. A few bodies of Thjoths bloodied the waves with several shafts embedded in each. The Dweorg trudged forward, squelching through lapping water and mud and praying to the ancestors that no arrows would find him.

Gnorn struggled to keep up with Orvandil and King Vols, who led the charge into Guthfrid's troops. As Vols ran towards their right, the Dweorg glanced at the enemy's left flank. Bravery aside, if it was intact, they were all as good as dead. His heart danced to see the Torrlonder formations churning in complete disarray. Vols' gamble had paid off: King Fullan had come over to their side. If they could win their way over to the right flank, they would squeeze Duke Guthfrid's men in a vise between Thjoths and Ellonders. And one Dweorg.

In front of Gnorn, the foremost Thjoths crashed into Torrlond's soldiers. Men screamed and steel rang. Gnorn rushed headlong into the fray, yelling the battle cry of the Dweorgs of the Fyrnhowes, "Hza-atarku Kheendwunok!"

And then he was in it. Whirling to dodge a blow, he spun around and hacked off his attacker's sword arm, which fountained red. A blade flashed down on him, but it rang when the Dweorg parried it with his axe. Proving quicker than his adversary, he shattered the man's ribs with a forward thrust. To his right, he caught a glimpse of Orvandil and Vols, who cut deep into Guthfrid's ranks without looking back.

Gnorn recognized the danger of the king becoming surrounded as another blade swept down on him. He caught it with his axe, but the large grey-kirtled man who wielded it pressed down on him. Gnorn found his footing and pressed back, and the big man's eye's widened as the Dweorg grunted and forced him backwards.

But the big Torrlonder squinted as he glanced behind Gnorn for a fraction of a moment. Sensing movement behind him, Gnorn jerked backward and thrust his axe haft into the gut of the grey-kirtled soldier about to cut him down. The man groaned and buckled, and Gnorn hefted his axe forward to fend off a blow from the large soldier still in front of him.

Sword clanged on axe, but a sudden pain burned across his face as the blade's edge bit into the Dweorg's cheek and nose. Blood welled from the wound as the big man grinned. With a deep-throated growl, Gnorn moved with cunning speed, using his size and weapon to his advantage.

Jumping closer and dropping to the ground feet first, he landed on his hip and took the soldier's legs out from under him with a savage kick behind his knees. The big man fell backwards with arms flailing.

Just when he tried to raise himself, Gnorn swung his axe straight into his face, cleaving through his skull in the space between his helm and his nose and splattering out chunks of its greyish, bloody contents.

The Dweorg wasted no time gloating. He rose and sprinted in the direction he had last seen King Vols and Orvandil. The two blond Thjoths towered above a swarm of Torrlonders like an island in a sea of grey kirtles. Sheer numbers would overwhelm them. Gnorn ran as fast as his stout legs would take him.

Something slammed into his side and sent him reeling. Even before he landed, some part of the Dweorg's mind knew he had been careless in his haste. The ground rushed up at him. He dropped his sharp axe, grunted with the impact, and rolled. When he stopped, he craned his head up seeking his weapon. A few feet away, between struggling pairs of legs pushing against each other, metal gleamed on the sand. Ignoring the pain blooming all over one side of his body, he scampered up and dove for his axe.

Too late. A grey-kirtled soldier reached the weapon first and stomped a large boot on it. He also had a big sword raised aloft. The Dweorg lunged to one side, but the Torrlonder anticipated the move and adjusted his swing. The blade arced straight for Gnorn's head.

Steel clanged and the Dweorg winced, but his head felt no impact. A tall form stood between him and his attacker. Twice more blades clashed. The next time, the Thjoth who had saved Gnorn slipped under the Torrlonder's guard and ripped through the man's thigh. Droplets of blood flew from the sword as he swung it again and smashed in the foe's helm and skull. The Torrlonder flopped down and planted his face in the sand.

Gnorn grabbed his axe and rose to glimpse his savior. When the tall man turned around, the Dweorg's eyes widened with recognition.

It was Halvard, the young Thjoth he had bested in the wrestling match by slamming his head into the lad's gut. This was a generous payback. The big fellow grinned at the Dweorg.

Gnorn gave him a slight bow. "King Vols is surrounded. Shall we help him?"

Halvard nodded. "Where?"

"This way."

The young Thjoth ran behind him. As the Dweorg had feared, a throng of grey kirtles surrounded Vols and Orvandil, who fought back to back. While soldiers circled them like a pack of dogs, they thwarted every attempt the Torrlonders made to cut them, sending down in death or agony each attacker foolish enough to venture close. But the pack was sensing blood, and they were on the verge of overwhelming the two Thjoths.

Gnorn ducked his head and barreled straight into the grey kirtles, jarring his already sore body in more places than he could count but tackling four Torrlonders to the ground in a tangle of limbs and shouts. Halvard and several other Thjoths followed into the gap he made. Bouncing to his feet, the Dweorg swung his axe and beheaded one of Torrlond's soldiers as he rose. The man's body lay back down where it was, minus its rolling, blood-spattered head. Oncoming Thjoths buried their blades in the others, who shrieked and lay still. Gnorn wheezed and tried to catch his breath, spinning around to make sure no one surprised him again. Resting his free hand on his knee, he watched Orvandil for a moment.

Many blows had shattered the Thjoth's shield, so he fought with his long dagger out. Whirling and cutting with dagger and sword, he moved as a deadly blur. Sweothol clove through one man's face, sending his teeth spinning out amidst a spray of blood. Dodging a downward cut, Orvandil drove his dagger in hilt-deep and out the other side of his next assailant's neck. A fountain of crimson followed when he yanked it out and swung around with Sweothol to parry another blow. Two drove at him at once. A clang rang out, and Sweothol ricocheted off one man's blade to carve through the other's neck. Before his spinning and spurting head hit the ground, Orvandil buried his dagger in the other one's heart, grinding it through broken mail and shoving the body into the sand.

Vols too parried blows and laid low several foes in mere moments. Halvard and the others fought like crazed beasts. More Thjoths joined them, and soon they pushed back the Torrlonders. Gnorn shrugged and took a deep breath, then he plunged back into the thick of it.

. . .

When the Thjoths reached the Torrlonders' right flank, King Fullan ordered his archers to cease and to make way for the foot soldiers. Pointing his sword at the tatters of Guthfrid's left flank, he shouted, "Forward! For Ellond!" and marched at the forefront of his shieldwall. Like a merciless spear thrust, the Ellonders in wedge formation smashed into the scrambling Torrlonders. Shields clashed and swords bit through steel, wood, flesh, and bone. Already in disarray and unable to form a line, the Torrlonders collapsed before their foes. The Ellonders drove ahead, their king in the lead.

Fullan flung himself forward with energy his soldiers strove to match. He parried a blow and hacked through an assailant's byrny and collarbone. Another blade swung near the king's face, but he dodged aside and thrust his sword through its bearer's byrny into his chest. A third blade nearly caught him, but one of his soldiers cut off the shrieking Torrlonder's arm in mid-swing, exposing bone and meat before blood spewed from the wound.

Fullan wheezed and grimaced when an unseen enemy's blow, or perhaps one of his own men's wild swings, sliced through the king's corselet and byrny into his ribs, knocking him aside. Gritting his teeth through the pain, he faced an attacker who swung at him. Fullan parried, and steel rang out with a jolt of pain on the king's wounded side. The grey-kirtled soldier rushed forward, but Fullan drove his knee into the man's stomach, buckling him over. He raised his blade, and a twinge lanced across his ribs, but he hacked at his attacker's neck. Not a clean blow as the helm deflected it, but the man shuddered and crumpled. Fullan winced and stumbled with the sharp sting of the wound on his torso. Breathing had become difficult, and he thought perhaps a rib was cracked. Someone else took the position at the point of the wedge, but the formation had lost most of its order anyway.

Someone cried out, "The king! The king's wounded!" Nearby Ellonders let loose furious screams. They swung their weapons and charged forward into the fierce melee, sweeping through the Torrlonders as a relentless force. Fullan's heart swelled with pride. He limped through the pain and mustered a throaty yell as he raised his sword and rejoined the fray.

. . .

GNORN KEPT PACE WITH ORVANDIL AND KING VOLS, GUARDING their backs as Grimrik's warriors pounded back the Torrlonders. The Dweorg spotted a Torrlonder as he tried to sneak at Vols from behind. Gnorn rewarded him with the sharp side of his axe, which cracked through his helm and skull right into the soft bits that spewed outside.

It was grim work, and blood mingled with sweat as the clanging of steel punctuated screams. But before long, the blue kirtles of Ellond appeared through the press. More and more Ellonders poured forward, and Gnorn perceived it would soon be over.

To their credit, Torrlond's soldiers fought on until the end. But, at length, the last succumbed to the blades of Ellond and Grimrik. Amidst screams and moans and slobbering whines of the wounded and dying, the Dweorg suppressed the urge to cover his ears. With the rush to stay alive over, he found the aftermath a hard thing to stomach, and he was covered with sweat and blood, most of the latter not his own. He clenched his teeth and watched as King Vols and King Fullan met face to face where the battle had been thickest. The Thjoth had cuts on both arms and one cheek, whereas blood ran down the Ellonder's side. Like Gnorn, both men were hunched over and breathing hard.

"Well met, Fullan of Ellond. I'm Vols, King of Grimrik."

"Well met, indeed, Vols of Grimrik. Though you and your ancestors have attacked our shores and pillaged our ships, you and your men have begun to make up for it today. But how did you know we'd take your side?"

Vols wiped his forehead and showed his teeth in a broad smile. "In Sundara I spoke to the wizard Galdor. He told me of your intentions while trying to convince me to join you. I found him persuasive."

A brief smile interrupted Fullan's tired grimace. "Then you had good reason. It was Galdor's plan to take Torrlond by surprise, though I didn't expect to this early. Still, we've managed to weaken Earconwald. But now, I expect Duke Guthfrid's demise will reach Earconwald and Bledla's ears. They'll come in numbers too great for us. It would be best not to linger."

Vols pointed out to the sound. "The rest of our ships are on their way. And it seems our men had company in their labor."

Gnorn turned toward the water. Just as Vols said, the Thjoths' dragon ships were not alone as they made for the shore. In addition to vessels the Thjoths captured from Torrlond and Farwick, ships of Sildharan approached. Their fleet must have sallied from Thulhan to aid the Thjoths, crushing their foes between them. Pressed from both sides, the sailors and soldiers aboard the ships of Torrlond and Farwick must have had a hard time of it. Gnorn guessed most of them ended up in the sound. Thjoths and Sildharae rowed alongside each other toward the armies of Ellond and Grimrik.

At that moment, a dozen horses with blue-kirtled soldiers astride them galloped toward King Fullan. They slowed as they advanced, and the young fellow at their head alighted after they arrived. Tall and handsome with bright eyes and brown hair, he took off his helm and smiled before he approached and bowed.

"Earl Elfwy," said Fullan, who stood straight but held his hand to his wounded side, "did you send Redwald on his way?"

"Your Majesty," Elfwy said between heavy breaths, "We took Redwald and his men before they reached anyone. We also intercepted soldiers who escaped the battle and sought to bring word to Earconwald. Three were our own." At this last word, the young earl bowed his head.

Gnorn nodded. It could not have been easy to slay men of their own kingdom, but many Ellonders had devoted themselves to the Way, or their interests lay with Torrlond. Such were the times. Such was war.

Elfwy looked at his king again, standing straight and at attention. "But we were too few to catch them all. Word will reach Earconwald soon. We have little time." The young earl's eyes widened and focused on the blood on Fullan's kirtle. "Your Majesty, you're wounded."

Fullan waved his palm. "The blade did not reach deep. There are many in far worse condition." He turned to King Vols. "With your consent, I would put all the wounded aboard your longships beached on the strand while we wait for the others to arrive."

Vols nodded his agreement, and they gave orders to find the

wounded and bring them to the ships. The warriors of Grimrik and Ellond set to work, picking up men who bled and groaned and screamed. Some could walk with a little help. Others had to be carried. Some did not make it to the ships. But by the time the Thjoths' other vessels and those of Sildharan arrived, some longships laden with wounded were rowing toward the city.

One of the first from the arriving ships to greet King Vols was Duneyr, who had led the sea battle. Gnorn was glad to see the red-headed Thjoth alive, for Duneyr had been kind to him. A bleeding cut on his right forearm did not prevent him from beaming his usual smile. Behind him came several persons: a grey-haired Sildharae wearing a silver breastplate and helm, an old man with a long white beard and brown robe, a beautiful young woman in a black tunic and breeches, and a squat fellow with a nasty scar across his face. Gnorn did not know who the Sildharae was, but his heart leapt to see Galdor, Sequara, and Abon again. A great grin crossed his face, which made him wince when it stretched the cut on his nose and cheek.

Duneyr laughed and shouted in the Northern Tongue, "King Vols! The gods have spared you for another battle. I'm glad of it. Here are friends from Thulhan: the esteemed wizard Galdor of Ellond; our favorite shaper, Abon of the deft fingers and golden tongue; Lady Sequara of Asdralad; and Lord Arveryd, who has the honor to be Admiral of King Naitaran's fleet." The last he introduced with a wink, no doubt in reference to how many of Sildharan's ships the Thjoths had raided over the years.

Vols replied, "Well met, friends. And greetings to you, Lord Arveryd. King Fullan, it seems you have your advisor back."

"So it seems," said Fullan with a grin.

The wizard approached and bowed. "Your Majesty, it's good beyond words to see you. But you're wounded, I see."

The King of Ellond clasped his chief advisor on the shoulder. "Not badly." He winced and then smiled. "You may take a look at the cut after we reach the city if you wish to assure yourself. I've missed your counsel, old friend."

"You've done well enough without me, and I couldn't have devised it better than it fell out, thanks to the Thjoths. But you're right: We must hasten from this shore. Word of your deeds will no doubt soon reach Earconwald and Bledla."

Wearing an uncomfortable frown, Lord Arveryd gave a curt bow to King Vols. "Your Majesty, I've not yet had the . . . ah, *pleasure* of meeting you in person, though, as a fellow seaman, I'm quite familiar with your . . . exploits."

Vols laughed at the admiral's difficulty, for the Thjoths were a perpetual menace to the Sildharae when they were not selling them thralls. "For now, we'll put such exploits aside, admiral. After we defeat Torrlond, we'll sort them out on the seas."

The old nobleman nodded. "Very well, though I confess I prefer you as an ally. And I thank you on behalf of King Naitaran and the people of Sildharan."

Fullan, Vols, and Arveryd directed a well ordered evacuation of the beach. With the captured vessels from Torrlond and Farwick, there was enough room for everyone. While the soldiers boarded, Gnorn and Orvandil spoke with Sequara and Abon.

The sorceress looked at the Dweorg's face with a serious frown on hers. "We need to heal that wound. It's a nasty cut."

Gnorn wiped blood off his cheek with his finger. "When we reach the city, my dear. The cut is not deep, and there are many with worse wounds."

"It's good to see you both," said Abon. "Your journey sped well, it seems."

"Thanks to Gnorn," said Orvandil. "But where's Dayraven? He didn't come with you?"

Gnorn had started to wonder about the same thing. Abon glanced at Sequara and waited for her to answer. Hesitating, she looked at Orvandil and then Gnorn.

A sudden dread tugged at the Dweorg's stomach. "He's not hurt?"

"No. I'd know if he were," said Sequara. "Dayraven's on his way."

After Orvandil and Gnorn exchanged puzzled looks, she said, "He parted from us on our way north from Sundara. He had to prepare himself. To defeat Bledla. We don't know where he is now, but he'll be here soon. He'll come."

"Yes," said Orvandil with a nod, "he will."

Gnorn stifled his anxiety. He placed no less faith in Dayraven than Sequara and Orvandil did. Still, the lad had better stay out of trouble and show up in one piece.

The friends boarded the last ship, Admiral Arveryd's, with Galdor and King Fullan, who insisted on seeing all his men aboard a ship before setting foot on one. Once aboard, Ellond's king went below deck, where a Sildharae sorcerer tended to his wound.

"It's best you and I be on the last one," said Galdor to Sequara as they stood on deck. "They'll come. Be ready for fire."

A SHORT WHILE AFTER THEIR SHIP LEFT THE STRAND, GNORN STARED back at the shoreline. Torrlond's mounted scouts appeared where their dead and wounded fellows lay. After they alighted from their steeds, a handful of arrows arced over the water, but the vessels were already out of bowshot, and the missiles splashed in the sound. The scouts could only watch the ships sail toward Thulhan.

Viewing the first Torrlonder arrivals from the stern of Admiral Arveryd's Sildharae vessel, the Dweorg chuckled in the safety of the ship. But he did not laugh too hard. With the chaos of battle over, his body seemed intent on reminding him of every bump and bruise it just suffered. The cut on his face was stinging like a wasp had bitten him, and his whole body ached like he had rolled down a slope strewn with sharp rocks. His ribs and right shoulder were especially sore. Gnorn was happy not to face another battle just yet.

At that moment, large dark shapes flashed over the horizon into the sky. Dragons. The Dweorg's breath caught as he realized what easy targets the ships would make for the serpents of the air. "Oh damn." He was far more afraid of the lingworms than he had been of dying in battle with honest soldiers. *It's being helpless*, some part of his mind reflected. *In battle, at least a man has a chance, some control over his fate.* There was nothing he could do about the serpents of the air.

Orvandil took up a spear he had picked up from the beach and pointed upward. "Here they come." He had that eager look in his eyes, like he was itching to fight the beasts.

Gnorn shook his head. "Lunatic," he muttered.

Galdor said to Lord Arveryd, "Reef the sails at once, and signal the other ships to do the same."

The Sildharae admiral stared at the wizard, eyes wide with bewilderment. "That would slow us."

"You won't outrun them. If you would save lives and ships, do as I say."

Admiral Arveryd hesitated, but then he nodded and hurried to obey, barking orders in Andumaic.

The wizard grasped Sequara's arm. "Redirect their fires. Hold them off until I'm ready."

The sorceress nodded. Galdor began chanting his spell. Gnorn had no idea what the wizard was up to, but he had seen Sequara redirect dragon flames before, and he reckoned it might be safest to remain near her. Not that there was anywhere far he could wander while stuck on the blasted ship.

The serpents of the air grew larger with every frantic heartbeat. Gnorn's fear was no less than the first time he was on the wrong end of a lingworm's attack. The feeling of desperate helplessness in their presence was all too familiar. The Dweorg gripped his axe and glanced at the sorceress as her eyes locked onto the approaching beasts. With her gaze fixed on them, Sequara sang a song of origin:

Agadatha ar hurolin tirion im dhornu
Ingkhatha in shalakhin dhanion an vardhu.
Shandulay ni danudon brinkhala targon,
Nonghalay di valanon sintala bardon.

The sorceress repeated the song several times before the first dragon arrived. Its dark red wings beat the air, and a mighty roar erupted from its throat. Men aboard the ships yelled and cowered. The vessels appeared small and impossibly slow. Gnorn's mouth hung open, and though he wanted to hide his face, he did not avert his eyes from the looming lingworm.

Swooping down toward the ship the Dweorg waited on, the great worm opened its jaws wide, showing its teeth like rows of swords. The beast disgorged a burst of flames toward the stern, where Sequara waited. With fire catapulting down onto them, Gnorn and the rest of the men screamed and flattened themselves on the deck.

Lying on his belly, the Dweorg watched as only three figures remained upright: Orvandil, Galdor, and Sequara, who stood like a slender silhouette against the wave of flames. Just before the torrent of fire engulfed the ship, Sequara swept her hands to her left. The flames followed her motion, swerving and smashing into the water with a deafening explosion of steam and a loud hiss. Drops splashed onto the ship like rain, and Gnorn grabbed at planks as a wave from the impact rocked the vessel, but all aboard were unharmed.

Orvandil lunged back and cast his spear at the beast's belly as it swooped overhead and darkened the ship with its vast shadow. The weapon snapped on impact without piercing its scales and plummeted into the waves.

Gnorn groaned and stood up. There was no time to celebrate the near miss, for the second dragon came close behind the first. It too spat fire at the rear ship, and the Dweorg flinched. Again Sequara commanded the flames into the sound. Seething steam erupted as droplets scattered all over, and the Dweorg teetered as the ship swayed.

The bursts of the third and fourth dragons too crashed into Quinara Sound while the fleet crawled closer to the safety of the city. The next dragons, however, circled above and waited for the first ones to regroup, and soon all twelve cunning beasts swooped down at once for an all-out assault on the ships. They spread out. Each hurtling serpent of the air targeted a different ship.

Sequara cried out, "Hurry, Galdor! I can't hold them all off at once!"

Gnorn cringed as twelve columns of flames poured from the sky. "May the ancestors grant that I die on dry land!"

Sequara screamed with the effort to control the bursts of fire. Nine wavered and veered off course, roaring into the water and unleashing huge fountains of steam amidst men's terrified shouts.

Staggering then falling into Orvandil's arms, Sequara blinked and shook her head to retain consciousness after her struggle.

Two ships had partially caught fire, and the largest dragon's flames had smashed straight into a Sildharae vessel. The entire ship exploded into a massive conflagration. Men engulfed in the blaze flailed about blindly until they fell or leapt into the water, disappearing with hisses under the waves. Their screams were so terrible that many in other ships clenched their hands over their ears. Gnorn held his stomach and suppressed the urge to retch.

Most of the men aboard the two vessels the dragons' breath had grazed helped each other shed their mail and armor before leaping into the water and swimming toward other ships. Their comrades pulled some out of the water by throwing over ropes and extending oars. Others did their best to swim for the city. Some who could not remove their armor in time plunged into the water and never appeared again.

While Sequara had fought off the dragon flames, Galdor was continuing his chant. Gnorn noticed a change in the air, which grew thicker and moister, with a tangier whiff of salt, even as a breeze began fingering his face. He looked up with sudden understanding and awe at the wizard's ploy.

The sky over the ships darkened with iron-grey clouds. Overhead, the wind picked up to a strong gust blowing north. At once, the gust escalated into a furious gale. As the dragons gathered above for another assault, Galdor raised his hands then threw them forward. Obeying his command, the gale erupted into a mighty force howling over the fleeing ships and concentrating on the dragons. The water churned and grew choppy with white-capped waves, heaving the ships to and fro.

Gnorn grabbed the railing on the deck to keep from toppling over and held on for dear life. "Not this! Better dragon fire than plunging into the cruel, cold depths!"

But it was the dragons that suffered the direct blast. Six smaller lingworms blew backwards, twisting round and round and becoming distant specks within heartbeats. Five larger ones strained, but their efforts proved futile when the wind whipped them away too, their roars receding with them.

The last and largest serpent of the air beat its wings furiously and made a little headway against the wind. But Galdor swept his hand down, and a bolt of lightning split asunder the sky, striking the dragon through its belly and back. Thunder cracked. The beast shrieked and writhed as the current illuminated it and snaked around it, and the gale swept it away even as the thunder rolled.

When the dragon was no longer visible, the wind died down. Sky and waves soon returned to normal.

Gnorn gazed at the old wizard with bewilderment and wonder unfastening his jaw wide, tugging at the cut on his cheek again. "By the ancestors' beards!" He slapped his face on the unwounded side and wiggled his fat fingers in front of his eyes. "Someone wake me! Am I burned or drowned?"

"Neither yet, friend Dweorg." Sweat poured down Galdor's brow, and he breathed hard as he leaned on the railing. "But they'll soon return, and we can't hold them back again. We must hurry to the city."

The men did not hesitate to obey orders to row hard for Thulhan. They straggled in through the river gates in haste and poured off the vessels, glad to be alive for at least a little longer. Some of the wounded, however, died on their way to safety, and even the hale showed little cheer. The city's people too did not rejoice when the ships returned. Gnorn did not blame them. The dragons' flames had slain many loved ones, and more had perished in battle at sea. They all knew the War of the Way had arrived in their kingdom.

22

WRATH AND DESTRUCTION

Following the vanguard of their soldiers, King Earconwald and the Supreme Priest Bledla arrived on Quinara Sound's western shore to find the shattered corpses of Duke Guthfrid's troops strewn all over like gruesome detritus after a violent storm. Thousands of dead and dying bloodied the sands, and the sticky, fecal stench of battle hung in the air while the wounded groaned or cried out. Few bodies belonged to Ellond or Grimrik.

In his wrath at the tidings, Bledla had sent the dragons ahead, hurling after their foes' fleeing ships. Too late did he sense the presence of Galdor and some other powerful sorcerer. Unable to counteract their spells in time, he watched as they thwarted Edan's instruments, but he assured himself he would not need to wait long for righteous vengeance. *At last, Galdor, I have you. This day's devilry was no doubt your work, but you'll not gloat over it for long. Run to Thulhan. Skulk there if you like. There's no escape now.*

The Way's enemies were all trapped inside Sildharan's chief city, just where he wanted them. The traitors of Ellond had revealed their true allegiance. Perhaps this was Edan's way of sorting the false from the true. *"By their deeds shall ye know who are the Eternal and who are not," wrote the Prophet.* It was a source of sorrow and regret that the twisted heretic had corrupted so many of the Torrlonders' kin in Ellond, including King Fullan. But the Eternal would prevail, and then there would be no more sorrow, no more pain. It would be as if such evil folk had never existed.

After he summoned the serpents of the air back and examined them for wounds, healing the one struck by lightning, he commanded them to depart and rest as he thought through the best course ahead. It would not do to allow his anger to lead him to carelessness. There was no need to rush. All the heathens and traitors in one place. One city, soon to be one vast tomb. He would meditate on Edan's will until clarity arose within him, but as he surveyed the carnage and considered the day's losses, he could not stifle his righteous wrath. One of Torrlond's strongest divisions was in ruins, and one of the Way's greatest supporters lay dead. It was Torrlond's first major setback in the War of the Way. *But it was only through treachery, the first and last resort of the wicked.* The supreme priest took several deep breaths and unclenched his fist.

At Bledla's behest, Earconwald ordered his soldiers to bury the many martyrs of that day, with Earl Guthfrid laid to rest in his own large mound. The few remaining bodies of Thjoths and Ellonders they threw in the sound. In truth, in addition to his pious desire to dispose of the dead in a fitting manner, Bledla needed time to gather his thoughts. On the threshold of complete victory, he would make no mistakes. Even as he performed his duties, he listened for the will of Edan.

When all was ready, the supreme priest conducted a solemn ritual honoring the fallen Eternal next to Guthfrid's fresh mound. King Earconwald and his other dukes and earls as well as King Ithamar and the nobles of the Mark stood nearby. While Torrlond's ranks and allies waited with hands folded and heads down, Bledla commemorated their comrades with words from the Book of Aldmund:

"'For, my beloved, when one of the Eternal passeth from the confines of his mortal body, it is no death. Rather, it is the movement of life into greater life. The Eternal die not, but live forever in Edan's bliss. And on the day of His kingdom's fulfillment, the Eternal will be together, dwelling in the light of their true Lord.' The words of the blessed Prophet Aldmund," declared Bledla.

He gazed upon the ranks with his fiery eyes, knowing he must strengthen them. "As we go forward to defeat the wicked, we'll carry the memories of our beloved brothers with us. Their blood calls to us to fulfill Edan's will. With His strength guiding us, we'll rid Eormenlond of these traitors and heathens and demon worshipers. The one true faith, the Way, will usher in the Kingdom of the Eternal, and our beloved brothers will live again. For this day's treachery and deceit, we'll punish the evildoers, showing that Edan works His will through us. Even now, His providence grows clear. For *our* sake He causes such imposters to expose themselves, lest they lie as serpents among us. It is Edan's will, for He will separate the false from the true, the wicked from the Eternal. We *must* not question! Today is merely a test of our love for Edan. We'll pass this test, my brethren. On the morrow, we'll obtain righteous vengeance. Blessed be the Eternal!"

A deafening chorus of "Blessed be the Eternal!" rang out from the Torrlonders and from a large number of the Markmen, who cheered and raised their fists as they swore revenge. Afterwards, their commanders marched them back to camp, where they would have time to seek Edan's comfort and guidance ere they slept before the next day's great test. The sky was aswirl with the setting sun's orange, pink, and red. It was too late to begin the assault on Thulhan until the next day. But Edan had revealed to Bledla a fitting way to move forward.

THAT NIGHT, THE SUPREME PRIEST REQUESTED THAT KING Earconwald call a council of his dukes and the chief nobles of the Mark. In attendance also were the five high priests of the Way in their white woolen robes. Inside Earconwald's large, sumptuous tent stood a round oak table. Around the table sat the kings, dukes, earls, and priests. Candles on the table cast a ruddy light on the assembled, and competing shadows wavered on the tent's inner walls. Guards stood without. An army larger than any ever brought together in Eormenlond waited all around. In spite of this fact, some of the angry and anxious faces around the table revealed the day's events had shaken their confidence. Torrlond was not supposed to lose battles.

Seated next to King Earconwald, Bledla waited for his sovereign to speak as the others slumped in grim silence.

Earconwald cleared his throat and put on his most solemn face as he looked at the only empty chair around the table. "First, we mark the passing of one of our truest and most faithful servants. But we do not lament Duke Guthfrid. For he died one of the Eternal. His place is with Edan, his reward great. But we must finish Edan's work. Through trickery and deceit, our enemies have delayed the inevitable." Earconwald pounded the table with sudden energy. "We will prevail!"

Duke Ethelred, Duke Walstod, Duke Siric, and the high priests grunted pious affirmations. Most of the other Torrlonder dukes followed suit. However, the Markmen seemed less enthusiastic. Earl Haereth of Farwick sat looking listless and forlorn, as if he had heard nothing. Most of the Mark's fleet came from his earldom, and he had lost a large portion of his ships and men that day. Earl Hadulac of the Hemeldowns concealed his thoughts behind a frown, Earl Stigand of Kinsford sat like a large stone, and young King Ithamar of the Mark appeared solemn. Bledla realized the betrayal of the Ellonders was weighing on their minds.

But it was Durathror of Norfast who looked most worried. The normally boisterous duke pulled at his blond beard and stared at the table. Raising his head, he said, "My lords, there's a matter I must bring before you, though I'm loth to. As you know, the men of Norfast are kin to you all, and you will never find any more doughty and loyal. But we're also kin to the Thjoths. We came here in faith to fight the easterners by your side, but we didn't know our cousins would be with them. I say it in plain words to you: My warriors will not raise their weapons against the men of Grimrik."

Bledla restrained himself from clenching his fists. *Faithless dog!* How could one of Torrlond's dukes dare to defy the direct orders of his spiritual and secular sovereigns? He would brook no more disloyalty, and there was no time for such nonsense. "Such kinships matter not at all next to the bond of the Eternal," he said in a tone that conveyed a clear warning. "There are only the followers of Edan and the wicked, and those who don't fight with us are the latter." He glanced at Earconwald, who beamed a benign-seeming smile at him. That smile said everything: 'Let me take care of this. I know what to do.' Bledla hoped some cunning idea would enter Earconwald's mind, and he resolved to see how the king would handle the situation.

"What sort of cowardice is this?" blurted out Duke Siric of Rimdale before Earconwald spoke. Siric pointed an accusatory finger at Duke Durathror. "Your first loyalty should be clear enough." He was no lover of his neighbor to the north and seldom lost opportunities to show his faith to Torrlond and the Way, though Bledla had grave doubts about the true depth of that faith.

Durathror rose from his seat to his full height and pounded the table. "*You* dare call me coward! I'll tear off your fat head with my bare hands!"

Siric shrank in his chair, raising a protective hand to his pudgy neck, but Earconwald shouted, "My dukes! Brethren! Please, let's not lose our heads — or tear any off just now." He smiled at Durathror, who resumed his seat while glaring at Siric across the table.

Earconwald continued. "There's a solution to this dilemma that will present itself shortly. In the meantime, let's make no accusations or threats against one another when we should be most united." He turned to the Duke of Norfast. "Durathror. My friend. As you well know, I lost twenty thousand swords this day. I could ill afford to lose another twelve thousand, especially those as brave as your lads."

"Perhaps," offered King Ithamar, "we could pit the men of Norfast only against the easterners. Keep them apart from the Thjoths on the battlefield."

Earl Hadulac shook his head. "Not possible, Sire. Though we plan them in meetings like this, battles are things of chaos. No telling who meets who in the midst of fighting, and often enough friend slays friend."

At once, a smile crossed Earconwald's face. "But there's one place where there'll be no Thjoths. Our scouts have reported the army of

Sundara approaches from the south. No doubt they'll attempt to break our siege around Thulhan. We were thinking of sending Duke Weohstan to hold them off. If we send the warriors of Norfast to engage them instead, there would be no chance of meeting their cousins of Grimrik, and they would retain their honor." At the end of his speech, the king glanced at Bledla with a slight widening of the eyes.

Bledla understood and nodded. *Yes. A way to use Durathror. And perhaps to punish his disloyalty.*

Durathror thought a moment, frowning. "This might be."

Earconwald spread his arms. "You see? A solution."

Bledla gazed at Durathror. "They'll outnumber you, but we only require you to hold them back. No doubt your courage will be up to the task. Nevertheless, I'll send three dragons to ensure your success."

"A splendid idea," said Earconwald. "Should you need reinforcements, send word to us, and we'll provide soldiers from the divisions south of the city. You must depart straight after this council to occupy the road leading south from Thulhan. Needless to say, your role is vital to our success. We want no more of the enemy to strengthen those already gathered in the city. In the end, of course, they'll all perish."

The Duke of Norfast nodded. "Very well. We'll do it. The southrons won't reach Thulhan."

"Excellent," said Earconwald. "Duke Weohstan, you'll put your men where we had stationed Duke Durathror's."

The fat duke with a bald, splotchy head and thick red beard nodded and said, "Yes, your Majesty."

"The rest of you," resumed Earconwald, "will maintain your positions in the ring around Thulhan. We sent our swiftest messengers to order more ships waiting in the Gulf of Olfi to replace those we lost in Quinara Sound. The Ilarchae will complete the ring from the east on the morrow. Their outriders have already reported their army will arrive early in the morning. Tonight, we wait. But we won't let Thulhan rest easily. Our supreme priest has something special for its occupants." Earconwald looked toward Bledla, who graced them all with his chilly smile.

"Edan's enemies have bought themselves a night," said the supreme priest. "But it will be a night of such terror that they'll long for their deaths. I'll unleash the dragons, whose fire heralds Edan's light. We'll cleanse Eormenlond. Thulhan will burn."

Everyone appeared satisfied. After reviewing their positions and orders for the next day, the nobles from the Mark and Torrlond bade King Earconwald good night. Holding up his index finger, the supreme priest signaled his five high priests. Obeying their master, Arna, Joruman, Heremod, Morcar, and Colburga waited.

Bledla gazed at them and let the silence stretch a little. "You know your duty. Prepare the priests. I don't want their demon-worshipping sorcerers to call down a single drop of rain. If Galdor thinks to toy with the weather, we'll show him what Edan's chosen can do. The wind must come from the dry south, for we must not allow them to use moisture from Quinara Sound. Begin the spell as soon as you convene the priests, and I'll join you shortly."

Arna and Colburga listened with earnest frowns, while Joruman, Heremod, and Morcar grinned. "Blessed be the Eternal," they all said with bows.

After he dismissed the high priests, Bledla faced Earconwald alone. Guards waited outside, so the supreme priest spoke in a hushed tone. "If Durathror calls for aid, perhaps it would be best to see that our supporting troops do not hasten. They should arrive to keep our perimeter intact, but they should intervene only if the Sundarae threaten to break through."

A grin spread across Earconwald's face as shadows from the flickering candles played across it, and he too kept his voice just above a whisper. "My thoughts exactly. If Durathror feels unable to comply with my commands, it's time I replaced him with a duke more ready to obey. Someone with less Thjothic blood, perhaps. At least he and his men will be ridding us of the Sundarae, which will spare us much effort when we march south. I assume your dragons will also be slow to aid our subjects of Norfast?"

Bledla kept his countenance like stone. "When the traitor Durathror and his men fight the Sundarae army, the dragons might need to clean up whatever's left. As the earl from the Mark said, battles are indeed things of chaos."

Earconwald raised his eyebrows, feigning surprise, then he smirked. "A fair bargain. Norfast has always been my most troublesome dukedom, and Durathror has often acted too independently. Far too much Thjoth in the lot of them." He stroked his beard. "No doubt we'll find the territory more submissive in the future with its warriors slain in such heroic fashion. I need only dispose of Durathror's heir and assign the dukedom to someone more compliant once the war ends. In the name of *Edan*, of course."

The supreme priest did not return the king's smile. "Of course. Now, if you'll pardon me, Sire, I must attend to tonight's matter. We must not let our foes rest."

Bledla left with the same repugnance he always suffered in Earconwald's presence, feeling an urge to bathe and rid himself of the man's moral stench. *Still*, he admitted, *he has his uses. He handled Durathror, and Norfast's warriors will serve Edan one way or another. Earconwald will too, though he thinks otherwise. Soon he'll see . . .*

Six white-kirtled soldiers of the temple guard waited for him outside the tent, but he waved them away. "Wait for me at my tent. I'll go alone."

Making his way through the vast encampment, Bledla walked west. When men noted him by the light of their campfires, they bowed and said, "Blessed be the Eternal." Lost in his thoughts, he acknowledged the courtesies with a bare nod and continued on his way.

Mighty Edan, he prayed, *I thank you for showing me the way. Today was a trial, a test your servant won't fail. The heathens and demon worshipers will perish on the morrow. We'll fulfill your will. I see your kingdom as a vision before me. We're on the verge of arriving. And then even those who believed us cruel will see our kindness, and Your mercy.*

Yet, even after assuring himself through his prayer, other thoughts troubled his mind. *Every failure springs from treachery. Vile betrayal! First Fullan, then Durathror. Such allies and subjects are fickle, their devotion* unequal to our calling. Fullan will suffer for today. Ellond's unfaithful will feel Edan's wrath. I should have seen it, though. And who is the traitor in our midst? Even with Arna's help, I've been unable to discover him.

But there was one matter that ate at the supreme priest above all others. He tried to press it to the bottom of his mind, yet it would never leave him in peace. The boy. Dayraven. Where was he? Twice he had escaped. So much power. When he fought Dayraven in Asdralad, the boy had shown little control over it. But what if he learned? If he mastered that much power . . . Was he in Thulhan? *No. I would sense him. He's not there. But where, then?*

He shook his head to rid himself of such thoughts. Edan would provide a way. *Faith. I must have faith, and the rest will come.*

Wending his way through the camp, Bledla kept pacing and thinking until the men and cook fires began to thin. After some time, he approached an outlying sentry. Wielding a spear and wearing a sword at his side, the grey-kirtled guard asked, "Who walks there?"

"The supreme priest of the Way," said Bledla in his deep voice.

The man bowed and went down on one knee. "Blessed be the Eternal, my lord."

"And the Kingdom of Edan. Be watchful this night for the wiles of the enemy."

"Yes, my lord. Thank you."

Bledla left the encampment behind. Wraith-like in his white robe, he walked alone in darkness with the confident strides of one who knew where he went and what he must do. In a while, he came to a hill, which he climbed without pausing. But when he arrived at the top, he looked back once on the myriad campfires dotting the plain. *A splendid thing, mighty Edan. The army of light. The ranks of your Eternal.* Even as he stood there, the breeze morphed into a southerly dry wind that tore moisture from the air. He could feel the change on his skin. *Excellent. My priests are doing their work. Galdor and the others won't squeeze a drop from the sky. Tonight, it will rain only fire.*

Pressing on, he descended the hill. On its other side was another foothill, for these were the first folds in the landscape at the Osham Mountains' northern end. In the valley between the two hills waited twelve enormous mounds, inky forms in the night that seemed to betoken some ancient burial place. A sulphuric scent of smoke mingled with the clear night air as Bledla approached. When he neared them, the mounds gleamed in the moonlight with sleek scales, and spikes longer than swords emerged from their tops. Closer still he came, and long tails coiling around them took shape. When he arrived within a few feet of the nearest one, a large amber orb with a black slit appeared just opposite him. Reflecting the moonlight, the huge eye glowed eerily in the darkness and focused on the supreme priest. His dragons awoke.

He stepped closer to the eye and put his hand on the dragon's head, stroking the tough, leathery scales and tracing the grooves between them. Emitting a deep rumble like tumbling boulders that vibrated the earth, the beast purred as its master gazed and slid his bony hand along its brow up to the sharp tip of its smooth horn. Bledla was tall, but next to the lingworm's giant head, the white-robed man appeared tiny and frail. It could have swallowed him in one bite. Yet the beast waited obediently with its head bowed low.

Bledla smiled. "Edan has a special purpose for you all tonight."

The other dragons raised their heads and arched their necks closer to their master. Several opened their jaws and hissed, their forked tongues vibrating in answer to the supreme priest. Twelve pairs of amber eyes stared attentively from the darkness, each glassy orb larger than Bledla's head.

"The enemy has gathered in their den. They think their stones will grant safety. But you'll show them how wrong they are. Nine of you will raze the city during the night. You must strike from the air in silence, for their strongest sorcerers will seek to subdue your flames."

Bledla turned his gaze toward three larger dragons. "For you three I have another task. Fly south of the city, and wait to attack until the right time."

The supreme priest instructed them in the details of their tasks. He had no need to speak aloud, for he had chained the beasts' minds to his own through the song of origin, which he repeated even as his thoughts seeped into the serpents of the air. They would do his bidding without question, with no will of their own.

At length, Bledla nodded with satisfaction, and the enormous creatures rose to their full height. Several roared, the heat of their breath blowing back strands of his white hair and beard even as he exulted. They flapped their wings, stirring up winds that grasped at the supreme priest's robe. Then, in groups of two or three, they leapt into the air. He watched their huge forms blend into the sky's darkness, blotting out huge swaths of the stars.

His mind followed them in their flight. Three broke off from the rest to fly south while nine dragons headed east to the city. As the nine cut through the night air, the wind parting before them, the campfires of Torrlond's army and allies winked below them. Fires in Thulhan's watchtowers also glowed in the distance. Able to see in darkness nearly as well as during the day, the dragons rocketed toward the city. Thulhan waited below, growing bigger every moment. The shadowed landscape streaked by in a blur, and soon enough tiny specks that were men appeared atop the city's wall.

The men on the wall watched for foes, but they had no hope of seeing the serpents of the air. Flying high over walls that were impotent to stop them, the dragons peered down at the city spread out beneath them. They wheeled in the sky, carefully picking their first targets. Then, simultaneously, they plummeted onto Thulhan like a pack of predators seizing their prey.

Fire fell from the night sky on the helpless city. Four tall towers burst into raging conflagrations, their wealthy inhabitants instantly burnt to death. The tower of King Naitaran's magnificent palace was one. Flames surrounded it and glowed off its gilded onion dome like a giant torch. Five catapults atop the wall were also among the first structures to go up in flames, for Bledla had instructed his pets to make the next day's assault on the city easier. For a brief moment after the first conflagrations broke out, there was dead silence. Screams of terror followed.

The dragons flew up again for the next wave, but now they did not attack all at once. Instead, they swooped down randomly, belching fire at unexpected times and in unexpected places. Blazes erupted on rooftops. Alleys filled with bursts of flame. The cobbled streets seemed paved with gold as they reflected the wavering light. From some structures wrapped in flames, human torches stumbled out drunkenly before succumbing to horrible deaths. Nowhere was safe.

Soon fires burned all over the city. Smoke filled the air, and people ran out of houses and shops coughing and weeping. The panicked citizens did not know where to flee, for the serpents of the air flashed down on them without warning. Blurs glowing ruddy in the flames passed by with great gusts, pouring more fire out of the night.

King Naitaran, Galdor, and Sequara led three score sorcerers into the streets and onto the walls of the city. Though Sildharan was the Kingdom of a Thousand Sorcerers, not even seventy were powerful enough to control flames with the song of origin of fire. The gift ran strong enough in few for such sorcery. These few fanned out over the city, and wherever they chanted their spells, the flames died out.

Normal citizens found conventional means of combating the blazes. From the River Nurgleth running through the city they brought buckets of water and passed them along lines spreading toward the fires. Beside them toiled the warriors of Ellond and the Thjoths. Many dragon ships of Grimrik now burned in the city docks along the river with the fires of their namesakes. The river itself seemed ablaze as flames reflected in it, but Thulhan's people and the many soldiers fought heroically. This alone took great courage, for the dragons' breath claimed many who dared to emerge.

Amidst the chaos of smoke and fire, Sequara gazed at the obscured night sky, listening in the realm of origins for the dragons to anticipate their attacks. One of the very few with strength enough in the gift to control the flames before they struck, she murmured a song of origin, keeping firm her bond with fire.

Even as she did so, a part of her mind dwelled on one far away. *Dayraven. Where are you?* He was always somewhere in her thoughts, and from memories of him arose a poignant combination of guilt and longing. Added to that now was worry for him gnawing at her. Strange that she should experience more anxiety for one person than she did for an entire city on the verge of burning to the ground. Never had she found it so difficult to focus. But she would do her duty. Sweat ran down her brow, and she coughed as smoke hung in the air. Peering down a wide street on which people huddled in corners or ran frantically, she felt an enormous presence looming closer.

A column of fire spat down behind her, transforming the shadowed cityscape into grotesque shades of orange and red. Spinning around, she flung her arms out protectively. The flames shot in sundry directions, sputtering out in thousands of tiny tongues that harmed no one. Darkness returned. Sequara breathed hard and braced herself for the next one. She knew she could not stop them all.

Just then, a high-pitched shriek pierced the air behind her, and a chorus of angry shouts followed. Sequara turned. A panicked girl clothed in what looked like an old sack ran barefoot down the street with a small mob pursuing her. The girl had light blonde hair, almost white, though the glow of the fires tinged it red. She must have been an Ilarchae slave left behind when the others fled from the city to join their kin in their bloody rebellion. The rage-maddened people of Thulhan would catch her in moments.

Sequara did not hesitate. Running down the street, she shouted at the mob, "Stop! Leave her alone!"

They did not heed her. Instead, after one large boy grabbed the girl by the wrist and threw her to the cobbled street, they surrounded her and began to kick her. Another shriek, and the girl wailed as they closed in and tore at her.

The song of origin came from Sequara's lips before she could even think of what to do. "Alakathon indomiel ar galathon anrhuniae! Vortalion marduniel im paradon khalghoniae!"

Currents of blue energy snaked and crackled around her hands, which she pointed toward a burning building near the mob. A bright streak of jagged almakhti shot from her fingertips and crashed into the building, splitting the air with a deafening crack and sending splinters of stone flying amidst sparks from the fire.

All thirty or so people in the mob flinched and cowered. Wide-eyed fear replaced anger in their faces as Sequara approached with almakhti still writhing and buzzing around her outstretched hands. With the wrath that had possessed them now dissipated, the citizens of Thulhan appeared more like their usual selves: ordinary people who were mothers, fathers, sisters, and brothers. With a deep frown, Sequara took in the layers of tragedy embedded in the scene before her. The people seemed more distraught and afraid than anything, and she lamented the madness that drove them to chase down an innocent girl. Their helplessness in the face of death made them so desperate and full of hate. The girl had become an easy target, a symbol they could destroy. But it would do them no good.

She spoke with more cold-blooded anger in her voice than she felt. "Leave. Her. Alone."

They stared at her as if dazed.

With a snarl on her face and a loud snap of the energy, Sequara allowed the almakhti to surge around her hands.

Their trance broken, the lot of them scrambled all over each other to escape and ran in every direction.

Sequara stood in the deserted street and wondered what she would have done if any of them had realized she could not bring herself to harm them. Regretting how much strength it had cost her, she released the almakhti and hoped it would not attract any dragons.

The Ilarchae girl lay alone on the street. Her eyes were closed, and blood from her forehead, nose, and mouth streaked her face.

At first, Sequara feared the worst. But then the body stirred, and the girl sat up, propping herself with her thin arms. She shook her head and put one trembling hand to her bloodied face.

Now that Sequara was closer, she judged the girl was about ten years of age. Amidst burning buildings that lit the night with their fires and billowed choking smoke, she crept toward her. But when the girl sensed movement, she looked Sequara's way and started. Bright blue eyes wide in fear, the girl scrambled backwards to increase the distance between her and Sequara.

"It's alright," said the sorceress. She held out her hands with palms upward to show she meant no harm. "I won't hurt you."

The girl wobbled to her feet, turned away, and ran down a nearby alley. Darkness swallowed her.

Torn as to whether she should pursue the girl, who would mostlike refuse her help, or combat the flames, Sequara stood for a moment in indecision. The girl would suffer a terrible death this night if the citizens of Thulhan caught her again, but how many lives could the sorceress save by putting out the fires? There might be people in the burning buildings around her. Her mind was too muddled to make a choice. She felt her exhausted body begin to sway.

"Lady Sequara, how do you fare?"

She pivoted toward the voice addressing her in High Andumaic. Through the smoke emerged King Naitaran with a dozen guards in gold tunics in his wake.

Sequara was surprised to see the monarch, and even more surprised he would trouble to ask after her. The Ilarchae girl was gone now, she realized. She stifled a curse. There was only so much she could do. There wasn't enough of her to save them all, and she nearly despised herself for it.

"I'm tired," she admitted. "It will be a long night."

Citizens ran by to pour sloshing buckets of water on a blazing house.

Naitaran murmured the song of origin and waved a hand. The flames dissipated into smoke. He turned to her with soot and sweat on his face, a look of disgust twisting his mouth. "This is dirty work. It would have been easier to bring the rains, but there are too many of Bledla's priests, and I can feel his power even from here. They've swept away every bit of moisture. We *must* last through the night if we're to offer battle at dawn. The fires have consumed our defenses, so we'll go out to meet them. There's little point in saving the city, but we'll keep as many alive as we can. Especially the soldiers. Torrlond must pay dearly ere we meet our fate."

Sequara gave a curt nod. "Yes, your Majesty. Keep as many alive as we can. That's why Anghara and Oruma provide the gift: to protect and to heal."

Naitaran frowned. "To destroy and avenge as well, Lady Sequara. Be sure of it. Look around you. This too is the work of the Mother and Father, for they are life *and* death. None can resist. But I wonder, where's your Dayraven? The city's aflame, and none of us can master the serpents of the air. If the boy is what you say, where is he?"

Sequara stood straight and gazed at Naitaran, but she said nothing since she feared her anger would come tumbling out if she opened her mouth. She could almost feel the almakhti forming on her fingertips. But this was not the time to put this idiot in his place. Lives were at stake.

The King of Sildharan beheld her with a crazed expression, eyes wide in rage or desperation. "I've seen the future, and it's dark. Doom is upon us. Our world will end!" A sneer twisted his face. "If your boy comes, he'll burn too."

The temptation to strike down the arrogant fool with almakhti trebled, and she gritted her teeth.

He gazed down the street at another blaze consuming a building. Sanity returned to his eyes. "But we must spread out now. There are few enough to control the fires. I bid you good night. May you face your end with courage."

The king disappeared into smoke and darkness with his guards. Realizing she had just seen a broken man, Sequara shook her head, perhaps with as much sorrow as anger. *Sildharan's not the world, ass.* She murmured the song of origin of fire again and brought her gaze to the sky.

GASPS AMONGST THE CITIZENS OF THULHAN GATHERED AT THE RIVER with their buckets crescendoed into alarmed cries when Galdor, continuously chanting his spell beneath his breath, lifted a vast portion of the river's waters into the air. Raising his hands above him, he winced with the strain as he gestured for the thousands of airborne gallons — writhing like a living creature and coruscating in the light of the fires — to disperse in a broad circle above him. Sweeping his hands down, he released the water to slap down like a giant fist, eliciting screams from the citizens and soaking them. The fires within the radius of the fist hissed in their final moment while smoke and steam curled from the remains of blackened structures.

Dripping and blinking water from his eyes, the wizard bent over with his hands on his knees and took a moment to steady his labored breathing while the citizens resumed filling their buckets from the river.

When he spotted a soldier in a golden tunic running up to him, Galdor stood straight again.

"My lord, have you seen the king?" The man coughed in the inescapable haze of smoke.

"He's on the eastern side of the city. What tidings do you bear?"

The soldier caught his breath with a grimace contorting his face. "Our scouts have reported new movements among the enemy. They surround us on the west, and a large army moves south along the road."

"No doubt they discovered the arrival of the Sundarae. What of the eastern side of the city? Have the Ilarchae come?"

"Not yet, my lord. They'll reach us just after dawn."

"And will our friends from the south arrive first?"

"I can't say for certain. Perhaps."

"Thank you. You may report to King Naitaran now. Cross the Bridge of Tears to the eastern side of the city, and keep your eyes up."

"Yes, my lord."

The soldier ran off, coughing as he went, and Galdor pondered for a moment. *It will take time away from fighting the fires, but I must tell them. I need a clever messenger.*

The old wizard turned his thoughts from fire and sang a new song of origin: "Tulimmin kharkanae vinyoro ar dwinnin. Dalnommin valdarae bahoro an gwannin."

After Galdor repeated the phrase several times, he sensed the presence he sought and formed a link to it. A smile crossed his face and he waited. Within a short while, a crow cawed and emerged from the smoke to flap above the wizard. It landed on the cobbled street two feet from him. He stooped and pointed his finger at the bird. "Avoid the dragons, little fellow. It wouldn't do for one to roast your feathers."

The crow cawed as if to declare it had no intention of letting dragons come near it. Galdor held out his hand, and the bird hopped on it. He brought its beady eyes close to his face and said, "Bring these thoughts to King Tirgalan, little friend."

Man's eyes and bird's locked for thirty slow heartbeats, after which the wizard blinked and smiled once again. "Very good. Now fly south, and may your black feathers and clever mind shield you from harm."

With a few flaps and an awkward leap from Galdor's hand, the crow shot up into the swallowing smoke, leaving the wizard behind with a squawk. Through black, curling clouds it flew while dim orange glows told where fires burned below. As it ascended, a sound like a gust of wind arose. A moment later, an enormous mass whooshed a few feet overhead, the draft in its wake sending the bird into a spin.

But the crow recovered, cawing once to scold the dragon that nearly collided into it. Again it flew up, too small to concern the serpents of the air. At once, as it emerged from the smoke, stars leaped into view. Above the fires and screams it ascended, leaving behind the reek billowing from Thulhan. South it flew, where the air was still and peaceful.

However, things were not peaceful below. Many men in clinking mail moved on the ground in long columns, the moonlight glinting off their weapons.

The crow went on as commanded.

Speeding past the warriors on the road paralleling the River Nurgleth below, it continued south. It flew through the night for several more miles, following the river as the shadowed land rushed by. In the moonlight, the river wound like a dark snake across the bluegrey landscape.

At length, more weapons gleamed on the road below. Far beneath the crow, a long line of soldiers extended south into the dark. Hastening through the night to reach the burning city, these troops marched north on a collision course with the other soldiers. Normally, the clever crow would have had another reason for hovering near two such armies, but something now compelled it to find the man who led the army below.

The bird descended and wheeled in a circle over the troops, cawing loudly. Making for the head of the line, it plummeted toward a group on horseback and cawed again.

One man wearing a dark robe extended his arm toward the crow, which made a perch of the limb, beating its feathers and crying out.

The crow's noise startled the man's armored companions, but the robed man seemed to expect the messenger.

"An ill omen, your Majesty," said one of the others as he looked

PHILIP CHASE

through the gloom at the dark bird hopping and cawing on his sovereign's arm.

"Not this fellow," replied King Tirgalan of Sundara. "Galdor sent him, no doubt to warn us. Let's see what he shows us."

Tirgalan murmured a spell. The crow sat on his arm as it gazed into his eyes. After some time, the king ceased chanting. A few heartbeats later, he sighed and said, "Thank you, little one. Be off now." The bird cawed and flapped away, eager to disappear after delivering its message.

"More than likely he'll be feasting on us soon enough," said one man nearby as he peered ahead at the burning city's glow.

"Perhaps," answered Tirgalan. "But we now have knowledge of our enemy's intentions, and we must put that to some advantage." He turned to two riders nearest him. "Find Lord Maglo and Lady Niona. Tell them I would speak with them concerning Galdor's message."

"Yes, your Majesty." The two spun their horses around and rode down the line.

A short while later, Maglo and Niona, the two most powerful sorcerers in Sundara other than King Tirgalan, approached on horseback, each with a train of mounted guards. The darkness hid their features, but their silhouettes revealed flowing robes like those King Tirgalan wore. Maglo was a short, slight man who bore himself with a stoop, while Niona was of middling height and slender and sat straight in her saddle. Both wore their hair long, like Tirgalan.

Tirgalan rode aside with his sorcerer and sorceress. While speaking in hushed tones out of earshot of their soldiers, Tirgalan's voice rose once in protest at something Maglo said, but the latter pressed his point. They argued a while longer in urgent tones, but, at length, Tirgalan relented.

As they rode back to their men, the King of Sundara said, "Very well. The diversion *is* necessary. But you must retreat as soon as we've all gone by on the eastern bank. Understood?"

"Yes. Don't worry, my king. You'll face the greater peril," answered Maglo.

Tirgalan sent scores of scouts along the Nurgleth to find places where they could ford it. Men rode off in haste. Niona left to give her captains their orders.

In the meantime, Maglo and his nobles gathered one sixth of Sundara's army, around three thousand men. Once they were ready to set out, the other soldiers made way for them, and Maglo's host marched north on the road.

They made their way unopposed for a while, but soon enough Maglo's scouts came riding back in haste. The enemy approached not far ahead. Lord Maglo and his captains ordered their men into battle formations. Men scurried to form their lines under the light of the moon. When all was ready, they moved ahead. It was imperative to engage the enemy to allow the bulk of Sundara's army to slip by on the Nurgleth's eastern bank. They did not need to wait long.

Norfast's warriors came surging out of the darkness, screaming their battle cries in the Northern Tongue. The ranks of Sundara answered with a hail of arrows. The sounds of arrows piercing wood, mail, and flesh filled the darkness, and cries of agony followed. At the command of their captains, the southern soldiers tossed away bows and unsheathed swords. Shortly after, the front lines smashed with a terrible din.

Men screamed in the night and slashed their blades at anything moving near them. In the chaos and darkness, it was impossible to tell friend from foe. Steel grated and shields clashed. Warriors slipped on blood and the bodies of the wounded and dying. Men died alone in the dark with madness and fear all around.

Then came the dragons.

As the two armies struggled, three serpents of the air swooped down on them. At once, fire exploded in the darkness, illuminating for an instant the hideous scenes of battle in shades of eerie red. Flames gushed from the three beasts' jaws, but one burst of fire transformed into flickering sparks as Lord Maglo sang a song of origin to save his nearest troops.

Others were not so lucky. Scores of men flailed and rolled on the earth in agony as flames consumed them, their dying screams echoing in the night. The dragons' breath did not surprise Maglo, but one thing did: The beasts did not care which men they destroyed. Warriors of

Torrlond and soldiers of Sundara alike perished in the flames. What was worse, the dragons would make the retreat difficult, if not impossible.

But the sorcerer did not have long to puzzle over why the dragons would slay Torrlond's troops. From before and behind him, flames filled the air. He drew upon the gift and strained to control both streams of fire. Then the third blaze surged down on him.

23

ASCENSION

Even as he slept, Dayraven knew it was one of the true-dreams, a memory of the future. Commonplace dreams, fantasies of displaced fear and desire that visited everyone's sleep, differed from the visions telling of events far away and yet to come. In the midst of true-dreams, while his body slumbered in the world of forms, he stood in the eternal present, the realm of origins, where there was no now or then. Past, present, and future were one, and time did not pass, but simply was. He also realized he had no control over what the true-dreams showed, and they happened no matter what he did. Of all the manifestations of the gift, this was the one he liked least, for knowing the future gave little comfort. Thus, a sense of desperation tugged at him as the inescapable vision unfolded.

Dawn's light was blood red with dust and smoke hanging in the sky. A smouldering city straddled a river that poured into a larger body of water. The city was in ruins, the desolate carcass of a once mighty dwelling place bristling with proud towers. But the towers were charred, gaping mouths with smoke curling up from them to the heavens.

Outside the ruined city, two enormous armies gathered in concentric rings, and the one surrounding the other was much the larger.

Hundreds of thousands of tiny specks glinted with armor and weapons. Larger flecks of red circled in the air over the armies, and bright spouts of flame poured down from them onto the smaller army as the two forces rushed toward each other. *Bledla's dragons. Thulhan.*

The two armies clashed, their ordered ranks succumbing to chaos as they dashed against one another. Nearly a hundred bright flashes of white-blue energy snaked like jagged lightning between both sides, burning and flinging the bodies of those hapless enough to be in their path. Dayraven had never seen so much wizard's fire in one place. *Many strong with the gift in this battle.*

The tiny specks slew each other in numbers never seen before in Eormenlond. Soldiers of nearly every kingdom must have been present, but one side was clearly the stronger. The larger army enveloped the smaller, which shrank into itself.

Then the vision shifted, sucking him in close to the carnage. He flew past many unfamiliar faces, all twisted in fear and rage and struggling to kill and live amidst the clashing weapons and flying missiles, the smoke from dragon fires, the blood and sweat and spit and piss and puke, until the vision brought him before one who wielded the gift. Wearing clothes as dark as her hair, she held her hands before her as she chanted a song of origin, her face taut with concentration. Behind her eyes dwelled controlled fury as she wove her spell. *Sequara.*

A thick current of wizard's fire, or *almakhti*, burst from her hands, but thirty feet in front of her it exploded in a blinding flash that sent thousands of fragments of forked light hissing through the air.

When Dayraven could see again, he realized the sorceress contended with another who wielded magic. A huge man with red hair and beard grimaced then laughed as he approached. He wore a priest's white robe, and from his hands a bolt of energy writhed as it met Sequara's. *The High Priest Heremod. One of Queen Faldira's killers.*

The two streams of energy twisted and entwined in a dance of death, and where they met light erupted. Sequara kept her current of energy strong even as sweat ran down her brow and her teeth clenched. Yet the large priest beat her back with his ferocity, and she staggered as her garments smoldered in places. Soldiers fought around them, but Dayraven focused on the two wielders of magic.

As Sequara backed up, a huge shadow arose. A serpent of the air loomed behind her and swooped down, approaching at wondrous speed. It opened its jaws. Fire poured out toward the sorceress, who was oblivious to her bane rushing toward her in the form of eager, red flames. Down they roiled, eclipsing the sky behind her.

Dayraven jerked awake with his heart pounding and his hands outstretched, ready to cast a spell.

As in his vision, it was dawn. But there was no city nearby. Instead, jagged mountains surrounded him on every side, their snow-covered peaks pink as morning light seeped down them. Further down, the gloom still cloaked their rugged shoulders in blue-grey half-light, and shadows crept deep in the sharp valleys between them.

Dayraven took deep breaths and gathered a measure of serenity, though he surrendered a sealed off part of his mind to worry for Sequara. She was always somewhere in his thoughts, but the vision in the true-dream had added tenfold to the weight of his anxiety for her. When the image of the dragon flames behind her small form came before his eyes again, urgency pounded in his mind. He needed to reach her. He had to find a way to stop it.

But such a thought was futile, and he knew it. In the realm of origins, there was no future, and true-dreams were glimpses not of what must be but what *is* in the eternal present. Besides, he was far away from Thulhan, and it would not do to hasten too much in the place where he was now, for one wrong move could lead to death. Dead he would do her no good. The best course was to accomplish what he was there to do, and he could not do that if he allowed his emotions to get the better of him. He breathed and calmed himself again. The elf-shard's steady hush wrapped his mind in cold shadows and reminded him that all would unfold as it should.

When he gained control over his emotions, he glanced around. Two forms slept near the ashes and embers of a dying campfire. Thick furs like the one he slept under covered each. A third man also wrapped a cloak of brown pelt around him, but he was sitting up, his back turned to Dayraven. Relieved that no one saw him startled out of sleep, he reflected on the vision he beheld. *Another dawn, not this day's. Yet it will come soon. We must hurry as best we can.*

As Dayraven stirred, the man squatting under his cloak turned around. Beneath the fur, Captain Uthron of Golgar faced him. He scratched at the black stubble covering his face, and a small mist curled out of his mouth as he smiled. "Good morning, though it's a cold one. We won't be long now. If we make good time, we'll reach the foot of the Wyrmberg by nightfall."

"Good. Then we'll make good time."

It was the morning of the ninth day he had followed Uthron and his two men through the wild, unconquered Osham Mountains. It did not take long to understand why Uthron picked Tiran and Sorn as companions from his best rangers. Sorn was short and wiry, nimble as a mountain goat, and able to climb where no one else could, which was why the other rangers called him Spider. He said little, but Tiran made up for that. Tall and slender, Tiran was never shy about offering his gloomy opinions. Yet he too was among the best of Golgar's foresters, and both had earned Dayraven's trust. Over the last days, his ears had grown accustomed to the form of Andumaic the Golgae spoke while the men he traveled with became friendlier.

Captain Uthron had supplied Dayraven with a thick woolen tunic and breeches that he wore over his clothes, leather gloves lined with fur, and the fur cloak he slept in, as well as dried food, water, and other items he carried in his pack, such as rope, iron spikes and hammer, a small canvas tent, and fur boots with iron studs embedded in their soles.

Uthron had told him it was daunting for even the hardiest of the Golgae to climb the Wyrmberg, but it was impossible without such equipment. Dayraven was grateful, and he realized he would have never found his way without Uthron and his two rangers. The landscape they journeyed through was harsh and unforgiving towards anyone foolish enough to wander into it without knowing what they were doing. Forests of scraggly mountain pines survived in the lower elevations, but little else was strong enough to hold on to life in this raw, wild place.

We approach the top of the world, reflected Dayraven. *There's little between us and the vast, cold heavens, where only the gods of our imaginations dwell.* Even the blood in his veins sought to hide from the cold, to burrow someplace warm deep inside him. Flapping his limbs and rubbing his hands together, he forced his blood to circulate. He hugged his fur cloak closer to his body and moved nearer the fire, which Uthron began to rekindle.

Over the last eight days, they had trudged up and down craggy folds in the land. They took few rests and walked past nightfall. Ever climbing higher, into the heart of the Osham Mountains they meandered. The air thinned and the temperature dropped. For the first three days, they had walked on trails through pine forests. Used by elk, wolves, catamounts and other mountain creatures, the trails saved much time. The Golgae knew them, and though Dayraven was a good woodsman, he respected their knowledge.

After the fourth day, they had emerged from the pine forests and walked over paths no horse could have climbed, not even the sturdy mounts the Golgae used. Bare and rocky were these paths, and often they had to scale sheer faces of rock by using the rope and iron spikes they carried. Most often Sorn led the way. With a rope bound around their waists linking the climbers, Spider pounded spikes into the rock with his small hammer and secured the rope on them. Dayraven appreciated the precaution. Even if he survived the initial fall, a slip could mean death in this inhospitable realm. Also, as the least experienced climber by far, he was grateful the rope provided a clear marker to the best path.

Knowing he must claw his way up the Wyrmberg alone, he tried to learn from his companions. He proved an apt pupil, and Captain Uthron and the others were patient teachers. At the end of each weary day, Uthron told Dayraven what he knew of the path ahead, and he imparted all he knew of the Wyrmberg. Unfortunately, it was not much. Even if they were not convinced she truly existed, the Golgae were wise enough to avoid the lair of the legendary Gorsarhad, eldest of the serpents of the air.

Nevertheless, with each passing day, Dayraven grew more confident. The mountain he saw in his vision called him. As he lay awake for a while each night rubbing his aching legs and balling up beneath his fur cloak, he sensed the growing presence of something ancient and vast. The elf-shard's ceaseless whisper seemed to speak of it, and though it never again formed a word as it had in his vision, he knew it spoke of the dragon Gorsarhad. The great beast's presence was still dim, but Dayraven did not doubt the truth of her legend. He was also not blind to the harsh beauty of the place around him. *Whatever else happens, I'll never forget these mountains. Merciless and indifferent, but they command respect.*

When the revived fire licked the wood and crackled, Uthron's men bestirred themselves and laid out breakfast. They carried hunting bows, with which Tiran and Sorn had slain a mountain elk two days before. They broke their fast on what was left of the meat, some hard cheese, dry bread with crust so tough they had to suck on it, and four half-rotten apples.

Shaking his water bottle to break up a thin layer of ice, Dayraven took a deep draft. Cold wormed its way down his throat and spread to his chest. He ate his fill, knowing he would need energy for the day ahead. His tired, stiff muscles still told of yesterday's labor. He had always been slender, but now his body was more lean and muscled than ever under the layers he wore. Resigning himself to another day of scrambling over rocks, he swallowed the last of his bread, which stuck in his throat and grudgingly went down. Then it was time to pack. Ere dawn's light crept into the lee of the boulder they had sheltered under, they were on their way.

The day proved little different from the previous ones. They toiled over rocks as the sun rose higher and warmed their bodies, stopping occasionally to drink and less often to eat. The going was slow, and almost all the time they trudged upward. But late in the afternoon, they started a steep descent, which was a relief until Dayraven's knees started aching under the weight of his pack.

Towards evening, Sorn stopped ahead of the others atop a stony outcrop. When Dayraven stood beside him, his breath coming hard, he saw why the ranger had paused. On the other side of the outcrop, the hillside plunged downward as a scarp, almost a cliff, until it ended where it met a large valley. A forest of dark green pines blanketed this refuge and invaded the lower portions of the rugged hills ending the valley on the opposite side.

But far above the tree line loomed a giant among giants dominating the entire valley. Sheer and grey were the rocky heights jutting miles above the realm of mortals, above which a mantle of snow glistened in the evening sun. Only the wind dared to sport so high, where it tore away snow in a white wisp extending like some ancient woman's hair tossed in a breeze.

No one said anything while the small party drank in the scene. As he gazed at the mountain, a vision flashed in Dayraven's mind. A deep, dark cave loomed behind a tarn somewhere high up. The tarn was placid and still, its water clean and blue. The darkness of the cave seemed to echo the elf-shard's slithering murmur in his mind. Inside the cave lurked scales, bright eyes, and fire.

"The Wyrmberg," he said.

Captain Uthron glanced at him. "Yes. How did you know?"

"I've seen it before. Not in this realm, and not with my eyes. But I know this place." He looked at Uthron. "Can we cross this valley before dark?"

The captain squinted at the way ahead and frowned. "If we hurry, perhaps. It will likely be dark when we emerge on the other side of the forest, but then we'll arrive at the foot of the Wyrmberg. That's where we part. From there, if our lore holds true, you can reach Gorsarhad's lair within three days."

Tiran squinted as he gazed down at the valley, his hand shading his eyes. "No doubt the old lady's ready for a visitor. I hear dragons fancy visitors, especially around dinner time. I'll wager we won't be the only ones lurking in that forest either. Best not linger in there after nightfall."

"Nothing that dwells in those trees will harm us," said Dayraven calmly.

"Let's move then," said Uthron.

Dayraven adjusted his pack, sliding the straps away from where they had been digging into his shoulders. He forced his tired legs to descend the scarp. So steep was the way that he leaned back as he walked, and at times the incline forced him to sit back and crawl along on hands and feet. The sharp slope was stony and treacherous, and they kicked loose rocks that tumbled down it. Sometimes these sent other rocks bouncing until they started a small, dusty avalanche, and once Dayraven feared the entire hillside would buckle under them. But they made it without serious incident to the bottom, where a pile of loose stones announced the scarp's end and the forest's beginning.

Though it was no proper forest like the Southweald or Orudwyn, the shadows between the pines were deep and dark. A bed of dry, brown needles covered the forest floor, and the air carried the scent of sap. Moss and lichen clung to the gnarled, rough trunks and branches, and nothing but the wind stirred as the trees enveloped the men. Nevertheless, Dayraven sensed many eyes. He kept his mind alert.

At first, they forced their way through thick branches that scratched at them and left sticky pitch on their hands. But before long Tiran found a trail, and the going became easier. Useful for predator and prey, the trail served the small party, for it led north, the direction they needed to go. They knew such trails rarely followed one direction for long, so they relied on the sun for guidance too. They needed to clear the forest before dark, lest they lose their way under the trees, where it would be difficult to see the stars. Dayraven looked up through gaps in the branches to the sky, where the sun was a yellow-orange glow in the west. He picked up the pace. Uthron and his men followed without a word.

They marched on in silence. Their way was for a while quick and flat, but as the sun fell, the land grew hilly again, and Dayraven reckoned they had reached the foothills of the Wyrmberg. Shadows elongated as they climbed up and down tree-clad hills. The shadows merged into the gloom of twilight, and Dayraven beheld no end to the trees. It was growing difficult to see. *Can't be much further. I'm certain we made no wrong turns. I must reach the other side to begin the climb first thing on the morrow. No time to lose.*

But a short while later, when Dayraven tripped on a tree root he could not see even after he looked for it, he knew they would not reach the other side. Glancing behind, he could not make out his three companions through the murk. He waited until footsteps crunched closer. "I'm here," he said to alert them.

Uthron's voice answered from the darkness. "It's no good. We'll be bumping into trees and losing our way soon."

"Shall we make camp here then, my lord?" asked Tiran from somewhere behind his captain. "Right now this spot looks as lovely as any other, though this whole forest has an ill feeling."

Dayraven too misliked the place, but there was little else to do.

A long, mournful howl broke into the night before Uthron replied. Another haunting cry answered from a different direction. Then a third from yet another place.

"Mountain wolves," said Uthron. "They're larger than common wolves. And less afraid of men. By the sounds of it, they're all around us, and they know it."

"Best make a fire. Shall I get started, my lord? There's plenty of wood, at least." There was no fear in Tiran's voice, but they all understood the urgent need for fire to keep the wolves away.

But even as he asked, an idea came to Dayraven. "No. The Southweald too holds these big wolves. We name them *wargs* in the Mark. I have a use for them, so let's not make them nervous with fire. Wait a moment, and don't fear when you hear them come. They'll do us no more harm than your own hounds would."

"My hound bit me once," said Tiran.

Dayraven smiled in the darkness. "No more harm than your mother would, then."

"In that case, that's the end of all of us."

The men laughed, and Dayraven knew they trusted him with their lives, even if they were not enthusiastic about inviting wargs into their company.

There was no need for him to chant a song of origin, but he decided it would put the men more at ease if he did since that was the way they expected sorcery to work. So, he sang the words, "Voldhaliae curchalon im saloshar brunil. Dwindoniae rukhalon ar mindolar ardil."

His voice rang out clear as he repeated the song, but it was only a show. The real sorcery was happening within him as he entered the realm of origins and succumbed to the elf-shard, allowing it to blaze forth. With it, Dayraven's energy exploded in every direction, and he wandered free of his body. It was still a jarring experience, but he rode the energy instead of resisting it or trying to control it. So vast was it that he felt like a flickering candle flame in the midst of a storm. But his presence, the energy that was Dayraven, was still there, mingled throughout it. It was fragile and tiny, but there was still a link to the sense of himself. Gone was his fear of the power and what it might do to him, though he perceived something new in the elf-shard, a sentience and a hunger that might have frightened him had he not already sacrificed himself to it.

He drifted through branches and needles, often sensing birds and squirrels along the way, until he perceived the wargs as they approached. Locking onto their presence, he extended his being toward them through the power of the elf-shard, which carried him to them. Through darkness his energy spread, and soon he was with the mountain wolves.

Claws dug through the forest floor as feet padded along, sure of step. Long legs loped while jaws with sharp, meat-shearing teeth hung open, dripping with saliva. The scent of man-flesh hung thick in the air, the wet blood under their soft skin calling. The wargs sniffed warily, gauging the distance and number of men by sorting each smell. Hackles rose and throats growled, but hunger drove them toward this dangerous prey. Perhaps they were few and helpless. Perhaps they had none of their sharp, shining sticks, and there was no scent of the bright destroyer that cracked when it devoured wood, mangled fur, and tortured flesh. Cunning humans were always using it, but there was none of the thick mist that stung eyes and choked throats, so perhaps these men were stupid, easy prey. Many brothers and sisters gathered for the hunt, their eager eyes glowing.

But, with a sudden change, this hunt took a different course from the wargs' hope. A strange thing happened, a thing none of them had ever sensed before. It was not a thing they could smell or see or feel with flesh, but it was so strong as to be tangible in a way they had never experienced.

A vast energy seeped into the wolves, and they had no way of understanding how a man's will came to dwell in them. Before long, they could not distinguish between their own desires and the will that merged with them. The entire pack fell under his sway within a couple heartbeats.

Their hunger forgotten, the wargs continued toward the man-flesh, but now in obedience to the voice permeating their minds and bodies. The voice became their will. When they arrived in a circle around the men, they waited for the voice to command them.

Dayraven looked around. Many eyes surrounded him and his companions, eyes that were of one mind with him. He peered through the gloom at the dark silhouettes of his three companions, who huddled close together.

"They'll lead us through the forest to the mountain's base. We'll each need some rope to serve as leashes."

The three Golgae paused for a moment. Uthron broke the silence. "Alright. Tiran, take out some rope."

"Mountain wolves leading us through a dark forest," said Tiran as he took off his pack and unfastened its ties. "Next, some trolls will invite us to a sing-along."

Four wargs stepped forward while the darkness swallowed the rest of the eyes. When one wolf approached each man, the latter looped his rope around the beast's neck. As Dayraven reached up to slip his rope around the warg's huge jaws and over its stiff ears, it waited obediently. A child of the forest, the beast's fur smelled musty like the trees.

Dayraven had never been this close to a live warg before, and part of him awed at the animal's size. Much larger than the biggest dog he had ever seen, it was almost big enough to ride on. His head might even fit inside its mouth. *Our enemies, but noble beasts. We're no less predators. Life raging against itself.*

He did not tighten the rope around the neck too much, for there was no need, and he stroked the beast's thick fur on its muscled shoulders as he waited for the others, who were less comfortable with their new guides.

"Nice doggy," said Tiran as he gingerly placed his rope around his warg's head.

The mountain wolves led the way on silent paws, the men struggling now and then to keep up in the darkness. Stopping once in a

PHILIP CHASE

while to glance back, the wargs let the men catch up. A light tug of the rope halted the beasts as if they had been tame all their lives.

They met with no incident on their way out of the dark forest. The four wargs emerged from the trees with the men trailing behind a short while after they first encountered each other, having walked a couple miles together. The moon shone brighter outside the forest, and for the first time they had a good view of the large, grey-furred beasts that aided them. The Golgae shrank back from them. Their wet noses glistened in the moonlight, and their keen eyes glowed with intelligence. "Not sure I would've cozied up to you if I'd seen you like this first," said Tiran to the one that led him.

"Not to worry," said Dayraven. "They could no more hurt you than they could themselves." He turned to his warg and patted it on the head. "Good lads." After he slipped the rope off the beast, his companions followed suit, though with a little more care. "You may go now," he said to the mountain wolves, "and I wish you good hunting."

"As long as they won't be hunting us," said Tiran.

Dayraven smiled as the beasts disappeared into the trees. "No. I've already asked them to see you safely through the forest on the morrow. You may not see them, but they'll be there to protect you."

They made camp, and Dayraven looked up at the mountain looming over them, a monstrous shadow blotting out a quarter of the night sky. *The real task begins.* After Tiran and Sorn made a fire, the four ate together. Buried beneath the warmth of their fur cloaks, they huddled around flames that crackled and sent up drifting sparks. Dayraven said little as he watched the sparks float and wink out, and then it was time to sleep.

When morning light came, the first thing Dayraven did after rubbing his eyes was gaze up at the Wyrmberg. Up and up it soared, threatening to invade the realm of the stars. It seemed impossible that any mortal could reach its snowy top. Fortunately, he did not have to scale the summit. According to Uthron, the legends told that Gorsarhad's lair was two-thirds of the way up on the south-facing slope, about where the snow line lay in summer. Still, two-thirds of the way up the mass of rock frowning down on him seemed more than enough.

"Lucky the weather's clear for you." Uthron approached from behind. "Were it not summer, it would be impossible. Oruma and Anghara are with you."

Dayraven turned toward the captain of Golgar. "They put me in your path. I thank you, and Tiran and Sorn. I could never have made it here without your aid."

"I came for my kingdom. We've heard much of Torrlond's conquests. King Veduir too knows Torrlond will threaten us should the rest of Andumedan fall. That's why he allowed me to lead you." The captain's face softened into a smile. "Yet, now that we're here, I wish you good fortune for friendship's sake. You're a quick learner, Dayraven, and you might have been a fine ranger, though I know yours is a different fate. I'm only a soldier, but I can see the Mother and Father gave you the gift for a reason. Were it not for my king's commands, I would even now go with you up the mountain."

"Perhaps one day we'll scale another mountain together."

"I'll hope for that day."

After the men broke their fast, Uthron, Sorn, and Tiran prepared to leave. Dayraven gave them most of his remaining food, leaving himself a little more than enough for the three days he needed to reach Gorsarhad's lair. Uthron insisted he keep enough to return to the Hidden City. Dayraven refused.

"If I haven't left the Wyrmberg with Gorsarhad in three days, I'll have no need of food. I doubt I could find my way back to Holurad anyway."

Before they parted, all three Golgae embraced Dayraven and wished him luck, and even Sorn cracked a smile as he gave a curt nod. They turned and walked back the way they had come. After the forest swallowed them, Dayraven gazed back at the Wyrmberg. He was alone at the foot of one of the Osham Mountains' largest peaks. Even without a dragon waiting on it, the mountain was death for anyone but the most prepared climber to scale. If the weather turned, even a seasoned ranger could perish. He adjusted his pack, sighed once, and made his first step forward.

The first of many. Though his legs were tired and the way steep, Dayraven ascended at an even pace, as Uthron had taught him. In the beginning, his path was almost pleasant, a steady upward walk that afforded many views of the valley below. For most of the first day, he had no need to scale difficult spots. He scurried up a few small cliffs, but his iron studded boots remained in his pack.

Near the end of that day, he arrived at the foot of a cliff around which he saw no way. For a moment, he debated whether to make camp at its base and leave the climb for the morrow, or scale it then find a suitable place to sleep. Sitting on a rock, he took off his pack and untied the fastenings. After he reached in, he took out his climbing boots.

With boots on and his pack on his shoulders, he put his hand to the rock's rough surface. He glanced behind him. The orange sun sank low on the horizon. He had little time before darkness descended. Pulling himself up, he began the climb. Uthron and the others had taught him well. Distributing his weight between his toes and hands, he made his way up the cliff face. It took him longer than he hoped, however, to scale near the top, and by that time it was almost too dark to see.

The light had failed when he dragged his body over the lip of the cliff onto a shelf not more than twelve feet wide. In front of and above him rose the wall of another cliff, whose top the gloom hid. There was no choice but to set up his tent and huddle on the small shelf between the cliffs for the night.

Pitching the little tent within such limited space in the darkness was not easy, especially with the wind clawing at him and the tent. But he needed the warmth the little shelter provided, so he drove iron spikes into cracks in the rock to secure ropes attached to the tent. When his hammer tapped the last spike into place, he sagged in exhaustion. Though he had never believed in them, he prayed to all the gods that a strong wind would not blow him off the shelf. He entered the little tent and wrapped his fur cloak around him. In tune with the empty darkness beneath and above him, the icy tendrils of the elf-shard's shadow-whispers clung to his awareness. He closed his eyes and fell asleep at once.

When his eyes opened, the morning light brightened the eastern side of his canvas tent. Hoping he had not slept overlong, he crawled out of his shelter on all fours. In his bleariness, he almost forgot he had pitched the tent far up on a small shelf overlooking a cliff. But the view that met him when his head emerged served as a quick reminder.

Reds and pinks and oranges painted the sky in broad strokes over the forested valley he had walked through the previous day. From his perch, the trees appeared as tiny blotches merging in an undulating, dark green lake with tall points poking out here and there. A hawk with outstretched wings rode the wind currents far below him, hardly more than a brown speck. It was a beautiful scene, but he had no time to admire it. Relieved it was still early, he ate food from his pack and washed it down with water. When he finished, he dismantled his tent, packed up, and began to ascend the cliff above him.

The remainder of the cliff proved easy enough to scale, for he had been closer to the top than he guessed. His climb was steady after that, but there were a few tricky spots that day. He methodically made his way up while the air thinned and cooled until his breaths grew ragged after every major exertion. Uthron had warned him not to climb too fast. His lungs needed time to adjust to thinner air.

Dayraven rested and used the meditation exercises Urd and Faldira had taught him to relax his body. Letting himself drift, he sent his energy to mingle with the crisp mountain air and the solid rock beneath him. His body found it easier to adjust to its surroundings, and soon his breathing returned to normal. Afterwards, he sat in peace and focused on the dragon's presence, which grew stronger with every step up. He was sure he was heading in the right direction, though he did not know what would happen when he arrived.

When he was ready, he started once again. It was not long before he met patches of snow and ice. The snow crunched as his boots left their imprints in it. His would not be a warm bed that night.

Darkness found Dayraven at a better place for pitching his tent at the second day's end. He chose a flat section of a gentle slope to sleep on, with a large rock on one side as protection against the wind. After his tent was up and secure, he wriggled inside and bundled up beneath his fur cloak.

His chief thoughts were on the urgency of his mission and the dragon awaiting him on the morrow. Sequara, Gnorn, Orvandil, Galdor, Abon, and thousands of other lives, including his father's, depended on him. For their sake he must think of nothing but the eldest of Eormenlond's beasts. His journey and his toil drove all else from his mind until he lived and breathed for the single purpose of finding Gorsarhad. Once he did, he would become a conduit for the elf-shard's power, and thus he would wield the ancient lingworm.

That night he dreamt of the cave behind the tarn. Within, a vast presence brooded.

On the third day he arose at dawn. Though the sun promised to be bright, he shivered when he emerged from the tent. Chill was the air, and like a dagger the wind cut at him. To lighten his load, he left the tent behind, sure he would never need it again. His food too was nearly gone — a few strips of salted meat, a chunk of moldy bread as tough as the rocks he trod on, and a slice of hard cheese to suck on — but he thought little on that. Forcing his stiff legs to raise his body once more, he trudged up the slope. More snow and ice greeted him, but the iron-studded boots made him sure-footed.

A short time had passed when a tingling sensation invaded his mind. It was the elf-shard. It seemed to be stirring on its own, waking with an eagerness to be free. Having tasted total freedom on several occasions since his vision in Orudwyn, was the elf-shard now yearning to escape him? Or was it trying to tell him something?

He stopped a moment, for he had just arrived at the base of an ice-coated cliff that rose some two hundred feet above him. Breathing hard, he dug out his water bottle from his pack and drank while he pondered the sensation. He allowed his mind to drift in the realm of origins. Upward soared his awareness until it brushed against something enormous in the realm of forms. Ancient and sentient, powerful and cunning, fierce and aware.

Dayraven's eyes widened with understanding. He glanced at the icy, glistening cliff. *Gorsarhad's lair is up there. It's the third day, but morning light's still golden in the sky. I have arrived sooner than I expected. May the gods guide my next steps. Sithfar make my way sure, and Bolthar lend me strength.*

Putting his hand on his brow, he gazed up towards the top of the bright cliff. The rising sun shimmered off its glazed surface, and the ice wept in places. *This will prove difficult to climb. Even Sorn would have a hard time, but the closer I get to her, the easier our encounter will be. Should I find a way around?*

Just after that thought, the vision of the cave behind the tarn returned to him, vivider than ever. *Here. At the top of this cliff. I slept not far beneath the dragon's lair last night. I must find a way up.*

He did not hesitate. Finding a foothold then a handhold above him, he hoisted himself up and did not look back. He crawled up the glazed surface. More glad than ever for the iron-studded boots of the Golgae, he knew it would have been impossible without them. Still, it was no easy ascent. The whistling wind tried to pry him from the rock and ice, and the slippery patches more than once defeated him, forcing him to backtrack and find a way around them.

After a while, he was breathing so hard he thought about resting. The problem was there was nowhere to rest, so he clung to the surface and closed his eyes. When he opened them, he looked down and found he was not quite halfway up the cliff. It was hard to say which assaulted him with more strength: the dizziness or the disappointment. *That's the last time I look down.*

Stretching his right arm up, he grasped a bit of rock poking out and tested it. When it felt solid, he pulled up, his muscles straining and his toes digging into ice to help push him further. His left hand found another hold not far away, and for another moment he was safe. *One hold at a time. Don't think beyond that.*

The sun moved higher, and the icy cliff shed more treacherous tears as he clawed his way up. At times gusts peeled off cold drops that shimmered in the sunlight as they spiraled down and pattered on his face. His exhausted hands and arms trembled when he was not using them. His stiff legs too felt like wood, and his lower back burned with a fierce ache as sweat ran down it. But he inched his way up, sometimes digging his fingernails into the ice or using his small hammer to chip away a hold.

His progress was agonizingly slow, but his goal drew nearer. Time lost meaning as he concentrated on his next grip. There was only the ice and rock of the cliff's surface and the bone, flesh, and muscle of his fingers and toes seeking their next resting place.

At length, he looked up and found he was only ten feet from the top. He paused to breathe and gauge his next step. On the one hand, his body was screaming with exhaustion. On the other hand, his nearness to the top spurred him on.

But he was in a difficult spot, for the cliff's top jutted outward two feet. In vain he searched above for a hold allowing him to use all his limbs. He looked to the left, where a slick patch of smooth ice met his gaze. To his right the rock appeared ready to crumble. He reached out to test it. Flakes of rock peeled off at the lightest touch, and he dislodged one large chunk. A long moment passed before a distant crack interrupted the silence far below. *Then it must be straight up. But how?*

He debated a while, but he was not getting any stronger, so he decided to use the studded toes of his boots to push him just enough to grasp the salient bit of rock a few inches out of his reach above. There would be a dangerous moment when his hands would hold nothing, but if he reached the rock, he would be alright. In his mind, he saw his legs dangling in the air beneath him, but he thought he had enough strength left in his arms to pull him up with one last effort.

He took a deep breath and closed his eyes. When he opened them, he coiled his legs and lurched up, his hands seeking above him as he stretched to his full height.

Perhaps it was the suddenness of his movement. Perhaps it was just ill luck. Whatever it was, the ice and rock Dayraven's studded boots dug into gave way just as he leapt. At once, there was nothing under his feet but air.

But his push was just enough to reach the bit of rock above him with his right hand. His fingers grasped with all their remaining strength, the nail of the index finger tearing and ripping off as it scratched against the rock's unyielding surface. He ignored the pain and held on, his legs swaying in the air. The falling rock and ice landed with a crash that echoed up the cliff, followed by several smaller clacks.

Dayraven's right hand began to slip. He grunted and pulled, raising himself until his left hand reached the rock. With a burst of effort, he managed to grasp the rock with both hands. There he clung.

His hands were slippery with sweat and blood, and the rock was wet from the weeping ice. The cold wind shrilled and buffeted his body. He kicked to reach the cliff face with his feet, but the toes of his boots only came away after digging out more loose rock and ice.

Dayraven reflected on how absurd it was to die after coming within ten feet of his goal. He did not think he could hold on for much longer. His shoulder sockets felt like they were ripping out, his frozen hands were cramping, and his arms were burning. Closing his eyes tight, he screamed in frustration, fear, and rage. He did not want to die yet. Even worse, he was failing Sequara and all the others, but his hands only slipped further on the wet rock.

"Help," he tried to say to the elf-shard, but it came out as a hoarse whimper. *You led me here. Why?* The elf-shard's dark murmur was as indifferent as ever.

His grip was failing, the skin of his palms and fingers sliding and scraping on the rock. It would be only a moment now. He saw his body plummeting and breaking on the rocks below. No one would ever find it. His eyes opened in alarm. A blur streaked by above him, something black.

24

DRAGONBANE

In the pre-dawn gloom, Orvandil grasped the cold shaft of the strange, short casting spear he had asked Gnorn to forge during the night of hell. With everyone else fighting the dragon fires ravaging Thulhan, it had taken some time to convince the Dweorg to undertake the task. But once Orvandil explained what it was for, Gnorn had given him a broad smile and nodded.

They had used the abandoned forge in King Naitaran's palace complex. As flames rained from the sky and kindled the city, the Dweorg toiled over a weaponsmith's fire with Orvandil operating the bellows. Even when the palace's tower with its gilded dome crashed in blazing pieces that cratered the nearby courtyard and filled the air with choking dust and smoke, they did not pause in their work. Amidst chaos and madness they labored as if it had been the only thing that mattered while the world was ending.

The shaft was iron, for it needed both strength and flexibility. A steel shaft would shatter. Fortunately, the royal forge was well stocked with iron rods, and Gnorn found everything he needed to shape one to the right width and length. Since iron was so much heavier than wood, it took some experimenting to determine the right size. Anyone who had seen Orvandil tossing iron rods in the courtyard while fire consumed the shattered remains of the royal tower would have thought him mad. Of course, the shaft they decided on would have proven far too heavy for most warriors to cast.

The blade they welded to the iron shaft was even more crucial. It had to be the finest hardened steel, sharp enough to split a hair. Gnorn made sure of that. Only a Dweorgish weaponsmith could have accomplished it, and Gnorn was among the finest of his kind.

Orvandil had marveled over his friend's skill at the forge and how he made each blow of the hammer, no matter how hard or soft, shape the folded steel according to his desire. The Thjoth paid close attention, but after observing his friend work, he knew he did not understand the smallest fragment of Dweorgish smith-lore. Dripping with sweat and smudged with soot, Gnorn had worked with furious speed but astounding efficiency — every movement had a purpose. Even with such little time, the spear tip was a work of excellent craftsmanship, the sharpest and most durable steel in Eormenlond.

Last, the Dweorg welded together the shaft and the blade. After the hammer's last clang, Gnorn dipped the finished spear in a barrel of dirty water, which hissed and steamed. When he drew it out, he declared the result satisfactory, though ugly, and far too heavy for an ordinary man to wield. Orvandil did not care how pretty the spear was, though he knew Gnorn's pride in not only the strength but also the beauty of Dweorg-wrought weapons.

As for the spear's weight, Orvandil was no ordinary man. When he first lifted the weapon in his right hand, he tested its feel and knew he could cast it far. Somehow Gnorn had made it lighter than he expected, and the balance was perfect. The ripples in the steel tip gleamed in the forge's ruddy light, and the iron shaft was blacker than a new moon night. The Dweorg knew his business. When Orvandil made a trial of it by thrusting it through a steel plate, mail, and several pieces of leather at once, the spear sheared through every layer. Strength and sharpness it had.

"Needs a name," said Orvandil as he withdrew the weapon from the punctured steel and leather.

The Dweorg looked up at his tall friend with a grim smile. "Then let the thing be called Dragonbane."

"That'll do."

By the time Dragonbane was ready, the dragons had gone. All that remained were their fires licking at ruined buildings all over the city. But the exhausted sorcerers contained the flames, and at length only smoke and an eerie silence surrounded Thulhan's people. Orvandil wondered why the lingworms had left their terrorizing, but he supposed even dragons needed rest. Certainly the beasts were mortal. At least he aimed to find out if they were.

He knew the serpents of the air would reappear. The Torrlonders never fought without their dragons in the vanguard. Without the lingworms, they would find their war harder going. If Dayraven did not come, he hoped to do something about it, though he wished Gnorn had time to make eleven more iron-shafted spears.

But there was no time. Dawn's light would soon seep into the sky, and then the battle for Thulhan, the kingdom of Sildharan, and all of Eormenlond would begin. One spear would never be enough. To prevail, those who opposed Torrlond would need a miracle. Perhaps Dayraven would come.

After the dragons abandoned the city, Orvandil slept. During that time, King Tirgalan had arrived with the troops of Sundara, though the southerners had suffered many losses along the way. They entered the city from the eastern gate, having crossed the Nurgleth under the cover of darkness. But Thulhan's people had no heart to cheer for their allies. Their city was a smoking ruin, and soon it seemed likely to become a vast pyre. Their friends from the eldest of the Andumaic kingdoms had come merely to leap in the pyre with them.

Then things had worsened. Just after the last Sundarae straggled in and the gates closed, the Ilarchae horde rode in from the east, which ended Orvandil's sleep.

The barbarians made no attempt to conceal their arrival. As one mass, the Ilarchae sang a grim song in their rough tongue. The song's words needed no translation: In the ears of the Sildharae and their allies, they promised death.

Cheering and bellowing at the smoking city, many savages galloped close under the cover of morning darkness. Risking arrows from the city wall, they flung the heads of Sildharae soldiers from Sirukinn's

Wall towards Thulhan. The Ilarchae seemed to regard the gesture as some sort of bold deed, an announcement of the imminent fate of the rest of the Sildharae. It served to further dishearten Thulhan's people, forced to imagine the heads of their loved ones and kin rotting outside the city.

None of that bothered Orvandil. He knew what war brought out in men. Sometimes he hated himself for knowing it too well, and he wished he felt sorrow, even fear, at such horrors. But he only felt the battle hunger coming, and the prospect of death was familiar now, almost an old friend. He expected to die in battle, and this was as good a day as any.

At least he had seen Grimrik one last time. And Grimrik's queen. Osynia was as beautiful as ever. Perhaps more, if that were possible. He had hardly been able to speak in her presence. And she had seemed content with her life. The old grief he caused had scarred over. He was glad. He wanted her to be happy. For the sake of her daughters, he hoped Dayraven would come. But even if he did not, Orvandil would fight until the end. Might be he would die while fighting a serpent of the air. That would be worth a song, if anyone lived to sing it.

The best plan they could come up with did not leave much room for hope. His cousin Vols had brought him and Gnorn as well as Duneyr and several other trusted warriors to what the citizens and soldiers called the Dark Council. As it took place before dawn, it was indeed dark, but the title reflected the mood more than anything.

In the ruins of the palace's throne room they had gathered, with guttering torches fixed on the columns providing dim light. Chunks of the ruined palace tower had broken through the ceiling in the corner furthest from the throne, and the torches and lamps revealed a thick coat of dust lying everywhere in the magnificent room, dulling even the gems set in the walls.

Though the chamber seemed unsafe to Orvandil, King Naitaran had insisted they meet there. Sitting atop his throne, Sildharan's ruler ranted to the gathered leaders and their trusted captains about the end of times and the dusk of civilization. Perhaps he was a great sorcerer, as some said, but he deemed the broken man a poor leader for a time such as this.

Fortunately, Galdor had more sense and more spine. The old wizard had laid out their situation and chances without flinching. Orvandil could still hear his words: "Three things will determine this battle. The first is magic. Bledla and his priests are well accustomed to battle magic. Thus, we will need all with the gift to face them. Second, the dragons. If I know Bledla, they will target the sorcerers among us. Should they succeed, they will next seek large concentrations of troops, so we must occupy them for as long as we can. Last, the armies. We are outnumbered, but, with our backs to the wall, we will fight all the more fiercely. However, all will be for naught if we cannot protect the soldiers from the dragons and from Bledla's priests. It may be that all who face the foe in battle will fall, but at least we may hope the citizens will live. If we remain behind the walls, the city burns in dragon fire and we all die: soldiers, sorcerers, and citizens. Our only option, then, is to sally forth. What's more, if we remain in large formations, the dragons will burn us before we can offer resistance, so we must close swiftly with the foe. Even Bledla will not sacrifice the Torrlonder troops to dragon fire just to get at us."

They had arrayed their troops under cover of darkness to meet the ring of their foes. Some of Sildharan's soldiers and most of their strongest sorcerers would face Torrlond's army to the west, for they knew the Torrlonders had brought at least two hundred priests of the Way as well as the high priests and the supreme priest, who were all accustomed to using the gift in battle. There would be a struggle of magic alongside steel, but there too the enemy outnumbered them, and no one matched Bledla. Also positioned on the west were the Ellonders under King Fullan and the Thjothic warriors of King Vols.

The troops of Sundara and the rest of the Sildharae army would face the Ilarchae on the city's eastern side. King Tirgalan of Sundara, who had turned grim since the loss of many of his soldiers and one of his most trusted sorcerers, a man called Maglo, was to take command of the troops on that side. Orvandil reckoned the Ilarchae would see a different side of the gentle king.

Then there was Sequara. He had never seen the sorceress of Asdralad so fierce. She spoke little, but the grim cast in her eyes said everything. *She seeks revenge. She'll have some before the end.* To be sure,

Sequara might never have spoken aloud of vengeance, but Orvandil knew that look. *She'll be in the thick of it.* And if dragons would be coming to her, he knew where he would be.

Later, it was not easy to refuse King Vols when he asked him to command a Thjothic division. But he had convinced his cousin when he told him his plan. Vols had many excellent commanders anyway. Duneyr, Grimling, Arinbjorn, Kialar, and Asgrim: All were good men. More importantly, the deed Orvandil had in mind appealed to Grimrik's king, who wished he had thought of it first.

"Fight well then, cousin," said Vols as he grasped Orvandil's shoulder. "If I don't see you after the battle, I know they'll sing of your deeds for ages to come."

Thus Orvandil waited in the dim greyness next to Sequara just outside Thulhan's western gate. The greys were lightening, however, and shades of color began to appear in their surroundings. They stood in front of a formation of golden-kirtled Sildharae foot soldiers, whose nervousness Orvandil could almost smell. *They'll hold. They fight for home. Warriors are fiercer with kin at their backs.* Gnorn too came with them.

"You'll need my axe behind you while you prance around with that hunk of iron you call a spear," the Dweorg had said.

Orvandil had smiled when he said it. He was glad to have his friend near him, and not only because the Dweorg was formidable with his axe. Strange it was that a Dweorg should understand him better than anyone else, but Gnorn was perceptive as well as wise. He had grown fond of the Dweorg, and he could think of no one he would be prouder to stand by while facing the end, unless it were Dayraven.

It would have been good to have Abon near as well. The shaper was at Galdor's side, where he belonged, with the rest of the Ellonders. They were not far to the right, but Orvandil could not see them in the half-light.

Soon enough, dawn bled into the sky. He had hoped they would join battle before light came, thus increasing their chances of surprising the foe, but the signal to charge had not come.

The light increased. He looked back at the city, or what was left of it. A pall of smoke hovered over row upon row of charred buildings. Not one of the many towers that once boasted of the noble families' power had escaped destruction. Most lacked their tops, and some had toppled over. Smoke and flame had blackened the stones outside the windows of all that remained standing. The palace's tower was a stub, the gilded dome a pile of rubble.

Less exalted citizens of Thulhan had lost their homes to the fires as well, their shops and businesses too. The city wall behind Orvandil bore black scars where the dragons breathed flames onto the catapults, which were now ashes. With all the dust and smoke hanging in the air, the dawn sky glowed the bloodiest red he had ever seen. *Fitting.*

They would not take the Torrlonders by surprise. Across from them, the foe's troops had nearly finished scurrying into battle formations. *Their scouts warned them of our movements. We never had a chance at surprise. At least we're out of the city.*

Row upon row of soldiers met Orvandil's gaze, their spears and helms shining as the sun's early rays bathed them. Vast was the army facing him, a sea of men ready to kill and die for the Way of Edan. On and on their ranks went in a curving arc, well beyond his field of vision, though he knew they encircled the city. With rows extending thirty deep in most places, their lines were not thin either. *Numbers don't mean everything. Discipline wins wars . . . and in their case, dragons.* Archers knelt in the front rows, their bows strung and waiting. And dispersed among the grey kirtles, a few white-robed priests stood out. Nowhere did the dragons appear. The Thjoth dared to hope they might engage the enemy before the beasts' fire rained down. *That signal better come soon.*

He gripped the upper strap of the round linden shield he wore on his left arm. Sweothol waited in its baldric hanging from his left shoulder, while his long dagger rested in its sheath on his right hip. Dragonbane's shaft felt cool in his right hand. Memories of other battles prodded at him, and he wondered where the Mercenary Company of Etinstone might be. *Ludecan still commands them, mostlike. I wonder how many who served under me live. Better not to meet them.* He would prefer not to kill men he once commanded, but he knew a warrior could not pick his foes in battle. *I've slain those I'd no wish to before.*

A war horn's blast shattered the air. More than a dozen others followed. *About time. Now come, big lizards. I have a gift for you.*

He did not need to wait long. Just as the ranks of Sildharan, Ellond, and Grimrik surged forth with their battle cries, the great lingworms tore over the horizon. They were distant, but their swift wings would carry them to the battlefield in moments.

Orvandil ran forward with Sequara on his left and Gnorn on his right. The sorceress had her curved blade sheathed, and she murmured something in magic's strange tongue. The Dweorg clutched his battle-axe. Soldiers around them hastened for Torrlond's front line, hoping the death awaiting them there was better than the fiery one that would soon pour from the sky.

In a chorus of whining buzzes, arrows began to shower down on them. The Thjoth edged in front of Sequara while holding his shield overhead to protect him and her. Two arrowheads dug into his shield with thuds. Several nearby men sprouted feathered shafts from their shoulders, legs, and chests before crying out and cringing to the dust. He could hear Sequara and Gnorn breathing hard as they sprinted, desperate to reach Torrlond's soldiers before the dragons descended on them.

As they neared the enemy's front line, casting spears flew at them. Orvandil side-stepped one, and Sequara leaped over it. But a Sildharae to his right caught one in his chest under the neck, his blood spraying as his limp body jerked back and collided with the ground.

Orvandil glanced overhead. The dragons were large now, their amber eyes visible as their tongues forked out in anticipation. They had only moments left. A wall of shields stood firm in front of them. It would be impossible to smash through the shieldwall in time for the Sildharae soldiers behind to engage with the Torrlonders. Those in the rear would be kindling for the lingworms.

Sequara pushed the tall Thjoth aside, surprising him. Sprinting ahead, she thrust forward her hands and yelled out a song of origin, "Alakathon indomiel ar galathon anrhuniae! Vortalion marduniel im paradon khalghoniae!"

Jagged blue wizard's fire streaked from her hands into Torrlond's front line. A deafening blast sent grey-kirtled bodies flying everywhere.

An acrid smell filled the air, and where Sequara's current of energy hit the shieldwall, there was curling vapor and a huge gap.

Orvandil rushed into the gap, thrusting Dragonbane's point through the torso of the first Torrlonder standing before him and lifting the man off the ground. He smashed the corpse into a grey kirtle behind it and blocked another soldier's sword blow with his shield. The next man thought to cleave Orvandil's spear shaft as the Thjoth held it up in defense. The attacker's eyes widened when the weapons sparked with a clash that notched his sword blade. Before the soldier recovered, the Thjoth swept his spear's steel tip through his neck, slicing through flesh, sinew, and bone.

Gnorn's axe flashed at his friend's side, cleaving through a man's shoulder. Orvandil pressed further in and swung Dragonbane into a row of Torrlonders, smashing them back and splitting open one's head. They needed to penetrate far into the Torrlonders' ranks to allow the Sildharae to mix with the foe. He hoped most had followed into the gap Sequara made. But when dragon fire roared above, men's terror-filled screams reached his ears from behind, and a wave of sudden heat struck his back.

Chaos reigned. Men cried out as they slashed. Blades sank into flesh. Steel clanged and gouged splinters out of shields. Punctuating the din were the crackling blasts of sorcerers channeling the energy around them into bursts of wizard's fire, or what the Andumae called almakhti. Blue currents flashed while red flames poured down. Amidst it all, Orvandil whirled and thrust Dragonbane, mowing down those who stood before him. He and Gnorn cleared a space for Sequara, who summoned her strength for another blast.

Thirty feet in front of the sorceress, a line of grey kirtles formed. Again she shouted her spell, and the current buzzed as it sprang to life around her hands. It split the air to seek the foe, and the flash on impact was twice as great as before as splinters of crooked light spun away and dissipated.

Where Sequara's current of energy had exploded, smoking corpses in grey kirtles littered the ground. But one figure still stood. A huge man in a priest's white robe loomed amidst the smoke. He laughed and sneered as he beheld Sequara. The man had a long red beard, and his eyes glowed with a look Orvandil knew well. This man liked to kill. The Thjoth recognized the High Priest Heremod, who raised his hands and unleashed a thick bolt of wizard's fire at Sequara.

The sorceress was ready with her own current of almakhti. After their explosive meeting, the two deadly streams snarled and twisted, scattering shards of bright, scorching energy. Sequara strained and stumbled, but she held on even as her clothes smoked in places. At the same time, five Torrlonders approached behind her.

Orvandil sped toward them and yelled to Gnorn, "Ward her back!"

Blows fell like hard rain, but the two friends parried with spear and axe and slashed at their attackers in a rapid series of clangs. Ropes of blood twisted in the air, and two grey kirtles went down. The others backed off.

Then Orvandil glimpsed the thing plummeting toward them from the sky. *It's come for Sequara while the white-robe engages her.*

"Dragon!" he shouted at the Dweorg as he planted his spear in the earth and tore off his shield. He spun the shield like a discus into one Torrlonder's face. Blood spattered and teeth shattered ere his back hit the ground.

"The other two are yours."

"Right!" Gnorn pounded his axe haft into his palm as Orvandil took up Dragonbane again in his right hand.

The Dweorg had little difficulty fending off the two attackers since the Torrlonders fled from the approaching lingworm.

"Seems I frightened 'em," said Gnorn with a chuckle as he raised his axe and chased them.

The Thjoth smiled but stared at the dragon, which grew more enormous with each passing moment. Red scales glistening in the morning light, the serpent of the air revealed yellowed teeth as its reptilian lips parted in a snarl. Men who had been fighting screamed and jostled each other to run out of the path of the imminent dragon fire. Orvandil stood his ground athwart the lingworm's path.

He cocked his muscled arm back, keeping his grip on Dragonbane tight. His gaze never moved as the dragon streaked closer. *Not yet,* he thought. *Wait for the flames.*

The great beast shifted its leathery wings and lashed its tail, sending its colossal, serpentine body swooping down. Still Orvandil abided the monster, not even blinking as his bright blue eyes peered up in concentration. *Not yet.*

Behind him, currents of energy crackled and flashed as Sequara and the big high priest fought on, but the Thjoth did not look back. With its predator's eyes on Sequara, the serpent of the air thrust open its jaws to disgorge a torrent of fire.

Now.

Two slow steps and three quick strides gave him the needed momentum. Heaving iron and steel upward with all his might, Orvandil cried out then watched Dragonbane speed. The spear clove the air in a straight line toward its huge target, shrinking to a tiny black needle in front of the dragon's gaping jaws. When flames swept over it, the iron shaft glowed hot red for an instant before disappearing in the great lingworm's mouth.

A spurt of blood erupted behind the dragon's head, and its flames guttered out as it choked and thrashed its long neck. The roar of agony that escaped the monstrous beast's throat washed over the battle. Men everywhere looked up from their grim toil in wonder and fear.

The dragon's wings clenched in the air then shuddered as its long body writhed. Unable to control its flight, the serpent of the air flopped then plummeted towards Orvandil, who stood unmoving. Thirty feet from the Thjoth, the ground greeted the beast with a colossal, earth-shaking crash. A dust cloud flew up as the lingworm lashed and flailed with blood-chilling shrieks. Even as others covered their ears and fled, Orvandil leaped forward.

The Thjoth unsheathed Sweothol as he sprinted for the wreckage of scales and spikes twisting in agony. Bitter was its pain. Terrible were its cries. Orvandil ducked under a lashing tail then lunged past the dragon's jaws snapping in blind fury. A clawed forefoot struck out, but he let it tear the ground then leaped. Landing on the forefoot as if it were a stair, he sprang up and alighted atop the beast's spiked back. One, two, three strides over its long neck, and he stood over the lingworm's head.

Just behind the skull, Dragonbane's Dweorg-wrought tip jutted out a foot. Sizzling and steaming blood ran down the spear. In a flash,

Sweothol rose then arced down with Orvandil's full strength behind it. The ancient blade sheared through scales and bit deep into the skull. Again Sweothol rose and fell. A spray of crimson followed in its wake.

The great beast shrieked and reared its head, hurling and spinning Orvandil in the air. The warrior landed on his feet, ran forward, and leaped high with his blade aloft toward the ghastly head that was pivoting toward him. Sweothol plunged into the jelly of the dragon's amber eye up to the hilt. The lingworm shrieked and wrenched so hard that the Thjoth lost his grip on the sword and flew backwards. Hitting the ground hard, he grunted with the impact and rolled. He raised himself on all fours and crouched in readiness for the next attack.

But the dragon's massive head crashed to the earth. Its remaining eye gazed blankly. When the beast's giant body shuddered and twitched for the last time, Orvandil rose and strode toward it. He plucked Sweothol from the ruined, clouded eye, and a clear yellowish fluid seeped from the wound. A mournful sigh escaped the dragon's nostrils, a warm rush of air with a deep, gravelly rumble. No other breaths followed.

For a long moment all was still.

Loud cheers broke the air. Those allied against Torrlond — Ellonders, Thjoths, and Sildharae — shook their fists, and in their faces and angry smiles was something more than joy at the beast's demise: There was belief. Word of the dragonslaying spread like fire.

Gnorn and the Torrlonders he fought all stared with the same wide-eyed expression, their deadly quarrel forgotten. Above the din the Dweorg shouted, "It worked! Dragonbane pierced the beast's skull!"

Warriors of Ellond, Sildharan, and Grimrik overheard the Dweorg, but they seemed to take the name for the man, not the spear, and they took up the cry, "Dragonbane! Dragonbane!"

Even the Torrlonders stopped fighting and gaped in disbelief at the huge ruin of their most formidable weapon. As incomprehension and dismay swept over them, they ran from the carnage, abandoning that part of the field to their jubilant foes.

Like the god Regnor, who slew the primeval dragon Hringvolnir, Orvandil had cast his spear into the mouth of the monster. Now the tall warrior stood beside his fallen foe, dwarfed next to its enormity. He did not glory in his deed, nor did he roar, for he understood two things. One was that the dragon had never wished to slay humans in battle. It was a slave of the supreme priest. The other was that he would never again in his life face such a magnificent opponent as that. Never again would he taste such dizzying, heart-pounding fear. Never again would he feel so alive as he stared death in the face.

But there was still much work to do. A battle to fight.

With hot, dark dragon blood spattered over his body and running down his sword arm, Orvandil strode in the direction he last saw Sequara. But he could not spot her, for soldiers allied against Torrlond came running to gaze at the warrior who slew a dragon. Men with ecstatic smiles forgot the battle and rushed toward him.

"Dragonbane! Dragonbane!" came the cry, but the Thjoth's face was like stone.

As warriors surrounded him and pressed close, he looked for Gnorn. *He'll be near her.* Sildharae, Ellonders, and Thjoths crowded around to slap his back, their fists pounding the air. But Orvandil walked through the shouts as they rang in his ears. *Where is she? And where's Gnorn?* He pressed forward even as the cry of "Dragonbane! Dragonbane!" grew louder.

A gap in the crowd opened. He glimpsed something black on the level of the ground. He pushed a man out of his view and saw her prostrate form lying still. Gnorn kneeled over the body with tears streaming from his grief-filled eyes down his lined cheeks, cradling her head in his lap with one hand and tugging at his beard with the other. A knot of dismay seized Orvandil's chest. He rushed forward, knocking aside several men in his way.

The cheers fizzled out. The tall Thjoth stood over the fallen sorceress. Angry burn marks streaked Sequara's cheeks and forehead. Her hands too were burned in places, as well as her clothes.

Twenty feet from her lay an almost unrecognizable corpse, smoke curling up from it as flames still licked a piece of its tattered white robe. Some of his red beard still showed, though most of it had burned away along with his face, where blackened cheekbones protruded through charred skin and vacant eye sockets stared up at the sky. The stench of burnt flesh and hair was thick. Orvandil looked away in disgust. *She had some revenge, at least.*

He squatted by Gnorn and noticed another wound. An arrowhead that had pierced Sequara's back jabbed through her shoulder under the collarbone. Glistening blood soaked her torn tunic, though its dark color made it hard to see how much. Particles of dirt clung to the front of her tunic and one of her cheeks.

Gnorn sobbed. Grief choked the Dweorg's voice. "I just found her! Lying on her face in the dirt! In the name of the ancestors and all your mad gods, why didn't I stay by her side?"

"It was sorcery she faced," answered Orvandil. He was numb, and he heard his deep and level voice say, "You did your duty. You could do nothing more." Perhaps he was speaking to himself as well.

Orvandil took Sequara's hand. He held her wrist, which was still warm. A moment later, he felt a tiny throb in her veins. "Gnorn, you oaf, she still lives."

The Dweorg's eyes went wide as his sob broke off. "What?" He tore off his helm and held it in front of her lips. When Gnorn examined the helm, her breath had misted a small patch on it.

"She lives!" cried the Dweorg as he plunked the helm back on his head, though it was askew now. "She lives!" he yelled with his broad smile. He rubbed the tears from his eyes and sniffled.

"Yes," nodded Orvandil, "but we must bind the wound. It was the arrow, not the priest, that felled her. She defeated her foe. She'll live if we stop the bleeding."

The Thjoth turned to the crowd. "Warriors of Sildharan, Ellond, and Grimrik! Return to the battle. Eleven dragons remain, and the foe outnumbers us. Our friends are in need. Return to the toil of blades, and take heart."

Cheers erupted, and one man shouted, "Hearken to the Dragonbane! The enemy returns!"

Several arrows fell among them. One struck a blue-kirtled Ellonder through the neck. He opened his mouth to scream, but only blood rushed out, and he flopped down. As his blood pooled under him, the crowd raged forward against the line of Torrlonders.

Orvandil stayed by Sequara and Gnorn. "Tear strips from your kirtle and bind the wound," he said to the Dweorg. "Leave the arrow. If we draw it out now, she might bleed to death." The Thjoth handed his dagger to his friend.

Gnorn cut strips from his kirtle and wrapped them around the wound. They soaked in the blood and turned dark. Orvandil stood guard over them. When the Dweorg finished, the Thjoth sheathed sword and dagger and lifted Sequara in his arms. Her unwounded arm flopped freely, but Orvandil hugged the bleeding shoulder close. She was not a heavy burden for him.

"Watch my back."

The Dweorg patted his battle-axe. "We're right behind you."

Amidst screams and clashes of weapons, Orvandil carried Sequara through the battlefield, stepping over corpses and spilled entrails. Slippery blood and human waste as well as warriors in their death struggles made his path treacherous. He tried not to jar her, but twice he leaped aside as a Torrlonder and then a Markman slashed at him. Gnorn slew both assailants with his axe, crunching through one's helm and severing another's spine.

Closer to the city, rows of burned bodies lay all over the earth, their charred mouths wide in fear and agony and their withered limbs curled up as if trying to protect themselves. These victims of the dragons had not even made it to the battle.

Orvandil gazed overhead to make sure no serpents of the air swooped down on them. Five circled high, one holding a squirming object in its claws. Another swept down as it vomited flames, but they were all distant. The ring of the battle was constricting in many places. Those allied against Torrlond were retreating as their numerous foes beat them back toward Thulhan's blackened walls. It would not be long before the enemy overwhelmed them. *We're losing. But we'll take some with us.*

When he turned ahead, a line of ten Markmen stood between him and Thulhan. The northerners wore byrnies and helms, and most held spears and shields, though four bore swords.

Gnorn stepped in front. "I'll handle this lot. Get her to the city."

"You can't take them alone," said Orvandil.

An arrow ripped into the knee of one of the Markmen. He dropped his spear as he buckled and cried out.

"I won't have to," said Gnorn. "Here come friends. Now go!"

Four Ellonders and two Sildharae joined the Dweorg as he rushed at the northerners with his battle-axe.

Orvandil glanced at Sequara's shoulder. Blood dripped from Gnorn's bindings. He needed to hurry, or she would bleed to death. He would come back for the Dweorg. Hastening toward Thulhan, he looked back once. Gnorn's axe flashed in the melee, but he had no time to follow what was happening.

He ran towards the city's western gate. The battle had not neared the city, though it seemed only a matter of time. When he arrived, he kicked the great oak doors bound with thick iron bands. "Open the gate! Open at once!"

High above, a young woman's head appeared atop the wall, a spear's tip next to it. The head disappeared, but a series of loud clacks sounded from within, and the gate creaked open a few inches. Three women, two dark-haired and young and one grey-haired, met Orvandil and reached out for Sequara. In their wide eyes he saw fear, but they had not forgotten kindness. He handed the body over, and together they held her.

"The shoulder wound," he said in the Northern Tongue as he pointed, wishing he had troubled himself to learn more Andumaic when he was in Asdralad. "You must stop the bleeding. She's Sequara of Asdralad. Hide her somewhere. Keep her alive."

The eldest of the three nodded, and he hoped she understood. Knowing the easterners' respect for sorcerers, Orvandil reckoned they would give her the best care they could.

He turned back to the battle. The gate slammed shut as he sprinted towards where he had left behind Gnorn.

25
SEEKING THE ELDEST

As he struggled to hold on to the rock he dangled from, Dayraven recognized the raven that landed three feet above him with a loud chortle. The moment its beady eyes gazed into his, he knew in the midst of his desperation this was the bird that led him to the elf in the Southweald another lifetime ago. The raven seemed real enough. At least it had not turned transparent white yet. It grasped precariously onto a bit of rock as it stared down at him, its wings flapping to keep it in place as the wind ruffled its jet feathers. So close, it appeared a large bird.

Between clenched teeth Dayraven groaned, "Help."

The raven croaked in answer and bobbed its head, jabbing its shiny beak toward the rock beneath its toes, well out of Dayraven's reach.

"Too far. Can't."

His body swayed in the wind. His fingers slipped a little more. A spasm shook his aching arms, and he gasped at the pain in his strained tendons. He glanced down. The rocky bottom of the cliff two hundred feet below waited to receive him and make an end of it. A couple heartbeats of flailing terror, then it would be over when rocks shattered his flesh and bones. He looked up again. The raven still sat there, cocking its head aside as if measuring the distance of Dayraven's fall.

The bird chortled again, seeming to smile with its eyes. He sensed wisdom behind the tiny black orbs. As he watched the raven, his mind calmed. Something in its gaze assured him that, whatever the outcome of his struggle on this cliff might be, life would go on.

Staring into its glassy black eyes, he lost sense of his muscles tearing with the effort to hold on, the hissing wind toying with him, the fear of falling to his death, and the bitter frustration of not accomplishing his task. All of that receded as if it were someone else hanging on for his life. Instead, there was only the soughing of the elf-shard's dark whisper in his mind and the raven's eyes, which grew as in a vision until he beheld his reflection in them:

A desperate young man clung to a section of wet rock, one of his fingers seeping blood where a fingernail had ripped off, his sweaty hair sticking to his forehead, veins popping out of neck and temples, arms trembling with the effort to grasp onto the rock that meant the tentative difference between life and death. But it was not just *his* life and death at stake. The raven knew this better than the young man did.

At once, the raven's eyes became Dayraven's. The blue flecks of his irises surrounded the bird's inky little orbs, and for a moment he was uncertain as to which pair of eyes he was staring out of. The world shifted from empty dawn sky to a breathtaking view of the landscape below the Wyrmberg, a fine place to sport over. He gazed down at himself, understanding he had become the raven. He *was* the raven, and they had always been one.

As he peered down, he perceived a crevice the young man struggling below could not see. The crevice was inches above the young man's hands, a perfect handhold. Such a small crevice, but enough. The young man hesitated. Making himself believe in the existence of this small crack in the cliff face, a cleft his own eyes had never seen, he forced his left hand to release the rock it clawed onto. Crying out with the effort, he grasped at the crevice. His fingers found the rough fissure and dug in, and with that small success came a burst of euphoria and energy. The young man dragged his body inches up.

Giving an approving nod and croak, the raven tapped its beak toward the next handhold. He watched the bleeding right hand shake toward it, veins protruding and snaking over bones under slick flesh.

The hand grasped hard rock. The man hauled his body a few more inches away from death.

After the next handhold, the young man's toes found a place to dig into. The rest of the ascent went by in a blur as the raven's eyes guided him. All the while, the bird flapped and chortled with triumphant laughter. Even though the last few feet of cliff jutted outward, the raven's guidance gave the man courage. He scrambled up without thinking about anything but the next handhold and the moment he was in.

Getting a firm grip on the cliff's lip with both hands, he let his legs swing out as if his body were a pendulum. When they came back, he used the momentum to swing them up over his head, and his left knee found the top. With his leg and hands, he clambered and pulled the rest of his body up, scraping his knees on the rock through his wool breeches but not caring about the pain. He rolled over onto his back. When he lay atop the cliff panting with exhaustion and jubilation, the vision of himself from the raven's eyes disappeared. Dayraven returned to his body.

As his natural senses asserted themselves, the ache rushed back to his trembling arms and back, his torn knees burned, and his right hand's index finger throbbed. None of it mattered. He closed his eyes as he lay face up, the sun turning the darkness behind his eyelids blood red. He was alive. His chest heaved as he gulped in breaths. The air was cool and sweet. Even the mountain seemed less a foe and more a teacher now. The icy caress of the elf-shard's unchanging breath glided along the surface of his mind. It seemed to wait with infinite patience. The raven croaked somewhere to his right. He turned his head toward it as he opened his eyes.

Twenty feet away, the raven played in a patch of snow. Falling on its back, it rolled down a gentle slope. A jumble of black feathers tumbling and flinging bits of snow in its wake, the raven croaked with pleasure at its game. It disappeared with a plop when it rolled into a large pool. Ripples skimmed across the tarn's clear surface.

He recognized it at once. A wide eye gazing up at the sky, its clear blue water reflected a few wisps of cloud and the greys and blacks of peaks rising around it. One half of the mountain lake showed the mirror image of the vast black mass waiting just beyond it. *The cave.*

With a sudden splash, the raven shot out of the tarn's center, again disturbing the surface, where clouds and peaks broke into shimmers of white, grey, and black. As it flew up, it transformed from black to ghostly white, just as in the Southweald. *I knew it was the same one*, thought Dayraven as he followed the bird's flight. The ghost-raven changed course abruptly, diving straight for the cave's huge entrance. Darkness swallowed it.

He sat up. He kept his eyes on the cave as he rose, aching in every tendon and joint of his body. Fixing his gaze on the spot where the raven had disappeared, he waited for it to emerge. When it did not come, he studied the cave. A gaping hole forty feet high and just as wide, it seemed so deep it might lead to the Wyrmberg's core. *Did Gorsarhad make this lair, or was this abyss always here?* Surrounding it on every side were jagged rocks, and behind it loomed the last third of the mountain, all covered in snow gleaming in the morning light. He squinted and looked behind him. Though it felt like an eternity since he had begun to scale the cliff, it was not long after dawn. *I must hurry. This is the dawn I saw in the true-dream.*

He looked again at the cave, still hoping the raven would fly out. *Has the dragon devoured it?* But Dayraven smiled as a flash of insight came to him. He understood what the raven was and where it came from. *It will never emerge until I go in and come out again. I am the raven. I've played the game. Life hiding and leading itself on.*

He laughed, just as the raven had laughed when it rolled into the tarn. *I am the raven.* It all made sense, at least in the realm of origins. He had called the raven out of himself, and it came when needed. *The raven is me. Twice it has visited. Perhaps I can learn to call it and soar with it. But another task awaits.*

Dayraven walked closer to the tarn. When he reached it he knelt, his stiff legs bending until his raw knees rested on rock. As he peered into the little mountain lake, a ragged, gaunt version of himself gazed back. Sweat darkened his light brown hair, which stuck to his head, and his beard was long. His wind-chafed cheeks were hollow, and his blue eyes looked out of shadowed sockets. The skin of his lips was so dry and chapped it was flaking off.

Beneath his image rested silver stones on the tarn's bottom. His hands reached in, and his face dispersed with the ripples. The water sent icy needles into his skin, but he enjoyed the sensation as the blood on his index finger floated away in a tiny red cloud. He brought his face closer and splashed it, then he cupped his hands and raised the water to his cracked lips. When he swallowed, cold fingers slithered down his throat. It tasted clean and crisp. What was more, in the water he sensed the great dragon's presence. *Her drinking pool.* When he rose, his body shivered once. *Time to visit her lair.* "Gorsarhad, eldest of dragons. Our meeting is long due."

Dayraven slid his pack off his shoulders and let it lie next to the tarn, his thick fur cloak bundled inside along with his other belongings. He needed them no more. Staggering forward, he made his way around the tarn towards the cave's mouth, whence a sulphuric stench emanated. The iron studs of his climbing boots scraped rock as he forced his weary legs to take steps. Here and there among blackened rocks lay animals' bleached bones: a horse's thigh bone, a troll's rib cage, a cow's skull with curled horns, and other bits and pieces from Gorsarhad's past meals. As he trudged forward, he wondered if any of the white fragments had belonged to people.

The mouth of darkness grew in front of him. He prepared to unleash the inner darkness dwelling in his mind. Journeying to the realm of origins in an instant, he dissolved the barrier that kept at bay the presence of the elf. The shard quickened and surged with such intensity that his body rocked forward and his arms spread out as his energy exploded outward with the elf-shard. For a moment all was brightness. To the limits of creation it took him, and it seemed to flirt with the idea of passing beyond it. But the tiny, fragmented presence within it that was Dayraven kept it grounded. Some part of it recognized the fragile, fleeting body inhabiting the world of forms. It remembered that some purpose had brought it to that place.

The cave waited. Walking closer, he wondered if even now the dragon watched him approaching. Silence seeped from the murk.

Beyond any doubt, the beast was aware of him. He made his way toward her lair. When he reached the entrance's threshold, it dwarfed his body in its baggy clothes. It seemed to Dayraven that no light could penetrate the thick darkness within. He listened for some sound, but all was still. Contrasting with the cold wind at his back, heat brushed against his face from the cave accompanied by the pungent smell like brimstone. *She's within. She waits.*

He entered the darkness. It was warm and dry inside. As he stepped forward a few paces, his boots' iron studs sparked against the rock, their clacks echoing in the vastness. So black was the murk that, when he put his hands before his eyes, he could not see them. The heat from within the cave rushed toward him, but he reckoned its source was still distant. Putting one foot in front of another, he walked in the direction he thought was straight, though the darkness was disorienting. He kept his hands in front of him in case he bumped into a rock wall, but his mind was as calm as the still surface of the tarn outside. The huge presence of the eldest of dragons grew with each step forward. *She's within, but still some way off.*

Shuffling forward, he remained in the stillness of the elf-shard's energy, which connected him to something infinite. In that calmness he dwelled, perceiving the pulse of life all around and within him. His heartbeat was slow. His lungs expanded and contracted to a steady rhythm. His blood coursed. Even as the muscles, sinews, and bones of his legs brought him further into darkness, he became part of the unseen mountain around him and remembered its long story. Ancient rock, bones of the earth, stood solid beneath his feet. Old was the Wyrmberg, unfathomable years older than its name. Far below the rock, remote but powerful and larger than the imagination, hot fires churned among molten rivers. Vast as it was, the solid rock between him and the fires was only a layer of skin. But he sought a different fire.

His energy flowed into the darkness. Wandering high and deep, Dayraven reached out. Many were the years the mother of dragons had dwelled there. The darkness and bare rock still remembered the children she birthed and raised. More than twenty times she nurtured her eggs, laying two or three at a time after mating with the male that proved himself mightiest by defeating or slaying his rivals. The male always flew off, leaving her to raise the young. Each time, only one baby survived: the strongest, which devoured its siblings at the first chance.

The strong one grew until it could fend for itself. Then, after years of mothering, she drove it away to find its own territory to defend. If it came back, she would kill it just as soon as she would any other serpent of the air that dared to invade her mountain. More than a score of children she had set loose on the world, and these in turn gave birth to others, which did the same. But now Gorsarhad was alone. A dragon's life was solitary, and one as old and huge as Gorsarhad brooked no company. Dayraven locked onto her presence.

He stepped forward as the sense of steel-hard scales pushed away all else from his mind. Claws, teeth, wings, and predator's eyes entered his consciousness. He had felt dragons before, and the mortal part of him awed at the memory. But Gorsarhad dwarfed those. Before her enormity, they were mere children. Her limbs were more powerful, her fire hotter. Her wings were more expansive, her scales thicker. She feared nothing, but she had forsaken the world in which she lingered so long. Hiding her bulk deep in the darkness, she brooded over memories older than all but the eldest of Eormenlond's kingdoms.

He perceived Gorsarhad was not asleep. In fact, the cunning old serpent of the air knew he was coming. In the bowels of her dark lair she awaited him, laughing inwardly at a man so foolish as to enter her domain. Her surprisingly sophisticated thoughts formed in his mind as if she spoke them in words:

Foolish mortal. Why have you come to disturb my rest? I smelled your soft flesh in the night beneath my lair. I let you lie to see how far your madness would bring you. Many are the years since one of your kind wandered here. In my youth they sought to slay me. Some of the babblers tried to bring me under their power, but I was too strong for all. Whether they brought steel or sorcery, I devoured them. Do you imagine I'm so old now I can't defend myself? Do you think to find a dragon's corpse here? A pile of bones? Mortal, I'll burn you first, then I'll consume you.

In the darkness of the cave, Dayraven smiled grimly. *I've brought something older and bigger than you, dragon.* The power of the elf-shard radiated from him like a beacon made from the sun's fire.

Even as it blasted his spirit in infinite directions, he rode the vast energy. Once again the presence of the elf seemed sentient, something separate from him and voracious. But he felt no fear and he managed to hold on to an awareness of the tiny pieces of himself, like the glimmering of a star amidst the much larger darkness of the night sky. Pointing the way, this glimmering reminded him of his purpose in visiting the Wyrmberg. A dire need was unfolding in the world of forms, which seemed so remote in its smallness and fleetingness. The will that was Dayraven inside the enormity of the elf's power directed itself toward the beast awaiting him in the realm of flesh.

He opened his mind to Gorsarhad, reaching outward to put his thoughts in her mind: *Eldest of Dragons. Gorsarhad the Mighty. In the hour of need I come to you.*

So, thought she, *one of the babblers. I've met your kind before, mortal. You burn the same as the others.*

I'm not the same as the others. I've not come to harm you.

Puny fleshling, I reck not why you come. You've trespassed where it's death to walk. You're food, though little more than a bite, and I'll devour you.

Within the serene indifference and atemporality of the elf-state, Dayraven knew what the serpent of the air would do before she even thought of it. *Gorsarhad, though your fires are mighty, I'll tame them.*

Gorsarhad laughed in her mind. *Die, fleshling.*

A flash of red heat erupted and flooded the entire cave in an instant.

The sudden brightness was blinding, but he was ready. He held his hands before him. The dragon's breath parted before them, leaving a cocoon of safety within the rush of fire. Flames licked all around him, and his skin felt their heat, but none touched him as he calmly drew upon the power of the elf to command them. After a few moments, Gorsarhad must have been satisfied that the intruder was no more. The onslaught of flames ceased. But it did not take her long to realize her unwanted company still breathed.

I still smell your raw flesh, feeble man. Long has it been since any being thwarted my fire. I would know who you are before I slay you.

Very well, mother of dragons. I'm the raven that arises in the east and departs in the west.

You speak soothly, for ravens are ever foolish and noisy. Such birds are not even worth eating.

I'm the forest dweller.

Forests are full of little creatures hiding in trees. Such defenses are weak. My flames consume them.

I'm the friend of Dweorgs.

Dweorgs hide under rocks. They're tougher than most of your kind, but they burn easily enough.

I'm the commander of trolls.

Trolls are stupid creatures, and they taste foul.

I'm the bringer of waves.

Then you may bathe my scales ere I slay you. Water is naught to me.

I'm the master of wargs.

Wargs take little to master. They flee from my roar.

I'm the tamer of flames.

I've seen that already, but don't think it will save you, fleshling. Many are my weapons.

I'm the scaler of mountains.

My wings bring me high above the clouds. Mountains are my resting places.

I'm the wielder of lightning.

My scales bear scratches from the yellow fire. Fire can't slay fire.

I'm the thrice-born who sees with elf's eyes.

For the first time, the mother of dragons hesitated. Though she seldom spared a thought for them since they were nothing she could eat, elves were beings she did not understand. *Such boasting is madness. You're no elf, for I smell your mortal stench. Next to my years, your little life is the blink of an eye, the flicker of a flame.*

That may be, mighty Gorsarhad, but I've traveled over many kingdoms of Eormenlond and seen many things.

Foolish mortal. You've seen nothing. All this rock and dirt beneath us is only one land of many, and not even the greatest. My wings have taken me over many kingdoms of your kind far over the great water. But wherever you are, your kind is the same. You cower at my fire, and your years are brief. I've seen the coming and going of your kingdoms. You breed like maggots, and you destroy one another over and over again. Whoever you are, and wherever you come from, your people will be dust.

Mother of dragons, I have no people.

Liar. Only dragons dwell alone. Your kind is too soft and afraid. Only we are strong enough.

But I tell you truly, Gorsarhad, I left my people. I died to them, but I live for all. I came back from Oruma's realm to find you. Together, we'll set your children free and bring balance to Eormenlond.

I care not for your kingdoms, fleshling. They'll be gone soon enough. You're petty creatures of the moment.

Nevertheless, eldest of dragons, you will *help me. For you've seen much, but I've seen more. You've flown high, but I've flown higher. Above the stars I soared, to the beginning of all things, and there I witnessed the births and deaths of worlds. Before the life-tree Laeroth I stood, and I drank in its majesty for aeons untold. You and I are both its tools, and you'll go with me now.*

Mortal, your insolence stinks in my nose. I've had enough of you.

The cave's floor boomed and shook when a tremendous force crashed into it. Bits of rock and dust fell from the roof high overhead and cracked or settled all over. Ahead in the darkness, Gorsarhad brought down another foot, and the cave reverberated again. Boom! Boom! More pebbles and dust rained on Dayraven. The beast's clawed feet pounded the cave's floor one after another, each time growing louder until the noise threatened to burst his ears.

He had little time. Fortunately, his connection with her essence was already strong, for he had nurtured it throughout the exchange between their minds. All that remained was for him to assert his will within her. *No, Gorsarhad, we must go together.* In that instant, he was one with the dragon.

The thundering of Gorsarhad's feet slowed then stopped. The silence that followed was as complete as the darkness. When the giant serpent of the air snorted, her hot breath swept back his hair. The mother of dragons stood rigid, like an enormous statue. In the darkness high above, two huge orbs the color of amber glowed. Now, with his energy dwelling in her, he saw from those dragon eyes. The breathtaking vision that unfolded was different from the blackness his human eyes beheld.

Within the cave were long formations of rock dripping from the ceiling and sprouting from the floor, arching and twisting in sundry directions. Some of the formations put him in mind of the ornate spires and buttresses in great cities, only nature wrought these rocks into graceful shapes more whimsical and fantastic. Bits of silver sparkled all over the cavern's walls, while dazzling gemstones gleamed red and blue. It was as if the cavern had captured the stars in its bizarre walls. He marveled at the strange beauty of this world out of reach for human eyes. He also noted that Gorsarhad saw him well. He was a puny, pathetic thing far below her like a small rodent. He did not wonder why she dismissed his kind as fleeting fleshlings.

Even as he saw from her eyes, Dayraven probed the recesses of the lingworm's mind. There he found hot fury. This mortal had somehow commanded her to stop, and she had no choice but to obey, as if her limbs belonged to someone else. She strained to wrap her jaws around the fleshling, but something she did not understand held her back. She felt it dimly, like a gentle breeze unworthy of notice. But somehow, all her enormous power could not bring her one inch forward against this breeze wrapping around her. In her mind sprang to life something the mother of dragons had not known for a long time. She almost had forgotten what *fear* was, but now it held her in its grip.

What have you done to me, fleshling? thought she. *How can one so wretched and small have such power?*

Because I know who and what I am. I'm this mortal standing before you, whose body you could crush as easily as I might swat a fly. But I'm also the raven and the wolf, the water and the fire. I'm the oak and the ash, the elk and the bear. I'm the ray of sunlight and the frost it melts on the grass. I'm the trout and the eagle that devours it. I'm the troll and the sparrow, the wind and the rain. I'm the deer and the catamount that stalks it as prey. I'm the salty wave and the cliff it beats. I'm the newborn babe and the old man bending toward the grave. I'm this mountain standing beneath us. And, mighty Gorsarhad, I am also you.

So fear not, mother of dragons, for I wish you no harm. We have a task we must accomplish together, a deed to perform that will reverberate beyond my small life or even your long one. Now, come forth from your lair. We have need of your swift wings. Come forth, and fly like the wind to the great dwelling place of mortals. To the city of Thulhan we must journey, for even now things come close to the point of no return.

Using the dragon's eyes as a guide, the wizard Dayraven turned around and walked toward the cave's mouth. Gorsarhad's mighty feet pounded behind as they made their way by twisting formations of rock. Soon enough, his own eyes squinted at brightness seeping toward him from the entrance. He smiled when he emerged and the world's light bathed him once again. The cold wind buffeted his face and tugged his clothes. Clear was the tarn's blue water, and beyond it, sharp peaks and shadowed vales stretched further than he could see. The sun had not yet climbed high, for which the mortal part of Dayraven was thankful. But he also saw with the elf's eyes, and those eyes beheld things far beyond the world of forms. *There's still time, but we must hasten. Many have already perished.* Behind him, Gorsarhad came forth.

In the light of day, he regarded the largest living creature he had ever conceived of, the eldest of dragons. Her bulk just fit through the huge entrance to the cave as she folded her wings to her body. But when she fully emerged, she stretched them, sending out a great gust. The sky disappeared behind two colossal sails of a wine-red hue with dark veins branching all over them. From head to tail, she was easily seventy-five feet long, her wing span greater still. Her scales were such a dark red they appeared almost black, as if her body's heat had baked them over her long existence. Glistening, ebony colored spikes the length of casting spears ran down her spine. Sharp were the dark claws curling from her feet, and immense were the thick, muscled legs extending from a belly as big as a longship's. Her long, serpentine neck led to a head with bulging jaw muscles. The many fires that rushed from her huge throat had yellowed her teeth, but he knew they were harder than rock and sharp enough to shear through the strongest steel. Graceful, curving horns the color of ivory extended back from her brow, beneath which her fearsome, proud eyes gazed forth. Aswirl with shades of amber and slit down the middle with black, those eyes looked down in wonder at the ragged little thing that had mastered her.

The mother of dragons ceased to struggle against Dayraven. They thought with one mind when the greatest of lingworms bent low to allow the mortal to crawl on her back. Heat met his flesh when he touched the thick, crack-lined scales near the beast's neck.

He stepped on Gorsarhad's right forefoot and clambered up the huge limb like the trunk of a thick old tree. But the scales were smoother than bark, and far harder. The young wizard grasped a spike on the great worm's back and pulled his body up. Atop her back, he stepped toward the huge head. Just behind where the neck joined the body, the last of the tall spikes made a good rest for his back, so he settled in there with his legs astride the base of her neck. On Gorsarhad's neck were shorter spikes, and around the first of these he clasped his hands. Smooth it was, and as sharp at its tip as a dagger.

When he was thus secure, Gorsarhad stood. The dragon's memories of flight were part of Dayraven through the elf-shard's power. But for the mortal wrapped in that power, the sensation was dizzying and thrilling as he rose with her. His fingers tightened their grip. The dragon's majestic wings unfurled, and when she brought them down, their gust sent dust scurrying and formed ripples over the tarn's surface. Again she flapped, and her huge body rose. Another flap, and they jerked upwards as her forefeet left the ground. When she beat her wings again, her hind legs sprang, and Dayraven's heart leaped at the same time. Had it not been for the dispassion of the elf-state, he would have been terrified. As he looked down, the Wyrmberg receded below. He recognized this view of the mountain from his vision in Orudwyn. They were high in the air.

Gorsarhad caught a current and spread her wings. As they sailed through the heavens, the chill wind blasted his hair back and brought moisture to his eyes. But Gorsarhad's warmth kept him comfortable enough, and her upraised neck shielded him from the worst of the wind. Even with tears running down his cheeks, he would not have closed his eyes for anything.

Far below, the rugged landscape rushed by. White peaks reached up for them while patches of green forest blanketed the mountains' feet, where their roots went deep into the earth. Here and there, soft, billowing clouds streaked over the blue welkin. The clouds' giant shadows eased over mountains and valleys in dark swaths that morphed with the land's shape. As his mount flew north with speed greater than any creature could match, Dayraven awed at the stark beauty of land and sky. *Wondrous. Sublime. Eormenlond is beyond description. But I must reach the battle in time. Make haste, eldest of dragons. Make haste, lest there be no one to tell of Eormenlond's beauty, only its sorrow.*

26
THE PROPHET OF EDAN

With Sweothol and his long dagger drawn, Orvandil rushed headlong into the group of Markmen gathered around Gnorn, who, down on one knee, held his axe above his head to parry a sword blow. Three northerners went down before they knew what hit them: one hamstrung, one with blood streaming from his neck, and another, who had raised his sword to strike at the Dweorg again, missing an arm.

But the Markmen were not cowards or fools. As their comrade lay in a fetal tuck and screamed with blood pulsing from the stump of raw meat and bone where his arm had been, they re-formed their circle, this time enveloping Gnorn and Orvandil. They closed in, waiting to see who would rush first. The Thjoth stood with blade poised.

Mangled bodies from the earlier struggle lay here and there. Orvandil recognized the corpses of the Ellonders and Sildharae who had come to help Gnorn before, along with a dozen dead northerners. He reckoned he would add to the count before he went down.

"What took you so long?" Gnorn grunted as he tried to struggle up, but he remained kneeling and leaning on his battle-axe. Blood ran down his left thigh, his right arm, and his helmless head, washing over the earlier wound across his face. He managed a weak smile, though he wavered and seemed likely to teeter over.

Orvandil stood by him. "Sorry, my friend. I'm here now." *We put up a good fight. A good day to make an end of it.*

The circle closed. The Thjoth knew he could slay two or three at most before their blades struck. Poised to spring, he gazed at them and tried to gauge which would take the lead. Like wolves encircling a dangerous prey, the northerners stalked forward warily.

"To the Dragonbane! To the Dragonbane!" someone cried out nearby. A group of blue-kirtled Ellonders rushed toward them, and Orvandil half smiled to see several Thjoths among them. He lifted one eyebrow when he saw who led the Thjoths: the chieftain Eyolf, elder brother of Orvandil's slain foster-brother. For a brief moment, Eyolf's eyes met Orvandil's. The chieftain gave him a curt nod.

Most of the Markmen turned to face their attackers, but several lunged at Orvandil. Steel rang out, men screamed, and Orvandil fought for his life and Gnorn's.

He parried the first warrior's sword blow with Sweothol and sank his sharp dagger through the man's byrny into his chest. The next attacker jabbed with a spear, but he spun aside and closed in, rendering the longer weapon useless. Sweothol arced through the man's thigh, shearing off the leg and leaving him rolling in agony. The Thjoth ducked under another blade and plunged Sweothol forward, skewering the blade's wielder off the ground. The body crashed into another attacker, knocking him down under the corpse. Orvandil pressed down with sudden force, and Sweothol pierced the second man, who gasped as his dead comrade lay on top of him.

Two more attackers set upon Orvandil. The Thjoth threw the long dagger in his left hand, and it plunged into one man's neck. The foeman tumbled back hacking and clutching his ruined throat, but his comrade reached Orvandil. As the second man's sword came down, Orvandil tugged on Sweothol, but the blade stuck in the two corpses he had embedded it in. In the fraction of a moment before his attacker's sword bit, the Thjoth only had time to wonder where it would land.

Another blur of steel, and a battle-axe shattered the northerner's helm in a spray of blood, sending him down. Gnorn stood over the felled body, panting with a wild look in his eyes. He turned to Orvandil. "Always having to watch your back," he said with a grimace. He swayed before dropping his axe and collapsing.

On the edge of the battlefield, the Supreme Priest Bledla recovered from the jolt of bitter pain that had accompanied his dragon's death. *They are instruments of Edan,* he thought. *Like us all, they may perish in His service.* The agony was immense, for he had put part of his energy into the beast. A lesser man might have let the pain master him, but not Bledla. He clutched his temples for a moment and stifled a scream as he gritted his teeth. Receding pulses of hot torment still seared his eye and brain as if steel had punctured them. Afterwards, he focused and meditated on Edan as he held on to the other eleven dragons. It took time to gather his energy, but Edan gave him strength. Not long after his dragon's death, he was ready for revenge. *I'll make them rue their wickedness. As light scatters darkness, I'll destroy them. First, the heretic.*

Like an eagle stalking a rabbit from a mile above, Bledla sought Galdor's presence. He sensed the familiar energy of his high priests placed around the field of battle. Not far away, Joruman and one of the dragons beat down King Naitaran of Sildharan. But, like a familiar taste on the wind, Galdor was out there. *Let Joruman have his kill*, he thought as Naitaran redirected the dragon's flames and fell back trying to deflect the wizard's fire crackling from Joruman's hands. *Galdor's within my grasp.*

He knew the apostate's presence all too well, and with the white-kirtled temple guards surrounding him and two of his dragons defending him from above, he devoted his full attention to finding the weaver of deception. Following the scent, Bledla pushed through the melee.

There was a loud ping, and a temple guard went down writhing with an arrow through his helm. There were still about fifty of them nearby, all devoting their lives to the supreme priest's safety.

Sensing that Galdor was escaping him, Bledla made a tight fist and called a dragon to obey his thoughts. The beast swooped down and vomited its fiery breath on a broad swath of the battle. The flames withered shrieking and flailing soldiers of both sides, but Bledla's progress towards his enemy quickened with the path cleared. Such sacrifice was necessary for the fulfillment of Edan's will.

Through choking smoke and screams he hastened. The supreme priest stepped over the charred body of a Torrlonder with fragments of his grey kirtle still smoldering, mouth and eyes wide with the shock before death. *We're all instruments of Edan. His purpose is all that matters.* When Galdor's presence grew strong again, Bledla caught a glimpse through the press of a white-bearded old man in a tattered and patched brown robe. The old deceiver. *Servant of demons,* he thought as a cold smile crossed his face, *your time has come.*

"Alakathon gorghothae ar galathon khuldar! Vortalion bhurudonae im paradon bholdar!" boomed Bledla's deep voice. The air cracked and flared with a mighty explosion when the supreme priest called upon his power. A huge blue current of wizard's fire erupted from his outstretched hands and streaked towards Galdor, searing and instantly slaying soldiers of both sides in its path before ripping aside their bodies. Others started and shielded their faces.

A second flash of light and brilliant scattering of wizard's fire revealed that the cunning heretic had felt him coming and had sung a counterspell, creating a shield of wizard's fire that absorbed the shock and dispersed it. But now the supreme priest had a clear view of his oldest and most bitter foe, who stood fifty feet away at the end of a row of smoldering bodies. Combatants all around shook their dazed heads, rubbing their eyes and poking their ears. Several Torrlonder soldiers recovered and approached behind Galdor, but some squat, ugly fellow with a green bag slung over his back waved his sword and held them back, leaving the wizard free to face Bledla. *I'll beat him down. He can't last.*

Bledla lashed out again at Galdor with another enormous bolt of wizard's fire, a blast of energy that drowned out all other sounds and bathed the battlefield in light and shadow. The apostate countered with a large wheel of buzzing blue energy from his hands. White light exploded. The impact knocked the brown-robed wizard back and scattered his energy shield in flickering splinters of wizard's fire, but he stayed on his feet.

The grey-kirtled Torrlonders pressed hard on the stout man who covered Galdor's back. Three struck out at once. The squat fellow took a wound on his thigh. Another Torrlonder slashed his sword arm, and he dropped his blade. Galdor looked back as his helper collapsed. Bledla seized his chance.

The wizard's fire sprang with enormous violence from his outstretched arms, streaking toward the foe as a blinding and deafening column of jagged energy. At the same time, Galdor bent back low with blue tendrils of snake-like light writhing from his hands. Even as he fell backwards, the old man caught ahold of Bledla's current with the energy from his hands and slung the bolt behind him into the Torrlonders that had cut down his helper. Their bodies flew, limbs twisting as the searing heat granted them quick deaths.

The supreme priest's smile changed to a snarl. The cunning heretic had expected the strike and appropriated the supreme priest's energy for his ruse. He vented his righteous fury in a scream and prepared to assault the old deceiver again.

Galdor shook his head as he tottered up with trembling limbs. The heretic's last effort had drained him. Recognizing his old foe's weakness, Bledla grinned. "Now die for all your treachery, worshipper of demons!" Raising his hands, he channeled Edan's strength into the energy streaming from him.

ORVANDIL KNELT BY GNORN, WHOSE EYES ROLLED UP AS HE coughed. Blood covered the Dweorg's face from a deep cut on his forehead. The Thjoth glanced up to see if any threat approached. Seven Ellonders and Thjoths, including Eyolf, still fought, and they were pushing back the four remaining Markmen. Steel rang, and a northerner fell with blood on his neck.

A hoarse voice cried, "The Mark! The Mark!" Three more northerners rushed over to help their brethren. The tall, slender one leading them made short work of the Thjoth who tried to cut him down, dodging the blade then burying his sword in the Thjoth's face.

Whirling to slip past an Ellonder's blow, the northerner swung his sword's edge through the blue-kirtled man's sword arm below the elbow, shearing through muscle and bone.

Eyolf stood before the deadly Markman with his blade ready while the others fought.

"No," whispered Orvandil as he rose.

The northerner feigned a thrust at Eyolf, who hurried to parry the blow. Almost admiring the warrior, Orvandil rushed forward but knew he was too late to stop what would follow. The Markman side-stepped Eyolf's attempt to correct his blade and slashed at the Thjothic chieftain's neck, which yielded like wheat to a scythe. Orvandil stopped and watched the man who had once been like his elder brother fall to the earth, which soaked in his blood.

"Markman." Dragonbane stood with Sweothol poised.

The warrior he addressed turned his head toward him. His masked helm hid his eyes, but the beard below it was more grey than light brown. Yet his lithe body did not suggest old age. Though slender, his arms were knotted with muscles, and his stance testified he knew well how to wield his blade. He carried no shield, and blood stained the brown kirtle he wore over his byrny.

"Thjoth. Ready yourself," said the Markman. He left behind his fellows, who engaged with the remaining Thjoths and Ellonders, to rush toward Orvandil.

Orvandil did not wait for him. The two sprinted at each other with swords aloft. The northerner swung high. A fraction of a heartbeat before they clashed, he shifted his blade to strike lower. The skillful motion was a blur, and Orvandil just managed to swing Sweothol down before his opponent sank his blade in his thigh.

The swords sang as they clashed, and the warriors rushed by each other. Orvandil wheeled around, knowing this foe would waste little time. Sweothol rushed up to parry, and steel rang out again. His attacker was not as tall as he was nor as strong, but the man was no weakling, and he was quick as a cat. *A cunning old warrior. Be careful.*

He studied his opponent as they circled one another, legs spread in a wide stance and swords set before them. Each of them was taut as a bowstring and prepared to spring. Orvandil sought a weakness in the Markman. Nothing presented itself.

BLEDLA POURED HIS POWER INTO DESTROYING HIS ARCH-RIVAL, THE wizard Galdor. Wishing to make his victory against his oldest enemy a decisive decree of Edan's will, he kept his dragons behind him to guard his back. He alone would defeat the apostate and wipe away his heresy. The temple guards rushed out of the way as the supreme priest and the traitor grappled with one another in a lethal contest of magic.

Blinding explosions of light erupted. Wizard's fire droned and writhed and scorched the earth, spraying clods of soil and cratering the battleground. Everyone fled from the dueling wizards. Bledla cried out as his energy blazed at his foe, who met it with his current of power. After colliding, the streams of wizard's fire twisted then flashed with white heat, but each time the explosions grew closer to Galdor, filling the air with smoke and an acrid smell. The old deceiver was lasting longer than Bledla expected, but he was weakening. *I'll bring him down soon.* Burn marks streaked Galdor's forehead and cheeks, and his brown robe smoked in places. He staggered back as Bledla advanced.

There was a brief pause in their struggle as Bledla prepared to deal out the death blow. Through curling smoke and haze, he beheld his foe thirty feet in front of him. Galdor gasped for air, sagging like a tired old man and mumbling a song of origin. *He lacks the strength to attack. Now. Slay him now.* Standing tall and erect, the supreme priest prepared his spell.

Even as he did, something coiled around his feet and legs. His lips curling in a smile of contempt, Bledla glanced down at the roots snaking up his legs and torso. When he looked up, a berm of rock and soil was rising from the earth before Galdor, who disappeared behind it. "Just like you to cower, Galdor. But it will do you no good." He held his arms high then thrust them forward as he screamed the song of origin. A massive trunk of wizard's fire bleached the battleground and fractured the air.

Bledla's bolt smashed into the berm with an explosive splintering of light, sending rocks and clods of soil flying and spinning. When the dust and smoke cleared, an ecstatic smile crossed the supreme priest's face. The feeble barrier was no more, and the old heretic lay on his back, wheezing with ragged breaths and struggling to rise. His old hands clutched the air, and a groan escaped his throat.

Bledla placed his hands on the twisted roots that had reached his chest. He snarled as he sent a jolt of wizard's fire through them. The blackened roots snapped and crumbled away when the supreme priest advanced.

He watched in righteous jubilation as the apostate struggled to delay the inevitable. Rolling onto his stomach, Galdor tried to push himself to his hands and knees. But his arms trembled, and he collapsed onto his face. Though the screams and din of battle penetrated the smoke, Bledla was alone with his foe. It was a fitting end. The supreme priest gloried as his triumph approached. A gust passed overhead, and he looked up. One of his dragons vomited fire on the enemy troops, the flames glowing eerily through the reek. *Nothing can prevent Edan's victory.*

He strode within fifteen feet of his foe, who lay in a heap and struggled even to breathe. Bledla's fists closed in triumph. At long last, the moment had come. "You're finished now, Galdor. It's over. I always told you the Kingdom of the Eternal would come in my time."

Galdor's hand trembled and reached out feebly.

The supreme priest raised his own strong, wiry hands and brought them down. A massive bolt of wizard's fire erupted from them toward his vanquished enemy.

Again and again, Orvandil and the Markman came at each other in a flurry of sword blows. So powerful and graceful was their deadly struggle that warriors of both sides ceased fighting to gaze at the spectacle. Sweothol rang and vibrated as Orvandil parried, dove, and slashed. The Thjoth was tiring, but the northerner too had sweat glistening over his leathery skin and was breathing hard. Yet neither man slowed the pace.

The gathering crowd cheered like Orvandil and this tough northerner were the champions of their respective sides deciding the battle's outcome, just as the Ilarchae often had it in their tribal wars. Hardly aware of the shouting all around him, the Thjoth focused on his foe's eyes. They were blue and fierce behind the masked helm. Not since he was young had anyone matched him thus. He waited for the opportunity to deal a decisive blow, but this warrior was focused and wary.

The older fighter rushed forward and feinted to the left before shifting his weight and slashing down to the right. Anticipating the move, Orvandil thrust his sword to the right. For the first time in this duel his blade tasted flesh as the warrior jerked backwards. Cheers erupted from the gathered Thjoths, Ellonders, and Sildharae.

Sweothol's edge had opened a cut on the northerner's forearm, but the man ducked low under Orvandil's next sweeping blow, and the Thjoth leapt back to avoid the counterstroke. When they separated, blood seeped down the Markman's arm. *Good. He bleeds.* But the man's expression changed as he gazed at Sweothol, eyes wide as if in shock, focusing on the hilt's red jewel.

The Markman's mouth twisted in rage. "That sword. How did *you* come by it?"

Finding the question strange in the midst of their fight, Orvandil paused. Before he got out a word, the northerner yelled, "My son! What have you done to him?"

The warrior did not wait for an answer. With inhuman speed, he surged at Orvandil, raining such quick blows on him that even the Thjoth could not follow them all. Their blades clanged, then the Markman slashed Orvandil's byrny, shearing through the mail on his shoulder. His flesh stung, and his muscle ached where a bruise would form. Though the cut did not reach deep, Orvandil took it as a warning.

He sliced to keep his opponent back, but the northman spun low to avoid the stroke and sprang up. His blade opened up Orvandil's left forearm as he lurched to avoid it. The Thjoth was glad to feel a sharp burn, which told him the steel had severed no major nerves. He backed away with blood crawling down his arm while the furious Markman swung a series of blows at him. Even as Sweothol rang out while he parried, Orvandil understood who fought him with such wild fierceness. *Dayraven's father. Gods. Of all the warriors on the battlefield.*

But he hardly had time to think. The Torrlonders and Markmen cheered as Edgil of the Mark beat him back. The Ellonders, Thjoths, and Sildharae were silent and tense now, hoping their champion could somehow defend himself from the onslaught of fury and skill. Amidst the ringing of swords, Orvandil struggled to speak.

"*Dayraven* gave . . . the blade. He's . . . a friend. Dayraven! Damn you, listen to me!"

His mouth contorting in a teeth-baring snarl, the northerner seemed to hear nothing as his sword lashed out again and again. Orvandil struggled to keep up with it, dodging and warding as best he could. *Can't slay Dayraven's father,* he thought. But if he did not, Edgil would kill him soon.

JUST WHEN BLEDLA'S IMMENSE BOLT OF WIZARD'S FIRE ERUPTED from his hands to finish Galdor, a white-robed form rushed out of the smoke. The man dove in front of the old deceiver, leaping into the current's path as he finished chanting a counterspell. A spoked wheel of blue light sprang to life, but the shield of wizard's fire was incomplete and yielded with a crack and a violent scattering of light shards. Bledla's bolt punched through and collided into the newcomer's chest. He shuddered in agony a moment as the current shook his body and danced around him, illuminating his wide-eyed face with a ghastly hue of blue. In that instant Bledla thought he recognized the man. *It can't be . . . It mustn't be.*

The priest fell to his knees, his arms flopping, his white robe smoking, and his chest a charred ruin with a gaping, bleeding hole in it. He collapsed onto his face as Bledla rushed over. The supreme priest told himself he had not seen the man's features through the smoke. *It's someone else. One of the others . . .* He reached the body, almost not daring to look.

The hair around the bald top of the head was grey. Even before he grabbed the body by the shoulder and turned it over, Bledla knew he had just slain his only true friend left in the world. He knelt and laid the head in his lap. Arna's eyes were clenched tight in agony. His chest was a ruin of stinking, blackened, and sizzling flesh. White, blood-stained ribs protruded. The blackened organs beneath them were slick. Clots of blood seeped from the huge hole, and the white robe was spattered with gore.

The eyes sprang open and locked onto Bledla, who jerked back in shock. Deep lines creased the flesh around those eyes, which peered at him accusingly. The High Priest Arna's face trembled with the effort to speak while Bledla gazed at him. Words came out, not much more than a gasp: "All . . . wrong." The shaking ceased. His eyes froze open in death.

Bledla gawked at Arna's slack face, trying to understand what his friend's last words meant. He shook with grief and rage. "Why?" he asked with eyes wide. "Why!" he screamed at the corpse.

A weak, old voice answered, "Because he understood what you could not."

Bledla dropped the head from his lap and stood up. He stared at Galdor, who had struggled to his hands and knees but still could not rise. A pained and furious scowl leapt to his face, and the supreme priest understood at once. "The traitor in our midst . . . The one who handed you the song of origin of dragons . . . How could he? You . . . *perverted* him!" Spittle flew from his lips as he screamed. "After all these years, how did you seduce him again? We were to usher in the Kingdom of the Eternal!"

Tears streaming down his old cheeks, Galdor looked him in the eyes. "I *loved* him. And you . . . You haven't brought the Kingdom of the Eternal, Bledla. Only death."

"Foe of Edan! Slave of demons! I'll bring *your* death now!"

The supreme priest raised his hands to strike. At that moment, something huge blocked out the sun, casting its shadow over him and yanking his awareness toward some immense presence. He looked up. His mouth gaped as shock widened his eyes. "It can't be."

DROPS OF BLOOD FLEW FROM ORVANDIL'S THIGH AS THE EDGE OF Edgil's blade slid away. He grimaced, but he thanked fate the burning cut was not deeper even as he parried the next blow with Sweothol.

"Damn you! Listen! Dayraven . . . is . . . my . . . friend!"

But the clanging of steel drowned out the words, and the northerner only shouted, "My son! Where's my son?"

The Thjoth ducked as the crazed man swept his blade over his head. Edgil's knee cracked against his face. He tasted blood as he staggered back and swung up his blade to deflect a blow from above. Sparks flew when swords met. The Markman's left fist smashed into the Thjoth's eye. A flash of red, and the world spun. Orvandil reeled backwards, hoping he was fast enough to avoid the next blow. A blur of steel swept just under his neck. The ground reached up for him while the cheers of Torrlonders and their allies rang in his ears.

He rolled as soon as he hit dirt. Edgil's blade flashed and bit into the soil where his chest had been. He sprang up, sweeping Sweothol before him to deflect the next blow. After the clang of blades, the Thjoth shook his head. The world returned to focus.

When the Markman came at him again, something rose in Orvandil's chest. He recognized his warrior's instinct, and he no longer suppressed it. *He's going to kill me soon. If there are any gods, may they forgive me.*

As when he slew his best friend on the island of Vargholm, he made himself forget who fought him. It was a man with a blade. The only rule was kill or be killed. The man behind the masked helm was no longer Dayraven's father, only the foe. And he was a foe who had drawn too much of Orvandil's blood. The battle fury came upon the Dragonbane, and he clenched his teeth in a grim smile.

He silenced the cheers of the Torrlonders and Markmen by driving back Edgil in a furious hail of blows from Sweothol. He matched the smaller man's speed as their swords sparked and whirled. But Orvandil was the stronger. At every meeting of their blades, Edgil backed a pace or two. Shouts arose from those allied against Torrlond. Men's fists pounded the air as they yelled encouragement to their champion. Orvandil let it all wash over him. He was intent on the man before him.

Sweothol rose and fell, swept forward and arced around. Edgil struggled to keep up. The Thjoth swooped down his weapon in a massive blow. The Markman met it with blade raised. The clanging shock bent the northerner, but he stood with both hands on his sword's hilt, grunting and holding back Sweothol as his arms quivered. Steel whispered across steel while the blades locked.

It was time to finish it, but Orvandil frowned and hesitated. Edgil dropped and swept out one foot at the ankle of the Thjoth's injured leg. Wounded and tired, the bigger man did not move in time. He lost balance as the Markman's leg spun him around. He landed hard on his knees with his back turned to his opponent. The sun was also at his back, and the northerner's shadow wavered in front of him as he raised his sword aloft behind Orvandil's head for the deathblow.

Instinct brought Sweothol stabbing behind him in an arc over his head as he flung his body backward, springing from his toes with all his strength. He thrust the sword's tip into the source of the shadow behind him. Sweothol shattered mail and sank into flesh even as the edge of Edgil's blade fell inches from the Thjoth's shoulder. Orvandil turned and held on to the hilt, twisting the merciless steel further into his adversary, whose sword fell and clanged on the soil.

The Thjoth gazed at the warrior he had vanquished. He was again Edgil, Dayraven's father. Orvandil frowned at the blood seeping from the Markman's chest.

The crowd stood in gape-mouthed silence, still taking in what just happened. Edgil looked down at Sweothol, the sword that was his reward for saving a king's life and his gift to his son. A foot of its ancient steel was lodged in his body through his byrny. Its jeweled pommel gleamed crimson as his thick blood ran down the blade and dripped onto the soil. His eyes appealed to Orvandil, their fury extinguished.

"My son?" He spoke in little more than a whisper. "Where is Dayraven?"

No words came to Orvandil. He withdrew the blade. Blood pumped from the wound, and Edgil sank to his knees. His face paled. The Thjoth knelt and caught him in his arms.

A huge shadow passed over them. Every face turned up, including Orvandil's.

In the sky flew the largest dragon he had ever seen, far bigger than the serpents of the air Bledla controlled. Its scales were black, its wings so vast the mortals beneath it cowered. Atop it sat a man, his hair waving in the wind. A bright light surrounded the man, whom Orvandil recognized from afar.

"There," he said to Edgil. Removing the masked helm from his foe's head, he saw a face much like Dayraven's, only hardened and older. He pointed at the man astride the eldest of dragons as they whooshed by with a gust of wind. "There's Dayraven, your son. He lives, and he comes to end this madness."

Edgil smiled weakly. His eyes followed the enormous beast's flight and squinted at the light emanating from the figure riding it. His face froze when his last quiet breath escaped.

His big shoulders drooping, Orvandil shut the eyes of the man he had slain. He released a long sigh, eased the body down, and left it lying in the dirt to find Gnorn. Everyone else on the battlefield gazed upward.

SEQUARA'S EYES OPENED. SHE STARED UP AT A HIGH, FIRE-BLACKENED ceiling. All around her were the groans of wounded and dying people. Further away, dim but audible, was the roar of multitudes, the din of battle. Much fear surrounded her.

Her body was afire with pain. Burns stung her face and hands, but the worst agony was like a knife twisting in her back, and her chest just under her collarbone ached like someone was ripping the meat out of her and prying her bones apart. Even breathing was laborious.

It came back to her. An arrow had struck her just after she defeated and slew the High Priest Heremod. His death had not been pretty. She remembered nothing else after that. She must have blacked out. Someone must have carried her here. Thulhan. She was inside the city.

But the pain was not what had awakened her. She had seen him. A true-dream came to her, and she had beheld Dayraven. In the vision he was lost and did not know who he was anymore. *He's near now.*

Sequara tried to sit up. The pain spiked when she moved, and she gasped as she sank back down. The ceiling swam and dimmed.

"Lie still," said a woman's voice in Andumaic. "You must not move now. You've lost too much blood."

Sequara tried to catch her breath, which came in short huffs as the pain throbbed and racked her body. "He . . . needs me." She clenched her teeth. It was hard to get enough air to speak.

"Whoever he is, he'll have to make do without you, dear. You're not going anywhere like this."

A hand pressed her forehead. She sank down, down, down. Comforting darkness came for her.

THE WIZARD DAYRAVEN STREAKED THROUGH THE SKY ON THE BACK of Gorsarhad, mother of dragons. It was still morning when smoke hovering over the ruined city of Thulhan greeted him and his winged mount. War raged in a huge circle around the city.

While they soared over the chaos of battle, the power of the elf in him blazed forth. Its energy leaped from him, and mixed in with it were the tiny particles of *his* energy, which he clung to with the same desperation with which he had clung to the cliff below Gorsarhad's cave. He was not certain how long he could hold on, and he did not know what the elf-shard would do if he let go. It was so hungry. *Must hold on long enough to defeat Bledla.* And while they shone as a beacon above the battle, Dayraven understood what he was channeling.

It was a force all around him. The elf was a gateway to it. *He* was part of it, always had been, to be certain. But it was interminably large, the self-renewing, infinite life underlying the finite world of forms, and Dayraven knew it by several names. *Laeroth. Oruma and Anghara. Edan.* All faces of the same thing. The pure, raw essence of Edan — no mask, no skin, no covering — had found a focal point in him, a place of entry into the world of forms, and he beheld everything below as if it were all unfolding within the space of his mind. He perceived his father's final breath and Orvandil's sorrow. He knew others dear to his mortal self lay near death: Gnorn, Abon, and, most of all, Sequara. He sensed the last moments of so many coming to rejoin Edan, all while an ocean of fear and desire surged and swelled beneath him. But one presence concerned him most: the one he had come to reckon with.

Gorsarhad obeyed Dayraven's will as the young wizard directed her toward the Supreme Priest Bledla. Bledla's remaining dragons sped toward them, eleven red streaks seeking the larger, black one. The nearest flew towards the eldest of dragons and hissed its forked tongue in challenge. Flames sprouted from its jaws as the two serpents of the air careered towards each other, but Gorsarhad unfastened her jaws and met fire with fire. The smaller dragon's flames blew back as the massive torrent of heat from Gorsarhad enveloped them. Engulfed in fire far hotter than its own, the smaller lingworm flapped its wings and retreated with a shriek as its scales and wings smoldered.

While Gorsarhad repulsed the attacks of her smaller kindred, another struggle played out. Something was happening to Dayraven. The ravenous will of the elf-shard was too mighty to resist. The tiny fragments of his energy were diminishing. In moments, he would be lost. There was no panic, no fear. It was the simple truth. He always had been the elf, and now there was no more hiding.

But there was one last thing to do. He focused on Bledla. For the second time, he challenged the supreme priest for mastery of the serpents of the air. For the second time, he approached Bledla's massive will and heard his voice in the realm of origins as if they spoke next to one another. *Who do you think you are to oppose Edan, boy?*

Dayraven laughed even as the sense of himself amidst the elf-shard's vast energy slipped away. *You're confused, Bledla. I oppose you, not Edan.*

You've tried to stop me before. I'll shred you to pieces, and this time you won't return, Dayraven of the Mark.

At last, Dayraven lost his grip on the minute pieces of his energy, or perhaps they simply dissipated, and there was nothing left to hold on to. It was the power of the elf that spoke. *It's not Dayraven of the Mark who comes. He's no more.*

Fear quivered in Bledla's mind, but the supreme priest remained defiant. *Edan's power will strike you down!*

No, mortal. Edan comes to wake you from your nightmare.

As before in Asdralad, the two wizards vied for mastery of the dragons. But this time, the one who had been Dayraven waited in serenity like the surface of a clear, still pond on a star-filled night.

Bledla hurled his ferocious energy forward. The one who was the window to Edan abode him. The collision promised to be huge, but something strange happened instead. Bledla passed through the window into the indifferent chill on the other side. He wrenched back his trembling energy like flesh recoiling from hot metal.

The window to Edan stood in tranquility, a halcyon, celestial eye.

The fear this inspired in the supreme priest infuriated him, and he rushed to attack once more. But all his massive power did not avail him, for he swept through his adversary's energy for the second time. Bewildered and raging, Bledla rose up and swelled with all his might. It was then that the one who had been Dayraven reached toward the wrathful mortal.

The will that pierced the supreme priest like a spear thrust was so enormous it bent the fabric of the world. Waves of bright bluish light, what the Andumae named *almakhti*, emanated from the form atop the black dragon. The window to Edan could sense the emotions of all the mortals beneath it. Soldiers on the battlefield and citizens of Thulhan alike beheld its energy from afar with eyes frozen wide in disbelief. Like enormous sheets waving in a colossal wind, the light coruscated and washed over everything. All that it bathed bent and warped with it, and every mortal looked on in wonder and confusion as the world transfigured into glowing hues and flickering shadows. The one who had been Dayraven looked upon it all with half-lidded eyes. Deep peace fell over him. It was not the same for Bledla.

The power of the supreme priest snapped with a massive explosion and fled out of the dragons he had possessed for so long. His terror-filled scream hovered over the battlefield like a monstrous echo inhabiting the air. Men everywhere dropped their weapons and clasped their hands over their ears. Like a gust, a far stronger will blew his energy away from the lingworms as if it were withered leaves. The tatters of his power lashed and scattered in the wind dispersing them. When the world returned to normal, this new will controlled all the dragons. Bledla's body fell to the dust.

Now emanating a white light like an aura around it, the presence atop Gorsarhad directed the mother of dragons to land near the white-robed form lying on the earth. The eldest of dragons descended and flapped her huge wings as she touched down, kicking up a dust cloud. When the dust cleared, the presence, bound in a mortal body, alighted from his stooping mount by swinging his legs over her side and sliding down her scales.

Mortals in soldiers' garb gathered in a huge circle, though none dared come close to Gorsarhad or the presence that wielded her. Yet something drove them to linger, to peer in rapt fascination. They all wished to know who or what it was that rode the black serpent of the air. And there was something more.

Like ants drawn to honey, they came and stared at the presence because it was truer than they were, and it called them toward something they could not understand. It was not blind to eternity as they were, not limited by the illusion of existence, and something in them seemed to feel that truth calling them, whispering of sweet release.

All over the western side of the city, the battle ceased as word spread that some god had descended on the greatest dragon ever and struck down the supreme priest of the Way. More and more soldiers rushed to the spot even as the presence wrapped in mortal guise strode toward the stricken man in the white robe.

Wondering why it was clothed in flesh, the window to Edan glanced at its hands and then stared down at the prostrate form beneath it. *Why am I here?* it wondered.

To end the suffering, came the answer from within.

It gazed at the unconscious white-robed man, knowing what pain he had caused and endured in his quest to find Edan. It took in the thousands of mortals gaping at it in bewilderment, recalling how each of them had suffered and would suffer and would cause others to suffer. It looked down again at the open hands of the body it inhabited, and it knew how the body's former owner had grieved. Those the young man had known, those who had given him meaning, were gone. His mother was long dead, his father's blood had soaked into the battlefield, his brother from the south was far away – if he yet breathed – and his great aunt had sacrificed herself.

If I am here to make an end of suffering, there is but one way.

"Dayraven?"

The window to Edan turned towards the weak, broken voice. Near a bloody corpse in a white robe, a soot and sweat-covered old man in a patched brown robe was trying to raise himself from the ground and had managed to get to his knees. Some part of it recognized this mortal, though it could not have said why. The wizard Galdor. He too had suffered. The window to Edan tried to smile as mortals did to assure Galdor it would all be over soon, but in the old man's bulging green eyes it saw only naked terror.

That too will be gone, it reflected. *No more fear.*

"You . . . you've become . . . the elf?" the old wizard stuttered. It took a great effort for him to speak.

The window to Edan gave a slow nod. *Yes. That is how they think of it in their ignorance and trepidation.* It opened its arms, and the white light surrounding it expanded. Overhead, the sky darkened. The multitudes looking on screamed and trembled and cringed to the dust. But they awaited his embrace.

"Dayraven!"

The elf turned around at the sound of the new voice, which tugged at it with recognition. It belonged to a mortal woman, one who had met it before in the realm of origins. She stood some twenty paces from him, but she was hunched over and seemed about to collapse. She panted in short gasps as if her weak, pain-filled flesh could not imbibe enough of the air it depended on. A sleeve of her tunic was gone. In its place, a large bandage was wound around one of her shoulders and under her armpit. Blood spotted it just below her collar bone. Burn marks streaked her face. Yes, some part of it knew her. *Sequara.*

"Dayraven," she said again.

There was so much pain in her voice. The window to Edan approached her, and though she was afraid, she walked toward it. It could end her pain. As it beheld her, it saw into her mind, and there it found her many memories. There was the sorrow of leaving her loved ones when she was a girl, the greater sorrow when they passed on from the world of forms, the many sacrifices for duty, the agony of losing her mentor and her beloved home to the violence of foreigners. There was joy too, but always the sorrow outweighed it.

But there was something else. Another's memories had somehow come to reside in her. A northern landscape with green hills and forest and river appeared, and familiar people dwelled in it.

"Dayraven," she said. Her voice trembled. She stood before the window.

It reached out to embrace her and end Sequara's suffering. *No more.*

But when it touched her wounded shoulder, something happened. Like a sudden flood, something *filled* the window. Sequara gasped and stood erect as her memories and a young man's memories inundated it. Images of Asdralad and the Mark passed by. Inhabiting them were the many people who had touched them: Faldira, Urd, Imharr, Father and Mother, Brother, Grandmother, Jhaia, Ebba, Orvandil, Gnorn, Hlokk, Abon, Galdor, and hundreds more.

Their spirits mingled in the realm of origins. It remembered everything, most of all how excruciatingly dear and beautiful she was, especially in her sorrow. With sudden illumination, it realized what it was that filled it like the light of the rising sun. The thing that pervaded it along with the young man's memories and her memories was *desire*. Desire for her. Desire for life.

I want to live.

With that desire, he recalled who he was.

Like a man breaching the frozen surface of water from beneath to suck in sweet air, Dayraven emerged in his body. The white elf-light flashed and went out, and the mundane world of forms returned with its benign blue sky. The power of the elf-shard receded back to the depths of his mind, where it hissed and lodged like a piece of glass so cold it burned.

When it diminished, Dayraven stood as a burnt out husk. He felt not just hollow, but also insubstantial, even transparent. But he found he still wielded Gorsarhad as well as the eleven remaining dragons that had been Bledla's. Each was a distinct prisoner of his energy. The black dragon waited nearby while the younger ones wheeled in the sky, waiting for his commands.

Dayraven looked at Sequara, who gazed in his eyes. Tears rolled down both her cheeks. When his hand came away from her shoulder, he knew he had healed her. The burns on her beautiful face and hands were dim scars.

"Thank you," he said.

She glanced at her shoulder and smiled through her tears. "Shouldn't I be thanking you?"

"I said I would find you, but you found me first."

There, in front of the amazed soldiers of five kingdoms, they embraced. Dayraven held on to Sequara, pressing her against his body, and knew she was the most real thing he had ever touched.

Behind them, the wizard Galdor cleared his throat. Dayraven turned and found the old man was standing now. He extended his hand toward the wizard, who approached with a large smile across his face.

His green eyes gleaming with tears, the old wizard grasped Dayraven's hand and laughed. Then Galdor winked at the young man and released him. Turning away to face the gathered multitudes, he held up his arms in token that he would speak.

Soldiers of Torrlond, the Mark, Sildharan, Grimrik, and Ellond all murmured. Friend and foe stood side by side, waiting for some explanation to what they had all witnessed. When all were silent, the wizard Galdor proclaimed, "Behold! The *true* Prophet of Edan has come. Hearken to him. The Prophet has come to tell us Edan's will."

Is that who I am? thought Dayraven as thousands of faces stared at him in silence and expectation. No. There were no prophets. No gods. Not, at least, the sort that most people understood. Edan. Oruma and Anghara. Regnor and Hruga. Laeroth. All names that people clothed with their fleeting desires. People worshiped the clothes, and, attached to their selves, they would despair if ever they saw the blinding darkness beneath them. Religions were wrappings, and these wrappings were bound to decay over the centuries as the unending and patient truth abode beneath. If there was anything like a god, it was the eternal play between desire and the end of desire.

But how could all these people know? They were clinging to their desires with such desperate fervor. He looked around at them all, tired, sweaty, and bloody as they were, and he frowned at all the tragedy before him. *So much death. Life raging against itself. If I must be their Prophet to make it end, so be it.*

"Edan sent me to bear you a message. Hear me now, for Edan dwells in me."

The crowd murmured again, but Dayraven continued. "Edan dwells in *all* of you. You are all Edan's children, you are all gods, and Edan grieves when you raise swords against one another. Cease this destruction now. Cease this war. This is not the Way. The Prophet Aldmund came to spread peace to Eormenlond, but those who followed twisted his words and misled the people. They turned his humility into grandiosity. They made his message of hope a message of hate, and the blood that flows this day is the fulfillment of their madness. Edan *commands* you now: Cease this war. What say you, Torrlonders? What say you, warriors of the Mark?"

There was a long silence, and men looked about for someone to answer. One in gilded armor made a few cautious steps forward. He was not tall, but he was a broad man and proud of countenance. Nevertheless, he went to his knees as he glanced at the huge dragon then addressed Dayraven. He was not altogether successful as he tried to sound bold, but his voice carried far. "Prophet, if that's how we should name you. I'm Duke Ethelred of Etinstone, cousin of King Earconwald of Torrlond. Perhaps we've been blind. By the miraculous power you've shown, we may believe Edan sent you to command us. But we've sworn to follow King Earconwald. Let him decide whether we lay down our arms, and if he follows your counsel, we'll fain turn our backs to this place and return to Torrlond."

Dayraven thought a moment. "It shall be so. Fetch your king. I guarantee his safety for a parley. Tell him to hasten and render his decision before us. In the meantime, spread the word that there will be no more fighting until King Earconwald has determined his kingdom's future."

Duke Ethelred bowed his head and stood. Men parted before him as he headed west, in the direction where Earconwald waited outside the ring of battle. At the same time, thousands more arrived around the scene and jostled for a view of the prophet who descended from the sky. They had no difficulty seeing the huge black dragon, which roared once as she towered next to Dayraven. The gathered soldiers covered their ears and cringed at the heat of Gorsarhad's breath. The other eleven serpents of the air still circled overhead.

As murmurs passed around the swelling throng, Galdor leaned in close to the younger man. As he did so, Dayraven perceived some terrible grief behind the twinkle in the old man's eyes. Galdor whispered, "What if Earconwald refuses to back down?"

PHILIP CHASE

Dayraven kept all emotion from his face. "Then there'll be much more death. But I've met this man once before. He's a coward. A gifted coward who will retreat if we give him the chance to bow out with grace." He glanced at Sequara, whose face hardened even as she nodded at him.

Shouting broke out among the hosts of warriors, and voices cried out that Earconwald approached. It took a while for a sign of Torrlond's leader to appear, but, at length, a section of the crowd stirred. Bodies fought for room, and men sought a glimpse of the man who ruled Eormenlond's most powerful kingdom.

Captain Nothelm, commander of the king's bodyguard, arrived barking orders for everyone to make way. One hundred elite troops under Nothelm's command formed a wedge that split apart the mass of men, and soon enough the monarch strode through the gap they made. Wearing his crown and a gilded corselet with Torrlond's ensign embossed on it, King Earconwald frowned and puffed out his chest when he looked up at the enormous dragon. Duke Ethelred, the bearer of Dayraven's message, lingered a few paces behind his cousin and sovereign. He stopped as Earconwald strutted forward to meet Dayraven.

Perhaps he wished to show everyone he did not fear this Prophet of Edan. Perhaps he did not believe the tale his duke had told. Or perhaps it was pride that drove him. Whatever it was, the King of Torrlond walked up to Dayraven and looked him in the eye with a great smirk across his face.

"So," he said in a quiet voice that only Dayraven, Galdor, and Sequara could have heard. He glared at Dayraven. "The boy from the Mark has become the Prophet of Edan." He glanced back at Bledla's unconscious form lying in the dirt. "You defeated my supreme priest, I'll grant you that. But he was getting old, you know, and he was wearing on me. I was thinking he needs a replacement, and I've been waiting for someone likely. There would be, of course, many rewards for the man I choose. Together, we could rule all of Eormenlond. Who knows? Perhaps we would even go beyond these shores. I have a vision, Dayraven, and you can be part of it."

Becoming supreme priest of the Way was nothing he had ever

contemplated. This king's "vision" was a petty thing, but for a flickering moment, Dayraven thought of the good someone might do as head of Eormenlond's mightiest faith. With such power, a person could transform the Way into the dream of peace he felt certain the Prophet Aldmund had meant to offer.

No. Dayraven smiled. In response, Earconwald's eyes widened slightly, and his grin slipped a bit.

Dayraven looked at Bledla where he lay, and he thought of the Way's mighty temples, the white robes that denoted its priests' purity, and its solemn rituals that promised salvation to the faithful. All trappings and clothes. All expressions of desire. All doomed to decay. He thought of how Bledla must have been when he was young, and he knew the supreme priest had once been much like him. *The Way has grown into a mighty tree, but its heart is rotten, and it would rot me with it before I could change anything. Even with good motives, power would claim me, as it did Bledla. No prophet would become the supreme priest.*

With a face like stone, Dayraven looked King Earconwald in the eye. "Let's play no games, Earconwald. I have twelve dragons at my command. If you don't call off this war now, I'll permit you to leave this parley. But when the battle resumes, I'll direct those dragons to seek you, and only you, and to roast your body until it's a pile of ash and bone." He paused to let that sink in, noting the quiver in the monarch's lip. "However, if you would save face, you may declare it was Bledla who deceived you into this war. It was he who claimed to speak with Edan's voice, and you were one of the many he fooled into following him. But now, the scales have fallen from your eyes. You wish to repent and bring your troops home."

Earconwald's eyes widened and his nostrils flared. "And what prevents me from drawing my sword and cutting you down here and now? I'd have your head off before you could sing one of your spells."

Dayraven nodded toward the gilded hilt at the king's hip. "Move your hand one inch toward your blade, and that dragon will breathe fire on you before your sword's out." As if to confirm the threat, Gorsarhad's predatory eyes locked onto the King of Torrlond as she snorted a plume of smoke.

Earconwald glanced at the eldest of dragons, and he scratched his

PHILIP CHASE

beard as he pursed his lips. But when he turned back to the young wizard, his smirk had returned. "And you would die in the flames as well, fool."

Dayraven smiled back. "I've already died, so it matters naught to me. Besides, from my point of view, better we both go than allow you to take me alone. So, will you have peace and live? If you choose war, your death is certain, and you cannot win without the dragons on your side. Even if you could, your army is already overextended. You know it."

The King of Torrlond's face trembled as his eyes narrowed. But he subdued his features after clenching his jaw, and it was a different countenance that turned towards the thousands of onlookers. "Men of Torrlond!" he said as he stepped a few paces away from Dayraven with smiling benevolence and piety in his mien. "Warriors of the Mark!" He moved closer to Bledla's still form lying on the ground.

"We've fought long and hard to fulfill Edan's will. We sacrificed everything to bring the Kingdom of the Eternal. For there was one who promised great rewards to those who followed him. When he spoke to us, he said it was Edan's will that we fight to spread the Way. Behold!" Earconwald's hands flew out toward the white-robed old man. "Here he is, lying in the dust. This man, the wizard Bledla, used the holy office of the supreme priest of the Way to deceive us all. Drunk with his own power, he it was who told us to come east with swords in hand. *He* it was who said Edan commanded us to slay our neighbors. *He* it was who said death would lead to life. But defeat proves his falsehood. I, Earconwald, your king, tell you a new prophet has shed light on the darkness. No longer blind, I see now Bledla's counsels stemmed not from Edan but from his ambition and wickedness. I repent this war, and I extend an offer of peace to King Naitaran of Sildharan."

"Noooo!" It was not Naitaran who wailed in answer.

Bledla staggered up to his knees with a crazed, wild-eyed expression squirming across his face. "You cannot! False king! Thrice-damned traitor! Edan will punish you!" His trembling hand flashed out toward Dayraven, his bony index finger extending. "Slay him! Any soldier of Torrlond or priest faithful to me, slay that servant of demons!" The effort cost Bledla much, for he buckled over on hands and knees and gagged as vomit poured out of his mouth and splattered on the ground.

The High Priest Joruman stepped forward from the crowd. His cunning eyes met King Earconwald's long enough for the monarch to nod at Joruman. In that moment, Dayraven knew the two already had an understanding, though this might not have been the time they planned for.

Joruman raised his voice as Bledla continued retching. "Followers of the Way! Faithful of Edan! Our duty now is to our king, for he is the consecrated of Edan. You heard this man speak with hatred in his soul toward our monarch. His words condemn him. He is the deceiver. This war is his design. His only end is to destroy us, for *he* is the servant of demons, the enemy of Edan. Hearken now to King Earconwald, your rightful ruler, and to the true Prophet of Edan!"

Bledla extended his palm outwards and tried to protest, but he coughed and choked on his vomit.

Earconwald walked towards Dayraven again and faced him with a smile. "My people! If King Naitaran agrees, we will have peace. Let him come to this parley."

Cheers broke out from the weary soldiers of both sides. Bledla crawled on hands and knees toward Earconwald and Dayraven as Torrlond's monarch reached toward the jeweled hilt of his sword. In token of peace, he pulled the blade out of its scabbard with a hush of steel and extended it hilt forward to the young man. He held the shining metal with both hands and stared at Dayraven with a broad smile. The golden hilt waited for the completion of the gesture. The young wizard hesitated, glancing at the disgraced supreme priest, who quivered while raising his body.

Dayraven reached out. But before he grasped the hilt, Earconwald shifted. The King of Torrlond grabbed the hilt himself and moved with furious speed. Many in the crowd gasped. Everything happened in a blur as Sequara and Galdor rushed to interpose their bodies between Earconwald and Dayraven.

But they were in no position to stop the monarch. Nor was Dayraven. The only sound was steel shearing through cloth and flesh. Everyone stared with mouths frozen open. Dayraven's eyes were wide, for he had not expected the move. *What a pity for it to end this way*, he thought. He looked at Bledla with a hard frown, lamenting the loss of what might have been.

Earconwald had lunged at the supreme priest with precise ferocity. Bledla had just reached them and struggled up to his feet when the king plunged his golden hilted blade into the supreme priest's chest and out his back. A snarl writhed across the monarch's face as he drove the blade in deeper.

Bledla remained upright while a crimson circle spread over his white robe. The tall old man gazed at his sovereign with blue eyes narrowed in a grimace while Earconwald declared, "And peace can begin only with this vile traitor's death."

The supreme priest's eyelids fluttered. Breath seethed between his teeth, and he said in a strained but deep voice, "Your death will follow soon, and you'll suffer the torments of the damned." He coughed out blood that oozed over his lips.

Earconwald wrenched out his blade. Red flooded the old man's robe. He fell onto his face and lay still. Thus ended Bledla, Supreme Priest of the Way, ere the Kingdom of the Eternal came to Eormenlond.

The King of Torrlond wiped his blade on the supreme priest's robe, sheathed it, and gazed around at the multitudes. "Now, we have only to hear the response of King Naitaran. Will Sildharan have peace?"

A rumbling of voices emerged from one side of the ring of onlookers. Soon enough, with much jostling, another gap formed in the crowd, through which Naitaran walked with several of his soldiers surrounding him as guards. His beautiful robes singed in places and his face blackened with soot, Naitaran appeared haggard but still dignified. Narrowing his eyes above a proud frown, he commanded his guards to wait for him and walked toward Earconwald, Dayraven, Sequara, and Galdor. He glanced at Dayraven as if to size him up, and then a scornful sneer contorted his features when he stood face to face with King Earconwald. "Tell me, King of Torrlond, why should I cease fighting now that we have the advantage? The dragons are in our hands, and your true strength lies dead where you just slew him."

Earconwald's face reddened, but Dayraven raised a hand before anyone spoke. The young wizard looked at the King of Sildharan. "Your Majesty, the dragons are not in *our* hands but in *my* hands, and it's my intention that no one use them again as weapons after this day. I also remind you that your allies are even now fighting on your behalf on the eastern side of your city. The people of Sundara and your own troops are dying as they defend Thulhan from the Ilarchae. Instead of wasting more lives here, the course of wisdom would be to accept King Earconwald's offer of peace and go aid your brethren. You might repulse the Ilarchae from your lands, though they would never have been here had you and your ancestors not enslaved them for your profit."

Naitaran's eyes widened in surprise for a moment, and, with twitching mouth, he glared at Dayraven. But then he nodded and looked at Earconwald. "Very well. We'll have peace between our kingdoms. For now. But how do I know you'll keep your word if I withdraw my troops to the eastern side of the city?"

Dayraven answered before Earconwald could speak. "King Fullan and King Vols will remain here and ward the western side of the city with their soldiers until the Torrlonders and the others leave." He gazed at Earconwald as he added, "I'll stay here with the dragons. At the first sign of treachery, I'll set them loose. They'll be hunting for only one man."

Earconwald's face clouded, but he forced a smile. "I give my word. We'll return to Torrlond." He moved closer to Dayraven and lowered his voice as he kept his smile frozen in place. "And I vow to make you suffer for this, boy." He glanced at Sequara. His smile widened to a leer. "And *her* too."

Before Dayraven could reply, Torrlond's monarch turned to Duke Ethelred. "Send word to the other dukes and to King Ithamar of the Mark. Tell them to bury the dead and form ranks for a march. We're going home." Without looking back, he stalked past Bledla's corpse toward the gap in the crowd where his guards waited. He disappeared in the press with Captain Nothelm, Duke Ethelred, and the High Priest Joruman escorting him.

Galdor turned and shouted aloud, "Let it be known! There is peace!" After closing his eyes and sighing, the old wizard staggered toward the body of Arna and knelt by it. Glancing at each other, only Dayraven and Sequara perceived his grief.

The thousands of gathered soldiers hailed the tidings, and it did not take long for word to spread throughout the battlefield. The terms reached the ears of King Fullan and King Vols, who began organizing their men while Naitaran gathered his soldiers to march to the eastern side of Thulhan. Weary and relieved, many of the living set about the grim task of collecting the wounded and the dead. The survivors of Sildharan, Ellond, and Grimrik drifted toward the city while the men they had fought moved towards their encampment to the west.

Dayraven made Sequara promise to return to Thulhan and rest, for though he had healed her, she had lost much blood and was still weak. Galdor said he would find and care for Abon and others, though the old wizard with his palpable weight of loss looked in need of rest himself.

The Prophet of Edan walked in the direction of Thulhan and kept a watchful eye on the movements of Torrlond's army. The dragons wheeled in the sky as a warning to Earconwald. There were those whom the young wizard yearned to see and attend to, but he could not leave his post until he was certain Torrlond and its allies were truly gone. All the while, the sharp elf-shard strained in his mind. Its whispers of unending darkness were keener than ever, almost seeming to cut him. They refused to recede even when he focused on his body and the world of forms around him. The thing's hunger remained, and it strained at his sense of belonging in the realm of materiality, which seemed less substantial than it should have. Perhaps the disoriented feeling would subside.

As Dayraven stood beneath the city's blackened wall, nearby soldiers pointed at him and whispered in their various tongues. One of the straggling Sildharae, a young bowman with slouching shoulders and a scabbed over wound on his left arm, said loud enough for him to hear, "That raggedy fellow there? Doesn't much look like a prophet."

Dayraven smiled to himself. *Nor do I feel like one, now that it's over. I want to go home. But where's home?*

27
THE FINAL PARTING

The sun sank in the west over Quinara Sound, and with it sank all waning hope of an easy victory. The folk of the tribes were weary with the toil of battle. Many warriors bore wounds. Many no longer breathed. Their stories were over. What was a man or a woman after flesh yielded to steel and blood soaked in the earth? Meat and bones that would rot and go back to the dust. Food for crows and flies. Did the gods have a purpose for it all, or were they helpless too in the face of the darkness behind the chaos?

Munzil of the Grey Wolves turned his gaze from the darkening sky and watched Surt. The leaders of every tribe sat for the war-moot in a circle around a crackling fire, which reddened their grim faces, and while they spoke freely, they all looked to the war-leader of the Fire Dragons to decide their fate. The great man's stony face showed no sign of disappointment in the day's events.

After the Torrlonders had fled from the battle, the Sildharae had come in full force against the tribes of the Wildlands. The Torrlonder holy men had abandoned the Ilarchae, and so there was no one to oppose the Sildharae holy men and women. Many warriors died before the folk of the tribes retreated from Thulhan. Their foes seemed intent on surrounding them and pushing them into the sound, and they nearly did it. It was almost a rout, but Surt had organized and rallied the tribes, and they stood firm. The battle had raged all day, and only when evening approached had the Sildharae let up in their attack. Now, the folk of the tribes were dug in with the sound at their backs. Their enemies, whose camps surrounded the warriors of the Wildlands, would no doubt resume their attack in the morning and try to finish off the free tribes.

But none of this seemed to concern Surt. If anything, he looked more calm and determined than ever, and he even grinned as Rugnach, war-leader of the Strong Axes, spoke in favor of breaking through the Sildharae and escaping back to the Wildlands.

"The Torrlonders have betrayed us. They are weak outlanders, and they are nothing without their lingworms. But without them attacking the place of many stones, the Sildharae and their allies outnumber us. And they have their holy men and women. Their lightning slays many of our best warriors."

Gunburcha of the Stone Fists spat toward the fire. Some of the spittle glistened and ran down her scarred chin. "Running back to the Wildlands is a coward's deed," she declared in her rough voice. She gazed with hard eyes at the fire, but there was no mistaking whom she meant.

Rugnach's angry face jerked in her direction, but before he could protest, another voice joined in. "There's a difference between a coward and a wise man when his foe comes in numbers greater than his own." It was Bolverk of the Raven Eyes, a tall, grey-bearded warrior missing one eye. He was the most cunning and grim man Munzil had ever seen, one who hid his long memory and fierce heart well. "If we live to fight again, we may defeat the Sildharae some other time."

"We should *fight* the brown ones now!" yelled Graen of the Cleft Skulls, who pounded his huge fist into his open hand. "Death before retreat!"

"We could surprise them in the darkness," said Ogar of the Night Trolls. The huge man's grey teeth showed when he grinned, a look made all the more unnerving by his missing nose.

A few murmurs followed this comment, but Surt held up his hand, and everyone waited for the great man to speak.

"We will not retreat. Neither will we attack now."

A long silence followed. Everyone waited, and it was Gunburcha who asked, "What then will we do?"

"We wait."

"For what?" asked Bolverk. One of his eyebrows arched up.

Surt smiled. "A rider came from Folnir of the Tall Spears just before we sat down for the war-moot."

"The Tall Spears?" Rugnach's puzzled voice spoke for nearly everyone. "But they're back in . . ."

Surt stared at the other leaders as he finished telling the tidings. "The other twelve free tribes of the Wildlands are joining us. I sent them word of our victory at Sirukinn's Wall, and other messages besides. They wish to share in our glory. They bring forty thousand warriors. They're on their way, and they'll reach us before morning."

Silence, and then a chorus of exclamations. Surt held up his palm, and the voices died down. "I've ordered them to surprise the Sildharae from behind. When they attack, we'll strike with all our strength and drive the slavers back to their piles of stones. We'll keep fighting until we defeat them." He thrust his mighty fist in the air. "The folk of the tribes are strong." Then he pointed with his index finger at his head. "But we must also be clever to win. The cowards of Torrlond abandoned us, and we'll have revenge for that one day. But first, we *will* defeat Sildharan. Once we've ground them to dust, we'll not stop. The gods have awakened us and given the folk of the tribes a mighty fate. We need no weaklings as allies, for the gods have given this land to us. All of Eormenlond will be ours. All of it!"

As the leaders of the tribes broke out in cheers, Munzil allowed himself a proud smile. If only his wife and children could have seen this day. He had never doubted Surt since the time he found him, after the gods led him with the vision. For the sake of his lost people, not for himself, he was grateful the gods had chosen him to begin the awakening of the Ilarchae. The Grey Wolves would live in the memories of the folk of the tribes. They might all merge into one people someday, but they would always remember it was the last of the Grey Wolves who had come to Surt with the god-bestowed vision. Now that the folk of the tribes were facing their test, the man's greatness was evident. A warrior's true quality always emerged when his foes surrounded him, and Munzil knew Surt would lead them to victory. He was as sure of him as he was of the gods.

In the darkness of late evening, flames cast a ruddy light that danced as they devoured the funeral pyre of Edgil, son of Conwulf. Dayraven had said goodbye to his father when he lit the pyre with a torch. The warrior wore the mail, helm, and clothes he died in. Next to him lay Sweothol, its jeweled hilt gleaming and its bare steel reflecting the fire. Orvandil had insisted on putting the ancient blade to rest with its former owner, and all agreed the man was worthy of such honor. The eager flames licked the body and lapped the darkness. Hot blood sizzled as it seeped from his chest wound. Sparks crackled and hovered in the air while dark smoke billowed. At length, the head popped with the heat. Soon after, the greedy flames rose so high that only a vague shadow appeared within them. Later, when the flames died down, there would be only ashes and small pieces of bone. Over these they would pile a mound. As his father's body went up in smoke, Dayraven reflected that future travelers to Thulhan would go by the mound and wonder who or what lay beneath it. Perhaps a few would know his father's tale, but no doubt it would fall out of memory at some point in the future.

Next to him stood Orvandil, Galdor, King Fullan, and King Vols. For a time they all waited with hands folded in front of them, but the two kings had many duties, as did the old wizard. They left in silence, and only Orvandil remained with Dayraven. Neither spoke for a long time as they gazed at the burning pyre. But when the fire began to lessen, the Thjoth bowed his head low and said, "I knew he was your father when I slew him."

Dayraven glanced at his friend as shadows wavered on his face. "I know. After you tried to tell him." He paused for a long while. "We don't choose the paths fate puts before us. We only pick which one we take. You did your duty, as did he. There's often sorrow in that, but no shame. No shame in that."

"My duty? Was I made to kill?"

The young wizard looked at his friend's eyes, which seemed to plead with him for an answer he could not give. Even as he thought about how to reply, the voracious elf-shard hissed and called him toward its vast, dark indifference. As if he were one of a countless multitude of tiny specks, its infinite weight pulled him toward it with inevitable force.

He repeated the struggle of crawling back to his emotions and memories. The same struggle had played out many times that day since Sequara called him on the battlefield. When he recognized his body once again, he held on tight to the world of forms. Not knowing how long his recovery had taken, he hoped Orvandil had noticed nothing strange.

He remembered the Thjoth's question. After a long sigh, he spoke with as much authority in his voice as he could muster. "Perhaps, Orvandil Dragonbane, you *were* made to kill, though it's hard to say who or what did the making or why. But you have much else to do too. In the troubled days ahead many will need you. I'll be one of them. A strong friend is like the morning star that heralds dawn. You have uncommon strength, and you must decide how to use it. But of one thing I'm certain: Eormenlond will long remember your deeds. Make them as good as you can."

Orvandil stared at Dayraven, then he nodded in acceptance. Neither spoke again that night.

The next morning, several Thjoths and Ellonders piled the mound over Edgil's remains. After they finished, Dayraven said his final farewell to his father. When he parted from him, his last tie to the Mark remained under that mound.

IN THE DAYS AFTER TORRLOND'S ARMY LEFT SILDHARAN, MANY reports reached Thulhan. The chief tidings concerned the ongoing battle against the Ilarchae. King Naitaran led his army against the host of savages, who proved far more resilient and cunning than anyone had predicted. More barbarians from the Wildlands had joined them, and they nearly overwhelmed the Sildharae.

Many miles to the north of Thulhan, the two sides were in a stalemate. The city was safe for the moment. However, through his arrogance, King Naitaran had succeeded in offending King Tirgalan. Also, many Sundarae had lost their lives in defense of Sildharan. Thus, Tirgalan had decided to march his remaining forces home to Sundara. Since the Thjoths and the Ellonders had already made clear their intention to return to their kingdoms, King Naitaran and the Sildharae would have to fight the Ilarchae on their own. Naitaran was sure of his victory over the savages.

But that was not the only news. King Earconwald's defeat in Sildharan was just the beginning of his woes. The moment he had landed in the east with most of his strength, the newly conquered kingdoms of the southwest rose up against Torrlond's rule. Beginning in Caergilion and spreading to Adanon, the local people attacked the small garrisons the Torrlonders had left to guard the subject territories.

King Earconwald swept through the kingdom of Ellond before he hastened back to Torrlond, where he would gather his forces before heading south to quell the rebellions. While in Ellond, he ordered his soldiers to massacre villagers and destroy as much as they could of King Fullan's realm. But he had no time to linger, for the pleadings of his garrisons in the southwest were urgent. Thus, Earconwald could not have broken his word to retreat from Sildharan even if he wanted to. If he intended to hold the kingdoms of the southwest, he would be busy for some time. What was more, he would have little help.

Startled at the Torrlonders' conduct in Ellond and disillusioned with their war, King Ithamar of the Mark forswore his kingdom's alliance with Torrlond. The Markmen journeyed back to their northern homes in disappointment and anger, and they made oaths to keep to their own borders in the future.

Also, a few survivors among Norfast's warriors reported how the dragons had slain their people as well as the soldiers of Sundara when Earconwald sent Duke Durathror south of Thulhan to fight the southrons. The tidings created dissension among Earconwald's dukes, and the people of Norfast were intent on rebellion. With the king's blessing, Duke Siric of Rimdale tried to usurp the dukedom of Norfast and add it to his territory, but Norfast's people supported Durathror's young heir. Siric threatened war, and Earconwald announced his support for Rimdale. But the king of Torrlond was in no position to aid Siric, for he was engaged in the southwest.

And there were stirrings in Golgar. Rumors began to spread that the Golgae were preparing to pounce on Sildharan while their ancient foe was weakened and occupied with the Ilarchae.

The clouds of war loomed over Eormenlond. The War of the Way died with Bledla, but new conflicts arose from its ashes.

DAYRAVEN BROODED OVER ALL THE TIDINGS. HE HAD STRIVEN through one ordeal after another to avert death and destruction, but he likened his efforts to building castles of sand. The realms of mortals would not change, nor would the ambition and pride of those who led them. He began to share Gorsarhad's view of his own kind.

And he had a more immediate problem. Like a cold mist sending strangling tendrils around him, the insistent presence of the elf pulsed in his mind. Ever since his final battle with Bledla, the shard had remained sharp and eager. He fought to contain it. He strove to retain the sense of his identity. At times the elf-shard bled out of him, creeping until it surged with cosmic violence and broke him. A short or long period of time might have passed before he found himself in some part of the city staring at a wall or the sky, not remembering how he had come there. If people saw him in those moments, they hurried away in fear, as if they saw something in his eyes they could not bear.

He kept telling himself it would ebb, that he would get better and gain control. But he began to acknowledge the rising fear that something in him might have broken when he surrendered to the power of the elf. It might not ever be possible to come back. One of these times, he would not awaken.

In such moments of despair, he distracted himself by pondering the tidings of the Torrlonders, the Adanese and Caergilese, the Ilarchae, and all the others. There would be many tasks in the days ahead. He had unfinished business to attend to. Promises to keep. He could not leave the world of forms just yet.

From one place he longed to hear news, but the wind brought not even a whisper of the island kingdom of Asdralad. He wondered if anyone was alive there now, and his thoughts lingered on Imharr's fate. The idea that he had sent his friend to his death haunted him. No matter what, it would be painful to see Kiriath again. He sighed as he looked out into the empty sky from Thulhan's wall.

The previous evening, he had released the dragons into that sky after word came of Earconwald's difficulties. Such primal power did not belong in human hands, and he more than suspected that wielding the dragons for so long had colored Bledla's character, nudging him toward aggression in the name of the cause for which he had lived and died. In any case, the beasts were gone now. Last to recede into the distance had been Gorsarhad, who flew southwest to her lair on the Wyrmberg. The memory of her departure into the setting sun was so vivid that Dayraven saw it once again.

The gigantic beast flew toward the red orb until she receded into a black dot, and finally it swallowed her. He kept staring into the distance, where the sun grew and whitened until he saw only bright light. Timeless peace and rest called to him as the elf-shard erupted to sate its unending hunger. Dayraven yearned toward the light and drifted as if weightless.

With sudden awareness, he grew conscious of what was happening. He sought his body in the world of forms and clawed his way back, striving to recall who he was. Faces came to him — people he knew — and the sound of their names followed. Father, Imharr, Ebba, Urd, Gnorn, Orvandil, Faldira, Galdor, Abon. Sequara. He snapped back to the present and blinked his eyes. The sky above him had returned to its ordinary blue.

His body shook as sweat formed on his skin, and he drooped with weakness. It was time to admit it. His mind was slipping away with greater frequency, as if he could no longer keep the realm of origins from invading the world of forms. A barrier was shattered, and Dayraven did not know if he could repair it. His lack of control was frightening, especially since the episodes happened without warning. Perhaps they were only aftershocks from his effort to defeat Bledla. Perhaps they would cease if he rested and did not draw upon the elf-shard's power. If he was lucky, he would never need to draw upon it again. *Fool*, he thought. *You need help*. He shook his head and turned to the stairs leading down to the city, wondering when the elf-shard would strike again and where he would find himself.

The streets showed many signs of the dragons' fire. In places there were gaps where entire homes or shops burned or were torn down after sustaining too much damage. Laborers had already carted out much rubble and many bodies. Other buildings bore black scars on their walls. What was left of most of the noble houses' once elegant towers would come down in the next days. But already there were signs of rebirth. Lines of carts pulled by oxen brought in a stream of stones and wood, and masons reshaped some of the old, charred stones to use in new structures. Life crowded the city's busy streets as smiths banged out new tools, farmers sold produce, and Thulhan's citizens started over. *Thus it goes on.*

Amidst whisperings and fingers pointed his way, he wove through the bustle. Though he had trimmed his beard and wore his brown robe over a new white kirtle and black breeches, everyone knew he was the Prophet who had saved the kingdom. He did not enjoy such fame, but he had no choice but to endure it for the moment.

He walked to Naitaran's palace with its ruined tower. There were no guards at the gate, and a great deal of visitors flowed in and out of the open doors. The palace had become a temporary sick house for the many wounded soldiers. But Dayraven was not just any visitor. In fact, he had been living and sleeping in the sick house for the past few days, often going out for walks such as the one he had just finished. Though he feared to draw upon his power, attending to the wounded was a helpful distraction, and there was great need. His skills as a healer had saved more than a few lives among the hurt Sildharae, Ellonders, Thjoths, and Sundarae, though his exertions left him exhausted and often disoriented. And there were some among the wounded he wished to be near.

Negotiating through wide corridors cluttered with bandaged soldiers on sleeping mats, he arrived in a spacious hall that normally served to feast large numbers of guests. Now the guests all lay in rows on the floor, each one occupying a mat. It was hushed in the hall. Only a few whispers of visitors and those attending the wounded brushed across the silence.

Dayraven walked between the rows of sick and wounded, stopping to examine a few who teetered near death. One who no longer breathed he covered with a sheet. Two servants of the palace approached to haul the body away.

He turned away and walked among the rows of the wounded until he came to the corner where Gnorn and Abon lay side by side. Bandages no longer encircled the wounds on his friends, for he and Galdor had healed them. But they still required rest, for they had lost much blood, and healing always left the patient exhausted. Abon slept, but Gnorn's smile was broad when Dayraven approached. The scars across the Dweorg's forehead, nose, and cheek did not diminish the sparkle in his brown eyes. The young wizard picked up a small, three-legged stool and sat on it after he set it down between his two friends.

"How is he?"

Gnorn looked over at Abon, who slept with one hand on the harp next to him. Somehow, the instrument had come out of the battle less damaged than its owner. "Better," answered the Dweorg. "He keeps ahold of that harp like a babe clutching his mother's teat."

After Galdor had healed him, Abon's leg was well enough, but the wound on his right arm had become swollen and infected beneath the flesh, and a fever took him. One of the Sildharae healers had wanted to amputate the arm, but Abon raged and insisted they lop off his head if he could never play the harp. After the shaper threatened to cut off a certain member of the healer's body if he spoke of removing his arm again, Galdor and Dayraven intervened. Through their attention and the use of leeches around the wound, the infection had cleared, and the fever had broken that morning. Abon was one of the lucky, for many wounded soldiers had died from infections or loss of blood after amputations.

"He's through the worst now." Dayraven looked at Gnorn. "And what of you?"

"What of me? It would take more than scratches to keep me down for long. Dweorg skulls are thick — mine especially."

"Thick skull or not, you keep to your bed for another day or two at least."

The Dweorg smiled. "No need to worry for me, lad. My wounds

will heal." The smile changed into a thoughtful frown. "I'm more concerned about yours now."

"*My* wounds? I've hardly a scratch."

"Not the kind one can see."

Dayraven stared at his friend. The elf-shard hissed and slinked over the surface of his mind, pricking it with thousands of tiny, chilling needles. It called and pulled at him. "Ah. So you've noticed."

"You go blank sometimes. Then you snap out of it. Sometimes you wince and turn pale. You're fighting something. Even the big fellow's mentioned it."

"Orvandil?"

"Aye. Says your talk is strange sometimes, like there's another voice coming out of you. A frightening one."

"I didn't think anything could frighten Orvandil."

"Perhaps not. But he's concerned. So am I."

Dayraven gazed at the Dweorg. He did not want his friend to worry, and Gnorn could do nothing to help him. He tried to smile. "I'm alright. It's just the after effects of so much power passing through me. It'll settle down. And I have much to think about. I'll talk to Orvandil to put him at ease. Have you seen him today?"

"He was here just before you. Left to find Vols. The Thjoths and Ellonders will all be setting out soon, except for a few who'll stay with the worst off of the wounded. I expect he'll be back in the afternoon."

Dayraven rose from the stool. "Alright. I'll find him later, then. In the meantime, you rest. I have others to attend to."

"Very well, though perhaps I should be the one advising you to rest. Save some energy. I must make some notes regarding your adventures in the mountains. I expect a fuller account from you. Perhaps we'll begin on the morrow." Gnorn yawned and closed his eyes, and Dayraven smiled as he snuck away.

The young wizard checked on a few more of the most grievously hurt in the great hall before he exited into a long corridor housing still more of the wounded. When he came to its end, he turned down a smaller hallway, which was empty. Walking by several closed doors, he stopped at the hallway's end, where the last door waited. Turning the brass knob, he pushed the door and entered a small room into which light streamed through an open window. The only occupant of the room was even then rising from her bed. Dayraven smiled as he pretended to scold Sequara. "You're a terrible patient."

She was dressed in a simple white frock that did not quite cover the round scar beneath her collarbone. On her face and hands were also dim scars, the only remaining signs of her struggle against the High Priest Heremod. Dayraven grasped her bare legs and swiveled them back on the bed. After looking at him with an exasperated expression and rolling her eyes, she sank back into a reclining position. As he draped the sheet over her legs and stomach, Sequara said, "I should be out there helping to tend the wounded."

"You should be in here resting. You're too weak still to be of use to anyone, and you know it. Tell me, was I this stubborn when you were caring for me?"

Her smile lifted his heart. "You were unconscious nearly the whole time, but no doubt you would have been at least as impatient otherwise."

He grinned. "There you're wrong. I would have prolonged my bed rest as long as possible to keep you in attendance on me."

She smiled again, but then the smile faded, and her face slipped into an intense stare that conveyed longing to him. He sat on the bed and leaned in close. They kissed at first slowly but then with increasing eagerness, and she ran her fingers through his hair. When their mouths parted, she looked at him. "Your hair's greying. You're too young for that."

"But I sometimes feel I've aged a hundred years."

"It's the gift. You've seen and felt more than most people could in several lifetimes."

He took her hand and caressed it. After a long pause, he said, "And there are other . . . worries."

Her eyes hardened, and she nodded. "Asdralad."

He sat up and stared at her. "I'm afraid of what we'll find there."

"I know. As am I. We must expect the worst. The Torrlonders most likely still hold the island." She squeezed his hand. He knew how much she left unsaid. Sometimes it was better not to speak of fears. And yet, somehow, she mustered a smile for him. "And you would seek Imharr there."

He nodded. "Yes. It would be good to see him. Our last meeting was so brief, it seems like a dream cut short when . . ." He looked down, and his throat closed up, choking off anything else he might have said.

Sequara squeezed his hand again. "If anyone could have kept him and Queen Rona hidden, it would be our Jhaia. We must hope." Her voice was strained as she said the last few words, and they waited for a while in silence, holding each other's hand.

Finally, Dayraven sighed out a long breath. "I promised him we would seek his sister in Caergilion someday. I don't know if she even lives. Slavers aren't known for their kindness."

"That is true. But, when the time comes, you will seek her nonetheless." She smiled again, but this time the smile seemed sad. "I know you, Dayraven. No matter what we find in Asdralad, you will honor that vow, though, with the return of war, it will be dangerous in the southwest."

"I'll be careful. And as soon as I've found what I seek, I'll return to you. It will be our final parting. Never again will I leave you. I'll help you rebuild Asdralad."

Sequara gazed at him for a time, her frown full of unspoken sorrow. "We should not think too far ahead."

"But I . . ."

She shook her head. "My heart too longs for what you want, and I've thought on it. I don't know what will happen, yet one thing I know: No queen or king of Asdralad has ever wed before. But I have no room for such worries now. Please. One mountain at a time."

His heart sank, and a great part of him did not believe her words and what they might imply. "We could make a new beginning. A new Asdralad." It was impossible that they should not be together. He needed her. There was so little else holding him to the world.

Tears welled in her eyes, but she mastered her emotions. "There may be a way. But right now, I cannot forget my people. My duty. That must come first. I'm sorry." Only the slightest tremble in her voice betrayed the effort it took to control it.

When he realized his mouth was hanging open, he closed it. He tried to follow her example — to cut himself off from all his emotions. He took a few deep breaths and attempted to calm his mind the way Queen Faldira had taught him. "No. Of course. Duty first. It is I who should be sorry." He attempted a smile and hoped it did not look too broken.

She gazed at him, still mastering her features, though a single tear spilled down her cheek.

He released her hand and stood up. "I'm sorry. I'll leave now . . . let you rest. You should rest." He turned from her and walked toward the door, too numb to soak in what was happening. He reached for the latch on the door.

"Dayraven. Please stay."

He paused to take a deep breath, and then he turned around, unable to keep the relief and joy from his face.

Sequara was lying on her bed, the tear track glistening on her face, but she looked at him with calm eyes. And then she grinned. "Even with so much of the gift and so many of my memories, you still have much to learn."

Feeling more than a little foolish, he gave her a sheepish smile and nodded.

"Stay with me a while. Please. Whatever else happens, we can be together now." She reached a hand toward him.

The lump in his throat made it difficult to speak. He nodded and approached her.

When he stood next to her, her hand reached for his and pulled him close. She sat up. They kissed, and her tear moistened his cheek. When he opened his eyes, she was gazing at him.

The elf-shard struck with sudden ferocity, and Sequara's face disappeared in a bright light. In infinite directions the power of the elf exploded and tore Dayraven away. He soared far from flesh and pain. In the realm of origins he floated, to its very edges, beyond which there was silence. Rest. Nothing. There on that border he hovered, half fascinated and half repulsed.

A blurred voice echoed. "Dayraven? What's wrong?"

He blinked. When he opened his eyes, Sequara's beautiful face was before him again. The tear track was still wet on her cheek. Confusion and apprehension emanated from her narrowed eyes.

"Nothing. It's alright. I'm alright now."

The anxiety in her frown did not lessen. "I'm sorry. I'm so sorry." She shook her head as if trying to deny what she saw. "It's beyond me to heal this."

"I'll just . . . stay with you a while. I too should rest."

She nodded and moved over. He lay down next to her, and they stared at the ceiling. They said nothing.

She reached toward him. At first brushing his fingers as if posing a question, she took his hand in hers. They clasped each other. The feel of her flesh touching his grounded him. He listened to their breathing and held on for dear life.

***

THE SUPREME PRIEST JORUMAN SAT IN ONE OF HIS NEW CHAMBERS high up in Sigseld, biting his tongue as he listened to King Earconwald, who sat across the round table from him. The monarch was imparting his final instructions before he departed for the south to quell the rebellions in Caergilion and Adanon. His foul mood had grown only worse since the defeat in Sildharan.

"Damn that fool Siric. He's on his own. If he can't do it, I'll find someone else for the job. We must contain the rebellion in Norfast. And punish those half-breeds."

Joruman forced a smile. "My priests will preach in support of Siric, my lord. As you have observed, we can't spare a single soldier for the good duke now, but we might as well give him the weight of the Way behind him."

"What good will that do? The Way didn't win me Sildharan. Did it?"

"In time, your Majesty. In time."

Earconwald clenched his fists and opened his mouth as if he were about to shout. But his lip only quivered, and at length he said, "Fine. Send your fucking white-robes to Norfast. For all the good they'll do."

Joruman suppressed a sigh. "Your Majesty, the recent events are only a setback. Eormenlond will be yours. Look at where we are now. You are still the master of the southwest."

"Which is in open *rebellion*, fool!" His fist struck the table.

The supreme priest's smile was growing more strained. "You and your troops will crush the rebels. In the meantime, I'll take care of matters closer to home."

"You'd better. Unless you wish to join the last supreme priest who failed me."

The forced smile slipped away. *You can't afford to lose me, idiot. Lose me, and you'll lose your kingdom in short order.* Joruman resisted saying the words aloud. "There's no need to trouble yourself about that, your Majesty. A wise man knows where his interests lie. I certainly do." *And you'd best realize where yours are.*

"I think you do."

"By the time you return in triumph from the south, I will have corrected the rumors about your former queen's demise. I will also build support for Siric where it counts, among the people. My own house needs a little ordering as well. I must arrange the appointment of high priests who will be of most use to you. This may not be easy since Morcar and Colburga are both hostile, particularly the latter, but I'll manage it. Then there are the matters of diplomacy. I'll test the waters in Ellond — we must be wary of Fullan now — and I may even be able to smooth things over with the Markmen. Some of our priests there have the ear of King Ithamar. He needs a little time to cool down. You'll see."

"I don't need that young braggart."

Joruman almost rolled his eyes. "Perhaps not. But you do need a kingdom to our west that is at least not hostile to your ambitions. For now."

Earconwald grunted to concede the point.

"Fortunately, Ellond is in no state to resist us, and we still have support there, though it's in some disarray and will need some guidance. King Fullan remains, I think, a minor obstacle in the grand scheme. When the time comes, it will be easy enough to seize his realm. The real barrier is Sildharan, which is at present occupied with the savages. By the time they've bled each other, we'll be ready. It'll be easier to take the east than it was before. It will all work in your favor if we are patient and make the right moves at the right times."

The king's features calmed into something like a sulking frown. "That may be."

"It will fall out as I have said. And while you're putting down the rebels in the south, I will not be idle. Now that I'm back in Torrhelm with access to my predecessor's private libraries, I'm close to discovering something that could be of great advantage to us."

Earconwald scoffed. "Your experiments? Wizardry has failed us, Joruman. My armies will win the day. Stick to your politics and your machinations. That's what you're best at. And you're no Bledla."

The supreme priest almost lost his mask of control at the last remark. The spoiled ass had no idea. But it was best that the king remain ignorant. "As you say, your Majesty. I will work in your favor in all things."

"Very well." King Earconwald rose, and so Joruman rose as well. "I expect regular reports, as we discussed. I rely on you to keep the nobles in order. Keep an eye on Duke Ethelred especially."

"Yes, my lord. May Edan grant you victory."

Earconwald sneered in disgust, as Joruman knew he would at the mention of Edan.

When the monarch turned without a word and left the room, Joruman smiled. While the plans for conquest had stalled, his elevation had happened sooner than expected. A major obstacle in the form of Bledla was gone, thanks to Earconwald's impetuousness. All in all, the situation was favorable to his goals. The recently consecrated supreme priest glanced at the scores of books lining the shelves of his new chamber. Among them he had found tomes he sought for years, including Ishdhara's volume on the gift. Something of a heretic among the Andumae, she had even recorded songs of origin. *A kindred spirit.*

His smile broadened. There was power here. Power that Bledla had never dared to contemplate. No supreme priest had ever been bold enough, and over the long centuries they had hoarded their secrets in these chambers, allowing them to accumulate dust until the moment when Joruman would delve their depths. He would be bold enough. Combining what he had learned from the boy Dayraven with his unfettered access to knowledge of which he had heard only rumors before, he would go where no supreme priest or sorcerer had ever dared to go. Slowly but steadily, he would advance true learning. He would initiate the transformation of not only Torrlond and the Way, but of humanity itself. He would lead the greatest minds in innumerable quests for truth, all aimed at the defeat of mortality. No more cringing in the darkness. Finally, he had arrived.

After Sequara drifted to sleep, Dayraven quietly extricated himself from the bed. He needed to think, and she needed rest. He stood in the open doorway for a long while gazing at her sleeping form and the subtle rise and fall of her chest beneath the sheet. She was the most beautiful and wonderful person he had ever known, and the pain of wanting her was more sweet and overwhelming than he could put words to. Yet it was clear she had to return to Asdralad. And once it was free of Torrlond, what then? She would be queen. There was no question: She would sacrifice her happiness, and by extension his, for duty. The worst part was that it was right of her to do so, and he could not help admiring and loving her the more for it.

Yet there had to be a way. He would never know another person the way he knew Sequara. Besides that, she was the only thing keeping him alive. In her lay the possibility that he could recover his humanity. They would journey back to Asdralad together, and along the way they would think of something. There had to be some way they could be together and fulfill their duty.

He needed to think. With one last, longing look, he shut the door and walked down the empty hallway. On the way out of the palace, he did not stop to check on any of the wounded. He was tired in his mind, and he needed more energy before attempting to heal anyone. Allowing his feet to walk where they would, he ignored the people along the dusty streets and wandered until he reached the western gate, which workers were rebuilding with hammers and chisels clinking on stones. Out of the city his steps took him, away from all the noise and activity, and the whole time he pondered how he and Sequara could stay together and how he could return to his right mind.

Following the road paralleling the River Nurgleth, he entertained and rejected several ideas in succession until he decided it might be better to think of something else for a while. At least there was one thing he had settled on: He would keep his promise to Imharr to seek his friend's sister, even if Imharr was no more. He hoped Imharr would be with him. Seeking her would give him time to figure out how he and Sequara would proceed. It felt good, and it felt right. He missed Imharr. If he was gone, this was the best way he could honor him, and Caergilion was the place to begin. *Riall. He said her name was Riall. Not much to go on.*

So. At least he knew one thing for certain. He would be seeking Riall in Caergilion. He had no idea what he would do when he found her. *If* he found her. But a little bit of certainty helped to lighten his mood and gave him the illusion at least that certainty could arrive regarding other matters. In truth, there was much he needed to figure out.

When he looked around to take his bearings, he saw that he had wandered a couple miles from Thulhan. He did not remember walking so far. No one else was around. The only sound was the murmuring of the river not far from the road.

He stared at the shimmering water and let its sound lull him for a while. In contrast with all the recent events and his state of mind, the river seemed peaceful and steady, though it was deep and strong. Drifting closer to the riverbank, he watched the play of sunlight on its gliding, restless surface. Brightness flashed and danced in spots all over the river. There was no pattern he could discern, only the continuous, elusive fragmentation of light.

But then the spots of light blurred and grew until they merged into one another. Dayraven's mind slipped, and the elf-shard awakened as the light took over his field of vision. Eager and rapacious, the elf surged beyond the confines imposed by a mortal mind. All was brightness as the power of the elf shone like a beacon through his flesh, which dissipated at first into tiny fragments and then into nothing. Along with his flesh, his memories slipped away as minute particles that merged into the vast eternal energy constituting the world of forms and every other world. Beyond the realm of origins he floated, one with the first light to illuminate the darkness.

M‍unzil followed Valdur towards Surt's tent. The one-eyed chieftain had not told him why the war-leader wished to see him, and he did not stoop to ask questions of his silent companion. It must have been something important. The great man would never call a warrior from the front lines for no good reason. Also, he would not have sent Valdur unless it was a large matter indeed. So Munzil waited to find out what it was.

Perhaps there was some breakthrough. Since the twelve tribes had arrived from the Wildlands, they had fought the Sildharae to a stalemate. The folk of the tribes had the greater warriors by far, but the southern slavers had the advantage of their holy men and women. The Sildharae king himself often rode into battle wielding his lightning and slaying dozens of warriors at a time. It would be a great deed to slay the man, and Munzil spent much time trying to think of how to accomplish the task.

They arrived at the war-leader's open tent. Striding past the perimeter of guards, Valdur ducked inside. Munzil followed. When his eyes adjusted to the dimness, he beheld Surt sitting in a chair in the tent's center. Next to him on another chair sat a tall man, a warrior of the tribes to judge by his appearance. He was blond with a long beard, and he looked strong. His cheeks were red and chafed, and his cloak and boots were made from the fur of the white bear. He appeared to have seen around forty winters, so he must have been skilled enough to live that long. Munzil did not recognize him.

"Ah, Munzil." Surt smiled at him. He knew the look. It was the way the great man often smiled when he was thinking of something bold. "I wanted you to be the first to know. You've earned that."

"The first to know what, my lord?"

Surt gestured at the stranger. "This is Marg. He is of the Broad Eagle tribe."

"The Broad Eagles? But they're . . ."

"From Enga Isle."

Sudden understanding awakened in Munzil. "You mean . . ."

"Yes. The Broad Eagles are joining us. And so are the other two tribes on Enga Isle. And the tribes from the islands to the north, all the way up to the frozen lands."

Munzil's eyes widened. "How many?"

"Thirty tribes at least, with seventy thousand warriors," answered Marg. He spoke with a strange accent, but Munzil could understand him. "When messengers came with tales of your vision, most of our folk scoffed. But when word reached us that all the tribes of the Wildlands had come together as one under the war-leader of the Fire Dragons, we began to wonder. And we had long heard stories of the soft, warm lands here. When more messengers came, we decided to hearken to them."

Munzil gazed at Surt. "You sent messengers to the islands?"

"Why not? They too are folk of the tribes."

Munzil could not help but laugh aloud. Surt had done it again. This would turn the tide at last. He could feel the hand of the gods in this. He turned to Marg. "You are most welcome, brother. It's an honor to have you among us."

"No. The honor's mine. I wished to see with my own eyes the man the gods spoke to: Munzil of the Grey Wolves."

Munzil smiled and nodded. "When will they arrive?"

"Soon," answered Surt. "And when they do, Sildharan will fall."

EPILOGUE

A man awakened next to a river. Or rather, he opened his eyes and found himself standing next to a river. He did not think he had been truly sleeping since he was standing, but he was not certain since he could remember nothing from before the moment he opened his eyes.

He wondered who he was. Holding his hands before him, he gazed at them as if they could provide some clue as to his identity. He felt old in his mind, but his hands were not old. However, the nail on his right index finger was mangled. While he examined his hands, he noticed that to his north in the distance lay a city. The city made him uncomfortable. Some sorrow awaited him there, and he wanted to be away from people. There would be many people in that city.

Besides that, he had to go somewhere. He could not remember where, but it was not that city.

So he made his first decision. He turned away from the city and walked south along the river. He would keep walking until he reached the place where he must go. Perhaps there he would find out who he was.

THE END

ABOUT THE AUTHOR

Rather than write about myself in third person, allow me to thank you for reading my book, dear reader, and to introduce myself. A medievalist with special interests in Old English, Old Norse, and various mythological traditions, I teach English composition and literature and run a YouTube channel ("Philip Chase" or "PhilipChaseTheBestofFantasy") dedicated to the exploration of the fantasy genre. Feel free to visit me there and join the wonderful fantasy literature community that exists on YouTube. I can also be found puttering around on Twitter (philipchase90), and if you would like to hear from me occasionally about writing updates or whatever ponderings I might happen to be tapping out on my keyboard, you could wander over to my website, PhilipChaseAuthor.com. Until next time!

Printed in Great Britain
by Amazon